CYGNISEN
PROVINCE

MONTSERRAT

ESBEN MOUNTAINS

CHAKIR

BRAEVICK
PROVINCE

DUNNESS RIVER

SAMARA

ANCA

STONEWATER RIVER

ZOLYA (CLIFFSBANE)

SUMERTON

ESBEN MOUNTAINS

RESSON

POROMIEL

BAY OF
MALEK

THE
BARRENS

PAVIS

KROVLA PROVINCE

CORDYN

N

W   E

S

BookTok praise for

FOURTH WING

"I wish I could erase this book from my head just so I can experience reading it for the first time again—I loved it from start to finish!"
—@thebooksiveloved

"I knew the instant I finished *Fourth Wing* that it was going to be an instant new obsession of mine."
—@darkfaerietales

"A breathtaking reminder of what it feels like to fall in love with reading all over again: best book of the year."
—@tuesday.reads

"A true masterpiece of fantasy romance."
—@elitereading

"The world, the characters, the representation! And there's dragons? *Fourth Wing* is spectacular."
—@krystallotuslang

"Action, magic, angst, spice, DRAGONS! Hands down the top book of the year!"
—@fantasy_books14

"This intense story full of twists, turns, tension, battles, and morally gray enemies has me completely captivated! I need book two in my hands!"
—@bookswithsierra

"Wow! What a ride! Obsessed is an understatement."
—@mandy_bookingchaos

"I love this book. It's like *Hunger Games* but with passion and sassy dragons."
—@_kristarosee

"An exhilarating ride that will leave you breathless and demanding more by the end!"
—@witchlinghavilliard

Industry praise for

FOURTH WING

★ "Suspenseful, sexy, and with incredibly entertaining storytelling, the
first in Yarros' Empyrean series will delight fans
of romantic, adventure-filled fantasy."
—*Booklist*, **starred review**

★ "Readers will be spellbound and eager for more."
—*Publishers Weekly,* **starred review**

Picked as a book to read for Disability Pride Month
by Reese's Book Club

"The book of the summer."
—*The Daily Lobo*

"A fantasy like you've never read before."
—**Jennifer L. Armentrout, #1** *New York Times* **bestselling author**

"Smart-ass. Bad-ass. Kick-ass. One helluva ride!"
—**Tracy Wolff, #1** *New York Times* **bestselling author**

"Dragons and war, passion and power…*Fourth Wing* is dazzling. Rebecca
Yarros has created a world as compelling as it is deadly,
and I can't wait to see where she takes it next."
—**Nalini Singh,** *New York Times* **bestselling author**

"A rip-roaring, breathlessly exciting war school fantasy."
—*Grimdark Magazine*

"An exciting, whirlwind start to a fantastic new series that is
sure to become a firm fantasy favourite."
—**Culturefly**

"I urge every single person on this earth to run to their nearest
bookstore or library and get this book in their hands.
Reading it was an experience I'll never forget."
—**The Everygirl**

IRON FLAME

#1 *NEW YORK TIMES* BESTSELLING AUTHOR

REBECCA YARROS

Entangled Publishing, LLC
644 Shrewsbury Commons Ave., STE 181
Shrewsbury, PA 17361
rights@entangledpublishing.com

Red Tower Books is an imprint of Entangled Publishing, LLC.

Visit our website at www.entangledpublishing.com.

Edited by Liz Pelletier
Cover art and design by Bree Archer and Elizabeth Turner Stokes
Stock art by Peratek/Shutterstock, yyanng/depositphotos,
stopkin/Shutterstock, detchana wangkheeree/Shutterstock,
and d1sk/Shutterstock
Interior art by Elizabeth Turner Stokes
Interior endpaper map art by Melanie Korte
Interior design by Toni Kerr

HC ISBN 978-1-64937-417-2
B&N ISBN 978-1-64937-617-6
Indie ISBN 978-1-64937619-0
BAM ISBN 978-1-64937-620-6
Ebook ISBN 978-1-64937-585-8

Printed in the United States of America

First Edition November 2023

10 9 8 7 6 5 4 3 2 1

ℝ RED TOWER BOOKS™

MORE FROM REBECCA YARROS

THE EMPYREAN SERIES

Fourth Wing
Iron Flame

The Things We Leave Unfinished
Great and Precious Things
The Last Letter

To my fellow zebras.
Not all strength is physical.

Iron Flame is a nonstop-thrilling adventure fantasy set in the brutal and competitive world of a military college for dragon riders, which includes elements regarding war, psychological and physical torture, imprisonment, intense violence, brutal injuries, perilous situations, blood, dismemberment, burning, murder, death, animal death, graphic language, loss of family, grief, and sexual activities that are shown on the page. Readers who may be sensitive to these elements, please take note, and prepare to join the revolution…

FOURTH WING

All other Wings' structure is identical

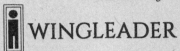 **WINGLEADER** **EXECUTIVE OFFICER,**
SECOND IN COMMAND

CLAW SECTION

 SECTION LEADER

 **EXECUTIVE OFFICER,**
SECOND IN COMMAND

SQUAD 1

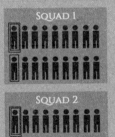

SQUAD 2

SQUAD 3

SQUADS = 15 – 20 PEOPLE

FLAME SECTION

 SECTION LEADER

EXECUTIVE OFFICER,
SECOND IN COMMAND

SQUAD 1

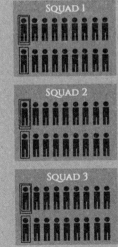

SQUAD 2

SQUAD 3

TAIL SECTION

 SECTION LEADER

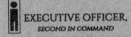 **EXECUTIVE OFFICER,**
SECOND IN COMMAND

SQUAD 1

SQUAD 2

SQUAD 3

DOUBLE OUTLINE = SQUAD LEADER
SINGLE = EXECUTIVE OFFICER, *SECOND IN COMMAND*

BWC
BASGIATH WAR COLLEGE

The following text has been faithfully transcribed from Navarrian into the modern language by Jesinia Neilwart, Curator of the Scribe Quadrant at Basgiath War College. All events are true, and names have been preserved to honor the courage of those fallen. May their souls be commended to Malek.

PART ONE

In this, the 628th year of our Unification, it is hereby recorded that Aretia has been burned by dragon in accordance with the Treaty ending the separatist movement. Those who fled, survived, and those who did not remain entombed in her ruins.

—Public Notice 628.85
Transcribed by Cerella Neilwart

CHAPTER ONE

Revolution tastes oddly…sweet.

I stare at my older brother across a scarred wooden table in the enormous, busy kitchen of the fortress of Aretia and chew the honeyed biscuit he put on my plate. Damn, that's good. Really good.

Maybe it's just that I haven't eaten in three days, since a not-so-mythological being stabbed me in the side with a poisoned blade that should have killed me. It *would* have killed me if it hadn't been for Brennan, who won't stop smiling as I chew.

This might go down as the most surreal experience of my life. Brennan is alive. Venin, dark wielders I'd thought only existed in fables, are real. Brennan is alive. Aretia still stands, even though it was scorched after the Tyrrish rebellion six years ago. Brennan is *alive*. I have a new, three-inch scar on my abdomen, but I didn't die. Brennan. Is. Alive.

"The biscuits are good, right?" he asks, snagging one from the platter between us. "Kind of remind me of the ones that cook used to make when we were stationed in Calldyr, remember?"

I stare and chew.

He's just so…him. And yet he looks different from what I remember. His brownish-red curls are cropped close to his skull instead of waving over his forehead, and there's no lingering softness in the angles of his face, which now has tiny lines at the edges of his eyes. But that smile? Those eyes? It's really him.

And his one condition being me eating something before he takes me to my dragons? It's the most Brennan move ever.

Not that Tairn ever waits for permission, which means—

"I, too, think you need to eat something." Tairn's low, arrogant voice fills my head.

"Yeah, yeah," I reply in kind, mentally reaching out for Andarna again as one of the kitchen workers hurries by, offering a quick smile to Brennan.

There's no response from Andarna, but I can feel the shimmering bond between us, though it's no longer golden like her scales. I can't quite get a mental picture, but my brain is still a little groggy. She's sleeping again, which isn't odd after she uses up all her energy to stop time, and after what happened in Resson, she probably needs to sleep for the next week or so.

"You've barely said a word, you know." Brennan tilts his head just like he used to when he was trying to solve a problem. "It's kind of creepy."

"Watching me *eat* is creepy," I counter after I swallow, my voice still a little hoarse.

"And?" He shrugs shamelessly, a dimple flashing in his cheek when he grins. It's the only boyish thing left about him. "A few days ago, I was pretty sure I'd never get to watch you do, well, *anything* again." He takes a huge bite. Guess his appetite is still the same, which is oddly comforting. "You're welcome, by the way, for the mending. Consider it a twenty-first-birthday present."

"Thank you." That's right. I slept right through my birthday. And I'm sure my lying in bed on the brink of death was more than enough drama for everyone in this castle, house, whatever it's called.

Xaden's cousin, Bodhi, strides into the kitchen, dressed in uniform, his arm in a sling and his cloud of black curls freshly trimmed.

"Lieutenant Colonel Aisereigh," Bodhi says, handing a folded missive to Brennan. "This just came in from Basgiath. The rider will be here until tonight if you want to reply." He offers me a smile, and I'm struck again at how closely he resembles a softer version of Xaden. With a nod to my brother, he turns and leaves.

Basgiath? Another rider here? How many are there? Exactly how big is this revolution?

Questions fire off in my head faster than I can find my tongue. "Wait. You're a lieutenant colonel? And who is Aisereigh?" I ask. Yeah, because *that* is the most important inquiry to make.

"I had to change my last name for obvious reasons." He glances at me and unfolds the missive, breaking a blue wax seal. "And you'd be amazed at how fast you get promoted when everyone above you continues to die," he says, then reads the letter and curses, shoving it into his pocket. "I have to go meet with the Assembly now, but finish your biscuits and I'll meet you in the hall in half an hour and take you to your dragons." All traces of the dimple, of the laughing older brother are gone, and in their place is a man I barely recognize, an officer I don't know. Brennan may as well be a stranger.

Without waiting for me to respond, he scrapes his chair back and strides out of the kitchen.

Sipping my milk, I stare at the empty space my brother left across from me, chair still pulled out from the table as though he might return at any moment. I swallow the remaining biscuit stuck in the back of my throat and lift my chin, determined not to ever sit and wait on my brother to return again.

I push up from the table and head after him, out of the kitchen and down the long hall. He must have been in a hurry, because I can't see him anywhere.

The intricate carpet muffles my footsteps along the wide, high-arched hallway as I come to— *Whoa.* The sweeping, polished double staircases with their detailed banisters rise three—no, four—more floors above me.

I'd been too focused on my brother to pay attention earlier, but now I blatantly gawk at the architecture of the enormous space. Each landing is slightly offset from the one below, as though the staircase climbs toward the very mountain this fortress is carved into. The morning light streams in from dozens of small windows that provide the only decoration on the five-story wall above the massive double doors of the fortress's entrance. They seem to form a pattern, but I'm too close to see the whole of it.

There's no perspective, which pretty much feels like a metaphor for my entire life right now.

Two guards watch every step I take but make no move to stop me when I pass by. At least that means I'm not a prisoner.

I continue to stride through the main hall of the house, eventually picking up the sound of voices from a room across the way, where one of two large, ornate doors is pitched open. As I approach, I immediately recognize Brennan's voice, and my chest tightens at the familiar timbre.

"That's not going to work." Brennan's deep voice echoes. "Next suggestion."

I make it through the massive foyer, ignoring what look to be two other wings off to the left and right. This place is astounding. Half palace, half home, but entirely a fortress. The thick stone walls are what saved it from its supposed demise six years ago. From what I've read, Riorson House has never been breached by any army, even during the three sieges that I know of.

Stone doesn't burn. That's what Xaden told me. The city—now reduced to a town—has been silently, covertly rebuilding for years right under General Melgren's nose. The relics, magical marks the children of the executed rebellion officers carry, somehow mask them from Melgren's signet when they're in groups of three or more. He can't see the outcome of any battle they're present for, so he's never been able to "see" them organizing to fight here.

There are certain aspects of Riorson House, from its defensible position carved into the mountainside to its cobblestone floors and steel-enforced double doors in the entryway, that remind me of Basgiath, the war college I've called home since my mother was stationed there as its commanding general. But that's where the similarities end. There's actual art on the walls here, not just busts of war heroes displayed on stands, and I'm pretty sure that's an authentic Poromish tapestry hanging across the hall from where Bodhi and Imogen stand in the open doorway.

Imogen puts her finger to her lips, then motions at me to join in the empty place between her and Bodhi. I take it, noticing Imogen's half-shaved hair has been recently dyed a brighter pink while I've been resting. Clearly she's comfortable here. Bodhi, too. The only signs that either has been in a battle are the sling cradling Bodhi's fractured arm and a split in Imogen's lip.

"Someone has to state the obvious," an older man with an eyepatch and a hawkish nose says from the far end of a table that consumes the length of the two-story room. Tufts of thinning gray hair frame the deep lines in his lightly tanned, weathered skin, his jowls hanging down like a wildebeest. He leans back in his chair, placing a thick hand on his rounded belly.

The table could easily accommodate thirty people, but only five sit along one side, all dressed in rider black, perched slightly ahead of the door, at an angle where they'd have to turn fully to see us—which they don't. Brennan paces in front of the table but not at an angle he can easily spot us, either.

My heart lurches into my throat, and I realize it's going to take some time to get used to seeing Brennan alive. He's somehow exactly the same as I remember—and yet different. But here he is—living, breathing, currently glaring at a map of the Continent on the long wall, the map's size only rivaled by the one in the Battle Brief lecture hall at Basgiath.

And standing in front of that map, one arm leaning against a massive chair as he stares down the table at its occupants, is Xaden.

He looks good, even with bruises marring the tawny-brown skin under his eyes from lack of sleep. The high slopes of his cheeks, the dark eyes that usually soften whenever they meet mine, the scar that bisects his brow and ends beneath his eye, the swirling, shimmering relic that ends at his jaw, and the carved lines of the mouth I know as well as my own all add up to make him physically fucking perfect to me, and that's just his face. His body? Somehow even better, and the way he uses it when he has me in his arms—

Nope. I shake my head and cut off my thoughts right there. Xaden may be gorgeous, and powerful, and terrifyingly lethal—which shouldn't be the turn-on it is—but I can't trust him to tell me the truth about…well, anything. Which really *hurts*, considering how pathetically in love with him I am.

"And what is the obvious thing you need to state, Major Ferris?" Xaden asks, his tone completely, utterly bored.

"It's an Assembly meeting," Bodhi whispers to me. "Only a quorum of five is required to call a vote, since all seven are almost never here at one time, and four votes carry a motion."

I file that information away. "Are we allowed to listen?"

"Meetings are open to whoever wants to attend," Imogen replies just as quietly.

"And we're attending…in the hallway?" I ask.

"Yes," Imogen answers with no other explanation.

"Returning is the only option," Hawk Nose continues. "Not doing so risks everything we're building here. Search patrols will come, and we don't have enough riders—"

"It's a little hard to recruit while trying to stay undetectable," a petite woman with glossy black hair like a raven counters, the umber skin at the corners of her eyes crinkling as she glares down the table at the older man.

"Let's not get off topic, Trissa," Brennan says, rubbing the bridge of his nose. Our father's nose. Their resemblance is uncanny.

"No point increasing our numbers without a working forge to arm them with weapons." Hawk Nose's voice rises above the others. "We're still short a luminary, if you haven't noticed."

"And where are we in negotiations with Viscount Tecarus for his?" a large man asks in a calm, rumbling voice, his ebony hand tugging at his thick silver beard.

Viscount Tecarus? That isn't a noble family in any Navarrian records. We don't even have viscounts in our aristocracy.

"Still working on a diplomatic solution," Brennan answers.

"There's no solution. Tecarus isn't over the insult you delivered last summer." An older woman built like a battle-ax locks her gaze on Xaden, her blond hair brushing just past her square alabaster chin.

"I told you, the viscount was never going to give it to us in the first place," Xaden replies. "The man only *collects* things. He does not *trade* them."

"Well, he's definitely not going to *trade* with us now," she retorts, her gaze narrowing. "Especially if you won't even contemplate his latest offer."

"He can fuck right off with his *offer*." Xaden's voice is calm, but his eyes have a hard edge that dares anyone at the table to disagree. As if showing these people they aren't worth his time, he steps around the arm of the massive chair facing them and settles into it, stretching his long legs and resting his arms on the velvet armrests—like he doesn't have a care in the world.

The quiet that falls on the room is telling. Xaden commands as much respect from the Assembly of this revolution as he does at Basgiath. I don't recognize any of the other riders besides Brennan, but I'd bet Xaden is the most powerful in the room, given their silence.

"For now," Tairn reminds me with the arrogance only a hundred years of being one of the most formidable battle dragons on the Continent can provide. *"Instruct the humans to bring you up to the valley once the politics are finished."*

"There had better be a solution. If we can't supply the drifts with enough weaponry to really fight in the next year, the tide will shift too far to ever hope of holding the venin advance at bay," Silver Beard notes. "This all will have been for nothing."

My stomach pitches. A year? We're *that* close to losing a war I knew nothing about a few days ago?

"As I said, I'm working on a diplomatic solution for the luminary"— Brennan's tone sharpens—"and we're so wildly off topic I'm not sure this is the same meeting."

"I vote we take Basgiath's luminary," Battle-Ax suggests. "If we're that close to losing this war, there's no other option."

Xaden shoots Brennan a look that I can't decipher, and I breathe deeply as it hits me—he probably knows my own brother better than I do.

And he kept him from me. Of all the secrets he hid, that's the one I can't quite swallow.

"And what would you have done with the knowledge had he shared it?" Tairn asks.

"Stop bringing logic into an emotional argument." I fold my arms across my chest. It's my heart that won't fully let my head forgive Xaden.

"We've been over that," Brennan says with finality. "If we take Basgiath's forging device, Navarre can't replenish their stores at the outposts. Countless civilians will die if those wards fall. Do any of you want to be responsible for that?"

Silence reigns.

"Then we agree," Hawk Nose says. "Until we can supply the drifts, the cadets *have* to return."

Oh.

"They're talking about us," I whisper. That's why we're standing out of their direct sight.

Bodhi nods.

"You're uncharacteristically quiet, Suri," Brennan notes, glancing at the wide-shouldered brunette with olive skin and a single streak of silver in her hair, her nose twitching like a fox, sitting next to him.

"I say we send all but the two." Her nonchalance skates a chill down my spine as she drums her bony fingers on the table, a giant emerald ring catching the light. "Six cadets can lie as well as eight."

Eight.

Xaden, Garrick, Bodhi, Imogen, three marked ones I'd never gotten a chance to know before we were thrown into battle, and...me.

Nausea rises like a tide. The War Games. We're supposed to be finishing the last competition of the year between the wings of the Riders Quadrant at Basgiath, and instead, we entered deadly battle with an enemy I'd thought were only folklore last week, and now we're...well, we're here, in a city that isn't supposed to exist.

But not all of us.

My throat tightens, and I blink back the burn in my eyes. Soleil and Liam didn't survive.

Liam. Blond hair and sky-blue eyes fill my memory, and pain erupts behind my ribs. His boisterous laugh. His quick smile. His loyalty and kindness. It's all gone. *He's* gone.

All because he promised Xaden he'd guard me.

"None of the eight are expendable, Suri." Silver Beard leans on the back two legs of his chair and examines the map behind Xaden.

"What do you propose, Felix?" Suri counters. "Running our own war college with all our spare time? Most of them haven't finished their education. They're of no use to us yet."

"As if any of you has a say in if we return," Xaden interrupts, earning everyone's attention. "We will take the advice of the Assembly, but it will be taken as only that—*advice.*"

"We cannot afford to risk your life—" Suri argues.

"My life is equal to any of theirs." Xaden gestures toward us.

Brennan's gaze meets mine, then widens.

Each head in the room turns toward us, and I fight the instinct to retreat as almost every set of eyes narrows on me.

Who do they see? Lilith's daughter? Or Brennan's sister?

I lift my chin because I'm both...and I feel like neither.

"Not every life," Suri says as she looks straight at me. *Ouch.* "How could you have stood there and let her overhear the conversation of the Assembly?"

"If you didn't want her to hear, you should have closed the door," Bodhi responds, stepping into the room.

"She cannot be trusted!" Anger might color her cheeks, but that's fear in Suri's eyes.

"Xaden has already taken responsibility for her." Imogen sidesteps, moving slightly closer to me. "As brutal of a custom as it may be."

My gaze whips to meet Xaden's. What the hell is she talking about?

"I still don't understand that particular decision," Hawk Nose adds.

"Decision was simple. She's worth a dozen of me," Xaden says, and my breath catches at the intensity in his eyes. If I didn't know better, I'd think he means it. "And I'm not talking about her signet. I would have told her everything discussed here anyway, so an open door is a moot point."

A spark of hope flares to life in my chest. Maybe he really is done keeping secrets.

"She's General Sorrengail's daughter," Battle-Ax points out, frustration clear in her voice.

"And I'm the general's son," Brennan argues.

"And you've more than proven your loyalty over the last six years!" Battle-Ax shouts. "She hasn't!"

Anger heats my neck, flushing up to my face. They're talking about me like I'm not even here.

"She fought at our side at Resson." Bodhi tenses as his voice rises as well.

"She should be confined." Suri's face turns downright ruddy as she pushes away from the table and stands, her gaze jumping to the silver half of my hair that forms my coronet braid. "She can ruin us all with what she knows."

"Agreed." Hawk Nose joins her with palpable loathing aimed in my direction. "She's too dangerous not to keep prisoner."

The muscles of my stomach tense, but I mask my expression like I've seen Xaden do countless times and leave my hands at my sides, close to my sheathed daggers. My body might be frail, my joints undependable, but my aim with a knife is lethally accurate. There's no fucking way I'm going to let them cage me here.

I scan each of the Assembly members, assessing which is the biggest threat.

Brennan rises to his full height. "Knowing that she's bonded to Tairn, whose bonds get deeper with each rider and whose previous bond was already so strong that Naolin's death nearly killed him? Knowing we fear he'll die if she does now? That because of that, Riorson's life is tied to hers?" He nods toward Xaden.

Disappointment tastes bitter on my tongue. Is that all I am to him? Xaden's weakness?

"I alone am responsible for Violet." Xaden's voice lowers in pure malice. "And if I'm not enough, there are not one but *two* dragons who have already vouched for her integrity."

Enough is enough.

"*She* is standing right here," I snap, and an unflattering amount of satisfaction courses through me at the number of jaws that drop in front of me. "So stop talking *about* me and try talking *to* me."

A corner of Xaden's mouth rises, and the pride that flashes through his expression is unmistakable.

"What do you want from me?" I ask them, striding into the room. "Want me to walk Parapet and prove my bravery? Done. Want me to betray my kingdom by defending Poromish citizens? Done. Want me to keep his secrets?" I gesture toward Xaden with my left hand. "Done. I kept *every* secret."

"Except the one that mattered." Suri lifts an eyebrow. "We all know how you ended up in Athebyne."

Guilt clogs my throat.

"That was not—" Xaden starts, rising from his chair.

"Through no fault of her own." The man nearest us with the gray beard—Felix—stands, blocking Suri from my sight as he turns toward her. "No first-year could withstand a memory reader, especially one considered a friend." He pivots to face me. "But you have to know that you have enemies at Basgiath, now. Should you return, you must know that Aetos will not be among your friends. He will do everything he can to kill you for what you've seen."

"I know." The words are thick on my tongue.

Felix nods.

"We are done here," Xaden says, his gaze catching and holding Suri's and then Hawk Nose's, their shoulders drooping in defeat.

"I'll expect an update on Zolya in the morning," Brennan says. "Consider this Assembly meeting adjourned."

The council members push in their chairs and file past the three of us once we step out of the way. Imogen and Bodhi stay at my sides.

Eventually, Xaden starts to walk out but pauses in front of me. "We'll head up to the valley. Meet us when you're done."

"I'll go with you now." This is the last place on the Continent I want to be left behind.

"Stay and talk to your brother," he says quietly. "Who knows when you'll get another chance."

I glance past Bodhi to see Brennan standing in the middle of the room, waiting for me. Brennan, who always took the time to help wrap my knees when I was a child. Brennan, who wrote the book that helped me through my first year. Brennan…who I've missed for six years.

"Go," Xaden urges. "We won't leave without you, and we're not going to let the Assembly dictate what we do. The eight of us will decide what to do together." He gives me a long look that makes my traitorous heart clench, and then he walks away. Bodhi and Imogen follow.

Which leaves me to turn toward my brother, armed with six years of questions.

It is the valley above Riorson House, heated by natural thermal energy, that is its greatest asset. For there lie the original hatching grounds of the Dubhmadinn Line, from which two of the greatest dragons of our time—Codagh and Tairn—descend.

—Colonel Kaori's Field Guide to Dragonkind

CHAPTER TWO

I shut the tall door behind me before moving toward Brennan. *This* meeting is definitely not open to the public.

"Did you eat enough?" He rests on the edge of the table like he used to when we were kids. The move is so...him, and as for the question, I ignore it entirely.

"So this is where you've been the last six years?" My voice threatens to break. I'm so glad he's alive. That's all that should matter. But I can't forget the years he's let me grieve for him, either.

"Yes." His shoulders drop. "I'm sorry I let you believe I was dead. It was the only way."

Cue awkward silence. What am I supposed to say to that? *It's all right, but not really?* There's so much I want to say to him, so much I need to ask, but suddenly the years we've been apart feel...defining. Neither of us is the same person.

"You look different." He smiles, but it's sad. "Not in a bad way. Just... different."

"I was fourteen the last time you saw me." I grimace. "I think I'm still the same height. I used to hope I'd get a last-minute growth spurt, but alas, here I am."

"Here you are." He nods slowly. "I always pictured you in scribe colors, but you look good in black. Gods..." He sighs. "The relief I felt when I heard you'd survived Threshing is indescribable."

"You knew?" My eyes flare. He has sources at Basgiath.

"I knew. And then Riorson showed up with you stabbed and dying." He looks away and clears his throat, then takes a deep breath before continuing. "I'm so damned glad you're healed, that you've made it through your first year." The relief in his eyes takes some of the sting out of my anger.

"Mira helped." That's putting it mildly.

"The armor?" he guesses correctly. There's something to be said for the delicate weight of my dragon-scale armor under my flight leathers.

I nod. "She had it made. She gave me your book, too. The one you wrote for her."

"I hope it was useful."

I think back to the naive, sheltered girl who crossed the parapet, and everything she survived in the crucible of her first year to forge me into the woman I am now. "It was."

His smile falters, and he glances out the window. "How is Mira?"

"Speaking from experience, I'm sure she'd be a lot better if she knew you're alive." There's no point mincing words if we only have a short time.

He flinches. "Guess I deserve that."

And I guess that answers *that* question. Mira doesn't know. But she should.

"How exactly *are* you alive, Brennan?" I shift my weight to one leg, crossing my arms. "Where is Marbh? What are you doing here? Why didn't you come home?"

"One at a time." He holds up his hands like he's under attack, and I glimpse a rune-shaped scar on his palm before he grips the edge of the table. "Naolin... He was—" His jaw flexes.

"Tairn's previous rider," I suggest slowly, wondering if he was more than that to Brennan. "He was the siphon who died trying to save you, according to Professor Kaori." My heart sinks. *I'm sorry your rider died saving my brother.*

"We will no longer speak of the one who came before." Tairn's voice is rough.

A corner of Brennan's mouth lifts. "I miss Kaori. He's a good man." He sighs, lifting his head to hold my gaze. "Naolin didn't fail, but it cost him *everything*. I woke up on a cliffside not far from here. Marbh had been wounded, but he was alive, too, and the other dragons..." His amber-colored eyes meet mine. "There are other dragons here, and they saved us, hid us in the network of caves within the valley, then later with the civilians who survived the city being scorched."

My brow furrows as I try to make sense of his words. "Where is Marbh now?"

"He's been in the valley with the others for days, keeping watch on your Andarna with Tairn, Sgaeyl, and—since you woke up—Riorson."

"That's where Xaden has been? Guarding Andarna?" That makes me a little less pissed that he's blatantly avoided me. "And why are you here, Brennan?"

He shrugs as though his answer is obvious. "I'm here for the same reason you fought at Resson. Because I can't stand by, safe behind the barriers of Navarre's wards, and watch innocent people die at the hands of dark wielders because our leadership is too selfish to help. That's also the reason I didn't come home. I couldn't fly for Navarre knowing what we've done—what we're *doing*—and I sure as hell couldn't look our mother in the eye and listen to her justify our cowardice. I refused to live the lie."

"You just left Mira and me to live it." It comes out a little angrier than I intend, or maybe I'm angrier than I realize.

"A choice I've questioned every single day since." The regret in his eyes is enough to make me breathe deeply and center myself. "I figured you had Dad—"

"Until we didn't." My throat threatens to tighten, so I turn to look at the map, then walk closer to take in more of the details. Unlike the one at Basgiath, which is updated daily with gryphon attacks on the border, this one reflects the truths Navarre is hiding. The region of the Barrens—the dry, desert-covered peninsula in the southeast that all dragonkind abandoned after General Daramor ruined the land during the Great War—is completely painted in crimson. The stain stretches into Braevick, over the Dunness River.

What have to be newer battle sites are marked with an alarming number of bright red and orange flags. The red ones mar not only the oceanic eastern border of the Krovlan province along the Bay of Malek but are heavily concentrated north into the plains as well, spreading like a disease, even infecting dots of Cygnisen. But the orange ones, those are heavily concentrated along the Stonewater River, which leads straight to Navarre's border.

"So the fables are all true. Venin coming out of the Barrens, sucking the land dry of magic, moving city to city."

"You've seen it with your own eyes." He moves to my side.

"And the wyvern?"

"We've known about them for a few months, but none of the cadets did. Until now, we've limited what Riorson and the others have known for their own safety, which in retrospect may have been a mistake. We know they have at least two breeds, one that produces blue fire and a faster one that breathes green fire."

"How many?" I ask him. "Where are they making them?"

"Do you mean hatching them?"

"Making," I repeat. "Don't you remember the fables Dad used to read to us? They said wyvern are created by venin. They channel power *into* wyvern. I think that's why riderless ones died when I killed their dark wielders. Their source of power was gone."

"You remember all of that from Dad reading?" He glances at me, bewildered.

"I still have the book." It's a good thing Xaden warded my room at Basgiath so no one will discover it while we're here. "Are you telling me you not only didn't know they're created but have no clue where they're coming from?"

"That's…accurate."

"How comforting," I mutter as electricity prickles my skin. I shake my hands, pacing in front of the large map. The orange flags are awfully close to Zolya, the second most populous city in Braevick, *and* where Cliffsbane, their flier academy, is located. "The one with the silver beard said we have a year to turn it around?"

"Felix. He's the most rational of the Assembly, but personally I think he's wrong." Brennan waves his hand in the air in a general outline of Braevick's border with the Barrens along the Dunness River. "The red flags are all from the last few years, and the orange are the last few months. At the rate they've been expanding, not only in their numbers of wyvern, but in territory? I think they're headed straight up the Stonewater River and we have six months or less until they're strong enough to come for Navarre—not that the Assembly will listen."

Six months. I swallow the bile fighting to rise in my throat. Brennan was always a brilliant strategist, according to our mother. My bet is on his assessment. "The general pattern is moving northwest—toward Navarre. Resson is the exception, along with whatever that flag is—" I point to the one that looks to be an hour's flight east of Resson.

The desiccated landscape around what had been a thriving trading post flashes in my memory. Those flags are more than outliers; they're twin splotches of orange in an otherwise untouched area.

"We think the iron box Garrick Tavis found at Resson is some kind of lure, but we had to destroy it before we could fully investigate. A box like it was found in Jahna, already smashed." He glances my way. "But the craftsmanship is Navarrian."

I absorb that information with a long breath, wondering what reason Navarre would have to build lures besides using one to kill us in Resson. "You really think they'll come for Navarre before taking the rest of Poromiel?" Why not take the easier targets first?

"I do. Their survival depends on it as much as ours depends on stopping them. The energy in the hatching grounds at Basgiath could keep them fed for decades. And yet Melgren thinks the wards are so infallible that he won't alert the population. Or he's afraid that telling the public will make them realize we aren't entirely the good guys. Not anymore. Fen's rebellion taught leadership it's a lot easier to control happy civilians than disgruntled—or worse, terrified—ones."

"And yet they manage to keep the truth hidden," I whisper. Sometime in our past, one generation of Navarrians wiped the history books, erasing the existence of venin from common education and knowledge, all because we aren't willing to risk our own safety by providing the one material that can kill dark wielders—the same alloy that powers the farthest reaches of our wards.

"Yeah, well, Dad always tried to tell us." Brennan's voice softens. "In a world of dragon riders, gryphon fliers, and dark wielders…"

"It's the scribes who hold all the power." They put out the public announcements. They keep the records. They write our history. "Do you think Dad knew?" The idea of him structuring my entire existence around facts and knowledge, only to withhold the most important of it, is unfathomable.

"I choose to believe he didn't." Brennan offers me a sad smile.

"Word will get out the closer those forces come to the border. They can't keep the truth hidden. Someone will see. Someone *has* to see."

"Yes, and our revolution has to be ready when they do. The second the secret is out, there's no reason to keep the marked ones under supervision of leadership, and we'll lose access to Basgiath's forge."

There's that word again: *revolution.*

"You think you can win."

"What makes you say that?" He turns toward me.

"You call it a revolution, not a rebellion." I lift my brow. "Tyrrish isn't the only thing Dad taught us both. You think you can win—unlike Fen Riorson."

"We *have* to win, or we're dead. All of us. Navarre thinks they're safe behind the wards, but what happens if the wards fail? If they're not as powerful as leadership thinks they are? They're already extended to their max. Not to mention the people living outside the wards. One way or another, we're outmatched, Vi. We've never seen them organize behind a leader like they did at Resson, and Garrick told us that one got away."

"The Sage." I shudder, wrapping my arms around my middle. "That's what the one who stabbed me called him. I think he was her teacher."

"They're *teaching* each other? Like they've set up some sort of school for venin? Fucking great." He shakes his head.

"And you're not behind the wards," I note. "Not here." The protective magical shield provided by the dragons' hatching grounds in the Vale falls short of the official, mountainous borders of Navarre, and the entire southwestern coastline of Tyrrendor—including Aretia—is exposed. A fact that never quite mattered when we thought gryphons were the only danger out there, since they're incapable of flying high enough to summit the cliffs.

"Not here," he agrees. "Though funnily enough, Aretia has a dormant wardstone. At least, I think that's what it is. I was never let close enough to Basgiath's to compare the two in any detail."

My eyebrows rise. A second wardstone? "I thought only one was created during the Unification."

"Yeah, and I thought venin were a myth and dragons were the only key to powering wards." He shrugs. "But the art of creating new wards is a lost magic, anyway, so it's basically a glorified statue. Pretty to look at, though."

"You have a wardstone," I murmur, my thoughts spinning. They wouldn't need as many weapons if they had wards. If they could generate their own protection, maybe they could weave extensions *into* Poromiel, like we've expanded our wards to their max. Maybe we could keep at least some of our neighbors safe…

"A *useless* one. What we need is that godsdamned luminary that intensifies dragonfire hot enough to smelt alloy into the only weapons capable of defeating venin. That's our only shot."

"But what if the wardstone isn't useless?" My heart races. We'd only ever been told there was one wardstone in existence, its boundaries stretched as far as possible. But if there's another… "Just because no one knows how to create new wards today doesn't mean the knowledge can't exist *somewhere*. Like in the Archives. That's information we wouldn't have wiped. We would have protected it at all costs, just in case."

"Violet, whatever you're thinking? Don't." He rubs his thumb along his chin, which has always been his nervous tell. Amazing the things I'm remembering about him. "Consider the Archives enemy territory. Weapons are the only thing that can win this war."

"But you don't have a working forge or enough riders to defend yourself if Navarre realizes what you're up to." Panic crawls up my spine like a spider. "And you think you're going to win this war with a bunch of *daggers*?"

"You make it sound like we're doomed. We're not." A muscle ticks in his jaw.

"The first separatist rebellion was crushed in under a year, and up until a few days ago, I thought it took you, too." He doesn't get it. He can't. He didn't bury *his* family. "I've already watched your things burn once."

"Vi…" He hesitates for a second, then wraps his arms around me and pulls me into a hug, rocking slightly like I'm a kid again. "We learned from Fen's mistakes. We're not attacking Navarre like he did or declaring independence. We're fighting right under their noses, and we have a plan. *Something* killed off the venin six hundred years ago during the Great War, and we're actively searching for that weapon. Forging the daggers will keep us in the fight long enough to find it, as long as we can get that luminary. We might not be ready now, but we will be once Navarre catches on." His tone isn't exactly convincing.

I take a step back. "With what army? How many of you are there in this revolution?" How many will die this time?

"It's best if you don't know specifics—" He tenses, then reaches for me again.

"I've already put you in danger by telling you too much. At least until you can shield Aetos out."

My chest constricts, and I sidestep from his embrace. "You sound like Xaden." I can't help the bitterness that leaches into my tone. Turns out, falling in love with someone only brings that blissful high all the poets talk about if they love you back. And if they keep secrets that jeopardize everyone and everything you hold dear? Love doesn't even have the decency to die. It just transforms into abject misery. That's what this ache in my chest is: misery.

Because love, at its root, is hope. Hope for tomorrow. Hope for what could be. Hope that the someone you've entrusted your everything to will cradle and protect it. And hope? That shit is harder to kill than a dragon.

A slight hum tingles under my skin, and warmth flushes my cheeks as Tairn's power rises within me in answer to my heightened emotions. At least I know I still have access to it. The venin's poison didn't take it from me permanently. I'm still *me*.

"Ah." Brennan shoots me a look I can't quite interpret. "I wondered why he ran out of here like his ass was on fire. Trouble in paradise?"

I flat-out glare at Brennan. "It's best if *you* don't know *that*."

He chuckles. "Hey, I'm asking my sister, not Cadet Sorrengail."

"And you've been back in my life all of five minutes after faking your death for the last six years, so excuse me if I'm not going to suddenly open up about my love life. What about you? Are you married? Kids? Anyone you've basically lied to for the entirety of your relationship?"

He flinches. "No partner. No kids. Point made." Shoving his hands into the pockets of his riding leathers, he sighs. "Look, I don't mean to be an ass. But details aren't anything you should know until you master keeping your shields up at all times against memory readers—"

I cringe at the thought of Dain touching me, seeing this, seeing *Brennan*. "You're right. Don't tell me."

Brennan's eyes narrow. "You agreed entirely too easily."

I shake my head and start for the door, calling over my shoulder, "I need to leave before I get someone else killed." The more I see, the bigger of a liability I am to him, to all of this. And the longer we're here… Gods. The others.

"We have to go back," I tell Tairn.

"I know."

Brennan's jaw flexes as he catches up to me. "I'm not sure going back to Basgiath is the best plan for you." He pulls the door open anyway.

"No, but it's the best plan for *you*."

...

I'm nervous as hell by the time Brennan and his Orange Daggertail, Marbh, as well as Tairn and I, reach Sgaeyl—Xaden's enormous, navy-blue daggertail, who stands under the shade of several even taller trees as though guarding something. *Andarna.* Sgaeyl snarls at Brennan, baring her fangs and taking one threatening step in his direction, her claw fully extended in a series of sharp talons.

"Hey! That's my brother," I warn her, putting myself between them.

"She's aware," Brennan mutters. "Just doesn't like me. Never has."

"Don't take it personally," I say right to her face. "She doesn't like anyone but Xaden, and she only tolerates me, though I'm growing on her."

"Like a tumor," she replies through the mental bond that connects the four of us. Then her head swings, and I feel it.

The shadowy, shimmering bond at the edge of my mind strengthens and pulls gently. "In fact, Xaden's walking this way," I tell Brennan.

"That's really fucking weird." He folds his arms across his chest and looks behind us. "Can you two always sense each other?"

"Kind of. It has to do with the bond between Sgaeyl and Tairn. I'd say you get used to it, but you don't." I walk into the copse, and Sgaeyl does me a solid favor and doesn't make me ask her to move, taking two steps to the right so I'm in between her and Tairn, directly in front of...

What. The. Fuck?

That can't be... No. Impossible.

"Stay calm. She'll respond to your agitation and wake in a temper," Tairn warns.

I stare at the sleeping dragon—who is almost twice the size she had been a few days ago—and try to get my thoughts to line up with what I'm seeing, what my heart already knows thanks to the bond between us. "That's..." I shake my head, and my pulse begins to race.

"Wasn't expecting that," Brennan says quietly. "Riorson left out some details when he reported in this morning. I've never seen such accelerated growth in a dragon before."

"Her scales are black." Yeah, saying it doesn't help make it feel any more real.

"Dragons are only gold-feathered as hatchlings." Tairn's voice is uncharacteristically patient.

"'Accelerated growth,'" I whisper, repeating Brennan's words, then gasp. "From the energy usage. We forced her to grow. In Resson. She stopped time for too long. We—*I*—forced her to grow." I can't seem to stop saying it.

"It would have happened eventually, Silver One, if at a slower pace."

"Is she full-grown?" I can't take my eyes off her.

"No. She's what you would call an adolescent. We need to get her back to the Vale so she can enter the Dreamless Sleep and finish the growth process. I should warn you before she wakes that this is a notoriously…perilous age."

"For her? Is she in danger?" My gaze swings to Tairn for the length of a terrorizing heartbeat.

"No, just everyone around her. There's a reason adolescents don't bond, either. They don't have the patience for humans. Or elders. Or logic," he grumbles.

"So, the same as humans." A teenager. Fabulous.

"Except with teeth and, eventually, fire."

Her scales are so deeply black they glimmer almost purple—iridescent, really—in the flickering sunlight that filters through the leaves above. The color of a dragon's scales is hereditary—

"Wait a second. Is she *yours*?" I ask Tairn. "I swear to the gods, if she's another secret you kept from me, I'll—"

"I told you last year, she is not our progeny," Tairn answers, drawing up his head as if offended. *"Black dragons are rare but not unheard of."*

"And I happened to bond to two of them?" I counter, outright glaring at him.

"Technically, she was gold when you bonded her. Not even she knew what color her scales would mature to. Only the eldest of our dens can sense a hatchling's pigment. In fact, two more black dragons have hatched in the last year, according to Codagh."

"Not helping." I let Andarna's steady breathing assure me that she really is fine. Giant but…fine. I can still see her features—her slightly more rounded snout, the spiral twist carved into her curled horns, even the way she tucks her wings in while sleeping is all…her, only bigger. "If there's a morningstartail on her—"

"Tails are a matter of choice and need." He huffs indignantly. *"Don't they teach you anything?"*

"You're not exactly a notoriously open species." I'm sure Professor Kaori would salivate over knowing something like that.

That shadowy bond wrapped around my mind strengthens.

"Is she awake yet?" The deep timbre of Xaden's voice makes my pulse skip like always.

I turn around to see him standing beside Brennan, with Imogen, Garrick, Bodhi, and the others flanking him in the tall grass. My gaze catches on the cadets I don't know. Two men and one woman. It's more than awkward that I went to war with them and yet I've only seen them in passing in the halls. I couldn't even chance a guess at their names without feeling foolish. It's not like

Basgiath is made to foster friendships outside our squads, though.

Or relationships, for that matter.

I'll spend every single day of my life earning back your trust. The memory of Xaden's words fills the space between us as we stare at each other.

"We have to go back." I fold my arms across my chest, preparing for a fight. "No matter what that Assembly says, if we don't go back, they'll kill every cadet with a rebellion relic."

Xaden nods, as though he'd already come to the same conclusion.

"They'll see right through whatever lie you're going to tell, and they'll execute you, Violet," Brennan retorts. "According to our intelligence, General Sorrengail already knows you're missing."

She wasn't there on the dais when War Games orders were handed out. Her aide, Colonel Aetos, was in charge of the games this year.

She didn't know.

"Our mother won't let them kill me."

"Say that again," Brennan says softly. He tilts his head at me and looks so much like our father that I blink twice. "And this time try to convince yourself that you mean it. The general's loyalties are so crystal-fucking-clear that she might as well tattoo *Yes there are venin, now go back to class* on her forehead."

"That doesn't mean she'll kill me. I can make her believe our story. She'll *want* to if I'm the one telling it."

"You don't think she'll kill you? She threw you into the Riders Quadrant!"

Fine, he has me there. "Yeah, she did, and guess what? I became a rider. She may be a lot of things, but she *won't* let Colonel Aetos or even Markham kill me without evidence. You didn't see her when you didn't come home, Brennan. She was…devastated."

His hands curl into fists. "I know the atrocious things she did in my name."

"She wasn't there," one of the guys I don't know says, putting up his hands when the rest turn to glare at him. He's shorter than the others, with a Third Squad, Flame Section patch on his shoulder, light-brown hair, and a pinkish, round face that reminds me of the cherubs usually carved at the feet of statues of Amari.

"Seriously, Ciaran?" The brunette second-year lifts a hand to her forehead, shielding her fair skin from the sun and revealing a First Squad, Flame Section patch on her shoulder, then lifts a pierced eyebrow at him. "You're defending General Sorrengail?"

"No, Eya, I'm not. But she wasn't there when orders were handed out—" He cuts off the sentence as two eyebrows slash down in warning. "And Aetos was in charge of War Games this year," he adds.

Ciaran and Eya. I look to the lean guy, who pushes his glasses up his pointed nose with a dark-brown hand, standing next to Garrick's hulking build. "I'm so sorry, but what is your name?" It feels wrong to not know them all.

"Masen," he replies with a quick smile. "And if it makes you feel better"— he glances at Brennan—"I don't think your mom had anything to do with the War Games this year, either. Aetos was pretty loud about his dad planning the whole thing."

Fucking *Dain*.

"Thank you." I turn toward Brennan. "I would bet my life that she didn't know what was waiting for us."

"You willing to bet all of ours, too?" Eya asks, clearly not convinced, looking at Imogen for support and not getting any.

"I vote we go," Garrick says. "We have to risk it. They'll kill the others if we don't return, and we can't cut off the flow of weapons from Basgiath. Who agrees?"

One by one, every hand rises but Xaden's and Brennan's.

Xaden's jaw flexes, and two little lines appear between his brows. I know that expression. He's thinking, scheming.

"The second Aetos puts hands on her, we lose Aretia and you lose your lives," Brennan says to him.

"I'll train her to shut him out," Xaden responds. "She already has the strongest shields of her year from learning to shut out Tairn. She only has to learn to keep them up at all times."

I don't argue. He has a direct link to my mind through the bond, which makes him the most logical choice to practice on.

"And until she can shield out a memory reader? How are you going to keep his hands off her if you're not even *there*?" Brennan challenges.

"By hitting him in his biggest weakness—his pride." Xaden's mouth curves into a ruthless smile. "If everyone is sure about going, we'll fly as soon as Andarna's awake."

"We're sure," Garrick answers for us, and I try to swallow the knot forming in my throat.

It's the right decision. It could also get us killed.

A rustling behind me catches my attention, and I turn to see Andarna rise, her golden eyes blinking slowly at me as she clumsily gains her newly taloned claws. The relief and joy curving my mouth are short-lived as she struggles to stand.

Oh…gods. She reminds me of a newborn horse. Her wings and legs seem disproportionate to her body, and *everything* wobbles as she fights to keep upright. There's no way she's making the flight. I'm not even sure she can walk across the field.

"Hey," I say, offering her a smile.

"I can no longer stop time." She watches me carefully, her golden eyes judging me in a way that reminds me of Presentation.

"I know." I nod and study the coppery streaks in her eyes. Were those always there?

"You are not disappointed?"

"You're alive. You kept us *all* alive. How could I be disappointed?" My chest tightens as I stare into her unblinking eyes, choosing my next words carefully. "We always knew that gift would only last as long as you were little, and you, my dearest, are no longer little." A growl rumbles in her chest, and my eyebrows shoot up. "Are you...feeling okay?" What the hell did I say to deserve *that*?

"Adolescents," Tairn grumbles.

"I am fine," she snaps, narrowing her eyes at Tairn. *"We will leave now."* She flares her wings out, but only one fully extends, and she stumbles under the uneven weight, careening forward.

Xaden's shadows whip out from the trees and wrap around her chest, keeping her from face-planting.

Well. Shit.

"I...uh...think we're going to have to make some modifications on that harness," Bodhi remarks as Andarna struggles to maintain her balance. "That's going to take a few hours."

"Can you fly her back to the Vale?" I ask Tairn. *"She's...huge."*

"I've killed lesser riders for that kind of insult."

"So dramatic."

"I can fly myself," Andarna argues, gaining her balance with the aid of Xaden's shadows.

"It's just in case," I promise her, but she eyes me with deserved skepticism.

"Get the harness done quickly," Xaden says. "I have a plan, but we have to be back in forty-eight hours for this to work, and a day of that is needed for flight time."

"What's in forty-eight hours?" I ask.

"Graduation."

There is no moment as rewarding, as stirring, as…anticlimactic as a Riders Quadrant Graduation. It's the only time I've ever envied the Infantry Quadrant. Now *those* cadets know how to hold a ceremony.

—MAJOR AFENDRA'S GUIDE TO THE RIDERS QUADRANT
(UNAUTHORIZED EDITION)

CHAPTER THREE

The flight field at Basgiath is still dark and appears deserted when we approach in the hour before sunrise, hugging the landscape of the mountains, the riot doing what they can to stay out of sight.

"That doesn't mean someone won't spot us landing," Tairn reminds me, his wings beating steadily despite having flown the last eighteen hours nearly straight through from Aretia. The window of time we have to get Andarna to the Vale without her being spotted is slim, and if we miss it, we'll put every hatchling in danger.

"I still don't understand why the Empyrean would ever agree to let dragons bond human riders, knowing they'd have to guard their own young not only against gryphon fliers but the very humans they're supposed to trust."

"It's a delicate balance," Tairn replies, banking left to follow the geography. *"The First Six riders were desperate to save their people when they approached the dens over six hundred years ago. Those dragons formed the first Empyrean and bonded humans only to protect their hatching grounds from venin, who were the bigger threat. We don't exactly have opposable thumbs for weaving wards or runes. Neither species has ever been entirely truthful, both using the other for their own reasons and nothing more."*

"It never occurred to me to hide anything from you."

Tairn does that weird thing that makes his neck appear boneless, swinging his head around to level slightly narrowed eyes at me for a heartbeat before turning his attention back to the terrain. *"I can do nothing to remedy the last nine months besides answer your worthwhile questions now."*

"I know," I say quietly, wishing his words were enough to cut through the acrid taste of betrayal I can't seem to wash out of my mouth. I'm going to have to let it go. I know that. Tairn was bound by his mating bond to Sgaeyl, so at least he had a reason to keep everything he did from me, and it's not like I can blame Andarna for being a kid who followed his lead. Xaden is another matter entirely, though.

"We're approaching. Get ready."

"Guess we should have worked on rolling dismounts earlier in the year," I joke, gripping the pommel of my saddle tight as Tairn banks, my weight shifting right with him. My body is going to punish me for the hours in the saddle, but I wouldn't trade the feel of the summer wind against my face for anything.

"A rolling dismount would tear you limb from limb on impact," he retorts.

"You don't know that," Andarna counters with what seems to be her new default form of conversation—telling Tairn he's wrong.

A growl rumbles through Tairn's chest, vibrating the saddle beneath me and the harness that holds Andarna to his chest.

"I'd watch it," I tell her, biting back a smile. *"He might get tired and drop you."*

"His pride would never allow it."

"Says the dragon who spent twenty minutes refusing to put on her harness," Tairn fires back.

"All right, kids, let's not argue." My muscles tighten, and the strap across my thighs digs in as Tairn dives, skimming the edge of Mount Basgiath, bringing the flight field into view again.

"Still deserted," Tairn notes.

"You know, rolling dismounts are a second-year maneuver." Not necessarily one I want to master, but that doesn't change the requirements.

"One you won't be participating in," Tairn grumbles.

"Maybe I'll take her if you won't," Andarna chimes in, the last word ending in a dragon-size yawn.

"Maybe you should work on your own landings before taking our bonded on a flight to meet Malek?"

This is going to be a long year.

My stomach plummets as he drops into the box canyon known as the flight field.

"I will drop Andarna in the Vale and then return and circle nearby."

"You need rest."

"There will be no rest if they decide to execute the eight of you on the dais." The worry in his voice clogs my throat. *"Call out if you even suspect it will not*

go your way."

"It will," I assure him. *"Do me a favor and tell Sgaeyl that I need to talk to Xaden on the walk in."*

"Hold on tight."

The ground rushes to meet us, and I reach for the strap across my thighs, my fingers working the buckle as Tairn flares his wings to rapidly slow our descent. My momentum throws me forward as he touches down, and I force my ass back in the seat before yanking the belt off.

"Get her out of here," I tell him as I scramble for his shoulder, ignoring every muscle that dares to ache.

"Do not take unnecessary risk," he says as I slide down his foreleg at the steep incline Andarna's position forces him to keep.

My feet slam into the ground and I stumble forward, catching my balance. "Love you, too," I whisper, turning long enough to pat his leg and Andarna's before running forward to get the hell out of their way.

Tairn whips his head to the right, where Sgaeyl lands with brutal efficiency, her rider dismounting in the same manner. *"The wingleader approaches."*

He'll only be my wingleader for another few hours if we live through this.

Xaden gives Tairn a wide berth to launch as he walks toward me.

Sgaeyl takes off next, followed by the rest of the riot. Guess we're on our own now.

I lift my goggles to the top of my head and unzip my jacket. July at Basgiath is muggy as hell, even this early.

"You actually told Tairn to tell Sgaeyl that you wanted to talk to me?" Xaden asks as the sun's first rays color the tips of the mountains purple.

"I did." I run my hands across my sheaths, checking to make sure my daggers weren't displaced during flight as we walk out of the flight field slightly ahead of the others, heading toward the steps that will bypass the Gauntlet and lead us back to the quadrant.

"You remember that you can…" He taps the side of his head and walks backward in front of me. I clench my fists to keep from brushing a lock of dark, windblown hair off his forehead. A few days ago, I would have touched him without reservation. Hell, I would have threaded my fingers through his hair and pulled him in for a kiss.

But that was then, and this is now.

"Talking that way feels a little too…" Gods, why is this so hard? It feels like every inch I sacrificed for in the last year when it comes to Xaden has been erased, putting us back at the starting line of an obstacle course I'm not sure either one of us ever chose to run. I shrug. "Intimate."

"And we're not intimate?" He lifts his brows. "Because I can think of more than one occasion that you've been wrapped around—"

I jolt forward and cover his mouth with my hand. "Don't." Ignoring the explosive chemistry between us is hard enough without him reminding me what we feel like together. Physically, our relationship—or whatever we are—is perfect. Better than perfect. It's hot as hell and more than addictive. My entire body warms as he kisses the sensitive skin of my palm. I drop my hand. "We're walking into what's certainly going to be a trial, if not an execution, and you've got jokes."

"Trust me—not joking." He turns as we reach the steps and heads down first, glancing back over his shoulder at me. "Surprised that you're not icing me out, but definitely no jokes."

"I'm angry with you for keeping information from me. Ignoring you doesn't solve that."

"Good point. What did you want to talk about?"

"I have a question I've been thinking about since Aretia."

"And you're only now telling me?" He reaches the bottom of the steps and shoots an incredulous look at me. "Communication is not your strength, is it? Don't worry. We'll work on it along with your shielding."

"That's…ironic coming from you." We start up the path to the quadrant as the sun steadily rises on our right, the light catching on the two swords Xaden has strapped to his back. "Does the movement have any scribes it can count as friends?"

"No." The citadel looms ahead of us, its towers peeking over the edge of the ridgeline the tunnel runs through. "I know you grew up trusting a lot of them—"

"Don't say anything else." I shake my head. "Not until I can protect myself from Dain."

"Honestly, I've considered scrapping the plan and just throwing him off the parapet." He means it, and I can't blame him. He's never trusted Dain, and after what happened during War Games, I'm about ninety-nine percent sure I can't trust him, either. It's that one percent, constantly screaming at me that he used to be my best friend, that's the kicker.

The one percent that makes me question if Dain knows what was waiting for us at Athebyne. "Helpful, but I'm not sure it will have the *trust us* effect we're going for."

"And do you trust *me*?"

"You want the uncomplicated answer?"

"Given our limited alone time, that's preferable." He stops at the tall doors that lead into the tunnel.

"With my life. After all, it's your life, too." The rest depends on how open he is with me, but now probably isn't the time for a state-of-our-relationship talk.

I swear there's a flash of disappointment in his eyes before he nods, then looks back for the other six, who are quickly catching up. "I'll make sure Aetos keeps his hands to himself, but you might have to play along."

"Give me a shot at handling it first. Then you can do whatever it is you think will work." The bells of Basgiath interrupt, announcing the hour. We have fifteen minutes until formation will be called for graduation.

Xaden's shoulders straighten as the others reach us, his expression shifting into an unreadable mask. "Everyone clear on what's about to happen?"

This isn't the man who begged my forgiveness for keeping secrets, and it sure as hell isn't the one who vowed to earn back my trust in Aretia. No, this Xaden is the wingleader who slaughtered every attacker in my bedroom without breaking a sweat or losing a minute of sleep over it afterward.

"We're ready," Garrick says, rolling his neck like he needs to warm up before combat.

"Ready." Masen nods, adjusting the glasses on his nose.

One by one, they agree.

"Let's do it." I lift my chin.

Xaden stares long and hard at me, then nods.

My stomach twists when we enter the tunnel, mage lights flickering on as we pass. The other door is already open when we make our way through, and I don't argue when Xaden plasters himself to my side. There's every chance we'll be arrested as soon as our feet touch the quadrant, or worse, killed, depending on what everyone knows.

Power rises within me, thrumming beneath my skin, not quite burning but ready if I need it, but no one appears as we cross into the rock-filled courtyard. We have minutes until this space fills with riders and cadre.

The first riders we encounter walk out of the dormitory and into the courtyard with cocky swaggers and Second Wing patches on their uniforms.

"Look who's finally here? Bet you thought you had the games locked down, didn't you, Fourth Wing?" a rider with hair dyed forest green says with a smirk. "But you didn't! Second Wing took it *all* when you didn't show!"

Xaden doesn't bother looking their direction as we pass.

Garrick lifts his middle finger from my other side.

"Guess this means no one knows what really happened," Imogen whispers.

"Then we have a shot of this working," Eya replies, and the sunlight glints in the piercing in her eyebrow.

"Of course no one fucking knows," Xaden mutters. He looks up to the top of the academic building, and I follow his line of sight, my heart clenching at the image of the fire blazing in the pit on top of the farthest turret. No doubt waiting for offerings to Malek—belongings of the cadets who didn't make it through

War Games. "They're not going to out themselves over us."

At the entrance to the dorms, we all exchange a look, then break apart wordlessly according to the plan. Xaden follows me down the corridor and into the little hallway I've called home for the last nine months, but it's not my room I'm interested in.

I glance left and right to be sure no one sees us as Xaden opens Liam's door. He motions at me, and I slip under his arm and into the room, triggering the mage light overhead.

My chest threatens to cave with the weight of grief as Xaden shuts the door behind us. Liam slept in that bed a matter of nights ago. He studied at that desk. He worked on the half-finished figurines on the bedside table.

"You have to be quick," Xaden reminds me.

"I will," I promise, going straight for his desk. There's nothing there besides his books and a selection of pens. I check his wardrobe, the dresser, and the chest at the foot of his bed, coming up empty-handed.

"Violet," Xaden warns me quietly, standing guard at the door.

"I know," I say over my shoulder. The second Tairn and Sgaeyl arrived in the Vale, every dragon would know they'd returned, which means every member of the quadrant's leadership knows we're here, too.

I lift the corner of the heavy mattress and sigh with relief, snatching the twine-bound stack of letters before letting the bedding fall back into place.

"Got them." I will *not* cry. Not when I still have to hide them in my room.

But what will happen if they come to burn my things next?

"Let's go." Xaden opens the door, and I walk into the hallway at the same moment Rhiannon—my closest friend in the quadrant—walks out of her room with Ridoc, another of our squadmates.

Oh. Shit.

"Vi!" Rhi's mouth drops open and she lunges, grabbing onto me and pulling me into a hug. "You're here!" She squeezes tight, and I let myself relax into the embrace for the length of a heartbeat. It feels like forever since I've seen her, not six days.

"I'm here," I assure her, gripping the letters in the crook of one arm and wrapping the other around her.

She squeezes my shoulders, then pushes me back, her brown eyes scanning my face in a way that makes me feel like complete shit for the lie I'm going to have to tell. "With what everyone was saying, I thought you were dead." Her gaze rises over my head. "Thought you both were."

"There was also the rumor that you got lost," Ridoc adds. "But considering who you were with, we were all betting on the dead theory. I'm glad we were wrong."

"I promise I'll explain later, but I need a favor now," I whisper as my throat closes.

"Violet." Xaden's tone drops.

"We can trust her," I promise, looking back at him. "Ridoc too."

Xaden looks anything but pleased. Guess we really are home.

"What do you need?" Rhi asks, concern furrowing her brow.

I step back, then push the letters into her hands. Her family doesn't always obey the custom of burning everything, either. She'll understand. "I need you to keep these for me. Hide them. Don't let anyone…burn them." My voice breaks.

She glances down at the letters, and her eyes widen before her shoulders curve inward and her face crumples.

"What are tho—" Ridoc starts, looking over her shoulder and falling silent. "Shit."

"No," Rhiannon whispers, but I know she's not denying me the favor. "Not Liam. No." Her gaze slowly rises to meet mine.

My eyes burn but I manage to nod, clearing my throat. "Promise you won't let them have these when they come for his things if I'm not—" I can't finish.

Rhiannon nods. "You're not hurt, are you?" She scans me again, blinking at the line of stitchwork on my flight jacket, where the hole from the venin's blade was repaired in Aretia.

I shake my head. I'm not lying. Not really. My body is perfectly healthy now.

"We have to go," Xaden says.

"I'll see you guys at graduation." I give them a watery smile but take a step toward Xaden. The more space my friends have from me, the safer they'll be for the foreseeable future.

"How do you do it?" I whisper at Xaden as we turn the corner into the crowded main corridor of the first-year dorms.

"Do what?" His arms hang loose at his sides as he continuously scans the people around us, and he puts his hand on my lower back like he's worried we might get separated. We're in the thick of the rush, and for every person too busy to notice us, there's another who does a double take when we cross paths. Every marked one we see gives Xaden a subtle nod, signaling that they've been warned by the others.

"Lie to the people you care about?"

Our gazes collide.

We pass one of the busts of the First Six and follow the flow of the crowd past the wide spiral staircase that connects the higher-years' dorms.

Xaden's jaw clenches. "Vi—"

I lift my hand and cut him off. "It's not an insult. I need to know how to do it."

We break away from the crush of cadets headed out the door to the courtyard, and Xaden strides purposefully for the rotunda, yanking open the door and ushering me through. I step away from the hand he places on my lower back.

Zihnal must be smiling on us, because the room is blessedly empty for the second it takes Xaden to tug me behind the first pillar we come to. The red dragon hides us from anyone who might pass through the space that connects all wings of the quadrant.

Sure enough, voices and footsteps fill the vaulted chamber a moment later, but no one sees us behind the massive pillar, which is exactly why this is our chosen meeting place. I glance around Xaden, noting the emptiness behind the pillars that flank us. Either everyone else is on the other side of the rotunda, or we're the first to arrive.

"For the record, I don't lie to the people I care about." Xaden lowers his voice as he faces me, the intensity in his eyes pinning my back to the marble pillar. He leans in, consuming my field of vision until he's all I see. "And I sure as hell have *never* lied to you. But the art of telling selective truths is something you're going to have to master or we'll all be dead. I know you trust Rhiannon and Ridoc, but you can't tell them the truth, as much for their sakes as for ours. Knowing puts them in danger. You have to be able to keep the truth compartmentalized. If you can't lie to your friends, you keep your distance. Understand?"

I tense. Of course I know that, but hearing it said so blatantly drives the situation home like a knife to my stomach. "I understand."

"I never wanted you put in this position. Not with your friends and especially not with Colonel Aetos. That was one of the many reasons why I never told you."

"How long did you know about Brennan?" It might not be the right time, but suddenly it's the *only* time.

He exhales slowly. "I've known about Brennan since his *death*."

My lips part and something heavy shifts, easing a weight in my chest that's been there since Resson.

"What?"

"You didn't dodge the question." Have to admit, I'm a little surprised.

"I promised you some answers." He leans forward. "But I can't promise you'll like what you hear."

"I'll always prefer the truth." *Some* answers?

"You say that now." A wry smile twists his lips.

"I *always* will." The sounds of boots shuffling behind us as students report for formation reminds me that we're not entirely alone, but I need Xaden to hear this. "If the last few weeks have shown you anything, it should be that I don't run from truth, no matter how hard it is or what it costs."

"Yeah, well, it cost me *you*." My whole body tenses and his eyes slam shut. "Shit. I shouldn't have said that." He opens them again, shaking his head, and the abject misery there makes my heart clench. "I know it was the *not* telling you. I get it. But when the lives of everyone around you depend on how well you can lie, it's not easy to realize it's the truth that will save you." A sigh moves his shoulders. "If I could do it all again, I'd do it differently, I promise, but I can't, so here we are."

"Here we are." And I'm not even sure where *here* is. I shift my weight. "But as long as you meant what you said about telling me everything—"

He flinches, and my heart sinks.

"You *are* going to tell me everything once I can properly shield, right?" It's all I can do not to grab onto him and start shaking. Hard. "That's what you promised in your bedroom." He is *not* doing this to me. "'Anything you want to know and everything you *don't*.' Those were your words."

"Everything about *me*."

Oh, fuck me, he *is* doing this to me. Again.

I shake my head. "That is *not* what you promised."

Xaden starts to take a step toward me, but I lift my chin, daring him to touch me right now. Smart man that he is, he keeps his feet planted.

He runs a hand through his hair and sighs. "Look, I will answer any question you want to ask about *me*. Gods, I *want* you to ask, to know me well enough to trust me even when I *can't* tell you everything." He nods like those words had been included in the original promise when we both know damn well they weren't. "Because you didn't fall for an ordinary rider. You fell for the leader of a revolution," he whispers, the sound so soft it barely carries to my ears. "To some degree, I'm always going to have secrets."

"You have to be kidding me." I let anger rush to the surface in hopes it will burn away the heartrending pain of his words. Brennan's been lying to me for six years, letting me mourn his death when he's been well-the-fuck alive the whole time. My oldest friend stole my memories and possibly sent me to die. My mother built my entire *life* on a lie. I'm not even sure what parts of my education are real and which are fabricated, and he thinks I'm *not* going to demand total, complete honesty from him?

"I'm not kidding." There's zero apology in his tone. "But that doesn't mean I won't let you in like I promised. I'm an open book when it comes to—"

"Whatever *you* want." I shake my head. "And that's *not* going to work for me. Not this time. I can't trust you again without full disclosure. Period."

He blinks as though I've actually managed to stun him.

"Full. Disclosure," I demand like any rational woman staring down the man who kept her brother's life a secret from her, let alone an entire war. "I can forgive you for keeping me in the dark before today. You did it to save lives, possibly even mine. But it's complete and *total* honesty from now on, or…" Gods, am I going to have to say it?

Am I really about to issue an ultimatum to Xaden-fucking-Riorson?

"Or what?" He leans in, his eyes sharpening.

"Or I'll get busy *un*falling for you," I spit out.

Surprise flares in his eyes a second before a corner of his mouth lifts into a smirk. "Good luck with that. I tried it for a good five months. Let me know how it works out for you."

I scoff, at a complete loss for words as the bells chime, announcing the beginning of formation.

"It's time," he says. "Keep your shields up. Block everyone out like we practiced on the way here."

"I can't even keep *you* out."

"You'll find I'm harder to block than most." His smirk is so infuriating, I ball my hands just to give my fists something else to do.

"Hey, I hate to interrupt what's obviously a moment," Bodhi whispers loudly from my left. "But that was the last bell, so that's our cue to get this nightmare started."

Xaden shoots a glare at his cousin, but we both nod. He doesn't do his friends the dishonor of asking if they accomplished their missions as all eight of us walk into the center of the rotunda.

My stomach jumps into my throat as the death roll sounds from the courtyard. "I will not die today," I whisper to myself.

"I really fucking hope you're right about this," Garrick says to Xaden as we face the open door. "It would be unfortunate to make it all three years and then die on graduation day."

"I'm right." Xaden walks out and we all follow, stepping into the sunlight.

"Garrick Tavis. Xaden Riorson." Captain Fitzgibbons's voice carries over the formation as he reads from the death roll.

"Well, this is awkward," Xaden calls out.

And every head in the courtyard turns our direction.

As dragons ferociously guard both their young and any information regarding their development, only four facts are known about the Dreamless Sleep. First, it is a critical time of rapid growth and development. Second, the duration varies from breed to breed. Third, as the name suggests, it is dreamless, and fourth, they wake up hungry.

—Colonel Kaori's Field Guide to Dragonkind

CHAPTER FOUR

My heart beats fast enough to keep time with a hummingbird's wings as we walk across the courtyard toward the dais, Xaden two steps ahead of the rest of us. He moves without fear, his shoulders straight and head high, anger manifesting in every purposeful stride, every tight line of his body.

I lift my chin and focus on the platform ahead as gravel crunches beneath my boots, the sound muffling more than one gasp from the cadets on my left. I might not have Xaden's confidence, but I can fake it.

"You're…not dead." Captain Fitzgibbons, the scribe assigned to the Riders Quadrant, stares with wide eyes beneath his silver brows, his weathered face turning the same pale cream of his uniform as he fumbles with the death roll, dropping it.

"Apparently not," Xaden replies.

It's almost comical how Commandant Panchek's mouth hangs open as he turns toward us from his seat on the dais, and within seconds, my mother and Colonel Aetos stand, blocking his view.

Jesinia steps forward, her brown eyes wide under her cream hood as she fetches the death roll for Captain Fitzgibbons. "I'm happy you're alive," she signs quickly before grabbing the roll.

"Me, too," I sign back, a sick feeling taking hold. Does she know what her quadrant is really teaching her? Neither of us had a clue during the months and years we studied together.

Colonel Aetos's cheeks grow increasingly red with every step we take, his gaze skimming our party of eight, no doubt taking note of who's here and who isn't.

My mother locks eyes with me for one heartbeat, a side of her mouth tilting upward in an expression I'm almost scared to call…pride, before she quickly masks it, resuming the professional distance she's maintained impeccably for the last year. One heartbeat. That's all it takes for me to know that I'm right. There's no anger in her eyes—no fear or shock, either. Just relief.

She wasn't in on Aetos's plan. I know it with every fiber of my being.

"I don't understand," Fitzgibbons says to the two scribes behind him, then addresses Panchek. "They aren't dead. Why would they have been reported for the death roll?"

"Why *were* they reported for the death roll?" my mother asks Colonel Aetos, her eyes narrowing.

A cold breeze blows past, and though it's a momentary relief from the stifling heat, I know what it really means—the general is pissed. I glance skyward, but there's only blue as far as I can see. At least she hasn't summoned a storm. Yet.

"They've been missing for *six* days!" Aetos seethes, his voice rising with each angry word. "Naturally we reported them dead, but obviously we should have reported them for desertion and dereliction of duty instead."

"You want to report us for desertion?" Xaden walks up the stairs of the dais, and Aetos backs up a step, fear flashing across his eyes. "You sent us into *combat*, and you're going to report us for desertion?" Xaden doesn't need to shout for his voice to carry across the formation.

"What is he talking about?" my mother asks, looking between Xaden and Aetos.

Here we go.

"I have no idea," Aetos grinds out.

"I was directed to take a squad beyond the wards to Athebyne and form the headquarters for Fourth Wing's War Games, and I did so. We stopped to rest our riot at the nearest lake past the wards, and we were attacked by gryphons." The lie rolls off his tongue as smoothly as the truth, which is both impressive…and infuriating, because he doesn't have a single fucking tell.

My mother blinks, and Aetos's thick brows furrow.

"It was a surprise attack, and they caught Deigh and Fuil unaware." Xaden pivots slightly, as though he's telling the wings and not leadership. "They were dead before they ever had a chance."

An ache unfurls in my chest, stealing my breath. The cadets around us murmur, but I stay focused on Xaden.

"We lost Liam Mairi and Soleil Telery," Xaden adds, then looks over his shoulder at me. "And we almost lost Sorrengail."

The general pivots and, for a second, looks down at me like she's not just my commanding officer, with worry and a touch of horror in her eyes. She looks at me like she's just…Mom.

I nod, the pain in my chest intensifying.

"He's lying," Colonel Aetos accuses. The certainty in his voice makes my head swim with the possibility that we might not pull this off, that we might be killed where we stand before we have the chance to convince my mother.

"I'm only behind the ridgeline," Tairn tells me.

"Breathe," Garrick whispers. "Or you'll pass out."

I inhale and focus on steadying my heartbeat.

"Why the hell would I lie?" Xaden tilts his head and looks down at Colonel Aetos with pure disdain. "But surely if you don't believe me, then General Sorrengail can discern the truth from her own daughter."

That's my cue.

Step by step, I ascend the stairs of the thick, wooden platform to stand at Xaden's left side. Sweat drips down the back of my neck as the morning sun beats against my flight leathers.

"Cadet Sorrengail?" My mother folds her arms and looks at me with expectation.

The weight of the quadrant's attention makes me clear my throat. "It's true."

"Lies!" Aetos shouts. "There's no way two dragons were brought down by a drift of gryphons. Impossible. We should separate them and interrogate them individually."

My stomach pitches.

"I hardly think that's necessary," the general responds, an icy blast blowing back the flight-loosened tendrils of my hair. "And I would reconsider your insinuation that a Sorrengail isn't truthful."

Colonel Aetos stiffens.

"Tell me what happened, Cadet Sorrengail." Mom cocks her head to the side and gives me the look—the one she used all throughout my childhood to unravel the truth when Brennan, Mira, and I would join ranks to hide any mischief.

"Selective truth," Xaden reminds me. *"Tell no lies."*

He makes it sound so fucking easy.

"We flew for Athebyne, as ordered." I look her straight in the eyes. "As Riorson said, we stopped at the lake about twenty minutes out so we could water the dragons and dismounted. I only saw two of the gryphons appear with their riders, but everything happened so damned fast. Before I could even get a grasp on what was happening…" *Hold it together.* I brush my hand over my pocket, feeling the ridges of the little carving of Andarna Liam had been working on before he died. "Soleil's dragon was killed, and Deigh was gutted." My eyes water, but I blink until my vision clears. Mom only responds to strength. If I show any sign of weakness, she'll dismiss my account as hysterics. "We didn't stand a chance beyond the wards, General."

"And then?" Mom asks, completely unemotional.

"Then I held Liam as he died," I state, quick to hide the quiver in my chin. "There was nothing we could do for him once Deigh passed." It takes me a second to shove the memories, the emotion, back into the box they have to stay in for this to work. "And before his body was even cold, I was stabbed with a poison-tipped blade."

Mom's eyes flare, and she jerks her gaze away.

I turn my focus to Colonel Aetos. "But when we sought help in Athebyne, we found the entire outpost deserted and a note that Wingleader Riorson could choose to keep watch over a nearby village or race to Eltuval."

"Here's the missive." Xaden reaches into his pocket and pulls out the orders from War Games. "Not sure what the destruction of a foreign village had to do with War Games, but we didn't stick around to find out. Cadet Sorrengail was dying, and I chose to preserve what remained of my squad." He hands the crumpled orders to Mom. "I chose to save your daughter."

She snatches the orders and stiffens.

"It took us *days* to find someone capable of healing me, though I don't remember being healed," I tell them. "And the second my life was out of danger, we flew back here. We arrived about half an hour ago, as I'm sure Aimsir can verify."

"And the bodies?" Aetos asks.

Oh shit. "I…" I have no fucking clue other than Xaden telling me they'd buried Liam.

"Sorrengail wouldn't know," Xaden answers. "She was delirious from the poison. Once we knew there was no help to be found at Athebyne, half the riot flew back to the lake and burned the bodies of both riders and dragons while I took the other half to find help. If you're looking for proof, then you can find it either about a hundred yards from the lake, in the clearing to the east, or in the fresh scars on our dragons."

"Enough." Mom pauses, no doubt confirming with her dragon, then turns slowly toward Colonel Aetos, and though he has a few inches on her, he suddenly appears smaller. Frost blooms on the surface of the dais. "This is your handwriting. You emptied a strategically invaluable outpost beyond the wards for *War Games*?"

"It was only for a few days." He has the good sense to retreat a step. "You told me the games were at my discretion this year."

"And clearly your discretion lacks common fucking sense," she retorts. "I've heard everything I need to hear. Correct the death roll, get these cadets into formation, and commence graduation so the new lieutenants can get to their wings. I expect to see you in my office in thirty minutes, Colonel Aetos."

Relief nearly takes my knees out from under me. She believes me.

Dain's dad stands at attention. "Yes, General."

"You survived a knife wound after being thrown into combat as a first-year," she says to me.

"I did."

She nods, a satisfied half smile curving her mouth for all of a heartbeat. "Maybe you're more like me than I gave you credit for."

Without another word, Mom walks between me and the edge of the dais, leaving us with Colonel Aetos as she heads down the stairs. The frost dissipates instantly, and I hear her footsteps on the gravel behind us as the colonel turns on Xaden and me.

More like her? That's the *last* thing I want to be.

"You will not get away with this," Aetos hisses but keeps his voice low.

"Get away with what, exactly?" Xaden responds, equally quiet.

"We *both* know you weren't taken off-mission by *gryphons*." Spit flies from his mouth.

"What else could have possibly delayed us and slaughtered two dragons and their riders?" I narrow my eyes and let all my rage shine through. He got Liam and Soleil killed. Fuck him. "Surely, if you think there's another threat out there, you'd want to share that information with the rest of the quadrant so we could adequately train to face it."

He glares at me. "You're such a disappointment, Violet."

"Stop," Xaden orders. "You gambled and you lost. You can't expose what you think the truth is without…well, exposing it, can you?" A cruel smile tilts Xaden's lips. "But personally, I think this is all easily solved by a missive to General Melgren. Surely he saw the outcome of our battle with the gryphons."

Satisfaction courses through me at the way the colonel's features slacken.

Thanks to their rebellion relics, Melgren can't confirm *anything* when there are three or more marked ones involved, and Aetos apparently knows it.

"I assume we're dismissed?" Xaden asks. "Not sure if you've noticed, but the entire quadrant is watching rather intently. So unless you'd like me to keep them entertained by retelling what happened to us—"

"Get. In. Formation." He grinds the words out through clenched teeth.

"Gladly, sir." Xaden waits for me to descend the steps, then follows. "It's settled," he tells Garrick. "Get everyone back in formation."

I glance over my shoulder and see Fitzgibbons shaking his head in confusion as he adjusts the death roll, and then I walk over to my squad between Imogen and Xaden.

"You don't have to escort me back," I whisper, ignoring the stares of every cadet we pass.

"I promised your brother I'd handle the other Aetos."

"I can handle Dain." A swift kick to the balls wouldn't be uncalled for, would it?

"We tried your way last year. Now we try mine."

Imogen lifts her eyebrows but doesn't say anything.

"Violet!" Dain breaks formation, moving toward us as we reach Second Squad, Flame Section. The worry and relief that etch the lines of his face make power prickle in my hands.

"You cannot kill him here," Xaden warns.

"You're alive! We'd heard—" Dain reaches for me, and I recoil.

"Touch me and I swear to the gods, I'll cut your fucking hands off and let the quadrant sort you out in the next round of challenges, Dain Aetos." My words earn more than a couple of gasps, but I don't give a shit who hears me.

"Violence, indeed." The hint of amusement in Xaden's tone doesn't reach his face.

"What?" Dain stops dead in his tracks, his eyebrows shooting up into his hairline. "You don't mean that, Vi."

"I do." I rest my hands alongside the sheaths at my thighs.

"You should take her at her word. In fact…" Xaden doesn't bother to lower his voice. "If you don't, I'll take personal offense. She made her choice, and it wasn't you. It will never be you. I know it. She knows it. The whole quadrant knows it."

Oh, just kill me now. Heat flushes my cheeks. Getting caught in his flight jacket before War Games is one thing. Outing us in public—when I'm not sure there *is* an us—is another.

Imogen grins, and I consider the merits of elbowing her in the side.

Dain glances left and right, his face flushing so scarlet I can see the color under the scruff of his light-brown beard as everyone looks on. "What else? You going to threaten to kill me, Riorson?" he retorts, the disgust on his face so similar to his father's that my stomach sours.

"No." Xaden shakes his head. "Why should I, when Sorrengail is perfectly capable of doing that herself? She doesn't want you to touch her. Pretty sure *everyone* in the quadrant heard her. That should be enough for you to keep your hands to yourself." He leans in, his whisper barely reaching my ears. "But in case it's not, every time you think of reaching for her face, I want you to remember one word."

"And what is that?" Dain seethes.

"Athebyne." Xaden pulls back, and the pure menace in his expression sends a shiver along my skin.

Dain's spine stiffens as Colonel Panchek calls the formation to attention.

"No response? Interesting." Xaden's head tilts to the side as he studies Dain's face. "Get back in formation, *squad leader*, before I lose all pretense of civility on behalf of Liam and Soleil."

Dain pales and has the decency to look away before stepping back into his place at the head of our squad.

Xaden's gaze meets mine for a heartbeat before he walks to the front of Fourth Wing.

I should have known going for Dain's pride would include a spectacle.

The squad shuffles, making room for Imogen and me in our usual places, and my face heats at the blatant stares from my friends.

"That was…interesting," Rhiannon whispers at my side, her eyes puffy and red.

"That was hot," Nadine comments from in front of us, standing beside Sawyer.

"Love triangles can get *so* fucking awkward, don't you think?" Imogen says.

I shoot a glare over my shoulder at her for going along with Xaden's implication—or assumption, but she shrugs unapologetically.

"Gods, I missed you." The blue streak in Quinn's short blond curls bobs as she shoulder-bumps Imogen. "War Games sucked. You didn't miss much."

Captain Fitzgibbons steps forward on the dais, sweat dripping down his face as he continues from where we interrupted, reading names from the death roll.

"Seventeen so far," Rhiannon whispers. The final test for War Games is always deadly, ensuring only the strongest riders move on to graduation—but Liam *was* the strongest of our year, and that didn't save him.

"Soleil Telery. Liam Mairi," Captain Fitzgibbons calls out.

I struggle to force air through my lungs and fight the sting in my eyes as the rest of the names blur together until the scribe finishes the roll, commending their souls to Malek.

None of us cry.

Commandant Panchek clears his throat, and though there's no need to magically amplify his voice over the small numbers we've been whittled down to over the last year, he can't seem to help himself. "Beyond military commendations, there are no words of praise for riders. Our reward for a job well done is living to see the next duty station, the next rank. In keeping with our traditions and standards, those of you who have completed your third year will now be commissioned as lieutenants in the army of Navarre. Step forward when your name is called to receive your orders. You have until morning to depart for your new duty stations."

Starting with First Wing, the third-years are named section by section, and each collects their orders before leaving the courtyard.

"It's kind of underwhelming," Ridoc whispers from my other side, earning a glare from Dain as he looks over his shoulder from two rows ahead.

Fuck him.

"Just saying, surviving three years of this place should come with a lifetime supply of ale and a party so good you can't remember it." He shrugs.

"That's for tonight," Quinn says. "Are they…handwriting those orders?"

"For the third-years they thought were dead," Heaton says from the back row.

"Who do you think is going to be our new wingleader?" Nadine whispers from behind me.

"Aura Beinhaven," Rhiannon answers. "She was instrumental in Second Wing's win for War Games, but Aetos didn't do too badly filling in for Riorson, either."

Heaton and Emery are called up from our squad.

I glance at the others, remembering the first-years who started with us but won't finish. The first-years who either lie buried at the foot of Basgiath in endless rows of stones or were taken home to be put to rest. The second-years who will never see a third star on their shoulders. The third-years like Soleil who were certain they'd graduate only to fall.

Maybe this place is exactly what the gryphon flier had called it—a death factory.

"Xaden Riorson," the commandant calls out, and my pulse leaps as Xaden strides forward to take his orders, the last third-year in formation.

Nausea grips my stomach, and I sway. He'll be gone by morning. Gone. Telling myself that I'll see him every few days because of Tairn and Sgaeyl's mating bond doesn't quell the panic quickening my breaths. He won't be here. Not on the mat, testing and pushing me to be better. Not in Battle Brief or on the flight line.

I should be happy for the space, but I'm not.

Panchek resumes his place at the podium, running his hands down the trim lines of his uniform as though smoothing away any wrinkles.

"I'll find you before I go." Xaden's voice cuts through my shield and spiraling thoughts, then fades as he walks out of the courtyard and into the dormitory.

At least we'll get to say goodbye. Or fight our goodbyes. Whatever.

"Congratulations to the new lieutenants," Panchek says. "The rest of you will report to central issue to turn in your uniforms—yes, you may keep your earned patches—and pick up your new ones. From this moment, seconds are now third-years and firsts are now second-years, with all the privileges that entails. New command designations will be posted in commons this evening. You are dismissed."

A resounding cheer goes up in the courtyard, and I'm grabbed into a hug by Ridoc, then Sawyer, then Rhiannon, and even Nadine.

We made it. We're officially second-years.

Out of the eleven first-years who came through our squad during the year, both before and after Threshing, the five of us are the only ones left standing.

For now.

After three consecutive deaths of prisoners during his interrogations, it is this command's opinion that Major Burton Varrish should be reassigned from an active wing until further notice.

—MISSIVE FROM LIEUTENANT COLONEL DEGRENSI, SAMARA OUTPOST, TO GENERAL MELGREN

CHAPTER FIVE

Riders party as hard as we fight.

And we fight pretty damned hard.

The gathering hall is more raucous than I've ever seen it by the time the sun begins to set that evening. Cadets gather around—or in Second Wing's case, on top of—tables overflowing with food and pitchers of sweet wine, frothy ale, and a lavender lemonade that clearly has its fair share of distilled liquor.

Only the dais table is empty. For this one moment, there are no wingleaders, no section leaders, not even a squad leader in sight. Other than the stars on the fronts of our shoulders that denote our years at Basgiath, we're all equal tonight. Even the newly anointed lieutenants who wander in to say their goodbyes aren't in our chain of command.

There's a pleasant buzz in my head, courtesy of the lemonade and the two silver stars on my shoulder.

"Chantara?" Rhiannon asks, leaning forward to look past me and lifting her brows at Ridoc, who is seated on my other side. "Out of every privilege that comes with being a second-year, that's what you're looking forward to? It's only a rumor."

The village that supplies Basgiath has always been open to second-years from the Healer Quadrant, Scribe Quadrant, and Infantry Quadrant, but not ours. We've been banned for nearly a decade after a fight led to a local bar burning down.

"I'm just saying I heard they might lift the ban finally, and we've been stuck with this dating pool for the last *year*," Ridoc states, using his cup to motion around the hall, which is mostly behind us. "So even the possibility of getting leave to spend a few hours in Chantara every week is definitely what I'm looking forward to the most."

Nadine grins, her eyes sparkling as she gathers the hair she dyed purple this evening in one hand so it doesn't fall into the pitcher, and leans over the table to clink her glass against Ridoc's cup. "Hear, hear. It is getting a little…" She wrinkles her button nose, glancing past Sawyer at the other squads in our wing. "Familiar around here. I bet by third year it will feel downright incestuous."

We all laugh, none of us stating the obvious. Statistically speaking, a third of our class won't survive to see our third years, but we're this year's Iron Squad, having lost the fewest cadets between Parapet and Gauntlet, so I'm choosing to think positively tonight and every night of the next five days, during which our only duty will be to prepare for the arrival of the first-years.

Rhiannon pulls one of her braids under her nose and furrows her brow like Panchek as she mock-lectures, "You do know that trips to Chantara are for worship only, cadet."

"Hey, I never said I wouldn't stop by the temple of Zihnal to pay the God of Luck my respects." Ridoc puts his hand over his heart.

"And not because you're praying to get a little lucky while the other cadets are in town," Sawyer comments, wiping the foam from his ale off his freckled upper lip.

"I'm changing my answer," Ridoc says. "Being able to fraternize with other quadrants *anywhere* in our downtime is what I'm looking forward to."

"What is this downtime you speak of?" I joke. We might have a few more empty hours here and there compared to first-years, but there's a slew of harder courses headed for us.

"We have *weekends* now, and I'll take whatever time we get." His grin turns mischievous.

Rhiannon leans forward on her elbows and winks at me. "Like you'll be using every second you can get with a certain Lieutenant Riorson."

My liquor-flushed cheeks heat even more. "I'm not—"

A resounding *boo* sounds around the table.

"Pretty much everyone saw you show up to formation in his flight jacket before War Games," Nadine says. "And after this morning's display? Please." She rolls her eyes.

Right. The display after he told me that he'd *always* keep secrets from me.

"Personally, I'm looking forward to letters," Rhiannon says, clearly jumping in to save me as Imogen and Quinn arrive, sliding in next to Nadine. "It's been way too long since I've been able to talk to my family."

We share a small smile, neither of us mentioning that we snuck out of Montserrat to see her family a few months ago.

"No chore duty!" Sawyer adds. "I will never scrub another breakfast dish again."

I'll never push another library cart with Liam.

"I'm going with his answer," Nadine agrees, sliding the pitchers of alcohol toward Imogen and Quinn.

A couple of months ago, Nadine wouldn't even acknowledge Imogen's presence because of her rebellion relic. It gives me hope that the new lieutenants who bear the same mark might not face discrimination at their new duty stations, but I saw firsthand at Montserrat how the wings look at marked ones—like they were the officers who perpetuated the rebellion, not their parents.

Then again, given what I know now, everyone is right not to trust them. Not to trust *me*.

"Second year is the best," Quinn says, pouring ale from the pitcher into a pewter mug. "All the privileges and only some of the responsibility of the third-years."

"But fraternizing between quadrants is definitely the best perk," Imogen adds, forcing a smile and wincing before touching her finger to the split in her lip.

"That's what I said!" Ridoc fist pumps the air.

"Did your lip get split while you guys..." Nadine asks Imogen, her voice trailing off as the table goes quiet.

I lower my eyes to my lemonade. The alcohol doesn't numb the ache of guilt that sits heavily on my shoulders. Maybe Xaden's right. If I can't lie to my friends, maybe I should start keeping my distance so I don't get them killed.

"Yeah," Imogen says, glancing my way, but I don't look up.

"I still can't believe you guys saw action," Ridoc says, all playfulness dying. "Not War Games—which were already scary as shit with Aetos stepping in for Riorson—but real, actual gryphons."

I grip my glass tighter. How am I supposed to sit here and act like I'm the same person when what happened in Resson has changed every single thing about what I believe?

"What was it like?" Nadine inquires softly. "If you guys don't mind us asking?"

Yes, I fucking mind.

"I always knew gryphon talons were sharp, but to take down a dragon..." Sawyer's voice drifts off.

My knuckles whiten and power simmers beneath my skin as I remember the angry red veins beside that dark wielder's eyes as she came for me on Tairn's back, the look in Liam's when he realized Deigh wasn't going to make it.

"It's natural to wonder," Tairn reminds me. *"Especially when your experience could prepare them for battle in their eyes."*

"They should mind their own business," Andarna counters, her voice gruff as though settling into sleep. *"They're all better off not knowing."*

"Guys, maybe now isn't—" Rhiannon starts.

"It fucking sucked," Imogen says before throwing back her drink and slamming her glass on the table. "You want the truth? If it wasn't for Riorson and Sorrengail, we'd all be dead."

My gaze jerks to hers.

It's the closest thing to a compliment she's ever given me.

There's no pity in her pale green eyes as she stares back, but there's no defensive snark, either. Just respect. Her pink hair falls away from her cheek as she tilts her head at me. "And as much as I wish none of it had happened, at least those of us who were there truly know the horror of what we're up against."

My throat tightens.

"To Liam," Imogen says, lifting her glass and defying the unwritten rule that we don't speak of the dead cadets after their name is read from the roll.

"To Liam." I lift mine, and everyone at the table does the same, drinking to him. It's not enough, but it has to be.

"Can I offer a word of advice going into your second year?" Quinn says after a quiet moment. "Don't get too close to the first-years, especially not until Threshing tells you how many of them might actually be worth getting to know." She grimaces. "Just trust me."

Well, that's sobering.

The shimmering shadow of my connection with Xaden strengthens, curling around my mind like a second shield, and I glance over my shoulder to see him across the hall, leaning against the wall next to the door, his hands in the pockets of his flight leathers. Garrick is talking to him, but his eyes are locked on mine.

"Having fun?" he asks, pushing through my shields with annoying ease.

A shiver of awareness rushes over my skin. Mixing alcohol and Xaden is definitely not a good idea.

Or is it the best idea?

"Whatever is going through that beautiful mind, I'm here for it." Even from this distance, I can see his gaze darken.

Wait. He's in flight leathers, dressed to leave. My heart slumps, taking a little of my buzz with it.

He nods toward the door.

"I'll be right back," I say, setting my cup on the table and wobbling a little as I stand. No more lemonade for me.

"I certainly hope not," Ridoc mutters. "Or you'll destroy all my fantasies when it comes to that one."

I roll my eyes at him, then make my way across the chaotic room to Xaden.

"Violet." His gaze rakes over my face, lingering on my cheeks.

I love the way he says my name. Sure, it's the alcohol overruling my logic, but I want to hear him say it again.

"Lieutenant Riorson." There's a silver line at his collar showing his new rank, but no other markings that could give away his identity in case he falls behind enemy lines. No unit designation. No signet patches. He could be any lieutenant in any wing if not for the relic that marks his neck.

"Hey, Sorrengail," Garrick says, but I can't peel my eyes from Xaden long enough to glance his way. "Good job today."

"Thanks, Garrick," I respond, moving closer to Xaden. He'll change his mind and let me all the way in. He has to.

"Gods, you two." Garrick shakes his head. "Do us all a favor and figure your shit out. I'll meet you at the flight field." He smacks Xaden's shoulder and walks off.

"You look…" I sigh, because it's not like I've ever been successful lying to him, and the fuzziness in my head isn't helping. "Good in officer flight leathers."

"They're almost exactly like cadet ones." A corner of his mouth lifts, but it's not quite a smile.

"Didn't say you didn't look good in those, too."

"You're…" He tilts his head at me. "Drunk, aren't you?"

"I'm pleasantly fuddled but not entirely sloshed." That makes exactly no sense, but it's accurate. "Yet. But the night is young, and I'm not sure if you've heard, but we have nothing to do for the next five days except prepare for the first-years and party."

"I wish I could stay to see what you do with all that time." He looks me over lazily, his gaze heating as though he's remembering what I look like naked, and my pulse leaps. "Walk out with me?"

I nod, then follow him into commons, where he grabs his rucksack from beside the wall and slings it over his shoulders casually, as if there aren't two swords hanging from the back of it.

A group of cadets hovers around the announcements board like the new leadership list is going to appear at any second and they might be erased from it if someone discovers they're not watching.

Yep, there's Dain in the center of them.

"You aren't waiting for tomorrow morning to leave?" I ask Xaden, keeping my voice low as we cross the stone floor of the expansive space.

"They prefer wingleaders to vacate their rooms first, since the new guys like to move in quickly." He glances at the crowd around the announcement board. "And since I'm guessing you're not offering a place in your bed—"

"I'm not nearly drunk enough to make that lapse in judgment," I assure him as he opens a door to the rotunda. "I told you, I don't sleep with men I don't trust, and if you're not offering full disclosure…" I shake my head and immediately regret it, nearly losing my balance.

"I'll earn your trust as soon as you realize you don't need full disclosure. You only have to have the guts to start asking the questions you actually want answers to. Don't worry about the bed. We'll get back there. The anticipation is good for us." He smiles—really fucking *smiles*—and it almost makes me rethink my decision.

"I tell you we're not together because you won't give me the one thing I need—honesty—and you counter with 'it's good for us'?" I scoff and walk down the stairs and past two of the marble pillars in the rotunda. "The *arrogance*."

"Confidence is not arrogance. I don't lose the fights I pick. And we're both allowed to have boundaries. You're not the only one who gets to set the rules in this relationship."

I bristle at the implication that I'm the problem here. "And you're picking a fight with me?" The world tips slightly when I look up at him.

"Picking a fight *for* you. There's a difference." His expression hardens as his gaze jerks left, toward the approach of Colonel Aetos and a rider wearing the rank of major.

"Riorson. Sorrengail." The colonel's mouth quirks into a sarcastic smile. "So *lovely* to see you both tonight. Leaving for the Southern Wing so soon? The front will be lucky to have such a capable rider."

My chest tightens. Xaden isn't going to a mid-guard wing like most lieutenants. He's being sent to the front?

"I'd say I'll be back before you can miss me," Xaden replies, his hands loose at his sides, "but word has it you pissed off General Sorrengail enough to be reassigned to a coastal outpost."

The colonel's face blotches. "I might not be here, but you won't be as often, either. Only once every fortnight, according to your new orders."

What? My stomach pitches, and it takes every ounce of control I have not to reach out and steady myself.

The major slides his hand into the breast pocket of his perfectly pressed dress uniform and pulls out two folded missives. His black hair is perfectly combed, his boots perfectly shined, his smile perfectly cruel.

Power rises within me, responding to the threat.

"Where are my manners?" Colonel Aetos says. "Violet, this is your new vice commandant, Major Varrish. He's here to tighten the ship, as they say. We seem to have gotten a little lax with what we allow around here. Naturally the quadrant's current executive commandant will still see to operations, but Varrish's new position only answers to Panchek."

"Cadet Sorrengail," I correct the Colonel. Vice commandant? Fucking *great*.

"The general's daughter," Varrish responds, looking me over in clear appraisal, his attention snagging on every dagger I have within reach. "Fascinating. I'd heard you were too fragile to survive a year in the quadrant."

"My presence would suggest otherwise." What a dick.

Xaden takes both missives, careful not to touch Varrish's hands, then gives me the one that has my name scrawled across the front. We crack Melgren's personal wax seals at the same moment, then unfold the official orders.

Cadet Violet Sorrengail is hereby given two days of leave once every fourteen days to be used only to fly with Tairn directly to and from Sgaeyl's current duty station or location. Any other absence from classes will be considered a punishable offense.

I grit my teeth to keep from giving the colonel the reaction he so obviously wants and carefully fold the orders, slipping them into the pocket at my hip. My guess is Xaden's say the same, and rotating our leaves puts us at every seven days. Tairn and Sgaeyl are never apart for more than three days. A week? They'll be in a near-constant state of pain. It's unfathomable.

"Tairn?" I reach out for him.

He roars so loudly it rattles my brain.

"Dragons give their own orders," Xaden says calmly, pocketing his papers.

"Guess we'll see." Colonel Aetos nods, then turns his gaze to mine. "You know, I was worried about our earlier conversation until I remembered something."

"And what is that?" Xaden asks, clearly losing patience.

"Secrets make for poor leverage. They die with the people who keep them."

What no one openly says is that while all four quadrants obey
the Code of Conduct, a rider's first responsibility is to the Codex,
which often overrules the regulations other quadrants live by.
By definition: the riders make their own rules.

—Major Afendra's Guide to the Riders Quadrant
(Unauthorized Edition)

CHAPTER
SIX

The churning in my stomach has nothing to do with the lemonade. I'm pretty
sure Colonel Aetos just insinuated he'd kill us.

"Good thing we're not keeping secrets," Xaden retorts.

Aetos's smile shifts to the softer one I've seen all my life, and the
transformation is eerie. "Do be careful who you share your war stories with,
Violet. I'd hate to see your mother lose either of her daughters."

What the fuck? Energy crackles in my fingertips.

He stares at me for a moment, making sure I get his point, then turns and
walks into commons without another word, Varrish following.

"He just threatened your life," Xaden growls, shadows whipping out from
behind the pillars.

"And Mira's." If I tell anyone what really happened, he'll target her, too.
Message delivered. Power burns through my veins, seeking an outlet. Anger
only fuels the energy that swiftly surges to an overwhelming wave, threatening
to rip me apart.

"Let's get you outside before you bring the place down," Xaden says,
reaching for my hand.

I give it to him, focusing on keeping the lightning at bay as we walk into
the courtyard, but the harder I fight to tame it, the hotter it becomes, and once
we're in the darkness of the courtyard, I rip my hand from Xaden's as power

tears from me, scalding every nerve on the way out.

Lightning illuminates the night sky, striking the courtyard about forty feet away. Gravel flies.

"Shit!"

Xaden throws up a shield of shadow, catching the rocks before they can hit any of the nearby cadets. "Guess alcohol doesn't dampen your signet," he says slowly. "Good news is it's all stone out here."

"Sorry!" I call out to the others as they scatter, grimacing at my utterly embarrassing lack of control. "Forget protecting me. The quadrant needs protection *from* me." Taking a deep breath, I turn to face Xaden. "Southern Wing? Is that what you chose?" Wingleaders always get their choice of duty station.

"There was no other choice by the time they handwrote our orders. I'll be at Samara. I spent today packing and shipping most of my things."

It's the easternmost outpost of the Southern Wing, where the borders of Krovla and Braevick provinces intersect, and a day's flight away. "They'll only have hours together every time they make the flight."

"Yeah. She's pretty pissed."

"Tairn, too." I reach out for Andarna in case she hasn't drifted off yet.

"You've lost all touch with reality if you think I'm getting close to him right now," she responds, her voice gritty from sleep. *"He's in a mood."*

"You should be sleeping." She's supposed to be settling in for the Dreamless Sleep. I still don't know exactly what that means, nor is Tairn open to questions on the parenting secrets of dragons, but he insists that sleeping away the next two months is critical to her growth and development. Part of me can't help wondering if it's simply a clever way to avoid a majority of the teenage years of moody dragons.

As if on cue, Andarna replies with a yawn, *"And miss all the drama?"*

"We'll only have hours to…" I whisper, looking away from Xaden's intense gaze. "You know. To pass information." The courtyard reminds me of a ballroom about two hours after everyone reasonable has left the party, full of drunkards and bad decisions. How the hell are Xaden and I going to fix whatever we are without time together?

"Pretty sure that's precisely the idea. They'll split us up for as long and as often as possible. We'll have to make the most of what time we get."

"I don't hate you as much tonight," I whisper.

"It's the alcohol. Don't worry, you'll despise me again tomorrow." He reaches out, and I don't retreat when he cradles the nape of my neck.

Warmth spreads over every inch of my body. The affect he has on me is as infuriating as it is undeniable.

"Listen to me." He lowers his voice and gently tugs me toward him, shooting a glance at a group of tipsy cadets watching nearby. *"Play along."*

I nod.

"I'll be back in seven days," he says for the benefit of the people passing by. *"Sgaeyl and Tairn won't be able to talk over the distance. They'll sense emotions, but that's it. Remember that leadership will read any missive we send."* He leans down, making it look to everyone else like we're locked in some kind of farewell embrace, which isn't far from the truth.

"A lot can happen in seven days." I understand what he's telling me mentally. "What am I supposed to do while you're gone?"

"Nothing that matters will change," he assures me for the benefit of onlookers. *"Don't involve yourself in anything Bodhi and the others are doing."* He has that look—the steely one he gets when he's sure he's right.

"You really aren't going to change, are you?" I whisper, my chest tightening.

"This isn't about us. Every eye will be on you, and you don't have a rebellion relic to hide your actions from Melgren if you're caught alone. Involving yourself endangers everything we're working for." Another group of cadets wanders closer, heading toward the rotunda.

It's hard to argue against that, especially when what I have planned requires being left to my own devices.

"I'm going to miss you." His hand flexes on the back of my neck as a couple of riders from Third Wing get a little too close. *"You can only fully trust those who were with us at Resson."*

"Think of all the spare time you'll have without having to constantly train me on the mat." I give in to the ceaseless urge to touch him, lifting my hands to his chest so I can feel the steady beat of his heart under my fingertips, and blame the alcohol for the utter lapse in judgment.

"I'd much rather have you under me on the mat than spare time." His arm wraps around my waist, tugging me closer. *"When it comes to the other marked ones, don't risk trusting them. Not yet. They know they can't kill you, but some of them would be happy to see you hurt given who your mother is."*

"Back to that, are we?" I try to smile, but my lower lip trembles. I'm not actually upset about him leaving. That's the lemonade talking.

"Never left that," he reminds me, keeping his voice low even though the others in the courtyard are now giving us more than enough privacy. "Keep yourself alive, and I'll be back in seven days." His hand slides to the side of my neck, and his thumb grazes my jawline as he lowers his mouth to only a breath above mine. "We managed to keep each other alive today. Trust me yet?"

My heart jolts. I can almost taste his kiss, and gods, I want it.

"With my life," I whisper.

"That's all?" His mouth hovers above mine, all promise and no delivery.

"That's all." Trust is earned, and he isn't even *trying*.

"Too bad," he whispers, lifting his head. "But like I said, anticipation is a good thing."

Common sense crashes through the fog of lust with embarrassing ease. For fuck's sake, what did I almost do?

"No anticipation." I outright glare, but my words lack bite. "We aren't happening, remember? That's your choice. I have every right to walk right back into the gathering hall and pick whomever I want to warm my bed. Someone a little more *ordinary*." It's a bluff. Maybe. Or alcohol. Or maybe I just want him to feel the same uncertainty I do.

"You absolutely have every right, but you won't." He gives me a slow smile.

"Because you're impossible to replace?" It does not come out as a compliment. At least that's what I tell myself.

"Because you still love me." The certainty in his eyes pricks every inch of my temper.

"Fuck off and leave, Riorson."

"I would, but you've got a death grip on me." He glances between our bodies.

"Ugh!" I drop my hands from his waist and step back. "Go."

"See you in seven days, Violence." He backs away, moving toward the tunnel that leads to the flight field. "Try not to burn the place down while I'm gone."

I glare in his general direction until I know he's far beyond my sight. And then I stand there another couple minutes, breathing slowly until I'm certain I have my emotions under some semblance of control. What the hell is wrong with me? How can I want someone who refuses to tell me his whole truth? Who makes a game out of it with his ridiculous *ask me anything* act? Like I'd have the first clue what to ask?

"He'll be back," Rhi says, coming up behind me, holding a missive of her own, excitement shining in her eyes despite the somber tone of her words.

"I shouldn't care." Yet I'm still wrapping my arms around my midsection like I need to be held together. "What has you fighting a smile?"

"Did something happen between you two?" She moves the letter to her pocket.

"What's the letter?" I counter. "Did you get orders?" Orders usually only mean one thing. I grab onto her shoulders and grin. "Did you?"

She grimaces. "I have good news and bad news."

"Bad news first." That's my new motto.

"Aetos is our new wingleader."

My face falls. "Should have expected that. What's the good news?"

"Cianna, our executive officer, moved up to being executive officer of the section." Her smile is brighter than any mage light. "And you're looking at our new squad leader."

"Yes!" I outright squeal in absolute delight and yank her into a hug. "Congratulations! You're going to be amazing! You already are!"

"Are we celebrating?" Sawyer asks loudly from the edge of the courtyard.

"Abso-fucking-lutely!" Ridoc shouts, ale sloshing over the sides of his mug as he rushes toward us. "Squad Leader Matthias!"

"What's your first order, squad leader?" Sawyer asks, Nadine racing to catch up to his long strides.

Rhi glances over each of us and nods as though coming to a decision. "Live."

I smile and wish it was that simple.

CHAPTER SEVEN

"I've never seen this room before," Ridoc says five days later, dropping into the seat next to me as the U-shaped amphitheater-style classroom on the third floor fills for Orientation. We're grouped in our sections and squads within our wings, putting us in the second row on the right-hand side, staring across the recessed floor at First Wing.

The noise outside is growing to a steady hum as civilians arrive for Conscription Day tomorrow, but it's still quiet within the walls of the quadrant. We've spent this week preparing for the first-years' arrival, learning our roles at Parapet, and drinking entirely too much at night. It definitely makes walking the hallways in the early morning interesting.

"We've never been second-years before," Rhiannon replies from my other side, her supplies perfectly aligned on her desk.

"Good point." Ridoc nods.

"Made it!" Nadine slides in next to Ridoc, shoving errant strands of her purple hair out of her face with a braced and wrapped hand. "How have I never been in this room before?"

Rhiannon just shakes her head.

"We've never been second-years before," I tell Nadine.

"Right. Makes sense." She grabs her things out of her bag, then drops it at her feet. "I guess none of our classes were this far down the hallway last year."

"What happened to your hand?" Rhiannon asks.

"It's embarrassing." She lifts the brace so we can see it. "I slipped and sprained it on the steps last night. Don't worry, the healers think Nolon might have an opening for me tomorrow before Parapet. He's been run ragged since War Games."

"That man needs a break," Rhiannon says, bobbing her head.

"I wish we had a break like the other quadrants." Ridoc taps his pen on the desk. "Even five or six days to just get away."

"I'm still recovering from the last six-day break I had away from here," I try to joke.

Rhi's face falls, and the rest of our squad quiets.

Shit. That was *not* the right thing to say, but I'm exhausted. There's no point trying to sleep when I can't quit dreaming about Resson.

"I'm around if you want to talk." Rhi's kind smile makes me feel like I'm two inches tall for not letting her in.

Do I want to talk? Absolutely. Am I able to? Not after Aetos made it clear not to share my *war stories.* He's already targeting Mira—I'm not putting my best friend in that situation, too. Maybe Xaden is right. If I can't lie, all my friends would be safer if I kept my distance.

"Good afternoon, second-years," a tall rider says, his voice booming as he strides to the center of the floor, quieting the room. "I am Captain"—he winces, scratching the trim beard that's a shade darker than his light golden skin—"Professor Grady. And, as you can tell, I'm new this year and getting used to the whole *professor* title, as well as being around twenty-one-year-old kids again. It's been a while since I've been in the quadrant."

He turns toward the end of the classroom—the one section where there are no seats—and crooks his fingers at the heavy wooden desk there. Lesser magic makes it screech across the floor until Professor Grady puts his palm out. Then it stops. He turns toward us and leans back against the edge of the desk. "That's better. Congratulations on living through your first year." He turns his head slowly, his gaze raking over each and every one of us. "There are eighty-nine of you in this room. From what the scribes tell me, you are the smallest class to walk this hall since the First Six."

I glance at the empty rows of seats above First Wing. We knew last year that we had the fewest number of dragons willing to bond, but to see how few of us there really are is…disconcerting.

"Fewer dragons are bonding," I say toward Tairn, knowing Andarna drifted into the Dreamless Sleep a few days ago. *"Is that because the Empyrean knows about the venin?"*

"Yes." I can almost hear the exasperated sigh in Tairn's voice.

"But we need more riders. Not fewer." It doesn't make sense.

"The Empyrean remains divided on whether or not we should get involved," Tairn grumbles. *"Humans aren't the only ones keeping secrets."*

But Andarna and Tairn have already made their choice—of that, I'm sure.

"…But the second year brings its own challenges," Professor Grady continues as I focus on class. "Last year, you learned how to ride the dragons who chose you. This year, you'll learn what to do if you fall off. Welcome to Rider Survival Course, or RSC for short."

"What the hell is that?" Ridoc mutters.

"I don't know," I whisper, writing the letters *RSC* in the blank book in front of me.

"But you know everything." His eyes widen.

"Clearly not." Seems to be the theme lately.

"Don't know what it is?" Professor Grady asks with a grin, staring straight at Ridoc. "Good—our tactics work." He crosses one boot in front of the other. "RSC is kept classified for a reason, so we get your genuine reactions to the situations at hand."

"No one wants my genuine reactions," Ridoc murmurs.

I bite back a smile and shake my head.

"RSC will teach you how to survive if you become separated from your dragon behind enemy lines. It's a staple of your second year, culminating in two full evaluations you must pass in order to continue at Basgiath—one in a few weeks…and the other *around* mid-year."

"What the hell do they do with a bonded rider who *doesn't* pass?" Rhiannon asks quietly.

Every member of my squad looks at me. "I have no clue."

Caroline Ashton raises her hand from her seat in First Wing across the room. A chill races down my spine as I remember how close she'd been to Jack Barlowe—the rider who'd been intent on killing me until I killed him instead.

"Yes?" Professor Grady asks.

"What precisely does '*around* mid-year' mean?" Caroline asks. "Or '*in a few weeks*'?"

"You won't know the precise date," he answers, lifting his brows.

She huffs, sitting back in her seat.

"And I won't tell you, no matter how many times you roll your eyes. No professor will because quite simply—we want you surprised. But we *do* want you to be prepared. In this room, I will instruct you in navigation, survival techniques, and how to withstand interrogation in case of capture."

My stomach turns over, and my heartbeat goes double-time. Torture. He's talking about being tortured. And now I carry information worth being tortured over.

"And you'll face trials on those at any time," Professor Grady continues, "taken from any place in the quadrant."

"They're going to abduct us?" Nadine gasps, fear lacing her tone.

"Sounds like it," Sawyer mutters in response.

"Always something around here," Ridoc adds.

"The other assessors and I will give you feedback during those trials, so by the time your full evaluations come around, you'll be able to withstand—" He cocks his head to the side as if choosing his words carefully. "Well, be able to withstand the hell we're going to put you through. Take it from someone who has survived it: as long as you don't break during the interrogation portion, you'll do just fine."

Rhiannon puts her hand up, and Professor Grady nods at her.

"And if we break?" she asks.

All traces of amusement leave his face. "Don't."

With my pulse still racing an hour after Orientation, I head to the one place that used to calm my fraying nerves—the Archives.

As I walk through the doorway, I inhale the scent of parchment, ink, and the unmistakable tang of book-binding glue and let out a long, calming breath. Row upon row of bookshelves span the massive chamber, each taller than Andarna but not quite up to Tairn, filled with countless volumes on history, mathematics, politics—what I'd trusted to be all the knowledge on the Continent. And to think, at one point in my life, I'd thought climbing their ladders would be the scariest thing I'd ever do.

Now, I'm simply existing with the ever-present danger of Vice Commandant Varrish, Aetos's threat hanging over my head, a secret revolution that could get us all killed at any moment, and now imminent torture from RSC. Kind of miss the ladders.

After five days of watching, Jesinia's name finally appeared on the scribes' schedule posted outside this morning, which means it's time to get started.

Fuck *not getting involved*. I'm sure as hell not going to sit around and do nothing while my brother and Xaden risk their lives. Not when I'm certain the answer to protecting both Aretia and Poromish civilians is right here at Basgiath. The revolution might not have a scribe in its ranks, but it has *me*, and if there's even a shot that we can win this war without the weapons the revolution hasn't made or *found*, then I'm taking it. Or at least investigating the possibility.

Only scribes may continue past the long oak table near the doorway, so I stand at its edge and trail my fingers across its familiar grain and scars as I wait. If training to be a scribe taught me anything, it was patience.

Gods, I miss this place. I miss what I thought my life would be. Simple. Quiet. Noble. But I don't miss the woman I was, the one who didn't know her strength. The one who believed everything she read with unfailing confidence, as if the simple act of writing something on a blank page made it gospel.

A slight figure wearing a cream tunic, pants, and hood approaches, and for the first time in my life, I'm nervous to see Jesinia.

"Cadet Sorrengail," she signs, smiling when she reaches me and flipping back her hood. Her hair is longer now, the brown braid nearly reaching her waist.

"Cadet Neilwart," I sign back, grinning at the sight of my friend. "We must be alone to warrant such an enthusiastic greeting." Scribes are strongly discouraged from showing emotion. After all, their job isn't to interpret but to record.

"We are," she signs, then leans to look past me. "Well, except Nasya."

"He's sleeping," I assure her. "What are you up to back there?"

"Fixing a few bindings," she signs. "Most everyone is off preparing for the new cadets coming tomorrow. Quiet days are my favorite."

"I remember." We'd spent nearly every quiet day at this table, preparing for the exam or helping Markham…or my father.

"I heard about…" Her face falls. "I'm sorry. He was always really nice to me."

"Thank you. I really miss him." I squeeze my hands into fists and pause, knowing that what I say next will either lead us closer to the truth…or get me killed.

"What is it?" she signs, biting her lip.

She's first in her year. That means she's probably trying for the adept path, the hardest of all degrees for scribes, and the one every Curator of the Scribe Quadrant has to have. It means not only does she spend more time with Markham than other scribes, but she'll almost never leave the Archives.

Nausea grips my stomach at the very real possibility that I can't trust her. Maybe there are no scribes within the movement for a reason.

"I was wondering if you had any older books about the founding of Basgiath? Maybe something about why they chose this location for the wards?" I sign.

"The wards?" she signs slowly.

"I'm prepping a defense for a debate in history about why Basgiath is here, instead of being built in Calldyr." And there it is, my first real lie. There's nothing selectively true in that statement. Nor any way to take it back. For better or worse, I am committed now to my own cause—saving as many people as I can from this war.

"Sure." She smiles. "Wait here."

"Thank you."

Ten minutes later, she hands over two tomes written more than a hundred years ago, and I thank her again before leaving. The answer to protecting Aretia is in the Archives. It has to be. I just have to find it before not even the wards can save us.

It is one thing to cross the parapet your first year.
But watching countless candidates lose their life to it feels a little
like dying, too.
Don't watch if you can help it.

—Page Eighty-Four, the Book of Brennan

CHAPTER
EIGHT

Conscription Day looks a little different on this side of it. I lean over the crenelations of the tower in the main war college and take note of the length of the line as the bells ring the ninth hour, but I avoid noticing the features of the individual candidates as they file in, starting up the long, winding staircase that will bring them to the parapet.

I don't need any more faces in my nightmares.

"They're starting up the stairs," I tell Rhiannon, who stands poised with a quill and the roll.

"They look nervous," Nadine says, leaning recklessly far over the edge of the tower to see the candidates lined up stories below.

They aren't the only ones. I'm four steps away from Dain and his memory-stealing hands that could pluck every secret from my head.

I lock my shields in place just like Xaden taught me and fantasize about shoving Dain off the tower.

He's made one attempt to talk to me, which I quickly shut down. And the look on his face? What the hell kind of right does he have to look…*heartbroken*?

"Weren't you nervous?" Rhiannon asks Nadine. "Personally, I wouldn't have made it across without Vi here."

I shrug and hop onto the wall, taking a seat to the left of Rhi. "I only gave you a little more traction. You had the courage and balance to make it across."

"It's not raining like it was during our Parapet." Nadine looks up at the cloudless July sky and wipes the sweat off her forehead with the back of her hand. "Hopefully more of them make it across." She glances my way. "You'd have thought your mother would have held off the storm last year, considering you were crossing."

"Clearly you don't know my mother." She wouldn't call the storm to kill me like a coward, but she sure as hell wouldn't stop it to save me, either.

"Only ninety-one dragons have agreed to bond this year," Dain says, leaning back against the wall beside the entrance to the parapet. He's in the exact position Xaden was in last year and has the same exact insignia on his shoulder—wingleader. The asshole gets Liam and Soleil killed and is promoted as a reward. Go figure. "More candidates making it across isn't going to equal more riders." He glances my way but quickly averts his gaze.

Nadine opens the wooden door at the top of the turret and glances down the stairwell. "They're about halfway up."

"Good." Dain pushes off the wall. "Remember the rules. Matthias and Sorrengail, your jobs are only to take the final roll before Parapet. Don't engage—"

"We know the rules." I brace my hands on the wall beside my thighs and wonder for the tenth time since I woke up this morning when Xaden will arrive today.

Maybe then I can address the three books on the craft of weaving fabric into traditional Tyrrish knots he left for me—strips of fabric included—on the desk of my new room on the second-year floor. It's not like I need a hobby.

But the note Xaden left on the stack of books? The one that read *I meant what I said on the parapet. Even when I'm not with you, there's only you.* That needed no explanation.

He's fighting.

"Fine," Dain says, drawing out the word as he stares at me. "And Nadine—"

"I don't have a job." Nadine shrugs and picks at the strings of her uniform where she cut the sleeves off. "I was just bored."

Dain frowns at Rhiannon. "Running a tight ship there, squad leader."

What an ass.

"There are no regulations about four riders on the turret during Parapet," she counters. "Don't even get me started this morning, Aetos." She looks up from her perfectly numbered scroll and raises a finger. "And if you even *think* about telling me to call you *wingleader*, I'll remind you that Riorson did a hell of a job without needing everyone to supplicate themselves to him."

"Because he scared the shit out of everyone," Nadine mutters. "Well, everyone except Violet."

I fight my smile and lose as Dain tenses, clearly at a loss for words.

"Since it's only us," Rhiannon says, "what do you know about the new vice commandant?"

"Varrish? Nothing besides the fact that he's a complete hard-ass who thinks the quadrant has gone soft in the years since he graduated," Dain answers. "He's friends with my father."

Figures.

"Yeah, it's a real daydream around here," Rhiannon responds sarcastically.

After Resson, I'm starting to realize that there's a purpose to pushing us to the point of breaking. Better to shatter in here than get your friends killed once we leave.

"Here they come," Nadine says, moving out of the way as the first candidates reach the top, their chests heaving from the climb.

"They look so young," I tell Tairn, shifting my weight on the wall and wishing I'd been a little more careful wrapping my left knee this morning. Sweat has already loosened the brace, and the slipping fabric annoys the shit out of me.

"So did you," he replies with a low growl. He's been pissy for the past two days, and I can't blame him. He's torn between doing exactly what he wants—flying to Sgaeyl—and seeing me punished for his actions.

The first candidate's gaze swings from Nadine's purple hair to the crown of mine, showing all its silver in my usual coronet braid. "Name?" I ask.

"Jory Buell," she says, struggling to catch her breath. She's tall, with good boots and what looks to be a balanced pack, but her exertion is going to work against her on the parapet.

"Step up," Dain orders. "Once you're on the other side, you'll give your name to the roll keeper."

The girl nods as Rhiannon jots her name down in the first slot.

All of the advice Mira gave me last year races through my mind, but I'm not allowed to give it. This is a whole other kind of challenge, to stand by and do nothing while these candidates risk their lives trying to become…us.

For many of them, we'll be the last faces they see.

"Good luck." That's all I'm allowed to say.

She starts across the parapet, and the next candidate steps up to take her place. Rhiannon takes down his name, and Dain waits until Jory is a third of the way across before letting the boy start.

I watch the first few candidates, my heart in my throat as I remember the terror and uncertainty of this day last year. When a candidate slips at the quarter mark and falls, the ravine below swallowing the last of his screams, I stop watching to see if they make it to the other side. My heart can't take it.

Two hours in, I'm asking their names with zero intention of remembering them, but I take note of the especially aggressive ones, like the bull of a guy with a deeply cleft chin who charges across, tossing the scrawny red-haired candidate struggling at the midway point without hesitation.

A little piece of me dies watching the cruelty of it, and it's a struggle to remember that every single candidate is here by their own choice. They're all volunteers, unlike the other quadrants, which take conscripts who pass the entrance exam.

"Jack Barlowe Junior," Rhiannon notes under her breath.

I don't miss the way Dain flinches and looks my way.

Blowing out a slow breath, I turn toward the next in line, trying to forget how Barlowe put me into the infirmary last year. I shiver at the memory of the way he forced pure energy into me through his hands that day on the mat, rattling my bones.

"Nam—" I start, but the word dies on my tongue as I stare in shock at the candidate standing far above me. He's taller than Dain but shorter than Xaden, with a muscular build and strong chin, and though his sandy-brown hair is shorter than the last time I saw him, I'd recognize those features, those eyes, anywhere. "Cam?"

What the hell is he doing here?

His green eyes flare with surprise, then blink with recognition. "Aaric... Graycastle."

His middle name I recognize, but the last? "Did you just make that up?" I whisper at him. "Because it's awful."

"Aaric. Graycastle," he repeats, his jaw flexing. He lifts his chin with the same arrogance I've seen in every single one of his brothers and especially his father. Even if I didn't recognize him from the dozens of times our parents' lives have tossed us into the same room, those startling green eyes mark him the same way my hair does me. He's not going to fool anyone who's ever met his father or *any* of his brothers.

I glance over at Dain, who openly stares at Cam—*Aaric*.

"You sure about this?" Dain asks, and the concern in his eyes gives me a glimpse of *my* Dain again, but it's short-lived. That version of Dain, the one I could always depend on, died the day he stole my memories and set us on a collision course with venin. "You cross that parapet, and there's no going back."

Aaric nods.

"Aaric Graycastle," I repeat to Rhiannon, who writes it down but clearly knows something is up.

"Does your father know?" Dain murmurs to Aaric.

"It's none of his business," he replies, stepping up to the parapet and rolling his shoulders. "I'm twenty."

"Right, because that's going to make a difference when he realizes what you're doing," Dain retorts, ripping his hand through his hair. "He'll kill us all."

"Are *you* going to tell him?" Aaric asks.

Dain shakes his head and looks to me like I have an answer for any of this when he's the fucking wingleader.

"Good, then do me a favor and ignore me," he says to Dain.

But not me.

"We're Second Squad, Flame Section, Fourth Wing," I tell Aaric. Maybe I can convince the others to keep it to themselves if they recognize him.

Dain opens his mouth.

"Not today," I tell him, shaking my head.

He snaps his mouth shut.

Aaric adjusts his pack and starts across the parapet, and I can't bring myself to watch.

"Who was that?" Rhiannon asks.

"Officially? Aaric Graycastle," I tell her.

She lifts a brow, and guilt settles in my stomach.

There are too many secrets between us already, and this is something I can give her. Something she deserves to know, since I just directed him to our squad. "Between us?" I whisper, and she looks over at me with an arched brow. "King Tauri's third son."

"Oh shit." She looks over her shoulder at the parapet.

"Pretty much. And I can guarantee his father doesn't know what he's doing." Not with how he felt after Aaric's older brother died during his Threshing three years ago.

"Should make for an easy year," Rhiannon says sarcastically, then beckons the next person without missing a beat. "Name?"

"Sloane Mairi."

My head whips in her direction, and my heart jumps into my throat. Same blond hair, though it's currently tangling in the breeze past her shoulders. Same sky-blue eyes. Same rebellion relic winding around her arm. Liam's little sister.

Rhiannon stares.

Dain looks like he's seen a specter.

"With an 'e' on the end," Sloane says, moving toward the steps and tucking her hair behind her ears nervously. It's going to blow right back in her face with the next gust of wind, temporarily blinding her on the parapet, and I can't let that happen.

I promised Liam I'd watch out for her.

"Stop." I jump off the wall, then yank out the small leather band I keep in the front pocket of my uniform and hand it to her. "Tie your hair back first. Braid is best."

Sloane startles.

"Vi—" Dain begins.

I glare over my shoulder at him. He's the reason Liam isn't here to protect Sloane himself. Rage courses through my veins, heating my skin. "Don't you dare say another word, or I'll blast you off this turret, Aetos." Power crackles through my hands without being called and erupts overhead, streaking across the sky horizontally.

Oops.

He sits, muttering something about losing every fight today.

Sloane takes the leather from me slowly, then braids her hair—simple and quick—tying it with the band and eyeing me the entire time with the three inches she has on me.

"Arms out for balance," I tell her, nausea rolling through me at the risk she's about to take. "Don't let the wind sway your steps." They were Mira's words, and now they're mine. "Keep your eyes on the stones ahead of you and don't look down. If the pack slips, ditch it. Better you lose it than your life."

She glances up at my hair, then down at the two patches sewn onto my summer uniform right above my heart. One is the Second Squad patch we won during the Squad Battle last year and the other is a bolt of lightning that branches off in four different directions. "You're Violet Sorrengail."

I nod, my tongue tying. I can't think of the right words to say about how sorry I am for her loss. Anything that comes to mind isn't enough.

Her expression shifts, and something that looks a lot like hatred fills her eyes as she leans down, her voice quieting so that I'm the only one who hears her say, "I know what really happened. You got my brother killed. He died for *you*."

I can actually feel the blood drain from my face as I blink away the memory of Deigh crashing into the wyvern who'd come for Tairn, sending Liam flying across my saddle. He'd been so heavy that my shoulders had almost dislocated trying to keep him from falling.

"Yes." I can't deny it and I don't look away. "I'm so sorry—"

"Go straight to hell," she whispers. "And I really mean that. I hope no one commends your soul to Malek. I hope he rejects it. Liam was worth a dozen of your kind, and I hope you spend eternity paying for what you cost me, what you cost *all* of us."

Yep, that look in her eyes is *definitely* hatred.

My heart abandons my body and lands somewhere in the vicinity of her recommendation.

"It wasn't your fault," Tairn says.

"It was." And if I don't pull my shit together right now, I'll fail Liam all over again. "Feel free to hate me," I say to Sloane, stepping aside and clearing the way

to the parapet. "Just do me a favor and put your fucking arms out so you don't see Liam before I do. Do it for him. Not me." So much for the caring, gentle mentor I'd hoped to be for her.

She jerks her gaze from mine and steps up.

The wind kicks up and she wobbles, sending my heart rate spiking.

"What in the angry-Mairi was that about?" Rhiannon asks.

I shake my head. I just...can't.

Then the stubborn girl finally extends her arms and starts walking. I don't look away. I watch every damned step she takes like my future is tied to hers. My breath freezes when she stumbles halfway across, and my lungs don't fully expand until I see her reach the other side.

"She made it," I whisper up to Liam.

Then I take the next name.

Seventy-one candidates fall from the parapet, according to the rolls. That's four more than our year.

An hour after the numbers are calculated, the quadrant assembles in typical formation—three columns per wing—and the roll keeper calls name after name, dividing the first-years into squads.

Our squad is nearly full and there's still no sign of Sloane.

I looked for her in the courtyard earlier, but either she's hiding from me... or she's hiding from me. That's the only logical answer.

Nadine, Ridoc, and I wait behind eight first-years shifting their weight, the living embodiment of anxiety. Aaric stands with impossibly perfect posture but keeps his head down next to a red-haired girl whose complexion is full-on green in the row ahead.

The fear radiating off them is palpable. It's in every drop of sweat sliding down the stocky guy's neck two rows ahead, in every bitten nail the brunette spits out onto the gravel next to him. It's coming out of their pores.

"Is it me, or is this fucking weird?" Ridoc asks from my right.

"Fucking weird," Nadine agrees. "I kind of want to tell them that it's going to be okay—"

"It's not polite to lie," Imogen says from behind us, where she stands with Quinn, who looks downright bored as she trims the ends of her blond curls with a dagger. "Don't get attached. They're all dragon fodder until Threshing."

The stocky-looking guy with deep umber skin looks over his shoulder, shooting a wide-eyed look at Imogen.

She stares him down and makes a circle with her forefinger, wordlessly telling him to turn around. He does.

"Be nice," I whisper at her.

"I'll be nice once I think they might stick around," she replies.

"I thought you said it's not polite to lie," Ridoc counters with a grin, shaking his head in a way that makes the collar of his uniform move, but not the tall spikes he's somehow gelled his dark hair into today.

I blink, then lean closer to him, staring at the side of his neck. "What is... Did you get a tattoo?"

He smiles and pulls at his collar, showing off the inked tip of a swordtail on the warm brown skin of his neck, ending near the base of his collar. "It wraps to my shoulder, to Aotrom's relic. Badass, right?"

"Badass." Nadine nods in appreciation.

"Absolutely," I agree.

Visia Hawelynn is called to our squad. Her name is oddly familiar, and when she appears, moving into formation two rows ahead, I remember why. A burn scar sprawls from her collar to her hairline, curving along the right side of her face. She's a repeat. She survived angering an Orange Daggertail at Threshing last year, but barely.

Sloane is called to First Wing.

"Shit," I mutter. How the hell am I supposed to help her in an entirely different wing?

"I'd consider that a blessing," Nadine says quietly. "She didn't seem to be a fan."

Dain steps forward on the dais to talk to Aura Beinhaven, the senior wingleader, and the daggers she has strapped to her upper arms glimmer in the sunlight as she nods her head in response. He glances my way, then crosses over to the roll-keeper at the edge of the dais and she pauses, lifting her pen to scribble something on the roll.

"Correction!" she calls out over the crowd. "Sloane Mairi to Second Squad, Flame Section, Fourth Wing."

Yes! My shoulders dip in pure relief.

Dain walks back to his position, ignoring the reproachful stare from Vice Commandant Varrish, and his composure slips for the second it takes for him to shoot me an indecipherable look. What? Is Sloane supposed to be some kind of peace offering?

The roll-keeper moves on, placing the first-years in their squads.

Sloane appears a minute or two later, and my relief is short-lived when she opens her mouth. "No. I refuse. Any squad but this one."

Ouch.

Rhiannon moves from her place at the front of our squad and gives Sloane a look that makes me glad I'm never on Rhi's bad side. "Does it look like I give a shit what you want, Mairi?"

"Mairi?" Sawyer looks back through the lines of first-years that separate us, and a new patch on his shoulder makes me smile. He's a fantastic choice for Rhi's executive officer.

"Liam's sister," I tell him.

His jaw slackens.

"No shit?" Ridoc glances between Sloane and me.

"No shit," I respond. "Oh, and if you haven't noticed, she already hates me."

"I cannot be in the same squad as *her*!" Sloane glares at me with pure hatefire in her eyes, but hey, her hair is still braided, so I'm calling that a win. She might loathe me, but maybe she'll listen at least enough to stay alive.

"Stop disrespecting your squad leader and get in formation, Sloane," Imogen hisses. "You're acting like a spoiled aristocrat."

"Imogen?" Sloane startles.

"Get. In. Formation," Rhiannon orders. "I'm not asking, *cadet*."

Sloane pales and steps into line in front of Nadine, taking our last first-year slot.

Rhiannon slides past Nadine and leans in close. "Pretty sure that girl wants you dead," she whispers. "Any particular reason I should know about? Should I see if we can trade her to another squad?"

Yeah. I got her brother killed. He was sworn to protect me, and he lost his dragon—and his life—keeping that promise. But I can't say that any more than I can tell her there are venin beyond our borders.

My stomach twists at the idea of having to lie to her.

Selective truths.

"She blames me for Liam's death," I say quietly. "Let her stay. At least if she's in the squad, Codex says she can't kill me."

"You sure?" Her brow furrows.

"I promised Liam I'd take care of her. She stays." I nod.

"Between Aaric and Sloane, you're collecting strays," Rhiannon warns quietly.

"We were strays once, too," I answer.

"Good point. Now look at us. Alive and everything." A slight smile curves her lips before she returns to her place in formation.

The noon sun beats down on the courtyard, and it hits me how far back we are from the dais, where the wingleaders wait with Commandant Panchek. Tufts of his hair catch in the morning breeze as he takes in the formation with wide, assessing brown eyes. This is the height of enrollment this year. We'll start dying pretty much immediately.

But not me. I've danced with Malek more than my fair share over this last year and told him to fuck right off every single time. Maybe Sloane is right and he doesn't want me.

"You're agitated." There's worry in Tairn's tone.

"I'm fine." That's what we're all supposed to be, right? Fine. Doesn't matter who dies next to us or who we kill during training—or war. We're *fine*.

The ceremony finally starts with Panchek's ominous-yet-pompous welcome to the first-years and our new vice commandant, and then Aura delivers a surprisingly inspirational talk about the honor of defending our people before Dain takes the lead, clearly trying to step into Xaden's boots.

But he's no Xaden.

The sound of wingbeats and the gasps of first-years fill the air, and I breathe deeply as six dragons—five belonging to the wingleaders and a one-eyed Orange Daggertail I don't recognize—land on the courtyard walls behind the dais.

That orange looks temperamental, his gaze darting over the formation as his tail twitches, but none of them are as menacing as Sgaeyl or as terrifying as Tairn. I glance down and pick a piece of stray lint off my dark uniform.

First-year shrieks echo off the stone walls as the dragons' claws flex, digging into the stonework. A heavy rock falls, missing the dais by a mere matter of feet, and yet not a single rider up there flinches. Now I understand how Dain was so blasé about all of this last year.

There's not a single dragon up there who would risk Tairn's wrath by torching me. Are they beautiful to behold? Absolutely. Daunting? Sure. There's even a slight elevation in my pulse. And yeah, Aura's Red Clubtail is eyeing the cadets like lunch, but I know it's mostly to see if she can weed out the weak—

The redhead directly ahead of me vomits, puke splattering the gravel, then Aaric's boots, as she bends at the waist and heaves, emptying the contents of her stomach.

Gross.

Sloane wobbles, and she shifts her stance like she's about to bolt.

That's a *bad* idea.

"Don't move and you'll be fine, Mairi," I say. "They'll torch you if you run."

She stiffens but her hands curl into fists.

Good. Pissed is better than scared right now. Dragons respect anger. They exterminate cowards.

"Let's hope the rest aren't sympathetic pukers," Ridoc mutters and wrinkles his nose.

"Yeah, that one isn't going to make it if she does that at Presentation," Imogen whispers.

These first-years would shit themselves if Tairn did so much as a fly-by. He's almost twice as big as any of the dragons perched on the wall.

"Didn't feel like loaning your sheer intimidation skills to this show?" I ask Tairn.

"I do not participate in parlor tricks," he responds, his derision making me smile as Dain prattles on about something. He's trying desperately for Xaden's charisma and coming up woefully short.

"What do you know about Major Varrish's orange? He looks…unstable." And hungry.

"Solas is there?" His tone sharpens.

"Is Solas a one-eyed Orange Daggertail?"

"Yes." He doesn't sound happy about it. *"Do not take your eyes off him."*

Weird, but all right. I can watch the orange glare at cadets out of his one good eye.

"A third of you will be dead by next July. If you want to wear rider black, then you *earn it*!" Dain shouts, his voice rising with each word. "You earn it every single day!"

Cath digs his red claws into the masonry and leans over Dain's head, swinging his swordtail behind him in a serpentine motion as he blows a hot breath of steam over the crowd that sours my stomach. Dain really needs to check Cath's teeth, because there has to be a bone stuck in there decaying or *something*.

Cries sound in the courtyard, and a first-year to the right—Tail Section—breaks out of formation and sprints back toward the parapet, racing through the aisles between cadets.

No, no, *no.*

"We have a runner," Ridoc mutters.

"Shit." I cringe, my heart sinking as two others from Third Wing decide to follow his example, their arms pumping wildly as they make a break for it from First Squad of their Tail Section. This isn't going to end well.

"Looks contagious," Quinn adds as they race by.

"Fuck, they actually think they'll make it." Imogen sighs, her shoulders drooping.

The trio nearly collides directly behind the center of our wing—our section—then bolt toward the opening in the courtyard wall where the parapet lies.

"Eyes on Solas!" Tairn shouts.

I look forward again, watching Solas narrow his one eye to a slit and swivel his head as he draws a full, rumbling breath. Lead fills my chest as I glance back over my shoulder and glimpse the runners nearing the parapet. The dragons didn't let them get that far last year.

He's toying with them, and at this angle…

Oh shit.

Solas extends his neck, tilts his head horrifyingly low, and curls his tongue, fire churning up his throat—

"Get down!" I shout, lunging for Sloane and tackling her to the ground as fire blasts overhead, the flames so close that heat singes every patch of exposed skin on my body.

To Sloane's credit, she doesn't cry out as I cover as much of her body as I can, curling over her, but the soul-rending screams behind us are unmistakable. I open my eyes long enough to see Aaric laying flat over the redhead under the endless stream of fire.

Tairn's roar fills my head as lava licks along my arched back.

A scream musters at the base of my throat, but I can't breathe in this inferno, let alone give it voice.

As quickly as it struck, the heat dissipates, and I fill my lungs with precious oxygen, gasping for breath before shoving off the gravel to my feet. I turn to face the aftermath as the other second- and third-years around me rise.

Those at the back of our section who acted when I shouted are alive.

Those who didn't, aren't.

Solas took out the runners, one of our first-years, and at least *half* of Third Squad.

Chaos erupts.

"Silver One!" Tairn demands.

"I'm alive!" I shout back at Tairn, but I know he can feel the pain my adrenaline is masking. The smell—*gods*, the smell of sulfur and the burned flesh of the dead cadets makes bile rise in my throat.

"Vi, your back…" Nadine whispers, reaching for me and withdrawing her hand. "It's torched."

"How bad is it?" I tug at the front of my uniform, and it comes off in my hand, the fabric burned clean through at my back. The armor beneath my uniform stays in place at least.

Ridoc runs his hands over the flattened, singed peaks of his hair, and my gaze darts around, checking on everyone else next. I note that Quinn and Imogen are safe behind us, already rushing to help Third Squad.

Sawyer. Rhiannon. Ridoc. Nadine. We all exchange quick looks that ask and answer the same question. We're all intact.

I let out a long breath, my head dizzy with relief.

"It didn't…it didn't burn through your armor," Nadine says.

"Good." Thank gods for dragon scales.

"Are you hurt?" I ask Sloane as she stumbles, staring in shock at the carnage of Third Squad as Aaric helps the redhead to her feet. "Sloane! Are you hurt?"

"No." She isn't shaking her head as much as she is flat-out trembling.

"Get back into formation!" Panchek's voice amplifies over the mayhem. "Riders do *not* balk at fire!"

The fuck we don't. Whoever didn't balk is *dead*.

Dain's wide eyes meet mine. He's either as surprised by what happened as I am or a really good actor. All the wingleaders must be, because they look equally stricken.

Looking back at what remains of Third Squad, I see Imogen staring at a pile of cinder. As if she can feel me staring, she slowly drags her numbed gaze to mine.

"Now!" Panchek demands.

She staggers forward and I meet her halfway, grabbing hold of her elbows. "Imogen?"

"Ciaran," she whispers. "Ciaran's dead."

Gravity, logic, whatever it is that keeps me grounded shifts. There's no way that was…intentional, is there? "Imogen—"

"Don't say it," she warns, glancing around us.

We make it back into formation as Major Varrish moves to the front of the dais, appearing completely unfazed that his dragon just took out riders who *hadn't* broken formation, some of them *bonded*.

"It is not only the first-years who earn their leathers at Basgiath!" he shouts, and I swear he's speaking directly to me. "The wings are only as strong as their weakest rider!"

Rage overwhelms my senses, scalding hot and undeniably *not* mine.

A girl with blackish-blue hair two rows ahead makes a run for it, running from our squad, and my heart stops when Solas leans forward again despite a snap from Cath on the right, the orange's mouth opening.

Oh. Gods.

I'm considering tackling her to the ground myself when a set of wingbeats as familiar as my own heartbeat sounds behind me. And the anger consuming my every breath, overruling my emotions, turns to something deadlier—wrath.

Tairn lands on the wall behind us, his wings flaring so wide one nearly touches the dormitory as he takes out the top row of stones next to the parapet. First-years scream, running for their lives.

"*Tairn!*" I shout with more than a little relief, but there's no breaking through the absolute fury coursing through him. My attention whips back and forth between Tairn and the dragons behind the dais.

The wingleaders' dragons all rear back, including Cath, but Solas holds his ground, his tongue curling when Tairn's chest expands.

"*You do not have the right to burn what is mine.*" His words consume all my mental pathways as Tairn lets loose an earth-shattering roar in Solas's direction. Everyone slams their hands over their ears, including me, my entire body vibrating with the sound, hot air blasting the back of my neck.

The wingleaders' dragons take a step to the side of the wall as the roar ends, away from the Orange Daggertail, but Solas stands firm, his eye narrowing to a golden slit.

"Holy shit," Nadine whispers.

That about sums it up.

Tairn extends his neck forward, high above our squad, then snaps his teeth together loudly in Solas's direction in a clear threat.

My heart races so fast it practically hums.

Solas lets loose a short, rasping snarl, then swings his head in a serpentine motion. His claws grip and ungrip the edge of the wall, and I hold my breath until he launches skyward, his wings beating quickly as he retreats.

Tairn lifts his head, watching the flight before he turns his attention to the dais and exhales a sulfur-laced gust of steam, blowing Varrish's thick black hair.

"I think he got the message," I say to Tairn.

"If Solas comes near you again, he knows I will devour his human whole and let him rot within me while his heart still beats, and then I'll take the eye I so graciously left him."

"That's…graphic." I'm not touching the question of their history with waves of anger still rolling off Tairn like a thunderstorm.

"The warning should be effective. For now." He retracts, drawing back for power before he leaps from the wall, his wingbeats kicking up the gravel around us as he takes off.

Panchek returns to the podium, but his hand isn't exactly steady as he swipes at the thinning hair on his head, the medals on his chest. "Well then, where were we?"

Varrish glares at me, his hatred a palpable taste in my mouth, and I know that even if he hadn't been an enemy before, he sure as Dunne is now.

And in the mountains of the Steelridge range, the green dragons of the Uaineloidsig line, known for their keen intellect and rational countenance, offered their ancestral hatching grounds for the good of dragonkind, and the wards of Navarre were woven by the First Six at what is now Basgiath War College.

—United Navarre, a Study in Survival
by Grato Burnell, Curator of the Scribe Quadrant

CHAPTER
NINE

The next morning, I wake in a cold sweat, the sky pale with early light through my east-facing window, my body flooded with adrenaline from the nightmare. Like every morning since Xaden left, I wrap my knees tight and dress quickly, pulling the flexible summer uniform meant for sparring over my armor and plaiting my hair in a single, loose braid as I head out of my room.

My heart still pounds as I jog down the spiral steps, my brain unable to shake the nightmares that come so vividly while I sleep. *When* I sleep.

I swallow back the bile rising in my throat. One of the venin got away in Resson, red veins spidering away from his malevolent eyes. Who knows how many more there are, making their way toward our border while we rest.

On the ground floor, first-years scurry to their newly assigned chore duties, but the courtyard is blissfully empty, the air thick with humidity yet mercifully cooler than yesterday thanks to the storm rolling in.

I hold the heel of my boot to the back of my thigh, stretching the muscle. Despite copious amounts of Winifred's ointment, the skin of my back is still tender from yesterday's burn, but it's a hundred times better than it was last night.

"Hasn't anyone told you that a perk of being a second-year is the extra hour of sleep you get to have without chores?" Imogen asks as she approaches, her footsteps light on the gravel.

"Yeah, which I'm sure is great for people who can sleep." I stretch the other leg. "What are you doing?"

"Going with you." She stretches, too, rolling her neck at the same time. "But what I can't figure out is why the hell you've been running every morning."

My stomach hollows. "How would you know that I've been running every morning? If Xaden thinks I need someone watching out for me this year…" I shake my head, unable to finish that sentence. He was supposed to visit yesterday but never showed, much to Tairn's aggravation…and my worry.

"Relax. Xaden doesn't know. My room is right above yours, and let's just say I'm not sleeping very well, either." Her gaze darts toward the rotunda as a group of cadets walks out.

Dain. Sawyer. Rhiannon. Bodhi. I recognize most as Fourth Wing leadership. Rhi and Sawyer spot us immediately and head our way.

"So, why are we running, Sorrengail?" Imogen asks, finishing her stretches.

"Because I generally suck at it," I answer. "I'm good in short bursts, but anything longer than that—and I won't make it." Not to mention it's hell on my joints.

Imogen's gaze snaps to mine, her eyes widening.

Bodhi's farther back and starts our way. His walk is so similar to Xaden's stride that I almost do a double take.

"What are you doing up?" Rhiannon asks, tucking a notebook under her arm as she and Sawyer reach us.

"I could ask you the same." I force a smile. "But I'm guessing it's a leadership meeting."

"Yes." Concern creases her brow as she studies my face. "Are you all right?"

"Absolutely. Good meeting?" It's a pathetic attempt at normal conversation, given the scenes from Resson still replaying through my head from my nightmare.

"It was fine," Sawyer answers. "They moved Bodhi Durran from Tail Section to Flame."

"We had to do some restructuring, seeing as most of Third Squad was torched yesterday," Rhiannon adds.

"Right. That makes sense." I glance over her shoulder and gauge I have about five seconds before Bodhi reaches us. If he knows I'm struggling, there's no doubt he'll tell Xaden, and I really don't need that conversation right now. "Listen, I have to get going."

"Going where?" Rhiannon asks.

"Running," I answer truthfully.

She draws her head back, her brow furrowing deeper. "You never run."

"Then it's a good time to start," I try to joke.

She glances between Imogen and me. "With Imogen?"

"Yep," Imogen replies. "Apparently we're runners now."

Bodhi arrives in time to hear that, his eyebrows rising.

"Together?" Rhiannon's gaze keeps bouncing—to Imogen, me, and back again. "I don't understand."

If you can't lie, you keep your distance.

"Nothing to understand. We're just running." My smile is so tight I think my entire face might fracture with the effort it takes to keep it there.

Bodhi's gaze narrows.

"But what if you don't make it in time for breakfast?"

"We will," Imogen promises. "If we leave right now." She glances at Bodhi. "I've got this."

"Let them go," Bodhi says.

"But—" Rhiannon starts, her gaze searching mine as if she can see right through me. Imogen's been training me since last year, but Rhi knows we aren't exactly friends.

"Let them go," he repeats, and this time it's not a suggestion but an order from her section leader.

"I'll see you later?" Rhi asks.

"Later," I agree, unsure I mean it as I turn without another word and jog across the courtyard toward the tunnel. The gravel is shit for traction, making it harder, but that's fine. I need harder.

Imogen catches me within a few strides. "What do you mean you won't make it?"

"What?" We pause at the doors.

"You said you won't make it." Imogen gets to the handle before I do and holds the door shut. "When I asked you why you're running. What did you mean?"

For a second, I debate not telling her, but she was there, too. She's not sleeping, either.

"Soleil didn't." My gaze locks with hers, but her expression doesn't change. Swear to the gods, nothing fazes her. I envy that. "She was on the ground when *she* killed her. The way she channeled…it drained everything from the land. Everything *touching* the land. Including Soleil and Fuil. I watched it happen. I watch it happen every night when I close my eyes. It spread so quickly, and I know…I can't outrun it. Not if I'm too far from Tairn. I'm not fast enough for any considerable distance." I try to swallow the tightness in my throat, but the knot seems to live there lately.

"Yet," Imogen says, yanking the door to the tunnel open. "*We're* not fast enough yet. But we will be. Let's go."

. . .

"It's weird as hell to be all the way up here," Ridoc says from my left as we sit in the first Battle Brief of the academic year later that day, looking down at where the first-years take up more than a third of the room.

It's standing-room only in the giant, tiered classroom for the third-years behind us. This is the only place in the quadrant besides the gathering hall designed to hold all the rider cadets, but it will take a few weeks of death rolls before we can all sit in front of the stories-tall map of the Continent.

It reminds me of the one in Brennan's briefing room in Aretia. He thinks we only have six months until venin challenge the wards, and yet there's not a single indication on this map.

"View is a little better," Nadine remarks from his other side.

"Definitely easier to see the higher portions of the map," Rhiannon agrees at my right, taking out her supplies and setting them on the desktop before her. "Did you have a good *run* this morning?"

"I'm not sure I'd call it good, but it was effective." I put my notebook and pen on the table, wincing at the pain shooting up my shins, and reinforce my shields. Keeping them up at all times is harder than I thought, and Tairn loves to remind me when they slip.

"Look at all those first-years with their quills and ink," Ridoc remarks, leaning forward to look down at the underclassmen.

"There once was a time we didn't have lesser magic to power ink pens," Nadine retorts. "Stop acting superior."

"We *are* superior." He grins.

Nadine rolls her eyes, and I can't fight my smile.

Professor Devera walks down the narrow set of stone steps on our left that follows the tiers of seats, her favorite longsword strapped to her back. Her black hair is a little shorter since I saw her last, and there's a fresh, jagged wound along the rich mahogany skin of her biceps.

"I heard she spent last week with the Southern Wing," Rhiannon says quietly.

My stomach tenses and I wonder what, if anything, she saw.

"Welcome to your first Battle Brief," Professor Devera announces. I tune out as she gives the same speech as last year and warns the first-years not to be surprised if the third-years are called into service early to man the mid-guard posts or shadow the forward wings. Her gaze rakes over them before she raises her attention to the seconds, her eyes crinkling for a heartbeat as she flashes a proud smile at me before continuing upward as she explains how necessary it is for us to understand the current affairs of our borders.

"This is also the only class where you will not only answer to a rider as your professor, but a scribe, as well," she finishes, lifting her hand toward the stairs.

Colonel Markham lifts the corner of his cream-colored robes as he descends, heading for the recessed floor of the lecture hall.

My muscles lock, and I fight the urge to flick one of my daggers into his traitorous back. He knows everything. He has to. He wrote the fucking textbook on Navarrian history that all riders are taught from. And until last year, I was his star pupil, the one he'd handpicked to succeed in the Scribe Quadrant.

"You'll respect Colonel Markham as you would any other professor," Professor Devera says. "He is the foremost authority at Basgiath when it comes to all matters not only of our history but current events as well. Some of you may not know this, but information from the front is actually received at Basgiath before it's sent to the king in Calldyr, so you'll be hearing it first here."

I glance down the tiers to where Aaric sits beside Sloane in the row with our squad's first-years, and to his credit, he doesn't flinch or even fidget in his seat. One good look, and Markham will know who he is, but with that haircut, if he keeps his head down, he's got a shot at blending in.

At least until his father sounds the alarm that he's missing from his gold-plated bed in Calldyr.

"First discussion point," Markham says when he reaches the floor of the hall, his silver eyebrows knitting. "There were not one but two attacks on our border by drifts of gryphons in the past week."

A murmur goes through the hall.

"The first," Professor Devera says as she lifts her hand and uses lesser magic to move one of the flag markers from the side of the map to the border we share with the Braevick province of Poromiel, "was near the village of Sipene, high in the Esben Mountains."

An hour's flight from Montserrat.

The only sound is pen and quill against parchment as we take notes.

"Here's what we can tell you," Markham says, folding his hands behind his back. "The drift attacked two hours past midnight, when all but a few villagers were asleep. It was unprovoked, and because Sipene is one of the villages that lies beyond the wards, the violence went undetected by the Eastern Wing for some matter of hours."

My shoulders dip, but I keep writing, pausing only to look up at the map. That village is at eight-thousand feet, an altitude unpleasant for gryphons. What were they looking for? Maybe I should have spent last night reading about what's in those mountains instead of six-hundred-year-old political ramifications of establishing our war college here and not in Calldyr to the west.

"The drift was routed by three dragons on patrol from the local outpost, but by the time they arrived, most of the damage had been done. Supplies were stolen, homes were burned. The last gryphon flier was found in some of the local caves above the village, though neither he nor his gryphon could tell us the motivation for attack, as they were both burned on sight."

Hard for prisoners to talk about the venin they've been fighting if they're dead.

"That's what they get," Ridoc mutters, shaking his head. "Going after civilians."

But were they? Markham didn't mention civilian casualties, only destruction.

I look up over my shoulder at where Imogen stands with Bodhi and Quinn, her arms folded over her chest. She glances down at me, her mouth tightening before she gives her attention back to Markham.

Shit. I want to be standing up there with them, asking what they really think, or even with Eya, who's with her third-year squad up in the corner. We might not be close, but at least she knows the truth. More than anything, I want to talk to Xaden. I want answers he's not willing to give me.

"As for the second," Professor Devera continues, moving another flag, this one to the south. My breakfast churns in my stomach when she puts the flag in place. "The outpost of Athebyne was attacked three days ago."

I gasp and the pen falls from my hand, hitting the desk loudly in the quiet room.

"Are you all right?" Rhiannon whispers.

"Something you have to say, Cadet Sorrengail?" Markham asks, cocking his head and looking at me in that characteristically unreadable expression he's so fond of. But the challenge I've often seen when he used to try and dig a correct answer out of me is there in the simple lift of his brow.

I know he's well aware of what is happening beyond our borders, but did Colonel Aetos tell him that *I* know, too?

"No, sir," I answer, grabbing my pen before it can roll off my desk. "I was startled, that's all. As far as I know from what you taught me in preparation for the Scribe Quadrant, outposts are rarely ever attacked directly."

"And?" He leans back against the desk in the center of the floor, tapping a finger along the side of his bulbous nose.

"And Montserrat was also directly attacked in the last year, so I can't help but wonder if this tactic is becoming more commonly used by our enemy?"

"Interesting thought. It's something we're considering among scribes." The smile on his face is anything but friendly as he pushes off the desk, clasping his hands behind his robes as he nods at me.

"We usually start with first-years," Professor Devera says, cutting a look at Colonel Markham. "Finishing the details we can give you about the Athebyne attack, it occurred a little before midnight, while nine of the twelve dragons stationed there were still out on their patrols. The enemy totals were around two dozen from what we can tell, and they were defeated by the three present dragons, with help from the infantry. Two gryphon riders made it into the lower level of the outpost before being caught and killed."

"Shields," Tairn growls, and I build them back up.

"I didn't even notice they'd slipped."

"They should be like clothes at this point," he lectures, snapping a little more than usual.

"I'm sorry?"

"Surely you'd feel a breeze were you to forget putting them on."

Point made.

"Isn't that where you guys were sent?" Rhiannon asks. "Athebyne?"

I nod, hoping none of those fliers were the ones who fought with us at Resson.

The first-years start when it's time for questions.

What was the gryphon's chosen formation for the attack on Athebyne?

A typical V.

Are the two attacks connected?

We have no reason to believe so.

The questions go on and on, and none of them are getting to the heart of the matter, which makes me look at the cadets below us with a healthy dose of skepticism that they aren't the critical thinkers they need to be. Then again, maybe the other years felt that way about us last year.

Finally, Devera opens the floor to the other years.

Rhiannon's hand shoots up, and Devera calls on her.

"Do you think it's possible that the enemy knew the outpost had been emptied for War Games and was trying to take advantage of the situation?" she asks.

Exactly.

Professors Devera and Markham share a look. "We do," Professor Devera finally answers.

"But the delay would show a lag in the timing of their information, correct?" Rhiannon continues. "The outpost was only empty for what? A few days?"

"Five days, to be precise," Markham answers. "And this attack occurred eight days after it was reoccupied." His gaze skates over mine, then lifts to the rows above. "The Poromiel trading post nearby, Resson, was leveled by Poromish unrest a couple of weeks ago, and we think that may be helping disrupt their communication lines about our outpost."

Poromish unrest?

Power rises within me so quickly that my skin heats.

Devera glances sideways at Markham. "We also don't usually give you the answers."

Markham chuckles and dips his head. "My apologies, Professor Devera. I must not be at my best today. Too little sleep in the last few days."

"Happens to the best of us."

I raise my hand, and Devera calls on me. "Where in the outpost were the gryphon riders found?"

"Near the armory."

Shit. I nod. They were raiding the outpost for weapons. Our wards might not reach that far, but I'd bet my life a cache of daggers was moved there if leadership knew venin were in the vicinity. Brennan can't supply even a fraction of the drifts. Of course they're going to fight to steal weaponry. We need to smuggle more out.

"What would you do were you in command of the riot at the Athebyne outpost?" she asks the room, then calls on Caroline Ashton when she raises her hand.

"I'd double the patrol for the next few weeks in a show of force, and maybe consider razing a few Poromish border villages," she suggests.

Rhiannon scoffs quietly.

"Remind me to never get on her bad side," Ridoc mutters.

"In retaliation?" Dain interrupts. "That's not our way. Read the Codex about the rules of engagement, Ashton."

Says the man who sent me to my death.

"He's right," Devera agrees. "We defend our borders with lethal force, but we don't take war to civilians." We just don't bother saving them, either. But does she know that? Shit, can I trust *anyone* around here?

But…maybe the whole report is wrong. Maybe it was wyvern and venin attacking, not gryphons. Maybe this entire presentation is a well-crafted lie.

"How many riders were wounded in the Athebyne attack, given that one was killed?" I ask.

"Four of us," Devera answers, pointing at her arm. "Including me. This is courtesy of a rider with an excellent aim of her bow."

So much for the not-gryphon idea.

We're excused after another half hour of current events, and I ditch my squad in the crowd, searching out Bodhi.

He's nearly to the steps of the briefing room before I catch up to him.

"Sorrengail?" he asks after we make it through the bottleneck of the doors.

"I want to help," I whisper. Maybe I can do more than just read.

"For fuck's sake." He takes my elbow and pulls me into an alcove, towering over me with a look of exasperation. "I have direct instructions to keep you as far away from *helping* as possible."

"He's not even here, and he's still giving you orders?" I adjust the strap of my bag on my shoulder as most of the quadrant funnels past.

"That tactic isn't going to work on me, because yes." He shrugs and scratches a pen into the cast on his arm.

"And I thought you were the most reasonable of the group." I sigh. "Look, if I can help, then maybe we can prevent what I'm assuming are…supply runs." Talking in code is ridiculous, but anyone could be listening. "Give me a job."

"Oh, I *am* the most reasonable in the group." He flashes a grin, leaning back on his heels. "I also don't have a death wish. Survive second year and strengthen your shields, Sorrengail. That's your job."

"She trying to talk you into letting her join the shenanigans?" Imogen asks, stopping alongside us.

"'Trying' is the precise word," Bodhi says. "Only trying." He walks off into the crowd.

"How are we expected to go back to class like nothing happened?" I ask Imogen as we walk out into the flow of cadets headed for the main staircase of the academic wing.

"You're supposed to *act* like nothing happened," Imogen says quietly, waving at Quinn, who's waiting ahead with Rhiannon. "That's the deal we all made when we came here." She moves her bag, twisting her wrist so her rebellion relic is front and center between us. "And like it or not, you're one of us now. Well, as close as you can get without one of these."

I shift my heavy pack on my shoulder and nod, realizing I know too little to actually help the marked ones and too much to speak frankly to my friends.

"Hey," Imogen says to Quinn. "Lunch?"

"Absolutely," Quinn answers.

The two walk ahead while Rhiannon falls back to keep pace with me.

"Doesn't Quinn usually eat lunch with her girlfriend?" Rhi asks.

"Yes, but she graduated."

"Right." She sighs and lowers her voice. "I wanted to talk to you before breakfast but didn't get a chance. I think the school is hiding something from us."

I nearly trip over my own boots but catch my balance before I can make a fool out of myself. "I'm sorry?"

She can't know. She just can't. I barely survived losing Liam… I can't fathom anything happening to her.

"I think there's something going on in the Healer Quadrant," she says, lowering her voice. "I tried to take a first-year to see Nolon yesterday after formation turned into a firepit, and he looks like absolute shit. I mean, the man could barely stand. And when I went to ask him if he was all right, the new vice commandant said he had more important things to do than talk to cadets and basically escorted him to that little door in the back of the infirmary, which is now *guarded*. I think they're hiding something back there."

I open and shut my mouth a couple of times, torn between confusion and relief. "Maybe they brought some of the injured riders from one of the outposts for mending," I offer. The backlog would explain why Bodhi is still in a cast.

She shakes her head. "Since when do a few broken bones wreck a mender?"

"Maybe they brought in a prisoner from Poromiel." Ridoc forces his way in between us. "And Nolon keeps healing them as Varrish breaks them. I heard one of the third-years say that's what Varrish is known for—torture."

"And you're known for eavesdropping." Rhi shakes her head.

Instead of eating lunch with my friends, I make a quick excuse and take my tray to the little library alcove in commons to finish reading *United Navarre, a Study in Survival*.

Sadly, after an hour hunched over the tome, I realize I already know most of the facts it regurgitates about the triumph of unification and the sacrifices made by both humans and dragons to establish peace. Disappointment stings like a paper cut. Naturally the secrets of ward-building weren't going to be in the first book I researched, but it would have been a pleasant surprise for *something* to be easy.

I contemplate asking Jesinia for a volume more focused on the First Six riders as I change for assessment back in my room, then head to the gym and meet my squad on the edge of the mat.

"I hate assessment day," I mutter, taking the spot between Rhi and Nadine.

"Can't blame you after the way yours went last year," Ridoc teases as he steps up next to Sawyer.

The first match begins between two of our first-years, and I can't help but notice Rhi glancing my way every few minutes. By the end, Visia—the repeat— has trampled the brutish girl with shocking red curls who'd thrown up on Aaric yesterday, and Rhi's all but frowning at me.

And she's not the only one. Sloane is staring like she might actually be capable of glaring me to death as she shifts her weight continuously on the left side of the mat.

"Baylor Norris and Mischa Levin!" Professor Emetterio, our squad's combat teacher, shouts at the first-years beside Sloane, then tilts his shaved head down at the clipboard in his beefy hands.

Shit. I really didn't want to know their names. The stocky guy with nervous eyes faces off against the brunette who couldn't stop biting her nails yesterday.

"You all right?" I ask Rhi as the brunette somehow flips the muscly one onto his back. Impressive.

"Should I be asking you that?" Rhi responds, lowering her voice to a whisper. "Are you mad at me?"

"What?" I rip my attention from the way the girl is handing that guy his ass to look at her. "Why would I be mad at you?"

"Between the running and not eating lunch with us, it kind of feels like you're avoiding me. And it's ridiculous, but all I can think is that maybe you're pissed that I chose Sawyer as executive officer yesterday instead of you, and if that's the case, then let's talk about it—"

"Wait. *What?* No." I shake my head, my hand holding my stomach. "Not at all. I am the *worst* possible choice for executive officer, considering I have to fly off to Samara every two weeks so Tairn can see Sgaeyl."

"Right?" She nods, relief softening her brown eyes. "That was exactly my thought."

"Sawyer is a great choice, and I have zero aspirations to leadership." I'm only trying to get by unnoticed over here. "Not mad in the least."

"So you're not avoiding me?" Rhi asks.

"I would have made a kick-ass executive officer," Nadine interrupts, saving me from having to answer. "But at least you didn't choose Ridoc. He would have seen the whole thing as a platform to crack more jokes."

Guess we're not being as quiet as we think we are.

Mischa firmly trounces Baylor, and Emetterio calls the next pair to the mat. "Sloane Mairi and…" he reads from his roll. "Aaric Graycastle."

"I want *her* instead," Sloane says, pointing a dagger at me.

She has to be kidding. But she's not. Sighing, I cross my arms and shake my head at Liam's little sister.

"Gods, Sloane." Imogen snorts, laughing off to the right, where she watches with Quinn. "You really feel like dying on your first day?"

"Did she compliment you?" Rhiannon whispers.

"Oddly enough, I think so."

"I can take her," Sloane fires back, white-knuckling her knife. "From what your letter said last year, her joints pop right out. How hard can it be?"

"Seriously?" I shoot a reproachful look at Imogen.

"I can explain." Imogen puts her hand over her heart. "You see, I didn't like you last year, remember? You're kind of an acquired taste."

"Great. I appreciate that," I quip back sarcastically.

"I couldn't care less about whatever grudge you think you hold against Sorrengail, Mairi." Emetterio sighs like this year has already exhausted him. "I know who trained her, and I'm not unleashing her on a first-year." He lifts a dark brow at Imogen. "I, too, made an error last year." He turns back to Sloane, the corners of his mouth slashing down. "Now disarm and take your place against Graycastle."

Sloane hands off her weapons and faces Aaric, who easily has about five inches and years of private combat tutoring on her. But she's Liam's sister, so there's a chance she'll be able to hold her own.

"Did someone say Sorrengail?" a deep voice asks from behind us.

Our line of second-years all glance over shoulders at the bullish first-year who threw the scrawny one off the parapet. There's a Second Wing patch on his shoulder as he lumbers forward, his hands at his sides.

"Popular today, aren't you?" Nadine whispers with a smile, pivoting playfully toward the first-year. "Hi. I'm Violet Sorrengail." She points to her purple hair. "See? Like my hair. Do you have a message for—"

He grabs hold of her head and twists, snapping her neck.

It is not unheard of that a candidate enters the Riders Quadrant having been paid to assassinate a cadet. I'm sorry Mira was targeted but proud to say she dispatched the threat quickly. You have enemies, General.

—OFFICIAL NOTICE FROM COMMANDANT PANCHEK TO GENERAL SORRENGAIL

CHAPTER TEN

I stare in shock for the length of a heartbeat as the first-year drops Nadine's body to the ground. It falls with a sickening thud, her head twisted at an unnatural angle.

She's dead.

No. Not again.

"Nadine!" Rhiannon yells, rushing to kneel at her side.

"Nadine?" the first-year asks, his thick eyebrows knitting into one.

"What the hell do you think you're doing?" Emetterio barks.

"No one interferes," I demand, and two of my daggers are in hand before I even realize I've reached for them.

The giant jerks his gaze from Nadine's body to my daggers, to my hair.

"I'm Violet Sorrengail." My heart pounds, but no one else will die in my name. Using a pinch grip, I don't wait for his response, flinging both daggers. But he's fast for someone his size and throws up his arms—where both my blades sink to the hilt.

Damn it.

"Violet!" Andarna shouts.

"Sleep!" I slam my shields up to block everything—everyone out. Xaden's gone. Protecting me is what killed Liam.

It doesn't matter *why* this guy is trying to kill me right now. Either I'm strong enough to survive or I'm not.

The first-year rips the bloodied daggers out of his forearms in quick succession with an angry grunt, letting them clatter to the ground. His mistake. He might be almost a foot taller, but he'll need those blades if he wants to kill me. His build, though…that's going to be hard to overcome.

Stop going for bigger moves that expose you. Xaden's words from last year ring in my head as if he is standing right beside me. I have to use what I have — my speed — to my advantage.

I charge toward him at a run, and he swings meaty fists at my head, but I drop to my knees before they can make contact. Ignoring the shattering pain in my legs from impact, I use my momentum to slide by, clipping the tendons alongside his knee as I pass.

He yells and falls forward like a fucking tree, slamming into the floor.

"Violet!" Dain shouts from somewhere behind me.

I scramble to my feet and turn back to the giant, who has already flipped himself onto his back as if impervious to pain, but he can't stand with what I've done to him. He can, however, reach for one of the daggers he dropped and throw it at me.

Which he does.

"Shit!" I spin sideways to avoid my own blade, and he kicks out with the leg I didn't slice.

His boot catches me behind my thigh.

The blow cuts my feet out from under me, and all I see is ceiling as I fall back, smashing my hip with the full force of my weight. Pain blinds me for a heartbeat when my head smacks against the floor, white-hot and so sharp my ears ring. But at least I haven't stabbed myself with my blades. One is still in my hand, but my eyes blur and tell me it's really two.

The first-year grabs hold of my right thigh and pulls, dragging me with the distinct squeaking sound of leather against the shiny floor. If I put my dagger through his hand, I'll strike my own muscle.

So I swipe out at his arm instead, my reach only catching him with a cut across the forearm. My heart launches into my throat as people around me yell my name, but they can't interfere. I'm a second-year, and this asshole isn't in my squad.

His grip secure, he drags me feetfirst toward him, his puddled blood soaking the back of my neck and wetting my hair.

If I don't get free, I'm dead.

I bring up my left leg and kick as soon as I'm close enough, catching him in the jaw, but he doesn't let go. Tenacious bastard.

A crunch sounds with my next kick, breaking his nose. Blood flies, but he shakes it off, lurching upward and rolling onto me, pinning me to the floor with his incomprehensible weight.

Fuck, fuck, *fuck*.

I swing out with my knife, but he catches my right hand, pinning my wrist to the ground. Then he wraps his other hand around my throat and squeezes.

"Fucking die, already," he seethes, his voice blending into the ringing in my ears as he lowers his face to mine.

There's no air as his grip tightens on my windpipe.

"Secrets die with the people who keep them," he whispers, bringing his nose an inch from mine. His eyes are light brown but rimmed in red as though he's on some kind of drug.

Aetos.

Fear floods my mind, breaking past my shields, but it's not mine.

I can't focus on Tairn's fear. That way lies shock and death.

And I'm not about to die under some no-name first-year.

My vision tunnels as I grab one of the daggers sheathed along my ribs with my free left hand, draw quickly, and plunge the blade into the giant's back, angling right where Xaden taught me. His kidney. Once. Twice. Thrice. I lose count as I stab over and over and over, until the grip on my throat releases, until the first-year sags on top of me.

He's dead weight.

My lungs fight to expand as I put the last of my strength into shoving him off of me. He's heavier than an ox, but I manage to push him sideways enough to slide out from under him.

Air—beautiful, precious air—fills my chest, and I gasp for it, breathing past the fire in my throat, and stare up at the beams of the ceiling. Pain. My entire body is nothing but *pain*.

"Violet?" Dain's voice shakes as he crouches beside me. "Are you all right?"

Secrets die with the people who keep them.

No, I'm not all right. His father just tried to have me assassinated.

I force myself to the familiar headspace beyond the pain and roll to my hands and knees. Nausea sweeps through me in waves, and I breathe in through my nose and out through my mouth until I can push it back down.

"Say something," Dain begs in a frantic whisper.

I walk back on my hands until I'm kneeling, then arch my neck, wincing as I pull breath after breath.

"Vi—" He stands and offers me a hand, and the worry in his familiar eyes—

Fuck no.

I throw all my energy into my shields.

"Don't. Touch. Me," I grind out, my voice like sandpaper, and stand slowly, more than aware of the number of eyes on me. My head spins, but I fight the dizziness as I retrieve all five of my daggers. Everyone in the nearby area watches as I bend over and use the dead first-year's uniform to wipe the blood off my blades before sheathing them.

The fear flooding my pathways changes to relief.

"I'm all right," I tell Tairn and Andarna.

"Matthias and Henrick, take the bodies," Dain orders. At least I think it's him. The ringing in my ears muffles everything farther than twelve inches away.

Emetterio appears before me. "May I touch you?" he asks.

Clearly, I made that demand of Dain rather loudly.

I nod, making sure my shields are in place, and Emetterio grasps my face, searching my eyes. He blocks the light, then lifts his hand. A fresh wave of nausea churns in my stomach.

"You're concussed. Want to skip the rest of the session?" He drops his hand from my face and holds me steady by gripping my arms when I sway.

"No." I'm not leaving assessment day the same way I did last year.

"I've got her," Imogen says, taking my elbow.

Emetterio's mouth purses, his dark eyes narrowing.

"I'm not going to try and kill her this year. Promise." She draws me to her side but doesn't hold on to me, just lets me lean a little.

Fine, a lot.

"You were just strangled, Cadet Sorrengail," Emetterio reminds me.

"Not the first time," I respond, the razor blades in my throat making my voice raspy. "I'll heal. I'm staying."

He sighs but eventually nods and heads back to his place at the head of the mat, picking up the clipboard he'd apparently dropped.

"Aetos sent him," I whisper to Imogen. "I think we're being targeted." Gods, I hope that's not why Xaden didn't show yesterday.

Her green eyes flare a second before Ridoc appears at my other side, his shoulder brushing mine.

"Damn, Sorrengail," he mutters, offering me an arm I don't take.

"It's always something, isn't it?" I try to smile as the two of them walk slowly back to the edge of the mat, giving me enough support that I don't fall to either side.

"He was probably sent as a message to your mother," Emetterio says, shaking his head. "Same thing happened to your older sister during her years."

The first-years stare in wide-eyed horror as I glance around the bloody mat, noting that Rhiannon, Dain, and Sawyer are missing. Right. Because they have to take Nadine and the nameless first-year's body.

Nadine is dead because she said she was me.

Heavy, eye-prickling sorrow threatens to take me out at my throbbing knees, but I can't allow myself to feel it. Can't let it in. Not with everyone watching. It goes into the box where I keep every other overwhelming emotion.

Sloane and Aaric stand in the middle of the mat, watching me with varying shades of shock on their face. There's far more concern on Aaric's face than Sloane's.

"Is someone going to clean up that mess and fight, or what?" I ask, ignoring the drip of thick liquid down the back of my neck. Standing here covered in his blood is better than lying there soaked in mine.

"And you wanted to take her on, Mairi." One of the first-years scoffs from across the mat. He has deep-set brown eyes under angular brows and a wide square jaw, but I don't know his name. I don't fucking *want* to know his name.

I already know Sloane's and Aaric's, and that's too much.

I knew Nadine's.

We stand shoulder to shoulder as the first-years mop up the blood then finish their assessment, and I focus on cataloging every single thing that's wrong with Sloane's fighting style, which is…a lot. In fact, she looks like she's spent nearly no time training for the quadrant.

That can't be right. Liam was the best fighter in our year, and every marked one knows they have to report to the Riders Quadrant when they're of age. Surely she's trained.

"You sure she's Liam's sister?" Ridoc asks.

"Yep," Imogen answers with a long sigh. "But she sure wasn't fostered with fighters, and it shows."

Aaric puts her on her ass six times with little to no effort.

Well, shit. This complicates some things. Like keeping her alive.

An hour later, I make it through physics under Rhi's watchful gaze, more than aware of the first-year's blood drying on my skin and holding my head high when other cadets stare. It's easier once the ringing in my ears lessens, but I'm still nauseated as hell after class.

I beg off from dinner and turn down Rhi's offer of help to get to my room, slowly but surely taking the steps up to the second-years' floor. Every bone, every muscle, every fiber of my being aches.

A heartbeat before I reach for my door handle, I feel it, the familiar midnight-tinted shadow wrapping around my mind.

Relief courses through me as I push open the door and see Xaden leaning against the wall between my desk and my bed, looking ready to kill someone as usual, his arms folded over his chest.

"It's been eight days," I croak, wincing.

"I know," he counters, pushing off the wall and crossing the room in a few steps. "And from what Tairn showed Sgaeyl, I should have told my commander to fuck off and gotten here sooner." He takes my face in his hands in a way that feels completely different from the way Emetterio had earlier, and the rage shining in his eyes is at odds with the gentleness of his touch as he takes stock of my injuries.

"The blood is his." My throat feels like I swallowed fire.

"Good." His jaw flexes as his gaze drops to the bruises I know are around my neck.

"I don't even know what his name was."

"I know." His hands fall away, and I immediately mourn their loss.

"Colonel Aetos sent him."

He nods, the motion curt. "I'm sorry I couldn't kill him first."

"The first-year? Or Aetos?"

"Both." He doesn't smile at my attempt at a joke. "Let's get you clean and wrapped up."

"You can't go around killing cadets. You're an officer now."

"Watch me."

"What's it like at Samara?" I ask him hours later as I sit cross-legged on my bed, bathed and choking down the bowl of soup he brought up for me from the mess in the main campus. Every swallow hurts, but he's right—I can't afford to weaken myself by not eating.

"Look at you, asking questions." A corner of Xaden's mouth rises as he leans back, taking over the armchair in the corner of my room, sharpening his daggers on a strap of leather. He ditched the flight leathers while I was in the bath, but he somehow looks even better in his new uniform. I can't help but notice he didn't add patches to this one, either. He'd only ever worn his wingleader insignia and wing designation while he was in the quadrant.

"I'm not fighting with you about your question game tonight." I shoot a glare his way, spotting the two tomes Jesinia loaned me on the bookshelf next to him. But any thought of telling him about my research disappeared at his reminder that I'm not granted the full truth when it comes to him.

"Wanting you to ask what you want to know isn't a game. You and me? Not a game." He drags his blade over the leather again and again. "And Samara is... different."

"The one-word answers aren't going to cut it."

He looks up from his work. "I have to prove myself all over again at what's arguably the cruelest outpost we have. It's…annoying."

I crack a smile. Leave it to Xaden to be *annoyed.* "Do they treat you differently?"

"You mean because of this?" He taps the side of his neck with the flat of his blade, touching the relic.

"Yes."

He shrugs. "I think the last name does it more than the relic. The older riders are easier on Garrick, which I'm thankful for."

I set the spoon down in the bowl. "I'm sorry."

"It's nothing worse than what I expected, and my signet's enough to give most of them pause." He puts the leather strap into his rucksack, then sheathes his last blade as he stands. "You know what it's like. People judge you by your last name all the time."

"I think it's safe to say you have it worse."

"Only within the borders." He flips my armor over where it's drying on the back of my desk chair, then crosses the room to sit on the end of my bed. It's not as big as his was last year, but there's room for both of us if I ask him to stay. Which I won't. It's hard enough to be this close and not kiss him. Sleeping next to him? I'd break for sure.

"Fair point." I put the bowl on my nightstand and pick up my brush, my gaze drifting to the door when I hear Rhiannon's voice in the hallway a second before she shuts her door. Which reminds me… "Did you ward my room from visitors before you left?"

He nods. "It's warded against sound, too." He crosses his ankle over his knee, keeping his boots off my bed. "One-way, of course. You can hear what's going on out there, but they can't hear what's going on in here. Figured you might like your privacy."

"For all the people I *can't* bring in?"

"You can bring in whomever you want," he counters.

"Really?" Sarcasm drips from my voice as I drag the brush through my damp hair. "Because Rhiannon tried to walk in and ended up on the other side of the hallway."

The corners of his mouth lift into a glimpse of a smile. "Tell her to hold your hand next time. The only way in here is by touching you."

"Wait." I pause, then finish pulling the brush through my snagged ends. "So you didn't ward it for only you and me?"

"It's your room, Violet." His eyes track the movement of the brush through my hair, and the way his fingers curl in his lap makes me swallow. Hard. "The room is warded to let in whomever you pull through." He clears his throat and shifts his weight as I finish another pass with the brush. "And selfishly, me."

I fucking love your hair. If you ever want to bring me to my knees or win an argument, just let it down. I'll get the point.

My breath catches at the memory. Has it really only been a few months since he said that? It feels simultaneously like forever…and yesterday.

"You warded my room for complete privacy for me and anyone I want to bring in?" I lift my eyebrows at him. "In case I feel like…"

"Doing whatever you want." The heat in his gaze makes my breath catch. "No one will hear a thing. Even if you wreck an armoire."

I fumble the brush and it falls into my lap, but I quickly recover. Kind of. "This particular one seems pretty solid. Nothing like the flimsy piece I had in my room last year." The one we accidentally turned into firewood the first time we'd gotten our hands on each other.

"Is that a challenge?" He glances at the furniture. "Because I guarantee we can take it down once you're healed."

"No one's ever fully healed around here."

"Good point. Just say the words, Violet." The way he looks at me is enough to raise my temperature a few degrees. "It only takes three."

Three words?

Oh, like *hell* am I going to tell him that I want him. He already has too much power over me.

"*Can* and *should* are two different things," I manage to say. My willpower when it comes to Xaden is pure shit. One touch, and I'll be back in his arms, accepting whatever he deems as enough of the truth instead of the full access I deserve…no, need. "And we definitely shouldn't."

"Then tell me how your week was instead." He changes topics smoothly.

"I couldn't watch them all," I admit. "At Parapet. I tried, but I…couldn't."

"You were on the tower?" His brow furrows.

"Yes." I shift, tucking my sore knees to the side. "I promised Liam I'd help Sloane, and I couldn't do that from the courtyard." A sarcastic laugh escapes my lips. "And she fucking hates me."

"It's impossible to hate you." He stands and walks to where his rucksack is leaned up against the wall. "Trust me. I tried."

"Trust *me*. She does. She actually wanted to challenge me at assessment." I lean back against my headboard. "She blames me for Liam's death. Not that she's wrong—"

"Liam's death wasn't your fault," he interrupts, his body going rigid. "It was mine. If Sloane wants to hate anyone, she can aim it all right here." He taps his chest as he turns, setting his rucksack on the desk.

"It wasn't your fault." It's not the first time we've had the argument, and something tells me it won't be the last. I guess there's enough guilt for two to carry.

"It was." He opens the top and rifles through the bag.

"Xaden—"

"How many candidates fell this year?" He pulls out a folded paper, then closes the bag.

"Too many." Even now I can hear some of their screams.

"It's always too many." He sits on my bed again, this time close enough that my knees brush his thigh. "And it's okay that you couldn't watch the younger ones die. It means you're still you."

"As opposed to turning into someone else?" My stomach twists at the flat expression on his face, the wall mentioning Liam's death put solidly between us. "Because I feel like I am. I don't even want to know the first-years' names. I don't want to know *them*. I don't want it to hurt when they die. What does that make me?"

"A second-year." He says it matter-of-factly, the same way he'd declared that he couldn't save every marked one last year, only the ones willing to help themselves.

Sometimes I forget how ruthless he is.

How ruthless he can be on my behalf.

"I've seen death before," I respond. "I was practically surrounded by it last year."

"It's not the same. Seeing our friends—our equals—die on the Gauntlet, at Threshing, in challenges, or even in battle is one thing. Everyone in here is just fighting to survive, and it prepares us for what happens out there. But when it's the younger candidates…" He shakes his head and leans forward.

I grip my brush to keep from reaching for him.

"The first year is when some of us lose our lives," he says softly, tucking my damp hair behind my ear. "The second year is when the rest of us lose our humanity. It's all part of the process of turning us into effective weapons, and don't forget for a second that's the mission here."

"Desensitizing us to death?"

He nods.

A knock sounds at the door, and I startle but can't help but notice Xaden doesn't. He sighs and stands, heading for the door.

"Already?" he asks after opening it, blocking me from view. Or blocking the view *from* me.

"Already." I recognize Bodhi's voice.

"Give me a minute." Xaden shuts the door without waiting for a response.

"Let me come with you." I swing my feet over the side of the bed.

"No." He crouches in front of me, putting us at eye level, the parchment from his bag still clutched in his fist. "Sleep is the fastest way to heal unless you plan on seeking out Nolon, and from what I hear, he's hard to come by these days."

"You need sleep, too," I protest around the dread filling my throat. We only have hours, and I'm not ready for him to go. "You flew for half a day."

"I have a lot to get done before morning."

"Let me help." Shit, now I'm begging.

"Not yet." He reaches out to cup my face, then drops his hand as if rethinking the move. "But I need you to pay close attention to what happens when you leave in seven days with Tairn." He presses the paper into my hand. "Until then…here."

"What is this?" I spare a glance downward, but it only looks like folded parchment.

"You told me once that I was scared you might not like me if you got to really know me."

"I remember."

"Every time we're together, we're training or fighting. There's not a lot of time for long walks by the river or whatever passes for romance around here." He squeezes my hand gently, but I can feel every callus he's built from mastering his weaponry. "But I told you I'd find a way to let you in, and right now, this is all I have."

My gaze jerks to his and my heart flies into my throat.

"I'll see you at Samara." He stands and grabs his rucksack and the two swords leaned up against the wall next to the door.

"How do I find you once I'm there?" My fingers clench the folded parchment. I've never even seen Samara. Mom has never been stationed there.

He turns at the door and looks back at me, holding my gaze. "Third floor, south wing, second door on the right. The wards will let you in."

His barracks room.

"Let me guess—warded for sound and to let in you, me, and anyone you tug through?" The idea of him using that soundproofing for breaking armoires with someone else is enough to curdle the soup in my stomach.

We might not be together, but jealousy's not exactly a rational emotion.

"No, Violet." He lifts both swords overhead, then slips them into the sheaths on the pack behind him with practiced expertise and a hint of a smirk. "Just you and me."

He's gone before I can even think of a reply.

With trembling hands, I unfold the paper—and smile.

Xaden Riorson wrote me a letter.

Garrick has always been my best friend. His father was my father's aide, which in a way makes him my Dain, except trustworthy. After Liam, Bodhi was and still is the closest thing I have to a brother, perpetually tagging along a step behind.

—RECOVERED CORRESPONDENCE OF LIEUTENANT XADEN RIORSON TO CADET VIOLET SORRENGAIL

CHAPTER ELEVEN

A smile curving my lips, I brace my hands on the top of my head and walk off the stitch in my side as Imogen and I finish our post-run cooldown a few mornings later, entering the courtyard a full half hour before breakfast is set to be served.

He wrote me a *letter*, and I've read it so many times I already have it memorized. There's nothing remotely dangerous in it, no secrets of the revolution or clues on how to help, but it's not like he can risk those by putting them in writing. No, this is even better. It's just about *him*. It's little details, like the fact that he used to sit on the roof of Riorson House during the rebellion in hopes his father would come home and tell him it was all over.

"You've been grinning like a drunkard for the last three mornings," Imogen complains, ducking to check under the dais as we pass by. "How is *anyone* that happy at sunrise?"

Can't blame her. I've been on edge since assessment day, too. So are Bodhi and Eya.

"No nightmares the last few days, and no one's up at this hour trying to kill me." My hands fall to my side. I made it a little farther between walking breaks this time.

"Yeah, because *that's* the reason." She rolls her neck. "Why don't you take him back already?"

"He doesn't trust me." I shrug. "And I can't really trust him. It's complicated." But damn do I miss catching glimpses of him every day. Saturday can't get here soon enough. "Besides, even if two people have unmatched chemistry, that doesn't mean they should be in a relationship beyond anything physical—"

"Oh, no." She shakes her head, then tucks a strand of pink hair behind her ear. "I was finishing a conversation. Not starting one. I'm down for running and weight training with you, but you have friends to talk about your sex life with. Remember? The ones I'm watching you actively avoid at every opportunity?"

Not going there.

"And we aren't friends?" I question.

"We're…" Her face scrunches. "Coconspirators with a vested interest in keeping each other alive."

That only makes me smile bigger. "Oh, don't go getting soft on me now."

Her gaze narrows as she looks past me, toward the outer wall. "What in Dunne's name would a scribe be doing in the quadrant at this hour?"

I startle at the sight of Jesinia waiting in one of the shaded alcoves, tucked away like she's trying to hide. "Relax. She's a friend."

Imogen dishes out a heaping dose of side-eye. "You're pretty much hiding from the second-years but befriending *scribes*?"

"I'm distancing myself so I don't have to lie to them, and I've been friends with Jes— You know what? I don't owe you an explanation. I'm going to see what *my friend* needs." I increase my pace, but Imogen matches it. "Hi," I sign to Jesinia as we near the alcove. This particular one has a tunnel that leads straight into the dormitory. "Everything all right?"

"I came to find you—" Her brow puckers under her hood as her gaze shifts to Imogen, who's sizing her up like she would an opponent.

"I'm fine," I tell Imogen, signing at the same time. "Jesinia isn't going to try to kill me."

Imogen tilts her head, her gaze dropping to the cream satchel Jesinia carries.

"I'm not going to try to kill her," Jesinia signs, her brown eyes widening. "I wouldn't even know how."

"Violet knew how to kill just fine on a scribe's education," Imogen replies, her hands moving quickly.

Jesinia blinks.

I lift my brows at Imogen.

"Fine," she replies, signing as she backs away. "But if she comes at you with a sharpened quill, don't blame me."

"Sorry about her," I sign once Imogen turns her back to us.

"People are trying to kill you?" Jesinia's brow knits.

"It's Thursday." I move into the alcove so my back isn't to the courtyard. "I'm always happy to see you, but what can I help you with?" Scribe cadets almost never enter the Riders Quadrant unless they're assisting Captain Fitzgibbons.

"Two things," she signs as we both sit on the bench, then reaches into her satchel, pulls out a tome, and hands it to me. It's a copy of *The Gift of the First Six* and looks to be hundreds of years old. "You said you wanted an early accounting of the first riders when you returned the other books," she signs. "This is one of the earliest I could find that's allowed to be removed from the Archives. Preparing for another debate?"

I set it on my lap and choose my words carefully. My gut tells me I can trust her, but after Dain, I'm not sure I can depend on my intuition, and knowing isn't safe for her, anyway. "Studying. And thank you, but you didn't have to bring it. I would have come to you."

"I didn't want you to have to wait for me to be on Archives duty, and you told me you run every morning…" She takes several deep breaths, which usually means she's composing her thoughts. "And I hate to admit it, but I need help," she signs before pulling a ragged tome out of the bag and handing it to me.

I take it to free up her hands, noting the worn edges and loose spine.

"I'm trying to translate this for an assignment, and I'm struggling with a couple of sentences. It's in Old Lucerish, and from what I remember, it's one of the dead languages you can read." Her cheeks flush pink as she glances back over her shoulder at the mage-lit tunnel, as if another scribe might see us. "I'll be in trouble if anyone knows I'm asking for help. Adepts shouldn't ask."

"I'm good at keeping secrets," I sign, my face falling as I remember using the language to pass secret messages with Dain when we were kids.

"Thank you. I know almost every other language." Her motions are sharp, and her mouth tenses.

"You know far more of them than I do." We share a smile, and I flip open the tome to the bookmark, taking in the swirling strokes of ink that make up the logosyllabic language.

Jesinia points to a sentence. "I'm stuck there."

I quickly read from the beginning of the paragraph to be sure I have it right, then sign the sentence she's looking for, spelling out the last word—the name of an ancient king who lived a thousand years before Navarre existed.

"Thank you." She writes the sentence down in the notebook she's brought with her.

Ancient king. I flip to the first page of the book, and my shoulders sag. It bears a date from twenty-five years ago.

"It's hand-copied from an original," Jesinia signs. "About five years before the quadrant received the printing press."

Right. Because nothing in the Archives is older than four hundred years except the scrolls from the Unification. Sweat cools on the back of my neck as I translate a few more sentences for her from various pages, surprised at how much I still remember after not practicing for a year, then hand the tome back when I finish the last sentence she has marked.

If I hurry, I can bathe the sweat off and still catch breakfast.

"We're working on removing all the dead languages from the public section of the Archives and translating them for easier reading," she signs with an excited smile, then puts her things away. "You should come by and see how much we've accomplished."

"Riders aren't allowed past the study table," I remind her.

"I'd make an exception for you." She grins. "The Archives are almost always empty on Sundays, especially with most third-years cycling home for break."

A scream rends the air, and my head shoots up. Across the courtyard, a second-year from Third Wing is dragged from the academic building, between two older riders, followed by Professor Markham.

What in Amari's name?

Jesinia pales and sinks farther into the shadows of the alcove as he's hauled into the dormitory building, where the tunnels beneath lead across the canyon and into the main campus of Basgiath. "I think," she signs, starting to breathe raggedly. "I think that's my fault."

"What?" I turn to face her fully.

"That rider requested a book yesterday, and I recorded the request." She leans toward me, panic growing in her eyes. "I have to record the requests. It's—"

"Regulation," we both finish signing at the same time. I nod. "You didn't do anything wrong. What was the book?"

She glances toward the doors where the rider disappeared. "I should go. Thank you."

It's only the fear in her eyes that keeps me from asking her again before she rushes off, leaving me staring at the tome in my lap, realizing how dangerous my "research project" really is.

"**W**ait for me!" Rhiannon calls out later that day, jogging up through the crowd of riders as we reach the steps beside the Gauntlet, where most of us are bottlenecked as we wait for our turn to climb up to the flight field.

"We're still here!" I wave before my gaze returns to moving restlessly over the people closest to us, watching their hands, their weapons. I trust my squadmates implicitly, but no one else. All it takes is a well-timed stab in a crowd, and I could bleed out without even knowing who'd killed me.

"This isn't right," Sawyer mutters, refolding our homework map for RSC. "I can't get number four no matter how many times I count the little elevation lines."

"That's north," I tell him, tapping the bottom of the folded monstrosity. "You're looking at the wrong sector for question four. Trust me, I had to ask Ridoc for help last night."

"Ugh. This is some infantry bullshit." He shoves the map into his pocket.

"Why won't you just accept that I am a land navigation god and ask for help like everyone else?" Ridoc teases Sawyer as Rhi catches up to us. "Finally! You'd think leadership would be on time."

"Leadership was in a meeting," Rhi replies, holding up a collection of missives. "And leadership was given the mail!"

Hope leaps up, replacing the hypervigilance for a second before I can squash it.

"Ridoc," Rhiannon says, handing over a letter. "Sawyer." She turns, giving him the next one. "Me." She flips that one to the back. "And Violet."

He wouldn't, I remind myself before taking the letter from her, yet I can't help but hold my breath as I open the unsealed flap of the envelope.

Violet,
Sorry it took me so long to write. I only just realized the date. You're a second-year!

My shoulders droop, which is just…pathetic.

"Who's it from?" Rhiannon asks. "You look disappointed."

"Mira," I answer. "And no, not disappointed…" My words trail off as we move forward in line.

"You thought it would be a different lieutenant," she guesses correctly, her eyes softening in sympathy.

I shrug, but it's hard to keep the frustration out of my voice. "I know better."

"You miss him, don't you?" She drops her voice as we shuffle closer to the steps.

I nod. "I shouldn't, but I do."

"Are you two together?" she whispers. "I mean, everyone knows you're sleeping together, but something's off with you."

I glance ahead, making sure Sawyer and Ridoc are engrossed in their letters. This is a truth I can easily give her. "Not anymore."

"Why?" she asks, confusion etching her forehead. "What happened?"

I open my mouth, then shut it. Maybe the truth *isn't* that easy. What the hell am I supposed to tell her? Gods, when did this all become so complicated?

"You can tell me, you know." She forces a smile, and the hurt I see behind it makes me feel like total and complete shit.

"I know." Lucky for me, we start up the steps, giving me a chance to think.

We reach the top, walking into the box canyon of the flight field, and my heart swells at the sight of the dragons organized in the same formation we stand at in the courtyard. It's a beautiful, terrifying, humbling kaleidoscope of power that steals the breath from my lungs.

"This is never going to get old, is it?" Rhiannon says as we follow Ridoc and Sawyer across the formation, her smile overtaking her face.

"I don't think so." We share a look, and I break. "Xaden wasn't honest with me," I say quietly, feeling like I owe my best friend *something* true. "I had to end it."

Her eyes flare. "He lied?"

"No." My grip tightens on Mira's letter. "He didn't tell me the entire truth. He still won't."

"Another woman?" Her brows rise. "Because I will absolutely help you annihilate that shadow-wielding asshole if you guys were exclusive and he—"

"No, no." I laugh. "Nothing like that." We pass by Second Wing's dragons. "It's…" There go my words again. "It's…complicated. How are you and Tara? I haven't seen her around much."

She sighs. "Neither of us has enough time for the other. It sucks, but maybe it will ease up next year when neither of us are squad leaders anymore."

"Or maybe you'll be wingleaders." The thought makes me bite back a smile. Rhi would be a fantastic wingleader.

"Maybe." There's a bounce to her step. "But in the meantime, we're free to see whoever we want. What about you? Because if you're single, I have to say that a couple of the guys in Second Wing somehow got hotter after War Games." Her eyes sparkle. "Or we could secretly visit Chantara this weekend and hook up with some infantry cadets!" She holds up a finger. "Healers might be all right, too, but I draw the line at scribes. The robes don't do it for me. Not that I'm judging if that's your thing. I'm just saying that we are second-years and our options for blowing off steam are *endless*."

A random stranger might be what I need to flush Xaden out of my system, but it isn't what I want.

She studies my face like I'm a puzzle that needs to be solved as we continue down the field. "Shit. You're hung up on him."

"I'm…" I sigh. "It's complicated."

"You said that already." She tries to school her expression, but I catch the flash of disappointment when I don't elaborate. "Mira have anything to say about the front?"

"Not sure." I glance through the letter, reading it quickly. "She's been reassigned to Athebyne. She says the food is only a step above our mother's cooking." That gets a laugh out of me as I flip the page over, but it dies quickly when I see the thick black lines that eliminate entire paragraphs. "What the…" I flip to the next page, finding more of the same before she signs off, hoping to fly over to Samara during one of my upcoming trips.

"What's wrong?" Rhiannon looks up from her own letter as we continue walking, passing by Third Wing's dragons.

"I think it's been redacted." I flash it at her so she can see the black lines, then look around to make sure no one else notices.

"Someone censored your letter?" She looks surprised. "Someone *read* your letter?"

"It was unsealed." I stuff it back into the envelope.

"Who would do that?"

Melgren. Varrish. Markham. Anyone on Aetos's orders. My mother. The options are endless. "I'm not sure." It's not a lie, not really. I slip the envelope into the internal pocket of my flight leathers and then cringe as I button up the jacket. It's too fucking hot for these things down here, but I know I'll be grateful for the extra layer in a few minutes once we're airborne.

A red in the second row huffs a blast of steam in warning at a cadet from Third Wing who gets too close, and we all hurry along.

Tairn is the largest dragon on the field by far, and he looks completely and utterly bored as he waits for me, the metal of my saddle glistening against his scales in the sun. I can't help but sigh in disappointment that Andarna isn't with him as his forelegs come into view.

"Hey, has Tairn said anything about another black dragon in the Vale?" Ridoc asks me over his shoulder as we make it past Claw Section, coming to Tairn first, who's standing in the lead position despite Rhiannon and Sawyer outranking me.

It's all I can do to not trip over my feet. "I'm sorry?"

"I know, it sounds ludicrous, but when we walked by Kaori back there, I swear I heard him say something about another black dragon being spotted. The guy was practically jumping with excitement."

"Tairn?" If the professor of dragonkind knows about Andarna, we're screwed.

"Only a few dragons saw her before she entered the caves for the Dreamless Sleep. You try keeping her hidden and see how it goes for you."

Awesome.

"Maybe it's Tairn they're seeing," I say to Ridoc. Not a lie. "Or an elder?"

"Kaori thinks it's a new one." His eyebrows rise. "You should ask him."

"Huh." I swallow. "Yeah, I can do that." Still not lying.

The three continue on, mounting their dragons.

Tairn dips his left shoulder for me but then straightens. *"On your left,"* he warns as a shape approaches from behind.

I whip around quickly to face the threat and secure my shields in place.

Varrish saunters toward me, his arms locked behind his back, and the major must be inhuman because there's not a dot of sweat on his high forehead. "Ah, Sorrengail, there you are."

As if Tairn is hard to miss.

"Major Varrish." I leave my hands at my thighs, where I can grab hold of my daggers easily, wondering what his signet might be. I've never seen a signet patch on him. Either he's cocky like Xaden and thinks his reputation precedes him or he's part of the classified-signet club.

"Quite the necklace you have there." He points to the greenish bruises on my throat.

"Thank you. It was expensive." I lift my chin. "Cost someone their life."

"Ah, that's right. I recall hearing you were nearly done in by a *first-year*. Good to see that the embarrassment didn't finish the job he started. But I guess you're probably used to barely squeaking by alive, seeing how frail you're rumored to be."

I officially loathe this man, but at least I know Tairn will eat him whole if he tries to attack me on the field.

He leans left, making a show of looking around me. "I thought you were bonded to two dragons?"

"I am." Sweat slides down my spine.

"And yet, I only see one." He looks up at Tairn. "Where's your little gold one? The feathertail I've heard so much about? I was hoping to see her for myself."

A growl rumbles up Tairn's throat, and he angles his head over me. Saliva drips in giant globs, hitting the ground in front of Varrish.

The major tenses but maintains a perfect mask of amusement as he steps back. "Always has had a temper, this one."

"He likes his space."

"I've noticed he likes you to have yours, too," he comments. "Tell me, Sorrengail, how do you feel about the way he gives you…oh, shall we say, an *easier* path to take than your fellow cadets?"

"If you mean to ask how I feel about how he stopped the needless execution of bonded riders by your dragon after Parapet, then I'd have to say that I feel pretty good about it. I guess it takes one *bad-tempered* dragon to keep another civil."

"Remind him that I threatened to digest him alive."

"I don't think that would go well for me," I reply.

"It would be fun to watch him eat the pompous one." Andarna's voice is groggy.

"Go back to sleep," I lecture. She's not due to wake for another month, Tairn said.

Varrish's eyes narrow momentarily on mine, and then he smiles, but there's nothing kind or happy about it. "About your little feathertail—"

"She can't bear a rider." Not lying, since she hasn't flown since waking in Aretia. "I fly with Tairn, but she'll go through maneuvers on the easier days."

"Well, see to it that she flies with you next week, and you can consider that an order."

Another growl sounds from Tairn.

"Dragons don't take orders from humans." Power rises within me, humming beneath my skin and making my fingers buzz.

"Of course not." His grin widens like I've said something funny. "But you do, don't you?"

"Impudent human," Tairn seethes.

I lift my chin, knowing there's nothing more I can say about this without disciplinary action.

"It's ironic, don't you think?" Varrish asks, retreating one step at a time. "From what Colonel Aetos told me, your father was writing a book on feathertails—dragons which hadn't been seen in hundreds of years—and then you ended up bonded to one."

"Coincidental," I correct him. "The word you meant to say is 'coincidental.'"

"Is it?" He seems to ponder, backing away and passing by Bodhi.

My stomach turns. *"Is it?"*

"I know nothing of your father's research," Tairn promises.

But Andarna has gone silent.

"Riders!" Kaori projects his voice across the field as Bodhi reaches my side. "Third-years have joined us today for a very special reason. They'll be demonstrating a running landing." He gestures to the sky.

Cath is on approach from the west, the Red Swordtail blocking out the sun for a second as he dives for the field.

"He's not slowing down," I murmur. Part of me hopes Dain falls off.

"He will," Bodhi promises. "Just not by much."

My jaw slackens. Dain rides crouched on Cath's *shoulder*, his arms out for balance as Cath drops to fly level with the field. The beats of Cath's wings slow only slightly the closer he gets, and I hold my breath when Dain slides down Cath's leg to perch on his claw while his dragon is still *flying*.

Holy. Shit.

"This is unadvisable for you," Tairn says.

"For anyone *with a heartbeat,"* I counter.

Cath flares his wings subtly, enough to drop speed, and Dain jumps as he passes by the professors. He hits the sunburned grass at a run, dispelling the momentum from Cath's flight within a few yards, and comes to a stop.

The third-years cheer, but Bodhi remains silent at my side.

"And that is why Aetos is a wingleader," Kaori calls out. "Perfect execution. This approach is the most efficient landing for when we need to engage in ground combat. By the time this year is over, you'll be able to land like this on any outpost wall. Pay close attention, and you'll be able to complete this safely. Try your own method, and you'll be dead before you hit the ground."

The fuck I will.

"Adaptation will be necessary," Tairn decrees.

"For today, we're going to practice the basics of moving from the seat to the shoulder," Kaori instructs.

"How are we adapting to that?" I ask Tairn.

"I didn't say we would." He chuffs. *"The dragon-watcher will adapt his request, or I'll have an early lunch."*

This maneuver is totally, completely pointless in the kind of war we need to fight.

"Kaori doesn't know what's out there," I say softly to Bodhi.

"What makes you so sure?" He glances my way.

"If he did, he'd be teaching us faster ways to get *off* the damned ground, not land on it."

"Tell him that we're still working on the next shipment," Bodhi tells me as we walk through the moonlit flight field a little before midnight a few nights later.

"Shipment of what?" I ask, adjusting my pack on my shoulders.

"He'll know what I'm talking about," he promises, wincing as his fingers graze the dark bruise on his jaw. "And tell him it's raw. They've had the forge burning night and day, so we haven't been able to—" He flinches. "Just tell him it's raw."

"I'm starting to feel a lot like a letter." I shoot a glare at him for a second. That's all I'm willing to look away from the uneven terrain for. There's no chance I'm risking a sprained ankle before a twelve-hour flight.

"You're the best way of getting information to him," he admits.

"Without actually knowing anything."

"Precisely." He nods. "It's safer this way until you're capable of shielding from Aetos at all times. Xaden was supposed to continue teaching you last visit, but then…"

"I got strangled." At least I've only been attacked once so far this year, but challenges open back up in a week.

"Yeah. It kind of fucked with his head."

"I imagine that dropping dead randomly would have been inconvenient to him," I mutter, half listening. *Shit.* Challenges open up in a *week*. It's time to start checking the list the cadre keeps so I can go about my poisoning ways again.

"You know it's not like that for him," he says in a lecturing tone that reminds me of Xaden. "I've never seen him—"

"Let's not do this."

"—care like this—"

"No really. Stop."

"—and that includes Catriona."

My gaze whips toward him. "Who the hell is Catriona?"

He winces and presses his lips in a thin line. "What are the chances that you'll forget I said that between here and Samara?"

"None." I stumble on a rock, or my feelings, but manage to catch my balance. Physically, at least. My thoughts? Those are tripping over themselves down the path of wondering who Catriona is. An older rider? Someone from Aretia?

"Right." He rubs the back of his neck and sighs. "Not even the tiniest bit of a chance? Because the thing about the deal you two have with your dragons is that he'll be back here next week, and I'm not remotely in the mood to have my ass kicked after fending off another assassination attempt."

I grab his arm and stop walking. "*Another* assassination attempt?"

He sighs. "Yeah. Second time someone tried to jump me in the bathing chamber this week."

My eyes widen as my heart hammers in my chest. "Are you okay?"

He has the gall to grin. "I completely eviscerated some asshole out of Second Wing while naked and only got a bruise. I'm fine. But back to why you shouldn't mention that comment to my rather moody cousin you're sleeping with—"

"You know what?" I start walking to the middle of the field again. If he doesn't want to process assassination attempts, then we have nothing else to say. "I don't know you nearly well enough to discuss who I am or am not sleeping with, Bodhi," I throw over my shoulder.

He shoves his hands in his pockets and leans back on his heels. "You make a fair point."

"I made the *only* point." Tairn's silhouette blocks the moon for a heartbeat before he lands ahead of us.

Bodhi grins sheepishly. "Your dragon has arrived in time to save us from the awkwardness of this conversation."

"Let's get going," Tairn all but snaps. I try not to take it personally. He's been insufferable for days now, but I can't blame him. I can feel his physical pain like a knife to my own chest when he overpowers my emotions.

"He's in a rush," I tell Bodhi. "Thanks for walking me out—"

"Humans!"

"Well, fuck." Bodhi swears under his breath as mage lights flicker on behind us, lighting up the field the same way they had the night we flew for War Games.

"Cadet Sorrengail, you will delay your launch." Varrish amplifies his voice across the field.

We turn and see him flanked by two other riders, walking our way.

Tairn growls in answer.

Bodhi and I exchange a glance, but we both remain silent as the trio approaches.

"What do we do if they try to stop us?" I ask Tairn.

"Feast."

Gross.

"I didn't expect you to leave until morning," Varrish says, flashing an oily smile as the two other riders flank us. The stripes on their uniforms declare them as first lieutenants, the same as Mira, one rank above Xaden.

"It's been a fortnight. I'm on leave."

"So you are." Varrish blinks at me, then looks at the female lieutenant on my left. "Nora, search her bag."

"I'm sorry?" I put a step between me and the woman.

"Your bag," Varrish repeats. "Article Four, Section One of the Codex states—"

"That all cadet belongings are subject to search at the discretion of command," I finish for him.

"Ah, you know your Codex. Good. Your bag."

I swallow, then roll my shoulders, letting the pack slip off my back before holding it out to the left, never taking my eyes from Varrish. The first lieutenant takes the rucksack from my hand.

"You may leave, Cadet Durran," Varrish says.

Bodhi moves closer to my side, and the male lieutenant takes a step closer as well, the mage lights catching the signet patch—fire wielding—on his uniform. "As Cadet Sorrengail's section leader, I am the next in her chain of command. And as Article Four, Section Two of the Codex states, her discipline falls to her chain of command *before* being brought to cadre. I would be negligent in my duty were I to leave her in potential possession of…whatever it is you're looking for."

Varrish narrows his eyes as Nora empties my bag onto the ground.

So much for a clean change of clothing.

Tairn lowers his head behind me, angling slightly to the side and growling deeply in his throat. At this angle, he can scorch two of them without touching Bodhi or me, which would only leave one for us to dispatch if we have to.

Anger prickles along my spine, and I fist my hands like that's going to actually help me contain the burst of power crawling through my veins.

"Was that really necessary?" the other lieutenant asks.

"He said search," Nora replies before looking up at Varrish. "Clothing," she says, flipping the pieces over. Her hands tremble when she glances in Tairn's direction. "Second-year physics text, land navigation manual, and a hairbrush."

"Give me the book and the manual." Varrish holds his hand out to Nora.

"Need a refresher?" I ask, suddenly grateful I left my copy of *The Gift of the First Six* in my room, not that it's taught me anything besides the fact that the First Six weren't the first riders—they were simply the first to survive.

Varrish doesn't respond as he flips through the pages, no doubt looking for scrawled secrets in the margins. His jaw flexes when he doesn't find any.

"Satisfied?" I drum my fingers along the sheaths at my thighs.

"We're done here." He tosses the book onto the pile of clothing. "See you in forty-eight hours, Cadet Sorrengail. And don't forget—since your feathertail decided not to join you for formation again, I will be pondering your punishment for dereliction of duty while you are gone."

And with that threat, the trio walks away, the mage lights winking off one by one as they pass, leaving us in the dark again except for the circle of light directly above us.

"You knew that was going to happen." I glare at Bodhi before crouching in front of my discarded things, packing them back into the bag. "That's why you insisted on walking me out."

"In addition to the very real attempts on *all* of our lives—Imogen and Eya were attacked today, too, coming out of a briefing for third-years—we suspected they'd search you but wanted to confirm," he admits, dropping down to help.

They could have died. My heart stutters in my chest, and I quickly fold that fear into the box where I've decided to hide all my feelings this year. Well, all emotions except one: anger.

"You used me as a *test*?" I jerk the fastener on the pack closed and shove my arms through the straps, hoisting it to my shoulders. "Without even telling me? Let me guess—it was Xaden's idea?"

"It was an experiment." He grimaces. "You were the control."

"Then what the fuck was the variable?"

The bells ring out, the sound faint from here.

"Check Tairn. It's midnight. You should get going," Bodhi says. "Every minute you stay is one fewer that Tairn gets with Sgaeyl."

"Agreed."

"Stop using me like I'm some kind of game piece, Bodhi." Each word is sharper than the last. "You two want my help? Ask for it. And don't fucking start on me about my shielding abilities. That's no excuse to send me into something unprepared."

He looks abashed. "Fair point."

I nod, then mount the ramp Tairn creates by dropping a shoulder. Moonlight and what little mage light reaches this height is more than sufficient for me to find the saddle. I could navigate the spikes of Tairn's back in the darkest night. I proved that in Resson.

There are already two packs twice the size of mine secured behind the saddle.

"Good thing they didn't search me," Tairn says.

"Are we carrying…" I blink twice.

"We are," he confirms. *"Now get in the saddle before they change their minds and I'm forced to incinerate your leadership. Later I'll have more than a few words for the wingleader about not preparing you, trust me."*

Taking a second to secure my pack, too, I settle in for the flight, dragging the leather across my thighs and strapping in.

"Let's get to them," I say once I'm buckled.

Tairn backs up a few steps, no doubt to keep Bodhi clear, and then launches into the night, every wingbeat taking us closer to the front lines…and Xaden.

CHAPTER
TWELVE

The landscape around the Samara outpost is as severe as the command that
runs it.

We're high in the Esben Mountains, a mile or two from the eastern border
with Poromiel, and surrounded by peaks that are still tipped with snow in the
height of summer. The nearest village is a half-hour flight. There's not even a
trading post within walking distance. This is as cut off from society as it gets.

"Be careful," Tairn orders me, waiting behind me in the field where he landed.
"It's known to be…brutal as a first assignment."

So naturally, they'd send Xaden here.

"I'll be all right," I promise. *"And my shields are up."*

To be sure, I check the walls of my mental Archives, where I ground in my
power, and can't help the little bounce in my step when I see only a hint of light
from my bonds coming from the doorways. I am definitely getting better at this.

I head for the entrance to the mammoth fortress that rises before me,
its dark-red stone cutting into the crisp blue sky. It's probably laid out like
Athebyne and Montserrat, but it's easily twice as big as either. Two companies
of infantry and eighteen dragons and their riders are stationed here.

Something sways up high on the wall, and I look to see a man in infantry
colors sitting in a cage about four stories above me.

Well, all right then. It's a little after eight in the morning, so I can't help but
wonder if he's been up there all night.

There's a hum in my veins that only grows stronger as I walk up the ramp that leads to the portcullis, where two guards are stationed. A platoon passes by, headed out for a morning run.

"It's the wards," Tairn says.

"They didn't feel like this at Montserrat," I tell him.

"They're stronger here, and since your signet has manifested, you're more sensitive to them now." His tone is tight, and when I glance back over my shoulder, I note that all the soldiers give him a wide berth, taking a path off to the side of the field.

"You don't have to watch my back," I say, reaching the top of the ramp. *"This is an outpost. I'm safe here."*

"There's a drift on the other side of the mountains, a mile beyond the border. Sgaeyl just told me. You're not safe until you're behind the walls or with the wingleader."

I don't bother reminding him that Xaden isn't a wingleader anymore as my stomach jumps into my throat. *"A friendly drift?"*

"Define friendly."

Great. We're not *on* the front; we *are* the front.

The guards at the gate stand taller when they take in my flight leathers but remain silent as I pass by. *"They're not acting like there's a drift across the ridgeline."*

"Apparently it's commonplace."

Even better.

"There, I'm all safe behind the walls," I tell Tairn, walking into the bailey of the fortress. At least it's cooler here than at Basgiath, but I'm not sure I'd like to experience winter at this altitude.

Or Aretia's, come to think of it.

"Call if you need me. I'll be nearby." A second later, wingbeats fill the air.

Like hell am I going to call him for anything. In fact, I'll consider these next twenty-four hours a success if I can block him out altogether. I've been on the wrong mental side of the bond during one of his trysts with Sgaeyl, and no thank you.

I pass by several platoons of infantry standing in formation and note the infirmary off to the right, in the same location as Montserrat's, but I'm the only person in black.

Where the hell are all the riders? I stifle a yawn—there wasn't much sleep to be had in the saddle—and locate the entrance to the barracks that make up the southern side of the fortress. The corridor is dimly lit as I walk through, passing the office of the scribes, but I find the stairs at the end. A sensation of unwelcome familiarity crawls along my skin as I climb.

Breathe.

This outpost isn't deserted. There isn't a horde of venin and wyvern waiting to be spotted from the highest point, either. It's only the same layout because almost all outposts are built from the same plans.

I push open the door to the third floor without encountering anyone. Odd. One side of the hallway is lined with windows that open to the bailey, and the other with equidistant wooden doors. My pulse picks up as I reach for the handle of the second door. It swings open with a squeak, and I recognize the tingle of energy that rushes over my skin, leaving chills in its wake as I step through the wards into Xaden's room.

Xaden's *empty* room.

Shit.

I sigh in pure disappointment as I drop my pack near his desk.

His room is austere, with serviceable furniture and a door that probably leads to a neighboring room, but there are touches of him here and there. He's in the books that sit stacked along the shelves of the bookcase by the window, the rack of weapons I recognize from his room at Basgiath, and the two swords that sit near the door, like he'll be back any second to retrieve them.

The only softness to be found is in the heavy black drapes—standard issue in the room of a rider who might have to fly night patrols—and the plush, dark-gray blanket covering his bed. His very large bed.

Nope. Not thinking about that.

What the hell am I supposed to do if he's not here? The swords say he's not out flying, so I close my eyes and open up my senses, finding the shadow that's only present when he's near. If I found him that night on the parapet, surely I can do it here.

He's close, but he must have his shields locked, because he doesn't reach out like he usually would when I'm close. The bond feels like it's tugging me downward, like he's actually...under me.

I close Xaden's door on the way out and follow the tugging sensation, making my way to the staircase and then descending. I pass the arched entrance to the second floor, catching a glimpse of a wide stone hallway with more barracks doors, then the entrance to the first, and finally reaching the sublevel of the fortress where natural light ends with the staircase on a stone floor. Mage lights illuminate two possible paths along the foundation of the fortress, both dimly lit and as welcoming as a dungeon. The scent of damp earth and metal permeates the air.

Shouts and cheers come from down a corridor to the right, echoing off the walls and floor. I follow the pull of the bond that direction and find a pair of infantry guards about twenty yards from the stairs who take one look at my uniform and step aside, allowing me access to a room carved out of the very foundation.

Noise overwhelms every other sense when I enter the chamber, and shock halts my feet inside the doorway.

What in the gods' names is going on?

More than a dozen riders—all in black—stand along the sides of the square-shaped, windowless room that looks better suited for storage than occupation. They're all leaning over a thick wooden railing, intently watching something in the excavated pit below.

I take the empty space on the rail directly ahead of me, finding myself between a veteran rider with a grizzled beard on my left and a woman who looks a few years older than me on the right. Then I see who's below and my heart stops.

Xaden. And he is shirtless.

So is the other rider as they circle each other, their fists raised like they're sparring. But there's no mat beneath them, only a packed-dirt floor decorated with suspicious spatters of crimson, both old and fresh.

They're equally matched in height, but the other rider is bulky, built like Garrick, and looks to have about twenty pounds on Xaden, who's cut in deep, muscular lines.

The rider swings for Xaden's face, and I white-knuckle the rough railing, holding my breath as Xaden easily evades the punch, delivering one of his own to his opponent's ribs. The riders around me cheer, and I'm pretty sure I see money change hands across the pit.

This isn't sparring. This is straight-up *fighting*.

And the way Xaden hit him? He's holding back.

"Why are they…" I ask the silver-barred lieutenant next to me, my words dying as Xaden dips and spins, avoiding another attempted hit. There's a definite sparkle in those dark eyes as he deftly jumps back again, denying his opponent's strike.

My pulse jumps. Damn, he's *fast*.

"Fighting?" The woman finishes my question.

"Yes." I keep my gaze centered on Xaden, who lands quick, consecutive punches to the other rider's kidneys.

"There's only one pass for lieutenants this weekend," she says, moving a little closer. "Jarrett has it, and Riorson wants it."

"So they're *fighting* for it?" I peel my eyes from Xaden long enough to glance sideways at the rider beside me. She has short brown hair, sharp, birdlike features, and a thumbprint-size scar on her jawline.

"Leave and pride. Lieutenant Colonel Degrensi's rules. You want it? You fight for it. You want to keep it? You'd better be good enough to defend it."

"They have to fight for *passes*? Isn't that brutal?" And wrong. Extreme. Horrible. "And detrimental to wing morale?" He's fighting so Sgaeyl will have time off to spend with Tairn, so he'll have time with *me*.

"Brutal? Hardly." She scoffs. "No blades. No signets. It's just a fistfight. You want to see brutal, go and visit one of the coastal outposts with nothing to do but turn on one another." She leans forward and shouts as Xaden deflects the next punch, then grabs Jarrett by the biceps and throws him to his back. "Damn. I really thought Jarrett was going to take him in less time."

A slow, proud smile spreads across my face.

"He won't take him at all." I shake my head, staring at Xaden with more than a little delight as he waits for Jarrett to gain his feet. "Xaden's playing with him."

The rider turns toward me, her gaze scanning me in clear assessment, but I'm too busy watching Xaden land hit after carefully placed hit to bother with what the lieutenant thinks about me.

"You're her, aren't you?" the rider asks, her appraisal pausing on my hair.

"Her who?" Here we go.

"Lieutenant Sorrengail's sister."

Not General Sorrengail's daughter.

Not the cadet Xaden is stuck with because of Tairn.

"You know my sister?" That earns her a glance.

"She has a hell of a right hook." She nods, her knuckles grazing the scar on her jaw.

"She does," I agree, my smile widening. Looks like Mira left her mark.

Xaden lands a solid hit to Jarrett's jaw with a crack.

"It appears Riorson does, too."

"He does."

"You sound pretty confident." She turns her attention back to the fight.

"I am." My confidence in Xaden is almost…arrogance. Gods, he's *beautiful*. The mage lights illuminating the chamber highlight every carved line of roped muscle on his chest and abs and play off the angles of his face. And when he turns, the hundred and seven scars that mark his back catch the light under Sgaeyl's relic.

I stare. I can't help it. His body is a work of art, honed to lethal perfection. I know every inch of it, and yet I'm still gawking, transfixed like it's the first time I've seen him half-dressed. This should absolutely *not* be turning me on, but the way he moves, the lethal grace in each and every calculated strike…

Yep. Turned on.

Maybe it's toxic as hell, but it's pointless to deny that every single part of me is attracted to every facet of Xaden. And it's not just his body. It's…

everything. Even the darkest parts of him, the parts I know are merciless, willing to annihilate anyone and everyone who stands between him and a goal, pull me in like a moth to a fucking flame.

My heart pounds like a drumbeat and my stupid chest aches just watching him maneuver around the floor of the pit, toying with his opponent. I've missed watching him in the gym, sparring with Garrick. I've missed being with him on the mat, feeling his body over mine as he puts me on my back over and over again. I've missed the tiny moments in my day when our eyes would meet in a crowded hallway, the bigger moments when I've had him all to myself.

I'm so damn in love with him that it hurts, and for the moment, I can't remember why I'm denying myself.

The rider on my left shouts, and Xaden's gaze jerks upward, colliding with mine.

Surprise registers on his features for all of a heartbeat before his opponent swings, his fist slamming into Xaden's jaw with a sound that makes my stomach twist.

I gasp as Xaden's head snaps sideways with the force of the blow.

He staggers backward to the cheers of the riders around me.

"Stop playing around and end it," I say through our bond, using it for the first time since Resson.

"Always so violent." He thumbs a drop of blood off the split in his lower lip, his gaze flashing to mine, and I swear I see a hint of a smile before he turns on Jarrett.

Jarrett swings once, then twice, missing Xaden both times.

Then Xaden strikes with two quick punches, putting his full weight behind them unlike before, and sending Jarrett to his hands and knees in the dirt. Jarrett's head hangs as he shakes it slowly, blood dripping from his mouth.

"Damn," the rider next to me says.

"Exactly." Is it wrong to smirk? Because I can't seem to control my facial muscles.

Xaden stands back as the riders fall silent in the chamber, and then he extends his hand.

Jarrett's chest heaves for a tense minute before he looks up at Xaden and shoves away the offered hand. He taps the floor twice, and while some riders around me groan—and yes, that's money changing hands in the form of gold coins—others clap a couple of times. Jarrett spits blood onto the floor, then stands upright, nodding at Xaden respectfully.

The match—if that's what this can be called—is apparently over.

The riders head my way, filtering past me for the door.

Xaden says something to Jarrett that I can't hear, then uses the metal rungs embedded into the stone's masonry at the far end of the pit to climb out.

He reaches the top, then takes his shirt from where it's draped across the railing and comes in my direction, watching me with enough heat in his gaze to set my already humming body on fire. Yeah, definitely can't remember why I'm denying myself any part of this man.

"Looks like he won the pass," the woman next to me says. "I'm Cornelia Sahalie, by the way."

"Violet Sorrengail." I know it's rude, but I can't make myself look away from Xaden as he turns the corner, approaching from the left.

He runs his tongue over the small cut at the side of his lower lip as if testing it, then tugs his shirt on. Taking away the show should cool my blood, but it doesn't. Pretty sure dumping a bucket of snowy slush from the nearby peaks over my head couldn't lessen the heat, either. I'd probably just steam.

Gods, I'm *screwed* when it comes to this man.

It doesn't matter that he hurt me, didn't trust me.

I don't even know if I trust *him*.

But I want him.

"Good job, Riorson," Lieutenant Sahalie says to Xaden. "I'll tell the major to take you off the patrol roster for forty-eight hours."

"Twenty-four," he corrects her, his eyes on me. "I only need twenty-four hours. Jarrett can have the other twenty-four."

Because I'll be gone.

"Suit yourself." She clamps Jarrett on the shoulder in consolation as he walks by, then follows him out.

We're alone.

"You're early," Xaden says, but the look in his eyes is anything but condemnation.

I lift a brow and try to ignore the way my palms itch to touch him. "Is that a complaint?"

"No." He shakes his head slowly. "I just wasn't expecting you until noon."

"Turns out Tairn flies pretty damned fast when he's not being held back by a riot." Gods, why is it so hard to breathe suddenly? The air between us is thick, and my heart thrums as my gaze wanders to his mouth.

He's killed people for me before, so why is him fighting for a weekend pass stripping every ounce of self-control straight out of my bloodstream?

"Violet." Xaden's voice drops to that low, quiet tone he only ever uses when we're alone, and usually naked. Very naked.

"Hmmm?" Gods, I miss the feel of all his skin against all of mine.

"Tell me what's spinning around that beautiful head of yours." He moves closer, invading my space without touching me.

Fuck, I *want* him to touch me, even if it's a bad idea. A really, *really* bad idea.

"Does it hurt?" I lift my fingertip to the corner of my lip where his is split.

He shakes his head. "I've had worse. It's what I get for blocking with my shields to concentrate on the fight. Otherwise, I would have felt you. Look at me." He takes my chin between his thumb and forefinger and gently tilts my head back before searching my eyes. "What are you thinking? Because I can read a lot into the way you're looking at me, but I'm going to need the words."

I want him. How hard is that to say? My tongue ties. What would giving into this insatiable need for him mean?

That you're human.

"I'm about three seconds away from carrying you up to my bedroom to continue this conversation." His hand slides along my jaw, his thumb caressing my lower lip.

"Not your room." I shake my head. "You. Me. Bed. Not a good idea at the moment." Too tempting.

"As I remember—which I do, often—we don't always need a bed." His other hand palms my waist.

My thighs clench.

"Violet?"

I cannot kiss this man. I can't. But would it really be the end of the world if I did? It's not like it would be the first time. Shit. I'm going to break. Even if it's only for this moment.

"Hypothetically, if I wanted you to kiss me but *only* kiss me—" I start.

His mouth is on mine before I finish.

Yes. This is exactly what I need. My lips part for him, and there's no hesitation in the glide of his tongue against mine. He groans, and the sound reverberates through my very bones as I wrap my arms around his neck.

Home. Gods, he tastes like home.

I hear the door shut a second before my back is pressed against the rough wall of the chamber. Xaden slides his hands beneath my thighs, then lifts me so we're level as he lays expert claim to every line and recess of my mouth like this is the only time he'll get. Like kissing me is more vital than his next breath. Or maybe that's the way I'm kissing him back. Whatever. I don't care who is kissing whom as long as we don't stop.

I lock my ankles at the small of his back, bringing our bodies flush, and my breath catches at the heat of his skin radiating through the fabric of his uniform and my leathers, and suddenly it's too much and not enough.

This was a bad idea, a teasing taste of everything I want, and yet I can't bring myself to stop. There's nothing outside this kiss. No war. No lies. No secrets. There's only his mouth, his hands sweeping up my sides, his desire matching the fire of mine. This is where I want to live, where nothing else matters but the way he makes me feel.

"Like a moth to a damned flame." The lament slips from my mind, into our mental pathway. He's gravity, pulling me back to him by the force of his existence.

"I'm more than willing to let you burn me."

Wait, that's not what I meant—

He cradles the back of my head, protecting me from the coarse stone, and angles for a deeper kiss. Gods, yes. *Deeper.* More. I can't get enough. I'll never get enough.

Energy arcs between us, hotter with every kiss, every flick of his tongue. Flames of need dance across my skin, leaving chills in their wake before settling deep within me, burning dangerously, reminding me that Xaden knows exactly how to sate this unquenchable desire.

He has the maddening ability to addict and satisfy all in the same breath.

My hands slide into his hair as his lips slip down my throat, and my pulse leaps when he finds that sweet spot right above the collar of my flight jacket, then mercilessly worships it with his mouth.

I'm instantly liquid, melting into him.

"Gods, I've missed the taste of you." Even his mental voice comes across as a groan. *"The feel of you in my arms."*

I bring my hands to his face and pull him back to my lips. He sucks my tongue into his mouth, and I whimper because I can say the exact same thing about him—I've missed everything about his taste, his kiss, him.

If any of those buttons on my flight jacket come undone, they're *all* coming undone.

The slant of his mouth over mine again and again makes me feel alive for the first time since… Gods, I can't even remember. Since the last time he kissed me.

His hand squeezes my waist gently, then stretches up, the tips of his fingers reaching just beneath my breasts. Fuck it, the jacket can come off. So can the top. The armor. Everything that separates me from him.

I reach for the buttons.

But he eases his kiss, taking it from urgent and deep to thorough and deliciously slow. *"We should stop."*

"What if I don't want to?" The physical sound that leaves me is pure denial. I'm not ready for this to end, not ready to return to the reality where we're not together, even if I'm the one standing in our way.

"We have to, or I won't be able to keep to the only kiss *limitation of your hypothetical question."* His hand drifts to my ass as his mouth softens, drawing on my lower lip with one last, lingering kiss. *"Fuck, I want you."*

"Then don't stop." I look him in the eyes so he knows I mean it. "We can keep it to nothing but sex. We did last year… Not that it worked well."

"Violet." It's part plea, part moan, and the war in his eyes makes my chest tighten. "You have no idea how badly I want to peel these pants off your amazing ass and fuck you until you're hoarse from screaming my name, so limp from orgasms that you can't fathom leaving my bed ever again, and every tree around here goes up in flames from lightning strikes." His hand slides from behind my head to the nape of my neck. "Until you remember exactly how good we are together."

"I never forgot." It's a whimper. My body is still humming.

"I'm not talking about physically." He leans in and kisses me softly.

It's sweet. Tender. Everything I *don't* want to feel. Not when it comes to him. Heat and lust, I can cope with. But the rest? "Xaden," I whisper, shaking my head slowly.

He studies my face for a heartbeat and masks the flash of disappointment with a half smile.

"Exactly." He gently lowers me back to my feet, then steadies me, holding on to my waist when my knees wobble. "I want you more than my next breath, but I can't fuck you into looking at me like you used to. I refuse to use sex as a tool to get you back." He takes my hand and presses it to my chest. "Not when I want to be here."

My eyes widen, and apprehension knots my stomach.

"That's what I thought." He sighs, but it's not defeat tightening his mouth. It's frustration. "You still don't trust me, and that's all right. I told you I'm not in this for a battle. I'm winning the damned war. I'm a fucking fool for saying this, but when haven't I been a fool when it comes to you?"

"Excuse me?" I bristle. His memory must be faulty, because I'm the one who's been the fool for him.

"Let me get this out." He glances at my mouth. "I'll kiss you whenever you want because my self-control is shit where you're involved—"

"Whenever *I* want?" My brows shoot up. What the hell is happening right now?

"Yes, whenever *you* want, because I'll live with my mouth attached to yours if I do it whenever *I* want." He retreats a couple of steps, and I immediately miss the feel of his hands, the warmth of his skin. "But I'm begging you, Violet. Don't offer me your body unless you're offering me *everything*. I want you more than I want to fuck you. I want those three little words back."

I stare at him, my mouth dropping open slightly. He's not asking to hear that I want him. He wants to hear that I *love* him.

"It's new territory for me, too." He rakes his hands through his hair. "No one is more surprised than I am, trust me."

"I'm sorry, but weren't you the one last year who said we could have all the sex we wanted as long as we kept feelings out of it?" I fold my arms across my chest.

"See? Fucking *fool*." He looks up at the rough-beamed ceiling like it has the answers. "Last year, I would have used any method it took to win you back, but for those three days you were unconscious, all I did was sit there and watch you sleep, thinking of everything I would have done differently." Determination is etched on every line of his face when he brings his gaze back to mine. "This is me doing things differently."

Somehow in the last month, we've managed to switch roles.

"This is me proving myself to you." He steps back and pulls the door open, gesturing for me to walk out first, then rests his hand on the small of my back as we walk down the hall. "We're not there yet, but you'll trust me again at some point."

"Sure, as soon as you agree to stop keeping secrets from me." How the hell is this *my* fault?

His sigh sounds like it's ripped out of his very soul. "You need to trust me even *with* secrets for this to work."

I grab onto the stair railing and take the stairs two at a time. "That's not going to happen."

"It will," he says as we near the ground floor, then changes the subject. "Are you hungry?"

"I need to wash up first." My nose crinkles. "Pretty sure I smell like I've been flying eight hours."

"Why don't you head on into my room, and I'll bring food." His hand slips from my lower back as we make our way into his barracks room. He points to the left and says, "That door leads to a private bathing chamber."

"There's no way you got a private bathing chamber as a brand-new lieutenant," I sputter. "Mira doesn't even have one."

"You'd be amazed what you can get when no one wants to share space with Fen Riorson's son," he answers quietly.

My stomach sinks. I can't think of a single thing to say to that.

"Don't look so sad. Garrick has to share with four other riders. Go." He motions to the door again. "I'll be right back."

An hour later, I'm clean and fed, and Xaden is sitting at his desk, fiddling with something that looks like a crossbow but smaller, as I sit on his bed and run a brush through my damp hair. I can't help but smile at the steady feeling of what's becoming routine, Xaden preparing a weapon while I sit on a bed.

"But they didn't search Tairn?" he asks without looking up.

"Nope, just dumped my stuff on the ground." My gaze catches momentarily on a palm-size gray stone with a decorative black rune on his nightstand before I spot a piece of grass that made the journey here from the flight field and flick it off my arm. "Did they search Sgaeyl?"

He shakes his head. "Only me. And Garrick. And every other new lieutenant leaving Basgiath with a rebellion relic."

"They know you've been smuggling something out." I lean over the edge of the high bed and drop my brush into my bag. "Toss me a sharpening stone."

"They suspect." He reaches into the top right drawer of his desk, taking out the heavy, gray sharpening stone. He leans over to hand it to me, careful not to brush his fingers along mine, and then goes back to tinkering with his weapon.

"Thank you." I grip the stone, then take the first knife from my thigh sheath and begin sharpening. They're only as good as they are honed. But no amount of busying my hands is going to make the next question any easier to ask without feeling like I'm now the one keeping things from Xaden.

I choose my words carefully. "When we were at the lake, before Resson, you said the only thing that can kill a venin is what powers the wards."

"Yes." He leans back in his chair, one eyebrow raised, his bow forgotten.

"The daggers are made of the material that powers the wards," I guess. "The alloy Brennan mentioned."

Xaden opens the bottom drawer and moves some things around before pulling out a replica of the dagger I used to kill the venin on Tairn's back. He walks over to me and holds it out, hilt first.

I take it from his hand, and the weight and hum of power coming from the blade are instantly nauseating—whether from the energy or the memory of the last time I held one, I'm unsure. Either way, I breathe deeply and remind myself I'm not on Tairn's back. There's no one trying to kill me or him. I'm in Xaden's bedroom. Xaden's very warded bedroom. Safe. No safer place on the Continent, really.

The blade itself is silver, sharpened on both edges, and the hilt is the same matte black of the one I used in Resson, the same that had been in my mother's desk last year. I run my finger along the medallion in the hilt that's a duller gray and decorated with a rune.

"That piece is the alloy." He sits next to me on the bed. "The metal in the hilt. It's a specific blend of materials smelted into what you see there. It's not power in itself, but it's capable of…holding power. The wards themselves originate from the Vale, near Basgiath, but they only reach so far. These"—he taps the medallion—"hold extra power to boost the wards and extend them. The more material, the stronger the wards. There's an entire armory of them downstairs, boosting the wards. The details are classified, but that's why outposts are placed strategically, to keep our borders from developing weak points."

"But how could the wards ever falter if these power them constantly?" I brush my thumb over the alloy, and my own power rises, charging the air.

"Because they only hold so much power. Once it's used, it has to be imbued again."

"Hold on. Imbued with power?"

"Yes. Imbuing is a process of leaving power in stasis, in an object. A rider has to pour their own power into it, which is a skill not a lot of us have." He glances meaningfully at me. "And don't ask. We're not getting into how that works tonight."

"Have they always been placed in daggers?"

He shakes his head. "No. That started right before the rebellion. My guess is Melgren had a vision of how an upcoming battle is going to go and these were central to his victory. Once Sgaeyl chose me at Threshing, we started to work to smuggle out a few daggers at a time to supply what drifts we could make friendly contact with."

"Aretia needs a forge to smelt the alloy, to make more weapons."

"Yes. It takes a dragon to fire a crucible, which we have, and a luminary to intensify dragonfire hot enough to smelt," he says.

I nod, staring at the thumb-size medallion. How can something so small be the key to our entire continent's survival? "So you just put the alloy into a dagger and get an instant venin killer?"

A smile tugs at his mouth. "It's a little more complicated than that."

"What do you think came first?" I ask, studying the dagger. "The wards? Or the ability to boost them? Or are they intertwined?"

"That's all classified." He takes the dagger back and returns it to the desk drawer. "So how about we work on *your* shields instead of worrying about Navarre's?"

I yawn. "I'm tired."

"Aetos won't care." He slides into my mind easily.

"Fine." I lean back, bracing my weight on my palms, and build my mental shields quickly, block by block. "Do your worst."

His smile makes me regret the challenge.

Though the chain of command may be consulted, the final say in
any academic punishment or repercussion lies
with the commandant's office.

—ARTICLE FIVE, SECTION SEVEN
THE DRAGON RIDER'S CODEX

CHAPTER THIRTEEN

"**Y**ou *wouldn't happen to know how to raise wards, would you?*" I ask Tairn
as we approach Basgiath from the southeast the next day, squinting into
the afternoon sun. The headwind added an extra couple of hours onto the flight,
making my hips protest and almost outright rebel.

"*Despite what you may assume, I am not six hundred years old.*"

"*Figured I'd ask, just in case you were holding back secret dragon knowledge.*"

"*I'm always holding back secret dragon knowledge, but wards are not among
it.*" His shoulders tense, rising slightly, and the beats of his wings slow. "*We're
being ordered to the practice grounds. Carr and Varrish are waiting.*"

My stomach plummets even though our altitude hasn't changed. "*He
threatened he'd be pondering my punishment for not forcing Andarna to
participate in maneuvers. I should have taken his warning more seriously.*"

Tairn's low growl vibrates through his entire body. "*What are your wishes?*"

"*Not sure I get a choice.*" A deep sense of foreboding crawls into my throat.

"*There is always a choice.*" He maintains direction even though he'll have to
bank soon to change course to the practice grounds.

I can handle whatever he wants to punish me with if it means keeping
Andarna safe.

"*We go.*"

An hour later, I'm not so sure I'm *handling* anything as much as I am
enduring.

"Again," Professor Carr orders, his thin white hair flopping with every gust of wind as we stand on the mountain peak we use when training my signet.

And to think…this is only a *warning*.

Fatigue washes over me again, but I know better than to complain. I'd made that mistake somewhere around strike twenty-five, and it had only added another mark to the tab Professor Carr was keeping in his notebook while Major Varrish supervised from his side.

"Again, Cadet Sorrengail." Varrish repeats the command, smiling at me like he's simply exchanging pleasantries. Their dragons, Breugan and Solas, stand as far back as possible without falling off the mountain. Tairn had lunged for their necks, snapped, and pulled back with inches to spare around strike thirteen. It was the first time I'd ever seen dragons *scurry*. "Unless you'd rather spend the foreseeable future in the brig."

Tairn's chest rumbles in a low growl as he stands behind me, his claws digging into the bare rock of the mountaintop. There's only so much he can do, though. While he's bound by the Empyrean, I have to follow the rules of the quadrant or risk the brig—and I'd rather bring down a thousand lightning strikes than spend one night locked in a cage at Varrish's mercy.

When I don't move, Carr sends me a pleading look, his gaze darting to Varrish.

I sigh but lift my hands, my arms trembling as I reach for Tairn's power. Then, I ground my feet in the mental construct of the Archives in my mind so I don't slip away into the fire that threatens to consume me. Swift and fast, the power rises again, and sweat beads on my face and drips down my spine as I struggle to control it.

Anger. Lust. Fear. It's always the most extreme of my emotions that bring on the strikes. It's rage that fuels me now as I summon that sizzling hot energy and release it, cracking open the sky with another lightning strike that hits a nearby peak.

"Thirty-two." Carr jots it down.

There's no care for if I can aim. Not a single consideration for mastery or strength. Their only goal here is to wear me down, while mine is to hold on to whatever scraps of self-control I can muster so I don't wake Andarna.

"Again," Varrish orders.

Gods, my body feels like it's cooking itself alive. I reach for the buttons on my flight jacket and yank them open, letting some of the infernal heat escape.

"*Violet?*" Andarna asks sleepily.

Guilt slams into me harder than a lightning strike. "*I'm fine,*" I promise her.

"*Waking is dangerous to the growth process,*" Tairn lectures. "*Sleep.*"

"*What's happening?*" She's alarmingly alert now.

"Nothing I can't handle." Not quite a lie. Right?

"I've never seen her produce more than twenty-six strikes in an hour, Major. She's at risk of overheating and burning out if you continue to push like this," Carr says to Varrish.

"She can take it just fine." He looks at me like he *knows*. Like he was there at Resson, watching me hurl bolt after bolt at the wyvern. If he's the picture of control, then maybe I should be glad I don't seem to have any.

"All it takes is her slipping in her grounding, or exhausting her physically, and she *will* burn out," Carr warns, his gaze shifting nervously. "Punishing her for insubordination is one thing, but killing her is quite another."

"Again." Varrish lifts his brows at me. "Unless your golden one would like to fly up and say hello, since she failed to appear as ordered. If she joins us, we'll only task you with three more."

"This is about me?"

My shoulders drop and my stomach hits the ground.

"This is an example of what happens when dragons choose poorly," Tairn counters. *"Solas should never have given this barbarian more power."*

"I don't want to submit her for tests or anything barbaric," Varrish cajoles, as though he'd heard Tairn's words. "I just want her to understand that she is not above the structure of command."

"I fucking hate him," I tell Tairn.

"I can feel this draining you! I'll come—" Andarna starts.

"You'll do no such thing, or you risk every feathertail in the Vale," I remind her. *"Do you want someone who takes joy in the pain of others like Varrish bonding a hatchling?"*

Andarna growls in pure frustration.

Tairn angles his wing, directing the cooling wind over my scalding skin.

"Well?" Varrish asks, tugging his cloak around him as steam rises from my body.

Tairn snarls.

"Humans do not command dragons, and that includes you." I lift my impossibly heavy arms and reach for power again.

Around strike forty, my knees buckle and I crumple to the hard rock. The ground rushes up at me, and I throw out my hands, sending pain shooting through my left shoulder as the joint partially subluxates from the impact. My mouth waters from the instant nausea, but I cradle my left arm and force myself to my knees just to take the weight off the joint.

Extending his neck, Tairn roars so loudly at Varrish and Carr that the notebook blows out of Carr's hands and tumbles down the mountain, vanishing from sight.

"Silver One is done!" he shouts.

"They can't hear you," I remind him, breathing through the pain.

"Their dragons can."

"If she dies, you will summon the wrath of not only General Sorrengail but General Melgren. Her signet is the weapon generals dream of in this war." Carr glances between Varrish and me. "And if that's not enough to encourage a degree of caution, *Vice Commandant*, then remember her death will cost you two of the most powerful dragons on the Continent *and* Lieutenant Riorson's irreplaceable ability to wield shadows."

"Ah yes, that pesky mating bond." Varrish clicks his tongue and cocks his head to the side, studying me like I'm nothing but an experiment for him to play with. "One more. Just to prove that you can listen to orders if your dragon will not."

"Silver One—"

"I can do it." I stumble to my feet and pray my shoulder will hold if I tuck my elbow in tight to my body. For Andarna, for the other hatchlings protected in the Vale, I can do it.

My muscles shake and cramp, and my shoulder screams as though there's a dagger in the joint, but I raise my palms and reach for Tairn's power anyway. I make the connection and let the energy flood through me one more time.

I wield, and lightning crashes.

But my arms cramp as the strike hits the nearest peak, the muscles twisting and bunching in an unnatural way, causing me to physically hold the power I usually release right away.

Fuck! I can't let it go!

"Silver One!" Tairn shouts.

Power lashes through me, extending the strike, which cleaves a section from the northernmost ridgeline ahead of me. The rock crashes down the mountain's slope, and still the lightning flows like an incandescent blade, cutting away the terrain.

I can't move. Can't drop my hands. Can't even twitch my fingers.

This is going to kill me.

Tairn. Sgaeyl. Xaden. It's going to kill us all. Fear and pain roll into one, seizing my mind with the one emotion I can't afford—panic.

"Cut it off mentally!" Tairn bellows as the strike goes on and on, and in the distance I hear Andarna cry.

My very bones catch fire, and a scream rips from my throat as I shove mentally at the doors to my Archives.

The strike ends, and I stagger backward, falling against Tairn's foreleg and crumpling between his talons. Every breath is a struggle.

Carr swallows. Hard. "We're done for the day."

I couldn't stand if I wanted to.

Varrish examines the destruction I caused and turns toward me. "Fascinating. You'll both be indispensable once you come to heel." He turns then, his cloak billowing in the wind as he walks to Solas. "This is the only warning you'll get, Cadet Sorrengail."

The threat hits like a punch to the stomach, but I can't think around the blistering heat.

Carr hikes over, then puts the back of his hand against my forehead and hisses. "You're burning up." He glances at Tairn. "Tell your dragon to carry you directly to the courtyard. You won't make it from the flight field. Get food and a cold bath." There's something suspiciously close to sympathy in his eyes as he looks me over. "And while I agree that we do not command dragons, perhaps you could talk Andarna into making an appearance. You are a rare, powerful signet, Cadet Sorrengail. It would be a travesty to use your training sessions in this manner again."

I'm not a signet. I'm a person. But I'm too damned hot, too tired to make the words form. Not that it matters—he doesn't see me that way. Carr never has. To him, we are the sum of our powers and nothing more. My chest heaves, but even the cool air of the mountaintop can't touch the burn sizzling in my veins.

Tairn wraps his claw around me, securing a talon under each arm to lock my limp body into position, then launches, leaving Carr beneath us on the peak.

We're airborne in an instant. Or maybe it's an hour. Time has no meaning. It's all just pain, beckoning me to let go, to release my soul from the prison of my body.

"You will not let go," he orders as we fly toward Basgiath, moving faster than I've ever felt him go before. The air rushing by feels so damned good, but it's not enough to reach the furnace in my lungs or the molten marrow of my bones.

Mountains and valleys pass under me in a blur before I recognize the walls of the quadrant, but Tairn blows by the courtyard and then plummets to the valley below.

The river. Water. Cold. Clear. Water.

"I've already called for support."

My stomach lurches as he pulls up to a hover at the last second, my body swaying from the change in momentum.

"Hold your breath." It's his only warning before water covers me from head to toe, gushing with bone-crushing force, icy from the last of the summer runoff. The contrast threatens to crack every part of me, to peel me away layer by searing layer.

I've lived with pain my entire life, but this agony is beyond my capability to endure.

Soundlessly, I scream, air gushing from my lungs as I dangle from Tairn's claw, the water forcing the heat from my body, saving me with the same pummeling blows that tear at my skin.

Tairn yanks my head above water, and I gasp for breath.

"Almost there," he tells me, holding me in the rapids.

The water beats at me mercilessly but lowers the temperature of my body until the last of the flames in my bones extinguish.

"Violet!" someone bellows from the shoreline.

My teeth chatter as my pulse slows.

"There." Tairn walks to the bank—I hadn't even realized he'd been standing in the river with me—and deposits me in the long summer grass beneath the row of trees that grow along the Iakobos.

I lie limp, fighting for the energy to take my next breath as my heart beats slower and slower. Summoning all my energy, I force my lungs to expand, to draw in air.

"Violet!" Imogen calls out from somewhere to the right, then falls to her knees beside me a moment later. "What the hell happened to you?"

"Too. Many. Strikes." A rough blanket lands on my shoulders as I shake, water dripping from my nose, my chin, the unbuttoned edges of my flight jacket, which miraculously made the trip, too. Bone-shattering cold has replaced all the heat, but I'm breathing normally again at least.

"Oh shit." Bodhi settles at my other side, reaching for my shoulders, then retreating.

"You're so…red." That's Eya. I think.

"Glane says it's burnout," Imogen says, her hand surprisingly gentle on my back. "Tairn called for her. What do we do, Violet? You're the only lightning wielder I know."

"I. Just need." I twist to the side, my legs curling under me, the words punctuated by the chatter of my teeth against one another. "A minute." I look up at the trunk of the familiar sprawling oak tree in front of me and concentrate on holding myself together.

"Cuir says she needs food now that she's cooled down," Bodhi adds.

"A green would know," Eya says with certainty. "Food it is."

"How did this happen?" Imogen asks. "Carr?"

I nod. "And Varrish."

Bodhi's warm brown face appears in front of mine. "Fuck." He tugs the edges of the blanket closed around me. "This is because of Andarna?"

"Yes."

Bodhi's eyes widen.

"Are you fucking kidding me?" Imogen's voice rises. "He used your signet as a punishment for Andarna not showing for flight maneuvers?"

"That asshole," Eya seethes, shoving a hand through her dark hair as she exchanges a look with Bodhi.

After a minute, I find the strength to hold the blanket myself. At least my muscles are working again. Longing rips through me as I stare up at the tree, its wide trunk, which I know bears the scar from two knife marks.

I want Xaden.

It's illogical. He couldn't have stopped Varrish. I don't need his protection. I don't need him to carry me back to the dorms. I just…want him. He's the only person I want to talk to about what happened on that mountain.

"I think we need to get her back to the dorms," Imogen says.

"I'll handle it," Bodhi promises, capturing my gaze. "This won't happen to you again."

"*Tell the humans that I will handle dragon matters,*" Tairn says.

"*How—*"

"*You will trust me.*" It's an order.

"Tairn says he'll take care of it." I rock forward and force myself to my feet. Bodhi catches my shoulders gently, wincing when I grimace. "I'm ready. Let's go."

"Can you walk?" he asks.

I nod, looking past him to the tree. "I miss him," I whisper.

"Yeah. Me too."

No one carries me. They simply stay at my side, step by step, as we make our way up the hundreds of stairs that spiral through the foundation walls and back to the dorms, our footsteps the only sound breaking the silence around us.

Because no one wants to say what we're all thinking… If Andarna doesn't show up at the next formation, Varrish's second punishment might just kill me.

"You get your running landing yet?" Imogen asks on Friday.

Sloane is thrown to the mat again, and we wince from the side of the gym, our backs to the wall so no one can sneak up behind us. Sloane's back has none of that protection and is going to be black and blue tomorrow.

Unlike Rhiannon, who's in here leading the extra sparring time she negotiated for all of our squad's first-years against some others from Third Wing, Imogen and I are here in full uniform between classes for only one reason—Sloane—and her terrifying lack of skill. We were hoping to see that she's improved over the week. She hasn't.

"Tairn won't let me out of the saddle," I say quietly, like he isn't constantly in my head since my near burnout on the mountaintop.

"I heard that," he grumbles.

"Only because you're listening." When shifting my weight doesn't help, I take a step off the wall to relieve the pressure on my tight, red skin. At least the physical remnant of my near burnout has dimmed to nothing more painful than a sunburn, but it's annoying as hell.

"Strengthen your shields and perhaps you won't require monitoring."

"Not completing maneuvers? Refusing to bring Andarna to class?" Imogen gasps with mock surprise. "Aren't you just becoming the little rebel?" Her gaze darts over my face, then drops to my neck. "Your friends still think you lost control during a training session?"

I nod. "If they knew what really happened, they wouldn't leave my side."

"You'd be safer," she notes.

"They wouldn't be." End of subject.

"Keep your eyes on your opponent!" Rhi shouts at Sloane from the sidelines just as Sloane does the opposite, glancing down as she nears the edge of the mat, and that's all her opponent needs, the first-year landing a jaw-cracking punch that sends Sloane sprawling.

Imogen and I both flinch.

"This is sparring, not a challenge! Come on, Tomas!" Rhi snaps at a squad leader from Second Wing.

"Sorry, Rhi. Pull it back, Jacek," the squad leader chides.

"Damn." Imogen shakes her head and folds her arms. "I get that Jacek's channeling some serious anger, but I've never seen him hit that hard."

"Jacek? Like Navil Jacek?" The second-year from Third Wing Jesinia and I saw hauled away by Markham was listed on the death roll a couple of days ago.

"That's his younger brother on the mat," Imogen says.

"Shit." Now I feel bad for the guy, even though Sloane is in a similar situation. "I think Markham had him killed," I whisper.

"Because he didn't return a book on time?" Imogen's eyebrows rise.

"I think he asked for something he shouldn't have, and yes, I know that sounds absolutely ridiculous, but there's no other explanation for him being found in his room, beaten to death."

"Right," Imogen muses. "That only makes sense if he's one of us."

To others, it fits in with what Panchek is calling a *particularly brutal* start to the year. I'm the only one in our group who hasn't had another attempt made on their life.

"You'd better be *really* careful around your little robed friend if scribes are running out there ordering the death of riders."

"Jesinia isn't a threat," I protest, but my words die in my throat as I remember that it was her report that got Jacek taken in the first place.

"Let's end it," the squad leader from Second Wing suggests after Sloane gets knocked to the mat again.

"I'm fine!" Sloane staggers to her feet, wiping blood from her mouth with the back of her hand.

"Are you sure?" Rhi asks, her tone implying it's absolutely the wrong decision, which we all know it is.

"Definitely." Sloane takes a fighting stance against Jacek.

"Glutton for punishment, that one," Imogen says. "It's like she *wants* to have the shit kicked out of her."

"I don't understand." Aaric shifts ahead of me, his back blocking the view, and I maneuver to see the mat. "I thought everyone marked was trained to fight."

"Depends on where we were fostered." Imogen moves forward with me. "And after Xaden started to climb the ranks…well, some of the families in charge *stopped* training us, according to what I'm hearing from the first-years. Good thing she wasn't on the challenge board this week."

Jacek puts Sloane on the mat for what feels like the hundredth time, then brings his knee to her throat, making his point. If this were real, she'd be in a world of trouble.

"Her first is on Monday, and she's going to have her ass handed to her if not worse." I unsheathe a dagger and flip it, catching it by the tip, like my skills can in any way help her when she won't even speak to me.

"Monday?" Imogen turns slowly to look at me. "And how would you know that?"

Shit. Well, it's not like she isn't already holding almost every secret that could get me killed. "Long story, but…a book my brother wrote."

"Who is Sloane up against?" She pivots back toward the mat.

"You're not going to ask about the book I shouldn't have?"

"No. I, unlike some people, don't feel the need to know everything someone else deems private."

I scoff at the obvious dig. "Yeah, well, you're not sleeping with me."

"You *wish* you were my type. I'm phenomenal in bed." Her nose scrunches when Sloane face-plants into the mat. "Seriously. Who is she against?"

"Someone she can't beat." A first-year from Third Wing who moves like she's been sparring since birth. It had taken me the better part of an hour to find someone who could point the girl out earlier in the gym.

"I've offered to help her," Imogen says quietly. "She won't take it."

"Why the hell not?" I catch my knife, flipping it with total muscle memory.

Imogen sighs. "No fucking clue, but her stubbornness is going to get her killed."

I watch Liam's sister struggle under Jacek's weight, her face splotchy and red from the exertion, and blow out a slow, resigned breath, my fist closing around the hilt of the dagger. The unspoken rule of the quadrant is to let the strong weed out the weak before they can become a liability to the wing. As a rider, I should walk away. I should let Sloane rise or fall on her own merits. But as Liam's friend, there's no way I can stand by and watch her die. "Not on Monday, she won't."

"You suddenly develop Melgren's signet over there?" Imogen retorts, tucking a chin-length strand of pink hair behind her ear.

"I'm calling it!" Rhi shouts, ending the match, and I breathe a sigh of relief.

"Not exactly." Glancing around the gym, I locate Sloane's opponent for Monday. "I just need to do a couple of things after physics, but I'll see you for our gym session tonight." What muscles I have are all due to Imogen's dedication to torturing me at the weight machines since last year.

"How is that class going for you, anyway?" Imogen asks with a sarcastic smile, damn well knowing that I couldn't make it through without Rhiannon's help. I might lead our year in history, geography, and every other subject that crosses over with the scribes, but physics? Not my specialty.

"Hey, Vi—" A hand curls over the top of my shoulder from behind me, and my heart surges, beating painfully in my ears.

Not again.

Muscle memory takes over as I spin around, dislodging the grip, and push my left forearm against a leather-clad chest, catching the assailant off-balance and allowing me to shove him the few inches backward into the wall while whipping my dagger to his tattooed throat in one instinctual motion.

"Hey, hey!" Ridoc's eyes bulge as he throws his hands up, palms outward. "Violet!"

I blink quickly as the knot in his throat bobs, scraping the edge of my blade.

Ridoc. It's not an assassin. It's just *Ridoc.*

Adrenaline pours into my system, and my hand trembles slightly as I lower the weapon. "Sorry," I mumble.

"For nearly dissecting my jugular?" Ridoc sidesteps before lowering his hands. "I knew you were fast, but *damn.*"

Mortification deprives me of words as heat rushes into my face. I nearly slit my friend's throat. Somehow, I find the sheath.

"You should know better than to sneak up on someone," Imogen lectures, her calm tone at odds with the knife she clutches in her left hand.

"I'm sorry. Won't do it again," he promises, his gaze shifting to worry as he glances over my shoulder. "I just figured I'd see if you wanted to walk to physics. Sawyer's already by the door."

"Everything all right?" Rhi asks, walking to my side as she slips her satchel over her shoulder.

"All good," Imogen answers. "You're doing a great job as squad leader, by the way. It was a good idea to get the first-years extra sparring time."

"Thanks?" Rhi stares at Imogen like she's grown a second nose.

"See you tonight." Imogen sheathes her knife and looks at me with more understanding than I want either of us to have as she backs away. "I'm going to offer my help to Mairi. Again."

I nod.

"You sure everything is good?" Rhi asks as I pick up my pack from the floor and nearly drop it with my jitters. Stupid fucking adrenaline.

"Perfect." I force the fakest smile known to humankind. "Let's go to physics. Yay physics."

Rhi exchanges a look with Ridoc.

"She's probably just nervous about the quiz, and I didn't help by startling her like a jackass." He rubs the skin of his throat as we start toward the door, where Sawyer waits.

Rhiannon's mouth drops open for a second. "Violet! I thought you said you had it down? We could have studied again this morning. I can't help you if you don't tell me you need help."

Isn't that the truth.

"Just remember, you need two out of three elements when pulling any flight maneuver," she recites as Sawyer takes a bite out of an apple and opens the gym door for us. "Velocity, power, or…"

I scan the first floor of the academic wing as we walk down the hall, my gaze scouring every alcove, every classroom door for someone who might jump out at us.

"Violet?"

Wrenching my focus from the stairwell ahead, I find Rhi giving me an expectant look. Right. She's asking me about physics and aerodynamics.

"Altitude," Sawyer answers.

"Right." I nod as we step into the stairwell. "Altitude."

"You're killing me—" Rhiannon starts.

"Now!" someone shouts from behind us.

Before I can react, a bag is thrown over my head, and with one breath, I'm unconscious.

There is a natural distrust that must be overcome between
infantry cadets and riders. This exists mainly because riders will
never trust that infantry has the courage to hold the line when
dragons arrive, and infantry will never trust that the dragons
won't eat them.

—MAJOR AFENDRA'S GUIDE TO THE RIDERS QUADRANT
(UNAUTHORIZED EDITION)

CHAPTER FOURTEEN

I jolt awake as the scent of something acrid fills my lungs, and I swing my fist,
knocking a hand away from my face. Smelling salts.

"She's up," a woman in dark blue announces, backing away to confer with…
Professor Grady?

My head buzzes as I sit up, stretching my legs in front of me, and immediately
reach for Tairn. *"What's going on?"*

My eyes are slow to adjust to the bright light, but it looks like we're in some
sort of forest.

*"The course humans wouldn't have to take if they would simply stay seated,
known as RSC,"* he growls with surprising frustration, like he's the one whose
just been drugged and dragged out of the quadrant.

Rhiannon, Sawyer, and Ridoc are on my right, all looking as confused as I
feel. To my left are four second-year riders with Second Squad, Flame Section,
Second Wing designations, looking around the forest in bewilderment. Nice to
see we aren't the only ones befuddled.

"At least it's not an assassination attempt." If it was, we'd be dead, especially
as fuzzy as I feel.

"It will be if we aren't back at Basgiath when Sgaeyl arrives tomorrow."

Oh. Shit. *"This can't last longer than a day."* Can it? *"If it does, you should fly back alone."*

Across from us sit two groups of eight infantry cadets—if their blue uniforms are any indication—in hushed conversation. They're all…homogenous. The four men all have the same military-short haircut, cropped close to their skulls in a fade, and the women wear their hair slicked back in tight buns. Same dark-blue uniforms, same boots, same…everything. Only the name tags above their hearts are different, except for the one with a squad leader designation on their shoulder in each group.

The four of us are all dressed in our summer uniforms, but we've each made our own modifications. My lightweight black top has slits down the front that give me direct access to the daggers sheathed in my armor at my ribs. Rhiannon prefers a tunic with sheaths directly sewn in. Sawyer likes his sleeves short, weapons strapped to his upper arms, and Ridoc never took the time to see the uniform tailor—he just ripped his sleeves off. We aren't even *wearing* name tags, and the same goes for the squad from Second Wing.

"And leave you to fend for yourself?"

The forest floor is soft and muddy in patches, and the afternoon sun streams in between the branches at an angle, which means we've only been unconscious an hour, maybe two at most. It's nothing but trees as far as I can see.

"I think that's the point." I blink, fighting to bring my brain into sharper focus. *"Promise me, if I'm stuck out here on land nav, that you'll see her if you can. We can't be that far from Basgiath."*

Professor Grady hands each rider a waterskin. "Sorry for the abrupt change of scenery. Hydrate."

We all uncork our skins and drink. The water is crisp and cold…but there's something else there, too. Pungent. Earthy. And something bitterly floral that I can't quite place. I close the skin, cringing at the aftertaste. Professor Grady *really* needs to take better care of his skins.

"You all right?" I ask Rhi, who is checking her sheaths for weapons.

"A little dazed, but yeah. You?"

I nod, running my hands down my sides to make sure my daggers are exactly where I left them. They are. My bag is still strapped to my back, too.

"They took us in the stairwell?" I look over to see Sawyer rubbing his temples and Ridoc scratching the tattoo on his neck.

"That's my last memory." She nods in agreement, studying the squads next to and across from us.

"Anyone know where we are?" Sawyer asks the obviously more alert infantry squads.

The cadets look over at us, but no one answers. Or speaks at all.

"I'm going to take that as a no," Ridoc drawls.

"It's a no from us." The rider from Second Wing with a squad leader designation lifts his hand in greeting.

"Do you know where—" I start to say toward Tairn, but the usually crystal-clear connection is muffled, like someone has thrown a blanket over it. Panic clenches my heart as I realize the same is true for Andarna, though I don't risk waking her with questions. "I can't reach Tairn."

Rhi's gaze snaps to mine, and she cocks her head to the side. "Shit. Feirge, either. It feels like something is…"

"Smothering the connection," Sawyer finishes.

I set the waterskin down next to me, and the others catch on, doing the same. What in Dunne's name did we just drink?

"We're blocked out," a rider with a shoulder-length dark-blond braid whispers.

"Breathe, Maribel," the squad leader orders, shoving his tan hand into his dark curls, like he might actually benefit from that suggestion a little more. "It can't be for long."

Ridoc's hands fist. "This isn't right. I don't give a shit if it's for the course—we're not supposed to be cut off from them."

"Tomas?" Rhiannon asks, leaning forward to look past me.

"Hey, Rhi." The squad leader waves. "This is Brisa." He points to a woman with a shaved head, rich brown skin, and an observant, quick-moving gaze, and she gives us a curt nod. "Mirabel." He swings his finger to the blonde with pronounced flight goggle lines in her pale cheeks and a fire-wielder patch on her shoulder, and she waves. "And Cohen," he finishes. The rider closest to me, with a fast smile, short black hair, and warm russet-brown skin, lifts his hand in greeting.

"Hi." Rhiannon nods. "This is Sawyer, Ridoc, and Violet."

The pleasantries are cut short as Professor Grady marks something in a folder and clears his throat. "Now that you're all awake, welcome to the first joint land navigation exercise." He pulls two closed maps from the folder. "In the last two weeks, you've been taught how to read a map, and today you'll put those skills to use in a practical setting. Were this an actual operation with the makeup of an outpost, this unit would consist of the composition you see here."

He steps away from a woman who must be the infantry professor, revealing two cadets in pale blue sitting beside a scribe. Their hood is down, and they're wearing cream pants with a cream hooded tunic—not robes—but that's definitely a scribe.

"Riders and infantry for fighting, a scribe to record the event, and healers for the obvious reasons." He motions them forward, and all three move to stand at the end of the infantry lineup.

The infantry professor wearing captain rank walks up and stops beside

Professor Grady with impeccable posture. "Cadets, rise," she says.

The infantry squads practically jump to their feet, immediately standing at attention.

I draw back slightly, surprised at my first instinct, which is to tell the infantry captain to fuck off because I don't answer to her. No rider does.

Professor Grady glances our way and nods.

The eight of us stand, but we're not even *at ease*. We just are.

The infantry captain looks at us and barely refrains from rolling her eyes. "This is the shortest course you'll be conquering together this year, so try to get to know one another. Fourth Wing, you're attached to fourth squad." She looks around, and one of the cadets directly ahead raises his hand. "And Second Wing, you're attached to second squad, just to make it easy." A cadet raises her hand on the left. "Your objective is to find the location marked on the maps and secure it. Once you do, you'll be extracted."

It can't be that easy.

Professor Grady holds out the maps, and Rhiannon steps forward, taking both and handing one to Tomas.

One of the infantry cadets starts to step forward but stills.

"Two maps," Professor Grady says. "Two teams but one cohesive unit. You're not used to working together. You weren't even warned you would be. But keeping Navarre safe requires teamwork between the segments of our military. There are times in your careers when you'll need someone you can trust in the air or on the ground, and those bonds are forged here at Basgiath." He looks between our groups. "We'll see you tomorrow afternoon."

Tomorrow afternoon?

My stomach founders. Tairn won't see Sgaeyl unless he honors my request and leaves. And me...I'll miss the few hours Xaden is here. It will be another *week* until I can see him. The disappointment hurts more than it should.

"Just find the extraction point and secure it? That's our mission?" Sawyer asks, eyeing the map like it might bite him. This is not his strongest skill, for certain.

"No problem." Ridoc puffs out his chest.

"Oh. Right," Professor Grady replies. "You see, we have to level the playing field a little bit. Infantry has been doing land nav since their first year, so naturally, they might be a little better at it than you."

Ridoc stiffens.

The infantry cadets smirk.

"And you might notice that none of you eight"—Professor Grady looks us over—"has the ability to fully communicate with your dragons."

"Which is bullshit," Ridoc says at full volume.

A woman on the infantry side gawks.

"It is," Professor Grady agrees. "It's not something we do lightly, either, and your dragons loathe it just as much as you do. You've all been dosed with a particular mixture of herbs that dulls not only your connections but your signet as well. As frustrating as it is, we're actually pretty proud of the concoction, so let us know if you feel any side effects."

"Besides you cutting off the most important bond we have?" Rhi argues.

"Precisely," Professor Grady replies.

I reach for my power, but only a tingle fills my fingers. Gods, I feel... vulnerable, and it really fucking sucks. My mind flies over what the mixture could possibly be as the two professors walk between our groups.

When Grady reaches the end of our section, he turns, moving backward. "Oh, and did I mention that there are two groups of you out here? The other is on the far side of the forest, and while your dragons will be hunting them, their dragons are hunting *you*. A few unbondeds joined, too."

The fuck? My stomach hollows.

Almost every infantry cadet looks faint, and one wobbles where he stands.

"Infantry, the riders are going to need to lean on your land nav expertise, but you won't live without them should you encounter a dragon." Grady looks the eight of us in the eye as he backs away. "Try and see that most of them make it out of here, will you?" He flashes a grin and turns around, walking into the forest with the infantry professor, leaving us in the middle of the fucking woods without supplies or our dragons.

We stare at the infantry squad.

The infantry squad stares at us.

The healers look comically uncomfortable, and the scribe already has a notebook out, pencil at the ready.

"Well, this should be a good time had by all," Ridoc mutters.

"Did he insinuate that we could die?" the smaller of the healers asks, his olive skin paling.

"Piss off the dragons and find out," Sawyer replies.

"You'll be all right"—I look for his name tag—"Dyre." I offer him a smile as I pass on my way to the scribe. Soft red hair frames a creamy white face almost overcome with freckles as the short woman blinks up at me with even shorter brown lashes. "Aoife? They drag scribes into RSC?"

"Hi, Violet. I'm currently the first in my year training for the field and not to be an adept," she says. "You're the most powerful rider in yours. Dyre and Calvin are the best in their years." She shrugs. "Naturally they built the strongest team first."

Ridoc grins. "So you're saying we're the team to beat?"

"Something like that." The scribe fights back a smile.

"Then let's make sure we *don't* get beat," Rhiannon says before turning her attention to the map. "Tomas, what do you think?"

He hands a map to Brisa and consults on Rhi's.

Two hours and several arguments with the infantry later, we're four miles from our starting location with another six to go. Rhiannon and Ridoc examined our map—which marked where we'd been dropped and our extraction point but didn't label our location—discussed a route with Tomas, made sure we all saw it, and then handed it over to the infantry to agree on a route before we started walking.

"I'm telling you, we're in the Parchille Forest," Cadet Asshole—otherwise known as Calvin—argues with Rhiannon a few steps ahead. He's actually gone about fifteen minutes without reminding us that he's their ranking officer, so I'm sure we're due any minute now. "That map doesn't resemble any I've ever seen for Shedrick, which means we could be headed the opposite direction we should be. None of these landmarks match."

"And I think you're wrong," Rhiannon counters, keeping her tone even.

"I think we're in the Hadden Woods," Aoife says, holding her journal closely. She already has three pages of notes taken. "It's the only forest close enough to bring us all by horse, since I doubt your dragons flew us in."

I add, "It's also the only forest close enough for Tairn to stay behind and see Sgaeyl without causing either of us pain from the separation."

"Their squad leader is the infantry equivalent of Aetos," Ridoc mutters from my right side.

I nod but keep from chuckling.

Cohen throws his head back on Ridoc's right and doesn't bother suppressing his laugh. Guess Dain's reputation carries across the wings.

"Who is Aetos?" Cadet Quiet asks from Aoife's left. It's the first time the curvy brunette has spoken in hours, but her brown eyes are constantly moving, taking in our surroundings. I would bet that she's tied with Brisa—who is covering our flank with Tomas and Sawyer—for most observant in our group.

"One of our wingleaders," I answer. "Kind of like your battalion commander."

"Oh." She nods as Rhiannon and Asshole continue arguing ahead of us. "You guys function in sections, right?"

"Yep." The landscape hasn't changed. The forest is mostly flat, with a few rolling hills that have been easily scalable. But the heat? Damn, it's stifling. I tied my uniform top around my waist about an hour ago, leaving me in my armor. I have no idea how Aoife is surviving with her hood up, but she hasn't removed it. "Squad, then section, then wing."

"What do we do if we come across a dragon?" she asks.

"First we choose a sacrifice," Ridoc says. "And then we offer it and run."

Her eyes flare wide.

"Don't be an asshole." I elbow him in the arm. "Depends on the color, but a good rule of thumb is to lower your eyes and back away," I tell the infantry cadet. "But we can usually hear them coming."

"Then prepare to be digested," Cohen adds.

"Oh *gods*," the brunette whispers.

"You are now my favorite year-mate." Ridoc throws an arm over his shoulder.

"Can I see your map?" Brisa asks from the rear of the formation.

"Don't you have your own?" Calvin retorts.

Rhi's head whips toward him. "Give it to her or I cut it out of your hands."

He glares at Rhi but passes it back so we can get it to Brisa.

Gods, this grass is high. It's nearly up to my waist in the places where the trees don't shade the ground. I step onto an uneven knob, and my ankle rolls. Ridoc grabs ahold of me before I can fall, then steadies me without a word as we continue the climb. "Thank you," I say softly.

"Are your knees wrapped?" Ridoc asks, concern lining his forehead.

I nod. "Yep. Didn't do the ankles, though, since I wasn't exactly expecting a hike."

"I have cloth if you need to wrap something," Dyre calls out from behind us.

"I'll keep that in mind, thank you," I answer.

A guy behind me asks, "Are all scribes this quiet?"

"It's my job to record, not participate," she answers.

"Not participating will still get you eaten by a dragon," he argues.

I assure her, my eyes never leaving his, "I'd never let a *scribe* get eaten by a dragon."

Rhiannon's voice rises as the argument ahead of us heats. "Because there's no way in hell they hauled us out of our rooms and brought us that far away in four hours."

"Because your dragons can't fly that quickly?" Calvin is about an inch shorter than Rhi and has no problem glaring up at her.

"Because our dragons wouldn't carry *you*, dumbass," Ridoc responds.

Aoife snorts and Mirabel laughs, flanked by the rest of the infantry squad behind us.

Calvin turns and levels a look at Ridoc. "Have some respect for the rank." He taps his shoulder, where there's an open triangle embroidered beneath two oak leaves.

"Your rank means exactly jack and shit to me."

"What, like you're *so* above us infantry?" Calvin counters.

"I mean technically, when we're flying we're above *everyone*," Ridoc argues.

"But if you're asking if I'm better than you, then the answer is obviously yes."

I sigh and watch Calvin's hands just in case he decides to go for the shortsword sheathed at his side. It's not a bad weapon, but they all carry them. There's no variation for height or specialization. It's all so…uniform.

Then again, we were pulled straight out of the hallway, so it's not like Ridoc is carrying his preferred bow. Sawyer and Rhiannon are missing their favorite swords, too.

"Stop pissing him off on purpose," Rhiannon says, glancing back at Ridoc as we start trudging up another hill. Maybe this one will give us a better vantage point than the last. "We're going to need fresh water, or this is going to get ugly fast."

Ridoc grins. "But it's so much fun!"

She arches a brow.

"Fine." He puts his hands up. "I'll let him maintain his delusion of grandeur."

"Oh, so you'll listen to *her*—"

"She's my squad leader. You're not."

"So, you only respect rider squad leaders," Calvin prods.

Aoife furiously writes in her notebook.

"Shut it, Calvin," a cadet from behind me says with more than a little exasperation.

"You want my respect? Earn it." Ridoc shrugs. "Cross the parapet, climb the Gauntlet, survive Threshing, and then we'll be on equal footing."

"What, like we don't go through some shit in the Infantry Quadrant?" someone behind us challenges.

"See her?" Sawyer says, and I swear I can *feel* him pointing at me. "She bonded not only one of the biggest fucking dragons on the Continent, but a *second* dragon, and then went into combat against the gryphons a couple of months ago and came out alive. You go through that kind of shit in your quadrant?"

The cadets around us fall silent. Even Aoife's pencil remains poised above her notebook as she stares at me.

Awkward. And *wrong*. No one in our little group knows what we're really against out there. And my silence? It's starting to feel a lot less like self-preservation and more like I'm complicit.

"You're a Sorrengail, aren't you?" Mirabel asks. "The commanding general's daughter?" She winces. "The hair kind of gives you away."

"Yes." There's no use denying it.

"Your mother is terrifying," she whispers.

The scribe glances between us before putting pencil to parchment again.

I nod. "That's one of her more prominent qualities."

"Hey, guys?" Brisa raises her voice behind us. "I think I know why it feels like we're getting nowhere."

"Why is that?" Rhiannon asks over her shoulder.

"Calvin's right, but so are you. They gave us two different maps," she says as the first of us crest the hill…and freeze.

Even my heartbeat comes to a standstill as Rhiannon throws up her hand to stop the rest of the group.

An Orange Club—nope, that's a Scorpiontail—growls at us low in her throat from where she's been lying in wait on the other side of the hill. Our heads tilt to follow the movement as she rises to her full height, dominating the skyline, her tail whipping behind her.

Baide. Jack Barlowe's dragon. Or at least she was.

"Amari help us," Calvin whispers, his panic palpable.

I drop my eyes in deference just like Kaori taught us as my pulse leaps and my brain fights the urge to panic. "Oranges are the most unpredictable. Eyes down. Do *not* run," I whisper. "She'll kill you if you run. Try not to show any fear." Shit, *this* is what we should have been talking about instead of arguing about which quadrant is superior and which forest we're in.

My chest tightens when my immediate instinct—to reach for Tairn—is denied. With any other dragon, I would bet against risking the anger of our dragons by torching us, but the cadets behind us are a whole other story. And since I killed Jack last year? All bets are off.

She has nothing to lose, and given the hot blast of steam that levels the grass and makes my face sticky, she remembers exactly who I am.

"Riders!" Rhiannon calls out. "Take the front!" She's obviously thinking the same way. "Infantry, guard the healers and scribe!" She glances at me sideways, careful not to raise her eyes. "Violet, maybe you should—"

Keeping my head down, I push past Calvin to stand in the front, catching movement in my peripheral vision. "I'm not hiding."

"What are you doing? It's going to eat you," one of the cadets behind us hisses.

I look over and see a healer, Dyre, a few feet to my right, staring straight at Baide, his mouth agape.

A growl rumbles up the orange's throat, and I lunge, gripping the strap of Dyre's medical pack and yanking him behind us, passing him to Ridoc, who quickly shoves him to safety and moves to my side.

"No, she's not," Sawyer says, moving forward with Ridoc so the infantry is behind us. "That's why we're taking the front."

Baide swivels her head, then opens her mouth and curls her tongue, and I chance a quick glance, catching her hazy golden eyes narrowing to slits as she arches her neck, changing her angle instead of lowering her head to strike in the typical—

I inhale sharply. "Rhi, she's going to blast right past us just like Solas."

Rhi takes less than a second to assess and decide. "Second Wing," she calls back. "Halt and cover the infantry where you are!"

Movement behind us ceases as Baide flexes her claws in the ground and swivels again, choosing a target.

"It's... It's..." Calvin babbles.

"Drop your eyes and shut up," Rhi orders.

"Gods, they all *smell* scared," Ridoc whispers from my right.

"Exactly how pissed at you do you think she is?" Sawyer asks me from Rhi's left.

"She dropped a mountain on her rider." Ridoc sighs like we're all fucked, and I couldn't agree more.

My heart leaps into my throat as Baide prowls backward, lowering her head to our level. It's the perfect angle to torch us, but I resist the urge to look and keep my eyes trained on the grass in front of me.

Hot air gusts in our direction as she scents each of us, starting with Rhiannon and moving to Sawyer. There are a few muffled cries from the infantry cadets as she exhales a dank huff of steam, then breathes in again when directly in front of me.

I fight my racing heart. Last year, I might have accepted death. But this year...this year, I'm bonded to one of the deadliest dragons on the Continent.

That's right. You might hate me, but I belong to Tairn.

And while there's a good chance Tairn might die if I do, I'm not sure any dragon is willing to risk his wrath if he doesn't. Baide draws back, then darts forward with an open jaw, snapping her teeth shut directly in front of my nose and pelting my face with saliva.

Holy. Shit.

Someone behind us screams, then fucking *runs.*

"No! Gwen!" Calvin shouts as Cadet Quiet breaks to the left, sprinting through the grass.

Baide's head swings, tracking the movement, and my heart sinks as she drops her jaw, the side of her tongue visible ahead of me as it curls—

"Down!" Rhi shouts as the other squad leader, Tomas, runs after Gwen, catching her within a few strides and yanking her back by her uniform in the same way I'd snatched Dyre from the front, all but throwing her at Calvin as we drop as ordered. She stumbles to the ground at Calvin's feet just as Baide's nostrils flare.

Heat consumes the air around us at the same second my chest hits the ground, and I close my eyes like that can block out the sounds of screaming behind us.

"The Northern Esbens are believed to have been the hatching grounds of the orange dragon before unification, though, true to their unpredictable nature, they often chose new valleys in the same range," I whisper as fire rages past, fighting to keep my heart from seizing.

I haven't known this type of terror since Tairn began channeling, and definitely not since I manifested my signet.

The blast ceases, and Baide snaps her jaws shut, then swings her massive head in front of us one more time before crouching deeply and launching directly over us. I drop my gaze as her poison-barbed tail comes within a foot of me.

And then she's gone.

We all scramble to our feet, and riders run…toward nothing. Brisa is the first to reach the charred ground where Tomas had stood. Her hand shakes as she reaches toward the still-smoking earth. My mouth waters as nausea rolls through me, but I keep my breakfast down.

Mirabel isn't as lucky, retching in the grass a few feet away.

"Tomas…" Cohen kneels beside Brisa.

Rhi pivots to face the terrified infantry, her fists clenched at her side. "And that," she shouts, "is why you don't fucking *run*!"

There's a course second year that I can't tell you about, other than
to say that it's hell.
My only advice? Don't piss off anyone else's dragon.

—PAGE NINETY-SIX, THE BOOK OF BRENNAN

CHAPTER
FIFTEEN

When the sun sets the next day and we have yet to reach an extraction
point, it's clear we've failed our land navigation exercise.

All because we didn't stop to make sure the two fucking maps *matched* and
now have no clue where we are. Blisters have long since formed and popped on
my feet, my bones ache from sleeping on the ground last night, and the idea of
spending another night out here, just to wander aimlessly again in the morning,
makes me want to scream in frustration.

How could something as simple as land navigation fuck us up this badly?

We've backtracked, crossed two creeks that look like they could belong
on either of the maps, and narrowly avoided an encounter with an ornery Red
Daggertail who—lucky for us—decided a nearby cow looked tastier than weary,
hungry cadets.

As I sit against the trunk of a tree down the slight incline from our makeshift
camp, relieving Ridoc of watch, it hits me that I know a slew of new names. Not
that infantry dies at Basgiath at the same rate riders do, even though they're
the biggest quadrant, with over a thousand cadets at any given time, but once
they get to their units? The upcoming war will devour them at a far faster pace.

"Did you get dinner?" Ridoc asks, brushing grass off his pants as he stands.

"I'll grab some when I'm done." I slip my pack from my shoulders and set
it next to me. Not only have I been hiking for two days, I've carried textbooks
with me. We all have. "Infantry caught a good amount of rabbit that should be
done cooking any minute."

"They're way better at that than we are," he admits begrudgingly, ruffling his hair. "You don't think they'll let us meander out here forever, do you?"

"I think whatever they gave us has to inevitably wear off." I turn my head and see Cadet Dyre walking toward us with Rhiannon, carrying a plate. "And our dragons aren't going to let us perish over our inability to work together enough to compare two maps. Then again, maybe they will. We might deserve it, since our stubbornness cost Tomas his life."

"It's…" He sighs, waving to the pair as they reach us. "Hey, Rhi. I was just saying that this whole exercise is a little cruel, don't you think? Practicing torture, I get. Navigating land, I understand. Evading capture, sure. I'll even make an argument for having to learn what bugs are edible. But it's not like other dragons are waiting behind enemy lines to kill us."

"You'd be surprised," I mutter, exhaustion getting the better of my tongue.

"What?" Rhi questions.

"I mean, we really don't know what's out there, do we?"

"Hopefully not fire-breathing gryphons," Ridoc says.

"Right." Rhiannon tilts her head, studying my face, and I quickly shrug.

"Hi, Dyre." I muster a smile.

"I brought you dinner." He looks at me with a reverence I don't deserve.

"You didn't have to do that," I reply.

"I owe you my life, Cadet Sorrengail." He hands me a plate of roasted rabbit. "The least I can do is bring you dinner."

"Thank you." I set the plate in my lap. "Just do me a favor and keep your head down next time" Another thing infantry has on us? They carry a rudimentary set of survival gear—including a mess kit—in their packs at all times, like they might be deployed at any second. We definitely have a few things to learn from each other.

"Anything you need. I'm at your service. I owe you a life debt."

Before I can assure him that he doesn't, Ridoc claps him on the back. "I'm going to take Life Debt back to camp."

I nod in thanks, and the two walk back up the incline to camp. Dyre is sweet, but he's been underfoot the entire two interminable days we've been lost in these godsforsaken woods.

"You know what's out there," Rhi says as she sits next to me, pulling her braids over one shoulder.

"What?" I fumble and nearly drop the plate.

"You've been attacked by gryphons." She stretches out her legs and looks at me skeptically. "So you actually *do* know what's out there…right?"

"Right." I nod a little too quickly, then cover a jaw-cracking yawn with my hand. My body is at its limit, but I'm sure I can push another couple of hours to make it through watch.

Her frown is fast but unmistakable. "I've got the watch. Your body needs the extra sleep."

"I can do it," I protest.

"You can, but it's my job to manage the needs of my squad, and you need sleep. Consider it an order." There's no room for argument in her tone. This isn't my best friend speaking—it's my squad leader.

"Order it is." I stand, brushing the grass off my leathers with one hand and clutching the plate with the other, then give her a forced, tight-lipped smile before turning toward camp.

"Vi?"

I look back.

"Something is going on with you," she says quietly, but there's no mistaking the steel in her tone. "I haven't so much as seen Andarna since you returned, you're running with *Imogen* of all people, you won't open up about whatever's up with you and Xaden, and you won't talk about War Games. You might think that I don't notice that you're pulling away from everyone, but I do. You barely eat with us, and every chance we get to sneak into Chantara, you're holed up in your room reading." She shakes her head, running her hand along the grass. "If you're not ready to talk, to tell me what's going on with you, I want you to know that's all right—"

"There's—" My stomach twists as I try to deny it.

"Don't," she interrupts softly, her unyielding gaze holding mine. "I'll be here when you're ready because your friendship is precious to me. But please, for the sake of that friendship, don't insult me by lying."

She looks away before I can think of a response.

There's no sleep that night, but at least there aren't any nightmares, either.

A convoy of horses and wagons arrives the next morning, as do the professors, who have choice words for our failure.

"You were in the Hadden Woods, though none of you could work together long enough to figure it out. It's apparent that we have a lot to learn from each other." Grady hands each rider a waterskin and smiles as the infantry professor does the same for her cadets. "Seeing as you were our top squads, I can't deny that I'm disappointed, but at least most of you survived."

He's disappointed, but Tomas is *dead*.

I uncork and drink, tasting something sweet and hard to place as I drain it.

"Next time, we'll make sure you have supplies," he promises. "We wanted to see how you'd make do this first time out, and now we know."

First time out. Great. We get to do this again.

The blanket thrown over my dragon bonds lifts, and power rushes through my veins. I feel like *me* again.

"*Tairn.*"

"*Behind you,*" he answers.

Wingbeats fill the air, and the horses prance nervously as our dragons land at the edge of the trees, the ground vibrating with the force of their landings.

"Holy shit," Calvin says softly, backing away with the other cadets.

"You're going to have to get used to them." Ridoc pounds the squad leader's shoulder. "They'll be at the outposts you're all stationed at once you take your commands after graduation."

"Right...but so close?" he whispers.

"Probably closer," Ridoc whispers back and nods.

The seven of us in black say our goodbyes, then head to our dragons.

"Does it bother anyone else that they just took away our bonds? Our signets? And then handed them back like it wasn't..." Sawyer shakes his head. Even the rhythm of his steps is angry.

"Violating?" I suggest.

"Exactly," he agrees. "If they did it just then, that means they can do it whenever they want."

"*It's a new development this year,*" Tairn says, his eyes narrowing on Professor Grady. "*One I do not care for. I could hear you, sense you, but you could not reply.*"

"Tairn isn't a fan, either." Gods, I'm so *tired.* Why the hell would leadership be developing ways to weaken us? Because that's what it felt like, being weakened, being cut off not only from my greatest sources of strength and support—Tairn and Andarna—but the very power I've come to depend on.

"See?" Rhiannon says. "I know you don't believe me, but I'm telling you that things are *weird* this year. Guarded infirmary doors? Developing elixirs to muffle our bonds? You were nearly assassinated at assessment."

"Panchek thinks that was someone looking for revenge on my mother, and I didn't say I don't believe you," I counter with selective truths.

"You don't say much, period." She shoots a look at me.

Keeping secrets from her is going to shred our friendship. Already, I feel it pulling at the seams. She might be trying to be patient, but it's her nature to solve problems and I'm a huge one.

Tairn dips his shoulder at my approach.

"*Please tell me you got to see Sgaeyl?*" I ask, summoning the energy to mount.

Not sure how, but I manage to climb to his back and settle into the saddle.

"I did for a couple of hours. That's all the time I was willing to be out of range from you, and only after Baide left."

"And they're already gone, right?" Why does it feel like my heart is breaking all over again? Missing Xaden is illogical and annoying and kind of pathetic, but I can't make the feeling ebb.

"We will see them in a week."

So why does every instinct I have scream we won't?

My dad hoped I'd go into the infantry like he did. He thought riders were pompous pricks, and in his defense...we really are.

—RECOVERED CORRESPONDENCE OF LIEUTENANT XADEN RIORSON TO CADET VIOLET SORRENGAIL

CHAPTER SIXTEEN

We're back in enough time for me to visit the Archives, so I do just that. If I can't see Xaden, I may as well spend my time researching. It's late afternoon before I can get cleaned up and make my way down there, and it makes me smile to see Jesinia working at one of the tables with Aoife.

Aoife looks up at the sound of my bootsteps, prompting Jesinia to, as well. They both wave and I return the gesture.

I pause at the study table, setting down my book to return as the two have a quick discussion before Aoife rises and heads to the back of the Archives. Then Jesinia walks over, carrying what looks to be the notebook Aoife brought along during the land navigation exercise.

"What are you doing in here on a Sunday?" I sign as she reaches the study table.

She puts the notebook down on the scarred oak surface and lifts her hands to sign. "Helping Aoife transcribe her account into the official report to be filed. She's taking a quick break. Want to see what she chronicled?" She picks up the notebook and offers it to me.

"Absolutely." I nod, then take the notebook and skim Aoife's neat handwriting. It's amazingly accurate, with little details I'd missed, like the two infantry cadets who'd offered to be the healers' aides because that's their job for the squad. They have designated roles for each mission. I set it down on top of the book I'm returning to sign. "This is incredible."

"Glad to hear it's accurate." She glances over her shoulder, as if checking to see if we're alone, which we are. "The tricky thing is to capture the truth and not just an interpretation. Stories can change depending on who tells them."

If she only knew. How does someone like Jesinia graduate to become whatever Markham has evolved into? "Can I ask… What book did Jacek request that got him hauled away and killed?" I sign before I think better of it.

Her eyes widen. "He was killed?"

I nod. "A few days after we saw Markham take him."

Her face turns the same shade as her robes. "He was looking for an account of a border attack that doesn't exist. I told him there's no such record, but he came back three times, certain there was because he'd had family killed in the event. I recorded the request and sent it up my chain of command, thinking it would help him, but…" She shakes her head and drops her hands, blinking back tears.

"It's not your fault," I sign, but she doesn't respond, and it hits me that I could have been hauled away by Markham last year, but I wasn't. And there's only one logical explanation. I glance around us quickly to make sure we're still alone. "Last year, you didn't record when *I* asked for a book that doesn't exist in your records."

Her eyes widen.

"Did you?" My hands tremble as I sign. Shit. This is a bad idea. She'll be in danger if I bring her into this. But she's also the best person who can help me find what I'm looking for, and we only have *months*.

"No."

"Why?" I have to know. Everything hinges on her answer.

"At first, because I didn't want to be embarrassed that I couldn't find it." Her nose scrunches. "Then because…I couldn't find it." She looks over her shoulder at the empty Archives. "We should have a copy of almost every tome in Navarre here, yet you told me you'd read one that we don't have."

I nod.

"And then I looked up wyvern." She spells out the individual letters because there's no sign for the winged creatures. "And nothing. We have no recorded folklore like what you read."

"I know." My heart thrums faster. We're venturing into dangerous territory.

Her brow knits under her hood. "If you were any other rider, I would have considered that you have a faulty memory and got the title wrong, or even the subject matter. But you're…you."

I sign slowly so she doesn't miss a word. "The title wasn't wrong. I found my copy."

She takes a deep breath. "Which means our Archives are incomplete. There are books in existence we have no record of."

"Yes." And now we're talking treason. I can't tell her too much, not just for her own safety but in case…in case I'm wrong about her.

"I sent requests to other libraries looking for a wider collection of folklore, but the responses made it clear we have the most comprehensive selection." Her forehead wrinkles in concern.

"Yes." Gods, she's catching on without me even having to tell her. "Does anyone know what you were doing?"

"I implied that it was a personal passion to collect forgotten folklore from the border regions." She winces. "And then I implied that I was considering compiling a new tome as my third-year endeavor to graduate. I lied." Her mouth tightens, and she drops her hands.

"I'm doing a lot of that lately." Once I'm sure we're still alone, I continue. "Have you recorded any that I've asked for this year?"

"No."

Great Dunne. If she's caught breaking regulation, she won't just be denied the adept path; she'll be expelled from the college—or worse. She's already risking so much on my account, if she's telling the truth.

"You're looking for something. I knew it the second you lied about preparing for a debate." She searches my eyes. "You're a horrible liar, Violet."

I laugh. "I'm working on it."

"Can you tell me what you're looking for? I won't record your requests, not if you're thinking the same thing I am."

"Which is?"

"That our Archives are incomplete, either by ignorance…" She breathes deeply. "Or intention."

"Helping me could hurt you." My stomach sinks. "Get you killed. It's not fair to bring you into something dangerous."

"I can handle myself." She lifts her chin, and her next gestures are sharp. "Tell me what you need."

What can I tell her without endangering her further? Or risking our exposure? I have no idea if she's capable of shielding Dain or any memory reader from her mind. So clearly nothing about battles or venin. But that's not what I need, anyway. "I need the most comprehensive texts you have about how the First Six built the wards."

"The wards?" Her eyes flare.

"Yes." It's the simplest request that could be messily explained by wanting to research how to strengthen our defenses…if she tells. "But no one can know I'm asking, that I'm researching. More than my life depends on it. The older the text, the better."

She looks away for what feels like the longest minute of my life. She has every right to pause, to think, to realize just how badly this could go for both of us. This isn't a slip of memory, simply forgetting to record a request from a friend. This betrays her quadrant, her training. Her eyes meet mine. "I can't risk Aoife seeing right now, but I'll find you this week with the first tome I'm thinking of. One is all I can risk going missing. Saturdays are usually the day I work the Archives, when it's quiet. Bring it back then and I'll give you another if the first doesn't have what you need. Only Saturdays." She lifts her brows as she signs those last two words.

"When it's quiet." I nod in understanding, my stomach flipping with a mixture of hope and fear that I'm going to get her hurt...or worse. Glancing over her shoulder, I see Aoife walking our way. "Aoife is coming," I sign, keeping my hands where the other scribe can't see them. "Thank you."

"But there's something I want in return," she signs quickly, angling her back so Aoife won't see.

"Name it."

"You think Sloane has a shot?" Rhi asks on Monday as we watch the first round of challenges be called out.

My stomach churns with nausea like I'm the one who's going to be summoned to the mat. Fuck, I'd actually feel better if it was my name I knew they were going to call instead of Sloane's.

"She'll win," I answer truthfully.

I pocket the latest letter Xaden left me on my bed—I've already read it four times—as Aaric takes his place on the mat. I glance around and see Eya waiting with First Squad and offer a fast smile, which she returns. Ever since she helped me after my near burnout, we've developed a weird sort of relationship. We're friendly, if not friends, at least.

Turns out Xaden has known Eya since they were ten, according to the letter. Her mother was active in the government of Tyrrendor, holding a council seat even though she was a rider, which is uncommon. In fact, most of the aristocracy chooses to serve in the infantry, just like Xaden's father, because riders are discouraged from holding their family's seats. Not only are our commissions lifelong instead of the few years an infantry officer can agree to, but too much power in one person terrifies any king.

"You forgive him yet for whatever it is he lied to you about?" Rhi darts a meaningful look at my pocket, then folds her arms and glares at a pair of first-years shoving each other near the edge of the mat. "Stop fucking around!"

They instantly halt.

"Impressive." I grin, but it falls quickly. "And it's hard to talk something out with him when we only see each other once a week."

"Fucking first-years," she mutters, then glances over at me. "That's a good point. But you should get some time this weekend. Hey, did Ridoc tell you he saw Nolon yesterday?"

"He just said he had to take one of the first-years to the infirmary," I say, raising one eyebrow in question.

"Trysten." She nods. "He's the one with the floppy hair that never quite stays out of his eyes."

"Whatever his name is. The guy who shattered his forearm." I don't want to know his name. I already feel responsible for Sloane—who is currently swaying back and forth nervously across the mat. Emotionally attaching to any more first-years is just reckless. "Ridoc said that Nolon couldn't even *see* them until after dinner, and there were only a handful of other cadets in the infirmary."

"And when he walked out of that secretive room he's got with Varrish in the back of the infirmary, he was with an air wielder who looked just as haggard," Ridoc chimes in as he sidles up between us. "So clearly Nolon isn't doing his best work. Guy needs a month off."

Aaric delivers a punch to his opponent's jaw that makes the guy's head snap back.

"I give that a seven," Ridoc heckles from the sidelines.

"Out of ten? Solid eight," Sawyer counters from the other side of Rhiannon. "Perfect form." Then he lowers his voice and adds just for the four of us, "And I'm still going with the torture theory. I bet they've got gryphon riders in there or something."

"You think he's really torturing people back there?" Rhiannon says, lowering her voice even more.

"I have no clue." I blink as Aaric elbows his opponent in the throat with a quick jab that even Xaden would respect. "I would think they'd use the main interrogation chambers if they were doing something like that. The ones beneath the school."

"That's a fucking nine," Sawyer calls out.

"Nine!" Ridoc agrees, throwing up his hands with all of his fingers spread out except a thumb.

I laugh, then gasp as Aaric breaks his opponent's nose with the heel of his hand, ending the match. Emetterio declares him the winner, and the first-year has the decency to make it off the mat before dropping his hand away from his gushing nose.

That's a lot of blood.

Sawyer and Ridoc break out in applause, both shouting scores.

"Gods, can that one fight." Rhi nods slowly in approval as Aaric takes his place in the squad.

"Well, when you've had the best tutors," I whisper, grateful he's one secret she knows about.

"Daddy hasn't come looking for him?" She glances my way.

"Apparently not."

Challenges around us come to an end, and the professors call out the next batch.

"Sloane Mairi and Dasha Fabrren," Emetterio calls out.

"Hey, Rhi?" I swallow. Squads shift, but ours keeps our mat. That's the benefit of holding the reigning Iron Squad patch from last year.

"Hmm?"

"Remember how I said Sloane was going to win?"

"Yes, I remember a comment from ten minutes ago," she teases. A couple of our first-years pat Sloane on the back and offer what I hope are words of encouragement as she walks out onto the mat in front of us.

"Right. Well…" Shit, if I tell her, will she feel honor-bound to report me? She wouldn't, and that's the problem. She'd help me break into the fucking Archives if I wanted.

If you can't lie, distance yourself. But this is another thing I don't have to lie to her about.

Dasha joins Sloane on the mat, her shiny black hair braided in a single line from the tip of her forehead to the nape of her neck. She's petite and still has the pallor of a first-year who hasn't seen enough sun, but she's nothing close to the shade of green Sloane is turning.

There's a slight crimson tint to Dasha's lips that lets me know she had one of the frosted pastries from the tray I'd placed on her squad's breakfast table before they arrived this morning. Now that I'm looking, all of the members of her squad have that same hue to their mouths.

Oh well. It wasn't like I knew which one Dasha would eat.

"If you're going to change your mind and say she's going to lose, then don't tell me." Rhiannon shakes her head. "I'm nervous about this one."

"Me too," Imogen says, taking the empty spot on my right.

"That makes three of us," Quinn says next to her. "She's not just a first-year."

"No," I agree, noting that even Dain is watching from the next mat over. And to think, last year, I'd actually hoped I'd be in a *relationship* with him. "Rhi." I lower my voice. "She's not going to lose."

Her gaze narrows. "What are you going to do?"

"If you don't know, you don't have to feel guilty about reporting it. Just trust me." I slide my hand into my pocket as nonchalantly as possible and uncork the small glass vial as the two girls nod, each taking a fighting stance.

Rhi searches my eyes, then nods as well, turning back to the match.

The first-years circle each other on the mat, and I carefully turn the vial in my hand, letting what I know to be a colorless powder fall from the glass into the creases between my palm and fingers. I withdraw my hand in a fist, keeping it tight at my side as Dasha delivers her first blow, a punch straight to Sloane's cheek.

The blonde's skin splits.

"Fuck," Imogen mutters. "Come on, Mairi, hands up!"

Someone screams from the mat behind us, and we all look over our shoulders to see a first-year staring lifelessly up at his opponent. Shit. Killing an opponent during a challenge isn't cheered. But it also isn't punishable. More than one grudge has been settled on these mats in the name of strengthening the wings.

I suddenly feel a lot less guilty about my plans.

The girls circle again, and Dasha kicks high, catching Sloane on the unmarked side of her face so hard that her head snaps sideways, and then her body follows, turning as she falls to the mat, landing on her back.

"That was faster than I expected," Rhi notes, worry lacing her tone.

"Me too." I lift my closed fist to my mouth and shift my weight, making sure that I look as worried as I feel as Dasha follows Sloane down to the floor. The pair is only a few feet away, so at least I won't have to skirt my way around the mat. "Crouch," I say under my breath to Imogen.

She drops without question. "Come on, Mairi!"

I lower myself, too, panic creeping up my throat at the look on Sloane's dazed face as Dasha lands another punch, then another, and another. Blood spatters the mat.

Yeah, that's enough.

I wait for Dasha to exhale, then open my palm slightly and cough. Hard.

She breathes in and gets one more hit.

Then she shakes her head and her eyes glaze over.

"Get up, Sloane!" I yell, looking her dead in the eye.

Dasha falls back on her ass, blinks rapidly, her head wobbling as if she's been at the pub for the evening.

Sloane rolls to her side and plants her palms on the mat.

"Now," I order her.

Anger fills her eyes, and she lunges forward toward Dasha.

Dasha's fist curls, but her swing doesn't make contact as Sloane buries her shoulder in Dasha's stomach. At that angle, she had to have knocked the breath out of her.

Good. She only has another moment. Maybe two.

Sloane scrambles behind Dasha and then yanks her up and into the weakest chokehold I've ever seen. But hey, if it works.

"Yield!" Sloane demands.

Dasha bucks upward, her strength and focus returning.

"Yield!" Sloane yells this time, and I hold my breath.

Gods, if I judged wrong and Dasha gains the upper hand again…

Dasha finally drops her hand to the mat and taps twice.

My shoulders droop in pure relief as Emetterio calls the match.

"What did you do?" Imogen whispers without looking at me.

"What needed to be done." We both stand as the first-years do, but unlike them, we don't stumble as we gain our feet.

"You sound like Xaden," Imogen says.

My gaze swings toward her.

"Relax. It's a compliment." She smiles. "Liam is immeasurably grateful right now."

I swallow past the lump in my throat.

"Not half bad," Rhiannon says, glancing sideways at me before watching Sloane take her place with the rest of the first-years in our squad. "Not good, either."

"I'll give the match a six," Ridoc comments. "I mean, she didn't lose, so clearly that rates above a five."

The next pair takes the mat.

Once today's challenges are over, I look at Imogen and nod toward Sloane before heading that direction. "Give me a second," I say over my shoulder to Rhiannon.

Imogen jogs to catch up.

"Mairi," I say as we round the corner of the mat, crooking my finger at her.

Sloane lifts her chin in the air, but at least she comes. This isn't exactly the kind of discussion I want to scream across the gym.

"Ouch." Imogen points to her right eye as she approaches. "That's going to swell shut."

"I won, didn't I?" Her voice shakes.

"You won because I took Dasha out for you." I keep my voice low and spread my palm wide open, where there's a trace amount of the shimmering powder left on my skin.

"No." She shakes her head. "I won that fair and square."

"Gods, do I wish *that* were true." I huff out a breath. "Ardyce powder, when combined with an earlier dose of ground lillybelle, disorients someone for a minute—maybe two, depending on the dose. Similar to being drunk. Alone, they're mildly upsetting to the stomach. Together?" I lift my eyebrows. "They kept you alive."

Sloane's mouth opens and shuts once. Twice.

"Damn." Imogen grins, rocking back on her heels as cadets shuffle past, heading for the door. "Is *that* how you got through those first challenges last year? Devious, Sorrengail. Fucking brilliant, but devious."

"I did that for your brother," I tell Sloane, keeping eye contact even though the hatred shining through hers hurts like hell. "He was one of my closest friends, and I promised him while he was fucking dying that I'd look after you. So here I am, looking after you."

"I don't need—"

"Wrong tactic," Imogen lectures. "'Thank you' is appropriate."

"I'm not thanking her," she seethes, her eyes narrowing on me. "He'd be here if not for you."

"That's some bullshit!" Imogen snaps. "Xaden ordered—"

"You're right," I interrupt. "He would. And I miss him every single day. And because of the love I have for him, it's okay that you hate me. You can think whatever you need to about me if it gets you through the day, Sloane. But you're going to train. You're going to accept help."

"If it's Malek's will that I join my brother, then so be it. Liam didn't need help," she retorts, but there's a touch of fear in her eyes that lets me know most of this is bluster. "He made it on his own."

"No, he didn't," Imogen argues. "Violet saved his life during War Games. He fell off Deigh's back, and it was Violet and Tairn who flew after him and caught him."

Sloane's lips part.

"Here's the deal." I take a step closer to Sloane. "You're going to train so you don't get yourself killed. Not with me. I don't need to be part of your development era. But you will meet with Imogen every single day if that's what she wants, because I have something you want."

"I highly doubt that." She crosses her arms, but the effect is ruined by the rapid swelling of her eye.

"I have fifty of the letters Liam wrote for you."

Her eyes widen.

"Oh shit." Imogen's head jerks toward mine. "Seriously?"

"Seriously." I don't look away from Sloane. "And at the end of every week that you attend and participate in whatever Imogen thinks you need, I'll give one of them to you."

"All of his things were burned," Sloane sputters. "They were sacrificed to

Malek as they should be!"

"I'll definitely apologize to Malek when we meet," I assure her. "If you want his letters, you'll train for them."

Her face turns a mottled shade of red. "You'd keep my brother's letters from me? If they still exist, they're *mine*. You really are a piece of work."

"In this case, I think Liam would more than approve." I shrug. "It's up to you, Sloane. Show up, train, live, and get a letter a week. Or don't." Without waiting for whatever snarky response she can come up with, I turn and leave, walking back toward where Rhiannon is waiting with the upper years of our squad.

"You. Are…" Imogen shakes her head as she catches up to me. "I see it now."

"What?" I ask.

"Why Xaden fell for you."

I scoff.

"Truthfully." She puts her hands up. "You're fucking clever. Way more clever than I gave you credit for. I bet you keep him constantly annoyed." A smile beams across her face. "How glorious."

I roll my eyes at her.

"And you got Sloane to agree to show up tomorrow morning after chores," she tells me. "It was a risky move, but it worked."

Now I'm the one smiling.

Jesinia brings me *The Unabridged History of the First Six* the next day, which is not only a three-hundred-year-old text but marked CLASSIFIED in the endpapers, and I keep my side of the deal, handing over *The Fables of the Barren*.

Then I hide away at every available second to read her book, when we're not being lectured by Professor Grady about our inability to check our egos or getting what feels like pointless Battle Briefs.

But while it goes into detail about the complex interpersonal relationships of the First Six, and even a little of their battle experience during the Great War, it simply labels the enemy as General Daramor and our allies as the isle kingdoms.

Not exactly helpful.

The book Jesinia gives me on Saturday is *The Sacrifice of Dragonkind*, by one of Kaori's predecessors, and goes into why Basgiath was chosen for the location of the wards.

"Green dragons, especially those descending from the line of Cruaidhuaine, have an especially stable connection to magic, which some believe is a result of their more reasonable, defensive nature," I repeat in a whisper as I pack to head to Samara that night.

There's absolutely nothing that could ruin my evening. Not when I'm about to see Xaden in the morning.

My eyes widen when I open the door and find Varrish standing there instead of Bodhi, flanked by his two henchmen, and immediately remind myself to thank Xaden for the wards that deny him entry. A quick step backward puts me out of his reach.

"Relax, Sorrengail." He smiles like he didn't nearly kill me with his little punishment. "I just came by to check your pack and walk you out to Tairn."

I slip my pack from my shoulders and hold it out to him, careful not to let him touch my skin so he can't slip through the wards. Then I keep my eyes locked on his henchmen as they dump my belongings instead of glancing to my bookcase to be sure my classified tome is hidden.

"It's clear," the woman says, and she's *kind* enough to put my things away.

"Excellent." Varrish nods. "Then we'll just escort you to your dragon. You can't be too careful around here, given the rash of attacks these last few weeks." He tilts his head. "Funny that most seem to be focused on those of you who disappeared during War Games, don't you think?"

"Not sure I'd ever call assaults 'funny,'" I reply. "And I don't need the escort."

"Nonsense." He steps back and gestures into the hallway. "We wouldn't want anything to happen to the daughter of the commanding general."

My heart bolts at an unsustainable rhythm.

"It's not a suggestion." His smile slides.

I check my sheaths to be sure my daggers are in place, then walk into the hallway, feeling the tug of Xaden's wards as I leave their safety. Every step I take for the next fifteen minutes is careful, deliberate, and I make sure I'm never within arm's reach or striking distance.

"I noticed your squad didn't have flight maneuvers this week," Varrish says as we approach Tairn on the flight field.

"I'll snack if he makes a move," Tairn promises, and I start to breathe normally.

"We had a few injuries that needed to recover after running landings."

"Hmm." He gestures toward Tairn as if inviting me to ride my own dragon. "Well, it was noted, as you'll soon see. I guess I'll meet your little golden next week."

Andarna.

"She is safe within the deepest stage of the Dreamless Sleep. You should be able to see her in a few weeks," Tairn says.

"That's what you said last week." I mount quickly, my pulse settling as I strap into the saddle. *"Before last year, I never would have considered that the safest*

place in the world was on the back of a dragon."

"Before last year, I might have seen you as an appetizer." He rolls his shoulders and launches.

When I get to Samara, I understand why Varrish warned that I'd see why he'd noted our lack of flight maneuvers.

I might be here, but Xaden is on twenty-four-hour duty in the operations center.

And I don't have clearance.

Many historians choose to ignore the sacrifices made by both humans and dragonkind to establish Navarre under the first wards in favor of praising the spirit of unification, but I would be remiss not to mention the losses suffered, both in terms of the ancestral hatching grounds of each dragon breed and the civilians who did not survive the continent-wide migration that resulted from the opening of Navarre's borders…or those lost when we closed them.

—THE SACRIFICE OF DRAGONKIND
BY MAJOR DEANDRA NAVEEN

CHAPTER SEVENTEEN

"Bodhi can't keep moving maneuvers for our section, or more teachers than Varrish are going to notice," Imogen says on Wednesday as we walk toward Battle Brief, moving up the main staircase in a sea of black.

"Tairn is going to the Empyrean about Andarna, but absolutely nothing can be done until she wakes from the Dreamless Sleep anyway."

She sighs. "How are things with Xaden?"

I nearly trip on the last step before the doorway. "You want to talk about my relationship with Xaden now?"

"I'm only giving you however long it takes us to reach the Battle Brief room." Her face puckers like she's tasted something sour. "So if you need to…talk, this is your chance, since I've noticed you're still icing your friends out, which is a mistake."

Well, in that case.

"One, Xaden told me to keep my distance if I couldn't lie to them, and two, between the land nav course—which we *failed*—and his duty schedule, I think leadership is keeping us apart as a punishment for not producing Andarna. And it's coded, but he says the same in the letter he left on his bed for me." A letter that quickly became my favorite because it delves into what his life had been like before the rebellion. It also makes me wonder what he'd be like if that was still the reality he was living in.

"That's just…weird," Imogen says, her brow furrowing as her gaze scans the hallway for threats.

"It is." I do the same, watching every pair of hands I can see. "The timing of the last two weeks is just too coincidental for it not to be on purpose."

"Oh no, that part is completely understandable." She side-eyes me. "Separating you two would be my first move if I was in a position of power. On your own, you're both capable of terrifying things with those signets. Together? You're a fucking menace. I mean it's weird that he's writing you *letters*."

"Why? I think it's…sweet."

"Exactly. Does he strike you as a *letters* kind of guy?" She shakes her head. "He's not even a *talking* kind of guy."

"We're trying to work on our communication." It comes out a touch defensive.

"You're eventually going to let him off the hook for keeping you in the dark, aren't you?" She shoots me a look that says she clearly thinks I should and pulls two hairpins from her pocket. "Better answer quickly. We're almost there."

"Can you love someone who refuses to be open with you?" I challenge.

"One," she blatantly mimics me, "we're not talking about my love life. I have Quinn—my actual friend—for that." She pins back the longest section of her pink hair with quick, efficient movements. "Two, we keep information classified all the time. You'd have the same problem with any rider you dated."

"That's not…" Fine, she has a point, but she's missing mine. "All right, let's say that you're with someone, and one day a battle-ax comes hurtling out of his armoire—"

"An armoire? I *really* wish you'd go back to confiding in Rhiannon." She shakes her head.

"—and nearly kills you. Wouldn't you demand to see the rest of the armoire to make sure there are no other battle-axes poised to strike before getting back together with them?" We're almost to the lecture hall.

"There's always a battle-ax." As we pass the doorway, she nods to Eya, who is chatting with Bodhi, and my eyes flare at her black eye and what looks to be a broken nose.

"Because that's *normal*?"

"You didn't want normal. If you did, you'd be in a relationship with Aetos." She shudders. "Or hell, anyone else in this place. But you wanted Riorson. If you didn't think the man was hiding more than a few battle-axes, then you're mad at the wrong person, because you lied to *yourself*."

I open and shut my mouth as we funnel through the wide doors into the Battle Brief room. Without windows to let the hot sun in, the hall is a welcome refuge from the sticky August heat.

"Oh, look, our time is up." She sighs in obvious relief.

"Helpful." I miss talking to Rhi.

"You want actual, meaningful advice?" She takes my elbow and tugs me to the side of the staircase, where the third-years stand. "Fine. Everyone fails land nav the first time. We're egotistical assholes who can't handle being wrong. The instructor just wants you to feel bad about it, which is clearly working. Not to mention that you have bigger issues to worry about than a man, like how you're going to survive the rest of RSC, including the interrogation portions where they will beat the shit out of you for fun, or like, I don't know…going to war. And you asked if I wanted to talk about your relationship, which implies that you damn well know you're still in one—"

I bristle. "That's not—"

"I'm still speaking." A third-year from First Wing gets too close, and she shoves his shoulder. "You don't have to freeze out everyone you can't be completely honest with just because Riorson thinks that works for him—it doesn't, hence *all* of your issues, and it damn well looks like your friend needs *you*, so go." She motions toward the staircase behind me, and I turn, catching sight of Rhi leaning against the wall.

Worry pinches her features as she reads the parchment she's clutching next to Tara, oblivious to the cadets passing by on the wide staircase.

I start down the steps, dodging more than one overeager first-year on my way to Rhi.

"I'm sure it's nothing." Tara rubs Rhi's shoulder as I reach them. "Show it to Markham after brief. I'm going to get going." She tucks her black hair behind her ears and smiles again when she sees me. "Hi, Violet."

"Hi, Tara." I wave as she leaves, making her way to First Wing's seats. "Everything all right, Rhi?" I ask, knowing she has every right to shut me out the way I've done to her.

"I don't know." She hands me the parchment. "I got this with a letter from my parents this morning. They said they're circulating around the village."

I open it, and my eyes widen for a heartbeat before I school my expression. It's the size of the public announcements the scribes nail to posts in every village in Navarre, but there's no official announcement number at the top.

BEWARE OF STRANGERS SEEKING SHELTER.

"What the hell?" I mutter softly.

"My thoughts exactly," she replies. "Read the rest."

IN THIS TIME OF UNPRECEDENTED VIOLATIONS OF OUR SOVEREIGN BORDERS, WE COUNT ON YOU, OUR BORDER VILLAGES, TO

BE OUR EYES AND EARS. OUR SAFETY DEPENDS ON YOUR VIGILANCE. DO NOT TAKE IN STRANGERS. YOUR KINDNESS COULD KILL.

"'Your kindness could kill,'" I repeat quietly as cadets shuffle past. "And what border violations?"

"What do we have here?" Markham says, snatching the paper from my hands.

"It came from my village," Rhi explains.

"So it did." He glances up at me and then over to Rhiannon. "Thank you for bringing this to class." He continues down the stairs without another word.

"I'm so sorry," I say to Rhi.

"Not your fault," she replies. "And I would have taken it to him after class anyway. If anyone could explain that, it would be him."

"Of course." I force a smile. "Let's take our seats."

We make our way to the seats beside Ridoc and Sawyer, then take out our things.

"How are your parents?" I ask Rhi, trying to make the transition sound natural.

"Good." She smiles softly. "Their shop is booming right now, since they moved another company of infantry into Montserrat."

I blink. That puts the outpost at more than capacity.

"Good morning," Markham says, his voice booming over the hall as he holds up the paper from Rhiannon's letter. "Today we're going to talk about the battles that aren't quite so obvious. One of your classmates received this notice." He reads it aloud, his intonation changing what's obviously a warning to a passionate plea.

Professor Devera stands with her arms crossed, her eyes downcast as he finishes reading.

"This is a regional notice," Markham explains, "which is why it does not carry a public announcement number. We have seen an alarming number of attempted border crossings in our mountain villages near our most strategic outposts. Why is this dangerous?"

My grip on my pen tightens. Are the Poromish civilians fleeing a new offensive? Nausea rolls through my stomach. Wards could protect so many more people, but I'm no closer to an answer than I was when we got back to Basgiath from Aretia. Every book I've read mentions the glorious accomplishment, but none say *how* it was accomplished. If the answer is in the Archives, then it's well hidden.

"Because we can't know their intentions," a first-year answers. "It's why we keep our borders closed."

Markham nods.

But when *did* we close our borders? As soon as we unified? Or closer to 400 AU, when I think we wiped the history from the books? I shift in my seat as power rises in direct proportion to my frustration. Answers are supposed to follow questions. That's how my life has always worked. Until now, there's never been a question I couldn't answer after a few hours in the Archives, and now I'm not sure I can trust any answers I *do* find there. Nothing makes sense.

My fingertips buzz, and heat quickly follows.

"Silver One." There's a note of warning in Tairn's tone.

"I know." I breathe deeply and fight to shove the feelings back into the neat little box that holds all my inconvenient emotions, tugging my shields tight around me.

"This could be a new tactic," a third-year calls out from behind us. "Infiltrating our outposts under false pretenses."

"Exactly." Markham nods again.

Devera shifts her weight and then lifts her chin, looking up at us. Does she know? Gods, I want her not to know. I want her to be as good of a person as I think she is. What about Kaori? Emetterio? Grady? Are any of my professors actually trustworthy?

"What's more disturbing is the propaganda these Poromish people bring with them, falsified announcements from their own leadership of cities destroyed in what they claim to be violent attacks." He pauses, like he's debating telling us the rest, but I know it's for dramatics. "Attacks they claim come from dragons."

Fucking. Liar. Heat stains my cheeks, and I quickly avert my gaze when he looks my way. The buzzing rises to a hum as energy gathers, pushing at my skin, looking for an outlet.

A disgruntled murmur rises from the cadets around me.

"As if dragons would ruin cities," Rhiannon mutters, shaking her head.

They wouldn't, but wyvern would…and do.

Markham sighs. "This notice does not mean we are without compassion. In fact, for the first time in hundreds of years, we authorized classified missions— now completed, of course—to reconnoiter those very cities."

My pen casing groans and power ripples along my skin, lifting the hair on my forearm.

"Are you all right?" Rhiannon asks.

"Fine."

"You sure about that?" She stares pointedly at my hand.

And the tendril of smoke rising from the pen. I drop it, then rub my hands together, like that's going to help dispel the energy coursing through my body.

"Those assigned riots have reported back that the cities inside Poromiel are intact, leading us to the same conclusion you've drawn—this is a new tactic that plays on our compassion." He says it with such certainty that I nearly applaud his acting. "Professor Devera?"

She clears her throat. "I read the reports this morning. There was no destruction mentioned."

Whose reports? The scribes can't be trusted.

"There you have it." Markham shakes his head. "I think this is a good time to focus our discussion on the efficiency of propaganda and the role civilians play in supporting a war effort. Lies are powerful tools."

He would know.

Somehow, I make it through the rest of the briefing without setting the map on fire, then pack my things in a hurry and force my way past the other cadets to get the hell out of there as quickly as possible.

I break into a run down the hallway, pulling the straps of my heavy pack tight so it doesn't slam into my spine when I race down the steps. Agonizing heat spirals tight, building in preparation to strike, and when I finally push through the doors into the courtyard, I stumble forward and throw up my hands to release it.

Power rips through me and lightning strikes near the outer walls, far enough away that the flying gravel only impacts the wall.

I feel Tairn hovering on the edge of my mind, but he doesn't lecture.

"Violet?" Rhiannon steps in front of me, her chest heaving from obviously having run after me.

"I'm fine," I lie. Gods, that's getting so fucking easy, and it's the one thing she asked me not to do.

"Obviously." She gestures to the courtyard.

"I have to go." Step by step, I back away from her, a knot the size of the entire quadrant forming in my throat. "I'll be late for RSC. Will you take notes?"

"Because that's *definitely* the class you should be late for," she says sarcastically. "What could possibly be more important than learning interrogation techniques?"

I shake my head, then pivot and run before I tell another lie. Into the dormitory. Down the steps. Through the tunnels. Across the bridge. Into the Healer Quadrant. I don't stop running until I'm almost to the Archives, and then only my body slows, not my thoughts.

The guard stands but doesn't challenge my right to walk straight past the large, circular door and into the Archives. Paper and glue and Dad. The scent fills my lungs, and the knot in my throat loosens as my heartbeat calms.

Until I realize at least two hundred scribes are seated at the tables, and every single one of them is staring at me. Then the organ beating in my chest picks up the pace again.

What in Amari's name am I doing?

"You've apparently lost all common sense with your control and regressed to where you think you can locate it," Tairn growls.

Fair point. Not that I'm telling him that.

"Just did."

A tall figure in cream robes turns in her seat and looks me up and down. "The Archives are not open to riders at this hour."

"I know." I nod. *And yet I'm here.*

"What can we do for you?" the professor asks in a tone that suggests I find somewhere else to be.

"I just need…" What? To return the book I shouldn't have?

Three rows back, a scribe stands, then walks forward, shooting me an incredulous look before lifting her hands to sign toward her professor. Jesinia.

The professor nods, and Jesinia heads my way, her eyes flaring in unspoken what-the-fuck as she approaches.

"I'm sorry," I sign.

She turns to my right in front of the study table, and I follow, noting that the stacks block us from the class's view. "What are you doing?" she signs. "You can't be here right now."

"I know. I accidentally ended up here." I slip my pack from my shoulders and rummage through for the book, handing it over to her like this was some planned meeting.

She glances from me to the book, then sighs and steps back a few feet, cringing when she slides the book onto a shelf it absolutely doesn't belong on. "You look upset."

"I'm sorry," I repeat. "Are you going to be in trouble?"

"Of course not. I told her you are an impatient, arrogant rider, and it would be less disruptive to our studies if I helped you, all of which is true." She glances toward the end of the stacks. "This couldn't wait until Saturday?"

I start to nod, then shake my head. "I need to read faster."

She studies my expression, and two lines appear between her eyebrows. "I asked what you were looking for, but I should have asked what will happen if you don't find it."

"People will die." My stomach sinks lower with every word I sign. "That's all I can say."

She sits with that for a few seconds. "Have you at least told your squadmates whatever it is you're too scared to tell me?"

"No." I hesitate, struggling to find the words. "I can't let anyone else die because of me. I've already put you in too much danger."

"You gave me a choice. Don't you think they deserve the same?" She levels a disappointed look on me when I don't answer. "I'll bring you a new selection tonight. Meet me on the bridge at eight." She steps into my space. "Saturdays, Violet. Or you'll get us caught."

I nod. "Thank you."

It was only when we pushed the wards to their true limits, extending them far past what we first thought possible and to what I now question as sustainable, that we defined the borders of Navarre, regretfully knowing not every citizen would benefit from their protection.

—The Journey of the First Six, a Secondhand Account by Sagar Olsen, First Curator of the Scribe Quadrant, Basgiath War College
—Translated into the common language by Captain Madilyn Calros, Twelfth Curator of the Scribe Quadrant, Basgiath War College
—Translated and Redacted for Academic Consumption by Colonel Phineas Cartland, Twenty-seventh Curator of the Scribe Quadrant, Basgiath War College

CHAPTER EIGHTEEN

"You're early!" I blurt when Xaden opens my door Saturday morning to find me on the floor of my room, surrounded by every history text I own and the two Jesinia loaned me.

Shit, I'm supposed to meet her in less than an hour.

He blinks and shuts the door behind him. "Hello to you, too."

"Hi," I respond, my voice softening. The elation of seeing him is tempered by the shadows under his eyes. "Sorry, I just wasn't expecting you to make it until noon, if they even let you come and— You look…exhausted." Even his movements are slower. Not by much, but I notice.

"That's what every man wants to hear." He sets his swords by the door and drops his pack right next to them. Like it's where they go. Like this room is partly his, too. Like his room at Samara feels like it's mine. Neither of us has ever asked for separate quarters.

Maybe I can't fully trust him, but I also can't stand to be away from him.

"I didn't say you aren't beautiful. I implied that you need a nap." I nod toward my empty bed. "You should sleep."

His slow smile stops my heart. "You think I'm beautiful?"

"Like you don't already know that." I roll my eyes and flip the page in *The Journey of the First Six, a Secondhand Account*, averting my gaze. "I also think you smell like you've been flying for twelve hours." It's not exactly true, but maybe it will check the already enormous ego I just inflated.

"Gods, I missed you." He laughs and rips off his flight jacket, revealing the short sleeves of his summer uniform and indecently toned arms.

I breathe through the impulse to forget every single worry for a couple of hours by laying *him* out over this floor and try like hell to concentrate on the text in front of me.

"Think anyone will report me for using the bathing chamber?" He's already rummaging through his pack.

"I don't think anyone would report you for cold-blooded murder around here, let alone taking a bath."

"Lieutenants aren't exactly supposed to be sleeping in cadets' quarters when they visit," he tells me. "We're breaking a few rules."

"Never bothered you before." Letting his assumption that he's sleeping here slide, I glance up from the book and immediately regret it when I see that he's shirtless. Gods help me if he strips off anything else.

"Didn't say it bothered me now." He stands, his arms full of fresh clothes from his pack. "Just don't want to see you punished for my actions. I thought they were going to find a way to send you on maneuvers today, or just lock you away."

"Me too." Awareness spreads through every part of my body as I lock eyes with him. "I'm sure they'll find a dark cellar for you next week, so we should try to enjoy this one."

"You and I have different definitions of the word 'enjoy.'" He gestures to the books scattered on my floor.

"Not really." I scan the page quickly and flip to the next. "I think spending the day tangled up in that bed together would be *enjoyable*, but since you drew your line, here I am with boring, sexless books."

"Say those three little words, and I'll have you naked in *seconds*." He looks at me with so much heat that I do a double take when I glance up, my breath catching.

"I want you." All day. Every day.

"Those are not the three words I need." He slides into my mind like a caress. *"And why aren't your shields up?"*

"Well, those are the words you get without full disclosure." I rip my gaze away. "And it's just us in here."

"Hmmm." He gives me a look I can't decipher. "I'll be right back."

"You don't really smell," I whisper, loath to let him out of my sight for even a second.

"Get any closer, and you'll take that back." He leaves, and I do my best to concentrate on the book in front of me and not the thought that he's about to be naked down the hall.

All I have to do is be honest with him about how I feel, and I can have him. His body, at least. But isn't that all I really had before? Ironic that it's my truthfulness that can put me out of my own misery when it's his candor I crave. I guess in that way, we're alike, both wanting more than the other person is willing to risk.

A few minutes later, he walks back in and the room feels instantly smaller, or maybe it's the jump in my heart rate making it feel harder to breathe and not the lack of air.

"That was quick." I've only read another twenty pages or so but I don't bother hiding the two books I need to return. It's not like he'd know which are mine and which are borrowed. The less I have to hide, the better.

"I could make so many innuendos, but I'll refrain." He tosses his things into his pack, then sinks into the armchair and leans forward, bracing his forearms on spread knees. He picks a book up off the floor. "Where are all the books from? You didn't have this many last year."

"Mostly from my old room in the main college." I skim the current page and sigh. This book is mostly scribe-centric stories about the Great War that are heavily redacted, with one vague passage about discovering the ability to extend the wards. "I crated them before Parapet and thought my mother would have shipped them off to storage, but it appears she is more sentimental than Mira or I thought. They were right where I left them." It had been a surprising discovery. Nothing had been touched in my old room, like I was expected back at any minute. "Really, you should get some sleep."

Jesinia will be pissed if I miss our appointment.

"*Colonel Daxton's Guide to Excelling in the Scribe Quadrant*," he reads from the spine.

"That one wasn't as useful as I thought it would be the first time I read it," I joke.

"I would say not." He sets the book down and then tilts his head, reading the book I have open in front of me. "*The Journey of the First Six, a Secondhand Account.*"

"Yes." My pulse leaps, and my stomach gets the same weightless feeling that usually comes when Tairn makes a steep dive. I should have hidden the damned books.

"Or maybe you want him to know," Tairn interjects.

"Go...be busy."

"A class assignment?" Xaden's eyes narrow when I don't answer.

"For research." For some reason I can't fathom, I draw the line at outright lying to him.

"I don't remember anything about the First Six being..." A tick of his jaw later, his gaze jumps to mine. "You're hiding something from me."

Shit. He knows. Or he guesses. That was fast.

"Violet?" It's practically a growl. He definitely knows. "Why are you researching the First Six?"

"For Aretia." I shut the book. There's nothing in it that's going to help, anyway.

Xaden draws a deep breath, and shadows extend from under the chair, rolling over his feet like a dark fog.

"For you, really." The admission is soft.

He stills so completely that I'm not sure he's even breathing.

"Brennan told you we have a wardstone." His words are clipped, controlled. The shadows begin moving like hands, gathering all the books around me but the one I'm holding and stacking them. "I'm going to fucking kill him."

"Why? Because he's more forthcoming with me than *you* are?" I close the book. "Relax, it's not like he gave me your journal or something."

"I don't keep one, but that would have been far preferable," he snaps. "Digging around for information on Navarre's most classified defense will get you killed."

"Civilians are fleeing for our borders, no one in Navarre knows the truth, and Aretia needs to defend itself—to protect the people I'm guessing you're prepared to take in when venin inevitably reach Tyrrendor." I clutch the old tome to my chest. "You *are* going to take people in, aren't you?"

"Of course we are."

"Good." At least my faith isn't misplaced. I glance over my shoulder at the clock on my desk. Twenty minutes until I have to return the book.

"But it's weapons that are going to defend Tyrrendor."

"I beg to differ, and I'll keep researching until I figure out how the First Six put these wards in place so we can duplicate the process in Aretia." I tilt my chin at him.

"No one knows how it was originally done, only how to maintain them." He rises from the chair, and his shadows follow as he paces, a barometer for his mood. "It's a lost magic, and you can't deny that it was probably *lost* on purpose."

"Someone knows," I counter, tracking his movements. "There's no chance that someone didn't leave a record somewhere in case they fail. We aren't going to destroy the only thing that could save us. We would hide it, but we wouldn't destroy it."

"And how the hell do you propose finding that record without letting the scribes know what you're up to?" he challenges, turning at the edge of my bed with his hands laced behind his neck and pinning me with a stare that might have sent me running last year.

The click of my teeth is audible as I snap my mouth shut.

He takes one deep breath, then another, closing his eyes. "The book you're clutching like a newborn. It's not one of yours, is it?"

"It's currently in my possession."

"Violet." I can practically feel him counting to ten in his head for patience.

"Fine. I borrowed it from the Archives. Are you really going to yell at me for trying to help?"

"Who knows?" The question is so soft that I almost wish he would just yell. He's always at his most lethal when he's calm like this.

"A friend."

His eyes snap open. "There's a reason we don't fuck around in the Archives. That's the beating heart of the enemy." His gaze bores into mine. "We don't have any friends there."

"Well, I do." I stand slowly. "And I'm going to be late to return the book if I don't head down there now. So why don't you get some sleep while I—"

"I'm coming with you."

"The hell you are." I slip the book into the borrowed bag. "You'll scare her witless. I haven't told her anything about you, or Aretia, or what's going on outside our borders, so relax."

Go figure, he doesn't. "She just knows you're researching classified material. I'm not going to *relax* knowing that you've put yourself in danger."

"You're in danger every single day." Anger flushes my skin.

Someone knocks on the door, and he sighs before jerking it open.

"Oh!" Rhiannon steps back, almost bumping into Ridoc. "I didn't realize you were here today, Lieutenant Riorson." She glances over at me. "Vi, we were going to ask if you wanted to come to Chantara with us—"

"She's busy," Xaden responds, clasping my hand.

"Don't be an ass." I yank my hand from his.

"Whoa." Ridoc's eyebrows rise as I turn toward Xaden.

"I've done exactly what you asked. I kept everything *from my friends."* I glare into the depths of his soul. *"So don't be an asshole to them."*

"Exactly what I've asked?" He leans down, bringing his face within a breath of mine. *"By keeping your research a secret?"*

My jaw drops. *"Are you really going to stand here and compare secrets with me?"*

"It's not the same." He winces.

"It's exactly *the same!"* I grip the strap of the bag to keep from jabbing him in the chest with my finger. How fucking *dare* he. *"I'm researching the wards for* you.*"*

"Why do you think I'm so angry?" The tension in his eyes, his posture, his tone equals mine.

"Because you don't like being on the other side of secrets."

"What the hell is going on?" Sawyer asks from the hallway.

"I...uh..." Ridoc scratches the top of his head. "I think they're fighting."

"That has... How long have you been hiding this from me?" Xaden questions.

"They're not even...speaking," Rhiannon mutters.

"I haven't hidden shit *from you. I've simply told you selective truths."*

He draws back like I've hit him.

"Sorry, guys." I turn to my friends. "Trust me, there's nothing I would rather do than go to Chantara with you, but unfortunately, I have to run an errand. Next weekend?"

"You'll be in Samara." Xaden folds his arms across his chest.

How is it possible to both love someone and loathe them all in the same moment?

Rhiannon looks between the two of us, then settles her attention on me. "Then the weekend after," she suggests quietly.

I nod.

Her brow knits in wordless question.

"I'm fine. I promise. You guys have a great time." I force a smile. "I'll let you know if I need your help burying a body later."

Ridoc sputters into a cough, and Sawyer pounds him on the back.

"I think she might mean you," Rhiannon says as she gives Xaden an arch look.

"I'm certain she does."

"Let's go," Sawyer says, leading the three of them out of the doorway.

"I'll do it, too," Rhiannon says over her shoulder. "I've never moved anything as big as you, but I bet my signet could put you in the ground without even disturbing the dirt if I'm pissed enough." She shoots a look at him before walking down the hallway.

Xaden sighs and closes the door. "You have some loyal friends."

"I do," I agree. "Just remember you said that when it comes time to tell them what's going on under their noses."

His answer is barely a grunt.

"I have to go—"

"I'm pissed that you hid it from me," he interrupts. "But I'm livid that you've put your life at risk *for* me. That's not something I can handle."

"It's not at risk. I can trust her." I reach for the door handle, and he steps aside. His mouth tightens with anger, but it's the flash of fear in his eyes that makes me pause. If I had a way of knowing he was just a little safer in Samara, I would want it. Even if he's being an ass. "Fine. You can come with me if you agree *not* to scare her."

"I can't control her feelings." He scoffs.

I arch a single brow.

"I just want to meet her." He lifts his hands, palms outward.

"So you can see if she's trustworthy? By looking at her? Even you aren't that powerful." I open the door and step out into the hallway. "Let's go."

"I'll know. I'm an incredible judge of character." He walks out after me, pulling the door closed.

"Your ego really is boundless." We start down the hall and turn right into the central corridor. *"And just because I'm letting you come doesn't mean I'm not still pissed at you."*

"Same." He puts his hand on the small of my back when we pass a group of cadets.

"You don't have to touch me for them to think you have a reason to be here. Everyone knows that we…"

"Knows that we what? You've been pretty damned clear that we're not together."

Wait…is that hurt in his voice? I hate the way my ire dulls. It's easier to live in the anger.

We head down the central staircase, winding our way past the ground floor, where most cadets branch off, and into the sublevel of the quadrant.

It's a maze of tunnels down here, but I know my way well enough.

"You would never sit here and do nothing when you could help. Asking me to do differently is just…insulting," I whisper to him once I know we're alone in the tunnels. "I'm smart enough to handle myself in the Archives."

"I never said you weren't brilliant. I never even said your plan wasn't brilliant. I said you're putting yourself in danger and I'm just asking you to be honest with me." Mage lights flicker on as we make our way toward the covered bridge that spans the canyon between the Riders Quadrant and the main college. "Varrish pushed you to near-fucking-burnout, and you didn't tell me that, either." His jaw works. "Or that you wielded in the middle of the courtyard after Battle Brief."

"How did you know?" I hadn't mentioned Varrish in the letter I'd left for him.

"You didn't think Bodhi would tell me?" His shadows stream forward, opening the door, and we head across the enclosed bridge. I don't think I'll ever get used to the casual way he uses his power.

"I hoped he wouldn't," I admit.

"That's the shit you need to tell me, Violet."

"What would you have done? Flown back here and killed him? He's the vice commandant."

"I debated it." He opens the next set of doors the same way.

"Bodhi has miraculously found reasons for our squad to miss maneuvers," I tell him as we walk into the main campus, passing the infirmary.

"And how long is *that* going to work? We're twice as likely to find a solution if you tell me what's going—" Xaden's head snaps forward and he grabs me by the waist, stopping in the middle of the hallway.

But we've already been seen.

"Put your shields back up."

"It's Nolon," I point out but raise them anyway as guilt nips at me for letting them fall in the first place. I keep hoping for the moment Xaden promises is coming, where it's second nature, but so far, it's maximum effort to keep them in place.

"Nolon?" My jaw drops at how much weight the mender has lost. His skin hangs as loosely as his black uniform, and his eyes are missing their usual spark when he tries to smile at me.

"Violet. It's good to see you." He glances at Xaden, his gaze falling to the arm wrapped protectively around my waist. "Did you draw back because you're under the assumption that I'm going to harm the young woman I've been mending for the last six years, Riorson? Or is it that you think no one knows that you two spend all your time together on the days either of you has leave? Because I assure you, I would never endanger Violet, and *everyone* already knows."

I step out of Xaden's arms. "What are you doing standing in the middle of the hallway? You look like you're ready to drop."

"You're on it with the compliments today."

Clearly, I need better shields if it's that easy for Xaden to slip in again.

"Waiting for someone." Nolon scratches a few days' growth of beard on his jaw. "And I suppose I could use some rest. It's hard work, mending a soul. Been at it for months now." His smile lifts on one side, but I can't tell if he's joking or not. "You've been well so far this year? I haven't been called to mend you."

"I'm all right. I subluxated my shoulder a couple of weeks ago and—" I don't know if he's as close to Varrish as my friends have hypothesized. The thought gives me pause and keeps me from mentioning the burnout. "And I've been really good about keeping my knees wrapped. No broken bones yet, either."

"Good." Nolon nods as the door behind us opens. "That's good."

"I'm here!" Caroline Ashton races forward, passing us on the left. "Sorry I'm late!"

"Punctuality is appreciated," Nolon lectures her before looking my way. "Do us both a favor and stay healthy, Violet."

"I will," I promise.

Caroline shoots a quick glare in my direction, and they disappear into the infirmary, the door closing softly behind them.

"She didn't look hurt," I note as Xaden and I start toward the Archives again.

"No, she didn't," Xaden agrees. "Must be visiting another cadet from First Wing. Nolon looks like he's about to burn out himself. Have there been more injuries than usual?"

"Not that I'm aware of. Ridoc thinks they're using Nolon for interrogations." My face crinkles. "But I'm not sure if he was serious or not. It's hard to tell with Ridoc."

"Hmm." That's all he says as we descend, the tunnels slanting downward toward the lowest point of Basgiath. The deeper we go, the cooler the air becomes, and the sharper a pang I recognize as grief resonates in my chest.

"What are you thinking? Your face just fell," Xaden notes quietly as we pass by the stairs that lead up to the main campus.

"Nothing."

"You can't expect more than one-word answers from me and not give the same."

He has a point.

"My father loved this place. He was ecstatic when my mother was assigned here because it meant that he'd have the full resources of the Archives." I smile at the memory. "Not that he didn't love maintaining the records and libraries at the outposts we were stationed at, but to a scribe, this place is the pinnacle of a career. It's their temple." We round the last curve, bringing the vault-style door into view. The circular entrance is ten feet across and guarded by a singular scribe, who's asleep in his chair.

"A well-guarded one." Xaden shoots a disgusted look at the sleeping scribe.

"Promise me you'll be on your best behavior." I grip his elbow so he knows I mean it. *"She's an old friend."*

"So was Aetos."

I narrow my eyes.

"If she's a true friend, then she has nothing to worry about."

"Look, if she was going to turn me in, she would have done it when I requested The Fables of the Barren *last year,"* I tell him as we cross into the Archives.

"You. What?" His jaw flexes, and he breathes deeply when we reach the table. The Archives are empty again, thank Zihnal, but that's why Jesinia chose Saturdays.

"Before Mira gave me the book at Montserrat, I requested it. And I didn't think anything of it at the time. But no one showed up at my door. No one hauled me off and divested me of my head. Because we. Are. Friends."

He remains silent as Jesinia approaches, her gaze widening as she looks between us.

Her steps slow.

"He's with me," I sign, offering a smile. *"Stop scaring her."*

"I'm just standing here."

"That's enough. Trust me."

"Did you find what you were looking for?" she signs back, nervously biting her lip, her focus darting to Xaden.

"No." I hand the bag over to her, and she slings the strap over her shoulder. "They're all too recent…and vague."

Her lips purse in thought.

"Maybe we should shift to something about the history of wards in general?" I suggest.

"Give me a couple of minutes. I have an idea."

"Thank you for helping us," Xaden signs.

Jesinia nods, then disappears into the rows of bookshelves.

"You can sign," I whisper at him.

"You speak Tyrrish," he replies. "One is far less common than the other."

We stand there in awkward silence, our argument still festering—at least on my part. I never know how he's feeling, which is one of our problems. By using that one word with Jesinia—*us*—he's linked himself to me. If she turns me in, he'll be dragged down, too.

"Try these two," Jesinia signs when she returns, then hands over the bag. "Also, I returned yours. Thank you for letting me read it."

"What did you think about it?" I ask, unnervingly aware that Xaden is watching.

Whatever she says next will seal her fate with him.

"Solid folklore with good stories." She tilts her head to the side. "It was a limited printing, clearly done on a press, but not so limited that there wouldn't have been one submitted to the Archives at publication." The look she gives me is full of expectation. "It's an…odd subject matter to leave out of the Archives, don't you think?"

I swallow hard. "I do."

Xaden tenses beside me.

"As I said," she continues. "Intriguing. I'll see you Saturday after next?"

I nod, and we leave after thanking her again, passing Nasya, who has started to snore in his seat.

We're halfway through the tunnels before Xaden speaks.

"Tell me what other book is in the bag." Guess the argument is still festering inside him, too.

"It's The Fables of the Barren.*"* There's no point lying to him.

"You gave that to her? Why?" Xaden's head slants in my direction, and he stops in the middle of the tunnel, grasping my elbow gently as fear flashes in his eyes.

"I loaned it to her, and because she asked."

"With that text, she could have turned you in." Anger burns in his eyes.

"And if I report that she's not recording my requests, she'll be at Markham's mercy." I grip the strap of the bag a little tighter. *"Trust has to go both ways to mean anything."*

"Both ways, but you're shutting me out while I'm trying my damnedest to open up to you."

Says the man who's never so much as told me he loves me. If he does. Gods, I'm so sick of having to make the first move when it comes to this man. And today isn't the day to open myself up to that rejection, too.

"Sure, as long as you can keep your *secrets. Has it ever occurred to you that this"* — I gesture between us — *"is all because you don't trust me?"* I take a step backward. *"You expect complete, blind faith without giving it. It. Goes. Both. Ways."*

"I'm the one who doesn't trust you?*"* Shadows curl around his ankles, following him as he pivots, heading up the tunnel. *"I'll see you later. I have to find Bodhi."*

He's heading off on revolution business, no doubt, and leaving me behind. Again.

"That's all you have to say?" I call out, frustration locking my muscles.

"No good can come of the things I want to say right now, Violet," he says over his shoulder. "So, instead of digging a deeper hole with words I'll regret later, I'm going to take some space and do something productive, because this isn't."

It's on the tip of my tongue to tell him that he doesn't get to choose when we have a fight, but he asked for space, and I can do the mature thing and give it to him.

When I wake in the morning, the other half of my bed hasn't been slept in and his things are gone. I can't stop my chest from tightening at the thought that he's headed back to the front lines, that either of us could be killed at any moment, and the last words we said to each other were in anger.

Dragons do not answer to the whims of men.

—COLONEL KAORI'S FIELD GUIDE TO DRAGONKIND

CHAPTER NINETEEN

My heart pounds erratically as I walk past First and Second Wings' dragons with the rest of my squad two days later for flight maneuvers.

Kaori stands in front of Fourth Wing, shifting his weight nervously beside Varrish, who watches me with a focus that makes my skin crawl, like he's mentally tabulating how many strikes he's going to make me wield in punishment for not producing Andarna. And the way Solas lurks behind him, his one golden eye narrowed on me, makes me wonder if Varrish will even wait until tomorrow.

Because obviously, from his angle, he can see that she isn't here, and worse, he looks *happy* about it.

I made it to twenty-seven strikes in an hour this morning with Carr before my temperature spiked, and he seemed disappointed. That makes two of us, considering I didn't hit a single point I aimed for. My arms feel like dead weight after all that wielding. If Varrish forces me up to that mountainside again today, I'm not sure I'll come down.

"There is *something* off about that orange," Rhiannon notes, adjusting the strap of her flight goggles as we approach Third Wing.

"You mean, like the fact that he torched Third Squad without a second thought?" Ridoc questions, buttoning his flight jacket.

"And Varrish seems so…controlled." Sawyer stretches his arm across his chest. "Kind of uptight, you know?"

Unlike me, Sawyer's only seen him at the surface level. I breathe in through my nose and out through my mouth, fighting off the nausea that threatens to expel my breakfast.

"It's definitely an odd pairing," Rhi agrees as we reach Claw Section's dragons.

There aren't any third-years on the field today, leaving more than enough room for the second-year dragons to spread out, but gods forbid Tairn not stand in the front row like the star of the show. I can already see his head above the others from here, and I'm pretty sure I just heard him chuff a sigh of annoyance.

Varrish's mouth quirks into a polished smile at me, but the glint in his eyes makes the hold I have on my Archives doors weaken, trickling power into my system in preparation to fight.

"And what's the deal with the way he stares at you?" Sawyer asks, shifting beside me to block Varrish's view. "He's always smiling at you like…" He shakes his head. "I can't quite put my finger on it."

"Like he knows something you don't," Rhi finishes, giving the Red Clubtail from First Squad a wide berth as we pass. "Is there some history with your mom, maybe? Some bad blood?"

"Not that I know of." They don't even know the half of it, but how could they when I haven't told them? "But he's obsessed with Andarna." There, there's some of the truth.

"She all right?" Sawyer asks. "I haven't seen her in a while."

"She's been resting a lot." I prepare myself for the utter misery of full leathers in the stagnant late-summer heat, then start buttoning as we approach Tairn. "She can keep up with simple maneuvers, but the stuff we're doing now? Formation flights and timed rolls? There's no point in putting her through this kind of stuff." Selective truths.

"Makes sense." Sawyer nudges me with his elbow. "See you up there!"

"You look a little queasy," Rhi notes once the guys are out of earshot. "Everything all right?"

"I'm fine." I force a quick grin and try to think of anything besides how much it's going to hurt when Varrish gets ahold of me. *"Varrish looks eerily delighted that Andarna isn't here."*

"I will handle this."

"Right. Of course you are." Rhi's mouth curves into a sad glimpse of a smile before she turns away, heading for Feirge, who waits on Tairn's other side.

"Fuck," I mutter, rubbing the bridge of my nose. No matter what I say right now, it's always the wrong thing. *"She's never going to forgive me for keeping all this from her once she finds out."*

"She will," he says, his head lowering slightly, but he doesn't dip his shoulder even as I reach his front left claw. *"Humans have the memories of gnats. Dragons hold grudges."*

"I'm going to forget you said that," I tease back.

"Be alert." His head swivels and I turn, unsheathing a dagger in the same moment.

"Surely you wouldn't think of attacking a professor, would you, Sorrengail?" Varrish glances at my weapon, keeping that same mask of a smile in place. "Let alone a vice commandant."

A low growl works up Tairn's throat, and he curls his lip just enough to bare the tips of his fangs.

"I attack anyone foolish enough to sneak up behind me this year." I roll my shoulder back and lift my chin.

"Hmm." He leans to the side and looks past Tairn's foreleg. "No little feathertail with you today?"

"Obviously." Fear slides down my spine.

"How unfortunate." He sighs, then turns his back on me, his boots crunching in the dry grass as he heads toward Solas. "There will be no maneuvers for you today, Sorrengail."

My stomach rolls. "I'm sorry?"

Tairn shifts sideways, sweeping his foreleg around me so I stand under his chest scales.

"Not yet," Varrish says over his shoulder, his brow puckering for a second as he notices Tairn's stance. "But you will be. Warnings have apparently not worked, and I am hereby charging you with dereliction of duty for your dragon's refusal to appear for maneuvers. You will mount and fly to your training location with Professor Carr to receive your punishment."

"That will not be happening." Tairn's head lowers fully, and his body crouches into a defensive position.

"What is going on?" Rhi asks, her gaze jumping between Varrish and me as she walks back over to me.

"Obviously, her first punishment wasn't enough to teach your subordinate, Squad Leader Matthias, so she requires another." He blinks, tilting his head. "And as the vice commandant, I don't owe you an explanation. Now mount up for maneuvers before you're punished alongside her."

"There will be no punishment!" Tairn roars, and from the abrupt head jerks of the dragons on the field, including Solas, everyone heard him. *"It is not within your power to summon a dragon."*

It takes a second for thoughts to relay through riders, and Varrish stiffens. "Your dragon may not fall under my command, Sorrengail, but you *do*. So unless you'd like to further explore that delicate space between burnout and death, you *will* mount and present yourself—"

"Even the smallest dragon does not answer to the most powerful of humans, which you are not." Tairn snaps his teeth, the sound carrying over the valley.

Feirge's head draws back, and her golden eyes widen.

"Andarna does not answer to you." Tairn stalks forward, his head and chest

so low to the ground that he nearly touches my hair, and Varrish retreats. *"I do not answer to you."*

Oh shit. This could go very bad very quickly.

"But you"—Varrish points at me—"answer to me!"

"Does she?" Tairn lunges forward, bypassing Varrish entirely and surging toward Solas with an ear-shattering roar, his morningstar tail lashing the air above me. Solas whips his head toward the ground to guard his most vulnerable area—his neck—but Tairn is faster, bigger, and far stronger. He's already there, his enormous jaw locked around Solas's throat.

I gasp as Tairn's massive fangs sink between the joints of Solas's scales, piercing his neck, and Kaori sprints to get out of the battleground.

Varrish turns and stiffens as crimson rivulets run over Solas's orange neck scales, dripping off several of the ridges.

"Tairn…" What will the Empyrean do to him if he kills Solas?

"Only a rider can be the vice commandant of Basgiath," Tairn warns, and Solas lets out a sound that's half roar, half shriek. *"Without a dragon, you are no rider."*

Oh *gods.* My heart lurches, the beat rushing to a gallop.

"Fine!" Varrish shouts, his fists balled at his side. "She will not pay a price for her dragon's refusal to attend."

"Not good enough." Tairn's teeth reach the edges of Solas's scales as I watch in slack-jawed horror. *"This is about you."*

Solas half roars, causing his blood to pour even faster down his exposed neck as he whips his tail toward Tairn, but he's half Tairn's size and has no hope of making contact, thank Dunne.

"All right!" Varrish staggers forward, and for a second, I feel sorry for him. "All right," he repeats, putting his hands up. "Humans have no authority to summon dragons."

Rhiannon sidesteps until her arm brushes my shoulder, and Feirge lowers her head, as do Aotrom and Sliseag. Hell, every dragon I can see in my peripherals takes the same stance.

"Apologize," Tairn demands, his voice low and sharp.

"I'm sorry!" Varrish's voice breaks.

"Apologize to the one Andarna deemed worthy of her bond."

I try to swallow, but my mouth has gone dry.

"Did he really just…" Rhiannon whispers.

"I think so." I nod. *"His apology isn't necessary to me, Tairn. Really. I'm happy to just not die today."*

"It is necessary to me, Silver One." His voice rumbles in my head. *"I speak for Andarna while she is in the Dreamless Sleep."*

Varrish pivots toward me, hatred and terror filling his gaze. "I am...sorry. It is not in my authority to summon any dragon."

"On your knees."

Rhiannon sucks in a breath, and Varrish hits his knees. "You have my most sincere apology—you *and* your dragon. Both of your dragons."

"I accept." My gaze darts frantically to Tairn's. "I accept!" I shout just in case he didn't hear me mentally.

Tairn dislodges his jaw with a wet, sucking sound as his fangs slip free of Solas's neck, and he retreats with arrogant footfalls, not even bothering to lower his head or protect his throat. Rhiannon and I fall into the shade as Tairn blocks out the sun overhead.

And Varrish stares at me with a hatred so bitter I can taste it on the back of my tongue as Solas launches behind him with a roar aimed in my direction—or Tairn's—leaving behind pools of blood on the grass below. Only once Solas is clear of the flight field does Varrish rise to his feet, and I don't need words to hear him loud and clear as he sends one last, lethal look my way and then strides for the end of the field and the Gauntlet steps.

"Problem solved." Tairn's head swivels, watching Solas's flight path, and the rest of the dragons in the field raise their heads again.

But my heartbeat doesn't calm or even slow at the dread that curdles in my stomach. Varrish may have been my enemy before, but I have a feeling this just made Solas my nemesis.

I thought for sure he'd cancel your leave after Tairn nearly slayed Solas," Rhiannon says, walking the path toward the flight field with me three nights later.

"Me too," I admit as the bells chime a quarter before midnight. "I'm sure when Solas is healed, he'll be right back in my face. Or worse."

"It's been a couple of days." She glances over at me, and even though there are only a few feet between us, the distance feels insurmountable. "Are you really going to make me use some of those new interrogation tactics we're learning to pry the truth out of you? Would you rather I go with the empathetic or more directly confrontational approach?"

"About?" I nudge her shoulder.

She shakes her head in frustration. "About Varrish's little comment that you'd already been punished once before?"

"Oh. Right." I take a deep breath and focus on my footsteps as we near the Gauntlet. "A few weeks ago, he got mad that Andarna wasn't feeling up to maneuvers and used my signet training as punishment."

"He *what*?" Her voice raises. "Why wouldn't you tell us that?"

"Because I didn't want you targeted." It's the simplest truth.

"And he's been targeting you?" She sounds incredulous.

"He doesn't like not getting his way." I adjust my pack on my shoulders and grimace as we approach the stairs alongside the Gauntlet. This is going to hurt like hell. I subluxated my knee yesterday during a challenge, but at least I won. "You really don't have to walk all the way out here with me. It's late." I change the subject before she can dig deeper about Varrish.

"I don't mind. I feel like I never see you anymore."

Gods, I feel so fucking guilty. And frustrated. And…lonely. I miss my friends.

"I'm sorry." It's all I can think to say. "Hard to believe that the first-years are about to start training on this thing." I look out over the Gauntlet, the five ascents of obstacles the first-years will have to complete in order to get to Presentation.

"More like dying on it." She bites out the words.

"That, too." My knee protests every step, threatening to buckle with each stair I climb, but the wrap holds it in place as I limp upward, my hand dragging along the rough stone that lines the staircase on either side.

"It's fucking pointless." She shakes her head. "Just another way to weed out the weaker—or worse, the unlucky."

"It's not." As much as I hate to admit it, the Gauntlet has its place here.

"Seriously?" She reaches the top of the stairs and waits for me.

"Seriously." I begin the walk down the flight field. "It made me look at everything differently. I couldn't climb it in the same way you did, the others did, so I had to find another way. It taught me that I *could* find another way and still survive." The moment on Tairn's back, fighting that venin, plays through my mind, and my hand curls around empty air as if still clutching that dagger.

"I just don't think it's worth the lives it costs. Most of what happens here isn't."

"It is." My rebuttal is quiet.

"How can you say that?" She halts, turning toward me. "You were right there when Aurelie fell. Is there any part of you that thinks she would have been a liability to the wing had she survived to Threshing? She was a legacy!"

I look up at the star-filled sky and take a breath before facing her. "No. I think she would have been a phenomenal rider. Better than me, that's for sure. But I also know that…" I can't get the words out. They lodge in my throat, held captive by the memory of Aurelie's eyes widening in that second before she fell.

"I wish that for once you would just say whatever you're thinking. I never know anymore."

"You don't want to know." It's the most truthful I've been with her since returning.

"I really do, Violet! It's just us out here. Talk to me!"

"Talk to you," I repeat, like it's really that simple, and feel something inside me snap under the weight of both our frustrations. "Fine. Yes, it's awful that Aurelie fell. That she died. But I think *I'm* a better rider for having been there, having watched her fall to her death and known that if I didn't get my ass moving, I was going to be next."

"That's…horrible." Rhiannon's lips part, and she looks at me like she's never seen me before.

"So is *everything* waiting out there for us." I swing my arms out. "That stupid fucking Gauntlet isn't just about physically climbing it. It's about overcoming the fear that we can't. It's about climbing *after* we see it kill our friends. Parapet, Gauntlet, Presentation—they seem excessive when we're here, but they prepare us for something way worse when we leave. And until you…" I shake my head. "You don't know what it's like out there, Rhi. You can't understand."

"Of course I don't know," she retorts, her body tensing more with every word. "You won't talk to me! You're running with Imogen, or locked away reading, or spending every possible Saturday with Riorson. And that's fine, I want you to get whatever support you need, but you're sure as hell not talking to me, so how would you expect me to know *anything*? Don't forget, Liam was my friend, too!"

"You weren't there!" My anger slips from the box I painstakingly built for it, and power whips through me, scalding my veins. "You didn't hold him, watch the light fade out of his eyes, knowing that there wasn't a physical thing wrong with him but he was dying because Deigh lay eviscerated just a few feet away. Nothing I did in those moments before mattered! Gods, I held on to him so tightly!" My hands curl into fists, my nails biting into my palms. "My shoulders almost dislocated, he was so damned heavy, but I held on! And it didn't matter!" Rage burns my throat, devouring me whole. "You haven't seen what's out there! What makes me run every fucking morning!"

"Vi," she whispers, her posture sagging.

"And the look on his face?" My voice breaks and my eyes burn with the memory of Liam's head in my hands. "You don't see it every time you try to sleep. You don't hear him begging you to take care of Sloane. You sure as hell don't hear Deigh scream…" I lace my fingers on top of my head and look away, waging war with the grief, the pain, the never-ending guilt, and as usual, I lose. There's only that box and the blessed emptiness I know is achievable if I can get a little control, but the words won't stop coming. It's like my mouth has disassociated from my brain and my emotions are running the show.

"And as horrible as it might be, as callous as it might make me, watching Aurelie fall, and Pryor burn, and even Jack-fucking-Barlowe get crushed under my landslide prepared me for the moment I had to leave Liam's body on the ground and fight. If I'd sat there and mourned like I wanted to, none of us would be here. Imogen, Bodhi, Xaden, Garrick—everyone—we'd all be dead. There's a reason they want us to watch our friends die, Rhi." I tap my chest with one finger. "We are the weapons, and this place is the stone they use to sharpen us." The energy in my body dwindles, and the heat dissipates.

My stomach hollows out at the utter devastation on Rhiannon's face.

Tairn's wingbeats grow louder as he approaches, and the sound helps settle my heartbeat.

"I'm sorry," I whisper. "And I'm glad you don't know what it's like." Blinking rapidly clears the blurriness from my eyes. "I'm grateful every single day that you don't have those memories, that you and Sawyer and Ridoc weren't there. I wouldn't wish that day on my worst enemy, let alone my closest friend, and even if I'm quiet lately, that's what you still are—my closest friend." But friends tell the truth. Telling her will put her in danger, but not telling her leaves her unprepared, just like we were. *Shit.* "And you're right. I should talk to you. You lost Liam, too. You have every right to know—"

"No." Tairn's voice blasts through my head and wind gusts at my back a second before he lands behind me. *"Solas's rider."*

"Good evening, Cadet Sorrengail," Major Varrish says directly from our left, mage lights popping on overhead as he walks around the boulders where he and his guards have been waiting only a dozen feet away. "Cadet Matthias. Sounds like I may have interrupted a discussion?"

His guards follow.

Oh *gods.* I almost—

"But you didn't," Tairn says.

"Sir?" Rhiannon's eyes widen as her gaze swings from me to the vice commandant.

"You know the drill, cadet." He closes the distance between us and points to the ground. "Or are you going to argue that you're not under my command at all now?"

Tairn lowers his head and rumbles a low growl.

Apprehension knots my throat, and I step to the side, taking Rhi out of Varrish's direct path. Indignation isn't going to help, so I swing my pack from my shoulders and open it, emptying the contents onto the ground. Then I shake the open bag to show him that it's empty. "Happy?"

"Not yet, but one day." His smile makes my stomach churn. "I'm patient."

The rider finishes the search, taking a look inside my bag just to be sure I actually emptied it before handing it back.

"Enjoy your leave while you have it." Varrish nods, that smile still frozen in place, and the three head off the field.

"Assholes." I crouch down and Rhi matches the movement, helping me repack the bag. "Thanks."

"Is that *normal*?"

"Yes." We stand once everything is tucked away. *"Are we glad they didn't search you again tonight?"*

"We are."

"But...why?" Confusion lines her forehead. "What is going on? That couldn't have been about Andarna."

"They'll never fully trust Xaden's last name." With good reason. I sling my pack over my shoulders and slip my arms through the straps. "I really am sorry for exploding on you back there. There's no excuse."

"Don't be." She offers me a sad half smile. "I'd rather you scream at me than pretend everything is all right with silence."

At least there's one truth I can give her.

"Nothing is all right."

In the years after my father died, I forgot what it felt like to be loved. Then I entered the quadrant and became the monster everyone needed me to be, and I never regretted it. But then you gave those words to me, and I remembered…and nearly lost you, too. I'm striving to be better for you just like I promised, but I need you to know that monster is still there, screaming to use every ruthless part of me to get your words back.

—RECOVERED CORRESPONDENCE OF LIEUTENANT XADEN RIORSON TO CADET VIOLET SORRENGAIL

CHAPTER TWENTY

The ground rushes up at us as Tairn flares his wings, slowing our descent as we land on the field at Samara. *"We will figure something else out,"* Tairn argues. *"Even if you move to my shoulder and successfully slide to perch…"* He shudders.

We've spent the better part of the last two hours arguing over whether or not I would ever attempt a running landing, which, if you ask Tairn, would be never.

"You can't change graduation requirements." I unbuckle from the saddle and wince at the twinge in my hips that tells me I went too long between breaks.

"I've never tried," Tairn lectures, and his head whips toward the edge of the clearing, tilting in excitement as he watches the tree line for movement.

I grin, knowing Sgaeyl must be close.

"Let's agree that we will come up with a solution that meets graduation requirements without breaking every bone in your body," he suggests quickly.

"Agreed." I should remember to only argue with him when he's got better things to do more often. Climbing to the back of the saddle, I unclip the packs and nearly lose my footing in my haste.

"We're all dead if you fall off my back and break your impatient neck."

"Because I'm the impatient one." I swing my small pack onto my back, then place one of the heavier packs on each of my shoulders. *"I can't believe you allowed someone up here to secure the bags. I'm impressed with your restraint."*

"The section leader attached the bags to the saddle before I put it on, naturally."

"And here I was thinking you'd evolved." My knee throbs as I navigate Tairn's back, but it's all but forgotten the second I lower my shields and feel that shadowy bond wrap around my mind.

It goes against my instincts to block him, but I force my mental shields back into place. After the way we left things last weekend, I have no idea what to expect from him, but he'll damn well expect me to have my shields up no matter how mad we are at each other. Bags secured, I slide down Tairn's leg and take the brunt of the impact on my good knee when I hit the ground.

"Go find Sgaeyl," I urge Tairn, heading across the field of trampled grass toward the looming fortress.

"I'll wait until you're inside as always."

"You're wasting time." I can feel his anticipation singing through my bloodstream, but I don't block it out. At least one of us is happy. The thing that happens later? That, I'll block out like my life depends on it.

"Then walk faster."

I laugh and trudge forward. Gods, these bags are *heavy*, and weirdly... vibrating with energy. Guess these ones have already been imbued with power.

An entire company of infantry jogs toward me from the arched entrance as I make it to the top of the stone ramp. Oh shit, I'm right in their way.

"Rider!" the commander yells.

Before I can step aside, the company splits down the middle and runs around me, so close I can feel the breeze from the air they displace like I'm a boulder in the middle of their rushing creek. I hold completely still to avoid impact, not even daring to breathe as they run by.

When the last of them pass, I exhale, then continue into the bailey. A group of healers crosses in front of my path, and when they clear, I see Xaden striding toward me across the courtyard, his face unreadable. My heart stutters, then pounds, but I make myself move forward.

Not sure how it's possible, but I simultaneously want to climb the man and kick him hard in the shins.

There's a group of riders in the courtyard behind Xaden, but they're only a blur of black because I can't look away from him, can't see past him. As complicated as our connection is, it's also undeniably simple. He's the horizon, and nothing exists beyond for me.

"I'm going to have to force your hand and I'm sorry," he says quickly as he

approaches, cutting through my shields like they're nothing but lace where he's concerned.

"*What else is new?*" I pause, noting that everyone between us gets out of his way.

"*You have about two seconds to decide if you want time to talk in private tonight.*" He's less than a dozen feet from me.

"*Not sure you want to be alone with me, considering what I'm carrying.*" I bristle. That's the first thing he has to say to me after the way he cut out last week?

"*Choose.*"

"*Yes. Of course I want to talk to you in private.*"

"*Tell me to kiss you. Even if it's just for show.*" There are only heartbeats between us now, and he's not slowing.

"*What?*"

"*Now, Violet. Or you'll be sleeping in someone else's room tonight.*" The look in his eyes demands an instant answer. Right. Because he told me months ago he'd only kiss me when I asked him to. He reaches for me, one hand sliding to the back of my neck and the other bracing my waist as our bodies collide.

The impact sends every sense reeling.

"*Kiss me.*" Just for show.

"I missed you," he says a second before his mouth crashes into mine.

"*You walked out on me,*" I accuse, nipping the soft skin of his bottom lip with my teeth.

"*Fight later.*" His hand slides along my face, and he presses his thumb just above my chin. "*Now kiss me like you mean it.*"

"*Since you asked so nicely.*" I part my lips under his and immediately regret every second I've spent *not* kissing him lately.

I whimper at the first stroke of his tongue along mine, and his hand flexes on my waist, gripping me tighter as he sinks into the kiss. *Yes.* One touch, that's all it takes, and the world around us ceases to exist. This is *everything.* The energy thrumming in the air around us pales in comparison to the power that floods my veins, the need that ignites within me as we both work to control the kiss.

He wins, consuming me, devouring every thought in my head besides getting closer. The bags slide from my shoulders, hitting the ground beside me with a thud, and I wind my arms around his neck, arching against him. I kiss him back like my life depends on his surrender and tilt my head for that perfect angle. He finds it without even trying, taking the kiss deeper, stealing little pieces of my soul with each swirl and slide of his tongue with an expertise I can't fight.

I can't remember why I ever wanted to.

Why would I deny myself the explosive pleasure of kissing Xaden? This is when we make sense. When nothing else matters but the feel of his lips, the flick of his tongue behind my teeth, the lust burning through me I know only he can fully sate. My heart gallops and my body floats as my hands slide into his soft hair.

Weightless. He makes me feel totally, completely weightless, like it's possible to fly on nothing but waves of sensation.

Gods, I fucking *want* him. Just like this. Just us.

"Violet." It's a mental groan as his mouth thoroughly lays claim to mine.

"Oh for fuck's sake." A familiar voice intrudes on my own little piece of heaven, and that's when I remember.

This is supposed to be for show, and here I am, completely losing myself in him. In the middle of the courtyard. In front of gods only know who. And that weightless feeling? It's because I'm anchored against his chest by one of his strong arms, my feet dangling off the ground.

"Good enough show for you?" I draw back slowly, dragging my teeth across his bottom lip before releasing him.

"Fuck the show." His eyes flare with the same heat that has me ready to combust. At least I'm not the only one losing control. I know that look on his face. He's just as turned on as I am.

He kisses me again, losing his polished finesse in favor of untamed demand, and I *melt.*

"Put my sister down, Riorson. You made your point." That familiar voice—

My head whips to the right, breaking the kiss. "Mira?"

She taps her fingers along her folded arms, but her stern expression—eerily close to our mother's—doesn't last more than a breath before her mouth curves into a smile. "Good to see you, Vi."

"What are you doing here?" I grin as Xaden sets me down. Then I step over the discarded bag to hug my sister.

"As of yesterday, I'm stationed here." She holds me tightly, just like she always does, then pushes me away by the shoulders to do her customary inspection for mortal wounds.

"I'm fine," I promise her.

"Are you sure?" Her hands move to the sides of my head, and she rises up on her tiptoes to look down at me. "Because I'm thinking you must have taken a pretty serious blow to the head to be involved with this one."

I blink. What the hell am I supposed to say to that?

"Play along, or you'll be in her room tonight. Not mine," Xaden tells me. *"She's been more than adamant."*

"Right, well…" Shit, I really don't want to lie to my sister any more than I have to.

"I'm going to take your bags to my room," Xaden says, helping me out of the pack on my back, then picking up the two I dropped.

"Thank you," I say mostly out of habit.

He leans in and brushes a kiss over my forehead. "I have duty today."

"No," I whisper, my stomach dropping in disappointment. That doesn't exactly leave us time to talk—which is probably the point. *"I guess we can't fight if we don't talk?"*

"We'll have time later," he promises. "Have fun with your sister. I'll see you tonight." He brushes a flight-loosened strand of my hair behind my ear and grazes his knuckles gently down the side of my cheek.

"All right." If it wasn't all for show, I'd be a puddle. And the heat in his eyes when they meet mine for a second? I'm instantly warm despite the mountain air.

"Don't let her set anything on fire," he says over his shoulder to Mira as he walks away, heading for the corridor near the southwestern staircase.

I scoff, but that doesn't stop me from watching him go.

"Keep your shields up."

"It's not like they help block you out."

"Told you, I'm harder than most," he replies. *"Keep them up anyway. It's not me you have to worry about."*

"He's…carrying your bags up to his room for you," Mira says slowly, moving to my side and glancing between Xaden's retreating back and me.

"He is." I nod. Or is he? The ache in my chest turns bitter. Maybe he's actually taking two of those bags to a drop point and leaving me with Mira to distract me. I hate that I can't trust him, that he can't trust me, that we're at this impasse.

"Oh shit," Mira mutters.

"What?" I sigh as he disappears into the building.

"You're not just fucking him, are you? You're falling for him." She stares at me like I've lost my mind.

My gaze swings to hers, and though I know I should, I can't lie to her. Not about this. "Not exactly."

"Who do you think you're fooling? He basically swallowed you whole, and now you're watching him with those big, soft eyes that are practically oozing with"—she gestures at my face, her nose crinkling like she smells something bad—"what even is that? Yearning? Infatuation?"

I roll my eyes.

"Love?" She says the word like it's poisonous, and something on my face must give me away because the disgust on hers morphs into shock. "Oh, no. You're in love with him, aren't you?"

"You can't possibly know that just by looking at me," I counter, my spine stiffening.

"Ugh. Let's go throw knives at shit."

*B*rennan is alive. *Brennan is alive. Brennan. Is. Alive.* It's all I can think as we empty our sheaths into the wooden targets that line the back of the outpost's small sparring gym on the north side of the first floor. It's a far cry from the pit on the south side of the fortress I first found Xaden fighting in.

Keeping secrets from Rhiannon is loathsome, but not telling Mira that Brennan is alive might just make me the worst person on the Continent.

"I'm the last person to judge who you sleep with—" Mira starts.

"Then don't." I flip my next-to-last dagger, catch it by the tip, and throw it, hitting the neck of the target.

"Regulations aside, because yes, what you're doing is fraternizing"—she throws her next dagger without even looking and hits the target mid-chest— "with an *officer*, I'm just saying that if it goes badly, you're stuck with each other for the rest of your careers."

"But you're not judging." I throw my last dagger, hitting *her* target in the neck.

"Fine, maybe I'm judging." She shrugs, and we walk to the targets. "But you're my only sibling. I'm allowed to worry."

I'm not, though. She and Brennan were inseparable as kids. If one of us should know that he's alive and healthy, it's her. "You don't have to worry about me." I yank my daggers out of the wood one by one and sheathe them along my thighs and at my ribs.

"You're a second-year. Of course I'm going to worry." She retrieves her own knives and looks over her shoulder at a pair of riders sparring on the mat behind us. "How is RSC going?" she asks, lowering her voice.

"We lost a rider in the first exercise. Two maps?"

"Yeah, it's a mindfuck." She presses her lips into a thin line. "But that's not what I meant."

"You're worried about the interrogation portion," I guess, sheathing the eleventh dagger at my ribs.

"They're going to beat you black and blue just to see if you can take it." She plucks my dagger from the throat of her target. "And the way you break—"

"I can handle pain." I turn toward her. "I live in pain. I practically built a house there and set up a whole economy. I can take whatever they dish out."

"After War Games, RSC is when the most second-years die," she admits quietly. "And they take one or two squads at a time for exercises, so you don't really notice the increase in the death roll, but it's there. If you don't break, they can accidentally torture you to death, and if you do break, they'll kill you for it." Her gaze drops to my dagger, and she looks concerned.

"It's going to be a shitty few days, but I'll be all right. I made it this far." Breaking bones is a Tuesday for me.

"Since when do you use Tyrrish daggers?" She holds mine up, examining the black hilt and the decorative rune at the pommel. "I haven't seen runes like these in…a while."

"Xaden gave them to me."

"Gave?" She hands it back.

"I won them from him during a sparring match last year." I sheathe it at my ribs beside the others as she lifts a skeptical eyebrow and chuckles. "So yeah, he pretty much gave them to me."

"Huh." She tilts her head to the side and studies me, seeing more than I want her to, like always. "They look custom."

"They are. They're harder to knock out of my hands than the traditional length and not as heavy."

She doesn't look away as we walk back to the throwing line.

"What?" I feel my cheeks heat. "He has a vested interest in keeping me alive. I know you don't like him. I know you don't trust him—"

"He's a Riorson," she says. "You shouldn't trust him, either."

"I don't." I look away after the whispered confession.

"But you're in love with him." She heaves a frustrated sigh and throws a dagger. "That's… I don't even know what that is, but 'unhealthy' is the first word that comes to mind."

"It's us," I murmur and change the subject. "Why did they station you here, anyway?" I choose a spot on the target in the upper abdomen, then hit it. "Samara is warded, and you're a walking shield. Kind of a waste of your signet." She's a *shield.*

Why the hell didn't I think of asking her about the wards sooner? Maybe the answer isn't in a book. Maybe it's in Mira. After all, her signet is the ability to extend the wards, to tug the protections with her even where they shouldn't be able to stretch.

She glances back at the sparring pair. "I think they're worried about attacks here because this outpost has one of the biggest power supplies for the wards. If this place falls, a giant portion of the border is vulnerable."

"Because they're set up like dominos?" I throw another dagger, wincing when I'm not as careful as I should be on my aching knee.

"Not exactly. What would you know about it?" She throws another without looking and hits the target true.

"Fucking show-off," I mutter. "Is there *anything* you don't excel at?"

"Poisons," she answers, flicking another dagger at the target. "Never had the aptitude for them like you and Brennan. Or maybe it's just that I could never sit still long enough to listen to Dad's lessons. Now tell me what you know about the wards." She shoots a sideways look at me. "Weaving isn't taught until third-year, and anything beyond is classified."

"I read." I shrug and hope to Zihnal it looks nonchalant. "I know that they originate from the wardstone in the Vale because of the hatching grounds located there, and that they're boosted with a power supply along our border outposts to expand their natural distance in places and maintain a strong defense." All common knowledge, or at least researchable.

She flings another knife. "They're woven to the ground out here," she says quietly as the pair behind us continues sparring. "Think of an umbrella. The wardstone is the stem, and the wards take the shape of a dome over Navarre." She motions with her hands, forming the shape. "But just like an umbrella's spokes are strongest at the stem, by the time the wards reach the ground, they're too weak to do much without a boost."

"Provided by the alloy," I whisper. My heart starts to pound.

"And the dragons." She nods, two lines appearing between her brows. "You know about alloy? Are they teaching that now? Or did Dad—"

"It's the alloy stored in the outposts that tugs some of those umbrella spokes forward," I continue, flipping my dagger in my hand by pure muscle memory. "Extending the wards twice as far as they'd normally reach in some cases, right?"

"Right."

"And what's it made of?"

"That's definitely above your clearance." She scoffs.

"Fine." It stings a little that she won't tell me. "But how do you weave *new* wards? Like if we wanted to protect places like Athebyne?" Flip. Flip. Flip. I keep moving the dagger and hope she sees it as casual.

"You don't." She shakes her head. "The extensions are what we weave. It's like continuing a tapestry that's been stretched too far. You're just adding threads to something that already exists, and we can't extend the wards to Athebyne. We've tried. But who told you—"

"Is that how your signet works?" I stop flipping. "Because you're basically a ward, right?"

"Not exactly. I kind of pull the wards with me. Sometimes I can manifest on my own, but I have to be close to an outpost. Kind of like I'm just another thread. What has gotten into you?" She flicks another dagger, and it lands dead center.

"Do you know how the wardstone works?" I ask, lowering my voice to a whisper.

"No." Her eyes flare. "Keep throwing before curious ears start listening."

I dutifully throw another.

"That information is way beyond my rank—and *yours*." Her next dagger lands right next to the first. "Why are you asking?"

"Just curious."

"Don't be. It's classified for a reason." Her wrist flicks another knife toward the target. "The only people who know are the ones who need to know, just like every other piece of classified intelligence."

"Right." I force a smile and throw my next dagger with a little more strength than necessary. Time to change the subject. Maybe she knows, or maybe she doesn't, but she's definitely not going to tell me. "Speaking of classified, were you on any of the missions to check the Poromish cities for damage?" I put my hands up when she gawks at me. "They told us about it in Battle Brief; it's not secret anymore."

"No," she answers. "But I saw one of the riots who did the flying while Teine and I were out on patrol."

My stomach twists. "Do you know anyone who was on the missions?"

"No." Another knife, another hit. "But I read the reports. Did they give those to you?"

I shake my head. "And you trust the reports?" It doesn't come out as casually as I'm trying for.

"Of course." She searches my eyes for answers I can't give. "Why wouldn't I? Why wouldn't *you*?" Her hands make a quick, outward motion, and the noise of the sparring pair disappears. It's a sound shield, just like she used in Montserrat—a lesser magic, but still a tricky one I haven't mastered. "Tell me what's going on with you. Now."

I was thrown into a battle with dark wielders, lost one of my closest friends, fought an actual venin on the back of my dragon, and then was mended by our very not-dead brother. "Nothing."

She gives me *the look*. The one that always loosened my tongue when we were kids.

I waver. If there was only one person on the Continent I could tell, it would be Mira.

"I just think it's weird that you wouldn't know anyone on the missions into Poromiel. You know *everyone*. And how do you know that what you saw was one of the riots tasked with reconnaissance?" I ask.

"Because there were over a dozen dragons in the distance to the south, over the border. What the hell else could it have been, Violet?" She gives me a skeptical look.

This is it. This is the opening to tell her the truth. The chance to bring her in so she fights on the right side of this conflict, so she can see our brother. Wyvern. She saw *wyvern*. But it's not just my life I'd risk by telling her. My heart sinks, but I have to.

Xaden could never understand—he doesn't have a sister.

"I don't know," I whisper. "What if they're wyvern?" There. I said it. Kind of. She blinks and draws her head back. "Say again?"

"What if you saw wyvern? What if they're destroying Poromish cities, since we both know it isn't dragons?" My hand clenches around the hilt of my last dagger. "What if there's an entire war out there we know nothing about?"

Her shoulders dip and sympathy fills her eyes. "You have to spend less time reading those fables, Vi. Have you been getting enough rest since the gryphon attack? Because you sound like maybe you're not sleeping." The concern in her tone breaks me down like nothing else could. "And it's hard to see combat for the first time, let alone as a first-year, but if you don't get enough sleep and present a stable, steady front… Riders have to be solid, Violet. You understand what I'm saying?"

Of course she doesn't believe me. I wouldn't either. But she's the only person in the world who absolutely, unconditionally loves me. Brennan let me believe he was dead—would still let me believe it. Mom has never seen me as anything but a liability. Xaden? I can't even go there.

"No." I shake my head slowly. "No, I'm not sleeping very well." It's an excuse, and I take it. Heaviness settles in my chest.

She sighs, and the relief in her eyes eases a little of the weight in mine. "That explains it. I can recommend some really great teas that will help. Come on, let's get these daggers out and get you to bed. You've had a long flight, and I have duty in a few hours, anyway." She leads me to the targets, and we remove the daggers once again.

"You're on duty with Xaden?" I ask to fill the silence as we pull blade after blade from the wood.

"No. He's in the operations center, which is—"

"Above my clearance. I know."

"I have a patrol flight." She puts her arm around my shoulders. "Don't worry. We'll get to spend some time together when you're here next. Every two weeks, right?"

"Right."

· · ·

The sky is black when Xaden slides into bed shirtless, the movement waking me from a fitful attempt at sleep. Enough moonlight comes through the window to see the harsh, beautiful lines of his face as he turns toward me, both of us lying on our sides. Enough moonlight to see a silver scar across his heart I somehow missed in the fighting pits. Was he wounded at Resson?

"You're awake." He leans onto his elbow, propping his head on his hand.

"I don't sleep well anymore." I tug the summer-weight blanket up over my shoulder as if he hasn't seen me in less than the slip of a nightgown I'm wearing. "And I don't have it in me to fight tonight."

"Then we won't fight."

"Because it's that simple." Even my sarcasm is exhausted.

"It is if that's what we decide." His gaze wanders over my face, softening with every second.

"What time is it?"

"A little after midnight. I wanted to talk to you earlier, but there was an incident—"

"Mira." I jolt upright, fear stabbing deep.

"She's fine. Everything's fine. Just some civilians trying to cross the border and the infantry…wasn't pleased."

"They weren't *pleased*?"

"They killed them," he admits softly. "Happens all the time out here, just doesn't get briefed at Basgiath. Lie back down." The suggestion is gentle. "Mira's perfectly fine."

We kill *civilians*? That information goes straight to the box.

"I almost told her today." I whisper the confession as my head hits the pillow, even knowing no one can hear us in here. "For all my anger, you're right not to trust me, because I almost told her. I even hinted, hoping she'd catch on." A bitter laugh slips free. "I want her to know. I want her to see Brennan. I want her to be on our side. I just…" My throat threatens to close.

Xaden reaches out and cups my cheek. There's no reproach in his gaze, or even judgment, though I've just given him reason to shut me out for the rest of our lives. His silence, the quiet acceptance in his eyes, keeps me talking.

"I just feel…heavy," I admit. "I don't have anyone who knows who I really am anymore. The guy I considered my best friend nearly got us killed. I'm keeping secrets from Rhiannon, from my sister, from…you. There's not a single person in this world I'm entirely truthful with."

"I haven't exactly made it easy for you to trust me," he says, stroking his thumb over my cheek. "I'm still not making it easy. But you and I are not *easy* people. What we build together has to be strong enough to withstand a storm. Or a war. *Easy* isn't going to give that to us."

What we build together. The words make my reckless heart clench.

"I should have told you I was reading into the wards." I rest my hand on the warm skin of his arm. "I knew you'd tell me not to, and I'd probably do it anyway, but mostly I didn't tell you because…" I can't even say it.

"Because I don't tell you everything, either." His thumb strokes across my cheek again. "You put it between us on purpose. Gave yourself a secret because I wouldn't share all of mine."

I nod.

"You're allowed to have secrets. That's the point. I'd prefer they not risk everything I've worked toward for the last few years—or your life. And yes, I'm still not happy about the scribe, but we're not fighting tonight. I just need to know the important things. I won't withhold information that could change how you make decisions, and I ask the same of you." His thumb continues the same soothing, lazy pattern.

I don't want us to have secrets, but he's already made it clear that's not changing. So maybe it's time to try another tactic. "How long will you hold on to the weapons for?"

A corner of his mouth tugs upward. "I won't meet up with a drift for another couple of weeks."

Holy shit, it worked. "You answered."

"I did." He smiles, and an ache wakes in my chest. "How did it go with Varrish?"

"Tairn nearly ripped out Solas's throat, which worked for getting Andarna out of maneuvers but may end up causing me bigger problems in the future." A small smile spreads across my face. Look at us: having a conversation without fighting.

"We'll keep an eye on the situation. I'm slightly worried I'll kill Varrish if he pushes you to burnout again." There's no teasing in his voice, and I know he'll do it.

"What's with the weaving book you left me after graduation?" I change the subject with a small, confused shake of my head. "And the strips of fabric? Do you think I'm suddenly going to start crafting?"

"Just thought you might like to keep your hands busy." He shrugs with one shoulder, but the devious glint in his eyes says it's something more than that.

"So I keep them off other cadets?"

"I just thought you might like to explore an aspect of Tyrrish culture. I can weave every knot in that book." He flashes a smile. "It'll be fun to see if you can keep up with me."

"In fabric knots?" Has he fallen off Sgaeyl recently?

"Culture, Violence." His hand slides to the base of my neck, and his gaze turns serious. "Do you have nightmares about Resson? Is that why you can't sleep?"

I nod. "I dream of a million different ways we could have lost. Sometimes I dream it's Imogen who dies, or Garrick…or you." Those are the ones that make it impossible to sleep afterward, the ones where their Sage takes him from me.

"Come here." He wraps his arm around my waist and tugs, rolling me toward him.

My back settles against his chest as he tucks me in close. Gods, he hasn't held me like this since the night we destroyed my room. Warmth infuses every inch of my exposed skin, pushing the cold from my bones. The ache in my chest expands.

"Tell me something real." It comes out as a plea, just like it did last year.

He sighs and curls around me. "I know who you really are, Violet. Even when you keep things from me, I know *you*," he promises.

And I know enough about him to be a real liability with the interrogation portion of RSC coming up.

"I'm still not strong enough to shield you out." Right now, with his arm draped across my waist, I'm not sure I want to.

"I'm not a good measure of your skill," he says against the bare skin of my shoulder, and a shiver of awareness ripples through me. "The day you can successfully block me all the way out is the day I'm dead. We're both dead. I can't block you out entirely, either, which is how you found me in the sublevel even when my shields were up. You might not be able to barge through, but you're aware I'm there. Just like you can muffle Tairn's and Andarna's emotions but you can't lock them out forever."

My breath hitches. "So I might be strong enough to block Dain?"

"Yes, if you keep the shields intact at all times."

"What's alloy made of?" I ask, heady with the knowledge that I can keep Dain out.

"An amalgamation of Talladium, a few other ores, and dragon egg shells."

I blink with surprise, both at his answer and the fact that he told me. "Dragon *egg shells*?" Well that's…weird.

"They're metal and still carry magic long after the dragons hatch." His lips skim the back of my neck as he inhales, then sighs. "Now go to sleep before I forget all my honorable intentions."

"I could remind you of some very fun, very dishonorable ones." I lean back into him, and he throws his leg over mine, locking me down tight.

"You want to give me those three little words?"

I stiffen.

"I thought not. Sleep, Violet." His arm tightens around me. "You love me," he whispers.

"Stop reminding me. I thought we agreed not to fight tonight." I snuggle in deeper, his warmth lulling me into that sweet middle space between wakefulness and oblivion.

"Maybe you're not the one I'm reminding."

The Migration of The First Year is one of the crowning achievements of Navarre's unification. What a celebration of the human spirit, to leave a life of war and enter one of peace, blending people, languages, and culture from every region of the continent and forming a cohesive, united society, whose only goal is mutual security.

—NAVARRE, AN UNEDITED HISTORY
BY COLONEL LEWIS MARKHAM

CHAPTER
TWENTY-ONE

I've decided rolling dismounts might be the death of me yet.

Thursday morning begins with my arm in a sling that's secured around my ribs with a strap, immobilizing my shoulder, thanks to yesterday's maneuvers. Turns out Tairn was right, and though I'm capable of making it to his shoulder, my body doesn't take the impact of the actual landing very well. We both agreed this time—accommodations will need to be made before graduation.

"How is it feeling today?" Rhiannon asks as we walk into the history class we share with Third Wing on the second floor.

"Like Tairn set me down and I just kept going," I answer. "It's not my first sprain. Healers say it should be about four weeks in the sling. I'm giving it two. Maybe." I'll be the first on the challenge board after Threshing if I give it much longer than that.

"You could ask Nolon—" Ridoc starts, then stops when he sees the look on my face. "What? Don't tell me Varrish won't let you get mended."

"Not that I'm aware of, no," I counter as we find our seats. "I put my name on Nolon's list, but I was told he likely wouldn't have an opening before it healed naturally."

Rhi shoots me a look that says told-you-so but I just give my head a quick shake. This is not the place to explore her conspiracy theories—even if they're starting to feel more and more like there might be some truth to them. I've never known a mender with a waiting list *a month long*.

Thursdays are my second favorite day of the week. No maneuvers, no RSC, no physics. I unload the heavy textbook and the notes I took on today's assigned reading, which is more like review for me. There hasn't been a single thing in this class I hadn't already studied with my father or Markham—or that I don't have trouble believing is true now.

Then I take out a few strips of the bright blue fabric Xaden left me and put them in my lap. I've got two of the knots in the book down already, and I'm determined to have two more by the time he gets here on Saturday. It's a ridiculous thing to challenge me on, but that doesn't mean I'm willing to lose. Even a sling won't stop me.

"Wonder who's actually here to teach," Sawyer says, stepping over the back of his chair from the row behind us and sitting next to Ridoc on my left. "Pretty sure I just saw most of the leadership making a run for the flight field."

My heart stops. "What?" Only a major attack would empty Basgiath of leadership. I turn in my seat to look out the window behind us, but the view of the courtyard isn't helping.

"They were running." Sawyer makes a running motion with his first two fingers. "That's all I know."

"Good morning." Professor Devera walks in, her smile tight as she passes three rows of tables and chairs to get to the front of the room. "I'll be filling in for Professor Levini. He was called away due to an attack on the Eastern Wing." She makes a quick study of his cluttered desk, then picks up the book on top. "You'll hear about it in Battle Brief tomorrow, but so far there's only one death." Her throat works before she looks up from the book. "Masen Sanborn. Some of you may have known him, since he's a recent graduate."

Masen. Oh my gods, *no.* His face flashes through my mind, smiling as he pushes his glasses up his nose. It could be coincidence. There's no logical way an attack would be used to cover up a single death…right?

"Unless they assassinated him *during* the attack," I mumble under my breath. We weren't even friends. I didn't even know him that well, but out of the ten of us who flew into Resson, now only six are still alive.

"What?" Rhi leans into my space. "Violet?"

I blink quickly and clutch the fabric in my lap. "It's nothing."

Rhi's brows lower, but she sits back in her seat.

"I see he has you discussing the second Cygni incursion from year 328." Devera rubs the back of her neck. "But I honestly don't see how that has any practical application."

"That makes most of us," Ridoc comments, tapping his pen against his textbook, and those around us chuckle.

"But just to say we did," Devera continues, running a hand up and down a faded scar marring the warm brown skin on her upper arm. "Everyone should know that the end result of the four-day temper tantrum was Cygnisen being absorbed into the Kingdom of Poromiel, where they've been for the last three hundred years. History and current events are tied because one influences the other." She glances up at the map on the wall that's about a fifth of the size of the one in the briefing room. "Can anyone tell me the differences between Poromiel's provinces and ours?"

The room is quiet.

"This is important, cadets." Devera moves to the front of Professor Levini's desk and leans back against it. When no one answers, she gives me an arch look.

"Poromiel's provinces maintain their individual cultural identities," I answer. "Someone from Cygnisen is more likely to label themselves as a Cygni instead of Poromish. As opposed to our provinces, who unified under the protection of the first wards, chose the common language, and blended the cultures of all six provinces into one cohesive kingdom." I recite it nearly verbatim from Markham's book.

"Except Tyrrendor," someone from the left remarks. Third Wing. "They never quite got the 'unified' message, did they?"

My stomach sinks. *Asshole.*

"No." Devera points her finger at the guy. "That's what we're not going to do. It's comments like that that threaten the unity of Navarre. Now, Sorrengail brought up a good point that I think some of you are missing. Navarre chose the common language, but who was it common to?" She calls on someone from Tail Section.

"The Calldyr, Deaconshire, and Elsum provinces," the woman answers.

"Correct." Devera's gaze sweeps over us just like it does in Battle Brief when she expects us to not only think through the answers but come up with the questions ourselves. "Which means what?"

"The Luceras, Morraine, and Tyrrendor provinces lost their languages," Sawyer answers, shifting in his seat. He's from Luceras, along the bitterly cold northwestern coastline. "Technically they *gave* them up willingly for the good of the Unification, but other than a few words here and there being assimilated, they're dead languages."

"Correct. There is always a cost," Devera says, enunciating every word. "That doesn't mean it's not worth it, but not being aware of the price we pay to live under the protection of the wards is how rebellions happen. Tell me what the other costs have been." She folds her arms and waits. "Come on. I'm not telling you to commit treason. I'm asking for historical facts in a history class of second-year riders. What was sacrificed in the Unification?"

"Travel," someone from Claw Section answers. "We're safe here, but we're not welcome beyond our borders."

Nor is anyone welcome past ours.

"Good point." Devera nods. "Navarre might be the largest kingdom on the Continent, but we are not the only one. Nor do we travel to the isles anymore. What else?"

"We lost major parts of our culture," a girl with a rebellion relic winding around her arm answers from two rows ahead. Tail Section, I think. "Not just our language. Our songs, our festivals, our libraries... Everything in Tyrrish had to be changed. The only unique thing we kept were our runes because they're in too much of our architecture to justify changing."

Like the ones on my daggers. The ones on the columns of the temple in Aretia. The ones I'm currently weaving in my lap.

"Yes." Somehow Devera makes that word sound both sympathetic and blunt at the same time. "I'm not a historian. I'm a tactician, but I can't imagine the depth of what we lost knowledge-wise."

"The books were all translated into the common language," someone from Third Wing argues. "Festivals still happen. Songs are still sung."

"And what was lost in translation?" the Tyrrish girl ahead of me asks. "Do you know?"

"Of course I don't know." His lip rises in a sneer. "It's a dead language to all but a few scribes."

I drop my gaze to my notebook.

"Just because it's not in Tyrrish doesn't mean you can't walk into the Archives and read whatever translated Tyrrish book you want." It's his haughty, arrogant tone that pricks my temper.

"No, actually you can't." I drop the fabric in my lap. "For starters, no one can just walk into the Archives and read whatever they want. You have to put in a request that any scribe can deny. Secondly, only a portion of the original scribes spoke Tyrrish, meaning it would have taken hundreds of years to translate *every* text, and even then, there are no historical tomes older than four hundred years in our Archives that I know of. They're all sixth, seventh, or eighth editions. Logic dictates that she's right." I gesture up to the girl a few rows ahead. "Things are lost in translation."

He looks ready to argue.

"Cadet Trebor, if I were you, I would consider the fact that Cadet Sorrengail has spent more time in the Archives than anyone else in this room, and then I would carefully consider an intelligent response." She arches a brow.

The guy from Third Wing shoots a glare in my direction and sits back in his chair.

"We lost our folklore," Rhiannon says.

Every muscle in my body locks.

Devera cocks her head to the side. "Go on."

"I'm from a border village near Cygnisen," Rhiannon says. "A lot of our folklore came from the other side of the border, probably as a result of the Migration of The First Year, and as far as I know, none of it's written. It only survives as an oral history." She glances my way. "Violet and I were actually talking about this last year. People raised in Calldyr or Luceras or other provinces aren't raised with that same folklore. They don't know the stories, and generation by generation, we're losing it." She looks left, then right. "I'm sure all of us have similar stories, depending on where we grew up. Sawyer knows stories Ridoc doesn't. Ridoc knows stories Violet doesn't."

"Impossible," Ridoc counters. "Violet knows everything."

Sawyer laughs and I roll my eyes.

"All excellent points." Devera nods, a satisfied smile curving her mouth. "And what did the Migration of The First Year give us?"

"A more unified culture," a girl from Tail Section answers. "Not only within our provinces but throughout the Continent. And it allowed those in what's now Poromiel a chance to live under the safety of the wards if they chose to move."

One year. That's all Navarre gave before we closed our borders.

And if you couldn't afford to move your family, couldn't risk the treacherous journey… Nothing about war, or the aftermath, is kind.

"Correct," Devera says. "Which means there's every chance that when you fly against a drift, you could encounter a distant relative. The question we must all ask ourselves as we enter service is: are our sacrifices worth it to keep the citizens of Navarre safe?"

"Yes." The answer is muttered all around me, some riders saying it louder than others.

But I keep quiet, because I know it's not only Navarre paying the price—it's everyone outside our wards.

The gym buzzes with anticipation that afternoon as the combat professors call the first names of the day to the mats. These will be the last challenges for months. The first-years will have the Gauntlet to worry about starting next week, then Presentation and Threshing. And the second-years will start disappearing by the squad for a few days at a time so they can teach us how to take torture.

Fun times.

A squad from Tail Section is called to our mat.

"I really hope I get called to the mat today." Ridoc bounces on his toes. "I'm in the mood to kick some ass."

"That makes one of us." I tighten the strap of my sling over my armor. Looking across the mat, I nod to Imogen, lifting my eyebrows as she talks with Sloane.

She nods back with a smile, telling me wordlessly that Sloane is ready to take on her opponent today. Rhiannon and Sawyer are doing the same with the other first-years, checking in as names are called out around the gym. I glance Aaric's way, but as usual, he's completely, totally focused, tuning out everything around him as he stares at the mat.

"How bad do you think the attack on the Eastern Wing is? It has to be something massive to call out half the leadership all day long," Ridoc muses.

Big enough to kill Masen.

"Speculating is only going to fuel rumors," Dain says, taking the empty place on my left side.

Fuck. I've managed not to have to interact with him for weeks. I step closer to Ridoc and lock every brick of my shields in place.

"As opposed to not noticing that most of the professors flew out of here like the wards have fallen?" Ridoc asks.

"The wards haven't fallen." Dain barely spares him a glance, crossing his arms. "You'd know if they had."

"You think we'd be able to feel it?" Ridoc asks.

"We would have been called out, too," I say. "And the dragons would have told us."

"Can't you ask your mom?" Ridoc tilts his head.

"The woman who knew I was missing for a week, then told me to get back in formation when she realized I'd survived my first combat mission? Yeah, I'm sure she'll be forthcoming with all the information." I give him a sarcastic thumbs-up.

The first pair is called to the mat, and I'm simultaneously horrified and grateful I don't know the first-year's name.

"You finally going to talk to me?" Dain asks.

"No." I don't give him the courtesy of even looking at him and, to be sure he gets the point, I move to Ridoc's other side, putting him between us.

"Come on, Violet." He walks behind Ridoc, then squeezes in between Quinn and me. "You have to be ready at some point. We've been friends since you were five."

"We're no longer friends, and I'll be ready to talk when the sight of you doesn't make me want to bury my knife in your chest all the way to the fucking hilt." I walk away before I act on the urge to stab the memory-stealing asshole.

"You cannot keep running away from me!"

I lift my middle finger and round the corner of the mat, taking the spot next to Rhiannon.

"What was that about?" she asks, wincing when our first-year takes a punch to the kidneys.

"Dain being an asshole, as usual." Sometimes the best answer is the simplest.

Our first-year kicks out, catching Tail Section directly in the mouth, and blood sprays.

"I don't get it." She shoots me a confused look, leaning in to murmur so Dain doesn't overhear. "I figured the thing at graduation was him and Riorson dick-measuring, but you don't speak to Aetos anymore. I thought he was your best friend. Sure, you two grew apart last year, but to not even be on speaking terms?"

"Was." My gaze tracks Dain as he walks around the mat to Professor Emetterio. "He *was* my best friend." For fifteen years, there was no one closer. I'd thought he was going to be my everything.

"Look. I'll hate him on principle if that's what we're doing. No problem with that. But I know you, and you don't cut people out like that unless they hurt you. So tell me, as your friend: Did he hurt you?" she asks quietly. "Or is this something else *we* aren't talking about?"

My throat clenches. "He stole something from me."

"Seriously?" Her gaze pierces mine. "Then report him for a violation of the Codex. He shouldn't be our wingleader."

If only she knew what her last wingleader had been stealing.

"It's more complicated than that." How much can I tell her without it being *too* much?

Our first-year pulls off a quick comeback, getting his opponent's leg into a bow-and-arrow submission maneuver. It's a quick tap-out after that.

We all clap. So far, we're looking like the squad to beat again this year, especially with the way Aaric is racking up the wins.

Emetterio looks at Dain, then clears his throat. I breathe deeply, waiting for him to call Sloane's name. "You're sure?" Emetterio asks.

"It's within my rights as wingleader." He disarms, unclipping his sheaths and dropping them at the edge of the mat.

What the actual hell?

"Not denying that." Emetterio rubs a thick hand across his shaved head. "Next match is Dain Aetos against Violet Sorrengail."

My stomach hits the floor. If my shields slip, I could doom *everyone* in

Aretia and every marked one in the quadrant.

Imogen's eyes aren't just wide—they're huge as she looks at me, backing away from the mat before quickly disappearing. Where is she going? It's not like she can run and get Xaden to interfere like last year. I'm on my own.

"No fucking way." Rhiannon shakes her head. "She's wounded."

Maybe not entirely on my own.

"And since when does that matter?" the other squad leader counters.

Breathe. I need to breathe.

"This is bullshit." I look Dain in the eyes when I say it, and he simply folds his arms across his chest. There's no getting out of this. He's a wingleader. He can challenge whomever he wants whenever he wants, just like Xaden had last year. Ironically, I'd been in far less danger the first time Xaden had taken me to my back on the mat. Then, I'd been gambling with just *my* life, but this could get the people I care about killed.

"*Keep your shields in place,*" Tairn warns. His agitation rolls through me, prickling the hair on my neck.

Dain steps out on to the mat, completely disarmed, but I've seen him spar. He's not Xaden, but he's deadly enough without any weapons, and I'm down an arm.

"You shouldn't do this!" Bodhi shouts as he runs at us, skidding to a stop next to me. Imogen isn't far behind. Ah, she'd run to find the closest person to Xaden possible. Makes sense. "She's in a fucking sling, Aetos."

"Last time I checked, you're a section leader." Dain narrows his eyes on Bodhi. "And your cousin isn't her wingleader anymore. I am."

The muscles in Bodhi's neck bulge. "Xaden's going to fucking kill him," he whispers.

"Yeah, well, he isn't here. It's fine," I lie, reaching for my first dagger. "Just remember who trained me." I'm not talking about hand-to-hand, and from the look Bodhi gives me, he knows it, too.

"Keep the daggers if that makes you feel better, Cadet Sorrengail," Dain says, finding the center of the mat.

My eyebrows shoot up.

"You know she's good enough to kill you from here with those," Bodhi reminds him.

"She won't." Dain cocks his head at me. "I'm her oldest friend. Remember?"

"And this is certainly friendly behavior," Rhiannon counters.

Taking a fortifying breath, I secure every brick in my shields just like Xaden taught me and step out onto the mat, palming one of my daggers in my free hand. If it comes between killing Dain and saving Xaden, there's no choice.

Emetterio signals the beginning of the match, and Dain and I circle each other.

"Reach for my face, and I'll cut you open," I warn him.

"Deal," he responds a second before he lunges for me, going for the torso.

I know his moves and easily dodge the first attempt, spinning out of reach. He's fast. Being chosen as wingleader wasn't all nepotism. He's always been good on the mat.

"You're faster this year." He smiles like he's proud of me as we circle again.

"Xaden taught me a few things last year."

He winces, then attacks, swinging for my torso again. I flip my dagger so the blade runs perpendicular to my forearm as I duck under his jab, then punch upward, clipping him under the jaw without cutting him.

"Fuck yes!" I hear Ridoc cheer, but I don't take my eyes off Dain.

Dain blinks, then rotates his jaw. "Damn." This time, he comes at me faster. It's harder to duck and dodge his swings without my arm to balance, but I hold my own until he catches me unaware and sweeps my feet out from under me with his.

My back slams into the mat and pain erupts in my shoulder, so sharp that stars swim in my vision and I cry out. But damn if my blade isn't at Dain's throat when he pins me with a forearm at my collarbone a heartbeat later.

Shields. I have to keep my shields up.

"I just want to talk to you," he whispers, his face inches from mine.

The pain is nothing compared to the ice-cold fear of having his hands this close to me.

"And I just want you to leave me the fuck alone." I hold my knife steady right where he can feel it. "It's not an idle threat, Dain. You will bleed out on this mat if you even *think* of taking a single one of my memories."

"That's what Riorson meant when he said *Athebyne*, isn't it?" he asks, his tone just as soft as his eyes—those familiar eyes I've always been able to count on. How the hell did we end up here? Fifteen years of the closest friendship I've ever known, and my knife could end him with a flick of my wrist.

"You know damn well what he meant," I reply, keeping my voice down.

Two lines appear between his brows. "I told my father what I saw when I touched you—"

"When you *stole* my memory," I correct him.

"But it was a flash of a memory. Riorson told you he'd gone to Athebyne with his cousin." He searches my eyes. "Second-years don't get leave for that kind of flight, so I told my father. I know you were attacked on the way there, but I had no way of knowing—"

"You said *I'll miss you*." It comes out in a hiss. "And then you sent me to die, sent Liam and Soleil to their deaths. Did you know what was waiting for us?"

"No." He shakes his head. "I said 'I'll miss you' because you chose *him*. I told you I knew things about him, that he had reasons you don't know about to hate you, and you *still* chose him. I knew I was saying goodbye to any chance of us on that field. I had no clue gryphons were waiting to ambush you."

"If you expect me to believe that, then you sorely misjudged me, and I know *every* reason Xaden has to hate me, and none of them matter."

"You know about the scars on his back?" he challenges, and I contemplate cutting into his throat to get him off me.

"The hundred and seven for the marked ones he's responsible for? Yes. You're going to have to do better than—"

"Do you know who carved those wounds into his skin?"

I blink, and—fuck him—he sees it, the flash of doubt.

"Tap out!" Sawyer shouts from the edge of the mat.

"My hand is a little busy at the moment," I respond without looking away from Dain.

"Violet—" Dain starts.

"You may have been my oldest friend, my best friend, but that all died the day you *violated* my privacy, stole my memory, and got Liam and Soleil killed. I will *never* forgive you for that." I press just hard enough for the blade to scrape against the stubbled skin of his upper throat.

His eyes flare with something that looks like devastation. "Your mother did it," he whispers and slowly rises, first to his knees, removing his forearm from my collarbone, and then to his feet. "She wins," he says as he walks off the mat. "I tap out."

He didn't mean that. There's no way my mother sliced into Xaden a hundred and seven times. Dain's just trying to get under my skin. I lie there for a handful of breaths, calming my racing pulse. Then I sheathe my blade and roll, gaining my feet awkwardly.

Emetterio calls the next challenge, and I walk off the mat and take my place between Rhiannon and Bodhi like nothing happened.

"Violet?" The question in Bodhi's eyes makes me shake my head in reply.

"He didn't touch me." Every secret in my head is safe.

Bodhi nods, then leaves our mat as Aaric faces off against a guy from Tail Section who looks like he might actually have a shot of ending Aaric's winning streak.

"Walk with me," Rhiannon demands, her jaw tense. "Now."

"Are you pulling rank on me?"

"Do I have to?" She folds her arms across her chest.

"No. Of course not." I sigh, then follow her to the edge of the gym.

"Was that about the something he stole?" Rhiannon asks. "Because whatever it was, it wasn't about defeating you."

"Yes," I answer, rolling my neck as the aftereffects of the adrenaline roll through me, nausea taking the lead.

She waits for me to add to my answer, and when I don't, she sighs. "You've been off all day. Is it because of the attack?"

"Yes." I glance over her shoulder and glimpse Imogen watching us. Does she know Masen's dead?

"Are you really going to make me pry answers out of you?" Her arms fall to her sides. "I swear to Amari, if you answer with a *yes* one more time…"

I say nothing instead.

"I heard what you said in history, you know." She drops her shoulders. "You said something about an assassination."

Fuck. "Yeah, I guess I did."

She studies me, her gaze flickering between my eyes. "Who else besides Masen is dead that went to Athebyne with you?"

My gaze collides with hers, and my heart starts to pound. "Ciaran. He was in Third Squad." I'm not telling her anything that isn't easily answered by anyone else.

"And you were attacked on assessment day. Imogen's been targeted twice since Parapet, too. So were Bodhi and Eya." Her gaze narrows. "Dain has one of those classified signets," she whispers. "What did he steal, Violet?"

Gods, she's putting it together too quickly. She's also owed as much of the truth as I can give her. "A memory," I say slowly.

Her eyes flare. "He can read memories."

I nod. "No one is supposed to know."

"I can keep a secret, Violet." Hurt flashes across her features, and I feel another thread of our friendship unravel as though I'd pulled it myself.

A chorus of cheers goes up behind us, but neither of us looks.

"I know." It's barely a whisper. "And I trust you implicitly, but not every secret is mine to tell." Dread digs its claws into my stomach. She's going to figure it out—it's only a matter of time. And then her life will be in as much jeopardy as mine.

"Dain stole one of your memories," she repeats. "And now you think the other riders with you during War Games are being picked off."

"Stop," I beg her. "Do us both a favor and just…" I shake my head. "Stop."

Her brow knits. "You saw something you weren't supposed to, didn't you?" She tilts her head to the side, then looks away.

I stop breathing. I know that look. She's thinking.

"Is that the memory he stole?"

"No." I inhale. Thank gods she's off the mark with that one. Movement to the right catches my attention, and I glance over to see Aaric walking our way, cradling his left wrist. "Shit. I think he's hurt."

"What killed Deigh?" Rhiannon asks.

Suddenly, there's not enough oxygen in the room, on the entire Continent, but I manage to pull air through my lungs as I face her. "You already know that part of the story."

"Not from you," she says quietly, her brown eyes crinkling at the edges as she narrows them. "You were holding Liam, and then you had to fight. That's what you said. What. Killed. Deigh?" The whispered words cut me to the quick. "Was it another dragon? Is that what happened out there?"

"No." I shake my head emphatically, then turn as Aaric reaches us. "Finally lose?"

He scoffs. "Of course not. But I did break my wrist. I'm supposed to come tell you," he says to Rhiannon.

"I'll take him to the infirmary," I tell her.

"Violet—" she starts, her tone indicating that she doesn't think our conversation is over, but it is. It has to be.

"Stop." I turn my back on Aaric and lower my voice. "And don't ever ask me that question again. Please don't make me lie to you."

Her head draws back, and she stares at me in stunned silence.

"Let's go," I say to Aaric, then start walking to the exit, shoving what just happened with Rhi into what's quickly becoming an overfull box.

He catches up, his long legs covering the distance quickly. The corridor of the academic wing's first floor is deserted when we enter, and our booted footsteps echo against the windows.

"So where does your father think you are?" I ask as we turn toward the rotunda, trying to take my mind off everything I just let slip to Rhiannon and everything I didn't.

"He thinks I'm on my twentieth-birthday tour," Aaric answers, rubbing his hand over his square jawline and light-brown scruff, disgust curling his upper lip. "Drinking and fucking my way across the kingdom."

"Sounds like way more fun than what we're doing here." I push the door open with my good arm.

"What part of this isn't fun?" he asks, walking ahead and opening the next door with his unbroken hand. "Between the two of us, we have a full set of functioning arms."

I crack a smile as we enter the dormitory corridor. "Ever the charmer, aren't you, Cam—" I wince. "Aaric. Sorry. It's been a hell of a long day." And all I want is to tell Xaden about it, but he won't be here for two more days.

We head down the steps, and though Aaric is roughly the same height as Xaden, he shortens his stride so I can keep up easily.

"She's catching on, isn't she?" he says when we reach the tunnels.

The hairs on the back of my neck lift as I look up at Aaric. "Catching on to what, exactly?"

"They haven't hidden it all away as well as they think they have." His jaw flexes. "It's easy to figure out if you know what you're looking for. Personally, it was the daggers my guards started carrying that tipped me off." He shoots a look at me. "The ones with the little metal discs."

My heart pounds so loudly I can hear it in my ears. Daggers. Metal discs.

"The guards were the hardest to slip, too," he says with a grimace. "They won't tell my father they've lost me until they absolutely have to. I'm just hoping it's after Threshing. He can't do shit after Threshing. Dragons don't even answer to kings."

"Oh shit." My chest feels like it's caving in as I grab hold of his good arm, halting our steps before the tunnel. "You know, don't you?"

He lifts a brow, the mage lights catching on those royally green eyes. "Why else would I be here?"

At some point, probably during your second year, you'll realize the trust you feel for your friends and family has nothing on the loyalty you develop for your squad.

—Page Ninety-one, the Book of Brennan

CHAPTER TWENTY-TWO

Faster. I have to run *faster.* Fear holds my throat shut as a tidal wave of death chases me across the sunburned field to where Tairn waits, his back turned. Wind roars around me, stealing every other sound, even my own heartbeat. Tairn's going to die, and he doesn't even see it coming for him.

Gold flickers near the tip of his wing.

Gods, *no.* Andarna. She's here. She shouldn't be here.

The wave nips at my heels, transforming the ground beneath my feet into an ashen, desiccated wasteland.

"There is nowhere to run, rider." A hooded figure steps into my path out of nowhere, raising one arm.

I'm yanked off my feet by an unseen force and lifted into the air, completely immobilized. The wave of death halts and the wind falls silent, as if he's stopped time.

He shifts his staff to the other hand, then pulls back the thick maroon hood of his floor-length robes with gnarled fingers, revealing the white of his scalp under his slicked-back, thinning hair. Shadows mark the gaunt hollows of his cheekbones on an eerily youthful face, and his lips are cracked and dry, just like the land behind me, but it's his red-rimmed eyes, the distended veins spiderwebbing across his temples and cheeks, that have me fighting to open my mouth, straining to scream.

Venin.

"So disappointing," he lectures, as if he's *my* Sage and not the teacher of the dark wielder I killed on Tairn's back. "All of that power at your fingertips, and yet you insist on fleeing over and over, using the same failed tactics, and expecting what?" He tilts his head to the side. "To escape?"

My ribs tighten around my lungs as terror takes hold, and I force a garbled sound through my throat, but it does nothing to warn Tairn and Andarna.

"There is no escaping me, rider," he whispers, his fingers ghosting over my cheek but not quite touching. "Fight me and die, or join me and live beyond the ages, but you will never escape me, not when I've waited *centuries* for someone with your power."

"Fuck you." It comes out as a whisper, but I mean it with every bone in my body.

"Death it is." He looks so…disappointed as he lowers his hand.

Wind howls as I fall to the ground. A scream tears through my body as a wave of agony rolls over my skin and bones, leaching the very essence of my energy until—

I wake, my heart pounding, my skin clammy, my fingers wrapped around my black-hilted dagger.

Just a dream. Just a dream. Just a dream.

"**A**re you going to tell me where we're going?" I ask Xaden on Saturday as he leads me down the stairs from my dorm room.

"*To Basgiath's forge,*" he says as we emerge from the academic wing into the empty courtyard. It's finally the time of year when the temperature outside matches inside. Autumn is settling in.

My chest tightens as I realize he's taking me to see where they steal the weapons—and what that means. He's letting me in.

"*Thank you for trusting me.*" The words don't do the feeling justice.

"*You're welcome.*" He looks down at me, his expression shifting. "*Will I earn a little trust back now?*"

I nod, tearing my gaze away from his before I do something reckless like let those three little words he wants spill out just because we're having a moment. But I can share with him a secret of mine as well. "*I found a text that said the First Six didn't just establish the wards but personally carved the first wardstone.*"

"*We knew that.*"

"*Partially.*" We cross down to the tunnels to the flight field, and I nod at one of our first-years. Channing? Chapman? Charan? Shit, it's something like that. I'll learn it in a couple of weeks—after Threshing. "*The text said* first *wardstone,*" *which means if they carved the one here, there's a good chance they carved the one in Aretia. I'm on the right track."*

"Good point." He jerks open the door to the tunnels, and I walk inside.

"I know what I need to look for, but I'm not sure where it would even exist."

"Which is?" He asks as we move toward the stairs.

My pulse is thrumming with excitement to finally see the forge, get a look at the luminary that the revolution needs so badly, too.

"I need a firsthand account from one of the six. My father talked about seeing one once, so I know they exist. Question is if they've been translated and redacted into uselessness." We turn into the staircase and both stop abruptly.

Major Varrish blocks our path. "Ah, nice to see you, Lieutenant Riorson." His smile is just as greasy as ever.

Fear squeezes my heart. Xaden is carrying enough contraband to see him executed two dozen times.

"Wish I could say the same," Xaden retorts.

"Found her!" Varrish calls up the stairs. "Shouldn't you be headed over to the main campus, Riorson? Surely that's where officers lodge when visiting." His gaze flicks my way.

It takes all my willpower not to retreat.

"There you are, Cadet Sorrengail." Professor Grady offers me a genuine smile as he descends, his arm linked through Ridoc's, whose hands are behind his back.

Ridoc shoots me a warning look, and dread settles heavily in my chest.

No. Not today. We're being taken.

"Turns out, you're quite hard to catch by surprise," Professor Grady says, a note of admiration in his voice. "Your door doesn't allow anyone entrance." He glances at Xaden, his focus shifting to the exposed swirls of his rebellion relic just under his jaw. "I'm guessing she has you to thank for that, since second-years can't ward. Makes nabbing her for interrogation training a little difficult."

"I'm not going to apologize." Xaden's eyebrows lower as Varrish's riders—the ones who usually dump my belongings on the flight field—both turn the corner above Professor Grady. One escorts Rhiannon, and the other, Sawyer. Both of them have their hands bound behind their backs.

Looks like our squad is next for interrogation…and I almost just saw the mother of all secrets around here. I force myself to breathe, fighting to keep the nausea at bay.

"She's on leave." Xaden sweeps me to the side, putting me behind his back. "And recovering from an injury." Shadows race from the edges of the stairwell, rising to form a waist-high wall. *"He'll use this opportunity to kill you for the embarrassment Tairn put him and Solas through."*

"You can't possibly know that."

"His intentions are pretty fucking clear. Trust me."

"No, *you're* on leave," Varrish says, delight sparkling in his eyes. "Cadet Sorrengail is headed out for training." He jabs his finger at the wall of shadow and winces. "Well, that's fascinating. No wonder you're so coveted. The pair of you really are quite something."

"You can't protect me from this any more than you could Threshing," I tell Xaden, stepping out from the shelter of his body. *"You know it's true."*

"You weren't mine at Threshing," he counters.

"I'm not yours now," I remind him. "I'll be fine," I say out loud. "Drop the barrier."

"Do listen to your little girlfriend," Varrish suggests. "I'd hate to report that you disobeyed a direct order, or worse—cancel her leave for next weekend. There's really nothing you can do here."

Oh, fuck. That is *not* the way to deal with Xaden. Ordering him around only makes him push that much harder. And separating Tairn and Sgaeyl for two weeks is more than they can take.

"I'm not in your chain of command, therefore I'm under no obligation to follow your fucking orders, and there is *always* something I can do. She's in no condition to be tortured, and if her fucking wingleader isn't here to advocate for her, then I will."

"Sgaeyl!" I reach out through the one pathway I avoid at almost every cost. *"They're going to cancel next week's leave if he doesn't relent."*

"How hurt are you?" Grady asks, concern on his face.

"Dislocated my shoulder last week," I answer.

"I chose him for his inability to relent," Sgaeyl reminds me.

"Not helpful at the moment. Do I need to remind you of what he's carrying?"

"Fine. But only so this conversation ends."

"Her wingleader is otherwise engaged," Varrish says to Xaden. "And feel free to continue to argue with me. You're right. You're not under my chain of command, but as I had to remind her dragon, *she is*. Or did you not hear about her disciplinary session? I'd hate for her to have to repeat it simply for you to learn your lesson, Lieutenant. Then again, you could always join us."

Xaden smiles, but it's not the kind that warms my heart. It's the one that chills every cell in my body to ice, the cruel, menacing curve I first saw on the dais when he was my wingleader. "One day, Major Varrish, you and I are going to have words." He drops the shadow barrier and lifts a brow at me. *"You went to Sgaeyl?"*

"I make no apologies for saving your ass from your own stubbornness." I put out my good hand, and Grady steps forward, binding it mercifully to the one

protruding from the sling. At least he didn't wrench my hurt shoulder behind my back, but damn, the rope is tight. *"There's a book on my desk that needs to be returned to the Archives."*

Anger burns in the depths of his gold-flecked onyx eyes. *"I'll see that it's done."*

"See you next week," I whisper. *"Tell her page three hundred and four mentions a text I'd like to read next."*

"Next week," he responds with a nod, his fists clenched as Varrish walks by with the others in my squad. "Violence, remember it's only the body that's fragile. *You* are unbreakable."

"Unbreakable," I repeat to myself as Professor Grady leads me away.

The things that happen behind closed doors in the Riders Quadrant in order to turn young cadets into full-fledged riders are enough to turn even the staunchest of stomachs. Those prone to queasiness should not pry.

—Major Afendra's Guide to the Riders Quadrant
(Unauthorized Edition)

CHAPTER
TWENTY-THREE

The key can be found in my desk drawer.

As far as secret phrases go, that one is laughably uncreative, but nevertheless, it's the one I'm quietly given after we enter the training facility. The entrance is so well hidden in the cliffside under the foundation walls of the quadrant that I've never seen it in all the years I've lived here. It's remarkably accessible for its intended purpose.

The antechamber of the windowless, guarded cave isn't too bad as far as torture chambers come. It could even double as an office. A large wooden desk consumes the center of the space, with a high-backed chair on one side and two on the other. They disarm us as soon as we arrive, our weapons taking up a respectable amount of the desk's surface.

But it's the two chambers beyond that make me wish I hadn't eaten breakfast. Both doors are braced with steel, and both have a barred window currently held closed by a steel latch.

"You've all been given your classified information to protect," Professor Grady says, leading us into the chamber on the right. There's a scarred wooden table in the center of the dome-shaped room with six chairs, and along the cobblestone walls are five wooden beds with no mattresses and a door that I'm desperately hoping leads to a bathroom or things are going to get awkward over the next couple of days. "Have a seat." He gestures to the table.

We all do as we're told. Rhiannon and I take the chairs across from Sawyer and Ridoc, the wood scraping the stone as we sit, all managing it without the use of our hands.

"For right now, we're in what's called a classroom setting. Remember what that means?" Professor Grady reaches behind Sawyer, and a second later, Sawyer's hands are free.

"It means we're not in the graded scenario," Rhiannon answers. "We can ask questions."

"Correct." Professor Grady moves to Ridoc and does the same. "The purpose of this exercise really is to teach you how to survive capture," he assures us. "These next couple of days are instructional only." He reaches for my bonds next, untying the rope with surprising gentleness. "It's an assessment."

"So you know which buttons to push when it's the real thing," Ridoc says, rubbing his wrists.

"Exactly." Professor Grady smiles. "Is it going to be fun? Absolutely not. Are we going to show you mercy? Also, no." He moves on to Rhiannon once my hands are free. "And Vice Commandant Varrish seems to have taken an interest in your squad, no doubt because you have quite the legacy here in Cadet Sorrengail. So unfortunately, it looks like we'll all be evaluated in how we handle this."

Two riders walk in with trays of food and pewter mugs, setting them down on the table. There are more than enough biscuits for the four of us and a jar of what looks to be strawberry jam.

"Eat and drink," Professor Grady says, gesturing to the trays. "You won't have the opportunity once we enter the scenario. Also"—he flashes a grin— "there's a patch up for grabs if you manage to escape. Though from what I hear, no squad has managed it in the last decade."

"It's as good as ours," Ridoc responds.

"Confidence." Professor Grady nods at Ridoc. "I like that in a second-year." He moves toward the door, then turns. "I'll let you know when we begin the scenario. Until then, you all need to share a secret. Something no one else outside the four of you could possibly know. And yes, we're going to try and force it out of you, along with the secret phrases you've already been given. Remember the coping mechanisms you've been taught in class so far, and this will be over before you know it. Every rider who graduates has sat where you're sitting and made it through what you're about to experience. Have faith in yourself. We're doing this *for* you, not *to* you." He offers a final reassuring smile, then takes his leave, shutting the door behind him.

Rhiannon moves immediately to the door, examining the bars and sealed hatch. "It's not sound-shielded that I can tell, but if we keep our voices down, we should have a modicum of privacy." She tries the handle. "And we're definitely locked in."

Sawyer parcels out the food onto the four plates we've been given.

"It's all so…civilized," I note as he slides a plate in front of me.

Rhiannon checks the other door. "And that's a bathroom, thank gods."

"I wonder if they take it away during the actual test," Ridoc muses, slathering jam onto his biscuit with the lone knife we've been provided.

"Fuck, I hope not," Sawyer says, taking the knife from Ridoc. "Anyone else wondering if we're expecting company?" He nods toward the bed on the end.

"Statistically, five second-years are alive in each squad at this point," I say, reaching for one of the mugs on the tray. "We lost Nadine."

Silence falls for a second, then two.

"Well, we're not losing anyone else. The four of us will make it to graduation," Rhiannon says, grabbing a mug for herself, too. She sniffs at it, then sets it down. "Smells like apple juice. All right. We don't know how much time we have, so let's go. Pick a secret—any secret—and share with the group." The knife and jam go to her next. "I'll start. Last year while we were at Montserrat, Violet and I snuck out so I could see my family."

"You what?" Sawyer's brows rise.

Ridoc swallows his bite. "Badass. Didn't know you had it in you to break the rules, Violet."

"Oh, Violet's *full* of secrets, aren't you?" Rhiannon shoots a look my way and hands me the knife.

"Really?" I dish out the jam a little too aggressively.

"Whoa." Ridoc glances between us. "Am I picking up on some tension?"

"No," Rhi and I simultaneously answer, then look at each other. Both our shoulders sag, and she sighs, looking away. I guess that's where our line is drawn. This thing we're going through is just between us. "We're fine," she says.

Somehow that makes me feel a little better, but not much.

I bite into the biscuit and chew thoroughly just in case whatever they put us through makes me puke it up later. I need a secret I can share that won't get any of them killed.

"I didn't tell my parents I had to repeat," Sawyer says, his gaze locked on his plate. "They didn't even question my first letter this year. They assumed that Riders Quadrant cadets couldn't write for the first two years, and I let them believe it. I just didn't want them to be embarrassed of me."

"You're not an embarrassment," I say softly, reaching for my mug. "And I'm sure they're just glad you're alive. So many of us aren't."

"Agreed." Ridoc nods, his hands wrapped around his mug. "I'm terrified of snakes."

"That's a shitty secret," Sawyer counters, his mouth lifting into a smile.

"Surprise me with one, and you'll see just how shitty. Besides, you didn't know it, so I think it qualifies." Ridoc shrugs. "We're not supposed to have a weakness in the quadrant, right? That's my weakness. I scream like a toddler every time I see one."

Everyone looks my way. Here we go. "I'm in love with Xaden Riorson." Mira. Them. I seem to be able to say the words to anyone who *isn't* Xaden.

"Hate to break it to you, but that's not a secret," Ridoc says, shaking his head.

"Yes, it is," I argue, my grip tightening on the mug.

"No," Sawyer chimes in. "It's really not."

"Hasn't been for a while," Rhi adds, giving me the first real smile I've seen from her in weeks. "You're going to have to do better than that."

They're supposed to be my center, my backbone, my safe place. That's why squadmates are forbidden from killing each other. Venin. Wyvern. The daggers. The wards. Andarna. Brennan. Aretia. I have too many secrets to count, and none of them are safer for it—they're just blissfully ignorant.

"Can't my secret be the same as Rhiannon's?" I ask.

"No," they all answer.

One thing. There has to be one thing I can tell them that might help prepare them for what's coming. "Our infantry is killing Poromish civilians at the border."

"What?" Sawyer leans in, his freckles standing out as the blood drains from his face.

"There's no way," Ridoc argues.

Rhiannon stares silently at me.

"Happened while I was at Samara." I look them each in the eye. "Whether or not we're getting updated at Battle Brief, it's happening. Good enough secret?"

They all nod, and I look away when I catch Rhiannon studying me.

"Good," I say, lifting my mug. The others do the same. I breathe in, tilting the mug to drink— "Stop!" I hiss. "Don't drink it." I set it down like the poison it is.

"What the hell?" Ridoc asks, putting his mug on the table.

"It smells like the water they gave us before the land navigation course," I whisper.

Rhi and Sawyer set theirs down, too.

"They're trying to disconnect us from our dragons," Sawyer notes.

"Or dull our signets," Rhiannon adds. "Did anyone drink?"

We all shake our heads.

"Good. Don't tell them. Fake the disconnect." She rises quickly and we follow, each dumping the content of our mugs in the toilet. "We can survive for three days without water, and we should be out of here tomorrow. No matter how thirsty we get, we'll live. We hold the line."

Now I understand the biscuits. My mouth feels like I've been eating sand.

"We hold the line," Sawyer agrees as we return to the table and sit.

"Fuck tomorrow. I say we break out tonight," Ridoc whispers. "There have to be keys that you can transport, right?" he says to Rhi.

"Not through walls." She shakes her head. "I'm close but not there yet."

"Or you can bend the metal hinges?" That one is directed to Sawyer. "Hell, I can pull moisture out of the air and force ice through the lock." He turns to me.

"I'm of absolutely no use in this situation." I lean back in my chair.

The door swings open and Professor Grady walks in.

"We can't reach our dragons," Rhi says, lifting her chin. "You tricked us."

"Lesson number one." He holds up a finger. "We're always in scenario."

Ten minutes later, we find out what the second chamber holds—not much— when they chain Ridoc, Rhiannon, and Sawyer to the rock wall they've been ordered to sit against. They're close enough together that they can almost but not quite touch as their wrists are cuffed in hanging manacles. There are at least six other sets on either side of the trio, and the mage lights above us show every dried blood spatter on the stone.

"I'm guessing the seat is for me?" I ask Professor Grady, eyeing the stained wooden chair in the center of the cylindrical room and its shackles along each armrest and leg. My heart pounds like it has a chance of escaping my chest, escaping this room. There's a drain under the chair, but I refuse to even *think* about what it's for.

"It is." He motions, and I sit, ignoring every instinct to flee. Panic threatens to choke me as he locks my right arm into the shackle, then does the same with both of my legs, leaving my dislocated shoulder in the sling. "Here is where I leave you."

"You what?" Ridoc pulls against the shackles at his wrists, but they don't give.

"I'll read the reports and give you my advice before the exam," he tells us. "But we learned a long time ago that it doesn't exactly foster trust between cadets and professors if we're the ones doing the questioning." He looks at each of us in turn. "Remember what you've been taught. They'll try to separate you, turn you against one another, or make you think that talking is an act of mercy. Use the strategies from your reading. Lean on one another. I'll be just outside the entrance. You make it to me, you earn that patch. Good luck." He smiles like he didn't just serve us up to be beaten, then leaves.

"Is now a good time to admit that I haven't done this portion of the reading?" Ridoc asks once we're alone.

"No!" Rhiannon shoots him a glare.

"Violet, are you all right?" Sawyer asks.

"I'm the only one in a chair, so I feel like I'm one up on you guys," I joke, but it falls flat as the door opens behind me.

Two riders I've never seen before—one man, one woman—enter. The man offers us a smile. "Well, hello there. You are all prisoners selected for interrogation," he says, leaning against the wall, just out of reach from Sawyer. He's average, unremarkable in height, looks, even his hair. I could have passed him a dozen times in the halls of Basgiath, or any of the outposts, and not noticed him. Same goes for the woman. It's as if being unmemorable is necessary to the job.

The woman circles me, a vulture scenting for weakness. I lift my chin, determined to show none.

"You each have one piece of information we need," the man says. "Give it up now, and this all ends. It's as easy as that."

"My map is under my mattress," Ridoc says.

My jaw fucking *drops*.

"Ah, going with the start-lying-immediately-so-they-won't-know-when-you-tell-the-truth strategy." The man grins. "Good one. But unfortunately for you, my signet is similar to Lieutenant Nora's and has to do with your bodily functions. In layman's terms, I'll know when you're lying, and you are lying."

The woman lashes out, the back of her hand striking my cheek so hard that my head snaps to the side. Pain bursts and I blink rapidly, then run my tongue over my teeth. No blood.

"Silver One!"

"Not now." I slam my shields up to spare him this.

"Violet!" Ridoc shouts, surging against his chains.

"I'm all right," I tell him, tell *all* of them. I do what I always do, compartmentalize the pain and push past it, forcing a smile. "See? Fine."

Rhiannon quickly masks her horror, but Sawyer doesn't bother to hide his disgust with our captors.

"You're the weakest. That's why you're first up," the woman says, disdain dripping from her low voice. "We've read the files on all of you." She drops to a crouch in front of me, then looks me over, her attention catching on my hair, the sting of heat at my cheek that I'm sure bears her handprint, and finally the sling. "How did someone as *frail* as you survive your first year?"

"You three carried her, didn't you?" the man says, looking at my squadmates. "What an unfair burden to put on first-years."

"Don't tell them anything they can use against us," Rhiannon orders.

The woman laughs. "As if we don't know everything already." She stands slowly. "Tell us the secret you're keeping."

"Fuck off." I brace, and sure enough, her hand flies at my face. This time, I taste blood, but none of my teeth are loose. I build a mental wall around the pain, picturing it disappearing beneath the box I build for it, just like I do with my shields.

"Quite the mouth for a general's daughter," the woman sneers.

"Who do you think I got it from?"

Her facade slips, and she genuinely smiles for a heartbeat before masking it. "How about this? Any of you give up your secret, and I won't shatter her pretty little face."

"It's going to take a lot more than that to break us," Rhiannon says.

"I couldn't agree more. Don't watch," I tell my squadmates, then brace.

She hits from the other side, striking higher, and my cheek explodes. At least that's how it feels. The initial wave nauseates me, then dissipates into a dull throb. My vision in my right eye blurs and something wet trickles down my cheek.

"Maybe she's not the key," the woman says, backing away from me and heading for the others. "Maybe you're all sick and tired of having to carry her frail weight." She tips Ridoc's head up. "Or maybe she's only strong for herself." She closed-fist punches him in the face. Blood and saliva hit the wall next to him.

Rage overtakes the pain, and I try to rock forward, but not only are my arms and legs shackled, the chair is bolted to the floor.

She looks over her shoulder at me. "You have the power to make it stop." She hits again.

I close my eyes and wish I could close my ears when I hear his grunt after the next punch. And the next. And the next. When I open my eyes—correction, *eye*, we've all taken a hit.

"Let them sit with that for a minute," the man suggests. "They'll soften up in a couple of hours." The woman agrees and they leave us, shutting the door but not the hatch on the window.

"Well, this fucking sucks." Sawyer spits blood onto the floor.

"Violet, your eye…" Rhiannon says softly.

"It's swelling shut, not falling out." I shrug with my good shoulder.

"If that's their opening, what's next?" Ridoc asks. His cheek is split wide open.

"They'll try to turn us against one another," Rhiannon answers. "We don't break. Agreed?"

"Agreed." We all say it.

The worst part isn't the pain or the swollen eye. It's the hours of waiting, the not knowing when they're going to come back and dish out worse. And then worse comes and leaves us all with more bruises in various places.

I'm pretty sure that last blow left Sawyer concussed.

Without windows, it's impossible to know how much longer we have to hold out for when we don't know what time it—

"What time is it?" I ask Xaden, lifting my shields just enough to communicate.

"Almost midnight," he answers. *"Are you—"*

"Don't finish that question. You know what happens down here."

"Yeah. I do."

"It's almost midnight," I tell the others quietly. "We still have all night to go."

"Is Tairn listening for the bells?" Sawyer asks, turning his face against his shackled arm to clear some of the blood off.

"Not exact—"

The door opens and the man walks in carrying a pewter mug. "Who's thirsty?" He drops down in front of Sawyer, blocking my view of his face. "It's right here. And you don't even have to give me your secret. You just have to tell me one of their personal ones." He motions down the line. "It doesn't count as breaking. It's just a personal detail that doesn't mean anything."

"Fuck you."

"Pity." The man tilts his head. "You're just not thirsty enough yet. Don't worry. You'll get there." He moves to Rhiannon, then Ridoc, then me. Our answers are all the same.

"Tight-knit group, aren't they?" Chills race down my spine as Varrish walks in, eyeing us all with unfettered joy.

"They are, sir," the man says.

Varrish rubs his thumb across his chin. "Doesn't someone usually give up a personal detail by now?"

"They do, sir."

Pride flares behind my ribs.

Varrish leans down and flicks the green Iron Squad patch on Ridoc's chest. "I'm guessing that's how they earned this last year." He stands and sighs. "This is taking too long."

"Sir, we're using standard interrogation protocol," the woman says, entering the chamber.

"Then it's a good thing that I'm here." His cheery disposition scares me more than the woman's fist. "This is my area of expertise—interrogation. And I have just the thing to crack them in record time." He looks toward the hallway, then crooks his fingers. "Come on in. Don't be shy."

Rhiannon's eyes flare, her gaze jumping from the doorway to me. The fear I see there hits me like a punch to the stomach.

"I believe you all know Wingleader Aetos?"

Every few years, a squad comes along that defies all expectations.
They rise through the ranks, secure every patch, win every
challenge. And then…they inexplicably falter, then fall. They call
it the burnout effect: they flare too fast, too bright to sustain the
pace. Sad, really, but mildly entertaining to watch them turn on
one another.

—MAJOR AFENDRA'S GUIDE TO THE RIDERS QUADRANT
(UNAUTHORIZED EDITION)

CHAPTER
TWENTY-FOUR

Dain steps into view, and my heart hits the stone floor as he surveys my
friends, then turns toward me. His eyes widen as he takes stock of my
bruised and swollen face. "Violet."

"Dain is here." I reach for Xaden even as fear freezes me in place. This can't
happen. I'm unsure how much Dain knows, but it's definitely not as much as I do.

"I'm on my way." The tense tone of Xaden's voice is all it takes for me to
know how deep the shit is about to get.

"You can't do anything." I reinforce my shields, putting all my mental energy
into the task and drawing power from Tairn to bolster them, stacking the bricks
two deep around my mental Archives.

"I don't understand," Sawyer says. "Why is our wingleader here?"

"He's advocating for her like Riorson said a wingleader should," Ridoc
answers, hope in his voice. "Aren't you?"

"He's not," I answer, keeping my eyes on Dain and his hands.

"Regulations state that riders should be healthy before beginning
interrogation assessment," Dain barks, ripping his gaze from mine to address
Varrish. "Cadet Sorrengail is clearly *not* healthy."

I blink in sheer surprise.

"Such a rule follower." Varrish clucks his tongue. "Regulations say they *should*, not that they *have* to be. It's more realistic that a rider would be wounded when captured."

"What am I doing here?" Dain demands.

"Testing a theory." Varrish smiles. "But while we're waiting for our guest to arrive, you should practice on her." He points to me.

Guest? My fear is replaced with anger. *"Don't come. Varrish wants to see if you will. I think he's testing the bond-blocking mixture."*

"If he sees your memory, the entire movement is at risk."

"And if you come in here, whipping shadows around, he'll know I have something to hide, and this will become a real *interrogation. Your only option is to trust that you trained me well enough."* A rescue sounds great in theory but would fuck *all* of us.

"Violet—" The plea in his voice nearly breaks me.

I shove that last brick in place and block Xaden out.

"You want me to…" Dain lifts his brows.

"Yes. Use your signet on her. Only to draw out the secret phrase, of course."

"My signet is *classified*."

"And she already knows what it is," Varrish says, shaking his head like this is all no big deal. "Doesn't she? That's why she's so angry with you. She blames you for what happened to her friend." He walks forward. "It's amazing what you can learn by simply observing."

Dain shakes his head. "I'm not doing this."

"Then who are you going to practice on to extend your ability past recent events? We're running out of civilians around here for Nolon to mend, and if you think she hasn't told the rest of her squad your little secret, you're giving her far too much credit."

Holy shit. While Carr is my teacher, Varrish is Dain's. What the hell is our vice commandant's signet?

Dain stiffens, his eyes searching mine.

I don't deny it. I can't. I'm a shitty liar, and with the lie-finder—or whatever his signet is called—on the other side of the room, I'm better off keeping my mouth shut.

"This is what your signet is *made* for. You're the first line of defense, Aetos. She could be a Poromish spy or a gryphon rider. You could save the entire kingdom by just plucking her secrets from her memory." Varrish looks at me like I'm an animal made to be studied. "You can see what really happened that day when the two marked ones were killed by"—he cocks his head to the side—"gryphons, wasn't it, Cadet Sorrengail? The truth is waiting, Wingleader Aetos, and you're the only one who can see it."

Breathe in. Breathe out. I concentrate on steadying my heart rate and holding Dain's gaze.

"Holy shit," Ridoc mutters. "He can what?"

I keep my focus on Dain. How can someone be so familiar and yet such a stranger? He's the same boy I climbed trees with, the same one I ran to whenever anything went wrong. But he's also the reason Soleil and Liam are dead.

"You could learn what it is she sees in him," Varrish whispers, getting closer to Dain. "Why she chose him over you. Don't you want to know? All the answers are right there. You just have to know where to reach." Have to give it to him, he's convincing as *fuck*.

The war within Dain's eyes makes my throat tighten, and when he reaches for my face with both hands, I arch my neck, leaning as far back as the chair will let me.

"No." I force the word out.

"No." He repeats my refusal slowly, then drops his hands, his gaze falling from mine. "I will not participate in an interrogation assessment of a cadet with a prior injury," he says over his shoulder at Varrish.

Then he walks out.

I drag a breath in, air wheezing past the tightness of my throat and into my lungs.

Rhiannon's eyes meet mine, then slide shut slowly in relief.

"Well, that was disappointing and anticlimactic," Varrish says with the first frown I've ever seen on his face. "Fucking rule follower. Back to typical tactics, I guess." He draws back before I can brace and throws a hard punch to my dislocated shoulder.

Agony overwhelms every one of my senses.

Then there's only black.

Nolon hovers above me when I wake. I jolt up from the wooden bed, and he rears back.

"There she is," he says, settling into the chair next to the bed.

"What time is it?" I glance around the room, quickly spotting Rhiannon, Sawyer, and Ridoc sitting on bunks. They don't look any more injured than they did before I passed out.

Before Varrish punched my shoulder out of the socket. Gingerly, I rotate the joint, then look at Nolon. I'm mended. There's an ache but nothing more, and I can see out of both eyes.

He nods.

"It's morning," Rhi answers, worry lining her forehead. "I think."

I reach for Xaden, but the pathway is opaque again. He's gone.

"The vice commandant called me in to heal you." Nolon's voice drops, and he leans forward. "So he can shatter you again and again until you break. I'm on orders to remain in the antechamber for the rest of your interrogation, which he's extended until tomorrow."

Dread knots my empty stomach.

"Is that normal?" Sawyer asks, leaning toward me and bracing his forearms on his knees.

"No," Nolon answers, holding my gaze. "He wants whatever it is you know, Violet." He reaches for my hand and squeezes lightly. "Is it worth holding on to?"

I nod.

"Is it worth watching your squadmates tortured?"

I wince but nod again.

"I think I've had my head buried in other matters for too long." He sighs, then stands. "Why don't you walk me to the door?"

I swing my legs over the bunk, then do as he asks, following him to the chamber's door. Rhiannon isn't far behind. "You'd better find a way out," he whispers to me before speaking through the open window. "I'm done for now."

The door opens, and Nolon escapes. "I'll close it," he tells whoever is on the other side. His eyes meet mine through the window as he shuts the door, the lock audibly clicking into place…but not the window.

Rhiannon tugs me down, and we both drop into a crouch.

"I've been thinking about my other patient," Nolon says casually.

"What about him?" Varrish replies.

"He spent the night in the infirmary again. Sorrengail will have to sleep off the mending for another hour or so. Why don't you walk back with me and see if your particular skills could be of use? I might be overlooking something."

Rhiannon and I exchange the same confused look.

"You think the sessions are failing?" Varrish asks.

"I think I've done all I can for him," Nolon answers. "I'm not going to sit here all day and waste time while she's sleeping—"

"Fine, we'll go," Varrish replies. "We have to be quick. The others are fetching breakfast."

"Then by all means, let's make it fast."

A moment later, the antechamber door opens and closes.

Rhiannon and I stand slowly, then peer through the window.

"I think we're alone," she whispers.

"Agreed."

"We have to get out of here," Rhiannon says to the guys. "I really, honestly think Varrish might try to kill Violet."

My stomach flips. Oh Dunne, she actually *said* it.

"Are you serious?" Sawyer asks, his eyes bulging, but Ridoc stays quiet, his gaze jumping between Rhiannon and me.

"He's already pushed me to burnout once," I admit quietly.

A look passes between the guys, and they stand.

"Fine, I'll ask the obvious question," Ridoc says as they cross the chamber. "What the hell do you know that we don't?"

I glance between all three of them. "If I told you—and trust me, I've considered it—you would be the ones strapped to the chair. I'm not about to let that happen."

"Maybe you should let *us* decide what risks we're willing to take." Sawyer cracks his knuckles and rolls his shoulders, already looking at the door.

"Lesser magic isn't working on the lock," Ridoc mutters, his hand extended toward the door.

"Valid point, Sawyer. But this…" I shake my head. "It's not just about me."

"Right now it is," Rhiannon says. "It's all about saving you. We can figure the rest out later. Sawyer, do your thing."

"Already on it."

We move out of his way, and he puts his hands up toward each of the hinges. His fingers tremble and the hinges smoke, then melt. Hot metal drips down the edges of the door as he works.

"Quick, before you accidentally weld us in here," Ridoc lectures.

"I don't see you melting anything," Sawyer responds from where he's crouched, sweat beading his brow as he melts the last hinge.

Relief nearly takes out my knees. We're going to make it!

The door wobbles, and Rhiannon and I lunge toward the guys, both throwing up our hands over them. Wood smacks into my palms, sending a jolt of pain through my newly mended shoulder as we catch what feels like the heaviest door ever made.

"Move!" Rhiannon shouts.

The guys scurry out from under the door, then help us lower it to the floor.

"We should consider quitting the quadrant," Ridoc jokes as we walk over the door and out of the chamber. "We'd be kickass thieves."

"With dragons," Sawyer agrees.

"Unstoppable," Ridoc says with a grin.

We pause at the desk only long enough to retrieve our weapons. I feel a little less panicked, less vulnerable with every blade I sheathe.

"Ready?" Rhiannon asks, gripping her shortsword.

Guess I'm not the only one who disdains feeling helpless.

We all nod, then head for the main door. Hope lives for all of a millisecond.

"It's the same kind of lock. Lesser magic isn't working," Sawyer seethes, already putting his hands out.

"I don't—" Heat prickles along my ribs. It's the same feeling I get when I walk through the wards on my door. I look down and stare. The dagger closest to the door handle is hot and…tingling. I pull it from the sheath, bumping against the door handle as I brush my thumb over the decorative pommel.

Metal clicks against metal, and we all turn to look at the lock.

"What the hell?" Sawyer's eyebrows jump.

"I don't know. That's…impossible." Knives don't open locks. But the heat and the tingling sensation are gone.

"Someone stop staring and try the fucking door!" Rhi orders.

Reaching for the handle, I hold my breath as the latch depresses. I pull. The door opens. "Holy shit." It's coincidence. It has to be. Magic isn't tied to objects like that.

"Holy shit later, escape now," Rhi says. "Go!"

"Right." I sheathe the blade and yank the door open.

If we ever choose to invade enemy territory—which we don't—I would choose Zolya as my first target. Take out Cliffsbane Academy and you take out *years* of gryphon riders in one strike.

—Tactics, a Personal Memoir
by Lieutenant Lyron Panchek

CHAPTER
TWENTY-FIVE

We race out of the cave and into the morning air, the rising sun hitting us in the face. Throwing up our hands to shield our eyes, we run forward into the knee-high grass that spans the distance from the cliffs to the trees.

"Where did you get those knives?" Rhiannon asks when we're halfway to the line of oaks.

"Xaden." It doesn't even occur to me to lie. "He had them made for me—"

"Well, this is an unexpected delight," Professor Grady says from behind us.

We spin, and I draw two daggers. I'd rather visit Malek than go back into that chamber. But I will...for the final exam.

"Think about that later," Tairn commands.

"I'm fine, thanks for asking."

"Of course you are. I chose well."

Professor Grady grins and sets down his mug as he rises from the chair that sits a few feet away from the door against the rocky cliffside.

Rhiannon strides forward, lifting her sword in attack position with her right arm and extending her left hand. "We'll take that patch now."

• • •

Dain doesn't look me in the eye at any point over the next few days, and I don't make the effort to talk to him. What could I even say? *Thank you for doing the only decent thing and not violating my privacy?*

"I'm just saying that spending every weekend flying for Samara or holed up in your room with Riorson isn't good for you," Ridoc says as we climb the staircase of the academic wing with the crowd headed for Battle Brief.

"As opposed to…" I glance over at him and wince. His cheek is still black and blue.

Thanks to Nolon, there's not a mark on me. It's anything but fair.

We lost a first-year, Trysten, to Gauntlet practice while we were in interrogation and missed the formation where they called his name on the death roll, too. That isn't fair, either.

"Being a normal second-year and spending some time blowing off a little steam every now and then," Sawyer answers for Ridoc from my other side. Ever since the interrogation, my squadmates have barely let me out of their sight.

"I'm fine," I tell them both. "This is just what happens when mated dragons bond to riders in different years." Twenty-four hours from now, I'll be in the saddle on my way to Xaden.

"It's why they usually *don't* do it," Ridoc mutters.

"First Squad lost someone," Rhiannon says, coming up behind us as we reach the second floor. "They just came out of interrogation about an hour ago. Sorrel's name will be on the death roll tomorrow."

My heart drops. The interrogation assessment has now taken two second-years.

"The girl with the kick-ass bow skills?" Sawyer gapes at Rhiannon as she scoots between us.

"Yeah," she says quietly.

A scribe cadet walks by, but I can't see who it is with the hood up. That's odd. Usually they're only in the quadrant for death roll or whenever Markham needs extra people.

"Did she break?" Ridoc asks. "Or did they break *her*?"

"I don't—" Rhiannon's words stop short, and so do we when two First Wing squads move off the wall and into our path. "Can we help you?"

They're all second-years. I drop my hands to my sides, close to my daggers.

"You guys escaped, right?" Caroline Ashton asks, lowering her voice. "That's what people are saying about the new patch." She taps beside her own shoulder, where we now wear a circular, silver patch with a black key.

"It's a classified patch," Sawyer says.

"We just want to know how you did it," Caroline whispers as the crowd pushes by us on the side to get to the briefing room. "Rumor is, it took them an entire day to reset the interrogation room after you guys."

The fact that she calls it a room and not *rooms* lets me know no one is really talking.

"All we can tell you is the same advice you've already been given. Don't break," Rhiannon tells them.

"Stick together," I add, holding Caroline's gaze even when she narrows it on me.

"Shouldn't you all be in Battle Brief?" Bodhi asks, his voice booming as he comes up behind us. One look sends the other squads scurrying for the door.

"Tairn told me he felt Sgaeyl get *very* angry last night," I say over my shoulder to Bodhi as we continue walking. "Anything I should know about?"

"Not that I'm aware of." We separate as we walk through the wide double doors into the briefing room.

My squadmates and I start down the steps, but something is off. The usual hum of the briefing room is approaching a roar of murmurs and outright exclamations as cadets pick up what look to be leaflets lying on every seat.

"What's happening?" Ridoc asks.

"Not sure," I answer as we bypass the first cadets in our row and find our way to our seats.

I pick up the half sheet of parchment on my chair and flip it over as my squadmates do the same.

My knees weaken as I read the headline.

ZOLYA FALLS TO DRAGON FIRE

THE THIRD LARGEST CITY IN THE BRAEVICK PROVINCE HAS FALLEN TO THE BLUE FIRE DRAGONS AND THEIR RIDERS. THOUGH THE CITY AND ITS DRIFTS FOUGHT VALIANTLY, THE TWO-DAY BATTLE ENDED IN POROMISH DEFEAT. ALL WHO DID NOT EVACUATE HAVE PERISHED. AN ESTIMATED TEN THOUSAND LIVES HAVE BEEN LOST, INCLUDING GENERAL FENELLA, THE COMMANDER OF BRAEVICK'S GRYPHON FLEET. ALL TRADE ROUTES TO THE CITY HAVE BEEN BARRICADED TO PREVENT FURTHER LOSS OF LIFE.

Two days ago.

My hand trembles, and I twist around toward the back of the room, my gaze jumping from one third-year to the next until I find Bodhi and Imogen.

"Oh gods," Rhiannon whispers beside me.

Bodhi and Imogen exchange a panicked look, and then our gazes collide. What the hell are we supposed to do? Bodhi's tense shake of his head tells me he doesn't know, either.

Drawing the least amount of attention to myself seems prudent, so I turn back to face the map and slide into my seat.

"Is this real?" Sawyer asks, turning over the parchment to examine it.

"Looks…real?" Ridoc scratches the back of his neck as he sits. "Is this some kind of test to see if we can discern official proclamation leaflets from propaganda?"

"I don't think so," Rhiannon says slowly, staring at me.

But my eyes are locked on the recessed floor and Professor Devera, who has just been handed a leaflet.

Please be who I think you are.

Her eyes widen, but I only see them for a second before she turns to face the map, her head tilted back. I'd bet my life that she's staring right where I am now, at the little circle at the foot of the Esben Mountains along the Stonewater River that marks where Zolya stands—*stood*. It's maybe a four-hour flight from our border.

"Violet?" Rhiannon's voice rises, like it's not the first time she's called my name.

"What is all the commotion this morning?" Markham shouts over the briefing room as he descends the steps. Someone hands him a leaflet.

"What do you think?" Rhiannon asks.

I glance from my squadmate's furrowed brows to the leaflet and force the roaring in my ears to quiet as I make a quick study of the parchment. "Parchment looks like ours, but I've never personally seen any made outside the border. Typeset is standard to every printing press I've ever seen. There's no seal, Navarrian or Poromish." I run my thumb over the larger, scrolling block letters of the headline, smudging the ink. "It's less than twenty-four hours old. The ink hasn't cured."

"But is it *real*?" Sawyer repeats his earlier question.

"The chances of someone hauling in all these leaflets from the border are next to nothing," I tell him. "So if you're asking if it was printed in Poromiel—"

My head jerks up, and I see Markham's face blotch red as he says something to Caroline Ashton on the aisle. She jumps from her seat and runs up the stairs, disappearing through the door.

"It was printed here," I whisper, fear twisting my stomach into knots. Whoever did it is as good as dead if they left any trace.

"So it's not real." Sawyer lifts his eyebrows, the freckles on his forehead disappearing into the grooves of his skin.

"Just because it's printed here for public dissemination doesn't mean what's on it isn't real," I explain, "but it also doesn't mean that it is."

"We wouldn't do this," Sawyer argues. "There's no way we send a riot to annihilate a city of civilians."

"Attention!" Markham shouts, his footsteps thudding as he strides down the steps.

The noise doesn't dissipate.

"If someone was trying to get news out, they'd send one leaflet like this to the printing press to be approved by scribes," I tell my squadmates quickly, knowing our time is short. "Once approved, it would take hours to set the blocks to print unless multiple scribes worked on it. But this isn't official. There's no seal. So either it's fake and printed for just this class—which is *a lot* of work—or it's real…and not approved." It's exactly what I would say if I didn't know the truth, and to be honest, I'm not certain this leaflet *is* the truth.

"Riders!" Devera yells, turning to face us. "Quiet!"

The room falls silent.

Markham's at the front of the classroom now, his features schooled in a mask of serenity as he stands beside Professor Devera. If I didn't know him better, I'd say he was almost enjoying the chaos, but I do, and he's rubbing his forefinger against his thumb.

No matter what he says next, this wasn't his plan.

"Apparently"—he gestures to us, his palm facing upward—"we are not ready for today's exercise. We were going to follow up on our discussion about propaganda, but I can see now that I overestimated your ability to judge a simple printing like this without hysteria." The insult is delivered in unemotional monotone.

Suddenly, I feel fifteen again, my self-worth determined by this man's opinion of my intellect and control.

"Damn." Ridoc sags in his seat. "That's…harsh."

"That's Markham," I say quietly. "You think only riders can be vicious? Words are just as capable of eviscerating someone as a blade, and he's a master."

"On the off chance that we actually did this and someone leaked the information?" Rhiannon asks, glancing my way. "You know him better than we do. What's his next move?"

"First, I don't think we'd target civilians across the border." That's the truth. We just won't do anything to help them, either. "But if he didn't print the leaflets, he'll discredit, deflect, then distract."

"As it is, we have two much more pressing matters to discuss," Markham lectures, his tone still cool. "So, you will now pass all pieces of propaganda to the left, where they will be collected to discuss on a day when you're capable of being rational."

A ripple passes over the room as everyone hurries to do as he asks. I'm reluctant to let mine go, but it's not worth drawing attention.

Professor Devera folds hers with quick, precise movements and pockets it.

"Honestly." Markham shakes his head. "You should have been able to spot those leaflets as propaganda within seconds."

Discredit. I have to admit, he's good. The stacks reach the ends of the rows, and then the cadets hand them forward, the pile growing and growing as it descends toward the floor.

"When, in the history of Navarre, have we ever flown a riot comprised only of blue dragons?" He looks us over like we're children. Like we've been found wanting.

Clever. He's so fucking clever. With the leaflets collected, every cadet in the room will question the exact wording. Every cadet except the riders who know the meaning of that entire paragraph came down to the placement of the word *fire*.

"But as I said." Markham claps his hands together and sighs. "We'll return to this lesson when we're ready. Right now, our first order of business is here, and celebration is in order."

Deflection complete. Cue distraction.

"I wasn't sure this day would come, which is why I hope that you'll forgive us for keeping the months of Colonel Nolon's hard work a secret. We didn't want to disappoint you if he could not pull off what will arguably be the greatest achievement of any mender in our history."

Didn't want to disappoint us? I barely manage to keep from rolling my eyes.

Markham raises his hand toward the doorway and smiles. "He was crushed under the weight of a mountain a few months ago, but Nolon has mended bone after bone to return him to your quadrant."

Crushed under the weight of a mountain? It can't be. My stomach hollows, and the noise of the room muffles under the sound of my own blood rushing through my ears to the cadence of a drum.

"No fucking way," Ridoc says, breaking through my panic.

"Tairn?" I can't bring myself to look.

"Checking now." The clipped, tense tone reminds me of Resson.

"Join me in welcoming back your fellow rider, Jack Barlowe!" Markham claps. The entire briefing room joins in, the loudest cheers coming from First Wing as two figures walk down the stairs.

Breathe. In. Out. I force air through my lungs as Rhiannon grasps my hand and holds tight.

"It's him," Rhiannon says. "It's really *him*."

"You brought down an entire cliff on his unhinged ass." Sawyer claps slowly, but it's only for show. "How the fuck was there anything left to mend?"

Dragging my gaze left, I finally work up the courage to look.

Same bulky frame. Same blond hair. Same profile. Same hands that nearly killed me during a challenge last year…before I killed him during War Games the first time my signet flared.

He turns a few rows down, walking past other second-years as Caroline Ashton escorts him back to his squad. It all makes sense now. The secrecy. Her visiting the infirmary. Nolon's exhaustion.

Jack pivots as he reaches an empty seat, turning slowly and nodding as the applause carries on. The look on his face is almost humble, like a man who's received a second chance he definitely doesn't deserve, and then he pivots, looking up the rows to find me.

Glacial blue eyes meet mine. Any doubt I had dies a swift death. It's him. My pounding heart jumps into my throat.

"Maybe he learned his lesson?" Rhiannon's voice pitches high with empty hope.

"No," Ridoc says, letting his hands fall to his lap. "He's definitely going to try to kill you. Again."

Menders are not healers. Healers are bound to the Code of Chricton, sworn to aide all in time of need and never to harm a beating heart. Menders are riders. They're only sworn to the Codex. They can as easily bring harm as heal.

—MAJOR FREDERICK'S MODERN GUIDE FOR HEALERS

CHAPTER TWENTY-SIX

"Not helping!" Rhiannon hisses as we all stare at Jack-fucking-Barlowe. A small, almost soft smile curves his mouth for an instant, and we fall silent as he nods at me then looks away quickly before he takes his seat.

"What the fuck was that?" Ridoc asks.

"I have no idea." It's the first time since Parapet he's looked at me with anything but pure malice.

"It's him," Tairn growls. *"Baide has kept the truth hidden for these months."*

"I can see him." I'd ask how the fuck a dragon hides something in the Vale, but Andarna isn't exactly common knowledge, either.

"Be aware of him at all times," Tairn warns.

Rhiannon squeezes my hand as she shifts in her seat. "Maybe a few months of being dead has changed him."

"Maybe." Sawyer's eyes narrow as he stares holes in the back of Jack's head. "But I think we're better off killing him again."

"I'm down with that plan," Ridoc agrees.

"Let's focus on keeping an eye on him," I suggest, forcing my voice past the knot in my throat as the applause finally dies down, allowing me to put my thoughts in order.

Jack is alive. Fine. He's hardly the worst thing I faced last year. I brought down not only one but two venin. I destroyed an entire horde of wyvern with Xaden. Maybe Jack's changed. Maybe he hasn't. Either way, my signet and hand-to-hand skills have only improved, and I doubt he's been sparring in the infirmary.

Ridoc, Sawyer, and Rhiannon all stare at me like there's a chance I might grow a tail and start breathing fire at any second. "I'm all right," I tell them. "Seriously. Stop staring." I don't have the option of not being all right.

They shoot me skeptical looks of varying degrees, then face forward.

Markham clears his throat. "Now, to our second matter of business for the hour." He looks over at Professor Devera.

"Yesterday evening, there was an unprecedented attack on one of our largest outposts," she says, her shoulders straightening as she scans the room.

"Again?" Rhiannon mutters. "What the hell is going on out there?" She releases my hand and starts to take notes.

A murmur rises among the cadets.

Focus. I have to focus.

"And this, cadets, is no conjecture. No propaganda. No game." That last word is said with a sideways glance at Markham. "It's unprecedented not only in its proximity—we've never had outposts attacked this close together before—but also because it involved three drifts." She lifts her pointed chin.

I glance up at the map, forcing my mind to work. Pelham near the Cygni border is my first guess, but Keldavi—along the Braevick border—is a close second after it nearly fell last week. Maybe the fliers are recognizing our weaknesses.

"They attacked Samara a little after sundown, while most of the riot was wrapping up the day's patrol."

The breath freezes in my lungs and my heart stutters. She has my full, undivided attention. Who cares if Jack Barlowe is seated beneath me or if papers are flying around with Poromish news? None of that matters more than whatever Professor Devera is about to say.

They're alive. They have to be.

I can't begin to fathom a world without Mira…and Xaden? My heart can't comprehend the possibility.

Oh gods, Sgaeyl's anger. I drop my shields completely, searching for a bond I wouldn't be able to feel from this far anyway. Still, I search.

"Tairn?" I reach out, but anxiety floods my bloodstream, overpowering every logical thought. It's not mine, but it may as well be. My heart begins to pound, and my ribs close in on my lungs.

"The outpost was successfully defended by the three riders who were *not* on patrol. Their victory is nothing short of astonishing. While no riders were killed in the assault"—her gaze snaps to mine—"there was one rider severely wounded."

No. The denial is sharp and fast.

Rage and terror pump through my veins.

Professor Devera lifts her hand and scratches the left side of her neck before looking away. "What questions would you ask?"

The *left* side of her neck.

Right where Xaden's relic is.

Mira's all right, but Xaden… I can't be here. It's impossible to be here when I have to be there. There's no reality outside of me being there. Here doesn't mean anything. Doesn't exist.

"I have to go." I grab my bag from the floor and shove the strap over my shoulder.

"Was the outpost breached?" someone in front of me asks.

"Vi?" Rhi reaches for me, but I'm already standing, moving down the row toward the staircase.

"Cadet Sorrengail!" Professor Markham calls out.

There's no time to answer him as I climb the stairs. No world outside the impossible-to-ignore drive that propels me up. My body isn't even my own because I'm not here.

"Cadet Sorrengail!" Markham yells as I leave the briefing room. "You do not have leave!"

"Get to the courtyard," Tairn rumbles through my mind.

We're on the same page, neither of us willing to wait for me to walk to the flight field. It doesn't matter if the uncontrollable urge is coming from me or Tairn, not when we both need the same thing.

"Violet!" someone shouts after me. Bootsteps race down the hall.

Jack Barlowe is alive. I whip a dagger from my thigh sheath and spin toward the threat.

"Whoa!" Bodhi throws up one hand, the other clutching his rucksack. "I don't want you to freeze to death on the flight there." He yanks his flight jacket out of his pack and hands it to me.

"Thank you." I take the jacket with motions that don't feel like my own. He's right. I would have climbed onto Tairn without a jacket. At least I carry my flight goggles in my bag at all times. "I can't stay. I can't explain. I can't be here."

"It's Tairn." He nods. "Go."

I go.

By their third year, a rider must attain full and complete control over their shields. Otherwise, in moments of extreme stress, they are susceptible to being not only influenced by their dragon's emotions but controlled by them.

—COLONEL KAORI'S FIELD GUIDE TO DRAGONKIND

CHAPTER TWENTY-SEVEN

By the time we land at Samara just before nightfall, I'm a jittery, frantic mess. I can't bring myself to care about whatever retribution waits for me at Basgiath. I'll handle whatever punishment Varrish wants to dish out.

I've spent every minute of the eight-hour flight trying to separate my feelings from Tairn's, but I can't, and he's definitively in primal mode.

He has to be the reason there's a hollow pit in my stomach threatening to devour all logical thought if I don't set eyes on Xaden in the next minute. It's Tairn's desperation to see Sgaeyl unharmed making my heart pound, not my own concern for Xaden. After all, if he was at death's door, Sgaeyl would have told us once we flew close enough for them to communicate. At least that's what the barely functioning logical part of my brain is telling me.

This is all Tairn. But what if it isn't? How seriously has Xaden been wounded?

Sgaeyl may have told Tairn that Xaden lives and I could see how bad it was for myself, but I'm still counting every second it takes the guards to raise the portcullis. The increased security is protocol and completely reasonable given yesterday's attack, but every moment that ticks by grates on my last nerve.

Just because I logically know Tairn is still flooding my emotions doesn't mean I can control them.

The second the portcullis is high enough for me to duck under, I do so. For once, my size works to my advantage. I'm inside the outpost before it's even a quarter of the way open.

Organized chaos reigns within. Chunks of masonry ranging from half my size to double it lay scattered around the courtyard, and a quick glance upward is all it takes to see where they fell from. There are scorch marks on the northern wall, too. The fliers must have breached the perimeter.

The healers work a triage station on the southern end of the fortress, the area around them thick with wounded infantry. But there are no black uniforms among the blue. No cream, either.

"Violet?" Mira calls out, emerging from the northwestern staircase I know leads to their operations room. No limp, no slings, no blood that I can see. She's all right. Just like Devera said, only one has been wounded, and it's not Mira.

"Where is he?" I yank my flight goggles from the top of my head and shove them into my bag without breaking my stride.

"What are you doing here?" She grabs hold of my shoulders, looking me over with her customary inspection. "You're not supposed to arrive until Saturday."

"Are you unharmed?"

"Yes." She nods. "I wasn't here. I was out on patrol."

"Good, then tell me where he is." My tone sharpens as my gaze swings wildly, looking for him. Fuck, I can't even sense him with Tairn overriding everything.

"You don't have leave, do you? Gods, you're going to be so fucked when you get back." She sighs. Have to give it to Mira, she doesn't fight battles she can't win. "He's in the sparring gym. From what I hear, your man is the reason we still have an outpost."

He's not mine. Not really.

"Thank you." I turn away from her without another word and head for the sparring gym. I love her, I'm thankful she's all right, but all of that is buried underneath the desperation clawing at my soul to lay eyes on Xaden.

The fortress is busy with recovery efforts, but the hall to the gym is deserted. Why would they have taken him to the gym for recovery? Is he unable to climb the steps to his room? That pit in my stomach deepens. How badly is he hurt?

The mage lights more than make up for the dying evening light outside the three oversize windows when I enter the gym. But there's certainly no makeshift infirmary in here.

Wait. What? I blink.

Xaden is on the mat in his short-sleeved, muscle-hugging sparring uniform. He has both his heavy swords out, metal clanging against metal as he spars with Garrick.

"You're slow today," Xaden lectures, advancing mercilessly. He moves like he always does, with lethal expertise and complete concentration. There's zero chance he's even *close* to seriously wounded. The burst of relief lets me draw my first full breath since leaving Basgiath, but it quickly fades.

Hands on him. I need my hands on him.

"Not. Much. I can do. About. That!" Garrick argues, blocking Xaden's advances.

"Get faster." Xaden lands blow after deliberate blow, deftly avoiding taking any himself. Each swing of those swords shifts the worry, the abject terror that he'd been *hurt*, into rage.

He's unharmed, and I'm a fucking fool for letting my emotions run amok, for letting my love for him overrule my common sense. That's on me, not Tairn.

But the wildness I can't breathe through? That's a hundred percent black morningstartail, and I can't break free, can't raise my shields enough to own myself.

I step into Xaden's line of sight, my toes hitting the edge of the mat.

Xaden glances toward me, and his eyes widen for all of a heartbeat before he nails Garrick in the face with his elbow, sending him tumbling to the ground. *Ouch.*

Garrick sprawls across the mat, his swords slipping from his hands. "Damn!"

"We're done," Xaden says without even looking back, already headed toward me, eating up the half dozen feet that separate us with those long, prowling strides of his. "I had my shields up. What are you doing here?" His eyes widen, like he can feel the chaos within me. "Violence, are you all right?"

"What am I doing here?" I bite out each word as my eyes rake over him, looking for the wounds Devera spoke of. Did I misinterpret her gesture? Did I really just fly here for *nothing*? My hands begin to shake. "I have no fucking clue!"

"This isn't you." His gaze sweeps over me.

"I know that!" I shout, torn between weeping with gratitude that he's alive and seemingly unhurt and destroying this entire gym — this entire fortress — because he was ever put in danger. "I can't get him out!"

"Hold on." He shoves my pack off my shoulders, and it falls to the gym floor before he sweeps me up against his chest.

I wrap my arms around him and shove my face into his neck, breathing in deep. He smells like mint and leather and mine — For fuck's sake, am I scenting him?

Xaden walks us straight into the gym's bathing chamber, and I get a quick glimpse of polished stone walls; high, glazed windows partially cracked open; and a row of wide benches under the center of three lines of spouts, not dissimilar to the ones at Basgiath. With a flick of his fingers, the door slams shut, and then he works a lever on the wall. Water streams from the spout in the aqueduct overhead, soaking us both in what feels like *ice*.

I gasp, my body tensing with the shock of the bitter cold, and for that heartbeat, it's all I'm capable of feeling.

"Put your shields up," Xaden orders. "Now, Violet!"

I claw through the glacier of my mind and shove the bricks of my shields into place. Tairn's emotions dull enough for me to claim some semblance of control. "Fucking. Cold," I say, my teeth chattering.

"There we go." Xaden flips another lever and the water warms. "What the hell happened that they gave you leave to come early?" Concern lines the area between his brows as he sets me on my feet, water spraying down on us.

My mind is mine again, though I can feel the intensity of Tairn's emotions beating at my shields.

"They didn't give me leave—"

"You didn't get leave?" His voice lowers to that dangerous tone that terrifies everyone in the world besides me. "When you already know that Varrish is going to—" His words die abruptly as his focus drops to my shoulder. "Who the fuck's flight jacket are you wearing?"

"Really?" I throw my arms out, happily letting the warmth soak into me. "It has third-year rank, Fourth Wing insignia, and a section leader designation. Who the hell's jacket do you *think* I'm wearing?"

His jaw ticks, water streaming down his face.

"It's Bodhi's, you territorial asshole!"

That answer doesn't seem to help.

"Are you serious right now?" I unbutton the fucking jacket and tug at the sleeves, but leather is a bitch when wet, and it takes a moment to yank it free. "I ran out of Battle Brief the second Devera clued me in that you'd been *wounded*. Yes, I left without leave. Then I flew eight hours at breakneck speed with an absolutely irrational Tairn, who thought if you'd been hurt, then Sgaeyl could have been, too. And now you pull some possessive, jealous, *whose-jacket-is-that* bullshit just because your cousin knew I was so panicked that I wouldn't stop for my own flight leathers?" I flat-out glare at his nonsensical ass and drop the jacket to the floor. "You can fuck right off!"

A corner of his mouth turns up. "You were worried about me?"

"Not anymore, I'm not." I see *red*. How can he find this amusing?

"But you were." A slow smile spreads across his face, and his eyes light up. "You were worried about me." He reaches for me.

"Do you think this is funny?" I step back out of his reach only to find the water-slick wall at my back.

"No." He cocks his head to the side, his smile slipping. "You seem a little angry that I'm not at Malek's doorstep. Would you rather I be bleeding to death in the infirmary?"

"No!" Of course he doesn't get it. His life might depend on mine, but he doesn't feel the way I do about him. He wants me, even said he fell for me, but he's never said he loves me. "I'm not mad at you for not being hurt. I would *never* want you hurt. I'm pissed at myself for being so reckless, so wrapped up in you, having such little control over my emotions that I just ran after you like… like…" Like a lovesick little fool. "And you, you're *always* calm, collected, and in control. You would have waited for all the information, and you sure as hell never, ever would have let Sgaeyl's emotions take over—"

My words die as Xaden wrenches up the wet sleeve on his right arm, exposing a puckered, angry red line that stretches from the top of his shoulder to halfway down his biceps. It's an inch thick at the top and triple that where it ends. He's obviously been mended, and if the scar is still *that* raised, he must have almost lost his arm.

"You really were wounded," I whisper, all the anger falling out of my body. My chest clenches; it must have hurt like hell. "Are you all right?" The question tumbles out even though I've just seen him demolish an opponent.

"I'm fine. The scribe's report must have gone out before the mender arrived from the Eastern Wing." The scar disappears as he tugs the sleeve back down. "And you're wrong about me. I wouldn't have waited for all the information—or even proof—if I'd heard you'd been hurt." This time, I don't step away when he reaches for me. His arm winds around my waist, and his hand splays on the small of my back to guide us out of the water's direct spray. The inches between us are both a gift and a curse as he leans in. "I'm not always calm or collected, and I'm *never* in control when it comes to you."

My heart leaps at his words, at the ever-present tension that rises between us, at the awareness that spreads through me from that single touch. It's not just the water warming me.

"Even now, I'm not doing what I should." His words come out clipped.

"Which is?"

"Hauling your ass to the mat until you're a hot, sweaty, aching mess from a dozen rounds of sparring." His jaw ticks. "Because I warned you never to put your life at risk over something as trivial as talking to me, and yet you did just that. Again."

"I'm down with everything but the sparring." Shit. That comes out breathless. "And it's not up to you to punish me anymore. I'm no longer in your chain of command."

"Oh, I know. And somehow it was a hell of a lot easier on us both when you were. You want full disclosure when it comes to me, right? How is this for open?" His gaze drops to my mouth. "I would have done the same thing you did because I'm just as reckless for you as you are for me."

A sharp, sweet ache consumes my chest. Gods, I want to believe that. But I also want more. I want the same three words he demands from me. I run my tongue over my bottom lip, and his eyes flare as steam fills the room.

"You were worried for *me*." The first time he said it came out amused. The second sounded happy. But this time, his tone shifts as if it's a revelation.

"Of course I was worried for you."

He draws me forward slowly, giving me every chance to object before bringing our bodies flush. The heat of him soaks into every chilled part of me, and all the burning worry I'd felt on the flight here and the searing anger that followed transforms into an entirely different—and far more dangerous—form of heat.

Fuck, I want him. I want to touch every inch of his skin, feel his heartbeat against mine in assurance that he's really all right. I want his body over me, inside me, as close as humanly possible. I want him to make me forget there's anything beyond this room or the two of us.

"And you flew here without even stopping to get your leathers." He lowers his head inch by torturously slow inch.

I nod.

"Because you still love me," he whispers against my lips a heartbeat before he kisses me. Thank gods he doesn't wait for my denial, because I'm not sure I have it in me to give one, not with the way he toys with my bottom lip, nipping it gently, then stroking his tongue over the curve. It feels too good, too right, too…everything.

It's the first time since Aretia that he hasn't waited for me to ask. The first time his infamous self-control has slipped. The first time he's gambled with possible rejection, kissed me simply because he wanted to, and fuck, that's exactly what I need—for him to need *me*.

I part my lips in invitation not just because I want him, but because he's acting on a confession I didn't have to pry out of him or even ask for. He groans, his arms surrounding me, and the kiss becomes exactly what he called himself—reckless. The feel of his tongue flicking against mine, then claiming, stroking, is a flame to a tinderbox, and I catch fire.

Need, lust, desire—whatever it is—dances down my spine and gathers, becoming an insistent ache between my thighs. Rising on my toes to get closer, I loop my arms around his neck, but we're still not close enough.

His hands work the buttons of my uniform, and I reluctantly relinquish my grip so he can slide it off. It smacks onto the floor somewhere to the left. I tug on his shirt, desperate for the feel of him, and he obliges, grabbing hold of it behind his neck and dragging it overhead, revealing miles and miles of warm, wet skin.

I kiss the scar right above his heart and stroke my hands down his sides, my fingers tracing the hard dips and grooves along his stomach. There is nothing in this world that compares to him. He is complete, utter perfection, his body carved from years of sparring and flight.

"Violet." He tilts my head and kisses me hard and deep, then slow and soft, changing the pace, keeping me straining for more.

My hands trace the lines of his back as he spears his fingers through the wet, loosened strands of my braid, then tugs, arching my neck before setting his mouth to it.

He knows exactly where I'm sensitive and *damn* does he use every bit of that knowledge, sucking and laving that spot at the side of my throat that melts my knees and makes my fingers curl against his skin.

"Xaden," I whimper, my hands sliding over the curve of his ass. Mine. This man is mine—at least for right now. Even if it's just these next few minutes.

He nips at the delicate skin of my ear, sending a shudder of sensation down my spine, and then his mouth is on mine again, stealing my sanity and replacing it with pure need. This kiss isn't as patient, as controlled as the others. There's a wild, carnal edge to it that makes my mouth curve against his, makes me bolder. I sweep my hand between us, then sigh.

He's hard for me, the length of him straining against his waistband as I squeeze.

"Fuck," he growls, ripping his mouth from mine, his breaths as ragged as mine as I stroke him through the fabric. "If you keep doing that…" He slams his eyes shut and lets his head fall back.

"I'll actually get you?" My core clenches.

His gaze snaps to mine, and the conflict I see in those dark depths makes me pause.

"Don't make me fight for this. Not again." I retreat from the warmth of his arms, and every nerve in my body screams in protest. "I can't always be the one fighting for this while you invent new ways to hesitate or tell me no, Xaden. You either want me or you don't."

"You just had your hand wrapped around my cock, Violet. I'm pretty sure you felt how fucking badly I want you." He rips his hand through his wet hair. "Gods, I *am* the one fighting for this!" he argues, gesturing between us. "I told you, I'm not using sex as a weapon to get you back."

"You'll just weaponize it with your little rule to make me say the three words I'm not ready to give you." And that edge of maddening need he has me riding is just sharp enough that I might cave, I crave him that fucking much.

"Weaponize it against you?" He shakes his head. "You told me that you can't separate emotion from sex. Remember?"

I open, then shut my mouth. He's right. I did say that. *Shit.* "Maybe I'm learning how."

"Maybe I don't want you to." He takes a step forward and cups the back of my neck. "I want you exactly how you are, emotions and all. I want the woman I fell for. It kills me every time I have to keep my hands off you, every night I lie awake next to you, both blessed and damned with the memory of how hot, how wet, how fucking *perfect* you feel when I'm losing myself in you."

My lips part and heat flushes my skin as if his words are an actual caress.

"When I do sleep, I dream of the sounds you make right before you come and the way the blue in your eyes outshines the amber right after, all sated and hazy. I wake up starving for you—only you—even on the mornings you're halfway across the kingdom. This isn't me denying you or manipulating you. This is me fighting for you." He palms my hip, and his thumb strokes the bare strip of skin between my pants and my armor.

"You want to fight for me?" I reach up into my hair and pull the pins loose one by one, letting them fall to the stone floor. "Then take a chance *without* knowing how I feel. You want my heart back? Risk yours first this time."

"If I tell you how I feel right now, you'd never trust that I'm not just desperate for your body." His brow furrows.

"Exactly my point." The last pin falls from my hair. "Choose, Xaden. You can let me walk out that door, or you can be the one who takes what I'm willing to give this time." I shake my hair loose and run my fingers through the wet mass to unravel the braid.

"Are you trying to bring me to my knees? Or win the argument?" His hand flexes at my hip as his heated gaze sweeps over me.

"Yes," I answer, reaching for the ties at the small of my back that secure my armor. "I just spent eight hours terrified of what condition I'd find you in, and I'm telling you that I don't just want you. I *need* you. There are your three words." I tug the wet string, and it gives. "That's all you get. Take me or leave me."

The fight within him is palpable, the tension between us sharp enough to pierce dragon scale. And for a second, I think he might just be stubborn enough to walk away and keep us at this impasse.

But then—thank gods—he breaks, fusing his mouth to mine, and the fire that had banked during our argument flares back to life even hotter than before. He kisses me like I'm the answer to every question. Like everything we've been and will be hinges on this moment. And maybe it does.

His hands work the laces at my back while I undo the buttons of his pants. I win the race, sliding my hand beneath the fabric to stroke him from root to tip.

The guttural groan he gives me feels like a reward and hits straight between my thighs, the ache intensifying to a throb.

"Let go so I can get you naked." He punctuates that last word with a nip of my lower lip.

Yes, please. I free him, and he pulls my armor loose enough to tug it over my head. It smacks the ground, and a second later the sensitive peak of my breast is surrounded by his mouth, flicked by his tongue. I moan, my fingers tunneling through his hair to hold him right there. "That feels so damned good."

Wrapping an arm around my back and the other behind my knees, he lifts, then lays me onto a water-warmed stone bench in one smooth motion. "You sure you want this here, *now*?" he asks, rising above me, blocking the spray of water from my breasts, his eyes hooded and his hair mussed from my hands. "In five minutes, I can have you comfortable in my bed."

He's so beautiful that my heart actually hurts from just looking at him.

"Now." My hands stroke his wide shoulders and down the relic that winds from his jaw to his forearm.

"Now," he agrees. There's nothing practiced or polished about the next kiss—it's all need sweetened with a desperation that matches my own, and all the hotter for it. This is exactly what I need, to be pressed between his hard body and stone, devoured with the same urgency I feel for him.

His hand skims down my curves, following the dip of my waist before skimming my waistband and undoing the buttons of my pants one by one. There's no hesitation in his touch when his fingers delve and stroke from my entrance to my clit.

My back arches and I gasp with white-hot pleasure.

"Even hotter than I remember." His mouth moves down my neck, overwhelming me with sensation as his fingers tease with featherlight touches. "Fuck, you feel like silk. Hot, slick silk." His voice has that rough rasp to it that I've missed.

He moves lower to worship my breasts with his mouth, his teeth raking lightly over my nipple with the perfect amount of friction to build the pleasure coiling tight within me. Of course he knows what I like. This isn't our first time. It's not going to be our last, either.

Power swells under my skin and builds as he circles my swollen clit, denying me the pressure I need.

"Xaden," I beg, my nails biting into the tops of his shoulders, but I'm careful not to brush his new scar. Every stroke of his fingers and flick of his tongue feels like a jolt of lightning through my system, electrifying every nerve until I'm a hypersensitive bowstring drawn too tight but not tight enough.

"I know exactly what you want"—he skims my clit—"and what you need." Two fingers slide inside me.

Deeper. Closer. More. That's what I need.

"Then give it to me," I demand, my hips rolling.

"I've waited forever to touch you."

My breaths come in ragged pants and moans, and my skin flushes, heat prickling as he builds the aching pressure with tighter, faster strokes.

"Gods, look at you. You are all I'm ever going to want. Just you. Just this. Just us." His voice curls around my mind until he's all I see, all I hear, all I feel and think. He's everything, watching me like he thinks the same about me.

"I need you." Maybe need isn't the right word, but there's no other term that captures how essential he is to my existence. I shove my thumbs into the waistband of my pants and push. I need them off, *now*.

"Same." We're a frenzy of questing hands and mouths as we struggle out of the rest of our wet clothes. I have a whole new reason to curse these boots, but Xaden makes quick work of them, stripping me bare.

I ghost my lips over the new scar on his arm, more than aware of how close I came to losing him, and then he's over me again, bracing his weight on his forearms, his eyes studying mine with an intensity that makes me shiver with anticipation as he settles between my thighs.

Reaching between our bodies, I wrap my fingers around him, bringing the head of his cock to my entrance. I'll die if he makes me wait any longer. I won't survive another breath without him inside me.

"I need you more, Violet." He cradles the side of my face and rolls his hips, pushing inside, stretching me as he consumes those first sensitive inches. "However much you think you need this, need me—I need you *more*." He thrusts, filling me with one long drive, until he's so deep that my eyes flutter closed, and I moan with the sublime pleasure.

There's nothing like this in the world. I'm sure of it.

"So. Fucking. Good." He echoes my thoughts with a groan, and then he's moving, withdrawing only to slam home again and again, stealing my stuttered breaths with kiss after kiss. The stone at my back gives me the leverage to arch into his thrusts, taking him deeper. It's too much, too good, and not enough all at the same time.

Each powerful stroke has me greedy for more. This is where I want to exist, with him above me, moving inside me, his focus totally, completely mine. *"Harder. Deeper."* I'm breathing too hard to speak. *"Don't treat me like I'm breakable."*

"I know exactly how much you can take." He slides his hands under me, then holds me to his chest as he rises, pivoting to sit on the edge of the bench.

My cry echoes in the chamber as I sink onto him, my knees anchoring on either side of his hips, and he hits that sweeter, deeper angle that steals my breath. *"Yes. There. Gods, I feel you everywhere."*

"Right where we left off." His hands shift to my ass. *"With you riding me."*

I wind my arms around his neck and smile against his mouth. No one is coming through those doors to interrupt us this time. There's only the sound of water hitting the bench beside us and our bodies coming together again and again, our hearts pounding, breaths strained between long, drugging kisses.

Reality narrows to sensation, the exquisite feel of his chest against my breasts, his mouth worshipping mine, his cock filling every inch I have, stretching me for more. The pressure coiling in my core is so tight, the pleasure so sweet I can taste it. It vibrates through me as my power rises, transforming me into pure, rapturous energy, until I'm the very lightning I wield, crackling in anticipation of the strike.

"More," he growls. "I want everything, Violet."

"You have it." His stubble scrapes my palms as I cup his face and kiss him. Lightning courses through me, building to a dangerous peak, and I don't need to ask. I know he has me.

It releases with a snap, flaring bright outside the windows for a heartbeat before it's swallowed by shadows that stream out to smother it. Nothing shatters. Nothing catches fire. He knows how my body reacts, knows exactly how to push me to the breaking point, and he has me covered when I explode.

I love him. I love him. I love him. I'm not ready to give him the words, the power that comes with them, but I can keep them for myself, chant them like my own personal Codex, the only truth I'm certain of.

His body tightens beneath mine, his thrusts coming harder as he curls an arm around me, hooking my shoulder and pulling me into every thrust.

That spiraling pressure arcs to a breaking point, and I fight, holding it at bay. Not yet. I want more. Fuck, I want to feel like this every minute of every day for the rest of my life.

"Let go." He shifts his angle, rubbing against my clit with the next thrust.

"I don't want it to end." I can hear the note of panic in my voice, the sharp note of fear that this will be the only time I feel like this, the only time he's mine. But the waves are coming closer with every roll of our hips, and my muscles tighten to the point of locking.

"Violet." His hand slides from my shoulder to the back of my neck, fisting in the long strands of my hair as he looks into my eyes like he can see straight to my soul. "I can't give this up. I *won't* give you up. Now let go."

My thighs tremble, and at the next thrust, I fracture with a cry. Lightning flashes, power tearing through me with instant thunder as the waves crest over me again and again. All I can do is hold on to Xaden and ride them out, bliss flooding my body until I'm too limp to rock back against him.

"Perfect." His restraint vanishes in an instant. Gone are the measured, precise thrusts. He growls into my neck and drives wildly with his hips, consuming me with abandon, and I realize that this is what I craved beyond anything else, even

beyond his secrets—his loss of control.

I want to be the only person he unravels for.

Holding on to his shoulders, I push back into every thrust, swiveling my hips and savoring the shout he lets loose when he finally shudders beneath me, his shadows blasting through the room. Rock cracks and water bursts from the aqueducts.

My heart races as I grin.

"Fuck." His forehead rests against mine, our chests heaving as we fight to catch our breath. "Just when I think I can handle you, I completely fucking lose it."

"That's my favorite part."

"Why does that not surprise me?" He brushes his lips over mine, and he locks his arms around me, keeping me from melting off his lap. "Death of me, I swear."

"What do we do now?" The question slips out before I can stop it. After all, I'm the one who's been fighting this—whatever this is.

"We have options." He caresses the side of my face and studies my eyes. "First, we can stay right here and go again. Second, we can clean up, get dressed, and sneak up to my room, where we can go again. Or third…" He pauses. "We can clean up, find a water wielder to dry our clothes, get you into one of my flight jackets, and fly to the rendezvous to drop the daggers—"

I'm up and running, grabbing for my clothes before he can even finish. Of course I'm going with him.

"I'm guessing that's a no to options one and two?" he says with a disappointed sigh.

Though gryphon riders are not capable of producing signets, they are not powerless. In fact, some would argue that they've honed lesser magic, especially mindwork, into the deadliest weapon of all. Underestimating them is an error.

—Gryphons of Poromiel, a Study in Combat by Major Garion Savoy

CHAPTER TWENTY-EIGHT

The thing about being two riders in an assumed relationship who happen to be bonded to a mated pair of dragons is that no one thinks twice about a midnight flight to get away, and there is no better view of the stars on the Continent than from Tairn's back.

"I still do not approve," Tairn lectures as we cross the barrier of the wards a little after midnight.

"And yet, we're still flying," I counter, shaking off the feeling of *wrongness* that sinks further into my bones with every wingbeat. From experience, I know it'll pass once we've been out beyond the wards long enough for my senses to adjust.

"Only because I vowed to let you make your own choices after Resson, not because I agree with you." He follows the slope of the peak, banking left to skim the landscape. Tonight's full moon means keeping a low profile. *"This is an unnecessary risk."*

"One Xaden and Sgaeyl take all the time." I stop fighting the wind and lean forward as he dives, grinning into the wind.

"The shadow wielder is not my concern."

"Sgaeyl is." The saddle's straps dig into my thighs, a constant reminder that I can't keep my seat without it.

"Sgaeyl would never be taken down by something as puny as a gryphon."

He scoffs. *"And as for losing the shadow wielder, she would be emotionally inconvenienced, that is true."*

I scoff at his bluster. *"An emotional inconvenience? Is that what I am to you?"* If so, then we don't need to worry that my death would cause Tairn's, or Sgaeyl's and Xaden's.

"You're currently a prize annoyance."

The wind steals my laughter, and I brace as we approach what looks to be a forested valley. The edge of the nearest ridgeline glows with the light from a Poromish village, but I'm not sure which one.

Tairn flares his wings, and gravity catches up with us, forcing me deeper into the saddle in the instant before he lands at the edge of a dark lake, jostling every bone in my body. Before I can get my bearings, he swings, leaving me grasping for the pommel as he puts his back to the water, facing the open meadow.

"That was abrupt." Good thing I'm still strapped in.

"Next time, you fly and I'll ride." His head sweeps from left to right as Sgaeyl lands next to us, Xaden on her back.

"He's still pissed that I came along," I tell Xaden, reaching for the buckle.

"You've gotten strong enough to handle Aetos," Xaden says, already moving for Sgaeyl's shoulder. Moonlight catches on his swords as he dismounts.

"I'm more worried about the company the lieutenant keeps than Aetos," Tairn growls. *"And don't even think of dismounting, Silver One."*

"I'm sorry?" I pull the leather through the first loop.

"Undo that strap and I'll launch." His head swivels, eerily snakelike, to glare at me over his shoulder.

My jaw drops. "You can't be serious," I whisper in a hiss.

"Try me." His golden eyes narrow into slits. *"I agreed to come to the drop-off. I did not agree to endanger your life when we are easily within a wyvern's flight from Zolya. I, too, remember what happens to dismounted riders."*

"You're being an overprotective ass." Not that he doesn't have a point. Maybe I'm not the only one with bad dreams.

"I am a credit to my line." He swings his head forward, completely dismissing me.

"Don't worry, you'll be able to hear everything from up there." Xaden's voice carries from where he stands just ahead of Tairn and Sgaeyl.

"Says the guy whose dragon isn't putting him in the corner," I grumble.

"I could have refused the rendezvous. This is a compromise." Tairn chuffs. *"They're approaching."*

It's on my tongue to fire back, but I close my mouth when I hear the wingbeats of gryphons. The sound is softer than those of dragons, less enunciated. Like a gale wind instead of a drumbeat.

Seven gryphons—a full drift—land in the clearing ahead and walk forward, their formidable heads darting left and right as they glance between Tairn and Sgaeyl. The gryphons are about a foot taller than Xaden, and though I can't make out colors well in the moonlight, I can see their razor-sharp beaks just fine from here.

"Please tell me you recognize them," I say to Xaden, my heart pounding. Power rises under my skin and charges the air around me.

"I do. You will in a minute, too," he replies as if we're meeting friends at the local tavern.

Tairn lowers his head in a gesture I recognize as both a threat to them and a favor to me, allowing me to see the rest of the approach.

The gryphons, half eagle and half lion, halt about twenty feet away, and three of their fliers dismount, leaving the pairs at the edges ready to fly at a moment's notice.

Our trust is as thin as December ice. One misstep and the fracture will have deadly consequences.

The trio walks toward Xaden through the knee-high mountain grass, and I recognize the one in the center almost immediately as the veteran that came upon us at the lake, then fought with us in Resson. Her face is a little more drawn, and she has a new scar down the side of her neck that disappears into her uniform, but that's definitely her.

But the man on her left isn't the same. He's a little shorter, a little more wiry than her stocky companion had been, and there's no malice under those slashing eyebrows when he glances past Xaden and up to me before quickly looking away.

I can't help but wonder if the man she'd been with at the lake was killed in the attack.

"Riorson," the woman calls out, pausing about ten feet from Xaden.

"Syrena," Xaden says, lifting two bags and then setting them on the ground before him. The message is clear: if they want them, they'll be coming closer to Tairn and Sgaeyl.

Syrena sighs and then motions the others forward.

The younger woman walking on Syrena's right is dressed in a paler shade of brown than the others. She looks to be my age and shares enough of Syrena's features that they could be related—cousins, maybe…or even sisters. They have the same straight noses, full mouths, lithe builds, and glossy black hair that contrasts their fair skin, though the younger one's is plaited in a simple braid over her shoulder. Her eyes are slightly larger, and her cheekbones are a little higher than Syrena's. She's the kind of beautiful that would normally lead to positions in a king's court or on stage in the theaters of Calldyr.

My chest tightens. The way she looks at Xaden isn't just doe-eyed. There's an unmistakable longing there, a hunger that has me blinking. It's like she's been trudging through a desert and he's the oasis.

She looks…like how I feel.

"Good to see you made it through the unfortunate assault on Samara," Syrena says as they reach Xaden.

"You want to explain what the fuck that was about?" Xaden's tone ventures into less-than-friendly territory. "Because one of your gryphons nearly took me out. If we didn't have a mender nearby in the Eastern Wing, I'd be down an arm because I hesitated, thinking it might be one of you." He glances at the other woman. "I thought we were on the same side, but I won't hesitate if it happens again."

I lean forward in the saddle, but there's not much give. Being up here, where I can only guess at what his expression might be, is torturous. Energy crackles in my fingertips, but I hold steady, keeping ready in case this drop doesn't go according to plan.

"I can't control every drift, Riorson," Syrena responds. "And I'm not going to blame other drifts in other chains of command who have to follow orders. We need more weapons than what you can supply. There are enough daggers in that outpost to arm a hundred fliers—"

"Those are powering our *wards*." His hands curl into fists at his sides.

"*Our* wards? Since when do you sympathize as Navarrian? And at least you *have* wards, Xaden," the girl on the right argues.

"For now." Xaden looks in her direction for a split second before returning to face Syrena.

That tone. The way she used his name… They definitely know each other.

"The attacks have to stop, Syrena," Xaden continues. "In your chain of command or not, the second I hear of fliers actually stealing daggers from outposts or any Navarrian wards being weakened by flier thievery, I'll cut off what shipments we do have coming your way."

I suck in a deep breath at his threat.

"You'll condemn us to death." Her shoulders straighten.

"You'll condemn us *all* to death if you take down the only wards standing between the venin and the hatching grounds at Basgiath," I say. "It's our only forge for weaponry, and there's enough raw magic in that range to feed them for a century. They'd be unstoppable."

Every head lifts my direction.

"*You're drawing attention.*" Tairn growls at the fliers, and they immediately look away.

"*I never said I'd sit here silently.*"

"Nice to meet you without Riorson's face attached to yours, Sorrengail,"

Syrena says, her gaze diverted from Tairn. Smart woman. "Though I'm guessing he still doesn't trust us completely if he's got you on the back of that enormous dragon of yours."

Xaden remains quiet.

"I'm glad you made it through Resson," I respond with a smile. Not that she can see it.

But the younger flier does. She stares up at me in an unsettling mix of shock and...shit, I think that's malice narrowing her eyes.

"My last name isn't winning any friends to your left," I say to Xaden.

"Ignore her."

"We made it through thanks to you and that incredible lightning you wield," Syrena says.

Another rumbling growl works up Tairn's throat as his head pivots right and he bares his teeth.

Syrena glances at the younger flier and then blanches. "You know better than to stare at a dragon, Cat!"

Cat. It's a fitting name for the way she's sizing me up.

"Wasn't staring at the dragon," the woman replies just loud enough that I barely make out the words. But she shifts her glare, aiming it at Xaden. "She's striking, I'll give you that."

What the fuck?

"Don't," Xaden replies, his tone dipping to that icy calm before addressing Syrena. "Sorrengail is right. You take down our wards, and there's nothing stopping them from draining the hatching grounds. They'd be impossible to engage, let alone defeat."

"So you'd rather we die while you sit protected behind the very weapon that could save *our* civilians?" the man asks like he's requesting the weather report.

"Yes." Xaden shrugs.

My eyebrows hit my hairline.

"This is a war," Xaden continues. "People die in wars. So, if you're asking if I'd rather your people die than mine, then obviously my answer is yes. It's foolish to think we can save everyone. We can't."

I inhale sharply at the reminder that the man I get behind closed doors isn't the one the rest of the world knows. It's not the first time I've heard him express the sentiment. He feels the same way about the marked ones who won't work to save themselves at Basgiath.

"Still an asshole, I see." Cat folds her arms.

"We've lost riders to the venin, too," he counters. "We're fighting with you. But I'm not sacrificing the safety of our movement or our civilians for yours. If that makes me an asshole, then so be it. We're not just sitting behind our wards, either. I'm risking my life, risking the lives of the people I care about, to get you weaponry from Basgiath and to complete our own forge to keep providing that weaponry so we're ready when both dark wielders and Navarre inevitably come for us. Which they will."

"Completing a forge?" Cat chances another glare in my direction. "Viscount Tecarus would strongly argue with that statement. You've had not one but two chances to acquire the luminary, and it's not like you haven't had what he's asked for both times."

"Out of the question," Xaden bites out.

"You're willing to let our entire kingdom fall prey to these monsters because you're what?" Cat asks, cocking her head at Xaden. "Smitten? Please. I know you better than that."

"Cat!" Syrena snaps.

My stomach lurches. *"What the hell is she talking about?"* Ludicrous as it might be, I think…it's me. What the hell would I have to do with a Poromish viscount?

"Nothing of any consequence." Xaden's tone is anything but comforting.

Tairn chuffs.

"We'll be discussing this later," I warn Xaden, adding it to a never-ending list.

"You know nothing where she's concerned." Xaden shakes his head once at Cat before turning back to Syrena. "The forge is our highest priority. As soon as we secure a luminary, we'll be operational and able to supply you in full. We have the rest of the material we need to begin, and that's all you get to know, because you're right, Syrena. I don't trust you. Until then, there are twenty-three daggers in these bags." He points to the bags at his feet.

"Twenty-three?" Syrena asks, lifting a brow.

"I need one of them." There's no apology in his words or tone. "Take them or leave them. Either way, Garrick will see your next shipment is delivered at the appointed location." He backs away, keeping his face toward them. *"It's near Athebyne. I'm not hiding it from you, just not repeating it in front of the rest of her drift."*

"I appreciate the honesty." It's surprising and refreshing.

"You have maybe a year until they're on your border," Syrena says.

My stomach sours as I remember that Brennan thinks we have way less than that. I need to delve deeper into researching the wards as soon as I'm back at Basgiath.

"We're all that stands between them and you. You know that, right? Or are you still hiding your heads in the don't-tell-us-too-much-in-case-we're-interrogated sand like you were last year?"

"We know," Xaden responds. "We'll be ready."

Syrena nods. "I'll do what I can to lessen the attacks on the outposts, but until you can openly say you're supplying us, it's like asking our forces to believe in specters. They don't *trust* you like I do."

"How you stop them is your business. I meant what I said." He tilts his head. "Come for our wards, and I'll watch you die."

We need to get them under wards of their own. It's the most logical path.

Sgaeyl huffs a blast of steam, and the male flier startles, then comes for the two bags and pivots, handing one to Syrena on his way back to the remainder of the drift.

"Thank you," Syrena says to Xaden before glancing up at me. "Tell your dragon he's still the scariest fucking thing I've ever seen, Sorrengail."

"I would, but it would just inflate his ego," I reply, settling back in the saddle as Xaden runs up Sgaeyl's foreleg to mount. "Stay alive, Syrena. I'm starting to like you."

She flashes me a smirk of a smile, then turns toward the other flier. "Let's go, Catriona."

Catriona. Cat.

The way my stomach hollows has nothing to do with Tairn's sudden launch into the night sky and everything to do with remembering what Bodhi said weeks ago.

I've never seen him care like this, and that includes Catriona.

Oh gods. The way she'd looked at him wasn't just longing—it was memory.

Cadets who are found absent without leave will be subject to
court-martial by their chain of command,
if they are not executed on sight.

—ARTICLE FOUR, SECTION ONE
THE BASGIATH WAR COLLEGE CODE OF CONDUCT

CHAPTER
TWENTY-NINE

Air steals the heat from my cheeks, and I pull my goggles into place as
Tairn flies for the border with forceful wingbeats. *"To avoid jumping to
conclusions like last year, she's your ex, isn't she?"* I ask Xaden, hoping my mental
voice sounds a hell of a lot steadier than I feel.

"How do you— Never mind, that's not important. Yes." He speaks slowly, like
he's choosing his words with the utmost care. *"We were over before I met you."*

It shouldn't matter. I have exes, too. It's not like we've really discussed our
sexual or romantic history, right? Of course, neither of them is a gryphon flier
who looks like…that, but still. There's no logical reason for me to feel this ugly
twist of irrational—

Shit. What is this? Jealousy? Anxiety? Insecurity?

"All three," Tairn responds in utter annoyance. *"To which I will remind
you that not a single dragon chose her. You were selected by* two. *Pull yourself
together."*

His metric is sound but has little to do with what I'm feeling.

"But at one point Xaden chose her." I lean into the right bank as Tairn hugs
the face of the mountain, continuing to climb.

*"And at one point, you thought gruel was a satisfactory meal, until you grew
some teeth and found the rest of the world's food waiting. Now cease this line of
thinking. It does not serve to make you stronger."*

Easy for him to say.

Silence envelops me for the rest of the flight, and I breathe a little easier once we cross Navarre's wards. Then guilt settles like a stone in my gut. We're safe behind our shields, but the drift we just armed won't sleep with the same certainty.

We land in the field, and I dismount after unbuckling, sliding down Tairn's foreleg.

"Be ready to go in the morning," Tairn orders. *"Perhaps returning quickly will soften your inevitable punishment for leaving abruptly."*

Because no one punishes dragons.

"I doubt it, but we can try." I lift my flight goggles as Tairn walks off with Sgaeyl, their tails swishing in rhythm. It's a little thing, but it makes me smile.

Xaden approaches, then winds his arm around my waist and tugs me to his firm chest before tipping my chin up with his thumb and forefinger so our gazes meet. Worry lines the space between his brows. "Are we going to have to spend our last few hours together talking about Cat?"

"No." I wind my arms around his neck. "Not unless you'd like to spend them talking about my previous lovers."

His focus drops to my mouth. "I would much rather choose our previous option number two, where we head up to my bedchamber and use our time judiciously."

"Solid plan," I agree, my body heating at the mere suggestion. *"But we are going to have to talk about Viscount Tecarus."*

"Fuck." He looks away. "I'd almost rather talk about our exes." His focus shifts back to mine. "Who are your exes? Do I know them?"

"Tecarus." I arch an eyebrow. "Now. I know you want to keep your secrets, but you told me you'd give me information if it could affect my decisions, and I have a nagging suspicion what's going on has to do with *me*." I trail my fingers down the side of his neck with his relic, simply because I can't help but touch him. *"So I'm asking you: what does Tecarus want for the luminary—the one device that could complete your forge—that you're unwilling to give?"*

His grip tightens around my waist, pulling me even closer. *"Besides weaponry and a private army?"* He pauses, war waging in his eyes before he sighs. *"You're the first lightning wielder in over a century. He swears he'll let us take it to Aretia if he can see you wield."*

I blink. "That part seems easy enough."

"It's not. Our first deal fell apart when I discovered he was only willing to let us *use* the luminary, not take it, which would have meant stationing dragons in Cordyn. And secondly, I don't trust him to stop at seeing you. He's known for collecting precious things and keeping them against their will." His thumb grazes my lower lip, sending a shiver of awareness through me. "I won't risk it. Won't risk you."

"Doesn't seem like it's your risk to take," I say softly. He needs that luminary, but maybe if I can get the wards up, that will buy us some time.

"I told you in Aretia—I would rather lose this entire war than live without you." He skims my jawline with his fingers before dropping his hand.

"I didn't really think you meant it when you said that." The ache in my chest damn near explodes. I love this man with every beat of my reckless heart, which would be his if he'd simply stop keeping all his secrets and let me know him.

"You have to trust me again at some point." His mouth tightens. *"Going to Cordyn isn't up for discussion. Brennan is already negotiating for different terms."*

"But I'm right here. You cannot protect me from every—" I glance over at the weight he slides into the deep sheath at my shoulder, the sheath that's only there because I'm wearing *his* flight jacket. "What is that?" But I already know. The alloy in the hilt flashes in the moonlight before it disappears, tucked against my arm.

"I need you to be able to defend yourself no matter what happens. You're not the only one with bad dreams, you know."

My lips part. "Xaden," I whisper, sliding my hands to his face and scratching my palms on the stubble of his cheeks. "I'm a lightning wielder. I'm never defenseless against venin."

"You'll have to keep it hidden, of course." His voice turns gruff. "Sew a deeper sheath into wherever you're most comfortable."

I nod. Right now, there's almost no chance anyone could spot it unless it was facing outward or they knew where to look, anyway.

"Anything else we need to discuss?" he asks.

A grimace wrinkles my nose.

"Other than the battle of Zolya getting leaked in Battle Brief and Markham playing it off as propaganda?" My mouth twists.

He simply stares at me this time.

"Or the fact that Nolon's spent months saving Jack Barlowe's life?" I turn out of his arms, and we start walking toward the outpost with its burning torches along the outer battlements. "Oh, and Varrish punched my shoulder out of socket during interrogation after Dain refused to use his signet on me."

Xaden stops.

"Don't worry," I say over my shoulder, tugging him along. "We escaped. They tried using this new elixir on us that dulls our connections to our dragons and our signets, but I remembered how it smelled from land nav, so we avoided that one."

"Signet-blocking elixir?" His voice rises.

"It's fine. If I can get my hands on the solution, I can probably figure out an antidote." I glance at him. *"Or Brennan can."*

His gaze bores into mine. "What happened to us working on that whole communication thing?"

"I could make you ask questions for the information." I flash a sarcastic smile. "Did I mention that Dain challenged me?" I'm definitely not asking about the ridiculous statement he dropped on me about my mother. Dain doesn't deserve my headspace. "Shit, I should probably tell you about Aaric, too."

Xaden sighs. "So much for option number two."

There's an odd hope that fills me as Tairn and I land on the flight field at Basgiath the next afternoon. Maybe it's that I finally feel like Xaden and I are really, honestly trusting each other with more than just our bodies, even if he's not giving me full access.

And his body is most *definitely* a perk. I'm deliciously sore from more than just the flight as I dismount Tairn at the edge of the field to avoid the incoming landings as First Wing goes through third-year maneuvers.

Shit, I should have slipped the dagger into my pack before landing. Dragons and their riders are *everywhere*.

"With all these dragons present, I have no doubt that Varrish and Aetos have been alerted to your return," Tairn warns me.

"I'll face my punishment," I respond, scratching the dull scales of his chin. "You need to hydrate. You're all dried out from the flight."

"Our departure was more my fault than yours. I will not stand for you to bear my punishment."

"Stop being sweet. It's disturbing." I pat his scales one more time and heft my bag higher on my shoulder. *"It's been a couple of weeks. Do you think Andarna will wake anytime soon?"* I miss her.

"There's no way to tell," he says quickly. Too quickly.

Suspicion finds home between my brows. "Is there something you aren't telling me?"

"Every adolescent enters the sleep for whatever amount of time their body needs. Hers apparently requires more than most."

And until the last couple of weeks, she's been waking up every time I'm distraught. Fuck. *"Should I worry?"*

"Worrying changes nothing. She is guarded by the elders and is sleeping safely."

Hmm. *"I'll tell you if my punishment includes death or inconvenience."*

"I will already know, as I am continuously with you," he grumbles. *"Forced*

to bear witness to the awkwardness that is twenty-one-year-old humans."

"I'll strive to make it less awkward."

"Could you do so, I would think you would have done it already." He waits until I walk in front of him, heading for the stairs by the Gauntlet, and then he launches, his wings gusting wind at my back.

I can't help but look to the left as I descend the steps. Our squad is practicing the deadly obstacle course that cost Trysten his life while we were in interrogation practice.

Aaric and Visia have already made it to the top—no surprise there—but the others are struggling. I have yet to learn any more of their names, but so far, we've only lost two.

Sloane bites her lower lip as she watches a girl with blue-black hair fumble along the spinning log on the fourth ascent...and fall. My heart lurches into my throat, but she grasps one of the vertical ropes along the course.

"Take that one at a run," I tell Sloane as I walk by. "Hesitate and you'll fall."

"I didn't say I need your help," she mutters back.

"Your brother won the Gauntlet patch last year. No one expects you to fill those shoes, but try not to die, will you?" I say over my shoulder, not bothering to stop. It's not like she's going to let me help, and I can't save her from this. She'll make it or she won't.

Fuck, I feel like *Xaden* of all people.

"You've angered the leadership, Sorrengail," Emetterio says as I approach, the sun reflecting off his freshly shaved and oiled head.

"It couldn't be helped," I say quietly, pausing at his side.

He glances sideways at me. "I do not have favorites. That would be foolish in this place."

"Noted."

"But if I did." He lifts his forefinger at me. "And I'm not saying I do. But *if* I did, I would suggest to that favored student that she stresses the undimmable bond of her legendary battle dragon and forgets any mention that perhaps strengthening her mental shields could have saved her from such a rash decision when it came to departing without leave." He lifts both of his dark brows at me. "But, I would also hope that another favored student—were I to have such a thing—would be teaching you stronger shield techniques so it doesn't happen again." His gaze drops to my collar, where there's a single silver line of lieutenant's rank.

"I get the point." A smile curves my mouth. "Thank you for caring, Professor Emetterio."

"I never said I did." He turns his attention to the Gauntlet, where Sloane has just crossed the fourth ascent.

"Right. Of course not." I grin as I walk-away, taking the rocky path to the quadrant, then fight the fear of my upcoming punishment. If Varrish tries to kill me, I'll fight. If he wants to torture me, I'll deal with it. Or maybe I should go straight to Panchek?

The path is crowded as another squad passes by for their turn at Gauntlet practice, and I stop stressing about stashing the dagger in my bag. At this rate, I'll make it to my room without anyone seeing the alloy-hilted dagger.

By the time I reach the second-year floor, I've gone through about a dozen different scenarios of how to turn myself in.

Professor Kaori looks up from his book as he walks toward me in the main corridor, his brows furrowed in concentration, and I wave before turning into the little hallway that houses my squad's chambers.

I stop short, my heart seizing for the length of what should be two beats when I see them.

"There she is." Varrish's greasy voice lifts the hairs on the back of my neck as he and his two henchmen push off the wall and head my way. "We've been waiting for you, Sorrengail."

"I was going to wash the flight off and then present myself for judgment." Close. I'm so *fucking* close to the safety behind my door.

"Oh, so you *do* realize you were absent without leave," Varrish says, his smile anything but reassuring. The trio passes by my door and Rhiannon's across the hall, then approaches Sawyer's to my left and Ridoc's to my right.

"Of course." I nod.

Rhiannon's door opens silently, and she peeks her head out, her eyes flying wide.

I subtly shake my head in warning, and she nods, ducking back inside and closing her door almost all the way. Good. I don't want them looping her in on my punishment as soon as she inevitably tries to defend me as my squad leader.

"Bag," Varrish orders.

Oh. *Fuck*. At least I didn't stash the dagger in there. My mistake might just save my life.

Nora holds out her hand, and I slip my bag from my shoulder and hand it over.

"You couldn't be bothered to wear your own uniform?" Varrish eyes Xaden's rank on my collar. "You do know that impersonating a commissioned officer is against the Codex, do you not?"

Nora dumps my bag onto the stone floor, breaking the binding on my history book. Ouch. "Look, she has another one here." She hands Bodhi's jacket to Varrish.

"Collecting them, are we?" Varrish takes the jacket without looking my direction. His focus is on the bag with the other two riders'.

He's going to take Xaden's jacket. I fucking *know* it. Panic wells in my throat, threatening to cut off my oxygen. I glance up at Rhi, locking eyes with her through the slit she's left in her door.

She cocks her head to the side silently, and I look pointedly to the dagger sheathed at my shoulder before lifting my brows at her.

"It's just books, some flight goggles, and the jacket," Nora says.

"A jacket that isn't hers," Varrish corrects her. "Just like the one she's wearing."

Rhiannon's door squeaks, but she manages to close it before they swing their gazes her way.

Fuck. Fuck. *Fuck.* I'm on my own. The dagger is more than enough to implicate me if he knows what it is, and if he doesn't, Markham will. But worse, it will implicate Xaden. They'll kill all the marked ones for what they'll perceive as his betrayal.

"Check the one she's wearing," Varrish orders. "Since it's clearly not regulation."

"I'm sorry," Professor Kaori says as he comes up behind me. "Did I just hear you order your…aides, or whatever it is you're calling them, to strip a cadet?"

"It's a *jacket*. She's in violation of Article Seven, Section Three, which states that impersonating a commissioned officer—" Varrish starts.

"It's Article Two, actually," I interrupt, folding my arms across my chest. The shoulder has way more give to it than what I'd expect, but I'm not foolish enough to draw attention to it by glancing down again. "And it says *impersonating* a commissioned officer is a punishable offense, not wearing someone's flight jacket. As you can see, I'm not wearing anyone's name tag, nor am I claiming to be someone I'm not."

"She has you there, Vice Commandant." Kaori tucks his book under his arm. "And since when do we search cadets' bags?"

"Since I took over as vice commandant." Varrish lifts his head, standing to his full height. "This doesn't involve you, Kaori."

"Nevertheless, I'll be staying," Kaori retorts. "Power must always be kept in check, don't you think, Major Varrish?"

"Are you accusing me of abusing my power where this cadet is concerned, *Colonel* Kaori?" Varrish moves to step toward us, but my bag is in the way.

"Oh, no." Kaori shakes his head. "I think you abuse your power in general."

It takes every muscle in my body to keep my features schooled.

Varrish's eyes narrow on Kaori before turning to me. "I will have that flight jacket." He holds out his hand.

I undo the buttons, begging my fingers not to tremble, and hand it over.

Varrish goes through every. Single. Pocket.

I don't need to warn Tairn—I can already feel his quiet presence in the back of my mind.

"Hmm." Kaori leans my direction and cocks his head, sweeping his gaze over my uniform. "Her name tag here clearly says Sorrengail, and I note two of her squad patches. Doesn't seem to be impersonating anyone to me."

"She is…" Varrish's face blotches as he comes up empty on the jacket. "She is still due to face court-martial for departing campus without leave—"

"Oh." Kaori nods. "That explains it. You haven't talked to Panchek this afternoon. I turned in my expert opinion that Sorrengail not be punished for what was clearly the choice of her dragon. Her very powerful, very worried, very *mated* dragon. Panchek agrees. She's clear of all charges."

"I'm sorry?" Varrish drops Xaden's jacket on the floor on top of Bodhi's, and his henchmen stand.

"Come now," Kaori says as if he's talking to a child. "We can hardly expect a second-year to shield out the overpowering emotions of her dragon when even we struggle as officers, let alone one as strong as Tairn."

"Maybe you struggle," Varrish snips, losing his customary slick indifference. "Some of us do not bow to the whims of our dragons. In fact, we influence *them*."

"Well, that's certainly a theory worth contemplating." Kaori pauses, waiting for a reply that doesn't come. "Odd. Would that mean you influenced Solas when he set fire to that squad of bonded riders after Parapet?"

Varrish glances between us. "We're done here."

The trio sidesteps the mess they made of my things and pushes by Professor Kaori.

"You're making enemies, Sorrengail," Kaori says softly after waiting until they've left.

"Not sure I made that one, Professor," I tell him honestly, dropping to the ground and shoving my things back in the bag. "Pretty sure he came that way."

"Hmm." He watches me as I stand. "Either way, be careful there." He gives me a cautious look and then disappears down the hallway.

I squeeze the jacket between my hands, finding a very *empty* sheath.

Oh gods.

"Get in here!" Rhiannon hisses, all but yanking me into her room and slamming the door shut behind me.

Ridoc and Sawyer rise from where they're seated at the window and close their physics books, exchanging a look before coming toward us.

"I didn't want you caught up in—" My words die when she holds the dagger up, grasping the tip. "Holy *shit*!" My jaw drops, then rises in an awestruck smile. "You just pulled that through the wall! I thought you couldn't do that yet!"

"I can't!" she rebuts. "Well, couldn't, I guess. Not until right now. Not until I thought whatever this is had a chance of getting you killed from the look you gave me."

"You're incredible!" I glance at the guys. "She is, right?"

"Enough about the signet!" Her voice rises with tension. "What is this? And why did you need them *not* to find it?"

"Oh. Right." I take a single step forward, and she hands me the dagger. A thousand possibilities, all varying degrees of the truth, run through my mind. But I'm so sick of lying to her, to them. Especially when attacks are increasing and keeping them in the dark will only hurt them. "The dagger."

Gods, I hope Xaden forgives me for this.

She's my closest friend and she just saved not only my ass but the lives of every marked one in this college. She deserves better from me. She deserves the truth. They all do.

"Violet?" she pleads.

I swallow the lump in my throat and meet her gaze. "It's for killing venin."

Barring invasion, only riders and designated scribes are
permitted in the Riders Quadrant.
To enter uninvited as infantry or even healer is to
welcome a swift death.

—ARTICLE TWO, SECTION THREE
THE BASGIATH WAR COLLEGE CODE OF CONDUCT

CHAPTER THIRTY

I tell them everything.

Every moment that transpired from the minute I made the decision to leave
our squad with Xaden for War Games to the second I fell from Tairn's back after
being stabbed. But when it comes to revealing how and where I woke up, my
tongue ties. I just can't do it.

It's not because I don't trust them, but because it isn't my secret to tell, and
to do so betrays Xaden…and Brennan. It risks every life in Aretia.

So, I tell them *almost* everything that happened after Resson. Andarna, the
assassination attempts, the daggers, supplying friendly drifts, Jesinia sneaking
me classified books about the wards, even the theory that Navarre knows how
to lure the venin—the rest spills out of my mouth in a deluge of words as they
stare at me, their expressions varying from shocked to disbelief.

"I was right. Deigh wasn't killed by gryphons." Rhi sits on her bed, staring
at the wall, her eyes unfocused as she processes.

"Deigh wasn't killed by gryphons." I shake my head slowly, sitting beside her.

"And you let him—let Riorson—lie for you." Sawyer folds his arms across
his chest.

I nod, a pit opening in my stomach as I wait for them to condemn me, to
shout, to kick me out of the room, to end our friendship.

"And you're sure the dragons know?" Ridoc tilts his head to the side, and his eyes slowly widen as if he's talking to Aotrom. "The dragons *know*."

"Feirge does, too." Rhi grips the edge of her bed. "She's stunned that I do. That you do."

"Tairn says the Empyrean is split. Some of the dragons want to act, and others don't. Without the Empyrean taking an official stance, none of the dragons are willing to put their riders in danger by telling them if they don't already know."

"And people are dying beyond the wards. All that *propaganda* is real." Ridoc paces between the window and door.

"Yes." I nod.

"They can't keep a lie this big," Ridoc argues, rubbing his hand over his recently buzzed hair. "It's impossible."

"It's not." Sawyer leans against Rhiannon's desk. "Living in Luceras, I promise you the only news we got along the coast came from what the scribes put out as official announcements. It's as easy as Markham choosing which news gets published and which doesn't. We aren't even open to trading vessels from the isle kingdoms."

Ridoc shakes his head. "Fine, then what about the wabern, or whatever you called them?"

"Wyvern?" Rhiannon offers.

"Right. If you killed all those dragon-size monsters, then where are the bodies? They can't hide an entire killing field, and Resson is close enough to Athebyne that someone would see. Liam wasn't the only rider with farsight."

"They burned them," Rhiannon says quietly, looking away in thought. "The patrol reports from Battle Brief said the trading post was charred for miles and we'd have to find a new location for the quarterly trades."

"How long do we have?" Ridoc stops pacing. "Until those things are at the border?"

"Some say a year, some say less. A lot less." I turn to Rhi. "You need to get your family to leave. The farther from the border, the better."

She lifts her brows. "You want me to tell my parents to leave the business they worked their entire lives for and uproot my sister and her family without telling them why?"

"You have to try," I whisper. "I'm so sorry I couldn't tell you." Guilt threatens to swallow me whole. "And the truth of it is that you still don't know everything. There are things I *can't* tell you, at least not until you're all capable of shielding Dain out. And I know that sounds like a bunch of bullshit because I've basically been lying to you for the last few months. And you have every single right to be angry at me, or to hate me, or to feel however you want to feel…of course." A self-deprecating laugh slips free. "Because it's exactly why I've been so pissed at Xaden." I end on a whisper.

"Stop." She takes a deep, shuddering breath and drags her gaze to meet mine. "I'm not pissed at you."

I draw back, speechless.

"I'm a little pissed," Ridoc mutters.

"I'm stunned but not angry," Sawyer adds, shooting Ridoc a look.

"I'm not pissed at you, Vi," Rhiannon repeats, her gaze locked on mine. "I'm just really sorry you didn't feel like you could tell me. Am I disappointed and more than a little frustrated that you didn't trust me earlier? Absolutely, but I can't imagine how heavy this has been for you to carry."

"But you should be pissed." My eyes burn and a boulder forms in my throat as I look at them all in turn. "You *should* all be pissed."

Rhiannon lifts her brows at me. "So, I only get to feel however I want as long as I rip you apart for not telling me? Not sure that's fair."

Breathe. I have to breathe, but the boulder feels like a mountain, now. "I do not deserve you." Her reaction to my outright deception couldn't be more different from how I'd torn Xaden to shreds. "Any of you."

She yanks me into a hug, setting her chin on my shoulder. "Even if it makes me a target to know all of this, you put your own life at risk and shared your boot with me at Parapet when we were complete strangers. How can you think I wouldn't want to share this risk with you now that you're my best friend?"

I hold her tight, torn between the absolute relief of her knowing—them all knowing—and ice-cold fear that all I did was expose them.

"We don't run." Sawyer moves toward us, then clasps my shoulder, squeezing lightly.

Ridoc walks over slowly and rests his hand on my upper back. "The four of us stick together. That's the deal. We make it to graduation, no matter what."

"If there's a Basgiath to graduate from," Sawyer remarks.

"I do have one question." Rhiannon pulls back, and the others drop their hands. "If we only have months, then what are we doing about it?" There's no fear in her eyes, just a steely determination. "We have to tell everyone, right? We can't just let them show up at the border and start sucking the life out of people."

Leave it to Rhiannon to jump into problem-solving mode. For the first time since returning to Basgiath after Resson, I don't feel so alone. Maybe keeping his distance works for Xaden, but I need my friends.

"We can't. Not until we have everything in place to fight. They'll kill us all before we even get the chance to spread the truth, just like they did during the Tyrrish rebellion."

"You can't expect us to twiddle our thumbs while Riorson and his marked ones run around with the fate of the Continent in their hands." Sawyer rubs the bridge of his nose.

"He's right." Rhiannon nods. "And if you think that establishing a second set of wards is the way to save people, then let's do that. We'll leave the marked ones to their weapons smuggling and focus on helping you research."

"Solid plan," Ridoc agrees, picking up the alloy-hilted dagger and studying it.

"Are you guys really volunteering to spend your time reading dozens of classified books on wards?" I look between them with raised brows.

"If it means we get to spend time in the Archives, I'm in." Sawyer nods enthusiastically.

"And we all know why, my friend." Ridoc grins and claps him on the back.

A spark of hope ignites in my chest. We'll be able to read four times as fast, cover four times as many books. "There has to be a record somewhere about *how* the First Six created the first wards. Jesinia has been looking, but she doesn't have access to every classified tome, and everything I've read has been edited or redacted during translation, including an account from the first of the scribes. It's like they hid the knowledge when they changed our history, which I think happened about four hundred years ago."

"So we're looking for a book older than four hundred years." Rhiannon drums her fingers on her knee as she thinks. "One that hasn't been through a set of hands to translate or change."

"Exactly. And Jesinia has already given me the oldest book she has access to on ward-weaving curricula, and it only covers expansion, not creation." My shoulders fall as I sigh. "What we really need is a primary source, and I doubt the First Six sat around writing books after they founded Basgiath. They were a little busy."

"Not too busy to keep personal journals." Ridoc sets the dagger's hilt in the center of his palm and tries to balance it.

Our heads turn in his direction, and my heart threatens to stop.

"What?" Rhiannon asks.

"They kept journals," he says with a shrug, moving as he tries to keep the blade upright. "At least two of them. War—" He catches us staring and quickly grabs the dagger by the handle. "Wait. Do I actually know something about the Archives that you don't?" A grin flashes across his face. "I do, don't I?"

"Ridoc…" Rhiannon warns, leveling a look on him I want nothing to do with.

"Right. Sorry." He sets the dagger on the desk and then sits beside it. "Lyra's and Warrick's journals are here. At least according to a classified ledger in your mom's office, they are."

"My mom's office?" My jaw hangs.

"The ledger, not the journals." He shrugs. "I thumbed through it when we were looking for something to steal during the Squad Battle, but it listed them in a sublevel vault, and you'd already said the Archives were closed, and then you suggested the map—"

"There aren't any sublevel vaults." I shake my head.

"That you know of," he counters.

I blink. "Jesinia would know if we had those books, let alone a sublevel vault." My father would have told me…wouldn't he?

Ridoc scoffs. "Right. Because the scribes have kept the biggest secret in Navarre's history safe all these years by granting access to second-years."

"He makes a good point," Sawyer notes.

He does. "I'll ask her to look." And it hits me that I would have known this ages ago if I'd just trusted my friends. "But if I don't even know about the vault, then they're beyond classified. Retrieving them could definitely get us killed."

Ridoc rolls his eyes. "Oh, good. I was wondering when it was going to start getting dangerous around here again."

Jesinia knows nothing about a sublevel vault, so while she hunts, the rest of us pore over every book about ward-weaving and the First Six she can give us. Research goes a lot faster when four people are doing it. And I have to admit, it's nice to look across my room during the hours we study and see my friends again.

But we don't find answers. And Andarna remains suspiciously asleep. And Tairn kindly telling me not to worry feels like a giant trigger to do exactly that, so I do.

I never get a chance to tell Xaden about our discovery—or lack thereof. That next Saturday, our squad is pulled into another session of land nav with the infantry, this time with First Wing, and I spend two days wandering the steep terrain of the mountains near Basgiath, avoiding Jack Barlowe—who is weirdly nice to *everyone*—at all costs.

"It's like he met Malek and decided to come back a decent guy," Rhiannon observes when we catch him tutoring first-years on the mat. "But I still don't trust him."

"Me, either." The professors all seem to love him now, too.

The next week, Andarna is still sleeping, and Sawyer stumbles onto a three-hundred-year-old passage that confirms more than one wardstone was created.

On Saturday, not only is Xaden on duty in the ops room, but Mira is on patrol for the majority of my visit, and the weekend after, our squad is dropped into the Parchille Forest amid the changing leaves without supplies and told to walk our way out.

Message received. Tairn and Sgaeyl won't be denied, but Xaden and I only get to see each other when we play by the rules—Varrish has determined that we've broken too many.

The next weekend, I have to choose between my squad receiving a zero if I don't participate in a cat-and-mouse evasion operation against Third Wing in the Shedrick Woods and flying to Samara for Xaden.

It's the very scenario Mira predicted last year when she learned I'd bonded Tairn—being forced to choose between my education, my squad, and Xaden and Sgaeyl. Tairn makes the choice before I can bludgeon myself about it.

We stay, but he's fucking miserable the next day when Threshing comes, and I can't blame him. I might not have a mating bond, but I'd chew my own arm off if it meant I had five minutes to talk to Xaden. Nothing I need to tell him can be written in a letter.

"You look more nervous than you did when it was our Threshing," Rhiannon says, coming to stand next to where my squadmates have claimed a spot on the hillside across from where the Fourth Wing first-years wait with their newly bonded dragons.

"I haven't seen Sloane yet, and I need to leave to take over the watch soon." I sway back and forth nervously, like a mother with a colicky newborn. *I'll find time to get to temple if you could just be with her*, I promise Dunne, the goddess of war.

"She'll make it." The tension in Imogen's folded arms tells me she's not feeling quite as certain as she proclaims. In addition to the extra reps during our nightly workouts, she's been more than a little short with me since I had to tell her that I spilled our secret, which then pressured her to tell Quinn, too.

Quinn took it a lot like Rhiannon, with grace and a sense of resolve.

Xaden's going to lose his shit when I tell him, but I'll deal with that when he gets here on Saturday. If they actually let us see each other.

"All of Flame Section is looking strong. Bodhi should be proud," Quinn says with a hopeful smile.

"Visia bonded a Brown Daggertail," Rhi says, nodding across the field to where the first-year stands in front of her dragon. "Avalynn, Lynx, and Baylor all made it, too. But I don't see Aaric or Mischa." She glances at me. "She's the one who's always biting her nails."

"Oh. Right." Guilt clogs my throat, and I swallow, but there's no clearing it. While I've avoided getting to know anything about the first-years, Rhi hasn't had that luxury.

Wingbeats fill the air again, and we all look to the right as a Blue Clubtail approaches with sapphire-hued scales that contrast the changing colors of the sunset sky, and he is *beautiful*.

"We've always been the better-looking species," Tairn chimes in.

"Andarna?" I ask him every single day, and today, twice.

"She still sleeps."

"That can't be natural." I shift my weight on the hillside.

"It's…longer than expected."

"So you keep saying. You have the Empyrean gathered." I change the subject and glance back over my shoulder at the dragon-covered mountain, spotting Tairn high on the ridgeline above, just a little lower than the dragons I assume are their elders. *"Plan on discussing anything tonight?"* Without the cooperation of the Empyrean, we're stuck.

"If we were, I couldn't tell you."

"Figured," I say with a sigh, watching the blue land in the field directly in front of the dais where leadership, including my mother, watch.

"I'll be damned," Rhiannon mutters as Aaric dismounts from the Blue Clubtail like he's been doing it for years, with an ease that reminds me of Xaden and Liam. I smile as he keeps his head down while recording his dragon's name and makes it back without my mother recognizing him.

"There." Rhiannon points toward the end of the field.

A midsize red the shade of a strawberry flies in, whipping her daggertail behind her when she lands in the middle of the field.

"A Red Daggertail," I whisper, relief flooding my veins as Sloane clumsily dismounts, clutching her shoulder. "Just like her brother."

Sloane hugs Visia tight, and I smile. I'm glad she has friends, that their year has the chance to become just as tight as ours.

"It's hard not to loathe her for hating you." Rhiannon sighs. "But I'm glad she survived."

"I don't need her to like me." I shrug. "I just need her to live."

"Squad Leader Matthias?" A rider from Third Wing wearing a black sash with a gray messenger insignia approaches.

"Here." Rhi beckons him forward, then takes the folded parchment from his hand. "Thank you." He leaves, and she breaks the wax seal to open the missive. Her gaze darts to mine, and she lowers her voice as Ridoc leans in. "Jesinia requests we meet her by the Archives door in fifteen minutes. She has a tome we've requested." She reads our code phrase slowly, excitement growing in her eyes.

I inhale sharply, and my heart jumps as I grin. "She's found the vault," I whisper. "But I have the next watch, and Threshing is almost over. You have squad leader duties."

"I'll take your watch," Ridoc offers quietly.

"And give Varrish a reason for me not to see Xaden this weekend? No way." I shake my head.

"Then I'll meet Jesinia." He reaches for the missive, and Rhi hands it over. "Sawyer can cover us here."

We all agree, and Ridoc and I head toward the quadrant, keeping clear of the newly bonded dragons' flight path.

"Which tower are we keeping watch on?" he asks as we enter the courtyard. "Dormitory?"

"Academic." I point up to the turret where the never-ending fire blazes.

"Ah. The burn pit. It's going to be a busy night up there once the ceremony ends." He nudges my shoulder. "I'll come up right after I meet with her. And then I vote we join the Threshing celebration after your watch." His head tilts. "Or at least I'll be celebrating. Unfortunately, I think you limit yourself to celebrating with Riorson, now."

"Go find out if all our problems are answered." I laugh, and we part ways when I push open the doors to the academic wing. It's eerily quiet in the building as I climb the wide spiral stairs up to the top floor. Come to think of it, I don't think I've ever been alone in the academic building in all my years here. Someone is always around. My heart rate increases with every flight of stairs, but I'm nowhere near as winded as I was when I made this journey for Aurelie last year.

I open the door onto the flat-topped turret and am immediately enveloped in heat from the flames rising from the iron barrel in the center.

"Violet?" Eya smiles and hops off the edge of the thick stone wall on the other side of the barrel. "I didn't realize you were relieving me."

"I didn't realize you had watch before me. How have you been?" I make my way around the barrel and try not to think of how many of the cadets will have their things offered to Malek in the next day.

"Good—" Her eyes blow wide as she glances past me—and I turn, immediately drawing a dagger from my thigh and moving to her side.

Four grown soldiers in infantry blue rush out of the doorway, each brandishing a shortsword as they face us. My stomach drops to the bottom floor and crashes. They definitely don't look lost.

"Infantry is not allowed in the Riders Quadrant!" Eya snaps, flipping her hatchet over her wrist and gripping the handle.

"We're here with express permission," the one on the right snarls.

"And paid well for the specific message we're to deliver." That ominous line comes from the tallest one on the left as they spread out on the far side of the barrel, splitting in the center to come at us from both sides.

Four assassins and two of us. They have the exit, and we're pinned between the fire, the wall, and four stories of nothing. *Not good.* And they know it, especially by the slow smile the one closer to the center gives, the firelight reflecting off his blade as he raises it.

Fuck them. I did not survive the entirety of last year, or these last few months, to die on top of the academic wing.

"Kill them all," Tairn orders.

"Go left," Eya mutters.

I nod and unsheathe another dagger. "Let me guess." They take slow, coordinated steps toward us, and Eya and I pivot so we stand back-to-back. "Secrets die with the people who keep them?"

The one on the left blinks in surprise.

"It's not as original as you'd think." In rapid-fire, I flick two daggers at him, catching him in the throat and heart. Eya shouts behind me, charging at the two on her side as my first attacker falls like a damned tree, crashing into stone and driving my daggers deeper.

Blades clash behind me, and I lose sight of my remaining attacker in the high flames as I grab two more daggers. Shit, shit, *shit.* Where is —

Fire blasts toward my face and I dive to the left, narrowly missing the barrel that skids across the cobblestone floor and slams into the wall with a *thud* loud enough to wake the dead. My shoulder takes the brunt of the impact when I fall, and I grimace as I force myself onto my knees, ignoring the wide, unseeing eyes of the soldier I've already killed.

"I'm coming!" Tairn shouts.

Eya screams, and I make the mistake of looking back over my shoulder as one of the soldiers wrenches his sword from the middle of her chest.

Blood. There's so much *blood.* It slides over her leathers as she clutches her ribs, and I watch in horror as she falls to her knees.

"Eya!" I shout, stumbling to my feet, but I can't get to her with the barrel blazing between us. Pinching the edges of my daggers, I lunge forward, then hurl both at the assassin she hasn't slain, catching him in the chest.

I have two more out when I spin to face the only one left, but there's no time to throw them. He's used Eya's death to close the distance. I gasp as he grabs ahold of my waist, locking down with a grip I can't dislodge as he marches three quick steps to the edge of the tower.

No! I slice at his arms, but he holds fast despite the wounds. I kick hard in his stomach, and he sputters, and with the next kick, he releases me. My momentum sends me flying backward, and my daggers scrape both sides of the turret's crenellations as I skid toward the edge, my feet kicking under me and finding nothing but air.

Fast. It's happening too fast to do anything but react.

Instinct takes over and my hands splay wide against the sides of the crenellations, releasing the daggers. Clawing for purchase, I sail backward, my skin grating against the rock to slow me down as I do, and the tips of my boots hit the edge of the turret…then slip right off.

But the impact is enough to change the angle of my fall, and stone rushes up at my face for no longer than a heartbeat before my stomach collides with the edge of the turret, stealing what breath I have on impact.

My weight drags me the rest of the way backward, and I dig in with my fingernails and hold as my lower half kicks against the crevices in the stonework beneath me, looking for a foothold.

This can't be happening, but it is.

"It's nothing personal," the soldier says, crawling forward onto the three-foot-deep wall.

I gasp for breath and cough at the first full inhale. There has to be a foothold below. There just does. This isn't how I die.

My feet search and I can feel the ridges, but there's nothing substantial enough to support my weight.

"It's just money," he whispers from his knees and reaches for my hands.

Oh gods, he's going to—

"No!" Power floods my veins, but there's nothing to do with a strike this close.

"Just money," he repeats, lifting my hands from the stone.

Xaden. Sgaeyl. Tairn. This will kill us *all*.

The soldier lets go.

I scream, the sound so shrill it tears my throat, and I slide, scraping my forearms raw as gravity drags me down, the top of the turret fading from view, but my fingers grab hold of the tiny lip at the edge…and cling.

My heart lurches into my throat as my feet scramble.

No foothold.

Barely any handhold, and my shoulders start to *wail* as I dangle.

"Just let go," the soldier urges, crawling forward again. "It will be over before you—" His eyes bulge and he gurgles, grabbing for his throat and the dagger whose tip protrudes a few inches below his chin.

Someone has shoved their knife in through his spine.

Everyone thinks most Riders cadets die from dragon fire.
Truth be told, it's usually gravity that gets us.

—PAGE FORTY-SEVEN, THE BOOK OF BRENNAN

CHAPTER
THIRTY-ONE

I slip another precious inch as the soldier is yanked backward, then thrown forward, over my head, disappearing into the darkness.

It's Eya. It has to be. Maybe the wound isn't—

Blond hair and icy-blue eyes appear above me, and my heart plummets with the assassin's body. Jack Barlowe.

"Sorrengail?" He lunges forward, grasping my wrists with an unbreakable grip.

"I'm so sorry," I tell Tairn and prepare myself for the weightless moment that will be my last.

"I've got you!" Jack shouts, holding my wrists tight as he throws himself backward and hauls me up and over the edge.

My ribs hit stone, and he lets one hand go, then grabs my leathers and pulls, heaving me the rest of the way onto the tower wall.

I don't waste time, scrambling forward to safety. As soon as my boots land inside the turret, he backs up a few steps, his chest rising and falling quickly with exertion as he gives me space, dodging the fallen body to the left as fire rages to the right.

"You saved me?" I scurry backward, leaving my hands at my sides and close to my daggers.

"I didn't know it was you," he admits, falling back against the tower wall and catching his breath. "But yeah."

"You could have let me fall, but you pulled me up," I say, like I'm trying to convince myself.

"Do you want to climb back up there and we'll do it again that way?" he offers, gesturing to the wall.

"No!"

Wingbeats sound overhead, and we both look up as Tairn soars by. He would have been too late, and we both know it. The relief coursing through my body isn't just mine; it's his, too.

"Look." Jack shakes his head and peers over at Eya's lifeless form. "I was on the dorm's watch for First Wing and ran when I heard the screams. And…well… riders don't die at the hands of infantry."

"I killed you. You have every right to throw me off the tower." I reach behind me one hand at a time and collect two of my daggers, sheathing them slowly, bracing myself for anything.

"Yeah." He rubs his hand through his short blond hair. "Well, that death was kind of a second chance for me. You don't know who you really are until you face down Malek. So, the way I see this is I just gave you a second chance, too. We're even." He nods once, then walks away, exiting into the tower.

I move slowly around the edge of the turret, stopping to roll over the body of the first assassin I killed and remove my daggers, cleaning them on his uniform before sheathing them at my thighs. The fire slowly sputters in the barrel, and I lean against the hard stone wall before letting my back hit every ridge on the way down as I slide to sit.

I stare at the tips of Eya's boots—they're all I can see from this angle—and let my head fall back against the wall. Then I breathe and wait for the adrenaline to pass, for the shock to wear off, for the trembling in my aching hands to cease.

Eya's dead. That's half of us who flew into Resson. Aetos isn't going to stop until we're all gone. He'll pick us off one by one. I hug my knees to my chest. Who will he come for next? Garrick? Imogen? Xaden? Bodhi? We can't go on like this.

"Holy shit." I hear Ridoc's voice a second before I see him. "What happened?" He falls to his knees beside me, looking me over in obvious appraisal. "Are you hurt? Stabbed?" His glance skitters sideways. "Burned?"

"No." I shake my head. "But Eya's dead. Assassins. Aetos."

"Fuck."

I laugh, the sound tripping out of my lips hysterically. "Jack Barlowe saved my life."

"Are you kidding?" Ridoc rises up and cups my face, checking my eyes for signs of concussion.

"No. He said this makes us even, and I really think he failed math, because by my calculations now I owe him *two* lives: the one I took from him, and the one he just gave me."

"I should have come with you." His hands fall away.

"No." I shake my head, and my vision swims. "They could have killed you, too." Shivers rack my frame.

"What do you need?"

"Just wait with me while it passes."

Silence stretches between us.

"I saw Jesinia," he says quietly. "The good news is she knows where the vault is. There are wards, but she knows how to get through them, too. But the bad news is we need someone in King Tauri's bloodline to do it. They're not just in some sublevel vault. They're in the royal one." His shoulders dip in defeat. "I'm sorry, Violet."

I look over at Eya's boots. There's nothing I can do to protect her now, but I can protect what she fought for. "Then it's a good thing we have access to a prince who happens to hate his father."

Gods save us from the ambitions of second-years. They think they've experienced everything because they've survived their first year, but in reality, they only know enough to get themselves killed.

—MAJOR AFENDRA'S GUIDE TO THE RIDERS QUADRANT (UNAUTHORIZED EDITION)

CHAPTER THIRTY-TWO

Xaden stares down at me that Saturday, his eyes boring a hole through my soul, and a muscle in his jaw ticks once. Twice.

At least there aren't any shadows creeping out from under my bed, so he can't be *that* angry, right?

"Say something." I hold his gaze and shift my weight when the edge of my desk digs into the backs of my thighs.

His shoulders rise with a deep breath. At least one of us is getting enough oxygen. My chest feels like it's about to squeeze my lungs right out of it.

"Rhiannon saved my life. If she hadn't retrieved that dagger before Varrish took your jacket, I wouldn't be sitting here." It comes out like the plea it is. "They had to know eventually. She saw the dagger. She knew *something* was up."

Those beautiful eyes close, and I swear I can *feel* him counting to ten.

Fine, maybe twenty.

"Say something. Please," I whisper.

"I'm choosing my words carefully," he replies, then takes another measured breath.

"I appreciate that." I open my mouth to make another excuse, but there really is none to give, so I sit and listen to the clock tick and rain pelt the window while he composes his thoughts.

"Who exactly knows?" he finally asks, slowly opening his eyes.

"Rhiannon, Sawyer, Ridoc, and Quinn."

"Quinn, too?" His eyes flare.

I hold up a finger. "That was all Imogen."

"For fuck's sake." He drags a hand down his face.

"They don't know everything."

He lifts his scarred brow, looking anything but reassured.

"They don't know about Aretia or Brennan or the luminary issue." I cock my head to the side. "Which really isn't an issue if I can get a week away from this place to fly to Cordyn. It's what? A two-day flight?" The city on the southern coast of the Krovlan province can't be too far.

"Stop." He leans in, bringing his face right up to mine, bracketing my hips on the desktop with his hands. "Do *not* go there with me. Not right now. This asinine idea of breaking into the Archives tonight is more than enough for me to sweat about without worrying you're going to fly off and get yourself captured and killed in enemy territory."

"It's not an idea—it's a plan." I cup his cheeks. "And it doesn't feel like you're sweating to me."

A sound like a growl works up his throat as he pushes away, retreating a step. "You have *no* idea what I'm thinking."

"You're right. I don't. So tell me." I grip the edge of the desk and wait to see if he'll shut me out as usual.

He runs his thumb beneath the bottom lip I haven't had the chance to kiss and glances toward the books piled on my shelves. "I appreciate you waiting for me to do this, but there are holes in your plan."

"What holes?"

"You haven't secured the agreement of the key participant, for starters—" He lifts a finger.

"That's because—"

"No, no, it's my turn to talk right now. You asked what I was thinking, right?" He gives me the wingleader look—the shrewd, calculated one that used to scare the shit out of me—and I snap my mouth shut. He lifts a second finger. "Jesinia won't be the only scribe there, which means there's a high probability of being caught." A third finger joins the other two. "Not only do the books have to be stolen, they have to be returned before anyone notices. Or were you planning on staying overnight to read?"

"I wasn't borrowing tomorrow's trouble on that one," I admit.

"And you really think we can get in and out in under an hour? Because the alternative leaves us dead."

"We don't have much of a choice if we want those journals."

He sighs deeply, then closes the distance between us and takes my chin between his thumb and forefinger to gently tilt my face toward his. "How certain are you that the answers to the wardstone are in those books?"

"We've read through half the classified tomes on ward-weaving and repair in the last month, and whatever we haven't, Jesinia has. They only cover weaving into existing wards or repairing them. Those journals are our best shot at learning how the First Six built the first wards. Our only shot."

"You know they'll kill us if we're caught, right?"

Us. I slide my hands up his chest. "We're dead anyway if we don't get Aretia's wards up. We have *months* if Brennan's right, and he usually is. The truth is coming out. It's just a matter of time."

His attention drops to my mouth, and my pulse leaps. "If you're certain this is the only way, then I'm in. There's no chance I'm letting you do this on your own."

My smile is instantaneous. "You're not going to argue? Or tell me there's another way?"

"Me? Argue with you about books?" He shakes his head, sliding his hand to my cheek. "I only pick fights I can win." He lowers his mouth inch by slow inch, then stops a breath away. "It's your turn to talk now."

He hovers right there and waits, our mouths so close it would only take a whisper of movement to connect us. All it takes is his nearness, his touch, and my blood simmers. Anticipation flushes my skin, and he strokes his thumb along my heated cheek but doesn't take what I so desperately want him to.

My breath catches at the realization that he's giving me the choice not just to kiss him, but to call our night in Samara an exception.

But it wasn't.

Leaning up, I brush my lips across his, then kiss him gently as if it's the first time. This isn't heat and passion, though I know it will be in a matter of heartbeats. This is something else entirely. Something that scares the shit out of me, and yet I can't bring myself to pull away, even in the name of self-preservation.

I'm choosing him, choosing us. There will be no calling this a lapse in judgment, or the result of too much adrenaline, or even lust.

I love him. No matter what he's done or why he did it, I still love him, and I know he cares about me.

Maybe it isn't love.

Maybe after all he's been through, he isn't capable of that emotion.

But I mean *something* to him.

He kisses me long and slow, like we have all the time we want, like there's nothing more important in this world than the slide of his tongue against mine, the drag of his teeth across my lower lip.

It's a bone-melting, intense assault on every one of my senses, and by the time he lifts his head, we're both breathing harder.

"We have to stop, or we're not leaving this room tonight." He drags the backs of his fingers down my cheek and steps back when I force myself to nod in agreement.

I shake my head to clear it, and he moves toward the door.

Where the hell is he going?

"I didn't ask him to help us yet for a reason."

"Yeah. I gathered that." Xaden pauses, gripping the door handle, and looks over his shoulder at me. "I'm *with* you. I'll do this. But you have to know the consequences if he says no."

My stomach pitches. Telling him will expose us...

"He won't." I'm sure of it.

Xaden dips his chin once, then yanks open the door.

Ridoc and Sawyer stagger forward, then slam into the wards and fall to the hallway floor.

My hand flies to my face as I smother a laugh.

"It's soundproof when the door is closed, assholes," Xaden growls. "And what the fuck is *he* already doing here?"

"*He* doesn't know why he's here," Bodhi is saying. "I just ordered him out of flight lessons."

I hop off the desk and hurry to the door as Ridoc and Sawyer pick themselves up and split, revealing Bodhi, Rhiannon, Imogen, and Quinn across the hall.

Aaric stands between them all, leaning against the wall, his arms folded across his chest. "Figured you'd come for me sooner or later," he says, his eyes narrowing on Xaden, shining with nothing short of malice.

The energy between these two is anything but good, which I should have expected. Xaden's father started a war that Aaric's father ended.

One by one, I pull them through the wards into my room, including Aaric, who hovers just inside the doorway, but I leave the door open in case anyone needs a quick exit. I turn to Aaric. "We need your help. And you can say no and walk away right now, but if I explain why we need you and you say no..." I drag in a shaky breath, reluctant to say what needs to be said.

"If we tell you why and you decline, you won't be walking away," Xaden finishes when I can't.

"You think I'm going to lift a finger for *you*?" Aaric reaches for his sword hilt.

"Whoa, whoa!" Bodhi grabs for his sword, angling to step between them. "Everyone calm down."

"You know what's happening out there, and you came here for a reason, right?" I say to Aaric, putting myself in front of Xaden. "Help us do something about it."

"You have no idea what he did to Alic!" he seethes.

"Your brother was a craven, murderous prick." Xaden hooks his fingers into my waistband and tugs me backward, setting me slightly behind him before he shoves Aaric through the wards and into the hallway. "And I'm not sorry I killed him."

Oh *shit*. I did *not* see that coming.

Three hours later, we've gone over the plan until we know not only our parts but everyone else's, too. Bodhi's had to step in between Aaric and Xaden twice, but we're finally on our way to the Archives. Turns out the key to securing Aaric's participation was noting that he'd be stealing from his father. An hour from now, we'll either have retrieved the journals or we'll be dead. The Archives aren't kind to visitors after the vault-like door closes.

"You sure about this?" I ask Aaric quietly as we walk down the tunnel from the infirmary in pairs, eight of us covered in scribe robes embroidered with second-year golden rectangles. This entire plan hinges on him.

"Absolutely. The only person I hate more than Xaden Riorson is my father. Just keep your boyfriend the fuck away from me." He stares straight ahead.

"He'll keep his distance," I promise, glancing over my shoulder, past the others at where Xaden follows close behind, the only one who refused to wear a disguise. Then again, if I was a shadow wielder I'm not sure I'd walk around in anything but black, either.

"I'll be wherever you are," Xaden counters as the bells ring out six times, signaling the hour. "Remember, the goal is secrecy, not showing off. This isn't the Squad Battle," he says, his tone low.

We pass the stairwell on the right that leads up to the rest of campus and down to the brig, then round the last corner. The Archives door comes into view, and lucky for us, Nasya is exactly where I expect him to be: asleep at his post.

Bodhi moves quickly with Ridoc, slipping behind Nasya and hiding behind the door to keep watch.

First obstacle complete.

Jesinia surprises me, meeting us at the door. "No," she signs, appraising our group, the lines of her mouth tense. "Only four of you. Any more, and it'll be too suspicious." Her gaze sweeps over Xaden. "Especially you."

Fuck. Everyone here was chosen for not only their loyalty but their signets.

"No one will see me," Xaden assures, keeping his voice low as he signs simultaneously. "Aaric. Violet. Imogen."

Jesinia's gaze catches on Aaric, and I see the moment she realizes who he is. The blood drains from her face, and she jerks her attention to me.

"Is he that obvious?" I sign as the others start to argue quietly.

"Only if you're looking for it," she replies. "They have the same eyes."

"The wonder of heredity," Aaric signs.

"I can retrieve." Rhiannon whispers her argument at Xaden.

"And I can wipe short-term memory if we're seen," Imogen replies. "Classified signet, remember? Your power is impressive, Matthias, but I'm the last line of defense around here." She moves to Nasya, putting her hands lightly on his head. "Just in case."

"We'll stay close." Quinn steps away from the group and motions at Sawyer and Rhiannon to follow. "Just in case you need us."

Rhiannon looks between Xaden and me, clearly torn. "If something goes wrong—"

"Then you'll go back to your rooms and act like it didn't." I hold her gaze so she knows I'm serious. "No matter what. Stick to the plan."

Her shoulders drop and she nods, shooting me one last look of frustration before joining the others behind the massive door.

"Walk softly," Jesinia reminds us, and my heart pounds as we file into the Archives. "We have to be quick. The Archives close in exactly an hour, and if we're in here when that door seals shut…"

I swallow the nausea that's threatening. "I know. We'll die." The Archives are warded with the ultimate pest protection.

"Just show us the way. We'll do the rest," Xaden says. He disappears the moment we cross the threshold, sticking to the shadows along the dimly lit walls. I can just see the vague outline of his shape if I look closely, but it's almost shocking how well he blends into the darkness.

Or maybe it's that the rest of the space is so bright, mage lights illuminating the rows and rows of bookshelves and empty study tables that stretch to the back of the cavernous dome. Empty is good—and expected for a Saturday night—but there's no telling who might be within the stacks or in the workrooms deeper within the Archives.

I force myself past the pinch of hesitation when I walk by the oak study table, following Jesinia. The marble under my boots is familiar and yet completely foreign. As many years as I've spent here, this is the farthest I've ever walked into the Archives.

Aaric glances down each row as we pass, but I don't take my eyes off Jesinia, forcing my mannerisms, my posture, my pace to mirror hers. The quiet I usually find such peace in is unnerving under these circumstances.

Gods, so much can go wrong. What little dinner I ate threatens to reappear.

The three of us follow Jesinia as she turns left and cuts through the second-to-last row of tables, guiding us in the direction of the workrooms. The scent of bonding glue grows stronger, and my heart stutters at the sight of a scribe headed our way, coming from the same hallway we're headed for.

The single golden rectangle on his shoulder marks him as a first-year, and though the Scribe Quadrant educates twice as many cadets as the Riders Quadrant, it's still small enough that he *should* recognize us if we were what we're pretending to be.

"Cadet Neilwart?" he signs while speaking, glancing at us in confusion. I lower my head and see Aaric doing the same, shielding our features as much as possible.

"Cadet Samuelson," Jesinia answers, turning slightly so I can see her hands.

Fuck, we're going to be caught before we even get *near* the wards.

"I've got this." Xaden's voice soothes the sharpest of the anxiety but not all of it.

But he's here. He's exactly why we waited for this particular night.

Shadows creep from beneath the tables, racing for Samuelson's feet, and Aaric tenses beside me.

"I thought only you and Cadet Nasya were on duty tonight?" Samuelson asks.

"And yet you're here," she replies.

Tendrils of black rise up behind the first-year.

"Wait." The last thing we need is a dead scribe cadet.

"This is me being patient," Xaden answers.

"I forgot my binding assignment in Culley's room." Samuelson glances meaningfully at the cream satchel strapped over his shoulder.

"Forgetfulness doesn't become a scribe," Jesinia signs, and my eyebrows rise as I fight back a smile. "If you don't mind, first-year, we second-years have things to accomplish. Not everyone requires weekends off to study."

The first-year flushes in obvious embarrassment, then steps aside into the aisle.

Shadows fall back into place, and we walk forward as a group.

"I thought he might kill him," Aaric whispers once we're out of the first-year's range of hearing.

"Wouldn't have surprised me," Imogen replies. "Might have been more efficient."

We both whip our heads around to see her shrug.

Jesinia leads us out of the main library and down a well-lit hallway lined with windows and with a few classrooms on each side. The deeper we travel into the Archives, the tighter my collar feels.

Xaden catches up to us in a few strides, walking calmly beside me.

"Someone is going to notice all that black," I lecture quietly as Jesinia turns to the right. This place is a fucking maze, and it all looks exactly the same.

"There's no one here." Xaden's hands are loose at his sides, and he's exchanged the swords he prefers at his back in favor of a short one, which tells me he's prepared for close-quarters fighting. "At least not in this section."

"Your shadows tell you that?" Aaric quips.

"I thought we agreed not to speak," Xaden retorts.

Jesinia opens the third door on the left, and we follow her into what looks to be a classroom. No wonder the hallway is lined with windows; in here, it's dark. Two of the walls are made of stone, and the back one is lined with books. The rest of the space is sparse, filled with rows of long trestle tables and benches that face a lone desk at the front of the room.

"Everything from here is only what I've been told," she signs, worry pursing her lips. "I've never been farther. If I'm wrong about any of this—"

"We can handle ourselves," I promise.

She nods, then walks to the far corner of the room, toward the long bookcase.

"Imogen," Xaden orders, nodding toward the door.

She takes a lookout position, retrieving a knife from under her robes as Jesinia reaches for the back of the bookcase, moving several tomes out of the way before locating a lever.

She pulls down on the metal piece, and the corner of the room separates from the other stones. It rotates a quarter-turn with surprising near silence, revealing the opening to a steep spiral staircase.

Looking closely, I can see the faint lines of the metal track it spins on.

"Amazing," I whisper. How many of these little hidden wonders exist around here? "What?" I hiss at Xaden when I catch him looking at me.

"I feel like I'm looking at what could have been."

"And?" The secret entrance clicks into place, halting its rotation.

"You look better in black," Xaden whispers, his lips brushing the shell of my ear and eliciting a shiver of awareness despite our current situation.

"This is as far as I can take you," Jesinia signs. "If I'm gone much longer, someone may notice. According to the others, the normal Archives wards end here, so if you can't get back in time, you're safer down there overnight."

"Thank you," I reply. "I'll be in contact as soon as we can return them."

"Good luck." She offers us an encouraging smile, then leaves the four of us to it.

Xaden leans into the stairwell. "Watch your step," he tells us. "There's a little light coming from the bottom, but we'll need to keep the rest from turning on."

"We're down to forty-five minutes," Imogen says. Any longer and we're either stuck and court-martialed…or dead.

No pressure.

"Then we'd better move quickly," Xaden replies, lacing his fingers with mine before starting down the steps.

The first time you are caught in the Archives after the door seals for the evening will be the last. The complex magics put in place to preserve our texts are not compatible with life.

—Colonel Daxton's Guide to Excelling in the Scribe Quadrant

CHAPTER THIRTY-THREE

Shadows blanket the ceiling, blocking any mage lights that could flicker on at our presence, so I put my free hand on the wall as we descend the stairs slowly. Every step is a gamble in the darkness, but miraculously, no one stumbles.

Pale blue light blooms at the bottom of the staircase.

"A mage light?"

"There are two guards at the end of this hallway," Xaden answers, slipping his hand from mine. *"Wait here while I solve that problem."*

I put my hand up to signal the others to stop when we reach the final step. The space opens into what looks to be a hallway, but Xaden doesn't question which direction to take. He moves quickly to the right, lifting both hands. A crumpling sound follows.

"Now," he says aloud.

The hallway is maybe thirty feet long and little more than a glorified tunnel supported by carved pillars over a stone floor. It smells like earth and metal and feels dank with humidity. At one end, light shines through an open archway. Glancing over my shoulder, I see that only darkness consumes the other possible path.

"There isn't even a door?" Imogen asks as we hurry down the hall.

"No need with wards that strong," Xaden comments.

"I can feel them." The thrum of sharp, intense power grows stronger the closer we get. The hair on the back of my neck rises, and my own power surges in answer to what feels like a hell of a threat.

"We have a few minutes before these two will wake up. I didn't hit them that hard," Xaden says as he and Imogen drag the infantry guards to the side, clearing the path.

"Those wards are some uncomfortable shit." Imogen rolls her shoulders.

"There's a hum, but it's not that bad," Aaric replies as we stare through the warded archway with its intricately carved stonework to the shelves of the small, circular library that lies beyond it.

"That bodes well for getting past," Imogen remarks. "And you'd better hurry."

"You're looking for two journals," I nervously remind him, even though we've gone over this three times.

"There have to be at least five hundred tomes in there." Aaric's gaze skims the shelves, and he sighs.

"You'll have to search—"

"Violet!" Xaden shouts as Aaric grips my hand and strides forward through the archway, yanking me along.

Powerful magic ripples over me as I stumble through, pricking every inch of my skin and twisting my stomach with the feel of a hundred-foot freefall as he pulls me into the library.

He releases my hand and I hit my knees, falling forward and catching myself on my hands. Nausea overwhelms every other sense. My mouth waters and my head hangs as I fight back the urge to vomit.

"Why the fuck would you do that?" Xaden snaps from the other side of the wards. *"Tell me you're unharmed."*

"Queasy, but I'll live."

Aaric ignores Xaden, dropping to a crouch in front of me. "Are you all right, Violet?"

I force air in through my nose and out through my mouth. "Tell me you knew it would let me through," I bite out as the worst of the illness passes. "Because it sure as hell didn't want to."

"My father doesn't have anything warded that isn't worth showing off," he explains, holding out his hand. "So, I took a chance that you wouldn't smack into the wards like a wall. And I can't get through these books in the next forty minutes alone. You're the one who knows what to look for."

I ignore his hand and push to my feet despite the smarting pain in my knees from the impact. I turn in a circle, taking the library space in. There are six heavy bookshelves with glass doors lining the circular walls, and a pedestal of cabinetry in the middle decorated with a velvet tablecloth embroidered with the king's signet. Above us, mage lights emit a soft glow, the illumination catching on the curves and knot-like lines carved into the decorative ceiling about five feet above Aaric's head.

The scent of damp earth is gone, and it's considerably cooler in this room than the tunnel beyond the archway. I scour above me, but there are no windows for ventilation or any visible modifications I can see. It's not just the wards. There's magic in this room.

"Pull me in. Now," Xaden demands.

"No," Aaric replies without so much as glancing in his direction. "The only perk I'm getting out of this whole expedition is knowing how much it must pain you to realize you can't get to her."

"Stop antagonizing him and get to work, Aaric. You start to the left and ignore anything that's not handwritten." I peek through the archway to see Xaden in full *fuck-you* mode.

His hands are loose, and shadows rise around him, forming blades as sharp as the one he carries. But it's the cool, calculating wrath in his eyes that makes me worry for Aaric's health—which is why I don't insist he pull Xaden in. *"I'm fine,"* I promise him.

"I'm going to fucking kill him."

"Then you'd be responsible for the deaths of two princes."

"Warrick and Lyra, right?" Aaric questions, already pulling tomes from the shelves.

"Yes," I reply.

"Alic deserved it. He was a bully and forfeited his life by coming after Garrick during Threshing. Though I wonder who it was that told Aaric, since if his father knew I highly doubt I'd still be in possession of my head."

"Well, Aaric doesn't deserve it." I skip the right side of the shelves in favor of the cabinetry. If I had a six-hundred-year-old book that was worth our entire kingdom, I'd store it where it was least exposed to the elements. I pull open the first drawer, which stores two books—*The Study of Winged Creatures*, which looks to be at least half a century old, and *A History of the Island Wars*, which appears even older.

"These are all journals," Aaric says. "Looks like every commanding general of the armies since the Unification."

"Keep going." I check the next drawer, then the next, and so on, until I've opened three-quarters of the storage. It's an exercise in self-control not to open every book and devour its contents. There are tomes here on the early wars, the history of the individual provinces, mythology of the gods, and even what looks to be the earliest tome I've ever seen on mining practices. My fingers itch to turn the pages, but I know better than to damage the parchment.

"This shelf is all journals of the commanding generals of the riders?" Aaric lowers his hood and glances over his shoulder at me.

"They used to be separate positions." I move to the last section of the center pedestal. "Healers, infantry, or even scribes could be the General of the Armies until about two hundred years ago with the second Krovlan uprising. After that, the commander of the riders commanded all Navarre's forces."

"You know that no rider has ever been named king, right?" Imogen asks through the archway.

"That's not entirely true—" I start, opening the top drawer.

"If you're asking if I give a shit about being second in line, then the answer is no," Aaric says over his shoulder at Imogen. "It's Halden's destiny to be king. Not mine."

"Does Halden know?" I ask, reading over the titles in the top drawer. "About what's happening out there?"

"Yes," Aaric says quietly.

"And?" I look over at him.

Our eyes lock for a heartbeat before he replaces a tome and moves to the next. "I'm here, aren't I?"

Understood. Halden isn't going to help. "Guess we have that in common."

"I still can't believe you kept his secret all these months," Imogen says.

"I kept yours, too," I remind her, opening the next drawer. This entire section seems dedicated to historical records.

"I've known Violet longer, which is why I'm *not* surprised she kept yours." He looks my way and moves to the next set of shelves. "The rift between you and Aetos was what caught me off guard. You two were inseparable when we were kids."

"Yeah, well, kids grow up." I bark out the words, shutting the drawer with a little more force than necessary. "You can't trust him, you know."

"Figured that out by that little exchange that went down between the two of you on the mat." He pulls out another tome. "These are the generals of the healers."

"Useful but not what we need." I crouch to open the last drawer. "Fuck. More records."

"We're down to twenty minutes, and we need ten of those to get back to the door," Imogen warns, her tone tight with urgency.

The collar of my armor tightens a little more, and I tug it away from my throat.

"These are the scribes," Aaric says at the fourth case.

"As carefully as you can, glance through the earliest ones. Try to only touch the edges of the pages." I close the bottom drawer and stand. There are two more cases to search. "Look for anything that mentions wards or wardstones."

He nods and pulls the first one down.

My attention shifts to the sixth bookcase. "Half of these look like Tyrrish history," I tell Xaden.

"Fascinating. We'll come back and study up after we win this war," he replies. A guard rustles and we all pivot, but Xaden has him knocked out again before he so much as opens his eyes. "Hurry, before I do permanent brain damage over here."

"This is dated six AU," Aaric says, shutting the journal. "The wards were well in place by then."

"Shit." Frustration expands the knot in my throat. "Start the next one." I pull a promising, cracked-spined tome, but it's a fucking *weather* almanac.

"Arts and crafts?" Aaric shows me the painted cover of one.

"Violet," Imogen warns. "That giant-ass door is going to seal us in here in fifteen minutes!"

This is *not* how this was supposed to go, but isn't that the story of my life these last couple of months? The propaganda should have opened the eyes of other cadets. Mira should have believed me. Andarna should be awake.

"Take a breath," Xaden orders. *"You look like you're about to pass out, and I can't catch you."*

"What if this is all for nothing?" I concentrate on lowering my heart rate, on keeping the panic from consuming me, then tilt my head to the side and read the spines of the collection in front of me that pertains to the isle kingdoms.

"Then we'll know to look elsewhere. The only way to fail this mission is to be caught. You still have five minutes. Use them."

"Astronomy," Aaric says, dropping down to read the bottom row of titles.

I close my eyes, draw a deep breath, and find my center. Then I open them and step back from the shelves. "'In the storage of ancient documents,'" I recite from the Scribe Manual, "'it is not only temperature and touch that must be monitored—'"

"Glad to see you haven't changed that much." Aaric's mouth curves into the first smile I've seen from him in years.

"'—but light.'" I glance up. "'Light will steal ink's pigment and crack the leather of spine and cover.'"

"One time, I heard her recite the entire unification agreement while climbing the battlements in Calldyr," Aaric notes, moving to the top of the next bookcase.

Light. They'd have to be hidden from light. I start searching for track marks in the floor that might signal another hidden door, or cubby, or *something*.

"Thought we weren't talking," Xaden drawls.

"Wasn't talking to you." He glances at Imogen.

"So, it's not all marked ones you hate," she replies, folding her arms across her chest.

"Why would I hate you?" Aaric puts the tome back. "Your parents led a righteous rebellion, and from what I can tell, you're just trying to do the same. I hate *him* for killing my brother."

"Fair enough." Imogen starts to tap her foot.

"Where would your father keep his most precious possession?" I ask Aaric. "He'd want to show it off, right?"

"He'd keep it within easy reach," Aaric agrees. "And are you going to tell me what it is you guys are trying to ward? It's a rebel outpost, isn't it?"

Xaden's eyes meet mine as I prod the wood pieces between the drawers on the center piece, looking for a pop-out compartment.

King Tauri would keep the journals within reach.

"It's the only logical thing to do," Aaric says, dropping to the floor and looking under the center pedestal. "To establish your own wards that aren't dependent on Basgiath's because you know you'll be waging war on two fronts. There's nothing under here." He stands. "Where is it? Draithus? That's the most logical choice. Close to both the Navarrian border and the sea."

"Violet, we have to go," Imogen warns, walking toward the guards and rolling up the sleeves of her cream robes.

King Tauri would want to show them off.

I reach for the velvet tablecloth and pull it off.

"There!" I point to the circle of glass set in the top of the pedestal. "Aaric! Beneath the glass!" Two leather tomes, barely larger than my hand. Perfect for keeping in a rucksack...while riding the first dragons.

"Not glass. Another set of wards." He leans over the cabinet and reaches in, then lets out a sharp hiss, his face contorting in pain as he pulls out both books. "Fuck!" He sets them on the edge of the cabinet, then holds his hands up.

I watch in horror as blisters the size of my thumb swell over every inch of skin that passed through the wards.

"I think those wards know I wasn't him." He grimaces. "Let's go!"

I unbelt my robes and reveal the two cream satchels Jesinia gave me for this exact reason, then carefully put one tome in each.

"Two minutes!" Imogen shouts from where she's kneeled next to the guards, her hands on the larger one's head.

Xaden drops two wineskins into their laps, and I snatch the tablecloth from the floor, then throw it over the case.

"Zihnal may love you, but let's not test him," Aaric grits through his teeth, holding out a blistered hand.

"It's going to hurt—" I protest, tying my belt tight.

"And I'm not leaving you in here." He grabs hold of my hand and grunts in pain as he pulls us through the wards and into the hallway.

My hand is sticky when he lets go.

"We have to run." Xaden gestures down the hallway, and I do exactly that. Run.

When the robe gets in the way, I gather the fabric in my hands and sprint, following Xaden as he races up the stairs.

"Bet you're glad we've been running every morning!" Imogen calls from behind me as we turn and turn and turn, the staircase dizzying me by the time we emerge into the classroom.

Xaden reaches for the lever Jesinia used, and as soon as Imogen and Aaric are clear, he pushes. We wait only long enough to see that the entrance begins closing before taking off again.

My chest heaves as we run down the hallways, Xaden taking every turn Jesinia did, never once questioning himself. Either he's really certain of the path or he knows we can't afford the time to even debate.

We reach the main library and the bells ring out, signaling an hour has passed.

"Faster!" Xaden demands.

They peal once.

There is no *faster*, but I don't have enough breath to snap back at him. Our boots pound against the marble as we race between the tables.

Twice.

"Run!" Sawyer shouts from the entrance.

Oh *gods* the door.

Three times.

It's closing on its own, and the locking mechanism won't allow it to open until a full twelve hours passes. The muscles in my thighs burn in protest.

I skid as we turn at the last of the tables, sliding into the end of the bookshelf and hitting my shoulder hard enough to wince.

A fourth.

Xaden falls back to run at my side, but he's the faster of us.

"Take the books!" I shout between gasping breaths. "You can make it!"

A fifth.

"You stay, I stay!" He lifts a hand, sprinting with it outstretched, and shadows fly from the walls to push against the closing door as we pass the study table.

Sawyer clears the narrow path that remains between the thick steel of the door and its casing.

The bells ring out a sixth time.

Xaden pushes me through the doorway first, and once I'm in, I look back, my breaths ragged and my heart pounding so hard I can feel it in my head.

Imogen races by, and Xaden reaches into the doorway as the seventh bell peals.

Oh gods, he's going to lose an arm, and *Aaric*—

They're not going to make it.

My last words with my father before the Battle of Aretia were
spoken in anger, because he was sending me
away for my own safety.
I'm not sure I'll ever forgive myself for that,
but I like to think he forgives *me*.

—Recovered Correspondence of Lieutenant Xaden Riorson
to Cadet Violet Sorrengail

CHAPTER
THIRTY-FOUR

Xaden yanks Aaric through just as the door slams shut, shadows scattering along the floor like fallen leaves.

I sag, leaning over and bracing my hands above my knees as I gasp for air.

"You made it!" Rhiannon ducks her head to mine, smiling wide.

"And we have to keep making it," Xaden reminds us. "Robes off. Keep to the plan."

My heart slows somewhat, and I straighten, then shrug out of the scribe's robes, putting them in Quinn's outstretched palms.

Bodhi helps Aaric out of his, careful with his blistered hands.

"Did you get them?" Jesinia signs, hope lighting her face.

I nod. "Will they suspect you?" Nasya looks more unconscious than asleep against the wall.

"Not if I get us back to the dorms quickly," she replies.

"I'll take care of him," Imogen says, heading over to Nasya.

"He shouldn't remember much. I hit him from behind," Sawyer admits, stuffing the robes into a large cream laundry bag.

I translate for Jesinia.

"I'll just berate him for falling asleep," she signs back, offering Sawyer a smile, and I translate.

He blinks, pausing for a long second before taking the last robe—Aaric's—
and putting it into the bag. "Damn, your hands…"

The blisters that have popped are bleeding, and those that haven't look like
they might go at any second.

"That's a rebound burn," Bodhi says. "It will clear up overnight if treated."

"Change to the plan." I glance at Xaden, but he merely lifts an eyebrow.
"Ridoc, take Aaric to your room and keep his hands hidden. Rhi, go to the
infirmary and ask for Dyre. A mender will draw too much attention. It might
take him some time to report if he's not on duty, but he should keep quiet if
you call in the debt he owes me. You'll have to sneak him into the quadrant—"

"Good idea. I can do that." She nods to the guys. "C'mon. Now." The three
of them take off down the hallway.

"I'll take the laundry," Jesinia signs.

I translate for Sawyer, and he hands over the bag.

"Let's move," Xaden orders.

"Go," Jesinia urges. "We're clear here."

"Thank you," I sign, then head out with Xaden and the others.

"How did it go for you?" Xaden asks Quinn as we pass the stairs on our left
and continue toward the Healer Quadrant.

"I projected into commons and made it clear I was looking for lemonade
because we've all been drinking in Imogen's room." She grins, a dimple popping
in her cheek. "And then I managed to take a walk as Violet *and* Rhiannon."

My mouth drops and I nearly stumble. "You projected looking like someone
else?"

She nods. "I can distort my own features a little, but it's way easier in the
astral plane. My signet is stronger because Cruth was my great-aunt's dragon.
But she's not a direct descendant, so I don't have to worry about going mad like
those whose dragons bond in the direct familial line. Dragons aren't supposed
to even get close to family lines for that exact reason—like they listen to human
rules." She glances at Imogen. "I still can't quite get the right shade of pink for
your hair."

We fall quiet as we pass by the infirmary. It's the last obstacle before we can
split up in the quadrant as planned.

"Well, that was blissfully uneventful." Bodhi pushes open the door to the
bridge.

"Speak for yourself," Imogen replies, smacking him in the chest as she
walks by. "You weren't in charge of keeping Xaden calm while Aaric had Violet
trapped behind the wards with him."

I scoff, because we both know that's *not* how that went down.

Xaden's jaw ticks.

We part once we reach the other side of the bridge. Imogen and Quinn take the stairs to their rooms, Bodhi and Sawyer head to commons to make as much of a scene as they can in order to be remembered, and Xaden and I climb to the first floor and escape into the courtyard.

The October air cools my flushed cheeks.

"You feel all right?" Xaden asks as we pass a group of cadets.

"Thirsty from sprinting, but…" I don't bother fighting the smile that stretches across my face. "But good."

He glances my way, his gaze flickering to my mouth, then tugs me into one of the shadowy alcoves carved into the thick walls. "That smile," he murmurs before his mouth takes mine in a hungry kiss.

I arch against him, spearing my hands into his hair as I kiss him back with everything I feel. It's not slow and sensuous like the one we shared in my room. This is hard and fast and…happy.

We're both smiling when we break apart.

"*We did it,*" I say as my hands fall to his shoulders.

"*We did it,*" he agrees, resting his forehead against mine. "*I hate leaving before I really have to.*"

"*Me too.*" I pull back and lift one of the satchels from my shoulder, then remove the journal. "*But it's safer this way. You need to get one to Brennan.*"

I flip to the center of Warrick's journal and grin at the sprawling strokes of Old Lucerish, keeping my ungloved fingers to the very edge. What I read has me grinning, victory swelling in my chest. "'*After we placed the last rune, we placed the wardstone where the dragons felt the deepest currents of magic run,*'" I translate slowly to Xaden, then glance up. "*I might be off a word or two, but it's here!*" I flip another few pages. "'*That last step complete, the protections fell into place at…*'" My face scrunches as I work out the rest. "'*…at the birth of an iron rain.*'"

I spot at least three more mentions of that term before quickly putting the journal back in the satchel. "*This is it.*" I hand it to Xaden. "*Take this to Brennan. He should be able to translate it. They won't expect you to leave until morning, so you can get out of here without being searched if you head out now, and splitting up the journals means we can read them twice as fast.*" And ensures that one of them makes it out of this place.

He folds the cream canvas around the journal inside, then unbuttons his flight jacket and stores the bundle against his chest before rebuttoning. "I wish I could spend the night," he says in that gravelly tone that instantly turns me on.

"That makes two of us."

He stares at me with something like longing, then reaches into the shadows and grabs the pack he'd stored there earlier. Keeping his eyes locked with mine, he swings the pack onto his back, then reaches for my face and kisses me again.

The simple pleasure of it is perfect.

"You are astonishing," he says against my lips. "I'll see you in seven days."

"Seven days," I agree, fighting the urge to pull him into another kiss. And another. "Now go. We have to keep to the plan, remember?"

He kisses me hard and quick, then walks away, striding across the courtyard like he owns it. I rub my hand over my heart, hoping to ease the ache of watching him walk away, but the hurt is nothing compared to the triumph I feel.

I step into the courtyard, then look up, waiting to catch one last glimpse of him in the overcast sky as he flies southeast.

For the first time in months, it's hope coursing through my veins instead of dread.

We can do this—we're *doing* this. We have the firsthand account of how the First Six activated their wardstone, and I know I can talk Xaden into flying for Cordyn to secure the luminary with me. He won't like it, but he'll do it. I just have to figure out how to get the leave approved. And until then, we'll keep doing what we're doing, smuggling out weaponry and building from within Navarre until we can stand on our own. Aretia will have wards in a matter of days; I'm certain of it.

"Violet?"

I look over my shoulder and smile at Nolon as he approaches, carrying a wineskin in one hand and a pewter mug in the other. He looks so damned tired, like he's just come from a major session or twelve. "Hi, Nolon." I wave.

"I thought that was you. I was getting some lemonade when Jack told me he saw you out here, and I remembered that you're on my mending list." He hands me the mug, then stands at my side, looking up at the sky. "It's your favorite, if I remember."

"That's too kind of you." I lift the mug and drink deeply, slaking the thirst that's burned my throat since our little sprint through the Archives. "And don't worry about my shoulder. It's already healed. You know, I never got the chance to thank you for helping us during interrogation."

"I never like to see you hurt, and Varrish has it out for you." He drinks from his own skin, then scratches his stubbled cheek. "Where is Riorson, anyway? I don't often see you apart on Saturdays."

My stomach dips as Jack Barlowe walks across the courtyard, Caroline Ashton at his side with some other second-years from First Wing. It completely flips when he gives me a nod, which I awkwardly return.

"Violet?" Nolon prompts, following my line of sight to Jack. "Everything all right?"

"Everything is fine. And Xaden left earlier. We don't always get along." I take another sip of the lemonade, then glance down at the contents. The kitchen must have changed up the recipe, because it has a funny yet familiar aftertaste.

"I meant what I said," Nolon says quietly, glancing at the cream satchel I carry.

Cream. Not black.

My head blurs, my vision swimming momentarily as I swing my head to look at him.

"Tairn—" But Tairn isn't there. Every connection I have is fuzzy.

No. Oh gods, *no.*

But…but I've trusted Nolon with my life for *years.*

"I never like to see you hurt," Nolon whispers, apology crinkling his brow as the mug rolls from my hand, crashing to the gravel a heartbeat later. "But I can't protect you from the consequences of your own actions when you risk the safety of every civilian in this kingdom."

Bootsteps sound all around me and the world spins, but it's Varrish's face I see hovering above mine. "Why, Cadet Sorrengail, what *have* you gotten yourself into?"

The only signet more terrifying than an inntinnsic is a truth-sayer.
And yet we let *them* live.

—Major Afendra's Guide to the Riders Quadrant
(Unauthorized Edition)

CHAPTER
THIRTY-FIVE

I blink slowly, my vision coming into focus with all the urgency of a snail. Dull, throbbing pressure radiates forward from the back of my head, and the mass of gray clears slightly, revealing stones set in a spiral pattern—a patch of them charred from smoke. A ceiling?

"That's not our concern," a man says, his voice unfamiliar and raspy. "We follow orders."

Fear-laced adrenaline charges through me, but I lock my muscles tight, forcing myself to remain as still as possible so I can get a grip on what the fuck is happening.

"It is if she finds out," another voice—this one female—replies.

It smells like wet moss and iron, and the air is cool but thick. We're underground. A steady dripping sound fills the silence.

"She's in Calldyr. We have a week until she's scheduled to return," the raspy-voiced one says.

And I'm sitting; that's what's digging into the base of my skull—the back of a chair. The weight across my wrists and ankles is familiar. I'm strapped in, just like assessment.

"Tairn—" I reach out, but the connection is foggy, and my power doesn't rise.

The lemonade. The satchel. *Nolon.*

Fuck. I've been caught.

"Ahh, there she is." A grizzled face appears over mine, and the man smiles, revealing three missing teeth. "Major? Your prisoner is awake!" He retreats, and

I lift my head, taking in my surroundings.

The prison cell is wedge-shaped, and a door that looks exactly like the one in the interrogation chamber makes up the narrowest portion, but this cell isn't for instructional purposes. My jailer wears infantry blue, which means this must be the brig.

I assume the wooden shelf at my right is meant to be a bed, and at least there's a toilet on the other side of that. Fear pulses through my veins at the sight of the unwashed, bloodstained walls, and I quickly look away, scanning the rest of the cell as my head clears. Nora, the woman who always dumps my bag, leans against a wooden table, her arms folded, and her face puckers into lines of what I think might be concern as the door opens beside her.

The smile on Major Varrish's face forms a pit in my stomach as he enters.

Oh *gods*. The others. Are they here? Have they been hurt? A boulder lodges in my throat, making it nearly impossible to draw a full breath.

"Out," he tells the other man, who scurries like a spider into the main chamber but doesn't shut the door behind him, giving me a glimpse of a desk covered in my black-hilted daggers before Varrish blocks the view. "I promised you I'd try your way *once*," Varrish calls over his shoulder.

Terror expands the pressure in my throat. I can't reach Tairn or Xaden. Can't call on my signet or even my knife skills, since my hands are bound.

I'm alone and fucking *defenseless*.

Nolon walks in, his steps sluggish, his eyes heavy with sadness. "We just need you to answer a few questions, Violet."

"You drugged me." My voice cracks. "I trusted you. I've *always* trusted you."

"Clear this up quickly and we can return to trusting each other," Nolon says. "Let's start with why you stole Lyra's journal?" He reaches behind Nora and brings out the book.

Every interrogation technique I've been taught deserts me, and I stare… just stare at the journal, my mind scrambling for a way out of this when there clearly is none.

"I wanted to be wrong," he says gently. "But Markham had sounded the alarm that the royal wards within the king's private library had been breached, and then I saw you standing in the courtyard with a scribe's satchel—"

"Which is common to transport books from the Archives," I counter.

Damn it. We were stupid for not assuming tripping the wards would alert Markham.

"And had that been the case, you would have woken up in the infirmary with a headache and my most sincere apologies." Nolon holds up the scarred leather journal, the very key to protecting Aretia. "But you carried this."

"We're not here to argue that point." Varrish watches me with rapt fascination.

"Answer my questions, and we'll let you go sleep that headache off before class tomorrow. Lie—even once—and it's going to get messy."

So, it's already Sunday.

"Three questions." Nolon shoots a stern look in Varrish's direction. "We want to know how you did it, who you did it with, and most importantly, *why*."

The boulder in my throat loosens, and I fill my lungs completely, willing my panic to subside. They don't know who, which means no one else is chained up down here. Not Xaden, or Rhiannon, or Aaric, or any of the others. It's just me. Being alone just turned into a *blessing*.

And I'm not defenseless. I'm still in full possession of my mind.

"Let's start with how you breached a royal ward," Varrish suggests.

"It would be impossible for me to breach a royal ward, seeing as I'm not royal." I lift my chin and mentally prepare for the worst.

"She's telling the truth," Nora says, tilting her head to the side. "My signet detects lies. Tell one, and I'll know."

My heart jolts.

Truth it is, then. After this is over, I'll have to explain my answers—or lack thereof—to my mother. Every single word matters.

"Violet, please," Nolon pleads, setting the journal on the table. "Just explain. Was it an unsanctioned squad challenge? Some kind of dare between second-years? They're still trying to ascertain exactly what's missing. Help us. Tell us, and this will go much easier for you."

Trying to ascertain. They can't get in.

"You're jumping to the *why* part." Varrish rolls his eyes. "Honestly, Nolon, this is why you've never been suited to interrogation." His pale gaze locks on mine. "How?"

"How can you assume that book isn't a reproduction if you haven't verified the original is even missing?" I ask Nolon.

Nolon glances sideways at Varrish. "Markham said the coverlet wasn't disturbed."

"And yet we have the fucking journal." Varrish walks a slow circle around me. "Is it a reproduction?"

He's trying to catch me in a lie.

"I wouldn't know, seeing as I haven't examined it." There hadn't been time.

"Truth," Nora rules.

Varrish stops in front of me, and I look straight into those pale, soulless eyes. "I'm guessing you have no proof, Major Varrish, because none of you can cross a royal ward, and no one is volunteering to tell the king that there's been an alarm, false or otherwise. Please, let me remind you, the last time someone accused me of lying without proof, they found themselves assigned to the farthest outpost

Luceras has to offer."

"Ah, you mean Aetos." He doesn't even flinch. "No worries. I'll ferret out the evidence he needs while I have you here under my supervision, since you're proving to be combatant instead of helpful, as Nolon had hoped. Grady is such a stickler for rules, so our last encounter wasn't nearly as fruitful as I would have liked." He crouches, looking at me like I'm a shiny new toy he can't wait to break. "Who stole that book for you?" He looks pointedly at my hands. "Because we both know you didn't."

Selective truth. That's all I have within my arsenal to protect my friends.

"I alone put that particular book into its bag."

"She's telling the truth," Nora remarks.

I glance from Varrish to Nolon. "And I'm done answering your questions. If you want to put me on trial, then call a quorum of wingleaders and do so according to the rules put forth in the Codex."

Varrish stands slowly, then backhands me. Pain erupts in my cheek as my head snaps to the side under the force of the blow.

"Major!" Nolon shouts.

"Nora, order an immediate formation and check the hands of every cadet in the quadrant," Varrish says as I blink through the sting. "Nolon, you're dismissed."

I breathe deeply, preparing for the coming pain as Varrish rolls up the sleeves of his uniform. I try to focus on a misshapen brick in the wall, try like hell to dissociate from my body.

No matter what happens in this room, they can't change the fact that Xaden got out with Warrick's journal. Brennan will have what he needs to raise Aretia's wards. Whatever agony Varrish has planned will be worth it.

Violence, remember it's only the body that's fragile. You *are unbreakable.* I cling to Xaden's words.

"I'll call you when you're needed," Varrish promises, waving Nolon off.

When he's needed to mend me.

"Don't worry. I'll start small," Varrish tells me. "And you have all the power here, Cadet Sorrengail. This stops as soon as you talk."

I cry out when he dislocates the first finger.

Then scream when he breaks it.

Drip. Drip. Drip.
I pretend the sound is rain against my window, pretend the hard, unforgiving wood under my cheek is Xaden's chest, that the arm bent at an unnatural angle

in front of me, throbbing in time with my pulse, belongs to someone else.

"Sleep if you can." The suggestion is soft, the voice so achingly familiar that I squeeze my undamaged eye shut.

You're not really here. You're a hallucination from pain and dehydration. A mirage.

"Maybe," Liam says, and I open my eye just enough to see him sit on the floor beside me. He pulls his knees up, resting his elbow on the side of the bunk just beneath my fractured arm. "Or maybe Malek sent me as a kindness."

Malek doesn't do kindness. Nor does he allow souls to wander about. Kudos to my brain; he's an excellent hallucination. He looks exactly as he had the last time I saw him, dressed in flight leathers and wearing a smile that makes my heart ache.

"I'm not wandering, Violet. I'm exactly where I need to be."

Everything hurts. Unending pain threatens to pull me into the blackness again, but unlike the last two times, I fight to stay conscious. It's the first moment I've been alone in hours, and I no longer fear the chair in the middle of the room.

Now I know more bones break when Varrish takes me out of it.

"I know," Liam says gently. "But you're staying strong. I'm so proud of you."

Of course that's what my subconscious would say—exactly what I need to hear.

I run my tongue over the split in my lip and taste blood. Varrish hasn't taken a blade to me, but my skin has split from his blows in so many places that I feel like one giant, open wound. The last time I moved, my uniform crunched from dried blood.

"Bring in her squad," Nora suggests from the antechamber. "She'll break as soon as you start on them."

Liam's jaw flexes, and fear knots my empty stomach.

"She didn't during assessment," Varrish responds. Gods, I wish I didn't know his voice. "And bringing them in means they'll know what's happened, and given the relic winding around Imogen Cardulo's arm, I doubt she'll be willing to wipe their memories. Killing them presents an entirely different set of issues, too. You're sure none of the cadets have hand injuries?"

"I inspected them all myself," Nora replies. "Devera and Emetterio are asking where she is, as is the rest of her squad. She's missed class today."

It's Monday.

I reach for Tairn, but the bond is still fogged. Right, because they forced that solution down my throat once again between shattering my arm and snapping my ankle. He didn't even have to take off my boots to make that happen.

But it's only my body they've broken. I haven't spoken a single word.

"That means you've been here two days," Liam says.

It will be another five before Xaden realizes I'm missing. No doubt they're monitoring correspondence to make sure someone doesn't alert him. He can't react, Liam. If he does, he'll risk everything.

"You think he's not already losing his shit?" A corner of Liam's mouth rises into the cocky smirk I've missed so much. "I'd bet he already knows. Sgaeyl will have felt Tairn's panic. That dragon of yours might not be able to reach you this deep under Basgiath, but Xaden's going to rip this place apart brick by brick. You just have to survive."

He can't risk the movement. He won't. Xaden's priorities have always been clear, and damn if that's not one of the things I love about him.

"He will."

The door opens, but I don't have the energy or the ability to rise, to turn my head or even lift a hand. My heart jumps, pounding like it sees the chance to flee this hellscape of a body. I don't know how to tell it that Mira's armor will keep it safe long after it wishes it could just stop.

Varrish lowers himself to my eye level, no more than a foot away from Liam. "You must be in so much pain. It can all stop. Maybe Nolon was right. Let's forget how you stole the book. You're clearly not going to give up your accomplices. But I need to know *why*. Why would you need a journal from one of the First Six? I've been reading it. Interesting history. What are you trying to ward, Sorrengail?"

He waits, but I keep my words to myself. He's way too fucking close.

"We could just stop dancing around each other and have a true discussion," he offers. "Surely you have questions I could answer about why it is we don't involve ourselves in Poromish issues. Is that what this is? Righteous indignation? We could have an equal exchange of information, since we both know it wasn't gryphons that killed your friend's dragon."

I startle, and pain washes over me, fresh and violent.

"Don't fall for it." Liam shakes his head. "You know he's trying to play you."

"But how much *do* you know?" Varrish asks softly, like it's a kindness. "And what have you been doing with the marked ones? We've been watching them for years, of course, but until Cadet Aetos gave you up, all we'd had to go on was speculation. But then you didn't come back to Basgiath. No outposts reported you seeking a healer. So, I'm going to rephrase my earlier question. Where did you go, Cadet Sorrengail? *Where* are you trying to ward?"

This is so much bigger than me stealing the book.

"Gods, you're good. Or you're in too much pain to react." Varrish tilts his head, reminding me of an owl as he studies me. "Do you know what my signet is, Cadet Sorrengail? Why it is I'm so good in this room? It's classified, but we're all friends here, aren't we?"

I stare at him but don't reply.

"I don't see people." He tilts his head and studies me. "I see their weaknesses. It's a great advantage in battle. Honestly, you surprised me when we met. From everything I'd heard about the youngest Sorrengail, I expected to look at you and see pain, broken bones, or maybe shame for never living up to Mom's expectations." He skims his finger over the obvious break in my forearm but doesn't apply pressure. The threat is enough to make my chest tighten. "But I saw…nothing. Someone taught you to shield, and I'll admit you're very good at it." He leans closer. "Do you want to know what I see now that we've cut you off from your power?"

Hatred wells within me and I hope he sees it.

"By Dunne, must I carry all of the conversation? 'Yes, of course I want to know,'" he says, raising his voice in mock imitation. "Well, Cadet Sorrengail, your weaknesses are the people you love. So many people to choose from. Squad Leader Matthias and the rest of your squad, your sister, your dragons." A twisted smile curves his mouth. "Lieutenant Riorson."

My heartbeat skips.

"Hold steady, Violet," Liam says.

"She's triggered," Nora notes from the doorway.

"I know," Varrish replies. "And I bet you're thinking he'll be the one who comes for you, aren't you?" He admires the bruises on my forearm like they're artwork. "That come Saturday, when you don't show in Samara, he'll come looking, even if it means violating his leave policy. You're pinning your hopes that he'll break the rules for you. That he'll save you, since your own mother hasn't lifted a finger for you."

My throat moves even though I'm too dehydrated to swallow.

"He won't wait until Saturday," Liam promises.

"That's what I'm counting on." Varrish nods. "I waited all year for you to break a rule so I could question you under Codex. Your mom's a real rule follower that way. But you have no idea the joy it gives me to know that Fen Riorson's son will break Codex by abandoning his post to come to your aid, that he'll be strapped to this chair next. And he *will* give me the answers I seek."

Wait. What?

"Shit. He's not just questioning you. He's setting a trap for Xaden." Liam tenses.

My heart starts to *pound.*

"You have so much power here, Sorrengail. You alone can save Lieutenant Riorson from what awaits him should he arrive. Tell me what I want to know, and I won't hurt him."

For a heartbeat, I'm tempted. The thought of Xaden being tortured makes my hand curl and my nails catch on the rough grain of the wooden slab.

"Where are you trying to ward? What are the marked ones up to?"

"Hold the line, Vi." Liam rests his hand against my side, and gods it feels *so* real. "Talking would lead to the deaths of every living thing on this Continent. If they had *anything* on Xaden, he'd already be in custody. They're not going to hurt him. They can't."

Logically, I know that, but emotionally…

"No? You're sure? You can save him. Right here. Right now. Because I think he'll come, and when he does, I will break him—and I'll make you watch," Varrish promises in a whisper. "But don't worry. You'll be screaming your secrets in no time. Of course, by then I won't need them. I'll have who I really want."

His gaze drops to my neck, as if he can see my pulse skyrocketing.

"Ahh, you see it now, don't you?" Varrish grins. "I'm sure you think he's indestructible, but let me assure you, I was lucky enough to glimpse the *most powerful rider of your generation* fumble his shields like a novice once. It was for less than a second, but that was all I needed to see what it would take to shatter him. We'll have all the information we need in a matter of days. You're not the prize, Sorrengail. You're the tool."

Fuck him.

"Does Solas enjoy hiding?" My voice croaks, and I cough.

He blinks but quickly masks his surprise.

"Just because you've blocked my ability to talk to Tairn doesn't mean he doesn't know exactly what you've done to me." My lip splits again when I force a smile. "You're hunting Xaden. But Tairn is hunting Solas. You're the weaker on both counts. I *might* die in this chamber, but I promise you *will.*"

"Just because I can't kill you without losing my target doesn't mean I won't shatter you over and over until he arrives. We're going to have fun, you and I." He stands, then brushes his hands on the thighs of his uniform before walking out. I hear his faint words through the door: "Call Nolon in. We need to start fresh."

But Varrish is wrong. Xaden won't come. He'll choose the safety of the revolution. I'm now one of the people he can't save. I just have to hope that everyone is wrong, that he'll survive my death.

"Don't leave me," I whisper to Liam. I don't care that I'm far gone enough to hallucinate, that my brain is using Liam as a crutch as long as he stays, as long as I'm not alone.

"I won't. I swear."

. . .

*D*rip. *Drip. Drip.* I lose track of the hours, the beatings, the questions I refuse to answer.

Nolon visits twice, or maybe it's three times.

Life is varying degrees of pain, but Liam never leaves. He's there every time I open my eyes, watching, talking me through the torture, holding my sanity together while simultaneously proving it's already left.

At least once a day, they chain me into the chair and force the serum down my throat, blocking me from Tairn. I eat the food they provide because survival matters most, and I sleep after each mending session, only to wake and be broken again and again.

My ribs are cracked thanks to a well-placed kick, and my left arm snaps in the same exact place Varrish broke it the first time, which tells me that not only am I not at full strength, Nolon isn't, either.

"We could bring in Jack Barlowe if this doesn't work." Nora's voice rises, bringing me fully awake from where I've dozed off in the chair. "Gods know he's been waiting for retribution."

"Tempting," Varrish replies. "I'm sure he'd be happy to find new and inventive ways to motivate her, but we can't trust him not to kill her. Can't trust that kid for anything, really, can we? Too unpredictable."

"Still can't believe that fucker survived," Liam mutters from where he stands leaned against the wall to the right of the door.

Gods, I'm sore and swollen at the broken places, and discolored on the bits of skin I can see. Everything *hurts*. I'm not even sure I'm *me* anymore as much as I am pain encased in a failing body.

But Rhiannon isn't being put through this, or Ridoc, or Sawyer, or Imogen, or Quinn. Everyone I care about is safe. That's what I grasp onto.

"You know, Sloane hates me," I whisper.

"Sloane can be tough." Liam shoots me an apologetic half smile. "You're doing a good job."

"Yeah, I'm a great role model." It's all I can do to keep from rolling my eyes.

"You asked to see me, sir? Down here? There have to be a dozen guards in the stairwell."

That *voice*. Fear slides down my spine, leaving chills in its wake as Liam's head jerks toward the door.

Dain. I'm so fucked. We all are.

"I did," Varrish responds. "I need your help. *Navarre* needs your help."

"What can I do?"

I twist against the straps that hold me captive, but their buckles hold strong.

"Stay calm," Liam whispers, like any of *them* can hear him.

"We had a breach of security this week, and classified documents were stolen. We caught the perpetrator and prevented the loss of intelligence, but the prisoner…" There's a dramatic pause. "It's blatantly obvious by connection that this rider is working with what we suspect to be a second rebellion, intent on destroying Navarre. For the safety of every civilian within our wards, I need this prisoner's memories, wingleader. You must extract the truth, or our very way of life will be compromised."

Well, when he puts it that way. I pull against my bonds again, sending ricochets of agony through my nervous system. I have no shields. No way to block him out.

Everyone in Aretia is going to die, and it will be *my* fault.

"I'm going to warn you," Varrish says gently. "The prisoner's identity may come as a shock." The door swings open before I can fully prepare myself.

Varrish walks in, leaving Dain standing in the doorway, his eyes wide as his gaze sweeps over me, lingering on my swollen, purple-splotched hands, bound to the arms of the chair, and the face I'm sure matches them. He can't even see the worst of it under my uniform, the broken bones and contusions.

"Violet?"

"Please help me," I whisper, even knowing I'm begging a Dain that no longer exists, the one I knew before he crossed the parapet, and not the hardened third-year in front of me.

"You've been torturing her for *five days*?" Dain accuses Varrish.

Five days? It's only Thursday?

"Since she stole Lyra's journal from the king's private library?" Varrish sounds bored. "Absolutely. She might have been a childhood friend, Aetos, but we both know where her loyalties now lie—with Riorson and the war he's planning against us. She wants to bring down the wards."

"That's not true!" I mean to shout but it comes out more as a whimper, my voice hoarse from days of screaming. Varrish has twisted everything. "I would never hurt civilians. Dain, you know—"

"I don't know *shit* about you anymore," Dain counters, his face twisting in anger.

"There's a war out there," I tell him, desperate to break through before he breaks *me*. "Poromish civilians are dying, and we're not doing anything to help. We're just watching it happen, Dain."

"You think we should involve ourselves in their civil war?" Dain argues.

My shoulders slump. "I think you've been lied to for so long that you won't recognize the truth even when it hits you in the face."

"I could say the same for you." Dain looks toward Varrish. "You're sure she was trying to take down the wards?"

"I've had the journal sent back to the Archives for safekeeping, but yes. The book she stole gave detailed instructions on how the wards were built and could be used as a map to unravel them." Varrish clasps Dain's shoulder. "I know this is hard to hear, but people aren't always who we want them to be."

Liam pushes off the wall and walks around the pair, coming to my side and crouching down. "I don't think you're going to be able to stop this."

Me either.

"Try not to be angry with her," Varrish tells Dain, his expression shifting to sympathetic. "We can't always help who we fall in love with, can we?"

Dain stiffens.

"Riorson pulled her into something she couldn't possibly understand. You know that. You saw it happen last year." He sighs. "I didn't want to have to show you this, but"—he pulls my alloy-imbedded dagger from his own sheath—"she was carrying this, too. That metal you see is what powers the wards. We think they've been smuggling them out to wherever they're planning to stage this war from, weakening our wards little by little."

"Is that true?" Dain's gaze flies to mine.

I spot Nora leaning against the doorjamb and shudder. "I can explain. It's not how he's portraying it—"

"I don't need you to explain," Dain snarls. "I've been asking you to talk to me for *months*, and now I see why you won't. Why you're adamant I never touch you. You're scared I'll see what you've been hiding." He stalks forward, and I shrink back in the chair.

Xaden, forgive me.

"Remember your ethics, Cadet," Varrish instructs. "Especially given your attachment to Cadet Sorrengail. Search like you've been practicing but focus on the word *ward*."

"Lieutenant Nora," a voice calls from the antechamber. "All leadership is being ordered to assemble. There have been…incidents at the border."

"By whose order?" Nora demands.

"General Sorrengail's."

"We'll be there shortly," Nora replies, waving him off.

"We might already be too late," Varrish says, shaking his head. "Riorson deserted days ago, according to the reports we received this morning. We're gathering the marked ones now."

My breath seizes. He deserted. He could be safe in Aretia right now, raising the wards. But Imogen? Bodhi? Sloane? They're the ones leadership is gathering.

Liam's hand settles on my shoulder, steadying me. They'll kill them all, and once they know about Aretia, they'll hunt the rest. "He can search your memory," Liam tells me. "But logic says he'll have to muddle through what you're thinking first."

"What have you done, Violet?" Varrish asks. "Orchestrated another attack on an outpost? Find out what you can, Aetos. The safety of our kingdom depends on it. Time is of the essence."

Dain's eyes flare, and he lifts his hands.

"You killed Liam," I blurt.

He pauses. "So you keep saying. But I only searched your memory to prove my father wrong, Violet, and all you did was prove him right. If the marked ones died betraying our kingdom, then they deserved what they got."

"I hate you," I whisper, the sound strangled as my eyes prickle and burn.

"She's stalling," Varrish snips. "Do it now. And if you see something you don't understand, I'll explain it once we know where their army is hiding. Just trust me that we are acting in the best interest of every citizen of Navarre. Our only goal is keeping them safe."

Dain nods and reaches for me, hesitating at the last second. "She's bruised *everywhere*."

"Show him what you *want* him to see," Liam urges.

"She's nothing more than a traitor," Varrish retorts.

"Right." Dain nods, and I close my eyes the second his fingers push in on my tender, aching temples.

They may have blocked me from my power, but that stems from Tairn. The control over my mind? That's *mine*, and it's all I have left.

Unlike last year, I feel Dain's presence at the edge of my mind this time, right where my shields should be, and instead of recoiling from the assault, I grab hold of that presence and throw myself into the memory, dragging Dain with me.

"Do we have a riot nearby?" Liam asks.

Gravity shifts as I realize my worst nightmare is indeed a living, breathing monster.

Two legs. Not four. Wyvern.

They'd sent us here to die.

Venin with red veins distending from their eyes, killing helpless people.

Blue fire. Desiccated land. Soleil and Fuil falling.

We'll never be able to smuggle enough weaponry out to make a difference. They've kept us in the dark, erased our very history to avoid conflict, to keep us safe while innocent people die.

Liam— Gods...*Liam*. I dig my mental fingernails into Dain and hold him there, making him feel it with me again, the helplessness. The chest-crushing sorrow. The eye-blurring rage.

It's been my honor. Liam's last words to me.

My vengeance in the sky, fighting along Tairn's back, armed with the only weapon that will kill the dark wielder doing her best to slay my dragon and end me.

The moment the dagger slides into my side, I stop pulling Dain and start *shoving*, screaming both physically and mentally, filling my head with every ounce of pain that's been inflicted upon me in the last four days.

Dain gasps, and his hands fall from my temples.

I throw my eyes open, the sound of my scream still echoing in my ears as he draws back, horror etched on every line of his face.

"I'm here," Liam promises. "And I still don't regret it, Vi. Not one second."

Wetness tracks down my cheeks.

"Did you get what you wanted?" I manage to ask through my shredded vocal cords.

"You're smuggling weapons," Dain says slowly, searching my eyes. "Stealing our weapons to aid another kingdom?"

My stomach sinks at my complete, absolute failure.

Out of everything I showed him, *that's* what he took?

I wrench my gaze from his to look at Liam, memorizing the lines of his face and those trademark blue eyes. "I'm so sorry I failed you."

"You never failed me. Not once," he whispers, shaking his head. "We pulled you into our war. If anyone's sorry, it's me."

"As you should be." Varrish sneers.

If Dain has conquered my memory, seen the weapons runs I've helped with, then he knows it *all*. A wave of hopelessness rolls over, stealing my resolve, my determination not to break. All I have left inside of me is pain, and that isn't worth fighting for, not if I've just given up everything—everyone—that means anything to me.

"They want us *now*!" the man shouts from the antechamber.

"Varrish," Nora prompts. "It's a summons for *all* leadership."

"What did you find?" Varrish turns to Dain, losing his composure. "Where are they staging from?"

"Give me that knife," Dain demands, holding out his hand. "I want to compare it to the one I saw in the memory. The ones they're *stealing* from us."

"Just don't kill her. We need to find and question Riorson first, use her as leverage." Varrish hands my dagger over to Dain.

He glances over the weapon and nods. "This is the one. They're taking them out by the dozen, arming the enemy. I saw everything." Brown eyes meet mine. "There's at least one drift involved."

My heart plummets. He knows. He saw despite my best efforts.

They'll question me again—keep me prisoner to lure Xaden, even—but they'll never let me leave here alive. This place I called home, the halls I walked with my father, the Archives I worshipped alongside the gods, the field where I flew with Tairn and Andarna, the halls where I laughed with my friends, and the rooms where Xaden held me will be my tomb.

And the boy I used to climb trees with along its river will be my demise.

I sag, the last of the fight draining out of me in defeat.

"Good. Good. Now tell me where they are," Varrish orders.

Dain grips the dagger in his left hand, spinning it so the blade runs parallel to his forearm as he brings it to my throat. "You should have trusted me, Violet."

I don't dare to even swallow as I hold the asshole's gaze. I won't die afraid.

"None of this would have happened if you'd just trusted me." The hurt in his eyes only feeds my rage. How dare he look wounded. "And now, it's too late."

"Varrish!" Nora yells as shouts fill the antechamber.

Varrish turns toward her, and I feel the knife slip against my skin.

Dain is going to kill me.

"You're all right." Liam steadies my shoulder. "I'll be right here. I'm not going to leave you."

Tairn. Andarna. Gods, I hope they survive it. Xaden has to live. He just has to. I love him.

I should have told him every day, been honest about my feelings even through the fights and the doubt.

Now instead of giving those feelings back to Xaden, they'll die with me. My vision blurs, and tears streak down my cheeks, but I lift my chin.

Dain whips his arm back, and I wait for the forward surge, the cut, the pain, the flow of blood.

It doesn't come.

Varrish staggers backward, holding his side, his eyes bulging as a roaring sound fills my ears. Dain brings the bloodied knife to the straps at my wrists, cutting one free, then the other. "I don't know if we can fight our way out of here," he says quickly, dropping down to cut my ankles free. "Can you move?"

What the fuck is happening?

"Aetos!" Varrish snarls, falling back against the wall, then sliding down the stone. He leaves behind a fresh trail of red.

"Violet!" Dain shouts, forcing something into my hand. "You have to move or we're dead!"

I wrap the fingers of my unbroken hand around the familiar hilt as Dain draws the sword at his side, holding it at Nora's throat when she lunges into the cell. "Let us pass, and you'll live."

He holds the blade steady and hooks his other arm behind my back as I try to stand, holding me upright when my legs try to fail. They're not newly broken since Nolon's last visit, that I can remember, but I whimper at the pressure against my cracked ribs and the nausea as the room seems to spin.

"I make no such promises." The low, menacing threat weakens my knees a second before a hand with a dagger reaches around Nora's throat, slicing without hesitation.

She falls, a torrent of blood flowing from the gaping wound in her neck.

I look up into the wrath of Dunne in the form of gold-flecked onyx eyes.

The only crime worse than murdering a cadet is the
unfathomable act of attacking leadership.

—MAJOR AFENDRA'S GUIDE TO THE RIDERS QUADRANT
(UNAUTHORIZED EDITION)

CHAPTER
THIRTY-SIX

Rage shines in his eyes as Xaden holds his sword in his right hand and a
dagger in his left, both dripping blood, both aimed to strike Dain.

Oh *gods*.

"No!" I shout, lurching to put myself in front of Dain, but my feet don't
cooperate and the ground rushes up to meet me.

"Shit!" Steel rattles against the floor as Dain catches me with both hands.

The edges of my vision turn black as pain threatens to pull me under. Every
inch of my body screams in protest as I find my feet. But it's not just Dain's arms
holding me—there are soft bands of shadows at my hips and beneath my arms.
Two Xadens appear, then merge into one as I fight to stay conscious. "He saved
me," I whisper. "Don't kill him."

Stabbing Varrish earns Dain a chance…right?

Xaden's gaze flickers to mine, and then he does a double take.

"Gods, *Violet*." Shadows explode around us, cracking stone and decimating
the wooden slab of a bed marked with my blood.

Guess my face is just as beaten as the rest of me.

"You came." I stumble forward, and Dain is smart enough to let me go.

Xaden catches me, shadows grasping his sword as he splays his hand over
my back and cradles me against his chest with a light touch, like he's afraid I
might break. "There's nowhere in existence you could go that I wouldn't find
you, remember?" He drops his lips to the dirty, frayed, blood-spattered remains
of my braid and kisses the top of my head.

Leather and mint overpower the iron-and-moss scent of the cell and, for the first time since Nolon drugged me, I feel safe. Tears soak his chest—his or mine, I'm unsure.

"God*damn*," Garrick says from behind Xaden. "You took off running and then couldn't save a single one for me? Took me forever to clear the barricade of bodies in the staircase."

My smile splits my lip all over again as I turn my face to rest my cheek above Xaden's strong, steady heartbeat. "Hi, Garrick."

He blanches, dropping his swords to his sides, but covers it with a quick smile. "You've looked better, Violet, but I'm glad you're alive."

"Me too."

"It's chaos up there," Garrick tells Xaden, sparing a questioning glance for Dain. "Leadership is launching all over the place to get to the border."

"Then it worked," Xaden states.

Varrish groans and our heads all whip in his direction. "You're turning traitor?" he accuses Dain as he struggles to his feet, still holding the wound in his side.

"Oh, is that what's happening?" Garrick asks, looking between Dain and Varrish.

"Your father will be so disappointed," Varrish hisses through bloody, clenched teeth. Coughing up blood means he doesn't have long.

"If he already knows what Violet showed me, then I'm the one disappointed in *him*," Dain counters, picking up his sword and raising it at Varrish.

"No," Xaden snarls. "Not you." His hand flexes at my back, and shadows wrap around Varrish a second before they drag him across the floor. Horror widens his eyes as the strands of black dump him into the chair, then bind his wrists and ankles in place of the shackles. "That honor belongs to Violet, if she wants it."

"She does," I reply instantly.

Xaden shifts his grip, wrapping his arm around my waist and watching my reactions. *"I don't know where I can touch you."*

"That's fine," I promise, gripping the alloy-hilted dagger in my right hand as my left lies uselessly at my side.

Dain steps back, lowering his sword as Xaden helps me walk, my feet shuffling over dried patches of my own blood on the stone floor.

Varrish's eyes narrow despite the pallor of his skin, and Xaden holds me steady as I lift the dagger to his chest with a trembling, weak grip, resting the point above his heart, right between his ribs.

"I promised you'd die in this room," I whisper, but I'm shaking too hard to push the blade home. It's taking everything I have just to stay standing.

Xaden's hand wraps around mine, and he jabs forward, driving the blade into Varrish's heart. I memorize the look on Varrish's face as the life fades out of him, just so I can reassure myself that he's really dead when the nightmares inevitably come.

I stare, and stare, and *stare* as the weight of everything that's happened closes in on me, threatening to steal my air. My throat squeezes shut and my eyes burn with prickling heat as my thoughts spiral. I just killed the vice commandant of the quadrant.

What the fuck am I supposed to do now? Go back to class?

And Xaden…Xaden risked *everything* by coming here.

"Give us a second, and keep Aetos breathing for now," Xaden orders, and I hear the room clear before he carefully pivots to face me, turning us away from Varrish's body. "You're alive. No matter what happened in this room, what was said, you're alive and that's all that matters."

"I didn't break," I whisper. "Dain… He saw right before he stabbed Varrish, but I didn't break, I promise." I shake my head, and my vision blurs then clears as water trickles from my eyes.

"I trust you." He cradles the back of my head, his beautiful gaze boring into mine, swallowing me whole. "But it wouldn't matter to me if you had. We're leaving. I'm getting you the fuck out of here."

I blink. "We can't go now. They'll follow us, and Brennan's not ready." My face crumples. "You'll forfeit access to Basgiath's weapons—"

"I don't give a *fuck*. We'll figure it out once we're there."

"You'll lose everything you've worked for." My voice breaks. "Because of me."

"Then I'll have everything I need." He lowers his face, leaning in so he's all I see, all I feel. "I will happily watch Aretia burn to the fucking ground again if it means you live."

"You don't mean that." He loves his home. He's done *everything* to protect his home.

"I do. I'm sorry if you expect me to do the noble thing. I warned you. I'm not sweet or soft or kind, and you fell anyway. This is what you get, Violet—me. The good, the bad, the unforgivable. All of it. I am *yours*." His arm wraps around the small of my back, holding me steady and close. "You want to know something true? Something real? I love you. I'm *in* love with you. I have been since the night the snow fell in your hair and you kissed me for the first time. I'm *grateful* my life is tied to yours because it means I won't have to face a day without you in it. My heart only beats as long as yours does, and when you die, I'll meet Malek at your side. It's a damned good thing that you love me, too, because you're stuck with me in this life and every other that could possibly follow."

My lips part. It's all I've ever wanted, ever needed to hear. "I do love you," I admit in a whisper.

"Glad you didn't forget." He leans in and brushes his lips over mine lightly, careful not to hurt me. "Let's get out of here together."

I nod.

"We have to move," Garrick calls out.

"Clear the staircase!" Xaden orders. "And tell Bodhi to track down whatever antidote she and the rest of her squad need."

"On it," Garrick says.

"My squad?"

Xaden looks back at me. "They're fine, but they were put under guard in the interrogation classroom after they tried to mount a rescue mission yesterday. Can you walk out of here?"

"I don't know," I answer truthfully. "I lost track of what's broken and what Nolon mended. I know my left arm is fractured, plus at least three of my ribs on my right side. My hip feels like it's not entirely where it's supposed to be, either."

"He'll die for his part." He pivots and walks us out of the cell, past Nora's body and into a fucking bloodbath. There are at least half a dozen bodies between us and the stairwell. He makes quick work of sheathing all my daggers where they belong but doesn't take the one I still have clutched in my hand.

Dain passes him supplies from a nearby locker, and Xaden splints my arm as quickly as possible. I bite down on my torn lip to keep from crying out, and he wraps my ribs over my armor.

"Xaden!" Garrick calls out from the stairwell. "We have a problem!"

"Fuck," Xaden mutters, glancing between the swords leaned against the wall and me.

"I can carry her," Dain offers.

Xaden shoots him a look that promises a slow, painful death. "I haven't decided whether or not to let you live yet. You can bet your ass I'm not trusting you with her."

"I can walk. I think." But the second I try, the room tilts. And for the first time in my life, I *feel* weak. That's what that monster did to me in this room. He took my strength.

"But he didn't break *you*, Violet," Liam says softly from the corner of the room, and my chest squeezes tight as he takes a step back toward the shadows. Then another.

"How about this—I promise the next time I'm beaten for five days straight, I'll let you carry me out of the prison," Xaden says, sheathing his swords behind his back.

"Thank you," I say—to both men.

Xaden lifts me into his arms, tucking me tight against his chest without putting pressure on my ribs. "Follow me or die. It's your choice, but make it now," he tells Dain as shadows surround us, forming a circle of blades as Xaden moves, carrying me up the mage-lit staircase.

My head falls onto his shoulder and I wince, but what does the pain matter if we're leaving? If we're both alive? He came.

"What kind of problem, Garrick?" Xaden asks as we round the corner of the staircase.

"A general-size one," Garrick answers, his hands in the air.

My mother's blade is at his throat.

Oh shit.

I lift my head, and Xaden stops cold, his body tensing against mine.

Her eyes meet mine from where she stands on the step above Garrick, the lines of her face strained with…wait, is that *worry*? "Violet."

"Mom." I blink. It's the first time she's said my name since before Parapet.

"Who did you kill?" She directs the question at Xaden.

"Everyone," he responds unapologetically.

She nods, then drops her blade.

Garrick breathes in deeply, moving away from her and putting his back to the wall.

"Here." She reaches into the rib pocket of her uniform and draws out a vial of clear liquid. "It's the antidote for the serum."

I stare at the vial, and my heart speeds from a dull thud to a gallop. How do I know that's what's actually in there?

"I would have come sooner if I'd known," my mother says, her voice softening along with her eyes. "I didn't know, Violet. I swear it. I've been in Calldyr for the last week."

"So your return is just what? Coincidence?" I ask.

Her mouth purses, and her fingers curl around the vial. "I'd like a moment alone with my daughter."

"That's not happening," Xaden counters.

Her eyes harden when she looks at him. "You of all people know the lengths I'll go to in order to protect her. And since I'm pretty sure you're the reason we're getting reports of dragons dropping wyvern carcasses at every outpost we have along our border, the reason this college is emptying itself of most of the leadership in a rush to *contain* the problem, the least you can do is give me a chance to say goodbye to her."

"You what?" My gaze swings to Xaden's, but he keeps his locked on my mother.

"Would have done it sooner, but it took a couple of days to hunt them down and kill them," Xaden replies to her.

"You've threatened our entire kingdom." Her eyes narrow.

"Good. You allowed her to be tortured for *days*. I don't give a shit whether it was by your absence or your negligence. It happened on your watch."

"Three minutes," she orders. "Now."

"Three minutes," I agree.

Xaden's gaze flies to mine. "She's a fucking monster." His voice is soft, but it carries.

"She's my mother."

He looks like he might fight me for a second, but then he slowly lowers me to stand and braces me against the wall. "Three minutes," he whispers. "And I'll be at the top of this staircase." That warning is given to my mother as he starts up the steps with Garrick leading the way. "Aetos, did you decide to follow?"

"Apparently," Dain says, waiting a few steps beneath me.

"Then fucking follow," Xaden orders.

Dain grumbles, but he marches up the steps, leaving my mother alone with me.

She's the picture of composure, her posture straight, her face expressionless as she holds out the vial. "Take it."

"You've known what's happening out there for all these years." I white-knuckle my weapon.

She steps forward, her gaze jumping from the dagger in one of my hands to the splint on the other, then selects a pocket in my uniform top and slides the vial in. "When you have children, we can discuss the risks you'll take, the lies you'll be willing to tell in order to keep them safe."

"What about *their* children?" My voice rises.

"Again." She hooks her arm around my upper back, sliding her hand under my shoulder, and hauls me against her side. "When you are a mother, talk to me about who you're willing to sacrifice so your child lives. Now *walk*."

I grit my teeth and put one foot in front of the other, fighting the dizziness, the exhaustion, and the waves of pain to climb the stairs. "It's not right to let them die defenseless."

"I never said it was." We take the first turn, climbing slowly. "And I knew you'd never see it our way. Never agree with our stance on self-preservation. Markham saw you as his protégé, the next head of the scribes, the only applicant he thought smart enough, clever enough to continue weaving the complicated blindfold chosen for us hundreds of years ago." She scoffs. "He made the mistake of thinking you'd be easy to control, but I know my daughter."

"I'm sure you think that." Each step is a battle, jarring my bones and testing my joints. Everything feels abominably loose yet so tight I might split open from the pressure.

"I might be a stranger to you, Violet, but you are far from a stranger to me. Eventually, you'd discover the truth. Maybe not while in the Scribe Quadrant, but certainly by the time you made captain or major, when Markham would start bringing you into the fold, as we do with most at those ranks, and then you would unravel *everything* in the name of mercy or whatever emotion you'd blame, and they would kill you for it. I'd already lost one child keeping our borders safe, and I wasn't willing to lose another. Why did you think I forced you into the Riders Quadrant?"

"Because you think less of the scribes," I answer.

"Bullshit. The love of my life was a scribe." Steadily, we climb, twisting along the staircase. "I put you into the Riders Quadrant so you'd have a shot at surviving, and then I called in the favor Riorson owed me for putting the marked ones into the quadrant."

I stop as the door at the Archives level comes into view. "You did what?" She didn't just say what I think she did.

She tilts her head to look me in the eye. "It was a simple transaction. He wanted the marked ones to have a chance. I gave him the quadrant—as long as he took responsibility for them—in return for a favor to be named at a later date. You were that favor. If you survived Parapet on your own, all he had to do was see that no one killed you outside of challenges or your own naivete your first year, which he did. Quite a miracle, considering what Colonel Aetos put you through during War Games."

"You knew?" I'm going to be sick.

"I discovered it after the fact, but yes. Don't give me that look," she chastises, pulling me up another step. "It worked. You're alive, aren't you? Though I'll admit I didn't foresee the mated dragons or whatever emotional entanglement you've involved yourself in. That was disappointing."

It all clicks into place. That night at the tree last year when he should have killed me for catching the meeting of the marked ones. The challenge where he had every opportunity to exact his revenge on my mother by ending me—and instructed me instead. Nearly intervening at Threshing...

My ribs feel like they're cracking all over again. He's never had a choice when it came to me. His life—the lives of those he holds dearest—has always been tied to mine. And suddenly, I *have* to know. "Are those your knife marks on his back?"

"Yes." Her tone is bland. "It's a Tyrrish cust—"

"Stop talking." I don't want to hear a single explanation for such an unforgivable act.

But of course she doesn't listen. "It seems that by putting you into the

Riders Quadrant, all I did was hasten our own end," she remarks as we climb the last four steps, coming out in the tunnel by the Archives.

Xaden reaches for me, and my mother's arm falls away.

"I trust you'll use the chaos to get her out?" she asks him, but we both know it's an order.

"Planning on it." He tucks me in against his side.

"Good. Don't tell me where. I don't want to know. Markham is still in Calldyr with the king. Do with that information what you will." She looks at Dain, who waits off to the side with Garrick, his face ashen. "Have you made your choice now that you know?"

"I have." He squares his shoulders as a group of scribe cadets runs by, their hoods in disarray, panic written on their faces.

"Hmm." She dismisses Dain with a single sound, then looks at Xaden. "And so the war of the father becomes that of the son. It is you, right? Stealing the weaponry? Arming the very enemy trying to rip us apart?"

"Regret letting me into the quadrant yet?" He keeps his voice deceptively calm, but there are shadows rising along the tunnel walls.

"No." Her gaze drops to me. "Stay alive, or this all will have been for nothing." She skims the backs of her fingers along my swollen face. "I'd tell you to take arnica and see a healer, but you already know that. Your father made sure you'd know everything you needed or where to find it. You're all that's left of him, you know."

But I'm not. Mira has his laugh, his warmth, and Brennan…

She doesn't know about Brennan, and in this moment, I have no regrets about keeping that secret.

The smile she gives me is tight and so full of sadness that I wonder if I'm hallucinating. It falls as quickly as it appeared, and she turns away from us, headed back to the stairwell that will carry her up to the main campus. "Oh, and Violet," she calls back over her shoulder. "Sorrengails walk or fly off the battlefield, but they're never carried."

Unbelievable. I watch until she disappears up the stairwell.

"No wonder you're so warm and fuzzy, Violet," Garrick mutters.

"We're leaving," Xaden announces. "Gather the marked ones and meet us at the flight field—"

"No." I shake my head.

Xaden looks at me like I've sprouted a few more limbs. "We just talked about this. We can't stay here, and I won't leave you."

"Not just the marked ones," I clarify. "If Markham is gone and most of the leadership is flying for the border, then it's our only chance."

"To leave?" Xaden lifts his brows. "Good, then we're in agreement."

"To give everyone a choice." I glance at the empty tunnel. "They're going to lock this place down once the cadre returns, once they know they can't stop the spread of information, and our friends…" My head shakes. "We have to give them a choice, Xaden, or we're no better than leadership."

Xaden narrows his eyes.

"Dragons will vouch for the ones who want to leave for the right reasons," I whisper.

He grits his teeth but nods. "Fine."

"It won't be safe here for you. Not after what you just did." I look to Dain and lift my brows. It's one thing to protect me in private, or to face down my mother, whom he's known his entire life. It's another to be known as the rider who ripped this place apart.

"Not that it will be safe for him where we're going." Garrick glances between Dain and Xaden. "You can't be serious. We're going to trust this guy?"

"If he wants our trust, he'll earn it," Xaden says.

A muscle in Dain's jaw flexes, but he nods. "Guess my last official act as wingleader will be to call a formation."

That's where the leadership is now! Trying to hide the bodies of over a dozen dead wyvern!" Dain finishes, his voice carrying over the courtyard a half hour later as we stand on the dais in front of formation, the other wingleaders to his right. The sun has fallen beneath the peaks behind us, but there's more than enough light for me to see the shock, the disbelief on the face of almost every rider.

It's only the marked ones and my squad who don't begin to argue amongst themselves, some quiet, some outright yelling.

"Was this what you had in mind?" Xaden asks me, his gaze swinging over the crowd.

"Not exactly," I admit, leaning heavily on him but managing to stay on my feet. My uniform is clean, my rucksack packed, and I'm wrapped and braced from ankle to broken arm, but more than one cadet is staring at my face. After a quick look in the mirror, I understand why.

Nolon must have only mended the most severe of my injuries, because my face is a collage of new, purple-black bruises and older, greenish ones, and that pattern only continues beneath the cover of my uniform.

Xaden damn near shook the entire time it took for me to change.

"If you don't believe me, ask your dragons!" Dain shouts.

"If their dragons agree to tell them," Tairn says, on his way back from the Vale. I'd finally trusted my mother enough to drink the antidote about ten minutes ago—which Tairn had claimed was the only logical move, and he bonded me for my intelligence, after all.

"What has the Empyrean decided?" We aren't the only ones making choices tonight.

"It will be up to the individual dragon. They will not interfere, nor will they punish those who choose to leave and take their clutches and hatchlings with them."

It's better than the alternative, which was full-scale slaughter of the dragons choosing to fight. *"Are you really okay?"* I ask him again. The bond between us feels strange, like he's holding back more than usual.

"I lost Solas in a network of caves while I was hunting him, so I was unable to kill him and Varrish myself for their actions. When I do find him, I will prolong his suffering before death."

I understand the feeling. *"And Andarna?"*

"Being made ready for flight. We'll pick her up on our way out." He hesitates. *"Prepare yourself. She still sleeps."*

Knots of apprehension twist in my stomach. *"What is wrong? What aren't you telling me?"*

"The elders have never seen an adolescent remain in the Dreamless Sleep this long."

My heart plummets.

"You're lying!" Aura Beinhaven shouts, snapping my attention back to the current situation as she charges toward Dain, blade in hand.

Garrick steps into her path, drawing his sword. "I have no problem adding to my body count for the day, Beinhaven."

Heaton draws their axe at the base of the steps, the purple flames dyed into their hair matching the shade of my pinkie finger, and faces the formation alongside Emery, who already has his sword ready with Cianna protecting his back.

Xaden was busy for the five days I spent in that cell. He came back with every graduate who bears a rebellion relic and a good share of their classmates. But not all.

"We'd better hurry this along." I look up at Xaden. "The professors are going to be here any minute." The distraction Bodhi engineered in the flight field bought us time to meet without teachers noticing, but not much, especially considering that Devera, Kaori, Carr, and Emetterio are among those on campus still.

"By all means," Xaden replies, a look of boredom on his face. "Feel free to convince them."

"Share the memory of Resson but nothing further," I tell Tairn. *"It's the easiest way for them to all have the same information."*

"I loathe that idea." He's complained before that sharing memories outside of a mating bond isn't exactly comfortable.

"Have a better one?"

Tairn grumbles, and I can see the moment it happens. There's a ripple through formation of tilted heads and gasps.

"There we go." I shift my weight to the less injured knee, and Xaden's hand tightens around my waist, leaving his dominant arm free.

Xaden sighs. "I guess that's one way to accomplish the goal, though I wish you'd left some parts out."

Parts like Liam's death.

"It's true!" someone in Second Wing yells, stepping out of formation and stumbling in shock.

"What the hell are you talking about?" another shouts, looking at the rest in confusion.

"If your dragons don't choose—" Dain starts, but his voice is overpowered by the outbreak of mayhem within the ranks.

"How's it going there, wingleader?" Sarcasm drips from Xaden's tone.

"You think you can do better?" Dain turns a slow glare his way.

"Can you stand on your own?" Xaden asks me.

I nod, grimacing through the sharp bites of protest all throughout my body as I straighten.

He steps forward, raises his arms, and shadows rush in from the wall at our back, engulfing the formation—and us—in complete darkness. There's a glimmer of a caress across my cheek, right where it's split to what feels like bone, and more than one cadet screams.

"Enough!" Xaden bellows, his voice amplified, shaking the very dais under our feet.

The courtyard falls silent.

Shadows recede in a rush, leaving more than one cadet gawking at Xaden.

"Fucking show-off," Garrick mutters over his shoulder, still squared off with Aura.

A corner of Xaden's mouth rises. "You are all riders!" he shouts. "All chosen, all threshed, all responsible for what happens next. Act like it! What Aetos has told you is the truth. Whether or not you choose to believe is up to you. If your dragon has chosen not to share what some have seen, then your choice has been made for you."

Wingbeats fill the air, and a murmur rises among the formation. I lock eyes with Rhi where she stands at the head of our squad. She nods subtly toward the rotunda.

I glance that way and catch a trio of figures in cream, led by Jesinia, all carrying packs. Thank gods, they came. Now I just need three dragons willing to carry them.

"Already taken care of," Tairn promises. *"And only this once."*

This once is all we need to save their lives.

"Wars do not wait for your readiness," Xaden continues, "and make no mistake about it—we are at war. A war in which we are outmatched not only in strength of signet but air superiority as a whole."

"Is this your idea of a pep talk?"

"If they need to be roused, they shouldn't be coming with us."

Fair point.

"Whatever you decide in the next hour will determine the course—and perhaps the end—of your life. If you come with us, I cannot promise you'll live. But if you stay, I guarantee you will die fighting for the wrong side. The venin will not stop at the border. They will drain every ounce of magic in Poromiel, and then they'll come for the hatching grounds in the Vale."

"If we go with you, they'll hunt us down as traitors!" a voice from Third Wing calls out. "And we would be!"

"Defining yourself as a traitor requires declaring your allegiance," Xaden counters. "And as for hunting us down…" His shoulders rise and fall with a deep breath. "They won't be able to find us."

My heart starts to pound with the growing roar of wingbeats in the air.

The door to the Gauntlet and flight field flies open, and a dozen professors rush out, anger and shock lining their faces.

"What have you done?" Carr shouts, running for us, his wispy hair flying in all directions as he lifts his hands. "You'll end us *all*, over who? People you've never met? I won't allow it!"

"Bodhi!" Xaden orders as Carr reaches Third Wing.

Fire erupts from Carr's hands, streaming toward the dais, and my stomach drops.

Time seems to slow as Bodhi steps forward and twists his hand like he's turning a dial.

The fire dies, extinguishing like it was never there and leaving Carr staring at his hands.

"You taught us well, Professor," Bodhi says, holding his hand in place. "Maybe a little too well."

Damn.

"He can counter signets," Xaden tells me.

Well, that's fucking terrifying.

The rest of the professors look upward as dragons fill the skyline, their wings flaring on approach.

Green. Orange. Red. Brown. Blue. I look up, spotting Tairn's rapid descent. *Black.*

Xaden grabs my waist as the walls shake under the weight of the mass landing. Claws dig in, shredding the masonry as dozens of dragons—maybe more—perch on every available space. Some fill the mountainside behind us, and others claim the top of the turrets in the quadrant, hovering like living sculptures.

"We won't stop you," Devera says to Xaden, then shifts to where her own dragon perches beside the parapet. "In fact, some of us have been waiting to join you."

"Really?" Bodhi grins.

"Who do you think left the news about Zolya all over Battle Brief?" She nods.

A smile lifts my mouth. She's exactly who I've always thought she is.

"We're leaving within the hour," Xaden calls out. "Your choice is as simple as it is personal. You can defend Navarre, or you can fight for the Continent."

We're in the air less than an hour later, flying south in the biggest riot I've ever seen: two hundred dragons and a hundred and one riders—nearly half the quadrant—strong. And more are coming, taking a slower route with hatchlings.

Tairn had lain in front of the dais and begrudgingly allowed Xaden to help me into the saddle, but we made it. He hooked onto Andarna, the smaller black dragon's body frighteningly limp with sleep, and now we're flying. I sleep most of the trip, too, draped across the front of my saddle, my body claiming the rest it sorely needs to knit itself back together.

It was too hectic to catch every face, but I'm proud that every single member of my squad is with us, even the first-years who are still fighting to keep their seats. They hold them into the morning and all throughout the next day, the riot pushing itself to the limit.

Marked ones take position at the edges of the flight formation, hiding us from Melgren's sight should he decide to battle us, and we fly the least populated route possible, but it's hard to disguise a veritable cloud of dragons, even at this altitude.

It must not have been just leadership that were pulled to the border. We don't encounter a single patrol as we cross into Tyrrendor, flying high over the Cliffs of Dralor onto the plateau.

"We're almost there," Tairn tells me as we pass over the crystal waters of the Beatha River.

"I'm all right."

"Don't bother lying to me. I can feel it all. The exhaustion. The pain. The

crackling of unset bone in your left arm. The chapped wounds on your face. The throbbing in your left knee that only eases—"

"Point made." I shift in the saddle, trying to alleviate some of it. *"You're the one who hasn't stopped for water in twelve hours."*

"And I could fly another twelve if need be. You're an incredibly needy species compared to ours."

By the time we approach Aretia, I'm all but dead in the saddle.

Tairn and Sgaeyl fly ahead, breaking from formation as we fly over the town, heading for Riorson House while the rest of the riot flies for the valley high above.

"You cannot make the hike down in your condition," Tairn decrees.

I'm too fucking tired to fight him.

My body jolts in protest when Tairn flares his wings, the change in momentum sending me deeper into the seat as he lands gently in consideration of Andarna in the middle of the courtyard in front of Riorson House.

Tairn's head turns toward the door as it's thrown open, and mine follows, slow from weakness and lack of sleep.

"Violet!" Brennan shouts, running down the marble steps.

I undo the buckle of my saddle and force myself to dismount, despite the agony of feeling my bones grate against one another. Cradling my splinted arm, I slide down Tairn's foreleg, right into Xaden's arms, and nearly crumple on the spot.

"I've got you," he whispers against my hair, supporting me against his side as we turn to face Riorson House and the rapidly approaching furious face of my brother.

Tairn launches behind me before I can turn to see Andarna.

"What the *fuck* did you get her into this time?" Brennan shouts at Xaden.

"He got me *out*," I promise.

"Oh? Then why is it she's half dead every time you bring her to me?" The look Brennan levels on Xaden makes me reconsider which of them might be the more violent one. Brennan reaches for my face but stops just short of touching me. "Oh gods. Violet, you're… What did they do to you?"

"I'm all right," I say once more. I step forward, and Brennan hugs me carefully. "I could probably use some mending."

His head tilts as the sound of the wind approaches a dull roar, and I follow his line of sight as the massive riot approaches the town, en route to the valley. "What have you two done?"

"Ask your sister," Xaden responds.

Brennan looks down at me, his eyes wide with shock and a touch of fear.

"I mean…" I try to force a smile, but it only splits my lip yet again. "You did say that you needed riders."

PART TWO

Half palace, half barracks, but entirely a fortress, Riorson House has never been breached by army. It survived countless sieges and three full-out assaults before falling under the flame of the very dragons it existed to serve.

—On Tyrrish History, a Complete Accounting, third edition by Captain Fitzgibbons

CHAPTER THIRTY-SEVEN

"**B**old choice to move so far from what you perceive as the safety of the wards," the Sage says, holding me immobile, my feet just inches from the frozen ground of my own personal torture chamber.

I'm trapped in this fucking nightmare again, but at least I made it farther across the sunburned field this time.

"Of course, *again*," the dark wielder hisses, his face contorting into a sneer. "You will never be free of me. I will hunt you to the ends of the Continent and beyond."

Throat working, I struggle to relax, to calm my heart and change my breathing in hopes of waking myself up. But it's only my mind that knows this isn't real. My body is very much locked into the illusion.

"You can only hunt me to the wards," I croak.

"Yet you sleep beyond them." A grotesque smile tilts his cracked mouth. "And the longest night has yet to pass." He reaches for a poison-tipped dagger—

I blink, my heart slamming against my ribs for the second it takes for me to shed the vivid nightmare and recognize my surroundings.

This isn't a wind-torn field or a cold, blood-soaked cell in Basgiath—it's Xaden's light-filled bedroom in Aretia. Big windows, thick velvet drapes, wall-to-wall bookshelves, massive bed. I'm safe. Varrish isn't waiting on the other side of the door to break me again because he's dead. I killed him.

I'm still alive.

For the first time in days, there's no pain when I breathe in, or when I stretch under the thick down comforter, or even when I twist away from the sun-drenched window to face Xaden.

Now, this is a view I could be more than happy to wake up to for the rest of my life.

He's asleep on his stomach, his arms folded under his pillow, his hair falling over his forehead, his perfectly sculpted lips parted slightly. The covers only rise to the small of his back, leaving me with miles of inked skin to admire. I almost never get to see him like this, never get to simply look at him, and I take advantage of every single second, studying the angles of his muscled arm, up to his rounded shoulder, and across the faint silver of the lines that mark his back. He's always more than enough to elevate my pulse, but asleep and fully unguarded, he steals my breath.

Gods is he beautiful.

And he loves me.

The black fabric of my thin-strapped nightgown bunches slightly as I shift up onto my knees, and the comforter falls away when I reach for him. I trace the silver scars with my fingertips and don't bother counting the lines. There are a hundred and seven of them, representative of the marked ones he took responsibility for to give them a chance at life in the quadrant.

For all that he says he isn't soft, isn't kind, he's also the only man I know whose back is covered in promises made for other people. Even if his reasoning was preparing for this war we're about to wage, he still risked his own life by vouching for them.

He risked his life to free me. Dain and I never would have made it out of there alive without him.

Alive. I'm alive.

And that's exactly how I want to feel.

I lean forward and press my lips to his warm skin, kissing the scar closest to me, wishing I could undo the damage my mother did to him.

"Mmm. Violet." His sleep-rough voice makes my lips curve and my blood heat. His muscles ripple as he stirs awake, and I take my time, kissing a slow path up the expanse of his back.

He inhales sharply, his arms tensing when I reach the place his neck meets his shoulder. Rolling, he flips to his back and pulls me astride in one smooth motion.

"Good morning." I smile, settling my hips over his. My breath catches at the feel of him beneath me, hard and ready.

"I could get used to waking up like this." He looks at me with a hunger that mirrors my own, and his hand slides from my hip, over the curve of my waist, and up between the peaks of my breasts to cup the side of my neck gently, carefully.

"Me too." My pulse quickens as I lean down and set my lips to his throat. "But we shouldn't get used to it," I tell him between kisses, working my way to his chest. "They'll probably put me with the other cadets tonight."

Last night, this had been the most private place for Brennan to mend me, and I'd wanted to sleep next to Xaden too badly to argue against his suggestion of staying after I'd finally gotten the chance to bathe.

"This is my house." He spears his fingers into my hair, his other hand flexing on my hip when I ghost my lips over the three-inch scar above his heart. "And I sleep where you sleep, which is preferably in this very large, very comfortable bed. You should *still* be sleeping."

I slide down his body, my hands roaming and stroking as I kiss every ridge of the incredible abdominals that tighten beneath my mouth. His eyes are my favorite part of him, but damn if the chiseled line above his hip that disappears into his waistband isn't a close second. I follow it with my tongue.

"*Violet.*" Xaden's voice is low.

I melt, instantly liquid when he says my name like that, and right now is no exception.

"Good plan." I slide my hand under his waistband and wrap my fingers around the thick length of him. How is every inch of this man perfect? There has to be a flaw somewhere.

"You're not recovered enough for the things I want to do to you," he growls.

My core clenches at the warning, the promise—whatever it is, I want it. I want *him*.

"Yes, I am. All mended, remember?" The craving for him overpowers any lingering exhaustion. A heady sense of power floods my system when I stroke my thumb over the head of his cock and his hips buck in response. There's nothing sexier than watching his control fray, nothing hotter than knowing I'm the one who brings him to the breaking point.

And I need him to do exactly that—*break*—to lose the gentle kisses and cautious touches and take me with the full force of what he's capable of. No holding back. No soft and slow.

"Are you trying to kill me?" His grip tightens in my hair, and I drag my gaze to his, finding a satisfying, wild glint in his eyes.

Need coils low in my stomach, my body remembering what follows that kind of look. He hasn't even touched me and I'm already aching.

"Yes," I answer honestly, then lower my head, keeping our eyes locked as I swirl my tongue around his tip. His guttural moan sets my blood on fire, and I wrap my hand around his base and take him deep.

"Violet." His eyes slam shut, and he throws his head back, his neck working as it arches, his body tensing like he's fighting the pleasure of it even as his hips jerk for more. *"That feels so fucking good."*

I hum in approval and work him harder, flicking my tongue along the ridge where he's most sensitive with every bob of my head.

"Fuck, fuck, *fuck.*" He tugs at my hair, his breaths coming faster and faster. "You have to stop. Or I'm going to lose it on you." His stomach flexes as he lifts his head to watch me. *"And I'm not sure I can be gentle."*

"Lose it." Sounds excellent to me. *"I don't want gentle."*

"Mending bones isn't instant. You're still heal—"

I suck him deeper.

He growls. *"You really want this?"*

"I want you feral."

The thought barely leaves my head before he pounces, lifting me off him and rolling me to my back. Then his mouth is on mine, kissing me hard and deep. It's all tangled tongues and nipping teeth, carnal and fierce and exactly what I need.

He slides his hand up my inner thigh, and then his fingers are *right* there, pushing my underwear to the side to stroke and tease before dragging them down my legs. I yank my nightgown over my head as he strips his sleeping pants off.

Yes. Gods, *yes.* He's all I can see, all I feel as he settles back between my thighs, the head of his cock nudging my entrance. His hand strokes over my newly mended ribs and his eyes flare, his gaze jumping to mine. "We should—"

"Please, Xaden." I cup his cheek. "Please."

He lifts my hand and kisses the palm, then the place on my forearm that had been fractured. His brow knits for a heartbeat as he scans my body, like he's looking for the safest places to touch me, like he can still see every bruise, every break.

My stomach knots at the thought that he might stop.

"Feral," I remind him in a whisper.

His gaze finds mine, and the way he smiles, raising the corner of his mouth into that arrogant smirk I love so much, makes my heart pound. Gripping my hips, he flips me over, then yanks my ass into the air, setting me on my knees.

"You will tell me if it's too much." It's not a request.

I nod, my fingers tangling in the sheets.

Then he lines us up and rolls his hips, pushing in and in and in, until he's so deep that I can feel him *everywhere.* I moan at the stretch, the fit, the utter perfection of him, muffling the sound in my pillow.

He grabs the pillow and throws it to the floor. "I want them to hear," he says, withdrawing slowly, stroking every inch of me, then slamming home again. *"Gods, you're fucking perfect."*

I cry out. He feels so damned good. *"There are hundreds of people in this palace of a house."* How I can string together more than two words is beyond me.

He leans over my back, then drags his teeth across the shell of my ear. *"And I want them all to know you're mine."*

I don't argue with his logic. I can't. Not when he slides almost all the way out of me, then snaps his hips, driving out every thought. He sets a hard, deep rhythm, turning me into pure, burning pleasure.

This is exactly what I needed—for him to take me, to consume me, to breathe life into me.

His fingers dig into my hips, pulling me into every driving thrust, and there's no way to rock back, to gain leverage, to force him to quicken his pace. I can only accept what he gives, surrender completely, and simply *feel*.

He winds me up, building the coiling pressure within me tighter and tighter, my cries filling the room along with his growls and whispered words of praise.

It just gets better, hotter, sweeter, until there is no world outside him, no existence beyond us. All that matters is the next thrust.

"Xaden." His name on my lips is a plea as the tension spirals so tight it borders on pain, power rising within me, white-hot and uncontrollable.

His hand rises along my stomach to my sternum, then lifts me upright so my back meets his chest. I turn my head, tangling my fingers in his hair, and he fuses our mouths, kissing me breathless while he drives into me again and again and again, his movements growing less and less controlled.

He's close.

"You're alive." His voice wraps around my mind as his fingers dip between my thighs and slide over my clit. *"Alive and strong and mine."*

Gods, he knew what I needed without me even telling him. My thighs lock, then tremble. It's too much and exactly enough.

"And you're mine." I gasp for breath, my pulse racing as he strokes me right over the edge.

And I fall. I absolutely *shatter*. Light flashes and is quickly snuffed by cooling darkness as wave after wave of bliss rolls over me.

He locks his arms around me, holding me close as he shudders, tumbling into his own release.

We stay like that, wrapped around each other in every way possible, our breaths ragged as we come back to reality.

A reality in which I wasn't *remotely* quiet.

My cheeks flush even hotter.

"You want me to sleep in here with you?" I ask once I can form words.

"Every night." He kisses me softly.

"You might not be able to ward it yet, but you'd better sound shield this room *today*." I lift my brows so he knows I mean it.

His mouth curves into a heart-stopping smile. "Already done."

I roll my eyes. "Of course it is."

B y the time we emerge from Xaden's room an hour later, there are cadets *everywhere*.

"This is…" Words fail as we descend the right side of the sweeping double staircase to the foyer.

"Noisier than the last time we were here," Xaden supplies, glancing over the crowd. Some riders stand in groups while others sit along the walls.

Every single one of them wears an expression that's a variation of exactly how I'm feeling right now—what the hell did we do? Aretia wasn't ready for this, and yet I brought them anyway.

Xaden may have risked the revolution by coming for me, but I smacked a giant target on it.

"Can we even fit all these riders here?" I ask Xaden as we pick our way through the mayhem.

"There are a hundred barracks rooms between the top three floors," he tells me. *"And that doesn't account for the family quarters on the second. The question is if they're all serviceable. Not everything has been repaired and rebuilt."*

"Violet!" Rhiannon waves from where she stands with our squad, waiting in front of the archway that leads into the great hall. Her gaze sweeps over me. "You look better."

"I feel better," I assure her, noticing that Imogen isn't with them. "What's going on?"

"I was hoping you'd know." She glances over our squad, then leans in, lowering her voice. "They took a quick roll last night, put us in our rooms, and fed us breakfast this morning, but that was an hour ago. Now we're just…" She gestures to the foyer. "Waiting."

"I think we may have caught them off guard," I admit, guilt hollowing my stomach.

"Let's go find out exactly how off guard," Xaden says. "We'll get some answers for you, Rhiannon." He gestures toward a hallway. *"We need to meet with the Assembly."*

"If you could just make that sound a little less foreboding." I pause when

we pass Aaric.

He's standing off to the side of the squad, his arms folded over his chest, watching everything and everyone around him. "What now, Sorrengail?" he asks, his mouth tightening.

"He isn't asking about the schedule," Xaden says.

"Picked up on that." I glance from Xaden to Aaric. "Your secret is safe with us."

"So presumptuous."

I shoot Xaden a glare. "It's up to you if you want to tell anyone about your family. Right, Riorson?"

A muscle in Xaden's jaw ticks, but he nods.

"You swear it?" Aaric bites out.

"I do," I promise.

It's all I get to say before Xaden takes my hand and tugs me down the wide hallway, where the crowd finally thins.

"I think I may have fucked up," I whisper, apprehension growing with each step we take.

"We may have fucked up," he says, squeezing my hand and stopping us in front of a tall wooden door with more than a few angry, raised voices behind it. "Doesn't mean we weren't right."

"The last time we were here, the people in that room wanted to lock me up as a security threat." My chest tightens. "I'm starting to think maybe they were right."

"Only four of them did," he says, his fingers poised on the black metal door handle. "And I guarantee they're more pissed at me than they are you. I didn't exactly answer their summons last night after Brennan mended you." He pulls open the door, and the raised voices become almost shrill as I follow him in.

"You've exposed everything we've worked for!" a woman shouts.

"Without so much as a vote from this council!" a man agrees.

"I made the call," Xaden says once we're clear of the doorway. "You want to yell? Yell at me."

Six members of the Assembly look our way from their chairs at the long table, as Bodhi, Garrick, and Imogen stand in front of them as if on trial. We're all that's left of the squad that fought in Resson.

"We're happy to address your choices, Lieutenant Riorson," Suri says. "Though I'm not sure what the general's daughter is doing here."

"Well, the general's son is right here," Brennan counters from the other end of the table as Xaden and I walk forward, putting ourselves between Garrick and Imogen.

"You know what I meant," the woman fires back, shooting Brennan a frustrated look.

The massive, empty armchair Xaden had sprawled across at our last meeting has been moved near the others. Guess they're still waiting on someone. I glance at the high, intricately constructed back and the figure of a sleeping dragon perched on its pointed tip, then do a double take. In this lighting, I realize that one half is a rich, polished walnut, and the other has a black sheen to it, as if someone polished and sealed burned firewood…as if the chair has been half burned.

Because it probably was.

"And I think I know why she's here." Hawk Nose glares with his one eye like I'm something that needs to be scraped away from his boot, but at least he doesn't reach for the sword at his side when he looks pointedly at our joined hands.

I pull mine from Xaden's grasp.

He sighs like I'm his biggest problem and snatches it back. "What's done is done. You can stay in here and chastise us all day, or you can figure out what to do with the hundred riders we brought you."

"You didn't bring us riders—you brought us cadets!" Suri shouts, pounding her fist on the table. "What the hell are we supposed to do with them?"

"Such theatrics are above you, Suri." Felix scratches his beard and all but rolls his eyes at her. "Though the question is valid."

"I'd suggest you call a formation and divide them into equal wings, for starters," Xaden suggests, his tone dripping with boredom. "Though they may prefer to stay intact. From what I've seen, Fourth Wing has the largest numbers."

"Because you were their wingleader," Brennan states. "They were used to following you."

"And Aetos," Xaden replies begrudgingly. "He's the one who called the formation after killing the vice commandant."

"Aetos is another matter." Battle-Ax runs her finger over the flat side of her weapon like it's habit. "He's confined to quarters until we can ascertain his loyalty, as are the *scribes*."

"Cath is enough to vouch for Dain's loyalty," I argue. "And Jesinia is the only reason we have Warrick's journal." My hand tightens on Xaden's when all six of the riders startle with surprise. *"You do still have Warrick's journal, right?"*

"You have a journal from Warrick?" Battle-Ax leans forward. "As in First Six Warrick?"

"I do. Jesinia helped Violet and her squad steal the journal for instructions on how to use the wardstone," Xaden says, turning his gaze on Brennan. "And she was right. It contains cryptic instructions in Old Lucerish that need detailed, precise translation, but it's better than nothing. I was supposed to bring it to you but got sidetracked by her capture."

"Dad never taught me Old Lucerish, only Tyrrish," Brennan says to me, lines forming between his brows, and a quiet woman with shiny black hair and wideset eyes keeps her diamond-sharp gaze on him. "But if you can translate it, then there's a chance we can secure —"

"Secure?" Hawk Nose snaps. "You bring a hundred riders and *two hundred* dragons here and have the nerve to say that word?" His eyes narrow on me. "You may as well have handed Melgren a map of our location. Or was that what she was truly after?"

"Here we fucking go," Imogen says under her breath.

"Violet risked her life to help us," Xaden responds. "And nearly lost it doing so."

"She should be confined and questioned," Hawk Nose suggests.

"Go near my sister, and I'll cut out your other eye, Ulices," Brennan warns, leaning forward and glaring down the table. "She's been questioned enough for two lifetimes."

"That doesn't change the fact that she's ruined us!" Battle-Ax declares. "We've already doubled patrols to the border, which leaves no one here to fight should Melgren launch an attack on us." She swings a finger at Felix. "And don't start with your *Melgren doesn't know we're here.* All the rebellion signets on the Continent can't hide a riot the size of a thunderhead. We have no wards, no forge, and *children* running amok in the hallways!"

"Cadets who are acting with more composure than you are." Xaden tilts his head. "Get a grip."

"Melgren isn't coming. Even if he knew where we are — which he doesn't — he can't risk his forces coming after us when the kingdom is reeling from wyvern carcasses we left up and down the border. Half the riders he plans on having in three years are *here*. He might want to kill us, but he can't afford to. And as for Violet" — he lets go of my hand and rips at the buttons of his flight jacket, then tugs his neckline down, exposing the scar on his chest — "if you want to confine her, *question* her, then it's me you start with. I bear the responsibility for her and any decision she makes. Remember?"

Gravity shifts as I stare at that thin silver line and its precise edges. It's… *gods*, it's the same length as the ones on his back. Xaden isn't responsible for just the marked ones anymore; he's responsible for *me*. Responsible for my choices, my loyalties — not to Navarre, like the marked ones, but to Aretia.

Imogen tried to tell me that day on the flight field, but I didn't pick up on it. *"When did you do that?"* I ask.

"About two seconds after I put you in Brennan's arms after Resson."

My gaze falls to the floor as they continue to shout in Tyrrish. I brought the cadets here. I was the one who got caught stealing Lyra's journal. I'm the one who forced Xaden's hand, forced them *all* into this situation.

"Then you will consider them my guests." Xaden's words drag me out of my self-pity. Shadows fill the floor and curl around the dais. "I do not ask permission of you—of *anyone*—to bring guests into my own home." Xaden's tone cools to glacial.

Garrick swears under his breath and rests his hand on the hilt of one of his swords.

"Xaden—" Ulices starts.

"Or did you forget that this is *my* house?" Xaden tilts his head to the side and stares at them in the same way Sgaeyl studies prey. "My life is tethered to Violet's, so if you want me in that fucking chair, you'll accept her."

Ulices's skin blotches while I feel the blood rush from mine.

His chair. The empty one. He's the seventh.

Holy shit. I knew this was his house, of course, but it never really registered. This is all Xaden's. No noble has claimed the duchy of Aretia. They all think the land is ruined, or worse—cursed. It's *all* his.

"Fine," the quiet woman says, her voice soft and calm. "We will trust Violet Sorrengail. But that doesn't help us arm the drifts without an operational forge. In winning this first battle with Navarre by taking half the Riders Quadrant, you may have lost us this war."

"And what do we do with all these cadets?" Battle-Ax asks wearily, rubbing the bridge of her nose. "Gods, you brought us Aetos and *scribes*. It's not like we can send them out to battle wyvern and venin."

"I also brought you four professors, and it's not like you're without your share of knowledge," Xaden replies. "I've already questioned the scribes. They can be trusted, and Cath vouches for Aetos. As for the other cadets, I suggest you get them back into class."

Something…shimmers, curling around the Archives I keep in my head.

"Violet." Her soft voice rattles me to my very core, and I grasp Xaden's arm to stay upright. Relief, joy, wonder—it all weakens my knees and stings my eyes.

For the first time in months, I feel whole.

A smile spreads across my face. *"Andarna."*

With all we've sacrificed for this kingdom,
we'd better be able to defend it.

—THE JOURNAL OF WARRICK OF LUCERAS
—TRANSLATED BY CADET VIOLET SORRENGAIL

CHAPTER THIRTY-EIGHT

The valley above Aretia looks eerily similar to the last time I was here, as though fall at this elevation is meaningless, when there are clear signs of winter approaching in the town beneath us. But unlike last time, there are dragons *everywhere*—the jagged outcroppings of rock above us, the mouths of the caves to the west, the wide valley to the east…everywhere.

And two of the biggest stand before me like bookends with Andarna between them.

"I thought you said she was awake?" I whisper at Tairn as if my voice might wake her, like there isn't a giant brown stomping his way past the copse of trees where Andarna is napping, her body curved into an S-shape. Grass moves in front of her snout with every gust of her exhale, and she looks quite content with her scorpion tail curled around her. And kind of…green?

No, her scales are still black. It must be an adolescent thing that they're so shiny she reflects some of the color around her.

"*An hour ago.*" Tairn chuffs and I'm pretty sure Sgaeyl just rolled her eyes.

"It took me an hour to get out of that meeting, and then I had to hike that cliff of a trail." I shouldn't wake her. The responsible action would be none, to let her sleep off the remnants of her nearly three-month-long dragon coma. But I've missed her so damn—

Gold eyes flash open.

Relief nearly brings me to my knees. She's awake.

I grin and feel my world right itself. "*Hi.*"

"*Violet.*" Andarna lifts her head, and a puff of steam blows back the loosened strands of my long braid. "*I meant to stay awake.*"

"That's all right. Tairn says you'll be nodding off for the next week or so." Stepping forward, I reach up to scratch her scaly jawline. "You were out a *long* time."

"*It felt like nothing.*" She arches her neck so I can get the area beneath her chin.

"Trust me, it wasn't." I step back and really look at her. If I had to guess, I'd say she's almost two-thirds the size of Sgaeyl. "I think you're bigger."

"*Naturally.*" She huffs, digging her claws into the ground as she stands upright.

I retreat another couple of steps, looking higher and higher as she shakes off the sleep, her wings rustling as she swivels her head, taking in the valley. "What do you want to do? Fly? Take a walk?" There's so much I need to tell her.

"*Food. We should seek sheep.*" She flares her wings out and then stumbles forward just like she did in the height of summer.

Shit.

I scramble backward through the cumbersome grass, rushing to keep from being sliced by Andarna's claws as she finds her balance.

"*Could you not crush our human?*" Tairn barks.

"*I wasn't even close,*" Andarna snaps in return with a quick glare his direction as she flares her wings with the same result.

"*I told you to be patient,*" Tairn chides.

The look she levels on him makes Sgaeyl huff in what I think is appreciation, and Andarna rolls her shoulders, digs her claws in, and tries again to raise her wings.

My stomach drops, my mind spinning so quickly I can barely catch a whirring thought as my gaze flicks between the two wings. Her left one doesn't fully extend. It makes it halfway, but the remainder of the black webbing never pulls taut.

She attempts once, twice, then bares her sharp teeth and hisses steam when it doesn't snap into place on the third attempt.

Oh gods. Something's wrong.

I have no fucking clue what to say or do. I'm…speechless. Powerless to help. *Fuck.* Am I supposed to ask her if she's all right? Or do I ignore it as I would a battle wound on an adult? Is the wing broken? In need of mending? Or is it part of the growth process?

Andarna's head whips back toward mine and her eyes narrow. "*I am not broken.*"

My heart sinks.

"I never said you were," I whisper.

Shit, shit, *shit*. I hurt her feelings.

"Speech isn't necessary when I can hear your thoughts. I am no more broken than you are." Her lip curls and her teeth flash.

Ouch. *"I'm sorry. That wasn't what I meant to imply."* The thought is barely a whisper.

"Enough." Tairn lowers his head to her level. *"She is allowed to be concerned for you, as you are for her. Now go eat before hunger overpowers common sense."*

Sgaeyl stalks past me on the right, the ground lightly shuddering beneath my feet as she heads for the meadow to the east. Feirge gets out of her way.

"There is a herd that is far better hunted on foot," Tairn says, a soft growl vibrating in his throat. *"Follow Sgaeyl."*

Andarna tucks her wings, flexes her claws, then walks around me wordlessly, heading for Sgaeyl. I turn to watch them walk away.

"Adolescents," Tairn grumbles. *"They're insufferable when hungry."*

"Her wing," I whisper, wrapping my arms around my stomach.

His sigh ripples the grass around me. *"The elders and I will work with her to strengthen the muscles, but there are complications."*

"Like?" My chest tightens, and I glance up at him.

"Put your shields up and block her out as much as possible."

I focus, shielding out that pearlescent bond I now recognize as Andarna. *"Done."*

"There are many reasons younglings do not leave the Vale. The mass expenditure of energy in Resson forced her into a rapid rate of growth. You know that. But if it had happened here, or at Basgiath where she could have been quickly, safely sheltered for the Dreamless Sleep, perhaps she would have grown as usual." His tone is enough to raise the hairs on the back of my neck. He's never this careful with his words, never this careful with my feelings. *"But we flew that critical day between Resson and Aretia,"* he continues. *"And then we waited again to fly to Basgiath, and even then she woke several times. The elders have never seen a dragon remain Dreamless that long. And now her growth is unpredictable. There is a second set of muscles along the fronts of our wings that forms during our growth. Hers did not. The elders believe she'll still fly…in time. Once she's strengthened the existing muscle to compensate."*

"Can Brennan mend her?" It's my fault because I used her power in Resson. Because we'd flown that day. Because we'd had to return to Basgiath. Because she bonded when she was a juvenile and I interrupted her Dreamless Sleep. I could list reasons all day.

"You cannot mend what does not exist."

I watch her quicken her pace to catch up to Sgaeyl, snapping her teeth at a bird that immediately regrets flying too close with a squawk.

"But she'll fly?" I've learned enough about dragons to know that a life without flight is more than a tragedy.

"We believe she can eventually train the existing muscle to bear the weight of her wing," he assures me, but there's a note of something else in his tone that has me bracing.

"You believe." I turn slowly to glare up at the second-biggest dragon on the Continent. "Which means you've had time to discuss. How long have you known?"

"Since she woke here in the high summer."

My heart stops sinking and flat-out plummets to the grass. She hadn't fully extended her wing then, either, but I'd thought nothing of it, since she seemed generally...clumsy.

"What else aren't you telling me?" There's no way he'd have cut her out of the conversation unless he was worried about my reaction to the information—or hers.

"What she herself has not recognized." He lowers his head, his great golden eyes locking with mine. *"She'll fly, but she'll never bear a rider."*

She'll never bear a rider. Tairn's words repeat through my head for the next three days while we're tossed back into classes, headed by the professors who flew with us to Aretia, as well as a few members of the revolution and the Assembly. Even translating Warrick's journal can't keep the thoughts out, and every time his prediction runs through my mind, I immediately think of something else just in case Andarna is listening in.

"Iron...rain," I say, writing the words on parchment as I finish translating the passage for the third time. I've come up with the same process every time, no matter how...odd it is.

"Iron rain mean anything to you?" I ask down the bond, closing the notebook on Xaden's desk and reaching for my pack. I'm going to be late if I don't hurry.

"Should it?" Tairn replies.

"Clearly, or she wouldn't be asking." I can practically *feel* Andarna's eyeroll. *"Ooh...sheep."*

"They will not stay down if you keep stuffing them in like"—Tairn sighs—*"that."*

I bite back a smile and race to meet my squad.

Have to give it to Brennan and the Assembly. We might be sharing books and cramming ourselves into every open room on the first floor for lectures, but every cadet is clean, fed, housed, and learning.

History is held in what I think was Xaden's father's office, and we started a new unit on the Tyrrish Rebellion yesterday so everyone can know what really happened six years ago, but we've only gotten far enough to cover the political landscape of the years before the rebellion.

Instead of challenges and hand-to-hand, Emetterio has us running the steep, rocky trail to the valley every day until our aching lungs adjust to the altitude, but he's warned us not to get too comfortable slacking off. Pretty sure the number of cadets vomiting beside the trail would indicate we're not, but the urgency in his tone pushes us to run harder.

"Hawk Nose" Ulices has taken over physics, which only gives him another reason to spend an hour every other day glaring at me. And "Battle-Ax" Kylynn is set to take on flight maneuvers once the Assembly agrees we're safe enough to let the riot rise from the hidden protection of the valley, which means we have more than two hundred restless dragons.

Suri, the member of the Assembly with the silver-streaked hair who blatantly hates me, flew off with Xaden and the other lieutenants two days ago. Not knowing where he is, wondering if he's in danger, worrying every single second that he might be in battle, has me breathing through another wave of nausea as we file into the rebuilt theater in the northwest wing of Riorson House.

The sight is more than impressive. Not just that there's enough seating for every cadet, but that of all the things they could have rebuilt in the last six years... they chose a theater.

"Welcome to Battle Brief," Rhiannon says, leading us halfway down the steps on the right and into our seats.

"Good. Maybe they'll tell us what's happening in Navarre," Visia says from the row ahead of us. Besides Aaric and Sloane, there are four other first-years, whose names I have yet to learn.

Unlike our usual Battle Brief, we're seated as if in formation: by wing, section, and squad. And unlike the map at Basgiath, this one is the height and width of the large stage where the curtain would hang, and it includes the isles — the five large and thirteen smaller islands that surround the Continent in every direction.

"Those red and orange flags," Ridoc notes from my left, pointing up at the map. "Are those..."

"Enemy territory, I'm guessing," Sawyer remarks, sitting next to Ridoc.

"Not like Poromish enemy." Ridoc takes his pen and parchment out of his pack, and I do the same, balancing the bound notebook on my lap. "Like...dark wielder enemy."

"Right. Drained land, destroyed cities like Zolya. Red is old movement and orange is new." Nearly all of the Krovlan province remains untouched, but the enemy is just a day's flight from our border. The only movement I notice since viewing this map in midsummer is up the Stonewater River—toward Navarre. "Did you guys get letters to your families?"

My friends couldn't give out our location, but they could warn their loved ones to leave the border region, or just *leave*. I wouldn't put it past Melgren to start executing the families to punish those who deserted.

And it's all my fault. I'm responsible for Andarna's wing, for forcing the exposure of the truth before Aretia was ready to act, for bringing a hundred riders here without permission, for the worry etched in Brennan's forehead about boosting the sheep population for all the dragons I led here, and for putting a target on my friends' families' backs. I grip my pen so tight it groans under the strain.

How could I make every right decision last year and every *wrong* one this year?

They all nod, with Rhiannon adding, "I'm hoping it convinces them to move."

Aaric doesn't bother turning from his seat directly in front of me. "I declined the offer to correspond," he says over his shoulder instead.

"I bet you did." I force a small smile. His father would shit himself if he knew Aaric had not only joined the quadrant but turned against Navarre.

"Any luck on the wardstone?" Rhi asks, and every head turns. Even Aaric and Sloane look over their shoulders.

"I've translated the section we need three times, and I think I'm close." My smile echoes theirs because I think I might actually *have* it. "I know it's been three days, but I'm a little rusty, and it's the oddest form of magic I've ever read about, which is probably why it's never been done twice."

"But you think it will work?" Sloane asks with blatant hope in her eyes.

"I do." I nod, straightening my shoulders like the weight of their expectations is physical. "I just need to be sure it's right." And I'd better be right. Those wards are our best defense if wyvern crest the Cliffs of Dralor.

"Let's get started!" Professor Devera says from the stage, her voice carrying over the hundred of us easily, and everyone turns to face her.

"It's just like being at Basgiath," Ridoc says with a smile. "But you know… not."

Rhi leans in and whispers, "Odd magic?"

"I…" My face scrunches. "I think the First Six practiced some kind of blood magic," I whisper even quieter than she had. I've translated the passage three times and come up with the same words every time, but I've never heard of using blood in…anything.

Her eyebrows rise. "You sure?"

"As I can be. Jesinia came up with the same translation for the passage, but I think I should probably go over it one more time. Just in case."

"Yeah. Just in case." She nods.

"Welcome to your first official Battle Brief as traitors," Devera announces.

That gets everyone's attention. A pit forms where my stomach used to be.

"Get used to the sound of the word," she says unapologetically, her gaze scanning over us. "Because that's what Navarre now considers us. Whether or not that's how we feel about the choice we made to defend those who cannot defend themselves, that is how we will be seen by the friends and loved ones we left behind. But personally, I'm proud of every single one of you." Her eyes find mine. "It's hard to leave behind everything you know, everything you love, because your honor demands it. With that said, please welcome Lieutenant Colonel Aisereigh, who will take the place of the Scribe Quadrant Curator, since we don't have them here."

Markham's position. Will Jesinia or the two other cadets start their own quadrant here without anyone to teach them? The Assembly finished debriefing and clearing Dain for attendance this morning, so he's sitting in the front row with the section leaders. I'm glad he's out of isolation but also glad he's keeping his distance.

"We believe in sharing information here in Aretia," Brennan says as he takes the stage with Devera.

"Still can't believe he ditched your last name," Sawyer says under his breath.

My year-mates are the only ones who know who Brennan is, and it seems Devera and Emetterio are going along with the name change as well. Maybe Kaori would have, too, if he'd come with us, but he'd looked at me, clearly torn, and said his place was with the Empyrean.

Everyone who stayed had their reasons. At least that's what I'm telling myself.

"He had to. Besides, I like his name. It's Tyrrish for resurrected," I reply. He's still just Brennan to me.

"First," Brennan begins, "we've done as you've asked and kept you in your respective wings. Second Wing and Third Wing, you know that Eleni Jareth and Tibbot Vasant are now your respective wingleaders. We expect any missing section leaders or squad leaders to be replaced by tomorrow, and you'll notify Devera of your choices."

My eyebrows shoot up.

"You won't choose for us?" someone from First Wing asks. That's the protocol at Basgiath.

"Are you saying you're not capable?" Brennan challenges.

"No, sir."

"Excellent. Moving on." He turns our direction. "We double-checked the rolls to be sure, but it appears that not only does Fourth Wing currently boast this year's Iron Squad—"

The first-years seated in front of us holler, since that honor of boasting the largest number of surviving first-years after Threshing is ours for the second year in a row. Baylor, the stocky one with the skull-trimmed black hair, shouts the loudest, and the corner of my mouth rises when he shoulder bumps Aaric into joining in.

"—but Flame Section has the unique honor of being completely intact." Brennan looks down at Bodhi. "Durran, you brought every single cadet. I guess that would make you the Iron Section."

Holy shit. I don't even bother trying to suppress my grin, now. I knew that Fourth Wing brought the most cadets, but we kept our *entire* section together?

"I'm assuming you'd like a patch?" Brennan asks, a smile tilting his lips.

"Fuck yes, we do!" Ridoc shouts, coming out of his seat, and our entire section cheers loudly, even me.

"Yes, sir," Bodhi says once we calm, glancing over his shoulder at us like he can't take us anywhere nice.

"I'll see what we can do." Brennan glances up at me and grins. "Now to real business. We'll start with your update from Navarre. As far as we can tell from our sources, the public doesn't know."

What? How? Rhi and I exchange a look of pure confusion as a ripple of hushed comments rolls through the theater.

"To our surprise, the outposts have successfully dispatched with the wyvern Lieutenant Riorson gifted to them, and General Melgren has kept the news from reaching the general public, though obviously all present military now knows. And unfortunately, they are still turning away every Poromish citizen at the border."

My heart plummets, and the tiny part of me that had hoped our leaving would prompt action and reflection dies a painful, disillusioning death. But once we have wards, we'll be a safe option for the Poromish citizens Navarre still won't take.

"Our forces have doubled their patrols at the borders of Tyrrendor"—he rubs his thumb along the bottom of his jaw—"but we feel confident that our location is still secret."

"Even with flying the Continent's largest riot across Navarre?" someone from First Wing asks.

"Tyrs are loyal," Sloane says, her chin rising. "We lived through the last rebellion. Whatever we see, we'll keep to ourselves."

Brennan nods. "The good news is: as far as our extensive sources can tell, your families have not been targeted, and we are reaching out with not only your letters but offers of sanctuary. If they're willing to risk stepping into the unknown, we'll work to get them here."

The lump in my throat makes it hard to breathe for a second. Dad would be proud of him.

"What does this lack of troop movement tell us?" Devera asks, shooting Brennan a little side-eye. "Or do you not remember how Battle Brief works?"

"My apologies." Brennan puts his hands up and stands back. "Been a few years."

"They've been too busy cleaning up the mess Riorson dumped at the border to bother with us," Dain answers.

"For now," Brennan agrees with a nod. "They might be in shock, but don't doubt that we'll be fighting a war on two fronts as soon as they can get their bearings and decide how much they can risk the public knowing."

"When do we get to fight them?" a guy from Third Wing asks, pointing up at the map. "The dark wielders?"

"When you graduate," Brennan answers, lifting his brows in a no-nonsense expression that makes him look just like Dad. "*We* don't send cadets to die, and that's exactly what will happen to you if you try to take on a dark wielder before you're ready. You will die. Are you really so anxious to start a new death roll?"

"Sorrengail and the others didn't die," he responds.

"Two of us *did* die," Imogen snaps, and the rider slides down in his seat.

"When you wield lightning, come and talk to me," Devera counters.

"Before you graduate, you're going to learn how to take on a dark wielder and survive," Brennan promises. "It requires a different style of fighting, and honing your signets, which you may have noticed are a bit testy up here. Remember, magic is a little wild out here beyond the wards, but we're currently deciphering Warrick's journal in order to get our wards operational as quickly as possible. We're also working on getting our forge up and running to supply both our forces and the gryphon fliers with weaponry, which is part of our mission—"

A grumble of disapproval ripples through the auditorium.

"Knock it off," Brennan chastises. "Fliers are dangerous, but they are *not* the enemy you've been raised to fear, though some are still hostile toward us, as evidenced by the attack on Samara four days ago."

Fliers attacked Samara? My pulse stutters. *Mira.*

"Which brings us back to Battle Brief," Devera continues. "One dragon was injured, but no riders were lost in the attack, according to our sources, mostly because there was only one dragon present at the outpost during the attack— political turmoil, remember? The wards did not fail, but a drift of fliers infiltrated the post, killing a dozen infantry before two of them were killed in the lowest level of the fortress."

No riders were lost. She's all right. Once my heart falls out of my throat, I can think again.

"They were looking for weaponry," I whisper. "That's where the armory is." Navarre's citizens might not know that we're gone, but the drifts do.

"Say it," Rhiannon urges quietly.

I shake my head, unwilling to follow my thoughts to their logical conclusion.

"What questions would you ask about the attack?" Devera cuts in. "This one's been briefing officers for too long and doesn't remember the art of *teaching*." She cuts another mean side-eye at Brennan.

"Fuck it. I'll say it," Ridoc mutters. Then asks at full volume: "Were they looking for weaponry?"

"Absolutely." Brennan nods. "That's the *only* reason for fliers to attack Navarrian outposts directly." He glances at me like he *knows* the question was really mine, and then stares in that challenging look of disapproval he mastered before the age of fifteen, daring me to rise, to stop avoiding the consequences of my own actions.

Fine. "Did the fliers attack Samara before or after the news of our..." Gods, what are the right words for what we did? "Departure from Basgiath leaked into Poromiel?"

Brennan's stare softens in approval.

"After," Devera answers.

The lump in my throat swells painfully, threatening to rip apart what facade of calm I have left. They attacked because they know we can't supply them. They're defenseless.

"It's not your fault," Rhiannon whispers.

"Yeah, it is." I focus on taking notes.

Brennan turns to the map. "On to enemy movements. In the last week, venin have taken the town of Anca. Not surprising, given its proximity to the recently fallen Zolya."

I don't bother looking at Anca. My gaze is locked on Cordyn, where Viscount Tecarus has the only other known luminary. It's the next largest city between Zolya and Draithus, and still outside venin-controlled territory. The seaside city was a two-day flight from Basgiath, but from here? I bet Tairn could make it in twelve hours.

"*Ten*," he corrects me. "*But it's not entirely safe*," he states, but it's not an argument.

"*So Xaden says, but neither is being here beyond the wards without a forge to arm anyone, including ourselves.*" Good thing we'll have the wards up soon.

"*She makes a good point,*" Andarna agrees. "*Can you carry a luminary?*"

"That question insults me."

"Can you carry a luminary while insulted?" she prods.

Tairn growls.

"What's concerning is that it appears the town was drained, and then the dark wielders pulled back to reassemble in Zolya," Devera says. "What does that tell us?"

"They're organized and basing out of Zolya," Rhiannon answers. "It's like a supply trip for an ongoing campaign."

"Silver One!" Tairn's tone changes. *"A riot approaches!"*

My breath seizes as my head swings toward the back of the theater, as if the small windows there will give me any clue of what's coming.

"Yes. They're not just consuming but occupying territory for the first time. Good—" Brennan quiets, no doubt talking to Marbh, then focuses as the entire theater falls silent. "Everyone get to the great hall and wait there," he orders, turning to Devera as the auditorium descends into quiet chaos.

"How many?" I force myself to breathe through the terror and shove everything into my pack and stand as everyone around me does the same in a hushed panic.

"Are they coming for us?" Ridoc asks quietly. "Navarre?"

I thought we'd have more time. How can this already be happening?

"I don't know," Rhiannon answers.

"Can Tairn take Codagh?" Aaric asks as I throw my pack onto my back.

My mouth opens and shuts as I think of General Melgren's dragon. I don't even *want* the answer to that question.

And Tairn is suspiciously quiet.

"Shortest revolution in history." Sawyer mutters a swear word and yanks the drawstrings of his pack tight.

"Forty. Sgaeyl is approaching as well, but she's too far out to—" Tairn pauses. *"Wait. Teine leads the riot."*

Teine?

Mira. Fear knots my stomach.

Fuck waiting.

I push past Sawyer to the outer aisle of the theater and then *run*, ignoring every voice that calls after me, even Brennan's. Running every morning for the past three months has bolstered what advantage I already had on most of the riders in this room—speed.

"Ready the crossbolts!" Brennan shouts above the fray.

Mira will get herself killed. Or maybe she's come here to kill *us*. Either way, she'll have to look me in the eye before she does it.

Legs pumping, I race across the back of the theater, cutting First Wing off from the exit and sprinting through to the main hallway. Statues and tapestries blur as I run by, my lungs burning as I dart past the guards and riders flowing into the thoroughfare.

Please, Dunne, do not let her incinerate this house before I get the chance to talk some sense into her.

I sprint past Emetterio as he shouts for me to get into the great hall, then nearly slip turning into the foyer, not daring to break my stride even when my heart pounds hard, protesting the altitude. The guards hold the doors open, no doubt so riders can mount, and I fly straight through, my feet barely skimming the marble steps into the courtyard just in time to see Teine's wings flare directly in front of me to halt a rapid descent.

That knot of fear lurches into my throat, and I skid to a stop about thirty feet outside the front door, my feet making furrows in the gravel.

Rock flies in a dusty barrage from the impact of the Green Clubtail's claws, and I throw up my arms to cover my face as Teine lands directly in front of the courtyard doors, blocking the exit into the town, and two others flank him, their landings just as abrupt.

I cough as the dust clears and immediately spot an angry-looking orange and glaring red facing me, their teeth bared.

Fuck me, four more land on the outer walls, shaking the masonry. They're everywhere.

My stomach sinks. We've been betrayed. Someone's told Navarre our location.

"Tairn—"

"Here," he answers a moment before dropping out of the sky like a damned meteor. The ground shudders with the force of his landing to my left, and the shade of his wing blocks out the sun overhead. He roars so loudly my teeth rattle, then lowers his head, his neck only inches from my shoulder, and streams a river of fire in a clear warning shot across the legs of the dragons.

Heat blasts my face for the length of a heartbeat before he draws back, his head darting in a serpentine motion.

Teine steps forward, and time feels like it slows to milliseconds as Tairn lunges, opening his massive jaw and latching onto Teine's throat just like he had Solas's.

"Tairn!" I scream in raw fear. If Teine dies, so does Mira.

"For fuck's sake, Violet!" Mira shouts.

"I have his throat, but I have not broken his scales," he assures me like I'm the dramatic one here.

"Well, as long as it's just a threat," I reply sarcastically. "Dismount peacefully and Teine lives!" Others rush into the courtyard behind me, their feet loud on

the gravel, but I keep my eyes locked on Teine and Mira.

She dismounts with enviable ease and strides toward me. Her cheeks are red with windburn, and her eyes are wild as she lifts her flight goggles to the top of her head. "We all come peacefully. It was Riorson who came for us. How else would we have found you?" She glances up at the house without breaking pace. "Gods, I thought this place was ash."

Xaden?

"It's not." My fingertips brush the hilts of my daggers. I'm not sure I can lift them to kill my sister, but I sure as hell won't be killed *by* her.

"Sgaeyl confirms," Tairn says, releasing Teine's throat and drawing back to my side. *"They're in range."*

Oh, thank the gods. My breath rushes out in a sigh of relief a second before Mira wraps her arms around me. "I'm sorry," she says into my hair, squeezing me tight. "I'm so sorry I didn't listen to what you were trying to tell me at Samara."

My shoulders dip, and I relax into her, slowly returning the hug. "I needed you," I whisper, unable to keep the hurt from leaching into my voice. There are so many other things that need to be said, and yet *that's* what comes out. "I needed you, Mira."

"I know." Her chin bumps the top of my head before she pulls back, clasping my shoulders. For the first time since I started at Basgiath, she doesn't scan my frame to see if I'm injured. She looks me straight in my eyes. "I'm so sorry. I let you down, and I promise it won't happen again." A ghost of a smile pulls at her lips. "You really stole half of Basgiath's cadets? And killed the vice commandant?"

"Dain killed the vice commandant. I just finished him off. Well, Xaden helped. It was more of a team effort," I admit, shaking my head to clear it. "Did you know? When I tried to tell you and you said I needed more sleep, did you *know*?" The thought of her trying to convince me it was all in my head if she knew better is unbearable.

"I didn't know. I swear, I didn't know." Her wide, brown eyes search mine. "Not until the wyvern was dropped at the front gates of Samara. Mom arrived about ten hours later and told me the truth—told *all of the riders* the truth."

I blink through the shock. "She just...told you."

"Yes." Her chin dips as she nods. "She probably figured out there was no lying her way around a giant dead wyvern."

And we'd already been on our way here.

"Xaden." I reach out, not because I don't trust my sister, but because I trust him more.

"If she said your mother confessed, then she's telling the truth. We're at the edge of the city now, just flying with the stragglers."

"And what, she just let all forty of you leave?" I step out of her hug and gesture at the dragons perched on the walls around us. There's no way they'd let dozens of riders desert.

"She gave us an hour to decide, and half of us chose to leave. We flew into other riders on the way who'd been given the same ultimatum. Leadership decided letting us go was a safer choice than letting us stay and talk the others into leaving, or worse, leaking information, and besides, it wasn't really our choice, was it?" She glances back at Teine.

That's...not right. Why would Mom and Melgren let them just...go?

"I think she knew I'd find—" She looks over my shoulder and freezes, then starts to tremble as her pupils blow wide.

"Mira?" I glance back to the house and see exactly what's shaken her.

Brennan hurries down the steps, his mouth curving into a smile I can't help but mirror. All three of us are here, and there are no words for how *complete* it feels. My eyes burn, blinking back the bittersweet yet wholly joyous emotion that threatens to overwhelm me.

We're finally together again.

"Brennan?" Mira croaks, and I move back a couple of steps to give them room. "How?"

"Hey, Mira." He's less than a dozen feet away, his grin widening.

"You're alive?" She stumbles forward, shaking her head. "After... I mean... It's been six *years*, and you're...*alive*?"

"In the flesh." He opens his arms. "Gods, it's good to see you."

She draws back her fist and punches him straight in the face.

The blood of life of the six and the one combined and set the stone ablaze in an iron rain.

—THE JOURNAL OF WARRICK OF LUCERAS
—TRANSLATED BY CADET VIOLET SORRENGAIL

CHAPTER THIRTY-NINE

So. Much. Blood.

"Get to the great hall and tell Ridoc Gamlyn that I need ice now!" I shout at a guard as we pass through the foyer.

"I'm fine!" Brennan manages to say around the handkerchief stanching the river of blood trying to pour down his face. He tests the cartilage and cringes. "Damn it, Mira, I think you broke it!"

"I heard a distinct crunch." I glare at my sister over my shoulder as we walk into the office where we have history class. It's set up for cadets, with a dozen chairs surrounding a hastily constructed table.

"You deserve it," Mira calls out, shaking off the guard who reaches for her. "Don't fucking touch me."

"Leave my sister alone," Brennan orders, sitting back against the edge of the table. "It's a family matter."

"Family? Family doesn't let each other think they're *dead* for six years." Mira leans against the wall to my right, putting me square between them. "The only family in this room is Violet and me."

"Mira—" I start.

"Lieutenant Colonel?" Ulices interrupts, pushing through the guards, and this time his eye isn't narrowed on me.

"Lieutenant Colonel?" Mira's gaze swings from Ulices to Brennan, and she folds her arms across her chest. "At least playing dead for six years earns you rank."

Brennan shoots her a look before turning toward Ulices. "I'm fine. Everyone can relax. I've had worse injuries sparring."

"Wouldn't be the first time I broke his nose." Mira offers a saccharine-sweet smile to Ulices, whose eye narrows on my sister.

A guard squeezes past Ulices, handing me a piece of cloth wrapped around a thick icicle, and I've never loved Ridoc's signet more. "Thank you," I tell him. "And tell the same to Ridoc, please."

"Deploy every rider currently not scheduled to scout the Tyrrish outposts as quietly as possible," Brennan orders Ulices. "We need to know if other riders are deserting, or if they're surging here in preparation to strike."

"With all the extra riders we have," Ulices mutters.

"Switch." I issue an order of my own to Brennan, holding out the ice.

"What about the new riot?" Ulices asks. "Same procedure as the cadets' arrival?"

"Riorson vouches for them, according to Marbh, but make sure the dragons do as well. Get them up to the valley." Brennan nods, and blood trickles off his chin.

Gross.

"Switch," I say again, waving the ice so he sees it.

Ulices glances at Mira. "You're sure—"

"I can handle my own sister," Brennan assures him.

"Don't be so sure about that," Mira counters, arching an eyebrow as Ulices departs, leaving the doorway empty but guarded outside.

"I can't believe you *hit* me," Brennan mutters. "Do you know how hard it is to mend myself? You? No problem. Doing it for myself? A giant pain in the ass."

"Oh, do cry for me, big brother." Mira scrunches her face as she mocks him. "You know, the way we cried for you."

And suddenly, I feel ten again, the smallest personality in a room of giants.

"I knew you wouldn't understand." Brennan jabs his finger in Mira's direction and flinches. "Shit, I'm going to have to set the cartilage."

"Understand? Understand that you let us burn your things?"

"I've already had this fight with him," I assure her.

"Let us watch our mother become a shadow of herself?" she continues over me. "Let us watch our *father's* heart give out because your death broke him?" Mira pushes off the wall, and I hold up my hand, palm outward, like I have even a prayer of stopping her if she decides to hit him again.

"Maybe I didn't go quite *that* far." Not that she isn't speaking the truth, but *damn*, that's harsh.

"Our father would understand what I've been doing." Brennan's voice turns nasal as he moves the blood dam.

"Would you please switch cloths?" I ask, water dripping from my fist to the stone floor.

"And as for our mother." Brennan stands. "I hope my death haunts her every damned day. She was so willing to sacrifice my life for a *lie*."

"That's not fair!" Mira snaps. "I may not agree with what she did, but I understand how she thought it was best to keep us safe."

"*Us* safe?" Brennan's eyes narrow. "You weren't killed!"

They're screaming at each other like I'm not even *here*. Yep, definitely morphed back into the little silent sister.

"Neither were you!" she yells. "You hid up here like a coward instead of coming home when we needed you!" She gestures at me. "You chose complete strangers over your sisters!"

"I chose the good of the Continent!"

"Oh for fuck's sake! Stop it!" I shout, silencing them both. "Mira, he was a brand-new lieutenant, and what's done is done." Pivoting toward Brennan, I shove the ice into his hand. "Brennan, put the fucking ice on your face before you stain the floors, you stubborn ass!"

Brennan slowly lifts the ice to his nose, looking at me like he's never seen me before.

"And to think, I used to wish I had siblings," Xaden says from the doorway, leaned against the doorframe casually, like he's been watching us for a hot minute.

All the fight within me transforms to pure relief, and I walk straight to him, careful not to slip on the blood Brennan has left splattered all over the place. "Hi."

"Hi," Xaden replies, wrapping his arm around my waist and tugging me against him.

My pulse skips like a rock thrown across a glassy pond as I soak in every detail of him. No new cuts or bruises on his face, but who knows what's under his riding leathers. "You're all right?"

"I am now." His voice softens to that tone he only ever uses with me, weakening my knees as he lowers his mouth to mine, giving me all the time in the world to protest.

I don't.

He kisses me slowly, gently, and I lean up on my toes to get closer, cupping his stubbled cheeks between my palms.

This right here makes everything worth it. The world could disintegrate around us and I'm not sure I'd notice—or care—as long as I have him in my arms.

"Seriously?" Brennan remarks. "Right in front of me?"

"Oh, this is *tame* for them," Mira replies. "Wait until they decide to basically climb each other in a public place. You can't *burn* that shit out of your head, trust me."

I smile into Xaden's kiss, and he deepens the pressure but keeps his tongue firmly behind his teeth—much to my chagrin. He pulls back reluctantly, but there's more than enough promise in his eyes to make my blood heat.

"So what are the Sorrengail siblings going to do now that you're all reunited?" Xaden asks, lifting his head to look at my family.

"We're going to beat the shit out of our brother," Mira answers with a smile.

"Survive," Brennan chimes in.

I let my hands fall from Xaden's face, then glance at my brother and sister. Everything I really, truly love—everyone I can't live without—is here, and for the first time in my life, I can protect *them*. "I need the blood of the six most powerful riders."

Brennan's brows fly upward, and Mira's nose wrinkles like she's just swallowed sour milk.

"Ever? Or living now?" Xaden asks without batting an eye.

"Why?" Brennan asks, water dripping from his fist.

"In residence, I think," I reply to Xaden, then turn to face my siblings and take a steadying breath. "I know how to raise the wards."

Nine of us—the Assembly, Bodhi, and myself—walk out the back door of Riorson House five hours later and start up a path cut into the ridgeline above, climbing the trail in pairs.

"You're certain about this?" Ulices asks my brother as they walk in front of Xaden and me.

"My sister's certain, and that's good enough for me," Brennan replies.

"Yes, by all means, let's waste our time catering to the whims of a cadet," Suri calls up from where she walks with Kylynn.

"A cadet who can raise the wards," Xaden counters.

No pressure.

Shivering, I shove my hands into the pockets of my flight jacket to ward off the chill as the sun sets behind the mountain. Finally, the trail levels out and we approach a set of somber guards who step aside so we can pass, following the gravel path that leads into the mountainside, becoming a man-made canyon open to the sky above.

Mage lights flicker on as we pass through the chasm, and my stomach flutters with nervous energy. No, that's apprehension. Nope...nervous energy.

Whatever it is, I'm glad I skipped dinner.

"We should be using this time to discuss the negotiations with Tecarus, since we're all here." Ulices looks pointedly at my brother.

"Missive arrived today. He wants us to come to his aid when called," Brennan says. "The seaside drifts are to be armed first, and he says he'll let us bring the luminary back to Aretia—"

"He won't," Xaden interrupts.

"—if he can see Vi wield," Brennan finishes.

"Looks like we need to seek another luminary, because he'll meet Malek before Violet," Xaden says in that calm, icy tone he uses when his mind's made up. "Unless you're eager to never see your sister again. He'll keep her as a weapon. You and I both know it."

"I can talk him out of any thoughts that direction." Brennan's jaw ticks.

"If there was another luminary, don't you think we'd be negotiating for that one?" Kylynn retorts.

"Then offer him a full armory, because Violet isn't up for negotiation." Xaden looks back and levels a glare at her.

"I don't mind going." Our shoulders brush as the path narrows and the walls of the canyon rise even higher around us. *"You need it."*

"I mind it. The answer is no. There is always another way."

It's a good thing we're about to have wards, then. It doesn't solve our issue with protecting Poromiel, not until we can build extensions like Navarre, but at least everyone here will be safe.

About twenty feet in, the canyon opens into a circular chamber that could easily fit all ten of our dragons, and my eyes are immediately drawn upward, to where a series of runes lead to the sky. *"How have I never seen this while flying overhead?"*

"Very old, very complicated masking runes."

The riders in front of us part, and the wardstone comes into view.

My lips part, because…wow.

The shimmering black pillar rises to over twice the height of Xaden and would take all nine of us holding our arms outstretched to surround it. Etched in the very center, at least six feet across, is a series of circles, each fitting within the next and boasting a rune carved in along its path. It's almost the same pattern as on the pages of Warrick's journal.

I move toward it, soaking in every detail. "Is it onyx?" I ask Xaden. It's *massive.* Too heavy for even a dragon to carry. They had to have carved it in this very chamber.

"We can't say for certain, but my father thought it was polished iron," he answers.

Iron rain. My heart jolts. This is really it. We're about to have wards.

"Let's get this done." Ulices's voice booms through the chamber, echoing off the high stone walls.

"And what are we doing, exactly, to raise the wards?" Bodhi asks, taking my other side as everyone forms a half circle around the stone.

"One second." I pull Warrick's journal from the protective leather pouch inside my flight jacket and flip to the translated parchment I left at the passage before glancing up at the stone to compare the drawings. The symbol Warrick drew isn't identical, but it has the runes in the same positions, so that's a good sign. "Here we go. 'And we gathered the six most powerful riders in residence,'" I read from the parchment, "'and the blood of the six and the one combined and set the stone ablaze in an iron rain.'" I glance around the line. "Six"—I point to the stone—"and the one."

"You want us to bleed on the wardstone?" Felix asks, his silver brows rising.

"I'm just telling you how Warrick and the First Six did it." I hold the journal up. "Unless there's someone here more capable of translating Old Lucerish?"

No one speaks.

"Right." I dip my chin and study the rest of the translation.

"By our best calculations," Brennan says, rubbing his hands together to keep warm, "the six most powerful riders currently in Aretia are Xaden, Felix, Suri, Bodhi, Violet, and me."

"Looks like there's something to be said for family lines," Suri notes.

"According to Warrick, the First Six bled their life—" I start.

Every head swivels my direction.

"I don't think it means to death," I quickly clarify. "Clearly the six lived on after they constructed Basgiath's wards." There's a definite sigh of relief around me. "With any luck, it'll be a quick cut across the palm, place our hands on the wardstone, and we should have wards."

"In an iron rain," Bodhi says slowly.

Suri draws a knife from her side. "Let's get this done."

The six of us move to the wardstone, and I tuck the journal into my flight jacket.

"Anywhere?" Bodhi asks, lowering his own knife to just above his palm.

"The journal didn't specify." Brennan draws his dagger over his palm, then presses his hand to the wardstone, and we all follow.

Hope swells in my chest, rising with my pulse, and I hiss through my teeth at the bite of pain as I slice. Blood wells, and I push my cut palm against the stone in line with the others. It's colder than I expect, warmth quickly leaching from my hand as blood drips down the shimmering black surface.

The stone feels frozen. Lifeless. But not for long.

I glance down the line to be sure everyone has their palms flat against the stone and see six narrow streams of blood snaking their way down the iron.

"Is it working?" Bodhi asks, bleeding a couple of feet away.

My mouth opens, but I quickly shut it.

No one answers.

Come on, I beg the stone, like I can will the damn thing to life.

There's no hum, no sense of power—nothing but cold, black stone. It's nothing like the awareness that comes from being close to the wards at the outposts or even holding the alloy-hilted dagger in my hand.

There's…nothing.

My stomach falls first, then my heart, and finally my shoulders as my head droops.

"I'm done." Suri pulls her hand off the stone. "The rest of you can sit here and bleed all night, but this clearly isn't working."

No, no, *no*.

Felix, Brennan, and Bodhi drop their hands.

Failure clogs my throat, leaving a bitter taste in my mouth. I did everything *right*. I researched, and read, and stole a primary source. I translated and double-checked. This is supposed to be the solution. It's everything I've been working on for months, the key to keeping everyone safe.

Did we bleed the wrong six riders? Is there an element of magic I missed? Something more to the blood? What did I miss?

"Violence," Xaden says quietly.

Slowly, I turn my head to look up at him, expecting disappointment or censure but finding none in his eyes. But there's no pity, either.

"I failed," I whisper, my hand falling away.

He watches me for a heartbeat, then two before dropping his own. "You'll try again."

It isn't an order, though, just a fact.

"Violet, I can—" Brennan starts, reaching for my hand.

I shake my head, then stare down at the blood welling in the cup of my palm. If he mends a cut this fresh, I doubt it will leave a scar. I won't even have *that* to show for the last three months.

The sound of tearing fills the space, and Xaden tightly wraps a cut piece of his uniform around my palm to stanch the bleeding. "Thank you."

"You'll try again," he repeats, wrapping another strip of fabric around his own hand.

I nod, and he turns to talk to Kylynn, keeping his voice low.

"Now can we *please* discuss how we plan to actually acquire that luminary?" Suri's tone rises with annoyance.

I stare up at the blood-marked stone, searching for answers it won't give me.

"It's a lost magic," Bodhi says softly, appearing at my side. He rubs his thumb over his newly mended, scarless palm. "Maybe there's a reason this stone never worked. It might be broken."

I nod again, incapable of speech. Bodhi. Xaden. Mira. Rhi. Brennan. Ridoc. Sawyer. Imogen… The list of people I've failed goes on and on. We're only here because I made my friends steal the journal in the first place, and then… nothing? Anger sparks in my chest, and power rushes in, heating my skin.

I don't *fail*. I've never failed anything in my life. Well, that first RSC land navigation, but that doesn't count. That was everyone. This is *me*.

"Offer the viscount twice the number of weapons he asked for," Ulices says, his voice fading with his footsteps.

"I'll send a missive tomorrow," Brennan promises as the others walk out of the chamber.

We have no wards. No weapons. Almost no experienced riders. All because I acted recklessly.

Power builds, vibrating my fingertips.

Felix moves to my side, his somber gaze studying me before he holds out his hand.

I blink, glancing at his palm, then up to his face.

"Your hand." He lifts his brow.

I hold my uninjured one out, and instead of touching me, he tilts his head and watches the slight trembling of my fingers.

"I suppose we'd better start tomorrow." He sighs. "Skip the run. We'll be training your signet." His bootsteps echo in the chamber, and I turn, watching him walk out, my gaze catching on the tight lines of Xaden's mouth as Kylynn lectures him with quiet words, the mage lights reflecting on the steel of her battle-ax strapped to her back.

Xaden was right. War requires weapons.

"Take me to Tecarus," I demand.

His gaze flies to mine and his jaw flexes. *"I would rather die."*

"We all will if you don't."

"Not going to happen. Subject closed." He folds his arms across his chest and goes back to his discussion with Kylynn.

Fuck this.

I walk straight past him, taking the path out of the chamber. There's no way I'm going to leave my friends defenseless when I'm the reason they got dragged into this.

"Violet!" Brennan shouts, running to catch up with me.

"Go away," I snap at my brother.

"With that look on your face? I don't think so."

"What look?" I shoot a glare in his direction, even though I know this isn't his fault.

"The same one you had at eight years old, when you stared Mom down over a plate of squash for twelve straight hours."

"I'm sorry?" Rocks crunch underfoot as we make our way down the path to Riorson House.

"Twelve. Hours." He nods. "Dad said to let you go to bed, that you weren't going to eat them, and Mom said you weren't going to sleep until you did."

"What's your point?"

"When I got up the next morning, Mom and Dad were both asleep at the table, and you were snacking on bread and cheese. I know that face, Violet. When you dig in about something, you're more tenacious than all of us put together, so no, I won't be *going away*."

"Fine." I shrug. "You can be the tagalong sibling for once." Within minutes, we're in through the guarded back door of Riorson House, walking through the network of hallways to the main corridor. *"Tairn."*

"Oh, this should be fun," Andarna answers.

I feel Tairn's sigh long before I hear it.

"You know it's the only way." Another turn later, we walk into the overwhelming noise of the great hall. Long trestle tables line the space, and my gaze skips over each one, bypassing the one where my squad sits and locking onto the table of new riders who arrived today.

"I will consider it," Tairn begrudgingly agrees.

"Thank you." I move through the sea of black with Brennan on my heels, locking eyes with Mira as I approach where she sits at the end of her table with her friends.

"Violet?" Her gaze narrows on my bandaged hand before she sets her pewter mug down.

"I need your help."

His first true action of rebellion was to seek allies, the first of which was Viscount Tecarus of the Poromish province of Krovla.

—THE TYRRISH REBELLION, A FORBIDDEN HISTORY
BY COLONEL FELIX GERAULT

CHAPTER FORTY

Xaden vetoed my second pitch to head to Cordyn like an overprotective asshole, and then I happily took him to bed, content with my own plans. He was gone again to look for more Navarrian deserters before I woke up this morning.

If I didn't feel him in my swollen lips and every sore muscle in my body, I'd almost think I dreamed him coming back yesterday.

Guess this is our new normal.

"Well?" Felix folds his arms over his barrel chest and lifts a silver brow at me.

Crisp, snow-scented wind whips at my cheeks as we stand between our dragons, a thousand feet over the tree line on a bowl-shaped mountainside about a ten-minute flight from the valley above Aretia.

"Those boulders?" I point across the ridge to a stack of three boulders as Tairn shifts his weight, the snow crunching under his claws.

"Would it help if I painted them?"

I refrain from rolling my eyes. "No, it's just that Carr never cared where I struck, as long as I increased the number of strikes in an hour." I roll my shoulders and open the gates on Tairn's power, feeling it rush through my veins and heat my skin.

Felix looks at me like I've grown another head. "Well, I guess we'll see what that technique has gotten us."

"I can wield twenty-six an hour on a good day, and I've been pushed over forty, but that last strike broke that mountain and…" The memory steals my words.

"And you were nearly burned alive?" he asks. "Why in Malek's name would you ever push yourself to that limit?"

"It was a punishment." I lift my arms as power rises to a sizzling hum.

"For what?" He watches me with an expression I'm too jaded to call compassion.

"I ignored a direct order so I could protect my dragon." The sizzle heats to a burn, and I flex my hands, letting the strike rip free.

The cloudy sky cracks open and lightning strikes on the opposite side of the bowl, hitting far above the tree line, easily a quarter mile from the boulders.

Felix blinks. "Try again."

Reaching for Tairn's power, I repeat the process, letting it fill me, then overflow and erupt, wielding another strike that lands halfway between the first and the stack of boulders. Pride makes my lips curve. Not bad timing. That was a pretty quick strike after the first.

But when I look at Felix, he isn't smiling. He slowly brings his stunned gaze to mine. "What was that shit?"

"I did that in less than a minute after the first strike!" I counter.

"And if those boulders were dark wielders, you and I would be dead by now." Two lines knit between his eyebrows. "Try again. And this time, let's try the revolutionary tactic of *aiming*, shall we?"

His sarcasm fuels my frustration, and another strike rips free, hitting between us and the boulders.

"It's a wonder you haven't hit yourself," he mutters, rubbing the bridge of his nose.

"I can't aim, all right?" I snap at him, reevaluating my previous thoughts that he and Trissa—the petite, quiet one—were the nice members of the Assembly.

"According to the reports filed about Resson, you can," he retorts, his deep voice rising with that last word. "You can aim well enough to hit a dark wielder atop a flying wyvern."

"That's because Andarna stopped time, but she can't do that anymore, so I'm left with what got us through the other portion of the battle—the good old strike-and-pray method."

"And I have no doubt that in a field of that many wyvern, you did some damage with sheer luck." He sighs. "Explain how you hit that last strike in Resson."

"I… It's hard to explain."

"Try."

"I pulled it. I guess." I wrap my arms around my waist to ward off the worst of the chill. Usually, I'd be warming up right about now, not feeling my toes start to lose feeling. "I released the strike, but I wrestled it into place while

Andarna held time."

"What about smaller strikes?" He turns fully to face me, his boots crunching the rock beneath us. "Like those that flow from your hands?"

What the fuck? My face must read the same because his eyes flare.

"Are you telling me that you've only wielded full strikes"—he points upward—"from the sky? That you just started throwing around bolts and never refined the skill?"

"I brought down a cliff on a classmate—that didn't kill him—and from then Carr's concern was how big and how often." I lift my hands between us. "And lightning comes from the sky, not my hands."

"Wonderful." He laughs, the sound deep and…infuriating. "You just might wield the most devastating signet on the Continent, but you know nothing about it. Nothing about the energy fields that draw it. Instead of shooting your power like an arrow—precise and measured—you're just heaving it around like boiling oil, hoping you hit *something*. And lightning comes from the sky or the ground depending on the storm, so why not your hands?"

Anger reddens my skin, raises my temperature, prickles my fingers, and pushes the power within me to a roar.

"You are slated to be the most powerful rider of your year—perhaps your entire generation—and yet you are just a glorified light show—"

Power erupts, and lightning flashes close enough that I feel the heat.

Felix glances to the right, where a scorch mark still smokes about twenty feet away.

Fuck. Shame races in to overpower the last vestiges of anger.

"And not only can you not aim, but you have *no control*," he says without skipping a beat, like I didn't almost torch us both.

"I can cont—"

"No." He drops down to the pack at his feet and begins sorting through it. "That wasn't a question, Sorrengail. That was a fact. How often does *that* happen?"

Whenever I'm angry. Or in Xaden's arms. "Too often."

"At least we found something to agree on." He stands and holds something out to me. "Take it."

"What is it?" I glance at the offering, then pluck it gingerly from his outstretched hand. The glass orb fits comfortably in my palm, and the decoratively carved silvery metal strips that quarter it meet at what appear to be the top and the bottom, where a silver medallion of alloy the size of my thumb rests upright inside the glass.

"It's a conduit," Felix explains. "Lightning may appear from various sources, but Tairn channels his power through *you*. You are the vessel. You are the pathway. You are the cloud, for lack of a better term. How else do you think you can wield from a blue sky? Did you never realize it's easier for you to wield during a storm, but you're capable of both?"

"I never thought about it." My fingers tingle where they meet the metal striping.

"No, you were never *taught* it." He gestures around the mountainside. "Your lack of aim, of control, is not your fault. It's Carr's."

"Xaden only moves shadows that are already there," I argue, fighting down the rising emotions I'm worried will lead to another embarrassing strike.

"Xaden can control and increase what already exists. It's why he's more powerful at night. No two signets are alike, and you create something that was not there before. You wield pure power that takes the form of lightning because that's what you're most comfortable shaping it as. Apparently Carr never taught you that, either."

"Why wouldn't he?" I look from the orb up to Felix as the first flakes of snow flutter down. "If I was the best weapon?"

A corner of his mouth lifts into a wry smile. "Knowing Carr, I'd say he's scared shitless of you. After all, you just took half of their cadets without even a plan. You brought down Basgiath on a fucking whim, no less." His laugh is more incredulous than mocking this time, but it still rubs me the wrong way.

"I didn't do that." My fingers curl around the orb. "Xaden did."

"He hunted riderless wyvern, deposited them on Melgren's front door, and exposed Navarre's greatest secret to the border outposts before noon," Felix agrees. "But you were the one who demanded he give the cadets a choice. In that moment, you wielded *him*, our unyielding, uncompromising, headstrong heir apparent."

"I did no such thing." Energy buzzes, and I roll my shoulders as it vibrates through my limbs, building to a breaking point. "I presented a humane option, and he took it. He did it for the sake of the other cadets."

"He did it for you," Felix says softly. "The wyvern, the exposure, breaching Basgiath, stealing half its riders. All for you. Why do you think the Assembly wanted to lock you away in July? They saw what you were. In that way, I suppose you're just as much a danger to Aretia as you are to Basgiath, aren't you? Power isn't only found in our signets."

"I'm not powerful just because he loves me." The bitter taste of fear fills my mouth a heartbeat before power breaks free, cracking through me like a whip, but lightning doesn't flash. At least not in the sky.

I blink at the glowing orb, then marvel at the string of lightning that runs from where my forefinger rests against the metal strip to the alloy pendant inside. The bolt vanishes a breath later.

"No. You're powerful *and* he loves you, which is even worse. Your power is too closely tied to your emotions," Felix notes. "This will help. It's not a permanent solution, but it will keep everyone in Aretia safe from your temper for now."

"I don't understand." And I can't stop staring at the orb, like the tiny lightning bolt will reappear at any second.

"The runes etched into the conduit are woven to draw specific power. I wove these specifically for you the last time you were here, but you were forced to leave before I could teach you how to use it. I'd hoped you wouldn't need it, honestly, but it seems Carr hasn't changed much in the six years I've been gone."

"Runes?" I repeat like a bird, staring at the etched shapes.

"Yes. Runes. Wielded power woven for set purposes." He exhales slowly. "Which you know nothing about because Basgiath doesn't teach Tyrrish runes, even if the college was fucking *built* on them. Guess we'll ask Trissa to teach that class. She has the most patience out of the Assembly."

I yank my gaze from the orb to Felix. "This…siphons my power?"

"Somewhat. I made it as a simpler way to imbue power into alloy. It will draw it from you when it threatens to overpower you or when you choose to direct it. Hopefully"—he lifts his brows—"in small, controlled amounts. Practice this week. You have to learn control, Sorrengail, or you'll continue to be a threat to everyone around you. God forbid you're flying in the clouds with your squad the next time you lose your temper."

"I'm not a threat."

"What you want to be doesn't change what you are without work." He picks up his pack and slings it over his shoulders. "You never learned how to start small, like the rest of your squad, and then move to the bigger, harder strikes. You have to master the basics you were never taught. Small, precise strikes. Small strands of your power instead of"—he gestures to the sky—"whatever in Dunne's name that was."

"I don't have time to master small, precise strikes. I need help *today*," I argue. "We need Tecarus to give us a luminary or—" I cut myself off.

"Or you and Xaden fucked the entire movement on that whim I mentioned earlier?" He lifts both brows at me.

"Something like that. It was a lot easier last year when all I had to worry about was keeping myself alive, and not the entire Continent." And I failed.

"Well, they do say second year makes or breaks you." He delivers the joke with a straight face, but there's a definite light in his eyes. "As for Tecarus, he wants to see you wield, not necessarily see you wield *well*. Your biggest obstacle there is convincing Xaden to fly with you, since I hazard to guess he's not budging on the topic of you going. He already shut down the possibility in July." He shrugs. "But we're done for today. We'll meet again in a week, and I'll be able to tell by the amount of power stored in that alloy whether or not you've been practicing. Store enough, and I'll continue to teach you."

"And if I don't?" My fingers curl around the orb.

"I won't," he answers simply over his shoulder as he walks toward his Red Swordtail. "I'm not interested in wasting my time on cadets who don't want to be taught when there are over a hundred who do."

The scorch mark behind him. The untouched boulders. The blast sites across the ridge. They all capture my attention. He's right. I'm a light show with deadly consequences, and the amount of times I've unleashed while close to my friends, close to Xaden... My throat tightens. I'm the menace everyone *thinks* Xaden is.

He might be a weapon, but I'm a natural disaster.

And I'm done letting everyone around me suffer because I can't get my shit together.

"I want to learn," I call after him. *As soon as I get back.*

"Good. Show me."

"Are you sure about this?" Mira asks as we enter the valley under the brightest moon this month. Every blade of grass is coated with predawn frost, reflecting back at us like glittering gems.

"'Sure' is a relative term."

"How relative?" She lifts her brows at me. "Because what we're about to do could have some pretty major consequences."

"I'm sure this is the only way we'll be able to make the weapons we need." I fasten the top button of my flight jacket to ward off the late-October chill. "And sure that if we stay on task, we can be back in two days max. I'm definitely sure that this will stop the gryphon attacks on Navarrian outposts. But am I sure that we won't fail or end up permanent guests of Viscount Tecarus? No."

"Well, *I'm* sure Xaden is going to lose his shit when he finds out you went behind his back," Mira lectures as we make our way to our dragons.

"Yeah, well, Xaden will forgive me as soon as he realizes we're back in the venin-slaying business. I'm only doing it this way because he refuses to do what needs to be done in the name of protecting me."

"Just so you know, I'm only doing this because doing everything you ever ask for the rest of our lives still wouldn't make up for me not believing you. I happen to like protective Xaden. Makes me worry about you less."

I kind of miss when he wanted to kill me. At least then he didn't insist on *hovering*.

"And I'm only doing this to make sure neither of you die," Brennan chimes in from the right.

"Please." Mira scoffs. "You're only here because of the rank on your uniform."

"Neither of you can negotiate an arms deal on behalf of the Assembly. You both know this could go very badly, right?" He shoves his hands in the pockets of his flight leathers.

"Is there a risk?" I nod and ignore the jump in my heart rate. "Yes. But he wants to see me wield for a luminary. Even Xaden said the biggest threat is him keeping me, not killing me." And if I have to stay in Poromiel so my friends and family can be safe, then fine. As long as Brennan and Mira get to leave with the luminary, it's a fair trade.

"Feel free to stay in the place you've called home for six years," Mira challenges Brennan, then shrugs a shoulder. "I've always been better than you with a sword, anyway. I'll bring Violet home without a scratch."

"No." I glance between them. Have they always bickered like this? "We're not fighting the entire way there, and we sure as hell can't fight once we *get* there. This is dangerous enough as it is. Pull yourselves together and quit squabbling."

"Yes, Mom," Mira mocks.

Mom. What would she think of the three of us working together?

We all fall silent, the quiet only broken by the frost crackling beneath our boots.

"Too soon?" Mira asks.

"I'd say so," I answer, tightening the straps on my pack.

"Definitely," Brennan adds.

All three of us are faintly smiling when we reach the dragons.

"You sure you can find the way?" I ask Tairn after I secure my pack behind my saddle.

"I'm going to pretend you didn't ask that."

"And Sgaeyl?" I shift forward and buckle into the saddle, flinching as the cold seeps through my leathers.

"She's out of range, but her emotions are calm."

"And you promise not to tell her until we're back?" I clutch the pommel and glance around the valley, looking for any sign of Andarna, but she's nowhere to be seen.

"She's already gone, and the Hungry One has been seething since this afternoon when she found out she wasn't coming." Tairn crouches low, then springs into the sky. The ground falls away with every powerful beat of his wings, and I foolishly hold my breath as we pass over a sleeping Aretia, as if the sound of my inhale might wake my friends.

Rhiannon is the only one who knows we're going, and she'll cover for us as much as possible. But even though I might be dispensable for a day, I have no doubt someone will notice Brennan is missing.

My cheeks are numb before we make it past Aretia, and my legs lose feeling by the time we reach the Cliffs of Dralor a couple of hours later. Flying for any amount of time this late in fall isn't for the faint of heart.

Tairn flies through the morning, holding back his speed for Teine and Marbh as we glimpse Krovla's second most populous city, Draithus, to the south and continue into the darkness ahead. The feeling seeps back into my limbs the lower in elevation that we fly and the higher the sun climbs.

"Sleep, Silver One. It's not me Tecarus wants to see perform like some kind of pet."

I take his advice and get as much rest as possible, but my jittery nerves have me shifting in my seat as we fly over land I've only seen in paintings. Amber fields ready for harvest give way to pale beaches and blue-green sea as the day passes into afternoon.

The closer we fly, the tighter the anxiety in my chest coils. This is either the best idea I've ever had...or the worst. By the time a drift of three gryphons appears, flying directly toward us in a standard V attack formation, I decide that we're definitely leaning into *worst idea* territory.

Just because they're smaller doesn't mean they can't deal Tairn some real damage with those talons.

"It's all right. They're escorting us into Cordyn," Tairn tells me, but there's a shift in his tone that tells me he's not happy about the entourage or the speed he has to slow to in order to accommodate them. They spread out, flying in a formation that surrounds the six of us. *"See that sorry excuse for a fortress on the eastern side of the farthest peak?"* he asks as we follow the line of the beach. I've never seen water that color, like it can't quite decide if it's turquoise or aqua.

"You mean the palace that looks like it's glowing?" The structure is a sprawling, glistening combination of white pillars and blue pools that cascade in five distinct terraces down the gentle slope of the hills above the beach.

"It's just the sun reflecting off the white marble," he grumbles. *"The entire thing is ridiculous and indefensible."*

How...beautiful. What a luxury to build a place like this, designed purely for aesthetics. No high walls or portcullises. Tairn's right. It's utterly indefensible, and it will fall should venin choose to take it, but my heart clenches at the thought that I'll never experience peace long enough to live somewhere like it. I can even make out a vast, colorful garden as we approach over the riverside city beneath.

The gryphon ahead of us dips into a sharp descent and Tairn follows suit, tucking his wings and getting just close enough to the gryphon to let him know he's no match.

"Stop intimidating them." The last thing we need is an incident before we can even ask Tecarus for the luminary.

"I can't help their inferiority." There's a definite smile in his tone, but his mood shifts as we level out near a manicured lawn in front of the third terrace of the palace. *"You will not be happy with the welcome we're about to receive."* He lands behind the gryphon and his flier, who hops down to face us.

"I'm sure we'll be fine. You worry too much."

"We'll see about that."

I make quick work of removing my pack, but damn do my stiff joints ache as I slide down Tairn's foreleg to land in the soft, green grass.

"Are you all right?" Mira asks, already waiting for me because she's *that* much quicker.

"Just sore from sitting in one position for so long." Gods, it's *hot* down here.

"Maybe we should have sent word ahead. They look like they'd rather fight than negotiate." She turns her attention forward, to the line of three gryphons and their fliers, who all face down our dragons despite being drastically overpowered, forming a wall of feather and talons that blocks us from proceeding to the palace.

"They're certainly brave, I'll give them that," I mutter as Brennan reaches our sides, putting me between him and Mira. Some things never change.

"They're also expecting us," Brennan notes quietly as we start forward.

"You think?" Mira asks, her gaze scanning our surroundings.

I keep my focus on the fliers and their hands.

"There are at least three dozen people watching from the balconies above, and there's another group behind the gryphons," Brennan states. "They were waiting."

"Plus, no one's screaming at the sight of our dragons," I add quietly.

Mira grins. "True."

"Be careful what you say in here. Tecarus will hold us to whatever deal we make. He doesn't take kindly to broken words. And keep your shields up, though I'm not sure they'll do much good," Brennan orders when we're less than a dozen feet from the fliers. "Fliers might not wield signets, but most of their lesser-magic gifts involve mindwork, and it's the one area where they have the upper hand on us."

"Noted." I don't even need to check my shields. They've been locked into place since we left Aretia.

The gryphons stare down at us with dark, beady eyes as we approach and click their razor-sharp beaks in a rhythm that reminds me of speech. The aggressive snaps of the one on the right make me glad I can't understand what they're saying.

Two of the fliers wear the same brown leathers I've seen before on Syrena, but the guy on the left with the patchy beard has a lighter-colored one and different symbols embroidered on his collar.

"Cadet?" I ask Tairn.

"Yes." He pauses. *"According to the feathered ones, a third of their ranks took shelter here. Cliffsbane Flight Academy was in Zolya."*

Brennan says something in Krovlish, his tone changing into the curt one he uses when his rank is more important than his name.

"We know who you are," the tall flier in the center interrupts in the common tongue, studying the three of us as if assessing which is the biggest threat. His attention lands on my wind-ravaged coronet braid and his posture changes slightly, taking on the most casual of battle stances.

Guess I win.

Mira moves closer to my side and stares him down, her hand resting just above the hilt of her sword.

"And you speak Navarrian," Brennan notes.

"Of course. Not every kingdom thinks theirs is the only language that should be spoken," the flier on the left says, her fingers drumming along her sword.

Solid point.

"Give us one truth, and we'll allow you to meet with the viscount," the central flier says, his reddish brows knitting.

"You're a truth-sayer." Like Nora. It's a guess, but I know I'm right when his pale eyes flare. So, some of our powers are the same. Interesting.

"Unlike riders, we do not label ourselves by our abilities, but yes, I have the *gift* of telling when someone is lying," he corrects me.

"Noted," I say for the second time in the last five minutes. I fucking *hate* being disadvantaged by ignorance, but it's not like the Archives were stacked with tomes on fliers or what they've gone through for the last six hundred years.

"Seeing as you've arrived without invitation, we require you have honest intentions before traveling farther." His hands flex near his daggers, and Mira palms the hilt of her sword.

We're one misstep away from drawing weapons, and we all know it.

"I'm here to wield lightning in return for asking your viscount for help." May as well start us out.

He cocks his head to the side, then nods, glancing toward Brennan.

"I'm here to broker a deal for your luminary in return for weaponry," Brennan declares.

The flier nods and looks at Mira.

"Fine." She sighs. "Make one wrong move toward my sister, and I'll gut you like a fish. That goes for everyone in this city. How is that for honest?"

My mouth opens slightly as I glance sideways at my sister.

"Damn it, Mira," Brennan growls.

The flier's mouth curves into a toothy smile. "I can respect that." He glances up at the gryphon above him, and the trio parts, revealing the figure waiting directly behind them.

A figure dressed entirely in black.

His jaw flexes, his hands curl at his sides, and his beautiful face… Well, he hasn't looked at me with that much anger since discovering my last name at Parapet, back when he wanted to kill me. Guess I should be careful what I ask for, because I'm so *fucked*.

"You aren't where I left you, Violence."

Having refused every proposal from the isle kingdoms, Queen
Maraya has named her distant cousin, Viscount Tecarus of
Cordyn, as her heir. As the viscount is living in his fifth decade
and has no direct heirs of his own, the decision
has not been a popular one.

—ON THE ARISTOCRACY OF POROMIEL
BY PEARSON KITO

CHAPTER
FORTY-ONE

"Where you left me?" I whisper under my breath at Xaden as we walk
across the guarded lawn, passing by a half dozen more fliers on our
way to a row of open doors made entirely of glass. How utterly impractical and
sublimely gorgeous. "Like I'm some kind of pet who should stay curled up on
your bed because you said so?"

Fuck him.

"The thought isn't entirely unpleasant," he fires back.

I breathe in through my nose and out through my mouth to keep my power
from rising, refusing to unpack the conduit from my bag.

"Save it for behind closed doors, lovebirds," Brennan orders from directly
behind us. "We need a united front."

"I can't believe you brought her here," Xaden retorts, shooting an icy glare
at Brennan.

"I can't believe you think you outrank me," Brennan says, his tone sharpening.

"I do in every way but one." Xaden looks forward, anger radiating from
every line of his body.

"The one is *all* that matters," Brennan counters.

"They really grow grass ornamentally?" Mira changes the subject as we
approach two guards in crimson uniforms near the door.

"You should see the butterfly garden," Xaden says, nodding to the guard on the right as we pass through the open doorway.

Wait. Why aren't we being escorted by fliers? And how the hell does Xaden know this place has a butterfly garden?

"How long have you been here?" I ask, entering the palace.

And *holy shit*, what a palace.

Every surface seems to shimmer, the white marble interior reflecting not only natural light but a soft glow of white mage lights far overhead and deep into the structure, where I can make out several seating groups of low-backed furniture. The ceilings are the height of Sgaeyl, the space divided by not only columns thick as Tairn's legs, with murals intricately carved into each circular block, but a wide staircase that must lead to the next story.

Pretty sure if I were to call out my name loudly enough, it would echo back in here, if not for the crowd of people in many different forms of attire milling about near a set of graduated pillars in various shades of black. Brown is definitely the dominant clothing color, and we are *definitely* the topic of conversation as we pass by.

"We landed a few hours ago," Xaden answers. "We changed direction as soon as Sgaeyl felt Tairn on the move."

You will not be happy with the welcome we're about to receive. That's what Tairn said when we landed.

"You and I are going to have a discussion," I send his direction. *"You promised."*

"I promised not to tell, not that she couldn't sense me."

Fucking dragon semantics.

"Is that…a pool?" Mira stares at the winding turquoise path that curves around the staircase and disappears out onto the terrace.

"You get used to them," Xaden remarks, leading us over a flat, marble bridge wide enough for two people. "Just be careful if you've been drinking. No railings."

"We won't be here long enough to drink." Brennan's words slow with our steps as a group of a dozen people descends the staircase in front of us.

But Xaden's been here often enough to drink? To have fallen into this pool?

"Here we go." Xaden's voice lowers. "Try not to set the place on fire."

Two crimson-uniformed guards station themselves at opposite ends of the curling bannister, and a tall, dark-haired man in a deep blue tunic with gold brocade walks forward, looking over us with rapt fascination. His uniform is tight about the waist, his flushed cheeks soft and round.

"Viscount," Xaden addresses him. "This is Cadet Violet Sorrengail and her sister, Lieutenant Mira Sorrengail. I believe you and Lieutenant Colonel Aisereigh are already acquainted."

"We are." He flashes impossibly white teeth as he smiles at me, etching deep lines into his forehead and at the edges of his eyes. "But it's you I am most curious about, Violet." The unnerving amount of glee in his gaze makes it nearly impossible to stand still as he studies me, drawing out his words until he finishes his perusal. "Is it true that you call lightning from the sky?"

"I do." I keep my focus on the viscount, but I feel the weight of his entourage staring behind him.

"How wonderful!" He clasps his hands in front of his chest, his rings twinkling with heavy gemstones.

"Shall we—" Brennan starts.

"It's poor etiquette to discuss business until dinner. You know the rules, Riorson," Tecarus says, glancing Xaden's way. "They certainly can't attend as they are. They'll need to be dressed suitably, as will you."

Xaden nods once.

"You know the rules?" I ask Xaden. *"Exactly how many times have you been here?"* And what part of our uniforms isn't suitable for dinner?

"I don't exactly keep count."

"Don't worry if you haven't brought anything fit for the occasion," Tecarus says to me. "I took the liberty of having a selection of clothing pulled from my best collection once Riorson told me you were inbound. My niece will see you properly attired, won't you, Cat?" he calls back over his shoulder.

My stomach hits the sparkly marble floor.

You have to be *fucking* kidding me.

"Of course, Uncle." Catriona steps down from the front row of the entourage, dressed in a purple, long-sleeved gown that shows her elegant figure to its best advantage. I'd thought she was beautiful from a distance, but up close, her features are truly so flawless that she's completely, utterly…devastating.

Suddenly, I understand exactly why Xaden's been here too many times to keep count.

"I didn't expect you to be here," Xaden says to Cat in that clipped, cold tone he uses when annoyed as they lead us down another hallway two stories above where we entered.

"Where did you think I'd be after dark wielders destroyed Zolya and took up residence at Cliffsbane?" Cat questions, pausing in front of one of the dozen doors in this wing.

Mira shoots me a look, lifting her eyebrows as we stop in the middle of the hallway, Brennan only a few feet behind.

Later, I mouth at her.

Cat reaches for the golden handle. "Why don't you take Aisereigh to dress for dinner while these two wash up?" She gives Xaden a longing look, and my eyebrows rise. Is she seriously eyeing him up in front of me? "We kept your room exactly how you left it, of course." She opens the door, revealing a sizable bedchamber with two large beds and a matching gold brocade sofa between them, then walks inside, leaving Mira and me to follow.

Wait. He has a *room* here?

What else has he not told me? Or *what haven't I asked* might be the better question.

"Why don't you come get dressed in my room?" Xaden asks, and it doesn't sound like a suggestion.

"Your room? I think I'd like a little space." Heat simmers beneath my skin, and I breathe deeply to keep the power caged. Now is *not* the time to lose control, not that I have it to begin with.

"Violet."

I turn in the doorway to face Xaden and grasp the door handle, lifting my brows at him as Mira edges around me into the chamber.

"I'm the next door down," he assures me, then glances over my shoulder. "Close enough to hear you scream."

"Good to know." I force a smile and his eyes narrow.

"Surely you can't be worried that she's in any danger from me?"

I roll my eyes at the incredulity in Cat's tone.

"Violet can—" Xaden starts.

"Violet can handle herself," I interrupt, startling Xaden.

"I never wanted you to have to. Not here." He lowers his head and his voice, narrowing the conversation to the two of us, anger and all. *"Tecarus might want to keep you, but every other flier in this palace will happily slit your throat—and Mira's—in the name of revenge against your mother. Brennan's anonymity is all that saves him here. You have no idea how much danger you're in, the lengths I've gone to in order to keep you safe—"*

"Stop keeping me safe!" I immediately regret raising my voice with Cat in the room and try to steady my ire with a deep breath. "You never would have pulled this bullshit last year. You never held me back, never caged me in the name of *protecting* me. You were the one telling me to find another way on the Gauntlet, watching me fight off other cadets at Threshing—"

"I wasn't in love with you then." His hand grasps the nape of my neck, and his thumb skates over the pulse in my throat. *"During Gauntlet, Threshing...I had no idea what you would become to me."* And he couldn't kill me thanks to

the deal he made with Mom—the deal he still hasn't trusted me with. *"I sure as hell hadn't sat by your bedside for three days, knowing my life—if it even existed beyond yours—would mean nothing without you in it."* The gold flecks in his eyes catch the light, and I can't help but blink at what I see there.

"You're...scared, aren't you?" I grasp the door's edge to keep from reaching for him.

"Of losing you? More like terrified. And when Sgaeyl told me Tairn was headed this direction I nearly lost my fucking mind."

Shit. What do I say to that? *"My plan to raise the wards failed, and you need the luminary. I'm not going to sit tucked away in Aretia just because you're worried something will happen to me. If I did, I wouldn't be the woman you fell in love with."*

"Your first attempt at translation fails, so you sneak off with your siblings into enemy territory?" His anger is palpable, matching mine as he lifts his head. *"Make no mistake—this is enemy territory."*

"We both know we need the luminary, and I wouldn't have had to sneak if you'd been remotely reasonable. We could have had it months ago." I take a step back into the room, leaving him in the hallway. Months ago would have prevented the attacks on the outposts and so many deaths.

"Reasonable?" His voice drops to that icy-calm timbre. "For looking for another way before serving you up to Tecarus? Let's get one thing straight. If I *ever* see a way to keep you safe? I'll take it."

The *fuck* he will. "Do you know who you sound like right now?"

"Please, enlighten me." He folds his arms across his chest.

"Dain." I shut the door in his face.

"Thank you," I tell Zara, the lady's maid we've been assigned, as I smooth the lines of my waist, awestruck she was able to find multiple gowns in my size on such short notice. Even the lightweight black slippers on my feet fit. "You're sure this is how everyone dresses for dinner?"

"With the viscount? Every night."

How...impractically beautiful.

"Done." Zara motions to the opening, and I step out from behind the dressing screen.

Mira chose the black velvet gown with the square neckline and sheer, gauzy sleeves, but I know it was the deep pockets that sold her. I can't help but grin as I see her tuck two of her daggers into the folds.

"I don't think I've seen you out of uniform in years."

"Well, it's black, so close enough." She grins as I move to peek in the mirror. "You look gorgeous."

"The dress is spectacular." I've never worn anything like it, and it suits my mood perfectly. The bodice, which plummets in a deep V to the base of my ribs, is made of woven, black leaves, never bigger than the size of my palm, narrowing above the swells of my breasts to single vines that drape tiny leaves over my shoulders and down the sides of my back, leaving the majority of my spine and all of my relic exposed. "What kind of material is this?" I ask Zara, fingering the sheer black fabric that falls from my waist to the floor in a multitude of layers. Were it just the one, the gown would be see-through.

"It's Deverelli silk," Zara says. "So fine it's nearly transparent."

"From the isle?" It's softer than any fabric I've ever touched. "You still trade with them?" Navarre hasn't in centuries.

She nods. "We did until the last few years, but the merchants think it's too dangerous to come here now. Anyway, the viscount likes to keep the most exquisite of objects for himself."

"So, it's true the viscount collects rare objects?" Mira asks, coming to stand behind me.

"He does."

"What about people?" I ask softly.

Her eyes flare. "Only if they agree to be collected."

"Kidnapping isn't his thing?" I take the sheath and alloy-hilted dagger Mira hands me, then reach into the long slit at my thigh to fasten it against my leg. Hopefully one weapon is enough to make it through dinner. If the viscount doesn't abduct people, then why was Xaden so scared to bring me here?

Someone knocks.

"No." Zara shakes her head and walks toward the door. "He won't lock you away, but he will make you a proposal that will tempt you to be collected. Singers, weavers, storytellers—they all eventually remain," she says as she opens the door.

There's nothing Tecarus could offer me, but Xaden must think there is.

"You went with black?" Cat stares from the doorway.

"I'm a rider."

"Of course." She tilts her head to the side. "I just would have chosen something more colorful. Xaden always laments how…monotone everything is at Basgiath. There's still time to change if you would like." Her smile is anything but kind.

And that's it. I officially loathe her.

"Xaden doesn't *lament* anything." An ugly, insidious flame ignites in my stomach, and it takes every ounce of restraint I have to keep from flicking a dagger at her snide head. Or at least *close* to it. "And are you capable of having a discussion that doesn't revolve around him?"

"Sure. If it makes you more comfortable, we can discuss how your mother has perpetuated a lie that's cost thousands of Poromish lives, some of which your own sister is responsible for taking."

My brows rise. Did she really just—

Mira catches my eye, confirming that she *did*. "I was going to remind you that it's probably bad manners to stab our hostess, but you know what?" She shrugs. "Fuck it. We don't need a luminary."

Cat blinks at Mira.

"Stop being a wretch, Cat." Syrena steps into the doorway, dressed in a navy-blue formal tunic that's hemmed asymmetrically to a higher line in the front and embroidered with gold feathers. "Nice to see you off your dragon, Sorrengail. Is Riorson hiding somewhere in there, or did he actually let you out of his sight?"

"Good to see you, Syrena." A smile curves my mouth at her teasing tone, and the fire in my stomach dissipates a little. "And he does get a bit protective, doesn't he?"

"He wouldn't be if he thought you were strong enough to stand at his side," Cat counters.

Never mind. It flares brighter than ever, hot, nauseating, and annoyingly strong.

Syrena levels a look at Cat that almost makes me pity her.

Almost.

"Syrena, this is my sister, Mira." I change the subject.

Syrena's mouth tightens as she studies Mira. "Your reputation precedes you. I had friends at Strythmore."

Well, shit. From tense to…tenser.

"I have no remorse for winning battles." Mira sheaths the next dagger at her waist in plain sight. "And if you're Syrena Cordella, then your reputation reaches across the border as well."

"Dining amid hundreds of fliers that root for your death, and you choose to wear a gown?" Syrena arches a brow. "Where is the shrewd judgment I've heard so much about?"

"I can kill just as easily in a gown as leathers. Want to see?" Only a fool would call Mira's expression a smile.

Syrena laughs, her shoulders shaking. "Ah, I see why little Sorrengail is so tough if she had to grow up with you. Let's get going. The men are already there."

I shoot Mira a look once the fliers' backs are turned, and she shrugs unapologetically.

We move into the hallway, and regret stabs deep at my choice of gowns when I see Cat's in the light. Her hair is pinned in an intricate style and she's wearing a bold, red silk that leaves her shoulders bare and matches the color she's painted on her lips.

Suddenly, I feel a little washed out.

Doubt makes my steps unsteady. Maybe I should have gone with color. Maybe she was telling the truth and Xaden is sick of all the black. Maybe she knows him better than I do.

"You all right?" Mira asks as the fliers lead us down the hall, making us the most unlikely foursome to ever walk the Continent.

"Yes." I roll my shoulders, trying to shake off the feeling. What the hell is wrong with me? I never judge myself against other women when it comes to how we look. How we fight? Sure. Ride? Definitely. But nothing ever as shallow as...appearance.

Being pretty doesn't save you at Basgiath.

"I hear you have an older brother," Mira says to Syrena when we reach the first staircase.

I keep the marble bannister in a death grip as we start down. The last thing I'm going to do is trip and fall in front of Cat.

"You're thinking of Drake," Syrena says over her shoulder. "Same last name, but he's our cousin, and come to think of it, you're just his type. He likes women who might actually kill him."

"Too bad I don't go for gryphon fliers," Mira responds as we round the corner to the next flight of stairs.

"Yeah, he'd probably draw the line at a dragon rider." Syrena laughs, but it's short-lived. "He's with the nightwing drift in the north, along the Braevick border."

I don't know their unit terminology, but the Braevick border means he's on the front line.

We make it to the middle terrace—the one we first arrived at this afternoon—and they turn left, away from the winding pool of water and past a line of guards.

"Did Zara not know how to attend your hair?" Cat asks with a pitying glance back at me as we approach a guarded set of double doors. "Surely, she could have come up with something a little more refined than just leaving it down like that. I thought you always wore it up in case of a fight?"

How does she know that? I've had *enough*.

"It would be a pity to kill her now. I'm hunting ten minutes away and I'd miss the show," Tairn says.

Power surges within me.

"Control it. Now," Tairn demands, all trace of sarcasm gone.

Swallowing hard, my fingernails biting into my palms, I fight the urge to blast her. What is it about Cat that brings out the irrational in me? "How sweet of you to worry about me, but you're not the one I'm picking a fight with tonight," I assure Cat.

"With Xaden?" Her eyes narrow, then drip with false sympathy. "If you don't already know that he's not the kind of man who gets flustered or loses control, then there's really no hope for you. Save yourself the energy, because he'll simply think any fight you *pick* is childish."

Shit. She's right. What am I doing? Xaden doesn't get flustered, and definitely not by *me*.

Wood groaning as it splits, then shatters. The sound of daggers clattering to the floor. The feel of my heart pounding, my breath stuttering as bliss settles in the marrow of my bones. "I've never lost control like that." The flash of memory rocks me to my core, clearing my head just long enough to breathe around the insufferable jealousy I feel toward a woman I don't even *know*.

The guards nod at the fliers and move to open the doors.

"Give it a rest." Syrena's tone sharpens at her sister. "You're all of a year older than Violet, and it's been longer than that since you two were together. He's just a man, but she's the best weapon we have against the dark wielders."

"Are you all right?" Mira asks, her worried gaze skimming my face.

"No," I whisper. "But I don't know what's wrong, either."

The doors swing open, and we walk into the largest dining room I've ever seen. The glass doors that line the back wall are propped open to the terrace despite the threatening clouds darkening the sky. A humid evening breeze flickers the candles along the table as the guards shut the door behind us. There must be over fifty people at the long, ornately decorated table that runs the length of the space.

And every single one of them has turned to look at the four of us.

My gaze finds Xaden's in under a second, and it's not because he's seated at the center of the table, or because he's one of only two men dressed in black, or even because he's turned around as if he sensed me coming—which he probably did. I locate him within a heartbeat because he's the center of my gravity.

As pissed as I am that he lectured me, that he refused to bring me, that there are years of history behind both of us we haven't discussed, that the tunic he's walking toward me in isn't just tailored to perfection but obviously made for *him*, it doesn't change the fact he's a fucking magnet for my heart.

"That dress…" His gaze sweeps over me and heats with an intensity that makes my cheeks flush, my pulse race. *"You're playing dirty, Violence."*

But why is he headed for me when the obvious choice is the woman in red just a few feet away?

"I'm still really damned angry with you." I lift my chin, just as furious with

myself for getting into this position, for feeling whatever all this bullshit is.

"Feeling is mutual." He slides one hand into my hair, then sucks a breath through his teeth when his fingers meet skin at the base of my spine. *"But it's possible to be angry while still madly, wildly, uncontrollably in love with me."*

His mouth crashes into mine in the same instant the world goes dark around us, blocking out everything—everyone—but Xaden. We might as well be the only people in the entire province. My body *ignites*. Gods, the chemistry between us is the only thing stronger than the anger. There's only the press of his lips parting mine, the quick, thorough claiming of his tongue, the jolt of instant need that has me gripping the fabric of his tunic as he kisses me breathless.

Just like that, the hottest of my jealousy, the infuriating insecurity that had me second-guessing myself is gone. It's as if the wall of shadow he's thrown up—

"What did you do?" I break the kiss, breathing deeply, and he leans his forehead against mine, keeping us cocooned in total darkness.

"What I should have done the second I saw you this afternoon." His hand tightens in my hair, tugging slightly. *"And probably shocked Cat enough to make her stop fucking with your head."*

"What do you mean?"

"She has the gift of heightening the emotions of the people around her, and she's exceptionally powerful. If you hadn't blocked me out all evening, I would have told you sooner."

My jaw hangs for a heartbeat before I snap it closed. First at the knowledge that I actually managed to block him out, and second—no wonder I can't get a grip on myself. She's been waging a war I didn't even realize we were in. Wait. He would have told me *sooner*? He's had *weeks* to tell me.

"You win," Xaden whispers. Shadows fall away as quickly as they appeared as he lifts his head, locking his eyes with mine.

"I haven't even *started* fighting with you." I drop my hands from his chest and throw the new rush of power rising within me into my shields. How the hell did she get past them in the first place? If they blocked out Xaden, surely they're strong enough for her.

"Fine. We can fight as much as you want later tonight. Just know that you've already won. I heard what you were saying." His grip softens in my hair, and he slides his hand to the nape of my neck. "I'm sorry I didn't listen to you. Sorry that I've been overreacting since pulling you out of that interrogation chamber—hell, since Resson. When Sgaeyl told me they were torturing you, and I couldn't get to you…" His eyes close for a second, and when they open, the fear I spotted earlier is front and center. "I can't fucking breathe when you're in danger, but that's not your fault. I should have brought you here when you asked me to."

My lips part and I blink, certain I misheard him.

"Now it's your turn. Can you admit that you should have waited for me to bring you so we could have formulated a plan?" His fingers trail deliciously up my bare back.

"No." I shiver at the touch. "I'm sorry for not telling you but not sorry for coming. We need that luminary *now*."

A corner of his mouth quirks up. "Figured."

"If you two wouldn't mind joining us? You're essential to this evening's discussion," the viscount states over the hushed room, mild annoyance in his tone.

Oh. Every single person is out of their seats, waiting for us by the open glass doors.

"Be ready for anything," Xaden says before turning toward Tecarus. "I make no apologies." He laces his fingers with mine, and we walk around the table toward the crowd where Tecarus waits. "Maintaining control is nearly impossible around Violet."

My face heats. What the hell? Did he hear her out there? That's impossible.

Cat stiffens next to her uncle, her face falling like Xaden's just delivered a killing blow in a battle I hadn't realized *they* were in.

"So I've heard." Tecarus motions to follow him outside, and we do, stepping onto a marble patio, Mira and Brennan filing in closely behind us. "Word traveled fast when you ruined that little war college of yours for her." Tecarus tips his wineglass my direction as if saluting me. "Split your quadrant right down the middle. Bravo. Been trying to take that place down for *years*, and you did it in what? Six days?"

Guilt settles on my chest with the weight of a dragon.

"Five." Xaden's hand tightens on mine as we cross the patio, coming to the top of a wide staircase—no. Not a staircase: seats. The entire north side of the sloping hill has been carved into rows, forming an oval-shaped outdoor arena the depth of Tairn's height and twice his length.

"Five days." Tecarus shakes his head in disbelief, then turns to me. "Marvelous. Now, I assume you'd like to discuss acquiring the luminary I have in my possession?"

"And I assume you've brought us out here to see me wield before you open yourself to discussion?" I ask as the thick, rain-scented wind blows my hair back. We're minutes, if not less, from a downpour.

"It's only prudent that I see what you're capable of before entering into negotiations for such a valuable item." He motions toward the mage light–illuminated arena.

"Seems fair." My hand slips from Xaden's, and I reach for my power.

"Oh, not from up here." Tecarus shakes his head as others join us, lining the edge of the patio, drinks in hand. "Down on the field. It's a performance after all, isn't it? Would be a shame to waste the gaming arena, since it took me years to construct. It's quite special. All the stone was quarried from Braevick, from east of the Dunness River. Oh look, they're wheeling out your target."

Target? Oh *shit*.

A foursome of uniformed guards pushes a metal chest the size of an armoire into the middle of a grassy field in the base of the arena. I can't even hit the trio of boulders Felix pointed me at, and I'm supposed to hit that chest? This is going to be over before discussions even begin.

"You might recognize the Rybestad chest, Xaden. It's the very one your father brought me when we were in negotiations for what some might consider a greater treasure."

"That chest belonged to your father?"

"It was one of the most valuable items he owned." Xaden tenses. "I'll walk her down."

"No," Tecarus says, his voice devoid of emotion.

Both our heads turn in his direction.

"How would I know what she's capable of without you?" Tecarus's eyes narrow on Xaden. "My offer is simple. As long as you don't step foot into the arena, Riorson, and she doesn't leave the field until she strikes the target, we'll open discussions for your luminary. Take the deal or leave it."

"We'll leave—" Xaden starts, his voice clipped.

"Deal." I look up at Xaden. "You don't have to protect me from my own signet. If he wants me to blow up your father's chest, I'll blow up your father's chest."

His gaze narrows for a second, and then he sighs. "Point made."

I gather the layers of my skirts in my hands and start down the steps. Nerves tighten my ribs, but I shake them off. If I wield enough strikes, certainly *one* of them will hit.

Wasn't that what got us through Resson before Andarna arrived?

"I'm coming," Mira announces from behind me. "It's not like I have anything to do with her signet," she yells back at Tecarus as she catches up to me.

The viscount doesn't argue.

"And mine isn't effective this far from the wards," she finishes in a whisper. "I tried earlier and nothing happened."

"Don't worry. We don't need you to shield. Just dodge the chest if it explodes," I respond, giving her a tight smile. *"What greater treasure was your father negotiating for?"* I ask Xaden once we're about halfway down the sand-colored stone. I can't even imagine how long it would have taken to quarry enough stone to build this, let alone bring it back from the edge of Braevick.

"An alliance my father made that I officially denied last year. The chest is priceless. If he wants you to destroy it with lightning, then this is more a statement about me and less about you."

"Why am I not surprised?" My hands crush the delicate silk of my gown as I put the pieces of a sickening puzzle together. *"Would that alliance have anything to do with Cat?"*

The hesitation I feel along our bond answers before he does.

"Yes."

"That information would have been valuable before arriving." To say the fucking least. No wonder she despises me. I'm not self-centered enough to think I'm the reason he called off whatever alliance they had, but I'm definitely a barrier to resuming it now. Her uncle wants me to blow up the very symbol of whatever it is they'd agreed upon.

"Still fighting. Got it."

Mira and I reach the grass as the first raindrops fall.

"We should have worn leathers," she mutters, keeping pace with me.

"I can't aim," I tell her quietly, pausing what feels like twenty feet from the chest, just close enough to see runes carved into the thick doors. "Carr focused on quantity over quality, and Felix and I just started lessons, so this might take a while."

Two of the guards move to the front of the chest that's taller and thicker than both of them. Thank Amari it's huge. A bigger target will be easier to hit. A guard pulls a small item from his pocket that I can't quite make out from here.

"I don't think they're interested in how long it will take." Mira nods to the top of the arena. Dozens of bow-wielding gryphon fliers have surrounded the top row of seats, all with arrows nocked our direction. "They're probably worried you'll strike Tecarus instead of the target."

"Right. No pressure." Lifting my hands, I reach for Tairn's power. Funny how the normally brutal heat of it is a comfort after so many days under Varrish's torture without it. "You guys might want to move," I call out to the guards as the stocky one in front holds his fist to the front of the chest like he thinks he has a shot at stopping it if the giant iron box shifts and topples onto him...or like he has a key.

A shiver of apprehension skates along my spine.

"The Arctile Ocean to the south is known for calm, warm waters and what were once lucrative trade routes," I recite, calming my racing heart.

"You still do that?" Mira lifts her brows at me.

"Only when I'm—"

The double doors of the chest burst open, sending both guards sprawling across the ground with startling force as a man jolts forward and falls to his hands and knees on the grass. His maroon tunic and trousers are tattered, like he's been kept prisoner for *weeks*.

"What the fuck?" Mira mutters.

His head jerks up to look at us, and my heart seizes with pure, immovable terror.

Distended red veins branch out from bloodshot eyes.

"Violet!" Xaden roars.

Venin.

Though her extraordinary signet allows her to extend the wards around herself and her dragon, Cadet Sorrengail lacks the consistent ability to produce her own wards without extreme emotional distress. I'm sorry to report I doubt this ability will develop in time. I had such hopes for her.

—MEMORANDUM FROM PROFESSOR CARR TO GENERAL SORRENGAIL

CHAPTER FORTY-TWO

"I s that…" Mira whispers, already palming her daggers as the dark wielder digs his hands into the soft green grass of the arena floor, laughing maniacally. Breathe. I have to breathe. But there's no air.

Purple robes billowing. Soleil charging forward, Fuil running behind her. The spread of death and decay reaching them both. The fall. Their bodies becoming nothing more than husks, drained of power and life.

"Silver One!" Tairn's roar splits my head, ripping me from the past before it swallows me whole. Rain splatters the ground around us, falling in heavy but sporadic drops. This isn't Resson, this is Cordyn, and I have to protect Mira.

"Move!" I scream at the guards, two of whom run while one other scrambles backward, leaving the last to stare in frozen shock. "Get out of here," I order Mira, sizzling heat filling my veins as I open the floodgates on Tairn's power.

"I'm not leaving you with that thing!" She flicks her dagger.

"No!" I shout, but it's too late—the dagger lands in the venin's shoulder.

He hisses, ripping the weapon free and grabbing for the petrified guard in the same breath.

"Great, and now he has a knife!" I lift my hands and release the energy burning through my limbs.

Lightning cracks, so white it's almost blue, and I throw up my hand to shield my eyes as it strikes the iron chest as though drawn to it. Sparks shower the arena, one singeing the back of my hand before I can brush it off.

"Tairn, I need you!"

"On the way."

Panic threatens to grab hold of me, and I waste precious seconds looking over my shoulder at where Xaden is already lunging for the steps. *"Stay put and keep your emotions to yourself. We need that luminary."*

"Violence—"

"I can do this." If I can't take on one emaciated venin, then what chance does the Continent stand?

The wind shifts, blowing my hair into my face, and I twist to see the venin's hands wrap around the guard's neck, but I don't need to watch to know exactly what's about to happen.

"Only the alloy-hilted daggers can kill him," I tell Mira, yanking my dagger from its sheath and slicing through a strip of fabric in my hem. If I can't aim, this is coming down to hand-to-hand.

The screams of the guard cut straight through me.

"Holy shit… He's really… What's the plan, Vi?" Mira asks, gripping her other knife.

"Kill him before he kills us, and whatever you do, don't let him get his hands on you." I grab my hair into a low ponytail and wrap the fabric from my dress around it to secure it quickly. I'm dead if I can't see.

The venin holds the guard like a shield, blocking me from any potential knife throw. The screams stop as the man slowly desiccates before my eyes. At least two of the other three are already off the field.

Letting Tairn's power consume me, I wield again and again, scorching the grass around the venin without fucking hitting him. The guard falls to the ground, parts of him flaking off as the rain pelts harder and faster.

"Damn it!"

"It's you," the dark wielder says over the growing noise of the storm. "The one who commands the sky." His eyes widen in eerie excitement. "Oh, how I'll be rewarded when I return with *you*."

"And here I was thinking I was the only Sorrengail with a reputation beyond the border." Mira takes a fighting stance, keeping only inches between us.

"By your Sage?" I ask him, tracking his movements as rain falls in sheets. Shit, I can't chance throwing my dagger. If I miss, I'm defenseless, and it's not just me on this field. *"I need daggers."*

"Which Sage? I promise, you'll wish—" he starts, raising his arms.

"For death?" I interrupt. "Already heard it. I killed that messenger, too." But I wasn't in a cumbersome ball gown. This thing is a fucking liability.

"Behind you," Xaden says.

I glance back and see two alloy-hilted daggers embedded in the ground five feet away. "Mira!"

She follows my line of sight and is already moving when I flip my dagger to its tip and flick my wrist, throwing for the dark wielder's throat.

The dagger sinks into his side.

Shit, I didn't account for the downward pressure of the driving rain.

The venin shouts in pain, yanking the dagger loose as Mira hands me one of the two Xaden flung our way. My fingers grip the water-slick handle, and I prepare myself for the worst when the venin lifts his hands.

But it's not the daggers he throws.

The Rybstad chest hurtles toward us, coming so quickly that I barely have time to knock Mira to the ground before it passes by, close enough that I hear it split the air.

A dagger immediately follows, then another, missing me but pinning the left side of my dress to the ground. I use our momentum to keep rolling, the diaphanous silk tearing away as I'm pulled to my feet by Brennan—who's decided to join us, I guess.

Gods, no. I can't lose them both in this.

"We need to surround him," Brennan says, grabbing the alloy-hilted dagger from the sodden grass. Water collects quickly, soaking my feet, my hair, and what's left of my dress.

"And how would you like to do that if we can't see him through this shit?" Mira asks.

"I'm minutes out!" Tairn bellows.

We might be dead in those minutes, but we're *all* dead eventually if I don't secure that fucking luminary.

"We have to keep him on the field, no matter what. One of them is capable of draining everyone in the palace," I tell my siblings. Back-to-back, we scan the field, and my breath catches when the dark wielder comes into view, dropping to a knee about twenty feet away.

No. Time slows to sluggish heartbeats as I watch him reach for the ground. There's no time to run. We won't make it.

My worst nightmare is *seconds* away from becoming reality.

Our mission is going to kill my brother and sister.

"I'm so sorry." It's barely a whisper.

His fist slams into the ground, and through the storm, I watch in breathless horror as his eyes burn fire red, the grass around him shriveling into brown blades.

"Mira!" Brennan shouts. "Shield!"

"I...I can't this far from the wards!" Her mouth drops as death races for us, the ground rippling as it surrenders its magic.

"Shield or we're dead!" Brennan grabs onto us both and yanks us into a tight hold.

I tuck in, hoping to make our trio as small as possible, while Mira throws her arms up over us. Her body trembles, and Brennan and I wrap our arms around her back to keep her steady. She screams as though she's being ripped apart.

She's going to burn out.

Shadows stream toward us, but they won't make it.

I love you. I push the thought Xaden's way and wait for my power to bleed out, wait for my death to make the venin unstoppable.

But it doesn't come.

You will live! Xaden orders, as if it's that simple.

Mira collapses, and Brennan takes the brunt of her weight as I scan our surroundings.

The entire field is dead with the exception of the tiny circle we occupy. She saved us. But it's just the field that's drained. The spectators are all alive and well above the steps from what I can see through the downpour. *All the stone was quarried from Braevick, from east of the Dunness River.* Isn't that what Tecarus said?

I wipe the water from my eyes and stand to face the dark wielder.

He rolls his shoulders in satisfaction, a blissful smile distorting his features as he throws his head back.

"If you can't strike him with lightning, then we'll have to get close enough to engage. He can't take both of us," Brennan says, lifting an unconscious Mira into his arms.

How far are you? I ask Tairn. Rain doesn't strike the remains of the grass as much as it splashes into water that has yet to run off.

Less than a minute.

"I don't have to strike him," I whisper as the idea hits, scanning the flooded field. "Get Mira to the steps. You'll be safe there."

Brennan looks at me like I've just suggested our world is flat. "Until the next time he drains—"

"I need you to trust me. Get our sister to the steps." I glance up at my brother and soak myself in Tairn's power, giving it free rein, letting it fill every inch of my body.

"Violet—" There's so much love and worry and fear in his gaze that I can't help but force a smile.

"I know what I'm doing. Now, run." I take the alloy-hilted blade from Brennan and turn away from them both.

"What the fuck are you doing, Violence?" Xaden demands.

"Shh. I'm concentrating." I slam my shields up, blocking him out as the venin pivots.

The asshole smiles wider when he sees me.

"You'll be quite the prize," he calls out over the rain, striding toward me as if we have all the time in the world. "And to think, you'll bring a dragon with you! You can't be parted for long, can you?"

I grasp an alloy-hilted dagger in each hand and wait.

If I lose my temper, I'm dead.

Charge him and lose? I'm dead.

Wait too long and let him get his hands on me? Yep, dead.

The female I killed on Tairn's back watched my fighting style and instantly adapted, which means I have to wait until the last possible second to show my hand.

Rain sizzles as it hits my heated skin. If I reach for much more, I'll lose the ability to control it and burn out, so I hover on that edge as I hear another sound overpower the rain.

Wings.

"I don't need to stress the importance of timing, do I?" Tairn asks.

"My timing will be perfect." The pounding of my heart steadies with each step the venin takes, sure of my course. There's no room for error. I glance right just long enough to see that Mira and Brennan made it off the field.

"I expect nothing less."

The dark wielder is only feet away, his gaze raking over me, no doubt looking for my weaknesses, when I feel the gust of wind from Tairn's wings at my back.

Now. I throw the daggers at the venin simultaneously, this time calculating for the force of the rain. The instant I see them slice through his boots, pinning his feet to the ground, I whip my arms out to the side, releasing all my power in a scalding torrent of lightning.

I stiffen my arms and lock every muscle.

Tairn's talons wrap over my shoulders and grasp tight exactly as lightning strikes behind the enraged venin, lighting up the sky in a brilliant flash—and charging the water that covers the arena and the venin's feet with lethal energy.

The dark wielder shrieks in agony, then falls dead, splashing into the field as we fly overhead.

I did it. Dunne be blessed, *I did it.*

"You cut it close."

I roll my eyes and breathe deeply despite the rain that runs down my face as Tairn banks left, taking us along the curve of the arena, back to the palace.

Sgaeyl, Teine, and Marbh have all taken up defensive perches on the terrace above, positioning themselves to incinerate the crowd.

"I will devour anyone who makes a move against you. My patience has ended." Tairn's wings beat slower as we approach the patio.

"I'll be sure to warn them." Tairn waits until I have my balance on my soaked, slippered feet, then stalks forward through the crowd to the cries of fliers and aristocrats alike, cracking the marble beneath his claws until he reaches the grass and pivots, swinging his tail like the weapon it is and completing the four-cornered defense the dragons have structured.

Brennan falls into step with me, Mira propped under his arm but walking on her own beside him.

"You all right?" I ask under my breath as we pass nobles with *umbrellas.* This was fucking entertainment for them.

"We're not the ones you should be concerned for," Brennan mutters as the last line of aristocrats—including Cat and Syrena—parts, revealing a situation far more dangerous than the one I was just in.

Xaden's lifted hand is raised at his chest, clenched in a partial fist, and wrath chills his eyes as he stares up at the viscount, whose feet kick for the ground.

Tecarus tears ineffectually at the shadows strangling his neck and, from the garbled sound of his breathing, he's slowly asphyxiating.

"Xaden, please don't!" Cat cries.

Xaden's grip only tightens as the rain dissipates to a drizzle.

Tecarus gurgles, and fliers draw their weapons, but one growl from Sgaeyl is enough to keep them from advancing on Xaden.

I lower the portion of my shields that allows Xaden in, then send every ounce of my love down the bond. *"I'm all right."*

He tears his gaze from Tecarus, the barely caged fury in his eyes making him nearly unrecognizable.

"Loosen your grip on his throat," I say calmly. "He can't answer questions if he's dead."

Two lines appear between Xaden's dark brows, and his grip eases.

Moving to his side, I make sure that my shoulder brushes his arm, that he can feel me physically as well as mentally. "You're lucky you're not dead," I say up at Tecarus's blotchy face. "If you'd put Xaden in that kind of danger, I'm not sure I would have been as merciful."

"You call this mercy?" Tecarus asks through gasped breaths, still kicking for the ground.

"Yes," Xaden says softly.

"You quarried the stones from east of the Dunness River, the land that borders the Barrens. It had already been drained of its magic."

"Yes!" Tecarus shouts.

Xaden swears under his breath.

"You built a pit for them, which means you've captured more than just that one." Puffs of steam rise from my skin, but at least I don't feel like I'm burning alive.

"I'll tell you everything we know," Tecarus assures us. "Just let me down."

"And we're supposed to trust you?" Brennan asks from my other side.

"We were able to keep that one from feeding for days—"

"Because the runes on the Rybstad chest hold items placed inside suspended in midair," Xaden interrupts. "He couldn't reach the ground to drain it until you opened the chest. I don't need you to tell me things I already know." He drops his hand, and the shadows evaporate.

Tecarus slams into the marble patio, grasping for his throat.

Xaden crouches down. "If you ever want to have words about why I severed that alliance, then you come for *me*. Violet is beyond your reach. If you so much as look her direction with anything but the utmost kindness and respect, I'll kill you without a second thought and let Syrena take her place as your heir. Do you understand me?" His voice has that icy softness that sends chills up my spine.

Tecarus nods.

"Apologize."

"I'm fine." He's taking this too far. This man is second in line to the Poromish throne.

"You do not *take punishments designed for me."*

"You have my most sincere apology, Violet Sorrengail," Tecarus croaks through abused vocal cords. "Now where does this leave us, Riorson?"

Xaden stands. "Now we negotiate."

An hour later, we're fed and changed into dry flight leathers, the four of us sitting across the cleared dining room table from Tecarus, Cat, Syrena, half a dozen aristocrats, and one general immediately to Tecarus's left.

Every person in the room is unarmed with the exception of Xaden and me, but our signets make it so we're never defenseless.

"May I present my offer first?" Tecarus asks, tugging his collar away from the red welts across his throat.

"You may," Brennan answers.

Xaden's hand slides over my left thigh and stays there. He's had one hand on me since leaving the patio. It's amazing I managed to get into my flight leathers, but I get it. If I'd just watched him face down a venin, I'd probably be in his fucking lap right now.

"Your power is…astounding." Tecarus shakes his head slowly at me, as if awestruck. "And you're still untrained. Just think of what you'll be a few years from now, or even one."

Xaden's hand splays wide, and I lace my fingers over his.

"That doesn't sound like an offer." I keep my voice as level as possible, trying like hell to ignore that this man nearly killed not only me but Brennan and Mira.

Anger rises to boiling wrath swiftly — too swiftly.

I glance at Cat. "Stay out of my head or I'll start wielding *inside*."

She leans back in her chair, but that narrowing of her eyes isn't defeat. Oh no, she's sizing me up as a worthy opponent.

Game on.

"Do you know why I'm such a successful collector?" the viscount asks, practically vibrating with excitement. "I have a gift for knowing what it is people want, what motivates them to give up their treasures." Gods, he's Varrish's opposite. Our signets really aren't *that* different than mindwork. "I think you and I could strike a deal if you consider that I could deliver your wildest dreams."

Xaden strokes my thigh absentmindedly, but it helps keep me grounded. "And what do you think my wildest dreams are?" I ask.

"Peace." Tecarus nods, his movements growing more erratic the more excited he becomes. "Not for you, of course. That's not what motivates you. Peace for the people you love."

Xaden's fingers still.

"Peace for *him*," Tecarus finishes.

My next breath is shaky. "I'm listening."

He presents his offer, and I have to admit, for a second, it's tempting. Spending a few years as his personal guard dog, monitoring the riderless wyvern who have begun flying over routinely in patterns that look suspiciously like control, in return for living out the rest of my days with Xaden, our dragons, and my loved ones on an isle committed to peace sounds perfect. It's also the coward's way out and completely unfeasible. The isles don't accept Navarrians even as visitors.

"Running away from the Continent to whatever land you've secured from the Deverelli isn't going to help the people I like or the ones I don't even know. It's just that — running away."

Tecarus's jaw flexes, and I get the impression he's not used to being told no.

"Even if I give the luminary to Tyrrendor?" He glances at Brennan. "Word spread quickly that Navarre let your cadets go without so much as a drop of blood spilled. Though I do wonder why that is, don't you?"

Yes. Every day.

"Dragons owe you no explanation." Brennan shrugs. "And my sister just *earned* the luminary. Or are you going back on your deal?"

"I would never break my word." Tecarus glances Xaden's way and leans forward onto the heavily embroidered forearms of his tunic. "Everything we know about the dark wielders." He nods at the silver-browed general, who slides a leather-bound book across the table to Brennan. My fingers immediately itch to open the cover. "But I never said I would give you the luminary if she wielded. I said we would enter discussions."

You have to be fucking kidding me. My hand tightens over Xaden's, like that's going to stop him from strangling the viscount with shadows or me from losing absolute control of my power. I should have brought the conduit into the meeting.

"Then let's discuss. What do you want in exchange for us leaving with the luminary today? Weapons?" Brennan asks. "Because that's what we're offering. The luminary is useless here, but we'll put it to use supplying your drifts with the weapons they need for the venin you *can't* capture."

Hopefully the details of how they managed to catch that one are in the book.

"Weapons are a good start," Tecarus agrees with a nod, his gaze sliding to Cat. "And you take the hundred flier cadets I've given shelter to after their academy was destroyed back to Aretia with the luminary."

I'm sorry…what the fuck?

"And what would you like us to do with your cadets?" Xaden asks, tilting his head slightly. "Gryphons don't fare well at altitude."

"They've never been given the chance to adjust," Tecarus argues. "And I want you to educate them just as I assume you are doing with the rider cadets. Keep them safe, teach them to work together, and we might have a chance of surviving this war. We've seen riderless wyvern patrolling the skies, no doubt reporting what they see instantly to their creators, in the last few weeks. Our reports say they've ventured as far west as Draithus. It won't help the fliers to stay safe here in the south—not when they want to fight. And who better to teach the fliers how to kill wyvern than dragon riders?"

Train with gryphon fliers? Take *Cat* back to Aretia? I would rather face down a dozen venin. Unarmed. Without Tairn or Andarna.

"There's no way to fly them into Tyrrendor," Mira points out.

A muscle in Xaden's jaw flexes. "There is. But there's no guarantee they'll survive it."

"We'll take the chance," Syrena answers. "It's the cadets' best shot at living long enough to fight the dark wielders."

"This is my offer. Take it or leave it," Tecarus demands.

There's no way—

"Done," Brennan answers. "As long as each flier we take brings a crossbolt with them."

I'm going to *throttle* my brother.

From the dangerous waves of the Arctile Ocean to the lowest
plains of the Tyrrendor plateau, the Cliffs of Dralor rise to over
twelve thousand feet in places, making them unflyable by gryphon.
While there are three well-carved paths within Navarre to ascend
the plateau, along the Krovlan border exists only one…and it is
deadly to both gryphon and flier.
Do not attempt under any circumstances.

—CHAPTER TWO: THE TACTICAL GUIDE TO DEFEATING DRAGONS
BY COLONEL ELIJAH JOBEN

CHAPTER
FORTY-THREE

My neck aches as I stare up, and up, and *up* the Cliffs of Dralor to where they disappear into a thick layer of cloud cover.

It's been four days since we struck the deal with Tecarus. Three nights ago, we delivered the luminary—a ring nearly as tall as Sgaeyl of vibrant blue crystals—to an offshoot of the valley above Aretia where the new forge is located. Yesterday, all cadets were ordered to get a good night's sleep, pack for a three-day mission, and assemble for flight formation at four in the morning, and now we're standing in a field west of Draithus, eyeing the drifts gathered on the other side of First Wing as the sun burns off the early morning haze.

"He can't be serious," Ridoc says beside me in formation, his neck craned at the same angle as mine. Between the hundred Aretian cadets and an equal number of fliers packed into this grassy field, I'd guess ninety-five percent of us look exactly the same, gawking at the steep, barely visible, narrow trail my brother just pointed at with absolute incredulity.

The series of ledges and switchbacks carved into the granite cliff looks more suitable to a mountain goat than a gryphon and blends so well into the terrain that it's no wonder the Medaro Pass has been kept secret.

Until now.

"Agreed." Visia nods. "He has to be kidding. That's not a trail—it's a death trap."

The path Brennan's so excited about isn't wide enough to support a full wagon, let alone the width of a gryphon…and he wants them to hike it? For us to hike it with them while dragons fly patrol?

"Pretty sure he's serious or we wouldn't all be here," Rhiannon says over her shoulder.

"What the hell does he expect us to do besides climb with them?" Aaric asks, keeping his voice down.

"Catch them if they fall off?" Ridoc suggests.

"Right, because we're capable of catching a gryphon," Imogen remarks.

My brow furrows as I study the steep trail. It's not the narrow path or even the gryphon traps Brennan described that worry me, but my own endurance. Twelve hours of constant climbing is going to torture my knees and ankles.

"Watch your back," Xaden warns, his voice already fading as he flies east with Sgaeyl on a mission I'm not privy to. *"I didn't have time to question every flier about their intentions."*

As if his personal recommendation would help the lack of trust between our two colleges.

"You've already warned me," I remind him, feeling him slip away. *"Don't die. I'll see you in a few days."* There's a rush of warmth, and then it fades along with his shadowy presence in my mind.

Ahead of me, Baylor covers a jaw-cracking yawn with his fist as Brennan continues to lecture us about the length of the journey ahead from where he stands on a bound stack of crossbolts, amplifying his voice over the field. "The journey should take you twelve hours, though I recommend taking time to rest along the trail." His gaze scans over us, as if gauging our reaction, which is mostly…speechless.

The only sound is the fall breeze rustling the leaves from the scrub oak trees at the south end of the field. Even the dragons and gryphons fall silent around us, as if they can't quite believe what's being suggested, either.

"So they can push us off?" a rider from Third Wing asks, and I don't think he's joking.

"That question is exactly why you'll be going with them," Brennan says, avoiding my gaze entirely as Syrena climbs up the pile of bound crossbolts to stand with him. "Not only have the wingleaders been given the locations of the gryphon traps to disarm them, but you need to learn some mutual respect and trust before you can be educated together. No rider will respect a cadet who hasn't crossed the parapet." He gestures at the trail behind him. "Behold a parapet for them to cross."

"It's narrow, but it's not that narrow!" Ridoc calls out, earning a few scoffs of agreement from the riders around us.

"And if we were just risking ourselves, perhaps it would be appropriate to deem it inferior to your death bridge at Basgiath," Syrena states, clasping her hands behind her back and facing the riders' half of formation. Sunlight catches on the palm-size metal rings that fall at the fronts of her shoulders, connected to the leather above. "But consider while you climb, while you decide if you'll truly accept fliers into your ranks"—her gaze catches mine—"that while this trail is perfectly safe for humans, it's perilous for gryphons. And ask yourself if you would risk the lives of your *dragons* climbing a trail built specifically to kill them into hostile territory so you can learn how to better destroy your enemy with the very people you considered your enemy up until last week."

Riders all around me shift their weight.

"She's right," I tell only Tairn, since Andarna is more than a three-hour flight away, no doubt in the midst of her morning training with the elders. Yesterday she almost managed a full wing extension. Almost. *"I wouldn't risk either of you."*

"Of course you wouldn't. Why would you, when I'm quite capable of carrying you all over the world?" I can feel his eyes roll. *"You did not bond the inferiority that are gryphons. You bonded dragons. Take them for a walk and let them prove themselves."*

"The way the fliers look at us is more like they expect us to prove ourselves."

"You were chosen by dragons. That is enough."

"Each squad will be paired with a drift of equal strength to make the ascent," Brennan says. "Hopefully by the time you reach the top, you've found some mutual ground on which to build a framework of partnership."

This is all in the spirit of comradery?

"Highly doubt it," Ridoc mutters.

"In the meantime, your dragons will remain close," Brennan asserts.

"I'll never be more than a minute's flight away," Tairn promises. *"Have fun hiking."*

I hold him to it when we're given our assignment—Cat's drift.

Three hours later, my calves are screaming from the constant climb, and the silence in our small, forced group has grown from uncomfortable to painfully awkward. Removing my right hand from the sheer rock wall, I adjust the weight of my pack on my shoulders to ease the growing protest in my spine and check on Sloane. She's climbing steadily a few feet in front of me, giving the gryphon ahead of her plenty of room to flick its lionlike tail.

We're climbing single file, with Fourth Wing leading the way. Only Claw Section is above us.

The trail itself is challenging although not unpassable, and while up to six feet wide at parts, it narrows to a quarter of that in places where the path has disintegrated, leaving gaping holes that have the humans hugging the cliff wall to get by. Every time we reach one, the gryphons stretch their grappling talons across while balancing on clawed back paws, and I find myself holding my breath that they make it. Considering the ones we're walking with are easily a couple of feet wider than the path, I'm surprised only two have fallen that I know of. They're able to catch themselves for now, but at higher altitudes? It could get ugly.

I look back at Maren, the flier I've been paired with until evening, and her gryphon as we approach an already triggered trap, the battering-ram-size log now lying harmlessly along the cliff wall where the path narrows. "Be careful here."

"Right at chest height. Nice." She offers me a pressed-lipped smile. She's petite for a flier, though still taller than me, with a heart-shaped face under dark hair woven into a long single braid that falls along the bronzed ochre skin of her neck. Her dark, hooded eyes meet mine without hesitance every time I look back to make sure she's still following, which earns my respect, but she's also Cat's best friend, which has me watching my back in more ways than one.

I look back again to make sure they pass safely.

"I'm not going to fall off the cliff," she promises as we make the sharp turn of the fourth switchback. Or maybe it's the fifth. The curves are the only places on the trail wide enough to walk in pairs. "Neither is Dajalair."

The brown-and-white gryphon's front left claw slips off the trail, and her talon screeches against rock with the most godsawful sound I've ever heard as she regains her balance.

Sloane and I trade a look that's surprisingly empty of hostility.

"Are you certain about that?" I ask Maren as all three of us pause, watching to see if any stones break off the rocky terrain. Anything that falls can be deadly to those climbing below us.

The gryphon arches over Maren and snaps its beak in my direction.

Yeah, that thing could definitely crush my head.

"Got it, you're certain," I say, putting up my hands and praying to Dunne that gryphons don't punish humans for speaking to them like dragons do.

Maren nods and scratches the feathered chest of the gryphon. "She's sure-footed and a little temperamental."

The gryphon makes a chortling sound, and we begin walking again.

The narrow ledge is exactly why they aren't allowed to fly any portion of the cliff. There's no guarantee they'll be able to stick a landing without causing a rockslide and killing everyone beneath them.

"Even if she fell from this height, we'd just have to fly down and start again," Maren says like a peace offering. "It's the upper portion of the trail that worries me. Another five thousand feet, and she'll struggle to beat her wings. She's not meant for the summitwing drifts."

"Summitwing drifts?" I can't help but ask.

"Those best suited for altitude, for flying the summits of the Esben range," she explains. "Daja might not want to admit it, but she's a lowland girl." Her smile brightens even as the gryphon snaps her beak rapidly a foot away from Maren's ear. "Like you wouldn't rather be stationed with the seawing drifts after graduation?" She laughs softly, no doubt at something the gryphon said. "That's what I thought. Trust me, we don't want to be headed into Tyrrendor any more than you want us to be there."

"So why come?" Sloane asks, walking too close to the next gryphon and getting flicked in the face by its tail.

"Like Syrena said, it's our best chance of survival—not just for us but for our people, too."

After another few minutes of tense silence, I ask, "So where are you from?"

"Draithus," Maren answers. "I'd ask about you, but everyone knows you grew up moving outpost to outpost until your mother was assigned to Basgiath."

My footsteps almost falter.

Sloane glances back at me with raised eyebrows.

"You've been a hell of a ransom target," Maren explains as we come to a series of carved steps meant to deter wagons. "Honestly, most of us figured Riorson would nab you after harvest his first year and gift you to us."

"You mean Cat figured." Sloane's tone has suspicious bite.

"Cat definitely figured," Maren agrees.

"Harvest?" I ask, skipping over the whole Xaden-should-have-kidnapped-me insinuation. "You mean Threshing?"

"Right." Maren checks on Daja's progress on the stairs before continuing upward. "Whatever it is you call it. When your dragons either kill you or choose you."

"So, our entire first year." Sloane laughs.

"Imagine our surprise when he shows up ready to defend you to the death last year."

I look back at her because I don't hear the animosity I'd expect. There's none of it in her eyes, either. "Were you disappointed?"

She shrugs, the metal rings at her shoulder catching the sunlight with the motion. "I was disappointed for Cat, but I wasn't exactly rooting for that toxicity any more than you would for your best friend. She's the one up there with Cat, now, right? Your squad leader?"

I nod, moving forward along the narrowing stairs, keeping my body as close to the cliff wall as I can without scraping up my flight jacket. "Rhiannon doesn't want Cat trying to hurl me off the trail."

"She probably would have," Maren admits, a smile in her voice. "She's a little…"

"Unhinged?" Sloane offers, keeping a good ten feet between her and the gryphon ahead of her with Ridoc, Visia, and the flier. I think that one is Luella, but I'm not completely sure. "Hopefully she doesn't try any of her mindwork on Rhiannon, or she might find herself dangling off the edge. Rhi isn't someone to mess with."

My eyebrows rise.

"Shocked?" Sloane says over her shoulder at me, keeping her hand on the cliff wall as we reach the end of the stairs. "Don't be. Liam didn't hate many people, but Cat was on that list."

Right. Because he and Xaden were fostered together. He would have met her.

"Angry," Maren corrects her. "I was going to say 'angry.' And relax, Sloane— none of us would dare channel power from our gryphons when they need to stay completely focused on not falling to their deaths."

"At least it's not just me you hate." I bite back a smile at Sloane.

"I don't hate you," Sloane says so quietly that I almost question hearing it. "It's hard to hate you when Liam didn't." My confused look must be enough for her to continue. "I'm in the October letters now."

"Ah, when Xaden forced him to become my bodyguard." We turn at the switchback and start the next ascent, this one cut a little steeper into the harsh gray rock of the cliffside. I look up and immediately regret the decision, my stomach churning at the view that's nearly identical to the one below. It's cliff and more cliff.

"We both knew my brother well enough to say for certain that no one forced him," Sloane replies, her shoulders dipping. "I just wish Xaden had asked someone else. Anyone else."

"Me too," I admit in a whisper, focusing on my footing where the path has crumbled to nothing more than a few yards.

"Look out!" Panicked voices call out above us.

Our attention jerks up.

The sky is gray and falling rapidly toward us.

It's not sky. It's a boulder.

We're about to become debris thanks to a triggered trap.

"Take cover!" I shout, throwing up my hands and pushing back against the cliff wall, making myself as small as possible while I reach for Tairn's power as a boulder hits the edge of the ledge an ascent above and barrels toward us.

My heart beats in my ears. *It's just like turning a door handle. Just like twisting a lock. It's a lesser magic. I can do lesser magics...*

With a boulder the size of a feathertail?

I envision the boulder changing course and twist my hands—

Black streaks through my vision a second before an explosion sounds above me, and I cover my head with my hands as pebbles rain down.

Tairn pulverized the boulder with his tail.

"Thank you." I sag back against the rock wall and take a couple of deep breaths to slow my hammering heart.

"Vi!" Rhiannon yells from up ahead.

"We're all right!" I shout back.

"Holy shit." Maren leans next to me, her hand on her chest.

"Morningstartail?" Sloane asks.

"Morningstartail," I confirm, watching Tairn level out, then fly back our direction.

Within seconds, he's hovering in front of me with precise beats of his wings, his golden eyes narrowing.

Maren ducks her head, and Sloane looks away.

"Hey, that wasn't my fault. I didn't slip." I lift my brows at him.

"It would be a shame to have gone through the last year just to have you kill us on a measly hike."

I scoff. "Noted."

He flexes his wings, air gusting against my cheeks before he dives again.

"Is...um...that normal?" Maren asks as we resume the trudge, my heart pounding through the surge of adrenaline.

"Which part? Tairn saving my ass? Or being grumpy about it? Because yes, both are normal."

"When you walk your parapet, there are rocks thrown at you?" she clarifies.

"Oh." I shake my head. "No. You just have to cross it, which is harder than it sounds. What do you go through to be chosen?"

"We walk to the edge of Cliffsbane, look out over the river—it's about thirty feet deep at that point—and wait for the drifts to fly by." Her tone lightens, and when I glance back, she's smiling. "When they approach, we jump."

"You jump?" Sloane whips her head back, her eyes wide.

Maren nods, and a dimple forms in her cheek. "We jump. And if we can land on a gryphon, climb into position, and hold on, they bond us." She reaches up and scratches under Dajalair's chin where beak turns to feather.

"That's pretty badass," Sloane admits begrudgingly. "What happens if you miss? Do the bodies wash up on the shore?"

We both pause, turning fully to watch Maren respond. Have to admit, I'm curious, too.

Maren blinks. "Bodies? No one dies. It's just like cliff jumping. If we miss, we swim to shore, dry, and shake off the embarrassment—and pick another branch for service. Infantry and artillery are popular."

Sloane and I exchange another look. "You just…swim to shore," I say slowly.

"Yeah." Maren nods, then points between Sloane and me. "And before you ask, it's you all who are the weird ones, killing cadets on your conscription day."

I draw back, letting her words sink in.

"Technically, they're candidates," Sloane mutters. "We're only cadets once we cross."

"Well, I guess that makes it better," Maren quips sarcastically.

"Hey, are we moving or what?" Sawyer calls from behind us.

"Moving!" I answer, then turn and keep hiking up the incline as a pulse of star-bright energy courses down the bond from Tairn.

"Whoa," Sloane says, putting her hand over her heart. "What was that?"

"I felt it, too." Maren blinks.

"Aretia's first hatchling has chosen to emerge," Tairn tells me, his tone clipped, considering the news.

"We have hatchlings?" I grin. *"Why don't you seem happy about it?"*

"The hatchling's choice transforms the valley back into a hatching ground. It changes the magic. Every channeling creature within a four-hour flight of the valley will know."

"That's just us. We're on the edge of about three hours away." I glance around, noting that the others seem to be in conversation with their bonded ones, too. *"Well, us and the fliers, and they'd find out once we get there anyway."* My smile widens at the thought of an Aretian-born feathertail. *"We have to trust them for this to work."*

"I suppose we do."

By late in the afternoon, I'd rather commend my soul to Malek than take another fucking step up this never-ending trail. No wonder Tyrrendor never suffered an invasion from Poromiel. Their troops would either be exhausted or dead—picked off by patrolling dragons—by the time they reach the top.

Every muscle aches, somehow simultaneously burning with exertion yet stiff from how calculated my steps have become the higher we've climbed, a result of the dizziness I can't quite shake. Even reciting facts in my head isn't making it feel connected to my body anymore. My heart beats at a humming, stressed pace, and I would give almost *anything* to lean against the cliff on my right, stop, and rest for an hour. Or two. Or four.

We've halted at least twice in the last hour. The gryphons are slowing to a pace that's starting to make me worry about reaching the top at all, but at least none have fallen to their deaths.

And the fights breaking out between fliers and riders aren't helping, either. We've had to stop the march three times just to switch up where certain cadets are walking. Brennan might be right that we'll respect the fliers for having climbed, but a daylong hike isn't going to solve the *years* of hatred we've borne for each other.

The afternoon is extra fun as we enter a thick layer of cloud that only allows a dozen feet of visibility and our progress slows to what feels like a crawl.

"Hopefully these clouds mean that we're close to the top, right?" Maren asks, glancing with concern at Daja, whose steps have grown slower with each ascent. Her head hangs and her feathered chest rises faster, shallower with every step. Hypoxia. Maren's in the same condition, as is the pair in front of us, Cibbelair and his flier, Luella. His silver-specked wings aren't just tucked in at his side; they're drooping.

While we riders have been conditioned in the mountains surrounding Basgiath and often fly at twelve thousand feet, the fliers can't say the same. The highest mountain in Poromiel tops out around eight thousand feet, which explains why only the summitwing drifts would carry out the high-altitude village raids we heard about in Battle Brief.

Even Sloane looks worried.

"Let me check how much farther we have to go," I tell Maren, softening my tone. *"Please tell me we're almost off this damned cliff?"*

"You feel closer. Perhaps three or four ascents from the top," Tairn answers. *"But none of us can see a thing through the fog. Claw Section is cresting now."*

"I think we have less than an hour left." I offer Maren what I hope is an encouraging smile but probably looks like a weary grimace. *"You sure you can't just pick them up in your claws like the crossbolts and fly them to the top?"* I ask Tairn.

"They'd never tolerate the indignity of it. Besides, all they have to do is crest the cliffs. We have wagons waiting to carry the ones who will allow it."

Right. Because they can't fly to Aretia. Not in this condition.

"We can make it an hour," Maren says between huffed breaths. "Luella," she calls ahead. "It should be about another hour! Are you holding up?"

"We'll make it," a weak voice responds ahead of the silver-specked gryphon.

Sloane braces a hand on the cliff and looks back at me. "She and Visia have been arguing," she whispers. "It's getting quieter, but I can't tell if it's because they worked out their differences or because Luella can't breathe. And I think she just threw up."

"Altitude sickness," I respond just as quietly.

"And you don't have to whisper," Maren states. "Gryphons have remarkable hearing."

"Just like dragons," I mutter. "No privacy."

"Exactly." Maren scratches just above Daja's beak, reminding me of that spot above her nostrils that Andarna likes. "Gossiping busybodies," she says with affection. "Don't worry, Luella will win her over. She's the nicest of us."

"I wouldn't be so sure." Sloane slows, waiting for us to come up with her. "Visia's family was killed in the Sumerton raid last year."

"Lu wasn't even a cadet when that happened," Maren argues between shallow breaths.

"If riders torched Draithus," Sloane quips, arching a brow, "would you care if you were walking with someone from the Northern Wing? Or would you simply loathe all riders?"

"Good point," Maren admits. "But it's hard to hate Luella. Plus, she bakes *really* good cake. She'll win Visia over with butterscotch once we get to Aretia— just watch."

A flash of dragon wing appears through the fog, cutting through the cloud like a knife before disappearing again.

"At least they're still trying to do patrols," Sloane says as we continue forward.

"Brave, considering they can't see the cliff's edge," I add.

A wave of tension…of awareness barrels down my bond with Tairn. Guess he's not too happy about the lack of visibility, either.

"Not there!" a familiar voice shouts up ahead, and the line halts. "You'll trigger it!"

Dain.

"What the fuck is he doing back here?" Sloane mutters. It doesn't matter how many times I explain that Dain didn't understand the consequences of stealing my memories; Sloane still despises him.

There's an overwhelming part of me that still does, too.

Cibbelair begins moving, picking his way carefully up the path, and we follow, eventually coming to where Dain stands rigidly against the cliff wall, making himself as small as possible so the gryphon will be able to pass by.

"There's a pressure trigger," he warns, gesturing to a section of the trail just ahead of him with a map clutched in one hand and holding out his other arm so Ridoc and Luella don't continue. "We know it sends out arrows but don't know from *where*, so we can't disarm it. Hence why I'm standing here, warning everyone about that particular section."

I glance up the cliff wall, noting the numerous cracks in the face that could hide any number of munitions, then back to the trail, where a rope has been laid across the rock to mark the untouchable area. It looks to be five, maybe six feet across, which would already give me a little pause on the ground, but jumping an area that big on an unforgiving ledge, at our level of fatigue—let alone the gryphons'—is flat-out intimidating.

And I can barely see a damned thing past the rope in this fog.

"We have to jump," Ridoc says, eyeing the trail.

"Everyone's made it across so far." Dain nods.

"Luella?" Maren leans out over the cliff to see past Cibbelair.

A small flier with pale, nearly white hair and freckles that remind me of Sawyer looks back. "I don't know. It's farther than I've ever jumped before."

"She's the smallest of us." Maren doesn't bother whispering.

"Like you," Sloane adds, looking my way.

"Ridoc, can you and Dain throw her across?" I ask.

"You mean can I throw *you* across?" Ridoc asks with his typical sarcasm.

I snort. "I'll be able to jump it." Like hell is Ridoc going to throw *me*.

Luella's head draws back in offense.

Shit. "I'm used to the altitude," I remind her, hoping to cover my accidental insult. "What has everyone else done?" I ask Dain.

"Running leap," he answers. "We're just making sure whoever's on the other side is done recovering first so there's no impact."

Gods, I wish Xaden were here. He'd simply pluck Luella up with shadows and ferry her across. Then again, he just might let her fall. I never quite know when it comes to other people.

Rhiannon can't retrieve something as big as a person. Cianna, our executive officer from last year, is up there, but wind wielding isn't going to help here, either. Our signets are useless for this.

"You jump first, Ridoc," Dain orders.

"So I'm *not* throwing Luella?"

"She either makes it or she doesn't, just like Parapet," Visia says, tying her shoulder-length hair back. "I'll go first."

"Cibbe says he goes first," Luella announces, then all three flatten themselves against the cliff wall next to Dain so the gryphon can pass.

Sloane's right. Luella's physically similar to me, small and shorter than average. She's even my age, since fliers start a year after riders. But she's suffering from altitude sickness, and I'm not.

I'm just lightheaded, which might be a death sentence up here.

The tip of another dragon wing appears in the mist, the flight pattern coming from the opposite direction. A brown, maybe? "Is that Aotrom?" I ask Ridoc. At this point, I'm about to beg for his aid, flier pride be damned.

"No. He's up top with the others. They just finished carrying the crossbolts and complaining about being treated like packhorses."

A corner of my mouth rises. "Sounds about right."

Cibbelair rocks back on his fawn-and-ochre haunches, then launches forward, clearing the trap and skidding on his landing.

Luella sucks in a breath as Cibbe's talons skim the edge, but he quickly sags against the cliff, his back rising and falling with stuttered breaths.

I'm torn between sighing with relief that the gryphon made it and acknowledging the growing pit in my stomach that tells me there's no way Luella will.

"Mind asking him if he'd serve as a railing?" I ask the flier. "We're both going to have to run and leap, and he'd be good at keeping us both from falling off the cliff."

Cibbe's head cranes back at an unnatural angle, and he chortles aggressively in my direction.

"He…" A small smile tugs at Luella's mouth. "He reluctantly agrees."

"Visia and Ridoc, get over there," Dain orders. "We need to keep the line moving."

Visia backs up to where we stand, bounces up on her toes, and runs, pumping her arms and legs, then launches herself across the roped-off area and lands cleanly on the other side.

"See, if she can do it, we're fine," I assure Luella, hoping it's not a lie.

"She's six inches taller than us and not nearly as winded." Luella swallows. "And no offense, but you look like you're about to pass out."

"I'm not," I lie, taking a second to adjust the slipping wrap on my left knee. I haven't had enough water or enough time off my feet today, and my body is more than happy to let me know about the neglect.

Gods, I never would have made it through Gauntlet if I'd felt like *this* that day.

Gauntlet. An idea takes hold.

"I'll—" Ridoc starts.

"Wait a second." I brace my right hand on the cliff to keep from losing my precarious balance and study the area above the trap, noting one of the thinnest cracks in the rock. Ridoc's the best climber we have, so it just might work.

"What are you thinking?" Dain asks. "Don't tell me nothing. You have those little lines between your eyebrows."

"I'm wondering how attached Ridoc is to his sword." I breathe through the nausea that always accompanies the dizziness.

"It's standard issue," Ridoc replies, then follows my line of sight. "Oh. You're thinking…"

"Yep." I glance at Luella so he catches on, and he nods slowly.

"I can't guarantee it will hold."

"Try." I lift my brows.

Ridoc reaches for his sword.

"No." Dain draws his shortsword, leaving the long one sheathed. "Use this one. It has a longer pommel, and it will be easier to work in." He hands the sword to Ridoc, then looks over at me. "I still know how your mind works."

Sloane scoffs.

Ridoc takes Dain's shortsword and sheathes it in the empty spot at his left, then climbs up a few feet before scrambling horizontally across the cliff face.

"What is he doing?" Luella asks.

"Watch," I say quietly so I don't startle Ridoc.

Hand over hand, he carefully moves across the rock, then plants his feet on a foothold that I can't even see, let alone trust, about halfway across. He frees the shortsword, drawing his elbow back as far as he can without losing his balance, then jabs it into the cracked rock with full force. The screeching sound is worse than a pissed-off gryphon.

"Rock," he says to Dain, reaching back with his right hand.

Dain picks up a loose one the size of my fist, then stretches his long arms out toward Ridoc, handing it to him.

Ridoc slams the rock against the pommel, hammering it deeper into the cliff until almost every inch of the blade has disappeared, and I don't miss the slight flinch on Dain's face. Ridoc grips the hilt and tests it with one palm, then two.

I hold my breath when he drops all his weight onto it, and thank Dunne, it doesn't give. He rocks his body backward, then swings forward, letting go at the height of his arc and landing on the other side of the rope.

This might work.

"And suddenly this is the Gauntlet, not Parapet," Sloane mutters.

"Easy," Ridoc says, then pivots to face me and holds out his arms. "Let's go, Vi. I'll even catch you."

"Fuck off." I lift my middle finger but grin across the haze at him. "I'm really hoping you're right-handed," I say to Luella.

She nods.

"Good. That hilt is eight inches—"

"Seven," Dain corrects.

"Imagine a man actually shortening a girl's estimate," Maren teases.

I can't help but smile. "Right. Seven inches. Just have to jump far enough to grab it, then swing across like Ridoc."

Luella looks at me like I told her we'll be climbing the rest of this cliff by hand.

"Want me to go first?" I offer.

She nods.

"Please take the dizziness and I swear I'll build you a bigger temple in Aretia," I pray to Dunne. But maybe that plea should be aimed at Zihnal, because damn do we need some luck. Butterflies attack my stomach.

"You're sure?" Dain asks.

I level a glare at him.

"You're sure." He restates it as fact, then backs up to give me more room.

I bounce up on the balls of my feet, then spring forward, planting that last step just before the rope and leaping toward the hilt.

I feel every beat of my heart marking time as I'm airborne.

Reach it. Reach it. REACH IT!

My right hand makes contact first, and I grip hard, slamming my left into the available space and holding tight as my body swings so I don't fly forward and trigger the trap.

"You've got this!" Ridoc shouts, holding out his arms.

"I will kick you in the face if you try to catch me!" I warn.

He grins and backs up a few steps as I take breath after breath, pushing back the blackening edges of my vision with sheer will, refusing to let the dizziness win.

I will not fucking die today.

Rocking my body back, I start to swing just like I'm on a Gauntlet obstacle, whipping my feet forward and back. When I have enough momentum, I mutter another prayer and let go, flying toward that rope line.

I hit the other side, and pain explodes in my knees as I fall forward, catching myself with my palms. *You made it, you made it, you made it,* I chant, forcing the pain into a neat little box and shoving a lid over it and stumbling to my feet. A quick sweep of hands tells me I haven't dislocated my kneecaps, though the left argues that it came damn close to abandoning ship.

"See?" I force a smile to my face and turn. "You can do it."

Maren pats Luella on the shoulder, and whatever she says makes the smaller flier nod as I back up, moving toward the center of the ledge and giving her space to land.

She takes the obstacle just like I did, her feet kicking for distance before she reaches the hilt and holds tight.

"There you go!" I shout. "Now swing until you feel you have the force to carry you."

"I can't!" she cries out. "My hands are slipping!"

Shit.

"You can," Dain encourages. "But you'd better move *now*."

"Move, Luella!" Maren yells.

Luella starts the same rocking pattern Ridoc and I used, swinging her feet to gain momentum, then lets go.

I hold my breath as she hurtles toward the line of safety.

Her feet land just before the rope and her eyes lock on mine, widening with terror as she throws herself forward, like the trap won't notice her misstep if she's quick enough.

Oh, *fuck*. Maybe Dain's wrong. Maybe the trap is twelve inches *before* the rope line. Maybe she's in the clear. Maybe we all are.

But clearly I have prayed to the wrong god.

Everything somehow slows and yet happens at once.

Luella dives forward, hurling her body where she was looking—at me instead of Cibbelair—and I barely have time to open my arms before she impacts, driving me backward at an angle into Visia…toward the edge of the cliff.

"Vi!" Ridoc shouts.

I try to pivot, to heave as much of our weight toward the safety of the wall as I can, but there's not enough time or strength, and we flounder, tangled in one another.

Feet trip other feet, and I start to fall. We all do.

A hand grasps the waistband of the back of my leathers and pulls, changing the direction of my fall. *Ridoc.* My feet lose traction as my momentum shifts, and I hit my knees near the edge of the cliff just in time to see Visia and Luella start to slide over.

And I can no longer stop time.

"No!" I scramble forward, rock scraping over my torso, and throw out my arms, reaching for whoever is closest as a sound like gushing wind rushes over my head.

Visia grabs hold of my left hand and Luella grips my right wrist, the weight of both women nearly taking me to join them. My right shoulder pops from the socket, and agony rips from my throat with a scream.

Visia fumbles for a handhold along the cliff wall, but Luella has both hands locked on my wrist, her feet kicking for purchase.

"Pull me up!" Luella shrieks, and I'm in too much pain to verbalize that I *can't*.

"Ridoc!" I shout as the edges of my vision blur, then blacken. "Help me!"

Feet pound, but Luella's grip slips from my wrist to my hand, and I chance a look back over my right shoulder, hoping for rescue as Visia's weight disappears, plucked from the side of the cliff by a giant beak.

Cibbe.

Visia was in his way. The gryphon dumps the rider on the ledge and then cranes his enormous neck toward Luella as bootsteps race *down* the ascent.

But all I see is Ridoc, staggering backward toward the wall, two arrows piercing the side of his abdomen.

"I'm all right." He nods quickly, glancing down at the arrows, blood trickling from his mouth.

No. No. NO.

I scream up the cliff for the only person who can save him now.

"BRENNAN!"

When a gryphon bonds, it does so for life.
Guard your life as you would your gryphon's,
for they are forever intertwined.

—Chapter One, The Canon of the Flier

CHAPTER
FORTY-FOUR

Booted feet scurry toward me from both directions, and Sloane grabs hold of Ridoc as Dain hits his knees beside me, then lunges forward, reaching for Luella at the same moment Cibbe does.

I rip my gaze from Ridoc's and focus on Luella's hazel eyes as she slips down my limp fingers.

"Hold on!" I demand. They just need another second.

But she slips farther, and Cibbe's beak closes on nothing as she loses her grip and falls, the cloud swallowing her whole.

"Luella!" a woman shouts from the left.

Cibbelair screams, and the shrill sound vibrates through my chest as I stare and stare and stare at the space where Luella was, as if she'll somehow emerge from the mist.

As if there's any chance she's alive.

"Damn it!" Dain quickly pushes back onto his knees. "Vi—"

"I can't move." My voice drops to a whimper. "My shoulder's out." Any second, the adrenaline will wear off and the true pain of the injury will hit.

"All right." His tone immediately softens. "I've got you." His hands wrap around my rib cage, and he carefully lifts me to my feet, my right arm hanging uselessly at my side.

Cibbe's screams become a keening wail.

"Something feels wrong," Tairn says.

"It's all fucking wrong."

"You dropped her!" Cat charges toward us from the other side of Cibbe, fury rightfully etched in every line of her scowl.

"I never had her." My chest crumples under the unbearable weight of the guilt because she's partially *right*. I may not have dropped her, but I didn't save her, either.

"Cat, no." Maren hurries around us, putting her hands out as if to block her best friend. "I saw it happen. It's *not* Violet's fault. Luella almost killed both of the riders because she couldn't jump the trap."

"You fucking dropped her!" Cat surges against Maren. "Cibbe saved your precious rider, and you *dropped* our flier! I will *kill* you for this!"

"Knock it off!" Maren shouts. "You kill her, you kill Riorson. Everyone knows it."

Fuck, it *always* comes down to that, doesn't it?

"I can—" Cat starts.

"Take one step toward Violet, and I'll throw you off this fucking cliff myself," Dain warns, his voice low and menacing. "Unlike Riorson, I don't give a shit who your uncle is."

"I'll do it just for fun," Sloane adds.

"Ridoc," I manage to say around the pain that throbs from my shoulder then devours the rest of me.

"Alive," he answers weakly.

"Cat, let it go. Cibbe doesn't have long," Maren says, her hand trembling as she reaches for the gryphon.

Cat breathes deeply, then nods, moving to the gryphon's side.

"Gryphons die with their fliers," Maren explains, her tone softening as she strokes the line where feathers turn to fur.

Like Tairn and me.

Cibbe lets loose a stuttered, three-beat cry, and the entire cliff, both above us and below, echoes it, as though the gryphons grieve the loss of the flier as one.

The beat of wings approaches as Dain leads me back from the edge, and I watch the mist, waiting for a flash of orange, for Marbh and Brennan to arrive.

"Put my shoulder back in." My voice croaks as I glance at Dain.

"Shit. Are you serious?" He lifts his brows.

"Do it. Just like when I was fourteen."

"And seventeen," he mutters.

"Exactly. You know how to do it, and we don't have any healers nearby."

"You don't want to wait for Brennan?" Dain takes hold of my arm.

"Brennan will try to mend me first, and Ridoc is dying. Now *do it*!" I snap, bracing for the pain.

A strap of leather appears in front of my face. "Bite down," Maren orders over Cibbe's cries.

I can't look at him, can't watch his healthy body die just like Liam's had, so I face forward and bite.

"One." Dain lifts my arm slightly and adjusts. "Two." He brings my arm out to a ninety-degree angle.

My teeth mark the leather as I fight the scream working its way up my throat. Ridoc has been shot with two arrows. I can handle this.

"I'm so fucking sorry," Dain whispers, putting his other hand between my neck and shoulder. "Three!" He rolls my arm forward and I clench my jaw, my eyes squeezing shut as white-hot pain sends stars flashing across my vision and he puts the joint back into place.

The relief from the worst of the pain is instant, and I remove the leather from between my teeth. "Thank you."

"Never thank me for that." He lifts my arm above my head, making sure it's in place, rotates it back down, then bends my elbow, tucking my arm across my chest before sliding his belt off and fashioning a temporary sling. "How is he?" he asks over his shoulder.

"Losing blood," Sloane answers as an orange claw lands on the ledge where the trap had been and Brennan executes a perfect roll-on landing.

"Are you—" He comes running at me, scanning me for blood.

"I'm fine! Save Ridoc!"

"Fuck." Brennan levels a look at Dain's leg. "You're next."

"It's just a graze." Dain glances down at me. "It just caught the edge of my thigh."

Brennan crouches next to Ridoc and starts working.

"It's all right," Maren tells Cibbe as the gryphon collapses, his head hanging over the edge of the cliff as his cries grow softer. "You have earned an honorable death."

Another set of wingbeats fills the air, and I face the mist, waiting for Tairn's disapproving scowl. But I don't feel him any closer than before.

"You did not ask me to fetch you," he says sternly.

The mist parts like a scene from a nightmare, and gray, gaping jaws fill my vision, opening wide to reveal dripping teeth that snap closed around Cibbe's neck, snatching the gryphon from the ledge before falling back into the mist.

My heart stops.

"What the fuck—" Sloane whispers.

"Wyvern," I manage to whisper, my head swiveling toward Maren and Cat. They're the only people here who've seen one. "Wyvern, right?"

"Wyvern," Cat replies, her eyes wide with shock. Maren is still as a statue.

"Wyvern!" Dain bellows, and all hell breaks loose.

"We can't see anything in the cloud cover," Tairn growls.

"But they can see well enough to eat *us!"* I can already feel him on the move. Thank gods Andarna is in Aretia. "Get up the cliff!" I shout at Maren, grasping her shoulder with my uninjured hand and shaking her to snap her out of it. "Get Daja up the cliff!"

She blinks, then nods. "Daja!"

Dain yanks me out of the path as the gryphon charges forward, and I can only hope the adrenaline rush is enough to get them up the last couple of ascents.

"I can't move him," Brennan says, his sight solely focused on Ridoc's wounds. "I'm blocking most of his pain, but I can't move him, Vi."

"And we're sitting ducks here," Sloane mutters, looking at the mist as more riders and gryphons push by.

"Go," Ridoc whispers, opening his eyes and finding mine. "Get off this trail."

I kneel beside him and take his hand. "We made a deal, remember? All four of us live to see graduation. We. Made. A. Deal."

"Ridoc?" Sawyer pushes toward us, his eyes bulging with fear as he brings up the last of our squad and Tail Section begins.

"They can't see," Brennan says, his voice tensing as his hands move, snapping one arrow in half, and then the second. "Aetos, the dragons can't see!"

"On it!" Dain looks up the cliff, and I hold Ridoc's hand tight as Brennan slides the first arrow out of his abdomen.

"You're on *what* exactly?" Sawyer snaps at Dain.

"Cath is relaying to Gaothal that Cianna needs to wield some wind so the riot can see," Dain responds. "You can't do anything here, Henrick, so get the others to safety!"

Sawyer clenches his fists. "If you think I'm going to leave my squadmates—"

"Sounds like your wingleader gave you an order, cadet," Brennan says, his tone flat.

"Take Sloane." I look over at her as she draws back, clearly offended. "I had to hold Liam while he died, his dragon already eviscerated by the jaws of a wyvern, and I will not watch his sister suffer the same fate. Get up the fucking cliff!"

Sawyer all but lifts Sloane to her feet, and the two join into the steady, hurried march as the clouds begin to thin.

"How powerful is Cianna?" I ask Dain quietly, absorbing the pressure of Ridoc's squeezing hand as Brennan works the second arrow free.

His tense expression answers the question for him.

The visibility may be improving, but it's not nearly enough to see what we're up against, and even if it were, without crossbolts, I'm the best weapon we have.

"I've already come to that conclusion." Gusts of air hit my back from the

force of Tairn's wings.

"Right." I let go of Ridoc's hand and brush his hair back up his forehead. "You will not die. Do you understand?"

He nods, his dark brown eyes fluttering closed as I stand.

"Where do you think you're going?" Brennan asks, his concentration wavering.

"I'm the best shot you've got. We both know it."

"Fuck," Brennan mutters.

"Find every wind wielder we have," I tell Dain as I walk to the brink of the ledge, temporarily stopping traffic as Tairn swings his massive body around to face Poromiel. "I think there's a storm wielder in First Wing. Not as powerful as my mother, but if we can raise the temperature it should help clear the clouds."

"Violet!" Brennan calls out. "If we can't clear the clouds, then use them to your advantage! No one here is as powerful as General Sorrengail. Come up with another plan."

Ever the tactician.

"We could send the entire riot in," Dain suggests.

"And if there's *one* rider on that wyvern, we could lose the entire riot." I shake my head.

"You're wounded. You know that, right?" Dain questions me, glancing at his belt.

"And you're a memory reader."

His gaze narrows.

"Oh, were we not stating obvious facts?" I study the clouds around us, looking for any break, any sign of blue sky. "Hate to break it to you, but your signet isn't exactly helpful in this situation."

"No time for this." Tairn lays his massive tail beside the ledge while keeping a steady hover.

"Would Riorson let you rush off into a battle against gods know how many wyvern—or worse, the venin who created them—when you're *wounded*?" His eyebrows rise.

"Yes." I step out onto the midpoint of Tairn's tail, my stomach settling at the familiar territory beneath my boots as I look back over my shoulder at Dain. "That's why I love him."

I don't wait for his response, not when Tairn is a giant target. He holds remarkably steady as I walk forward, navigating his spikes and scales with ease.

"The flier's death is not your fault," Tairn tells me as I find my saddle and lower into the seat.

"We'll save that for another day." I fumble with the belt for precious seconds. This fucking thing is nearly impossible with one arm, but I manage by holding

the strap in my right hand and fastening with my left. *"You know I can't wield with one hand, right?"*

"You don't need me to tell you your limits." Tairn dives and I'm thrown forward in my seat as we plummet through thousands of feet of dissipating clouds.

"You can't feel them, can you?"

"I was aware something felt off, but if I could accurately detect wyvern—if any of us could—without seeing them, we wouldn't be in this position."

Fair point.

Wind bites at my face, and tears streak from my eyes, but I'm not going to waste precious arm movements on getting my goggles from my pack. We emerge from the cloud cover and level out just beneath it.

"The ascents are clear," Tairn says. *"We will not risk the high ground if there are no riders to defend."* With great beats of his wings, we jolt upward, back into the mist.

"Are there other dragons out here?" I reach for the buckle of Dain's belt and carefully pull the leather aside to slip my arm free. I'm going to need it as soon as we're done. *"I don't want to hit anyone by accident."* Even if hitting the wyvern would probably *be* an accident, given my aim.

"They're all above, guarding the riders."

"Good." We fly straight through the thickest parts of the cloud, but there's no trace of the wyvern.

Until they—as in *two* of them—fly by on either side of us, streaks of gray in the otherwise endless white.

"Shit."

Tairn flies high, pushing up into blue sky.

Clouds stretch from the cliffs over the surrounding landscape. No wonder the riot didn't see the wyvern. They have the perfect cover.

And Cianna isn't powerful enough to dissipate all this.

Use it. That's what Brennan suggested.

Wyvern aren't just alive…they're created. They carry a form of energy forced into them by dark wielders.

"I have an idea."

"I approve." Tairn sails into the cloud cover. *"I've told Gaothal to instruct his rider to stop eliminating the clouds and instead push them away from the cliff."*

"Just from where the path is. Until then, keep the wyvern distracted." I clutch the pommel of the saddle with my uninjured hand and shove my right hand into my flight jacket between the buttons to stabilize my shoulder as much as possible.

Then Tairn dives back into the mist.

"Only two that Aotrom can see," Tairn announces, his wings beating the

clouds into little swirl patterns behind us. *"The cover has thinned enough to the north to make out their shapes."*

"A patrol?"

"Riderless," he confirms.

"Thank you, Zihnal." I lean forward as tears streak from the corners of my eyes. *"I know, I know. Dragons pay no heed to our gods."*

Tairn snorts, following a pattern of swirls similar to his own. He's tracking the wyvern.

"You're faster than they are, right?" Fear licks down my spine.

"Don't insult me when we're headed into battle."

"Right," I mutter to myself.

"Feel like using the conduit?" Tairn asks as two tails appear ahead.

"Nope. Aiming is detrimental to the goal."

"Understood." His wings beat faster, propelling us to a speed that leaves my stomach behind and narrows my vision as he pulls up above the wyvern to catch their attention.

It works, and my stomach hollows as we switch from the predator to the prey.

"If there were only one, I'd rip his throat out and call it a day."

"I know." But there's no guarantee that there are only two.

"Hold on, Silver One."

I buckle down, making myself as small as possible and lying across the saddle to minimize air resistance as Tairn moves at a pace I've never experienced. It takes all my effort to breathe, to fight the night at the edge of my vision, to just stay conscious as he bolts out of the clouds, then plummets back into the cover a breath later.

"They followed."

"Great." My fucking teeth are rattling. *"How is that cloud cover? Because I can't wield if I'm passed out."*

"They are almost clear."

I grit my teeth and ignore the throbbing ache of my shoulder. The clouds have to clear the path, or there's every chance I'll kill Ridoc and Brennan if they're still on the trail.

"We're rolling," he warns me a second before he does so, executing a move that disorients me thoroughly, a move most riders can't hold their seat for.

My stomach lurches into my lungs as he levels out, flying back the opposite way and dropping us directly *under* the wyvern. *"I know we're not supposed to question dragons—"*

"Then don't."

A set of pointed gray claws falls rapidly toward us. *"Tairn!"*

He banks hard right, then climbs quickly. *"The clouds have cleared the trail."*

My heart speeds to a gallop. *"Make sure they're following us."*

"Don't turn around, or you might actually *pass out,"* he instructs, flying faster.

I slide my hand out of my jacket with a wince, then gasp with pain as I rotate my palms downward and open myself to Tairn's power. It flows through me, filling my muscles, my veins, the very marrow of my bones until I am power and power is me. My skin starts to hum, then sizzle.

We break through the clouds, and I throw my arms wide, pushing past the pain and screaming with it all in the same breath, setting the molten energy within me free, and for the first time in my life, I force the power *downward*.

Energy erupts through me, searing my skin on the way out as lightning strikes within the cloud below us, webbing out like the many branches of an overgrown briar patch, twisting and turning, drawn to the energy harnessed within the wyvern.

Four distinct shapes light up beneath us, two directly under and two closer to the edge of the cliff, flashing brightly with the endless stream of power.

"Break free!" Tairn demands.

I force my palms shut and shove the Archives door in my mind closed, blocking the endless torrent of Tairn's power before I end up in the same condition I'd been in at Basgiath under Carr and Varrish's punishment.

The flashing stops.

"Go!" I shout down the bond, clutching my right arm with my left as Tairn banks deeply to the left and dives for the ground.

This time, the wind is a welcome reprieve from the heat of my skin and the burn within my lungs as we pass through the cloud and emerge on the other side.

Four wyvern carcasses litter the ground, one in the middle of the very field we'd stood in this morning. Tairn flies over each just long enough to be sure that they are, in fact, riderless, and we're joined by four others in the riot on one last sweep of the area.

Then we climb again, soaring through the clouds and coming out at the edge of the cliff, where everyone has gathered. Some gryphons load into heavy wagons with stumbling steps while others appear to have lost consciousness on the ground, but the fliers are all standing, as are the squads of riders.

Tairn quickly locates ours, and riders scurry as he drops to an abrupt landing.

"You could have crushed someone," I lecture.

"Could have, but alas, they moved."

I spot Rhiannon and Sawyer with Ridoc braced between them, walking him toward Aotrom, and breathe a sigh of relief.

"What? You thought I'd let your friend die?" Brennan asks, folding his arms and tilting his head up at me from where he stands next to Bodhi and Dain to the right of Tairn's foreleg.

"Never doubted you for a second." I force a smile.

"Want to get your ass down here and let me mend that shoulder?" He wields the older brother disapproving stare like the professional he is.

"Not particularly." I grimace and haul Dain's belt back into position, refusing to take the chance that I won't be able to mount again if a mending session knocks me out.

"So fucking stubborn," Brennan mutters, shoving his hands through his hair. "How did you know you could kill them like that?"

"I didn't." I breathe through the wave of pain that threatens to pull me under as I let the weight of my shoulder fall into the makeshift sling. "Wyvern are created with dark wielder magic, and Felix said something to me about energy fields the other day. I took a chance that the lightning would be drawn to their magic, and Tairn agreed to try."

Brennan's jaw drops slightly and Dain bites back an uncharacteristic smile, reminding me of the years when he cared more about climbing trees than our curfew.

"Chance panned out," Bodhi says, flat-out grinning.

"It did." I nod. *"Aren't you going to tell me how brilliant that idea was?"*

Tairn scoffs. *"I chose you last year for that brilliance, and now you'd like to be congratulated like it's something new? How odd."*

"You're impossible to impress."

"I'm a dragon, a Black Morningstartail. The descendent of—"

"Yeah, yeah." I cut him off before he makes me recite his entire lineage.

"Cath said there were four of them in there." Dain deftly changes the subject. "At least they were riderless. Could you imagine if dark wielders knew we were joining forces with fliers and moving them into Tyrrendor? Where a dragon just *hatched*? They'd see us as a ripe little draining target."

Bodhi's face falls.

Oh shit. *"That's why you were worried."*

"There's no telling who is within a four-hour flight." Tairn bites out those last words.

"They already know." My stomach twists. "That's why they're using riderless wyverns to patrol."

Brennan stills completely, and the color drains from his face.

"What?" Dain glances between us.

"Venin share a collective conscious with the wyvern they create," Brennan says quietly. "That's what Tecarus's book says."

"The book you haven't let me read in the four days you've had it?" I touch my fingertips to my head as the dizziness returns.

"It's only been three days, and you apparently already know," Brennan counters. "And some things are beyond your clearance, cadet, especially information we haven't finished analyzing."

"I know because I read the book my *father* gave me," I argue, and I almost regret the emphasis when he flinches. He didn't just separate himself from Mom when he changed his name — he distanced himself from Dad. "And Bodhi knows because it's how I killed an entire horde of them at Resson."

"I didn't know," Dain interrupts. "So if one of them felt that energy pulse… If one of them knows what it means…"

"Whoever created them knows," I finish for him, turning my gaze to Brennan. "And you can bet they'll come for us now."

It was only in the last fifty years that we realized they were no longer solely coming from the Barrens. They'd begun to take recruits, teaching those who never bonded a gryphon to channel what was not theirs to take, to upset the balance of magic by stealing it from the very source. The problem with mankind is we too often find our souls to be a fair price for power.

—CAPTAIN LERA DORRELL'S GUIDE TO VANQUISHING THE VENIN
PROPERTY OF CLIFFSBANE ACADEMY

CHAPTER
FORTY-FIVE

"Coralee Ryle. Nicholai Panya," a newly pinned Major Devera calls out over the frost-covered courtyard, reading from what's become the new death roll. For the first time since entering the quadrant, the names called every morning for the last week haven't been cadets, but active riders—and fliers—on the front lines, fighting to fortify the villages along the Stonewater River. Trying to divert the venin's attention from our valley, where *four* new dragons have hatched.

Don't say Mira. Don't say Mira. Don't say Mira. It's become my personal prayer to whatever god will listen while standing in formation.

I feel so fucking useless. Unlike the last two weeks, there's no luminary to fetch, no wards to fail at. There's a real war down there, and we're up here learning history and physics.

"We lost *two* yesterday?" Aaric tenses in the row ahead.

Rhiannon glances back over her shoulder at me, sorrow haunting her eyes for a heartbeat before she composes herself with a grace I can never seem to manage and straightens her shoulders at Sawyer's side. Two riders in one day is unfathomable in active service. The entirety of the Aretian Quadrant will be dead in less than two months at this rate.

"I think that's Isar's brother," Ridoc says from beside me. "Second Wing."

We both glance left, past Third Wing. Isar Panya bows her head from the middle of her squad in Tail Section.

I blink back the burning in my eyes, and my fingers squeeze tight around the conduit in my left hand.

"He was a lieutenant," Imogen says quietly.

"Two years ahead of us," Quinn adds. "Great sense of humor."

"This is cruel," I whisper. "Telling us that our siblings, our friends are dead this way is fucking cruel." It's harsher than anything we've been put through at Basgiath.

"It's no different than morning formation," Visia says over her shoulder.

"Yes, it is," Sloane argues. "Hearing someone from a different wing died, or hell, even our squad, isn't the same as being told your brother's gone." Her voice cracks.

A lump swells painfully in my throat. Brennan is inside, no doubt arguing with the Assembly about where to find game for the tsunami of predators we've brought here over the last month or coordinating shipments from the now-functioning forge. He's safe.

Every commissioned rider that isn't here teaching has been sent in shifts to man the outposts along the Cliffs of Dralor, like Xaden, Garrick, Heaton, and Emery...or to hold the front, like Mira.

Devera clears her throat and exchanges the roll for the one Jesinia holds.

My shoulders dip, a breath of relief clouding the freezing air. Mira's alive. Or at least she was last night when the rotational rider brought the news in. Morning formation doesn't scare me when it comes to Xaden—I'd know instantly if he...

Gods, I can't even think it.

"Chrissa Verlin," Devera begins reading from the commissioned fliers' roll. "Mika Renfrew—"

"Mika!" A low, guttural scream erupts from our right, and every head turns to a drift near the center of the fliers' formation as a guy falls to his knees. The rest of his drift turns, covering him with comforting arms.

"I'm never going to get used to hearing them do that," Aaric mutters, shifting his weight.

"Hearing them what?" Sloane counters. "Have emotions?"

"Sorrengail knows what I mean. You've been out there—" Aaric says to me.

"And I cried like an infant while Liam died. Turn around." Shit, isn't that at odds with everything I told Rhiannon when we fought beside the Gauntlet? The deaths are supposed to harden us, so why do I agree with Sloane on this one? There's something infinitely more...human about the way the fliers react.

Even the way they conduct their own Threshing at Cliffsbane is considerably less cruel than what we endure at Basgiath. Now I can't decide if it makes us stronger...or simply harder.

"— and Alvar Gilana," Devara concludes. "We commend their souls to Malek."

I glance right—just like I do every morning—and see Cat's posture soften, her eyes close briefly from her drift on the closest edge of their formation. Syrena is still alive, too.

She looks over at me and I nod, which she returns, even if it's curt. It's our one daily moment of truce, the only time we seem to recognize each other as little sisters instead of enemies, and it's over in less than a heartbeat.

Her gaze shifts into a glare as formation breaks.

Swear to Amari, Cat's hell-bent on making my life as miserable as fucking possible every other minute of the day and tries twice as hard on the days Xaden is here. Her loathing makes Sloane look downright warm and fuzzy—and worse, her entire drift seems focused on our squad, with five of the remaining six—Maren being the exception—blaming me for Luella's death and loudly proclaiming that I chose the rider over the flier.

The tall guy with shoulder-length brown hair—pretty sure his name is Trager—swung for Ridoc on the valley's flight field two days ago and ended up with Rhiannon's fist in his face when he ran his mouth about her particular border village turning away refugees. His lip is still scabbed. Guess our little hike up the cliffs didn't bond us like they'd hoped.

"What did she do this morning?" Rhiannon asks, looking Cat's direction with a raised brow.

"Knocked on my door before dawn, then got all annoyed when I actually answered the damned thing." Just the thought of it has my hand warming along the conduit. Felix has replaced the alloy in my conduit twice this week, but at least my inability to control my own power is helping imbue alloy for daggers, so in a way, I'm helping the war effort, since my attempt at activating the wardstone failed. I roll my right shoulder, hoping to ease the ache now that I've ditched the sling, but it still protests.

"Is she running out of bullshit to pull on you?" Ridoc asks as we start to move toward the door. It takes twice as long to get out of formation here than at Basgiath, considering Riorson House was built for keeping people out, not letting them in. "That doesn't sound as bad as Saturday, when she posted that list of all the fliers Mira has taken out over the years."

That day had been a *treat* and definitely soothed relations between riders and fliers. We'd had at least a dozen more fights than usual break out in the hallways.

"She was wearing a Deverelli silk robe when I answered the door." I grab my pack from the ground and swing it over my shoulders, grimacing at the weight. "How do I know it was Deverelli silk, you ask? Because it was pretty much see-through."

"Oh, damn!" Sawyer cringes. "Why would she... Are you..."

Rhiannon, Quinn, and even Imogen stare at him as the first-years head inside.

"Think about where she sleeps!" Ridoc smacks the back of Sawyer's head.

"Ow! Right. You're still in Riorson's room," Sawyer says slowly, blatantly turning his back on Cat as she walks by with her drift. "I forgot. Roll has you listed in Rhiannon's room."

Bringing an extra hundred cadets here meant doubling up, and technically, I shouldn't be sleeping in a lieutenant's room—not that either of us care or leadership is going to say anything to the man who owns the house.

"Which I appreciate." Rhiannon rests her hand over her heart. "As it gives me a little privacy for whenever Tara and I actually get time to see each other."

"Happy to help." I crack a smile.

"Have to give it to the girl." Imogen shakes her head, sighing as she looks past me toward Cat and her drift. "She's tenacious."

Every head swivels in her direction.

"Hey." Imogen puts her hands up. "I'm Team Violet. Just saying that I bet if Xaden ever called it quits, you'd fight to get him back, too."

Ugh. When she puts it that way...

"Do not humanize that walking piece of terror," Rhiannon counters. "I climbed the *entire* cliff with her, and I'm starting to think we'd be better off having Jack Barlowe up here instead."

He's one person I'm glad stayed behind, no matter how nice he'd been to me. I still don't trust that guy. Never will.

"Is Cat being...Cat again?" Bodhi asks, walking over as the courtyard empties.

"It's fine. She's fine. I'm fine." I shake my head, lying through my teeth so he doesn't tell Xaden that I can't handle myself. "Rhiannon and I have somewhere to be."

"We do?" Rhi's eyebrows rise. "We do."

"Right." He turns to Rhiannon. "Well, Professor Trissa just chose your second-years for a new class. Tomorrow at two in the valley."

Trissa? She's the petite, quiet member of the Assembly.

"We'll be there," Rhi promises.

. . .

Snow falls in Aretia earlier than it does at Basgiath, and by the first week in November, a thin blanket of white covers the rapidly growing town but not the valley above, thanks to a combination of the natural thermal heat of the mountain range and the magic channeled by gryphon and dragon alike, which only seems to be increasing.

I glance toward the worn path at the end of the valley that leads down to Riorson House, anxiety churning in my stomach.

"This is awkward." Sawyer folds his arms and levels a bored look across the fifteen feet of valley grass that separate the second-year riders in our squad from the second-year fliers in Cat's drift.

Looks like we've both been summoned.

But if the line of dragons standing behind us and the gryphons behind the fliers can manage not to attack each other, surely we can be civil.

"Agreed."

"Civil is overrated," Andarna notes, flexing her claws in the grass. *"I've never tasted gryphon—"*

"We do not eat our allies," Tairn lectures. *"Find another snack."*

Looking right, I catch Sawyer glancing between Andarna and Tairn over and over, like he's comparing the differences. "Don't worry, I feel like I see double all the time."

"It's not that. Did she grow again?" he asks, pulling at his collar. "I feel like she grew."

"I think a few inches this week." I nod. "We had to add a link to her harness on each side."

"Soon I'll be able to fly without it," Andarna notes with a huff.

Ridoc pivots to make his own observations, smiling up at Andarna. "The little Mini-Tairn is becoming ferocious, isn't she—"

"I am no one's miniature." Andarna's head darts toward him, and she snaps her teeth less than a foot in front of his face.

My heart *bolts*. "Andarna!" I shout, turning quickly to put myself between her and Ridoc as she withdraws.

"Damn!" Ridoc throws his hands up, his hair blowing back from the force of what can only be described as the frustrated huff of Tairn's...sigh. "Big," Ridoc blurts. "Meant to say big."

"No more spending time with Sgaeyl." I point at her, stopping short of tapping her chin before looking up at Tairn, who's lowered his head over her like he might actually put her between his teeth and yank her off the field like a puppy. *"I mean it. She's rubbing off on you."*

"I could only be so lucky." Andarna lifts her head, preening, and Tairn grumbles something in his own language.

"Holy shit," Maren mutters from behind me.

"Sorry about that. Adolescents." I shrug at Ridoc.

"Still can't believe feathertails are kids," Sawyer says, taking a step away from Andarna. "Or that you bonded *two* black dragons."

"That one caught me off guard, too."

I glance toward the path again, but there's no sign of Rhiannon. If Professor Trissa gets here before Rhi, she'll be in major trouble. Trissa might be the softest-spoken member of the Assembly, but she's also the sharpest-tongued when pissed, according to what Xaden told me before he flew out for the border again this morning with Heaton and Emery. At least we'd had a night together.

The third-years went, too, patrolling the Cliffs of Dralor for wyvern and Navarrian riders.

Wyvern we wouldn't have to worry about if I hadn't failed to raise the wards.

"Which part's worse?" Ridoc muses, tapping the dimple in his chin. "Them silently glaring at us like we have any fucking clue why they're up here, too? Or their menacing escorts?" His gaze locks on the gryphons standing guard over their fliers.

Dajalair wobbles slightly, still clearly not adjusted to the altitude. I have yet to see a single gryphon fly in the week that they've been here.

"Both." Sawyer unbuttons his flight jacket. "Is it me or is it getting hotter up here?"

"Hotter," I agree, breathing a sigh of relief when Rhiannon appears, flashing me an excited smile as she hikes toward us from the other side of the field. I add to Ridoc, "And be nice. I like Maren."

"I like Maren, too—but her best friend needs to get tossed off this cliff," Sawyer notes under his breath.

"The gryphons are up and about faster than I thought," Ridoc observes. "Most of them were still sleeping off the altitude a few days ago."

The gryphon standing behind Trager, the guy with the shoulder-length brown hair and crooked smile—notices Ridoc's appraisal, and snaps his sharp, two-foot beak in warning.

Trager smirks.

Aotrom blows a hot gust of steam over our heads, blasting all three fliers in the face with not just steam but a healthy layer of…is that *snot*?

"In their defense, we brought our own escorts," I note as Andarna stalks forward, her claws sinking into the grass on either side of me in clear warning. Her talons grow sharper by the day, and she fully extended her wing for the first time this morning, making her extra bold this afternoon.

"Elders say I'll be flying within a few weeks." A growl aimed at the gryphon works up her throat, and his beady eyes flare, then blink.

"You're baring your teeth, aren't you?" I don't bother hiding my smile.

"I don't trust them," she answers. *"Especially the one in the center who looks to be plotting your death."*

"Don't let her bother you."

Cat's eyes are indeed narrowed on me as usual.

"She bothers you." Andarna takes a single step forward, putting her chest scales just over my head.

"And she'll get used to it, or she'll kill her," Tairn answers from behind us where the other three—no, four—dragons wait now that Feirge has arrived. *"Either is acceptable."*

"I thought you were against us killing allies?" I glance over my shoulder as his shade envelops me thanks to the afternoon sun. Maybe it's Sliseag moving closer on her right, but there's a reddish sheen to Andarna's scales, and I can't help but wonder when that shimmer will dull to a shade more like Tairn.

"She has yet to prove herself an ally," Tairn notes.

"She still blames me for Luella's death."

"Hey, while we're just standing here…" Sawyer rubs the back of his neck, and his cheeks redden. "I…"

"You…?" I lift my eyebrows at the clearly unfinished question.

"I was wondering if you…" He cringes, then sighs. "Never mind."

"He wants you to teach him how to sign," Ridoc finishes, rocking back on his heels in clear boredom.

"Ridoc!" Sawyer glares his way.

"What? You made that way more painful than it had to be. For fuck's sake, it was like you were leading up to asking her out or something." He visibly shudders.

"What if he had been?" I counter.

"Then I'd be stuck cleaning little pieces of him off our shared floor when Riorson ripped him to shreds." Ridoc shakes his head. "So messy."

"First, Xaden has more than enough confidence to survive me being *asked out*." I glance up at Sawyer. "And yes, I'll teach you to sign. Why would that be embarrassing?"

"I should have learned years ago." Sawyer drops his hand. "And…obvious reasons."

"I'm not fluent enough to make a good teacher, apparently." Ridoc rolls his eyes.

"You'd teach me the sign for *sex* and tell me it was *hello*, just to see what happened when I used it," Sawyer fires back.

"What? I'm not a total dick." A smile curves Ridoc's mouth. "I would have waited until you asked about the word for *dinner*—that way, when you asked her if she wanted to grab a bite with you—"

"Oh!" I blink, putting the pieces together. *Jesinia.* "Don't worry, Sawyer. I've got you. Rhi signs fluently, too. So do Aaric and Quinn, and—"

"Everyone but me." Sawyer sighs, his shoulders dipping.

"Almost didn't make it in time," Rhiannon says, slightly out of breath as she reaches us.

Trager's eyes narrow even further on Rhi as Professor Trissa rounds the corner behind her.

"How's the lip?" Rhiannon asks, winking at Trager.

He moves to step forward, but Maren blocks him, shaking her head.

"I would have covered for you. Did you get your family settled?" I ask Rhi.

They'd arrived late last night, travel-weary and with only the items they could fit in a narrow wagon capable of making it up the Precipice Pass, the winding trading route up the northeast side of the Cliffs of Dralor, bordering the Deaconshire province.

"Yeah." Rhi grins and drops her pack in the surprisingly supple grass next to mine. I swear, it's like the seasons are reversing up in this valley. "Thank your brother for me. He assigned their houses right next to each other near the market square, and they've already picked out a spot to set up shop."

"Will do. And Lukas?" Just the thought of her nephew's perfect, chubby cheeks has me smiling wide.

"Still the cutest boy *ever*." She unbuttons her flight jacket and shrugs it off her shoulders. "They're exhausted, but they're safe. And the fact that I get to see them whenever I want now? Amazing. Plus, I got to show off my signet, and they were appropriately awed."

"That's phenomenal. I'm really happy for you." My posture relaxes, and I take a truly deep breath. Families have been arriving in Aretia for the last week, led in small, unnoticeable groups by the members of the revolution who delivered their offers of sanctuary. Ridoc's dad should arrive any day, but we haven't had word from Sawyer's parents yet.

"You might be wondering why we're meeting in the valley," Professor Trissa says, her breaths perfectly even as she reaches into her pack and pulls out seven printed illustrations, then hands them out to the seven of us.

Another smile tugs at my lips. Jesinia and the others got the printing press up and running.

The illustration's a depiction of a Tyrrish rune, not unlike those in the weaving book Xaden left me when he graduated. After a closer look at the illustration, I recognize it. The series of graduated squares is nearly identical to the hilt of the dagger on my right hip.

"As you are currently the top squad and drift, we have chosen your group as our…test of sorts." Professor Trissa steps back so she can see both lines of us. "You can channel?" she asks the fliers.

"About half power since yesterday morning," Cat answers.

"Mindwork?" the professor asks with a tone of curiosity.

"Not yet," Maren answers.

"But soon," Cat says, staring straight at me. "The drifts are getting stronger every day."

As if I'd forget what it was like to have her running amok in my head.

"So, back to arts-and-crafts hour?" Ridoc asks, folding his arms.

"Who knows how mage lights are powered?" Professor Trissa asks, ignoring his question and reaching into her pack. She removes eight small wooden boards, no bigger than a plate. She puts them in the center of our little stand-off. "Well?"

"Lesser magic," Maren answers.

"The ones you create yourself." Professor Trissa nods. "What about the ones that run continuously in, say, the first-year dorms. The ones that work before you can channel?"

Every rider looks at me.

"They're powered by the excess magic both we and our dragons channel," I answer. "It comes off us naturally, like…waves of body heat, but it's such a small amount that we don't even notice it."

"Exactly," the professor agrees. "And what is it that makes that kind of magic possible? Magic tied to objects instead of a wielder?" She looks us over with expectant, dark-brown eyes, then rubs the bridge of her nose. "Gods, I thought Felix was joking. Sorrengail, you're practically *covered* in them."

I glance down, glimpsing the shimmer of my dragon-scale armor beneath the V-neck of my uniform top, then lock onto the daggers Xaden gave me. "Runes?"

"Runes," Professor Trissa confirms. "Runes aren't just decorative. They're strands of magic pulled from our power, woven into geometric patterns for specific uses, then placed into an object, either for immediate work or usage at a later date. We call the process 'tempering.'"

"That's not possible." Maren shakes her head. "Magic is only wielded."

"It's still wielded." Professor Trissa all but sighs in disappointment at our ignorance. "But just like we store food for winter, a wielder can temper a rune using as much or as little power as they choose, then place it into something." She bends down and picks up one of the boards and waves it in our general directions. "Like wood, or metal, or whatever object the wielder chooses. That rune will activate when triggered and perform whatever action it was tempered for. Unlike alloy, which houses power, runes are tempered with power for specific actions."

Rhi and I exchange a confused glance.

"I see we'll need some convincing." Professor Trissa drops the board and lifts her hands. "First you separate a strand of your power." She reaches forward and pinches air between her thumb and forefinger. "Which can be the most complicated step to learn, honestly."

"Is she pretending?" Ridoc whispers.

Professor Trissa shoots him a sharp-eyed glare. "Just because you can't see my power doesn't mean I can't. Or are you unfamiliar with the process of grounding? Like your shields, your power is only visible to you when you give it form, whether it's the shape of your signet as a rider, or lesser magics, which you are all capable of."

"Point taken." Ridoc puts his empty hand up in defeat.

"Power can be shaped." Her hands move quickly, pulling at pieces of air, then using her fingers to form invisible shapes. Circles? Squares? Was that a triangle? It's hard to tell when we can't see. "Every shape has meaning. The points where we tie the power change that meaning. All of which you will need to memorize." She reaches into the air again, then creates…a rhombus? "The shapes we combine layer the meanings, changing the rune. Will it activate immediately? Sit in suspended state? How many times can it activate before the rune depletes? It's all decided here." She seems to flip whatever she's working on, then pulls another string and does…something.

"Fucking weird," Ridoc mumbles under his breath. "It's like when you're little and you ask your parents to drink from the teacup, knowing there's no actual tea in it."

Rhiannon shushes him.

"Once it's ready"—Professor Trissa bends and grabs the board, then stands— "we place the rune. Until it's placed, it has no meaning, no purpose, and will fade quickly. It's tempering the rune that makes it an active magic." She grabs what I assume is the rune she's been tempering with her right hand, then pushes her palm into the wooden board. "This particular one is a simple heating rune."

"That was simple?" Sawyer asks.

The board smokes, and I lean forward, my eyes widening.

"And there you have it." She turns the front of the board toward the fliers, then shows us. "Once you understand which shapes combine to make what symbols, the combinations are nearly limitless."

My jaw hangs open for a moment. The shapes have been *burned* into what I would have said was a decorative rune about ten minutes ago. I glance down at the illustration in my hands and wonder what the hell the dagger on my hip is supposed to do.

Every shape has meaning. The points where we tie the power change that meaning. I take another look at the multifaceted shape before she flips the board, holding it to face skyward, and my eyes widen with realization.

"It's a logosyllabic language," I blurt. "Like Old Lucerish or Morrainian."

Professor Trissa lifts her eyebrows as she looks my way. "Very similar, yes." Her mouth curves into a smile. "That's right, you can read Old Lucerish, too." She nods. "Impressive."

"Thank you."

"She's ours," Ridoc says to the fliers, pointing at me.

Not sure I'm anything to brag about, considering I barely passed the *history* quiz this morning. At least I'm solid in math, but then again, math doesn't change overnight.

"You're an ice wielder, are you not?" Professor Trissa asks Ridoc.

He nods, and she holds out her hand.

Ridoc uncorks the skin strapped at his hip, then draws the water out from the mouthpeice in a frozen cylinder before walking it to Professor Trissa.

She places the ice on the board, and my gasp isn't the only one heard as the ice dissolves in a matter of seconds and water drips from the sizzling wood. "Be careful of the medium you choose to hold the rune. A bit more power and that board would have gone up in flames."

"Why does no one teach this?" Maren asks, glancing from her parchment to the board.

"It's a skill the Tyrrish once controlled and perfected, but it was banned a couple hundred years after the unification of Navarre, even though many of our outposts and Basgiath itself were built upon them. Why?" She lifts her brows. "I'm so glad you asked. You see, riders are naturally more powerful, given the amount of magic we channel and the signets we wield."

Trager rolls his eyes.

"But runes are the great equalizer," Professor Trissa continues, setting the board on the grass now that it's stopped sizzling. "A rune is only limited to how much power you choose to temper, how long you want it to last, and how many uses it has before it depletes. They banned runes so they wouldn't fall into the wrong hands." She glances at the fliers. "Your hands, specifically. Get good enough at runes, and you can compete with a fair amount of signets."

"So, you want us to…temper this?" Cat asks, studying the illustration with an arched eyebrow. "Out of…magic?"

I hate to admit it, but I'm with Cat on this one—and by the looks on the faces around me, we all are. Even Rhi is glancing at the drawing with trepidation. This feels…overwhelming.

"Yes. With the power you'll learn to separate from yourselves, just like I showed you." Professor Trissa opens her pack and dumps another pile of boards onto the first.

She made it look so *easy*.

"We're going to start with a simple unlocking rune. Easy to build, easy to test." She glances between our lines.

"We can all unlock doors with lesser magic," Trager notes.

"Of course you can." Professor Trissa sighs. "But an unlocking rune can be used by someone who doesn't possess lesser magic. Now let's go. I expect your first runes woven before sunset."

"There's no way we're going to learn how to do that before sunset," Sawyer argues.

"Nonsense. Every marked one has learned a simple unlocking rune the first day."

"No pressure," Rhi mutters.

"Sloane and Imogen can do this?" I ask.

"Naturally." Professor Trissa shakes her head at me.

This is why Xaden had me practicing runes with fabric. Is that man ever going to learn to just tell me things outright? Or am I always going to have to dig information out of him? "'I'll answer any question you ask,'" I mock under my breath. It's hard to ask questions I don't even know *exist*.

"You're supposed to be the best of your year, so stop gawking and get to work," Professor Trissa lectures. "The first thing you'll need to do is learn to separate a piece of your own power. Let it fill your mind, then reach in and visualize plucking a thread of it from the current."

Rhiannon, Sawyer, Ridoc, and I exchange a series of what-the-fuck glances that are echoed by the fliers across from us.

"Advice?" I ask Tairn and Andarna.

"Don't blow anything up." Tairn shifts his weight behind me.

"At least blowing something up would be interesting," Andarna notes, eliciting a growl from Tairn.

"Now," Trissa demands, then holds up a finger. "Oh, and be careful. Power gets temperamental when you pull from it. That's why your bondeds are here. The closer the source, the easier it is for the first time." She looks us over, then folds her arms across her chest. "Well, what are you waiting for?"

I shut my eyes and envision my Archives and the swirling power that surrounds it. The blazing, molten stream of Tairn's power that flows behind his giant door looks capable of consuming me, but the pearlescent flow of Andarna's power just beyond the windows feels…approachable.

Steadying my breath, I reach for Andarna's power—

Boom. An explosion sounds, and my eyes fly open, every head whipping toward Sawyer as he flies backward. He lands just short of Sliseag's claws, a scorch mark left smoking in the grass where he'd been standing.

"And *that* is why we're having this class outdoors." Professor Trissa shakes her head. "On your feet. Try again."

Ridoc walks back and helps Sawyer to his feet, and then we do just that.

Try again. And again. And again.

Before sunset, I manage to weave an unlocking rune, but I'm not the first.

Cat has that honor and, unlike the rest of us, no scorch marks beneath her feet.

CHAPTER FORTY-SIX

"Runes?" Xaden asks a few days later, leaning over my shoulder as I sit at the desk in his room, practicing today's assignment, a triangular piece of torture that's supposed to somehow boost hearing. He picks up one of my five discarded attempts, burned into hand-size wooden disks, and I breathe deeply, savoring the scent of soap on his freshly washed skin.

A private bathing chamber is definitely one of the perks of sleeping in his room.

"We're the trial squad. I meant to tell you last night." I take the delicate strand of pearlescent power and bend it into the third shape in the pattern Professor Trissa gave us for homework, then let it burn brightly in front of me while I gently reach for another. Now that I know what to look for, I see the flow of power clearly before me, somehow both solid and insubstantial, glowing strands that flex under my touch. Seeing it doesn't make pulling individual strands any easier, though.

"I meant to tell you a lot last night, too," he says, setting the disk back down on the desk with the others. "But once I found you in bed, my mouth was otherwise occupied."

My lips curve at the memory as I form the next triangle, this one smaller, and set it within the larger ones floating in front of me. He's been gone more than he's been home, running the weapons from our forge to the front lines near the Stonewater River and filling Tecarus's armory. This trip lasted an extra day when he and Garrick found themselves caught in an attack.

"Do you want my help?" he asks, skimming his mouth down the side of my neck.

"That is…" My breath catches when he reaches the collar of my armor. "Not helping."

"Pity." He kisses the side of my neck, then stands, leaving me to my homework. Good thing, too, since I have class in a few minutes.

"This is why you left me that book in Navarre, isn't it?" I take the next strand and form the circle that should stabilize the shapes within and place it around the rune. That should do it.

"I wanted you to have a head start," he says, picking up Warrick's journal from where I abandoned it on the desk and thumbing through it.

"Thank you."

"This is impossible to read," Xaden mutters, closing the journal and setting it back on the desk before walking to where his uniforms hang next to mine in the large armoire.

I grin at the domesticity of it. There's nothing I wouldn't do to keep it just like this between us. "My father taught me." I shrug, examining my rune for anything I might have missed. "And Dain and I used it as a secret code when we were kids."

"Never pictured Aetos as the Old Lucerish type," Xaden notes.

Picking up the wooden disk in my left hand, I gently move the buzzing strands of power, pressing them into the disk. Much better than the last five. "You put runes into my daggers," I say, turning in the wooden chair.

My lips part and I blatantly ogle Xaden as he pulls his uniform from the armoire, a towel wrapped around his hips. How did I not notice he'd been basically naked behind me this whole time? Such a missed opportunity…

"Keep looking at me like that and you're not making it to class," he warns, his eyes darkening as he crosses the floor and tosses his clothing on the bed.

I force myself to turn away. Brennan warned Xaden that the first time I was late for class because of my sleeping arrangements, I'd be back in my assigned room. "You put an unlocking rune into my dagger, didn't you?" I ask, sliding all the disks besides the one I just finished into my pack, ignoring Warrick's journal, which mocks me from the edge of the desk. "That's how we got out of the interrogation chamber."

"A variation of it, yes."

Holding the best rune of my attempts, I lift my pack to my shoulders and slip my arms through the straps as I stand, turning to face him. His torso is still gloriously bare, but unfortunately—or fortunately for my schedule—he has pants on. "Care to elaborate?"

To my consternation, he goes for his socks instead of a shirt.

"You can do the unlocking rune. It's simple enough." He shrugs. "I added an element of need into the rune. So, you can't walk up to any door and open it just because you want to, but if the dagger's on your body and picks up on the *need* for a door to unlock, it will. If you'd made it up to the forge at Basgiath, it would have opened to your need." Sitting on the edge of the bed, he puts on his boots.

"I had the key the entire time?" My eyebrows rise, and if I didn't already love him, I would have fallen right then.

"You did. Are you feeling adventurous with questions today?" A corner of his mouth quirks.

I grip the disk and sink my teeth into my lower lip. The problem with being happy amidst the utter chaos we've caused is that I'm terrified to ask even a single question that might jeopardize it. "What's the rune on the stone you keep by the bed? That's what it is, right?"

"Yes, a complicated one at that." He sits up and reaches for the little gray stone, then offers it to me as he stands. "There's not a person alive who knows how to replicate this. Colonel Mairi was the last."

Liam and Sloane's mom. I take the palm-size stone and study the intricate lines of the rune. "It had to have been giant when she tempered it."

"I assume so. She must have collapsed it to fit when placing them into the stones."

"Stones?" I look up at him. "As in more than one?"

"A hundred and seven," he answers, watching me with expectation.

The marked ones. He wants me to ask.

"What does it do?" I rub my thumb over the blackened design.

"*Did.* It's a protection rune, but it was only intended to be used once." He runs his hand through his damp hair and pauses. "As you get better with runes, you can pull elements into them. Things like strands of hair or even other full runes for locating things. Or protecting them. This particular rune was made to protect someone of my father's bloodline."

"You." I look up and hand the stone back. "You're his only child, right?"

Xaden nods. "Each of the children of the officers were given them before our parents left for the Battle of Aretia. We were told to carry them at all times, and we did, even to the execution." His fingers brush mine as he takes the stone.

I damn near stop breathing, keeping my eyes on his.

"It was designed to counter the signet of the rider whose dragon would kill them." He swallows. "But it could only activate when killed by dragonfire."

"Which is the primary method of execution for traitors," I whisper.

He nods. "I kept it closed in my fist—we all did—as we stood there, watching our parents put into lines for execution. And the second they were..." His shoulders rise as he takes a deep breath. "…burned, heat raced up my arm. The next time I felt anything like that was after Threshing."

My eyes widen, and I close my hand over his. "The rebellion relics?" That must be why the swirling marks always start on the marked ones' arms.

He nods. "Our parents knew they'd die one way or another, and the last thing they did was make sure we were protected. I keep it purely for sentimental reasons." Leaning toward me, he kisses my forehead, then turns away, putting the stone on his bedside table. "I like it when you ask me questions," he says, leaning over to grab his uniform shirt. "Anything else you want to know?"

It's on the tip of my tongue to question why he didn't tell me about the deal he made with my mother and ask if it influenced his feelings for me. But then he stands, and my gaze catches on those silver scars on his back—the scars she put there—and I just can't ask. He told me that he's loved me since the first time we kissed. That should be enough. I shouldn't need to know anything more about the deal than what she said to me… Or maybe I don't want to, not if there's any chance it could shake our relationship.

"Violence?" He tugs his shirt on and turns.

"Nothing else to ask." I force a smile.

"Everything all right?" Two lines appear between his brows. "Bodhi mentioned that Cat isn't making it easy on you, and you've had a couple of lightning strikes—"

"Bodhi needs to butt out." There's no chance I'm letting Xaden worry about me before heading out for multiple days. Rising up on my toes, I kiss him softly. "I'll see you tonight."

Disappointment flashes through his eyes right before he cups the back of my neck and slants his mouth over mine for another blissful second, then pulls back. "You're close, but you need a directional cue for that rune."

"My rune is great, and I'll ask for help if I need it." I kiss him quickly just because I can, then rush out the door so I can make it to class in time. The second I'm in the hallway, I lift the disk to my ear.

Noise rushes in. Bootsteps pounding above me, doors closing ahead of me, people shouting beneath me—there's too much input to make any sense of it.

"I hate it when he's right," I mutter as I skid into class.

Naturally, Cat has tempered her rune *perfectly* when I get there, which makes me almost want to ask for Xaden's help, but he's already gone before I'm done with my classes for the day.

· · ·

"**W**e've given you two weeks to figure out how to integrate peacefully, and you have yet to do so, much to our disappointment," Devera lectures us the next week from the side of the center mat, Emetterio and one of the flier professors by her side. The sparring gym is only a fraction of the size of Basgiath's—fitting nine mats total—and it's packed with every cadet in Aretia standing shoulder to shoulder.

Including the fliers.

Until now, we've only been put together for rune lessons in very small increments and mealtimes, which usually end with at least one thrown punch.

"What the hell do they expect?" Rhiannon folds her arms next to me. "We've been killing each other for centuries, and we're supposed to what…weave flowers into each other's hair and confess our deepest, darkest secrets all because they gave us a luminary and hiked a cliff?"

"It's a little tense," I agree, holding the conduit in my right hand and rolling my aching shoulder, hoping it will forgive me for daring to sleep on it wrong. I have a lesson with Felix in two days, and I'm cramming as much power into the little glass orb as I can.

My power's been flaring all too frequently, with the fliers hurling insults every chance they get, insinuating that I dropped Luella to her death instead of Visia.

There's a clear divide in our ranks: a sea of black on my right and a swath of tan on the left, with a wide strip of bare floor between us. More than a dozen cadets wear bruises from the brawl that erupted yesterday in the great hall between Third Wing and two drifts.

"Yesterday's outburst of violence was absolutely unacceptable," the fliers' professor starts, her auburn braid sliding over her shoulder as she turns her head, addressing all cadets, not just the fliers. "Working together is what's going to make a difference in this war, and it has to start here!" She turns her finger on the rider cadets.

"Good luck with that," Ridoc says under his breath.

"We'll be making significant changes," Devera announces. "You will no longer be separated for classes."

My stomach pitches, and a mumble of discontent rolls through the gym.

"Which means—" Devera raises her voice, quieting our side of the makeshift formation. "You will *respect* one another as equals. We may be in Aretia, but as of today, we've decided the Dragon Rider's Codex still applies to every cadet."

"And as their guests," the flier professor says, placing a hand on her ample hip, "all fliers will abide by it." A disgruntled murmur rolls through their half. "Is that clear?"

"Yes, Professor Kiandra," they respond in unison.

Damn. That's kind of impressive, even if they do sound like infantry.

"But we acknowledge that we cannot move forward without addressing the hostility among you," Emetterio says, his gaze shifting between the groups. "At Basgiath, we had a method for addressing grievances between cadets. You may ask for a challenge—a sparring match that ends when one of you is unconscious or taps out."

"Or dies," Aaric adds.

The fliers collectively gasp, and the majority of us roll our eyes. They wouldn't last a day at Basgiath.

"Without *killing* your opponent," Emetterio continues, talking directly at Aaric before moving on, "for the next six hours, every request—between cadets of the same year—for challenge will be granted. You will address your grievances *once* on these mats, and then you will put them behind you."

"They're going to let us beat the shit out of them?" Ridoc asks quietly.

"I think so," Sloane whispers in response.

"It's going to be a phenomenal afternoon." Imogen grins, cracking her knuckles.

"They've been trained to fight venin," I remind them. "I wouldn't underestimate them." When it comes to signets, we can blast them out of the fucking skies, but hand-to-hand? There's a good chance we're outmatched.

"You may only challenge one opponent, and each cadet may only be challenged once," Emetterio says, holding up his forefinger and lifting his thick brows. "So choose carefully, because tomorrow, the rider or flier you hold contempt for may be off-limits."

Oh shit. My stomach drops. There's only one reason someone couldn't call a challenge, but they wouldn't…would they?

"Challenges between squadmates are forbidden under the Codex," Devera explains to fliers, then turns to us. "And tomorrow each squad of riders will absorb one drift of fliers."

Guess they *would*.

Anger flushes my cheeks, and Rhiannon and I exchange a perturbed glance, which is mirrored by everyone in our squad, especially Visia.

"Note that I said *absorb*." Devera stares pointedly at us. "You will not be *teamed up* or *partnered with*. You will fuse, you will meld, you will *unify*."

This goes against everything we've been taught. Squads are sacred. Squads are *family*. Squads are born after Parapet and forged through the Gauntlet, Threshing, and War Games. Squads aren't merged unless they're dissolved due to deaths—and we're the Iron Squad.

We do not bend. And we definitely do not *blend*.

"And if you don't"—Professor Kiandra's tone softens as her gaze sweeps over the gym—"we will fail when it's time for combat. We will die."

"We'll take your requests now," Emetterio says, concluding the lecture portion of today's festivities.

Lines form for those requesting challenges, and it doesn't surprise me that most of the queue is wearing brown. They have far more reason to hate us than most of us do to hate them.

"We are the Iron Squad, and we'll act like it," Rhiannon orders as the last of the line approaches Emetterio. "We stick together and travel mat to mat with any challenge leveled on us."

All eleven of us agree.

The first challenges are called, and I'm not surprised when Trager names Rhiannon to come to the mat. No doubt he's still pissed about the punch she delivered on the flight field.

She wins in less than five minutes, and his lip is bleeding again.

The third-year leader from Cat's drift, the stocky one with the necklace of scars, Bragen, knocks Quinn unconscious with a punch combination that leaves my mouth hanging.

Once Imogen is called to the mat by Neve—another third-year in Cat's drift, with short strawberry-blond hair and deep-set eyes—I sense the pattern.

"This is about me," I say quietly to Rhiannon when Imogen lands a solid kick to the other girl's head.

"That makes it about *us*," she responds. "Please tell me you're wrapped and wearing your armor."

I nod.

Imogen and Neve exchange precise, calculated blows until Devera calls it a draw after they're both bleeding.

"Catriona Cordella and Violet Sorrengail," Devera announces. "Disarm and take the mat."

"Don't do this." Maren tries to talk Cat out of it, but there's nothing but determination in her narrowed gaze.

"Of-fucking-course." I hand the conduit to Rhiannon.

"Why am I not surprised, Cat?" Imogen glares across the mat before turning toward me.

"It's fine. Predictable but fine." One by one, I unsheathe all thirteen of my weapons and hand them to her.

"She's got at least five inches on you, so watch for her reach," Rhiannon says quietly.

"From what I remember, she's quick on the attack and won't leave you much time to react, so commit to your moves. Don't hesitate," Imogen adds.

"All right." I breathe in through my nose and out through my mouth, fighting like hell to steady the nerves that have my stomach doing somersaults. If I'd known this was where today was headed, I would have acted earlier, maybe laced her breakfast with the fonilee I saw growing on the ridge just beneath the valley.

"You've got this," Rhiannon says with a nod. "You were trained by the best."

"Xaden," I whisper, wishing he was here and not on the border.

"Me." She nudges me with her elbow and forces a smile.

"Violet?" Sloane moves to Imogen's side. "Do me a favor and kick her ass."

My mouth tugs into a real half smile, and I nod at her before stepping onto the mat. Guess nothing unites foes like a common enemy, and for some reason, Cat has decided I'm hers. The mat has the same density as the ones at Basgiath, the same feel under my boots as I walk to the center, where Cat waits with a malevolent smirk.

"Scratch her eyes out," Andarna suggests. *"Really. The eyes are the softest tissue. Just jab your thumbs in there—"*

"Andarna! Use some common sense," Tairn snaps. *"The kneecaps are a much easier target."*

"Quiet time, now." I slam my shields up, muting Tairn and Andarna as much as possible.

"No weapons. No signets," Devera says. "Match ends when one of you is—"

"Unconscious or taps out," Cat finishes without taking her eyes off me. "We know."

"Begin." Devera steps off the mat, and I block out the noise around me, giving all my focus to Cat as she takes a familiar fighting stance.

I do the same, keeping my body loose and ready for movement. If she's quick on the attack like Imogen said, then I'll need to play defense.

"This is for Luella." She comes at me with a combination of punches that I block with my forearms, shifting my body so the blows glance off without their full impact. It's…easy, like I know the choreography. Like it's muscle memory. Her stance adjusts, and I jump back a second before she kicks out. Connecting only with air, her balance falters as I land, and she stumbles sideways.

Holy *shit*. She fights like Xaden.

He trained both of us.

Defeating a dark wielder begins with knowing where they rank in age and experience. Initiates have reddish rings to their eyes that come and go depending on how often they drain. Asims' eyes fluctuate in degrees of red, and their veins distend when riled. Sages'—those responsible for initiates—eyes are permanently red, their veins perpetually distended toward their temples, expanding with age. Mavens—their generals—have never been captured for examination.

—Venin, A Compendium
by Captain Drake Cordella, the Nightwing Drift

CHAPTER
FORTY-SEVEN

So much for thinking I have the advantage.

Her eyes flare, like she's come to the same conclusion as we circle each other, and then they narrow in a way that makes my stomach clench. Devera may have set the rules, but something tells me Cat is about to break them.

"Does it bother you?" she asks, lowering her voice as she raises her hands. "Knowing he taught me first? That I had him first?"

"Not at all, since I have him now." I swallow the sour jealousy that rises with the burn of bile in my throat.

"Really?" She jabs, and I weave. "The thought that I know what he tastes like?" She throws another combination that I block, then retreats as if it was nothing but a test. "How his weight feels above me?"

I will not vomit on this mat. I refuse.

"Nope." But shit if that picture doesn't play out in my mind as vividly as a nightmare.

Her hands on his skin, her mouth on the curling lines of his rebellion relic. Envy and anger roar in my ears, dulling my senses, and I blink rapidly to clear the image, but heat prickles my skin as power rises within me.

She comes at me again, and I throw my forearm up in a block, but she shifts unexpectedly, and when I block for the cross, she nails me with a left hook.

Pain explodes in my cheek, right on the bone, and I stagger backward, touching my face reflexively to check for blood, but she hasn't split the skin.

"I think it does bother you," she says softly as we circle again. "Seeing me here, where I belong. Sleeping right down the hall. I bet it keeps you awake at night, knowing I'm a better match for him in every way, counting the seconds he tires of your frail excuse for a body and comes back to the woman who knows exactly what he likes and how he likes it."

Every word she speaks raises my temperature, but I refuse to take the bait, so I'm ready when she charges forward this time, twisting as she jabs for my face. I manage to counter, landing my blow in the same location she'd hit me.

Pain shoots up my wrist, but I'm happy for the sting.

"You know what bothers me?" I ask as she bounces back on her toes, cursing when the back of her hand swipes at her cheek and comes away bloody. "That you're obsessed with fighting over a man." Rage fuels my movements when I go on the attack, but she's ready for every combination I have.

Because they're all fucking *his*.

"You going to do something about this?" I hear someone ask from outside the haze of anger that's slowing my reaction time.

"She wouldn't want me to." The answer comes from the edge of the mat as Cat lunges toward me, and I'm too focused on her hands to block her feet when they sweep mine out from under me.

I'm airborne for a heartbeat, and then my back hits the mat, rattling my bones and stealing my breath.

Cat follows me down, leaning her forearm against my throat and cutting off my air supply as she leans in, her mouth right next to my ear. "You seem angry, Violet. Are you just now realizing you're nothing special? That you're just a convenient placeholder he can fuck?" Her laugh is low and cruel. "I know how good he is. I'm the one who taught him that little trick he does with his fingers. You know, the one where he curls—"

I see *red* and throw every ounce of my rage into the punch I deliver to the side of her ribs, right where Xaden taught me to stab, and then I draw back and do it again, savoring the dull sound of the *crack* of her ribs and the jarring pain that shoots through my hand, along my wrist, and up my arm because I know I just delivered ten times worse.

She cries out, falling off me to her uninjured side, and I gasp, filling my lungs before hurtling my body after hers, rising onto my knees and slamming my fist into the side of her face with a satisfying *thud* before she can recover. Now she has my mark on both sides.

"What the fuck is *wrong* with you?" I snap. "It is *not* my fault that he doesn't love you!"

"Of course he doesn't!" She grabs hold of my arm and rolls with astonishing speed, twisting it behind my back.

White-hot agony streaks through me, making my mouth water.

"He's not capable of loving *anyone*," she hisses in my ear. "You think I'm so petty that I'd attack another woman over *love*?"

"Yes." I force the word out through gritted teeth as she shoves me downward, controlling me by the arm she could easily break, the shoulder she's an inch away from dislocating in this position. The side of my face smashes into the mat.

Think. I have to think. But *fuck*, all I can do is *feel*. Anger and envy pound through my veins with every heartbeat, strangling logic until I'm nothing but rage.

"You're too short-sighted for him," she says quietly, like she's afraid of being heard. "He thinks ahead, just like me. Gods, do you even know why he didn't kill you that first year? I do. Because he trusted me to look ahead *with* him."

She knows about the deal with my mother. He told *her*.

My fingers tingle, and I know I'll lose feeling in the entire limb soon, but that doesn't stop my body from trembling with fury…with rising power.

Think. I have to think. She knows all my moves, at least the ones Xaden taught me.

"Look at where we are. *Riorson House.*" Her mouth is close enough to my ear that I can *feel* how hard she's breathing. "Who wouldn't love all that power and the case it comes in? But I'm sure as hell not fighting you over a *man's affections.* I'm going to war with you for a *crown.* That was the reason we were engaged. It was promised to me, and I'm not giving it to a damned *Sorrengail* who chose to drop the flier instead of her squadmate. Your entire family deserves to die for what you've put us through."

A *crown*? Engaged? My chest aches because it all makes sense. Two aristocratic families in need of an alliance. And I'm nowhere near nobility.

"And gods, get some control over your emotions, would you? You're so fucking weak it's pathetic." Her words are a string of hisses.

Fuck her.

Rhiannon trained me, too.

I rear back with my head as hard as I can, cracking cartilage from the sound of it, and the pressure vanishes from my arm and shoulder, freeing me.

She yelps, the sound slightly muffled, and I thrust my uninjured elbow backward, hitting the soft tissue of her stomach just like Rhi taught me.

Blocking out the pain, I burst up onto my knees, then twist, throwing my weight onto her. She topples backward, and I take advantage of the opening, driving my knee into her sternum, then reaching for her throat.

I'm going to fucking *kill* her. How *dare* she come after me, like I had a choice in Luella's fall? Like I had anything to do with Xaden's choice to leave her? Fuck that. How dare she come after what's *mine*. He isn't a crown. He isn't a stepping stool for power. He isn't a tool to elevate her standing. He's *everything*.

Her face turns a mottled shade of red, and her eyes widen with panic.

"Violet!" someone shouts. A woman. A friend, maybe?

Power sears my veins and lifts the hair on the back of my neck, rising with the force of a tornado. Her hands tear at mine, but I only squeeze harder.

"Damn it, Cat!" someone else yells from the opposite side. "Tap out!"

Tap out? I don't want her to submit. I want her to cease existing.

"I honestly don't care if you kill her, Violence." Xaden's voice filters through the rage that holds me with the same unbreakable grip I'm using to choke the life out of my opponent. *"But* you *will."*

I blink as his words clear just enough of the fog for me to feel the slowing of her pulse beneath my hands, but I don't release my grip.

"Tap!" multiple people shout.

"I respect whatever choice you make."

But I'm not making a choice. There is no choice. There's only the swirling, chaotic vortex of anger and jealousy and—

She's fucking *cheating*, using mindwork.

"Get out of my head!" I scream so loudly my throat burns.

Cat glares up at me, and the anger burns even hotter as she tries to work her thumbs beneath my hands, wrath burning in her eyes.

She's not going to tap out. She'd really rather die than lose to me.

"I don't want to kill her." I have to let go. But my hands don't get the signal.

"Then don't." His voice wraps around my mind, and the anger ebbs just enough to let me realize he's here. It's been a week since I've seen him, and he's *here*.

And I love him more than I hate her.

I yank my hands from her throat, but I can't make my body move any farther than that. *"I need your help."*

Cat wheezes for breath as heavy bootsteps approach from the left.

Xaden's arms surround me, lifting me to my feet, and I cling to the love I feel for him with my fucking fingernails to keep from letting the anger consume me.

"I didn't tap out!" Cat croaks as she scurries backward, her neck bearing my handprints.

"Riorson!" Devera snaps. "Why would you interfere in a chall—"

"Because she cheated!" Imogen shouts. "She used mindwork!"

"She's the one who's unhinged!" Cat's voice breaks multiple times, and she jabs her finger at me.

"*I'm* unhinged? I'll show you unhinged when I kill you for fucking with my head!" I lunge against Xaden's arms, but he holds tight.

"Let me know if you actually mean it." He lifts me off my feet.

"Catriona!" Professor Kiandra forces her way through the line of fliers. "Tell me you didn't…" She glances from Cat to me and back again. "Let go, Cat!"

"Fuck her!" Pure hatred emanates from every line of Cat's body and only fuels the fire beneath my skin. "And fuck her entire *family*. I hope you all die for what you've done to us!"

Surging against Xaden's strength does no good. He has me locked down. But power whips through me and releases with a searing *crack*.

Lightning strikes simultaneously with thunder, flashing white across my vision. Cadets scream and the scent of smoke fills the air.

Xaden flings a hand outward, and shadows stream toward the wooden bleachers, snuffing out the quickly growing flames.

"Bragen! Maren! Escort Catriona to her room," Kiandra orders. "Her gift is limited by—"

"Distance. I know." Xaden swings me up over his shoulder like I'm a bag of grain.

"Riorson!" Rhiannon calls out, catching his attention before tossing the conduit to him.

He catches it one-handed, nods, then strides for the exit.

Every instinct tells me to kick, to thrash, to beat him into letting me go, but I force myself to stay completely still as he carries me out into the hall, past the gaping faces of leadership who line the walls, waiting for the challenge period to be over.

"It will ease," Xaden promises.

And it does. The fog of Cat's power fades with every step, leaving me raw, like the ruins of a beach after a tidal wave recedes. Gods, how am I going to keep this from happening again?

Xaden doesn't even break a sweat as he walks past the great hall, then surprises me when he doesn't turn into the foyer. Nope, he carries me straight into the Assembly chamber, startling the four who are gathered there, including Brennan.

And I'm in control of enough of my emotions to feel every ounce of the embarrassment that heats my face, but my body still vibrates with anger. At least it's *my own* genuine anger this time.

"What are you—" my brother starts.

"Get out," Xaden demands, crossing the room and climbing the steps of a new dais, where the chairs of the Assembly sit behind the long, formal table. "All of you. Right fucking now."

They glance at one another, then shock me to my toes by doing exactly that—grabbing a stack of parchment from the corner table and leaving, shutting the door behind them on their way out.

Xaden tosses the conduit into the massive middle chair before lowering me, my body sliding against his until my toes touch the dais. When our gazes collide, he arches his scarred brow. "She got you good." He reaches for my face, turning my head gently to examine my cheek. "But I think you got the last word."

"And how many of those humiliating words did you hear?" I don't want the answer, but I need it.

"All of them."

Fuck.

As a result of the Treaty of Aretia, the power to represent the province of Tyrrendor in the King's Senarium has hereby been transferred from the House of Riorson to the House of Lewellen.

—PUBLIC NOTICE 628.86,
TRANSCRIBED BY CERELLA NEILWART

CHAPTER FORTY-EIGHT

"The things she said…" I clench my aching fists and notice I've busted the skin across my knuckles.

"I know." His gaze rakes over me in a look I know all too well—assessing me for injuries.

"She said I'm just a convenient placeholder for you to fuck."

"I heard. How hurt are you?"

"I'm fine." Unless he's asking about my pride. "My shoulder's a little pissed, but I think my face took the worst of it."

"All right." He wraps his arm around my waist, pulls our lower bodies flush, and moves forward, forcing me to step back so the backs of my thighs hit the chair behind me. "Sit."

"Sit? I just lost my shit and threw my control out the window in front of the entire quadrant because of the venom she spewed—the emotions she shoved down my throat—and all you have to say is *sit*?"

He lowers his head, invading my space. "Nothing I could say right now is going to erase her words from your head, so sit, Violence. We'll do the talking afterward."

"Fine." I sink down onto the thick cushion, and my feet come off the ground. This particular piece of furniture was definitely built for someone Xaden's height. Two of me could sit in this thing. "She wants you for your name."

"I know." He braces his hands on the arms of the chair and leans in, brushing his lips over mine. "And you love me in spite of it. That's one of the many reasons I will *always* choose you." He drops to his knees in front of me and works the laces on my boots with quick, efficient movements.

"What are you doing?"

His mouth curves in a wicked smile that instantly elevates my pulse and transforms the heat of anger simmering in my blood into an even hotter fire.

My lips part as one boot hits the dais, the other following immediately after.

"In here?" I glance over his head at the empty hall. "We can't—"

There go my socks.

"We can." He flicks his wrist, and the clicking sound of a lock echoes off the stone. "My house, remember? They are all *my* rooms." His eyes lock with mine, holding me willingly captive as his hands slide up the length of my legs, caressing my inner thighs, waking every nerve ending along their path before he reaches for the buttons of my sparring pants.

My breath catches.

"My house. My chair. My woman." He punctuates each claim with a flick of his thumb, popping button by button free. Need floods my body, flushes my skin with a heady, addictive rush.

He grips my hips with both hands and yanks me to the edge of the chair, then cups the back of my neck and pulls me into a devastating kiss. My lips part, and the second he licks into my mouth, his tongue stroking mine, my core fucking *melts*.

The kiss is slow and sensuous, our mouths meeting again and again as I weave my fingers through his hair and completely, totally surrender. He senses the shift, growling low in his throat, and the kiss spins out of control in less than a heartbeat, turning wild and urgent, tasting of that sweet madness that only exists between us.

He's the only person in this world I can't get enough of. The only one I constantly crave. Love. Chemistry. Attraction. Desire. Everything between us keeps me constantly burning like an ember; a single touch is all it takes to send us both up in flames. By the time he breaks the kiss, his breathing ragged as he orders me to lift my hips, I don't care where we are as long as he puts his hands on me. The whole Assembly could walk through those doors and I wouldn't notice, not with the way Xaden's looking at me. The heat in his eyes could melt iron.

He hooks his fingers into the waistband of my pants and my underwear, then tugs them down my legs, kissing the tops of my thighs, the curves of my knees, and every inch of skin he uncovers, drawing soft sighs and impatient whimpers from my lips.

Fabric hits the dais, leaving me bare from the waist down.

"Xaden." My fingers tug at his hair, my heart pounding so hard I can't help but wonder if he can hear it, if the whole world can.

Instead of rising so I can get my hands on him, he pushes my knees wide.

I gasp at the cold rush of air between my thighs, but an instant later, his mouth sets me on *fire* as he drags his tongue from my slick entrance to my clit. White-hot pleasure streaks through my body like lightning, and I cry out, the sound filling the hall.

"This is what I fantasize about when I'm away from you," he says against my heated skin. "Your taste. Your scent. The little gasps you take right before you come." He settles in, his hands splaying wide on my inner thighs, pinning me in place as he uses his tongue to rob me of every thought. He swirls around that sensitive bud over and over, teasing, arousing, driving me higher and higher, but denies me the very touch I need. *"Is this what you think about? My mouth between your soft thighs?"*

Gods, how can he *think*, let alone form coherent sentences?

He scrapes his teeth over me delicately, and I gasp at the sensation, then whimper when his tongue follows. I can only moan when he slides a long finger inside me, and his answering groan vibrates through every nerve in my body.

"Yes." It feels so exquisite that I muffle my next cry with my fist. *"More."*

It's always *more* when it comes to him.

He alternates between quick, teasing flicks and long, lazy licks, building an ever-tightening spiral of pleasure deep within me. Another finger joins the first, stretching me with a delicious burn, and my hips rock as he thrusts them in a slow, hard rhythm that makes me crave every part of him.

Power rises, scalding my already flushed skin, crackling in the very air around us.

Without stopping, he releases my thigh and reaches around my hip, then retrieves the conduit. *"Take it."*

"I want you." My fingers slide from his hair to grasp the orb, my hips chasing every stroke he gives me, my breaths coming in uneven pants.

"You have me." I whimper at the mindless pleasure that rushes up my spine. *"And I have you exactly where I need you."*

Even my hand can't muffle the primal sounds he drags from me as his tongue matches the rhythm of his fingers, pleasure whipping through me with every stroke, gathering, building, stringing my body tight as a bow.

Gods, the sight of him kneeling, fully clothed, the leather of his flight jacket against my bare thighs, pushes me all the way to the edge and burns itself into my memory.

My thighs tremble when he curls his fingers inside me, stroking that sensitive wall that makes stars blink in my eyes. "Xaden…" My breaths stutter.

"Right there. Those gasps. That's what I hear when I wake, already hard for you."

With the next caress, pleasure and power crest through me, over me, in simultaneous waves that crash again and again. There's no thunder, no strike, only the hum of energy in my hand that flares with the strokes of Xaden's mouth and fingers.

But there's no release, either. No gentle letdown. Only the waves of infinite ecstasy that come without breaking.

He lifts his head, keeping me in a suspended state of indescribable bliss as his eyes lock with mine.

"I can't take it," I manage to say as the waves come and come with no end in sight.

"Yes, you can. Look at where you are." He grasps my hip and surges upward, propelling me deeper into the chair until my back hits the blackened wood, and still, he keeps stroking, holding me prisoner with my own pleasure. Brushing his lips over mine, he smiles. "Look at how beautiful you are, Violet, coming for me on Tyrrendor's throne."

Holy shit. I'd known that's where we were, but I hadn't *known*.

He grasps one of my thighs and drapes it over the arm of the throne, then braces his knee at the edge of the cushion and lifts my other leg over his shoulder as he slides down my body, lowering his head as he works his fingers ceaselessly, beckoning the endless waves.

Oh *gods*. I'm going to die. Right here. Right now.

"Every time I have to sit with the Assembly, I'll be thinking about this, about *you.*" He slides his hand under my ass and lifts me to his mouth, then replaces his fingers with the thick stab of his tongue.

Searing pleasure rips through me, arching my back, and there's no time to muffle the cry he wrings from me, but he doesn't exactly stifle his deep moan, either.

"I can't." My heart has to give out at some point.

"You can and you will." He strums his thumb lightly over my swollen clit, and my hips jerk.

The pleasure is sharper than a knife.

Shimmering onyx wraps around my mind and *everything* intensifies. *A driving, pounding, uncontrollable need courses through me with every beat of my pulse, demanding an outlet, demanding I rip through the confines of the leather and trade her sweet taste for the incomparable perfection of sinking into her when she comes.*

Xaden. I gasp for breath, gripping the conduit so tightly I prepare for the sound of breaking glass. It's his desire flooding our bond, compounding my own. His desperation. His power brushing against mine.

I need to fuck her, to flip her over the arm of this throne and drive into her, but I can't. I need her nail marks in the wood, need her cries filling this whole fucking house, need her knowing what I can be for her—anything and everything she needs. She's heaven in my mouth. Flawless. Mine. And she's almost there. Gods, yes, her legs are shaking, her walls are fluttering around my tongue. I love her so fucking much.

I shatter, splintering into a million glittering shards of bliss as I scream out his name. Power and light course through me without burning, and I arch again and again, coming apart at the seams of what I think is me but might be him.

He untangles from my mind, and I mourn the loss even as my body slackens. It's my lungs I feel draw air, my own power that crackles through the orb in my hand before settling, my own heartbeat that finally slows as the last of the orgasm fades.

"What the hell did you do?" I lift my head, my eyes flaring when I realize Xaden isn't tangled with me.

He's three feet and a million miles away, backed against the Assembly's table, gripping the shadow-covered edges with white knuckles, his eyes squeezed shut so tightly I wince.

"Xaden?"

"Just need a second."

I manage the awkward task of sitting up and move to stand.

"Stay right there." He holds his hand out.

Every line of his gorgeous body is drawn tight, and his leathers… Gods, that has to be *painful*.

"Come here," I whisper.

"No."

My head draws back. "You can't possibly think I'm going to let you get me off *twice*, let alone whatever the fuck that last time was, and not—"

"That's exactly what's happening." His eyes flash open, and the heat, the longing, the desperation I see there feels like it could be my own…because a few seconds ago, it was.

"I felt how much you need me." I shift forward to the edge of the chair—throne—whatever. "You want me over the side of the throne, right? Grasping onto the arm so my nails scar it."

"Fuck." The table groans under his grip. "I should *not* have done that."

"Oh, you definitely should have. It was quite possibly the hottest moment of my entire life. You ever want to bring me to my knees or win an argument? That's a sure bet."

A tight smile curves his mouth at the reference to his words from last year.

My toes touch the dais. "You gave me what I fantasize about—"

"Please don't." The words are forced through gritted teeth. It's the "please" that stops me in my tracks. "I'm hanging by a thread, so I'm begging you. Please. Don't." He hangs his head, and shadows slip across the dais, pushing my clothes toward me.

Confused is an understatement, but I stand up and quickly get my clothes back on down to my socks, then pick up my boots. "Do you want to clue me in on why you're keen on torturing yourself?"

He exhales just a shade short of a sigh. "Because I need you to see I'm more than capable of worshipping your body without reciprocation. You're not a convenient placeholder for me to fuck."

This is about *Cat*?

"I know that." So much for the afterglow of the world's longest orgasm. I'm right back to pissed.

"But you don't." He releases his death grip on the table and points at the throne. "Sit."

"For a repeat performance?"

A corner of his mouth quirks upward. "So I can help you with your boots. You're too short for the chair."

"Well aware," I mutter, sitting back on the throne and letting my feet dangle. "I don't like…not reciprocating."

He lifts my left foot, slipping on my boot.

"I don't like you thinking you're not the center of my fucking world, yet here we are. And before you start another argument, I'll fuck you later tonight. Trust me. I'm making a momentary point, not a lasting vow of masochism." He braces my foot on his thigh and ties the laces.

The sight eases some of the tension in my chest. No one would ever believe that scary, badass Xaden Riorson would tie *anyone's* shoes.

"I thought you were going to kill her," he says quietly.

Right. Back to Cat.

"I almost did." I lower one foot, then raise the other at his cue. "Would that have been unforgivable to you?"

He finishes tying my boot, then lets go of my foot. "Nothing you could ever do would be unforgivable to me." Stepping back, he leans against the edge of the table again. "And I don't particularly care if Cat lives, but I'm not cheering for her to die, either. She's a necessary yet volatile ally, and Syrena would be a disastrous enemy to make. But I do care that you would have regretted killing her."

And in that rage, I would have if he hadn't shown up.

"How could you ever love someone like her?"

"I didn't." He shrugs. "You are the first and only woman I've ever loved."

"You were just engaged to her for…" I pause. "I don't even know how long you were engaged for." I feel…stupid.

"I would have told you if you'd asked. That's the problem here, Violet—you don't ask."

"It's not like you ask me about my exes." I cross my legs.

"Because I don't want to *know*, which I suspect is the same reason you continue to not ask me about the things that actually bother you, but let's just ignore that like we usually do. Seems to be working out for us." He lays the sarcasm on thick.

I look away because he's right, damn him. Avoiding the potentially devastating questions, like why he's never told me about the deal he made with my mother, seems prudent when there's a possibility of losing him over a wrong answer.

He moves on when I fall quiet. "Cat and I weren't engaged, we were betrothed—and yes, there's a difference to me."

"Now who's arguing semantics? Let alone on behalf of the woman who just warped all of my emotions and turned me into an abyss of rage." Some of which is creeping back in.

"We'll get to that in a second. The betrothal clause of the alliance kicked in when she turned twenty." The table creaks as he fully sits back against it. "We tried it out for about three-quarters of a year, but we weren't compatible, and it came to light that Tecarus was never going to let us have the luminary anyway. He wanted us to use it *there*. I ended the betrothal, which, as you know, caused some problems."

"Weren't compatible?" I can't blame the insidious stab of jealousy on Cat this time. That burning sensation in the pit of my stomach is all me. "That's not exactly what she implied about your sex life."

"You don't have to like someone to fuck them." He shrugs.

My jaw slackens, considering what we just did.

His head tilts as he watches me. "As I recall, you didn't exactly like *me* the first time—"

"Do *not* finish that sentence." I jab my finger in his direction.

"On the other hand, I was already in love with you."

My posture softens. That right there is why I'm hopelessly in love with *him*. Because no one else gets to see him like this. Just me.

"Hardly seems fair, now that I think about it." He drums his fingers on the table. "And I wanted you too badly to care that you didn't feel the same way about me, not that I'd given you *any* reason to. Fuck, I wanted you to *run* in the opposite direction."

"I remember." Our gazes lock, and my fingers curl with the need to touch him. I reach for the conduit instead.

"Good. Maybe you'll remember that the next time Cat goes digging around your head."

"Digging? She *made* me jealous!" The word is bitter on my tongue.

"She didn't *make* you anything."

Felix won't miss the conduit if I throw it at Xaden's head, will he? "Oh really? You heard what she said. How would you feel if one of my previous lovers had you on the mat for a challenge, then told you that he knows how I taste?"

He tenses.

"How I feel on top of him?" I lower my tone, letting sex slide over every single word. "How he had me first and insinuates that he plans on having me last, too?"

His jaw flexes, and shadows curl around the legs of the table. "She wasn't my first by a long shot."

"Not the point. You want me to ask more questions? Then don't avoid them."

"Fine. None of your previous lovers are riders, unless there's history I'm unaware of when it comes to Aetos, so they'd never have me on the mat. I'm guessing infantry, but again, I don't want to know, so I don't ask."

"I didn't sleep with *Dain*." But he's ridiculously on the mark with the infantry guess.

"I knew that the second he kissed you after Threshing. It looked awkward as fuck." He shoves his hand through his still-mussed hair. "And to answer the question, I'd feel jealous, which is something you have a unique ability to bring out in me. And then I'd kick his ass, partially because that's what I do when someone challenges me, and more importantly for implying there's any other future besides the one where you and I are endgame."

My breath abandons me in a rush I refuse to call a sigh. Gods, he *ruins* me when he says things like that.

"What else were you feeling on the mat?" he asks.

"Anger." I glance up at the high, beamed ceiling in defeat. "Inferiority. Insecurity. She threw everything she had at me, and it worked."

"Anger, I understand. She said a lot that pissed me off, too." He shakes his head. "But inferiority is something you'll have to explain, considering you're more powerful than any other cadet."

"It has nothing to do with signets." I gesture to the giant chair I'm seated on. "She pointed out that you're a Riorson."

"You've known that since Parapet." He taps the rebellion relic along his neck.

"That's not what I mean. You just called this chair a throne."

"Because it is. Or it was before the unification." Another infuriatingly casual shrug.

I blink as realization smacks me straight in the face. "Wait. Are you…are you the *king* of Tyrrendor?"

"Fuck, no." He shakes his head, then pauses. "I mean, yes, technically, I'm the Duke of Aretia by birth, but Lewellen's on our side and doing just fine at governing the province. Even if Tyrrendor became independent, I'm more useful on the battlefield than on a throne. We're off topic. I know damn well you don't feel inferior to me, so who? Cat?"

I press my lips between my teeth. "I think I liked you better before you decided that feelings were something we need to discuss."

"Sorry to inconvenience you, but this year the role of Violet Sorrengail"—he points to me—"will be played by Xaden Riorson"—he taps his chest—"who will drag her, kicking and screaming if he has to, into a real relationship with real discussions, because he *refuses* to lose her again. If I have to evolve, you do, too." He folds his arms across his chest.

"Is he done talking in third person?" I pick at the metal band around the orb. "Cat was right in one regard. She is the better match. She's noble by birth, brave for becoming a flier, driven, ruthless, and mean as hell, just like you." Fuck, they're pretty much the same person.

His eyes flare, then narrow. "Hold on. Do you somehow think that *I* find you inferior to her?"

My shrug isn't exactly nonchalant.

He shifts like he's about to move toward me, then stops himself, putting his hands firmly back on the table. "Violet, you were just in my thoughts. You know I think you're perfect, even when you frustrate the shit out of me. Now tell me about the insecurity. I thought we handled that last year."

"Sure, before I knew you were leading a revolution, and before you declared you'd always keep secrets, and way before some beautiful aristocrat who you used to be betrothed to but conveniently was never mentioned appeared with her big brown doe eyes and sharp-ass claws at our bedroom door half naked—"

"She what?" His eyebrows rise.

"—and then has the nerve to tell me I'm not special just because you like to fuck me."

"I do like to fuck you." A slow smile curves his mouth. "I love it, actually."

"Don't side with her!" My nails dig into the cushion beneath me. "Ugh!" The shout echoes off the rafters, and I cover my face with my hands. "Why does she turn me into such a fucking mess? And how do I make it stop?" I'll end up killing her before solstice.

I hear his bootsteps, then feel his warm hands gently clasp my wrists.

"Look at me."

Slowly, I lower my hands, and he holds them in his as I open my eyes. He's right where we started this chat, on his knees in front of me.

"I don't want to have this discussion again." He uses the wingleader voice, then softens. "But I will. You're about to get some hard truths, because I wasn't clear enough in Cordyn."

My shoulders straighten.

"You raged today because you were angry." He strokes his thumbs over my pulse. "You got jealous because you were jealous. You grappled with inferiority because for some reason I can't understand, you feel inferior. And you lashed out with insecurity because I think both of us are just figuring this out as we go. Own your feelings like you did last year and be honest with me. Cat can't plant emotions, warp them, or even sway them unless you are already headed that way. Cat can only amplify what you're already feeling."

I swallow, but the lump forms in my throat anyway. It's all...me.

"Yeah, it's a shitty realization. I've been there." He laces his fingers with mine. "She can take you from irritation to full-on rage in the span of a minute or two. And yes, she's really fucking powerful, but so are you. But the only weapons she wields are the ones you hand her. You want to keep control of your emotions? You need to have control in the first place."

"I can't..." A pit forms in my stomach. "I haven't been in control since Resson," I admit in a whisper. "I let Tairn's emotions take over. I'm carrying around a conduit so I don't set your house on fire with my own damned power. I failed at the wards and now nearly failed tests, making shit decisions, fucking up left and right, and people's lives are in the balance. I keep hoping I'll find my feet, but..." I shake my head.

He lifts a hand to my cheek, avoiding the swollen lump where Cat hit me. "You have to find your center again, Violet. I can't do it for you." He holds my gaze, letting his words sink in, before adding, "You are a creature of logic and facts, and everything you know got turned upside down and shaken. You'll never know how truly sorry I am for that. But you can't just sit there and hope. You want it to change, then you have to figure it out, just like Gauntlet. You're the only one who can." He says it a hell of a lot kinder than he did last year.

"But how do I find my center while in the middle of a Cat storm?" I moan.

He glances away. "Look, Cat got to you because you weren't wearing your daggers. The one with the intertwined Vs? It's runed to protect you from her gift. Keep them on until you find your feet, and she can't fuck with you. Same thing happened in Cordyn. You took them off to wear that lacy thing you called a dress. Fuck, I wanted to rip it off with my teeth." His jaw ticks.

"You gave the daggers to me last year." My hand slides to his wrist.

"I figured she'd find a way to make my life difficult for breaking the agreement, and that would inevitably involve you." He leans in. "I love you.

She will never sit in this seat. She will never wear a Tyrrish crown. She's *never* had me on my knees in front of her." His mouth curves into a wicked grin that makes me instantly ready for it to be tonight. "And I've also never fucked her with my tongue."

My lips part and heat stings my cheeks.

"Now, can we consider this matter discussed? Unfortunately, I have a briefing to get to."

I nod. "I have class."

"Right. Physics?" he guesses as we both rise to our feet.

"History." I take his offered hand and we walk off the dais. "Which I'm surprisingly awful at, it turns out. Something about having read all the wrong books."

"Maybe you should find the right ones." His smile mirrors mine, and for a blissful second, it all feels…normal. If that's a word that could ever apply to us.

"Maybe."

When we reach the bustling hallway, he cups the back of my neck and pulls me in for a quick, hard kiss. "Do me a favor?" he says against my mouth.

"Anything."

"Come to bed *early* tonight."

Fliers and riders are held equal in every regard with the exception
of wing structure.
Riders will maintain their wings, sections, and squads,
as well as retain their commands.
Every drift will be absorbed by a squad, and their leader will
replace the squad's current executive officer for unit
cohesiveness and efficiency.

—ARTICLE TWO, SECTION ONE
THE ARETIA ACCORD

CHAPTER
FORTY-NINE

"I feel like you're the only one who isn't surprised," Imogen says as we stand in the courtyard after formation the next morning.

"We're the strongest squad. They're the strongest drift. I don't know how the rest of you *are* surprised." I shrug, glancing over at Cat's drift, who all seem to be turning various shades of purple and green from yesterday's challenges.

Same goes for our squad.

"Here we go." Rhiannon hands six of us familiar green patches.

"Do we really have to give them these?" Ridoc's lip curls at the patch we worked our asses off for, the patch the first-years fought to hold on to.

"Yes," Rhiannon chides. "It's the right thing to do. As of this moment, they're part of our squad, whether we like it or not."

"I choose to not," Sloane remarks.

Laughing, I run my thumb over the patch.

"I'll take one to Cat," Rhiannon says quietly. "You don't have to—"

"I've got it." I give her what I hope is a reassuring smile. "Let's do this."

"Let's do this," she repeats. "Second squad, time to move."

We cross the frost-covered courtyard together, and I tap the dagger at my left hip, making sure it's right where I left it.

Xaden loves me. He chose me. I will be the most powerful rider of my generation.

Cat only has the power I choose to give her, with or without my dagger.

The six fliers tense as we approach.

"I think they've chosen to *not* as well," Sloane mutters to Aaric.

Cat narrows her eyes on Sloane, and I step between them, offering Cat the patch. "Welcome to Second Squad, Flame Section, Fourth Wing, also known as the Iron Squad."

Similar greetings are given around us, but I keep my eyes locked on Cat as she stares at the patch like it might bite her. "Take the patch."

"What are we supposed to do with them?"

"We sew them onto our uniforms," Ridoc answers from beside me, making a back-and-forth motion with his hand to simulate pulling a needle through his uniform—as though explaining a patch to children.

"Why…?" Her gaze sweeps over us, catching on the different patches like she's never noticed them before.

I point to my collarbone. "Rank." Then my shoulder. "Wing. Iron Squad. Signet. Patches are earned, not given. Riders, and fliers now, choose whatever location they want for every patch besides wing and rank, none of which are worn on flight leathers, which is probably why you never saw Xaden wearing them. He generally abhors patches." There. That wasn't so bad. I can be civil.

"I knew that." She snatches the patch out of my hand. "I've known him for *years*."

Rhiannon lifts a brow from my other side.

I note the twinge of jealousy that she's been privy to parts of his life that I haven't, but there's no rage, no sour jolt of insecurity, and no self-loathing. I fucking *love* my daggers for a whole new reason.

Her eyes widen slightly as if she senses that she can't touch me, then narrow into malicious slits. Civility is definitely not on her agenda.

"Like I said." I offer her a bright smile. "Welcome to the quadrant's only Iron Squad." Pivoting, I hook my arm through Rhiannon's, and we start to walk away with the rest of the riders in our newly enlarged squad.

"Being in the same squad doesn't change the fact that it's still my crown," she blurts.

"Let's feed her to Sgaeyl," Rhiannon whispers as we pause.

I look at Cat over my shoulder. "Did you know that Tyrrendor hasn't had a crown in more than six hundred years? Turns out they melted them all down to forge the unification crown, so good luck with that."

"It's going to be fun making your life as miserable as you've made mine."

Oh, fuck civility.

"Gods, she really can't help herself, can she?" Rhiannon says under her breath.

"Cat, stop it," Maren chastises. "You're being ugly. I've told you over and over that she didn't drop Luella. She fell. It's as simple as that."

"You're welcome to try and make me miserable," I tell Cat, letting go of Rhiannon to walk back to the flier. "Oh! And one more thing." I lower my voice just slightly, well aware of every head within our squad that turns our direction.

"What?" she snaps.

"That trick you mentioned? You know, with the fingers?" A slow smile spreads across my face. "Thanks."

Cat's eyes bulge.

Imogen laughs so hard she snorts as I walk back to Rhiannon.

"Damn. Just…damn." Rhi claps a few times.

"I fucking love you." Ridoc throws his arm around my shoulders. "Anyone hungry? I woke up somewhere I hadn't exactly planned on and missed breakfast."

"I would," I tell him, "but I have plans in the library."

"The library? Then me too," Sawyer chimes in, following quickly.

"I'll go with," Rhiannon says with a nod.

"If the three of you are going, then so am I," Ridoc adds.

"You guys don't have to come with me," I say once we're halfway through the foyer.

"Oh, we needed to get away from Cat." Ridoc waves me off. "You're just the excuse."

"Her abilities are…horrifying," Sawyer concludes. "What if she decides to make me hate you?"

"Make Xaden hate you?" Rhiannon's eyebrows rise.

"She can't." I shake my head.

"Or make you instantly horny for some random flier, and then you're not the only one in that bed when Xaden rotates back," Ridoc muses. "Her signet—or whatever they call it—is fucking terrifying."

"She can only amplify the emotions you already have," I explain to them.

"We could kill her." Sawyer reaches for the door handle. "All the fliers are still struggling with the altitude, and their gryphons are still sleeping half the day, according to Sliseag, so they're probably at their weakest."

We all fall quiet, not out of shock but because we actually consider it for a few seconds. At least, I do. "We can't kill her. She's our squadmate."

Wait, is that really the only ethical line there?

"You sure?" Sawyer tilts his head. "Say the word and we'll bury a body. We still have a couple of hours before we're due in Battle Brief."

"Good idea. I could use a snack." Andarna's tone is indecently excited.

"We do not eat our allies," Tairn lectures.

"You never let me have any fun."

I crack a genuine smile. "I appreciate the offer."

We walk into the library, and I breathe in deeply. The scent in the two-story room is different than the Archives. Parchment and ink still smell the same, but there's no earthy undertones because we're aboveground, with light streaming in through the windows. Only the shelves of the first floor are filled with books, but I've made it my personal mission to see that the second floor looks the same within the next decade.

Stone may not burn, but books do.

"What are we doing here, anyway?" Ridoc asks as I swing my pack off my shoulder, picking the first empty table I see to rest it on. He gestures at Sawyer, who is scanning the back of the library. "I mean, we all know what *he's* doing here."

"Finding my center." My answer earns me two very perplexed looks. "Tecarus sent some books back for me with Xaden after the weapons run yesterday, probably still hoping to get on my good side." One by one, I remove the six books he gifted, stacking them on the table and placing the protective bag with Warrick's journal on top. "Krovlish is not my strong suit."

"Krovlish isn't anyone's—"

I grin as Sawyer cuts off mid-sentence at the sight of Jesinia.

"Good morning," he signs at me. "Is that right?"

"You've got it."

He takes off in her direction.

"Would have been more fun my way. She's got a great sense of humor," Ridoc mumbles.

"He's learning to sign!" Rhiannon smiles and sits on the edge of the table. We shamelessly turn to watch Sawyer greet Jesinia.

"And he's already coming back?" Ridoc's brow furrows.

I glance at the clock. "He only knows about four phrases, but he's catching on."

"So is Krovlish Jesinia's specialty?" Rhi asks, picking up the top book, which is an accounting of the first emergence of the venin after the Great War. At least, I think it is.

"No." I shake my head as the library door opens exactly at seven thirty. Right on time as always. "It's his."

"Seriously?" Ridoc mutters as I walk away from the table.

"You asked to see me?" Dain folds his arms across his chest. "Of your own volition? No orders or anything?"

For a second, I hesitate. Then I remember that he stabbed Varrish, he called the formation to split the quadrant, and when the truth came to light, he chose exile with a group of people who despise him because it was the right thing to do. "I need your help."

"All right." He nods without waiting for an explanation.

And just like that, I remember why he used to be one of my favorite people on the Continent.

"That's not the word for rain," Dain says the next day, tapping a symbol in Warrick's journal with the bottom of his pen as we sit in the wardstone chamber, our backs against the wall, our legs stretched out in front of us. The noon sun beats down on us, but it's still cold enough to see my breath.

"I'm pretty sure it is." I lean in, studying the journal that's equally balanced on his leg and mine.

"Did you ask Jesinia?" he asks, turning from the ward-centered entries of the journal back to the beginning.

"She thought it was rain, too."

"But she specializes in Morrainian, right?" He tilts his head and studies the first entry.

My eyes widen, jumping to his profile.

"What?" He glances at me, then abruptly turns his attention back to the journal. "Don't look so shocked that I remember Jesinia's specialization. I listen when you talk." He flinches. "At least I used to."

"When did you stop?" The question leaves my mouth before I can catch it.

He sighs and shifts his position slightly, just enough to tell me he's nervous. Two years in the quadrant couldn't rid him of that tell. "I don't know. Probably when I said goodbye to you on Conscription Day. Mine, of course, not yours."

"Right. You said hello to me on mine." A smile tugs at my lips. "Actually, I think you asked what the hell I was doing there."

He scoffs, then leans his head back against the wall and looks skyward. "I was so pissed…and scared. I finally made it to second year, gained the privilege of visiting other quadrants so I might be able to see you, and instead of being tucked away safely with the scribes, you show up dressed in black for the Riders Quadrant on your mother's orders, so dizzy that I still have no idea how you made it across the parapet." His throat works as he swallows. "All I could think was that I'd just survived a year of hearing my friends' names called on the death roll, and I was going to make damn sure yours wasn't. And then you hated me for trying to give you what you'd always told me you wanted."

"That's not why I hated—" I press my lips in a tight line. "You wouldn't let me grow up, and you were so fucking pigheaded that you knew what was right for me. You were never like that as a kid."

He laughs, the self-deprecating sound echoing in the chamber. "Are you the same person you were when you crossed the parapet?"

"No." I shake my head. "Of course not. First year hardened me in ways…" I catch his look, complete with raised eyebrows. "Oh. Guess it changed you, too."

"Yeah. Living only by the Codex will do that to you."

"Part of me wonders if that's why they push it on us so hard. They transform us into their perfect weapons, teach us to critically think about *everything* except the Codex and the orders they give."

He scratches the brown scruff of his beard and looks down at the journal. "Where are your translations for the beginning? Maybe we can compare the symbols."

"I skipped ahead to the ward entries, seeing as that's what we needed."

He blinks. "You…skipped? *You,* out of all people, didn't read a book from start to finish?" The flash of a smile he tries to hide hits me somewhere in the vicinity of my stomach, reminding me of the days when he'd been my best friend, and suddenly this is too much.

I scramble to my feet, dust my leathers off, and walk toward the stone.

"Vi," he says quietly, but the cavernous space amplifies it so he may as well be shouting. "We finally going to talk about what happened?"

The stone is the same empty cold under my hand as it was the night I failed to raise the wards. "Do you know how to imbue?" I ask, ignoring his question.

"Yes." His sigh feels strong enough to knock the wardstone over, and when I glance over my shoulder, I see him set the journal down on my pack and rise to his feet. Seconds later, he's standing next to me. "I'm sorry, Violet."

"It feels like it should be imbued, don't you think?" I drag my fingertips over the biggest of the etched circles. "Reminds me of the way raw alloy feels. Empty."

"I'm sorry for the role I played in their deaths. I'm so fucking sorry—"

"Did you steal my memories every time you touched my face last year?" I blurt out, letting the cold seep into my palm.

Silence fills the chamber for a long moment before he finally responds softly. "No."

I nod and pivot to face him. "So just when you needed information you couldn't ask me for."

He lifts his hand and puts it against the stone mere inches from mine, splaying his fingers wide. "I did it by accident the first time. I was just so used to touching you. And you'd gotten close to Riorson, and my father had pretty much bragged about the way your mother cut into him. I knew he had to be after revenge, but you wouldn't listen to me—"

"He was never out for revenge. Not with me." I shake my head.

"I know that *now*." He squeezes his eyes shut. "I fucked up." A deep breath later, he opens them. "I fucked up and trusted my dad when I should have trusted your judgment. And there's nothing I can say or do that's going to bring them back—bring Liam back."

"No, there isn't." My eyes water, and I force out a grimace of a smile that quickly falls.

"I'm so sorry, Violet."

"It's not all right," I whisper. "I don't know how to even start making it all right. I just know that I can't think about Liam and look at you at the same time without…" I shake my head. "I don't want to hate you, Dain, but I'm not sure I'll ever be able to—" My attention shifts to my hand. My very *warm* hand next to his on the stone. "Are you imbuing the stone?"

"Yes. I thought that's what you wanted."

"It is." My head bobs. "How long do you think it would take to fully imbue something this big?"

"Weeks. Maybe a month."

I move my hand, then return to my pack and crouch to stuff everything inside. "I need your help with the journal. And that's not fair, because I need to know that we won't talk about this—about Liam and Soleil—again. At least not until I have a lot more distance." Once it's all put away, I stand, facing Dain again.

His shoulders droop, but his hand is still on the stone. "I can do that."

"Thank you." I glance up at the overcast sky stories above us. "I'm usually free for about a half hour this time of day."

"Me, too, and I'll work on imbuing the stone."

"I'll ask Xaden to help, too." I slip my arms through the straps and settle the pack on my shoulders.

His hand falls from the stone. "About Riorson—"

My entire body tenses. "Be very careful with your words."

"Are you in love with him?" he asks, his voice breaking on the last word as he pivots to face me fully. "Because Garrick and I heard the end of what he said in the interrogation chamber, and trust me, *I* might be in love with him after that declaration, but are you? Really and truly?"

"Yes." I hold his stare long enough that he knows I mean what I say. "And that's never going to change."

Dain's jaw flexes and he nods once. "Then I'll trust him as much as you do."

I nod back slowly. "I'll see you tomorrow."

"Tomorrow," he agrees.

Mastery of one's signet does not occur at Basgiath,
nor in the years directly after.
No rider alive truly believes they've reached the
limitations of their power.
The dead ones may feel differently.

—Major Afendra's Guide to the Riders Quadrant
(Unauthorized Edition)

CHAPTER
FIFTY

"Better." A week later, Felix pops a grape into his mouth, then motions to the stacked rocks and the tendrils of steam at the base that only last a second before they're whisked away by the wind and snow. "You almost hit it that time."

I clench the energy-warmed conduit in my hand. "I did hit it." I sway on my feet and shake off my exhaustion. Too many late nights have been spent translating Warrick's journal from the beginning, too many lunches have been eaten in that cold wardstone chamber, and I've definitely spent too much time with Dain.

I'd almost forgotten how good he really is with languages, how quickly he catches on.

"No." Felix shakes his head, then plucks another grape from the bunch. How are those things *not* frozen? The ground has accumulated about six inches of snow in the hour we've been out here. "If you'd hit it, the rocks wouldn't be there anymore."

"You said to use less power, remember? Smaller strikes. More control." I shake the orb in his direction. "What would you call that?"

"Missing the target."

Snowflakes sizzle into steam as they land on the bare skin of my hands, and it's all I can do to not glare at the professor.

"Here." He shoves the bunch of grapes into the pack at his feet, then reaches for the orb, plucking it from my hand. "Strike the conduit."

"I'm sorry?" My eyes bulge as I swat a loose tendril of hair from my face.

"Strike the conduit," he says like it's the simplest task, holding the metal-and-glass orb only inches away from my fingers.

"I'd kill you."

"If only you could aim," he teases, his smile flashing white. "You clearly understand how energy and attraction work, as evidenced by how you took those wyvern out, right?"

"I struck into the cloud." My brow crinkles. "I think. I can't really explain it. I just knew that lightning can exist within a cloud, and when I wielded, it was there."

Felix nods. "It's about the energy fields. It's quite similar to magic that way. And you"—he touches my hand with the orb—"are the greatest energy field of all. Summon your power, but instead of letting the conduit have it all, cut it off yourself."

I shift my weight and swallow hard, fighting the tide of fire that lifts the hairs on my arm. Imagining the Archives doors shutting all but the last few inches, I allow only a fraction of Tairn's power to reach my hands.

My fingertips graze the metal of the orb, and it crackles with the familiar sight of whitish blue tendrils of pure energy branching from my fingertips against the glass and gathering into a single, delicate stream at the alloy medallion in the center of the conduit. Unlike the shimmering strands I pull from Andarna's power to temper runes, this is physical, like a tiny, sustained lightning strike. A smile tugs at the corners of my mouth as I let the power flow from me into the conduit just like I do every night, imbuing stone after stone now that I know how to change them out once they're fully imbued. "I love watching it do that."

It's the only time my power is beauty without destruction—without violence.

"You're not watching it, Violet. You're doing it. And you're supposed to love it. It's better to find joy in your power than it is to fear it."

"I don't fear the power." How could I when it's so beautiful? So varied? I'm afraid of *myself.*

"You shouldn't be," Tairn lectures. He's been commenting off and on the last hour—whenever he hasn't been trying to get Andarna to stop chasing the two new flocks of sheep Brennan had moved into the valley. *"I chose you, and dragons make no mistakes."*

"What's it like to go through life so self-assured?"

"It's…life."

I manage not to roll my eyes by keeping all my focus on limiting Tairn's power.

"Good. Keep going. Let it flow, but think trickle, not flood." Felix slowly draws the conduit away. "Don't stop."

Every muscle in my body tenses, but I do as he asks and don't cut the stream of power. Tendrils of that same white-blue energy stretch the inch of airspace between my fingers and the orb.

"What…" My heart starts to pound so hard I can feel it in my ears, and the five separate filaments of power pulse in time with its beat.

"That's you," Felix says softly, gentler than he's ever been with me as he draws the orb away another inch, then another. Then again, I'd be careful with me right now, too, if I were him. "Increase slowly."

The doors to my Archives open just another foot or so, and the power stretches with no pain and only moderate heat, evaporating any unlucky snowflakes in its path.

"You're starting to get it now, aren't you?" Felix retreats a full step, and my hand begins to tremble as I fight to amplify the power just enough to reach the conduit but not strike.

"Get. What?" My arm is full-on shaking now.

"Control." He grins, and I startle, my gaze swinging back to his.

Power bursts through the doorway and rips through me in a streak of scalding heat, and I throw my hands up—and away from Felix—a second before the strike splits the clouded sky, singeing the mountain on impact less than thirty feet up the ridge.

Felix's Red Swordtail puffs steam in agitation, but all I feel from Tairn is pride.

"Well, you *had* control." Felix hands the conduit back to me. "But at least that means you're capable. For a while there, I wasn't sure."

"I wasn't, either." I study the orb as if I've never seen it.

"You wield your power like a battle-ax, and sometimes that's exactly what's needed. But you of all people"—he gestures to the daggers sheathed in my flight jacket—"should understand when a dagger is called for, when only the precise cut will do." He lifts his pack from the ground and slings it over his shoulder. "We're done for today. By Monday you'll be able to keep that power flowing from—shall we say ten feet?"

"Ten feet?" There's no fucking way.

"You're right." He nods, turning toward his antsy dragon. "Make it fifteen." His head tilts to the side, and he pauses as if he's talking to his dragon. "When you get back to the house, tell Riorson we'll need both of you in the Assembly chamber at five o'clock."

"But Xaden isn't—" I lower my shields and sure enough, there he is. The shadowy pathway between our minds is strong with proximity and heavy with... weariness?

"You're home early. Everything all right?"

"No." He doesn't give any details, and his tone doesn't invite further questions.

"Is Sgaeyl all right?" I ask Tairn as I walk up the forearm he's dipped for me.

"She's unharmed." Frustration and anger simmer, then quickly scald our bond, and I swiftly shield him out to keep from losing control over my own emotions.

A half hour later, after flying back to the valley and watching Andarna show off her developing ability to extend her wing while counting to thirty with enthusiastic applause, I walk into the chaotic halls of Riorson House and head straight for the kitchen.

Once I have a plate of what I need, I start up the sweeping staircase and find Garrick, Bodhi, and Heaton talking on the second-floor landing. The look on Garrick's soot-covered face matches the ominous weight of Xaden's mood, and when Heaton turns their head, I nearly fumble the plate.

The right side of their face is one giant contusion, and their right arm is splinted from the elbow down.

"What happened?"

Garrick and Bodhi exchange a glance that makes my stomach sink, even knowing that Xaden is alive—and not in our bedroom on this floor, but four stories above me.

"They took Pavis," Heaton tells me quietly, looking to see that we're not overheard.

I blink. That can't be right. "That town is only an hour's flight east of Draithus."

Heaton nods slowly. "Took seven of them and a hoard of wyvern. Town was overrun before we even got there. Your sister—she's all right, just taking Emery to the healers for a shattered leg. She ordered us out after—" Their voice breaks, and they look away.

"After Nyra Voldaren fell during our mission today," Garrick finishes.

"Nyra?" She was the quadrant's senior wingleader last year and was damn near invincible.

"Yeah. She went in to defend a group of civilians that had taken shelter near the armory, and..." His jaw works. "And there was nothing left of her or Malla. It was just like Soleil and Fuil, completely drained. I'm sure they'll update everyone in Battle Brief tomorrow, but they recalled all first and second lieutenants to Aretia to regroup."

"I think they're going to change the wing structure," Heaton adds.

"They have to," Garrick agrees. "Leaving the less experienced riders back from the front doesn't do a damn thing when the front is this fucking fluid."

"Did they take Cordyn?"

Garrick shakes his head. "Skipped right over it and hundreds of other miles. They targeted Pavis and stayed there."

"It's a good staging point"—Bodhi drops his voice when a trio of fliers out of First Wing walk by—"for Draithus. Has to be."

They're coming for us.

Many of our most esteemed tacticians have tried to estimate the approaching tipping point—where the outcome of the war may have been decided even though we still fight. Many believe it will come in the next decade. I fear it will arrive much sooner than that.

—Captain Lera Dorrell's Guide to Vanquishing the Venin
Property of Cliffsbane Academy

CHAPTER FIFTY-ONE

We split as the hallway grows too crowded, and I continue up and up the stairs, climbing to the fifth floor, then nodding to Rhi and Tara as I pass by the open door to Rhi's room. Clearly, by their wide smiles, they don't know yet, and I decide to give them a few more minutes of blissfully ignorant happiness and keep walking down the long hallway to the back stairs.

The service stairway is dark, but mage lights wink on as I climb the steep, wrought-iron spiral staircase to its end. I open the door with lesser magic, then step out onto the narrow walkway that runs along the apex of the roofline and close it behind me.

Xaden sits on the edge of the small defensive turret thirty feet away, and the only shadows surrounding him are the ones the dying afternoon light casts. If I didn't feel his turmoil saturating the bond between us, I'd think he was up here for the view, the very picture of control.

Step by careful step, I cross the eastern line of the roof, careful not to let the breeze rip the plate from my hand or screw with my balance.

"What did I tell you about risking your life in order to talk to me?" he asks, his gaze focused on the town below.

"I'd hardly call that risking my life." I set the plate on the wall, then climb up to sit next to Xaden. "But I do now understand how you're so damn good at Parapet."

"Been practicing since I was a kid," he admits. "How did you know I was up here?"

"Other than being able to track you through the bond? You told me in a letter that you'd sit up here waiting for your father to come home." I reach for the plate, then hold it in front of him. "I know chocolate cake isn't going to fix this, but in my defense, I got it for you when I'd just thought you'd had a shit day, before I knew what really happened."

He glances at the slice, then leans in and brushes his mouth over mine before grabbing it. "I'm not used to people taking care of me. Thank you."

"Get used to it." The cold seeps into my leathers from the wall beneath us, and I note the heavy gray clouds moving in from the west. "It's already snowing up the pass. I bet we get seven inches tonight."

"Maybe more if you're good." A corner of his mouth lifts as he cuts into the cake with the fork.

"You're making dick jokes?" I brace my hands on the top edge of the wall.

"You're talking about the weather." He takes a bite, then cuts another one and hands me the fork.

"I was being considerate and giving you the option of not talking about what happened. Would you rather I talk about how translating is going with Dain?" I take the offered bite and give the fork back. Damn, no wonder he loves this cake. It's better than anything we had at Basgiath.

"I'd rather you stop being considerate and ask." His gaze locks with mine.

I swallow, getting the feeling he's not just talking about today's loss. "Were you there?"

"Yes." The fork clicks against the plate as he sets it in his lap.

"Tairn didn't tell me."

"I think Sgaeyl somehow blocked him out." He cocks his head to the side. "Pretty sure we're *both* blocked out right now, which means—"

"They're fighting." There's a hard wall beyond my own shields.

"Garrick and I flew in from Draithus once Emery put out the call, but by the time we got there…" He shakes his head. "Imagine Resson, but about ten times the size. Ten times the number of civilians."

"Oh." The cake settles in my stomach like ash, and we both fall quiet. A long moment passes before I rise to the challenge in his eyes and ask, "What are you up here thinking about?"

"We're outmatched." He looks away and flexes his jaw. "Outmatched and spread too fucking thin to be anything but a nuisance to them. We can't communicate fast enough. We aren't effective or any kind of real barrier when we're sending out riots of three." His gaze shifts eastward. "They can take the rest of Poromiel—take us—whenever they want, and I have no clue why they don't. We have no idea how many of them are assembling in Zolya or where the fuck all these wyvern are hatching from. There's no plan except hold the line, and the line isn't holding."

"We weren't ready." I look out over the rapidly growing town, noting the dozens of new roofs under construction and the uncountable number of chimneys letting out smoke from the homes within.

"We never could have been ready," he counters, lifting the fork, then stabbing it into the cake. "So don't go adding this to the list of things you blame yourself for. Even if we'd waited to come after the forge was running, after we had enough riders to imbue the alloy and temper runes for the daggers…" His shoulders dip in a sigh. "I'll never say this in front of the others, but we're fifty years too late."

The next breath I take is heavy and strained by the tightness in my ribs.

"What do we do about it?" Besides the obvious—Dain and I have to translate faster, just in case there's any actual hope of raising the wards. We already know that one of the symbols I translated originally was incorrect. Rain isn't *rain*. It's *flame*. Which, of course, helped us not at all.

"What we do isn't my decision. Your brother's the tactician, and Suri and Ulices command the army." He shoves a bite into his mouth.

"It's *your* city." His province, really.

"The irony is not lost on me." He hands me another forkful of cake, but this bite has lost its sweetness and goes down like sand. "Your sister *ordered* me off the field."

My eyebrows rise.

His laugh has a hard, sarcastic edge. "She ordered *me*. I had killed one of them and was retrieving my dagger—another problem, I might add—when the second one channeled right behind Sgaeyl. If she'd launched a second later, this cake would have gone to waste." He sets the fork down.

My heart starts to pound erratically. There's not a mark on him, and yet I'd almost lost him without even knowing he'd been that close to never coming home again. The thought is so unfathomable that I'm stunned silent.

"She swept me up in a claw, but your sister saw what happened and that's when she called it a loss. Not because Nyra died, or the three fliers from the footwing drift, or because we only had five dragons left." He shakes his head. "She called it because I was with them, and she wouldn't risk you."

"Is that what she told you?" The first flakes of snow descend.

"She didn't have to tell me. It was pretty fucking obvious."

"Then you don't know—"

"I do," he counters, then immediately closes his eyes. "I know. And through the anger and the horror of watching all those civilians flee, watching them *die*, I realized she treated me like every marked one has treated you since Threshing. Like you're just a vulnerable extension of me."

"I don't think anyone would ever mistake you for vulnerable." I reach for his hand and lace our fingers. "But yes."

He finds my gaze and closes his hand around mine. "I'm sorry."

"Thank you, but as annoying as it is, I get it. We're tethered." I shrug.

He kisses me quiet, hard, and quick. "For the rest of our lives."

B y the time a week passes, no one bats an eye at the sight of Dain and me huddled at a library table long after most cadets have found their beds for the night. We're still meeting at noon as well, and Xaden stops in when he can to help imbue the stone. And that little strand of lightning Felix has pushed me to sustain? Turns out that can imbue, too.

Desperation sinks her claws into me by the week after. We have nearly the entire journal translated, but the passage about raising the wards still isn't different enough from my first, failed interpretation to act on. We definitely get that Warrick insists that once the blood from one of the six powerful riders is used on one stone, it can't be used on the other he's referenced carving.

"Have you noticed his phrasing is so much more casual in the rest of the journal compared to the one section we actually need to understand?" Dain rubs his eyes and sits back in his chair beside me. "Like he's deliberately fucking with us from the grave."

"True." There are only four entries left. What in Malek's name will we do if the answer isn't in one of those? "He has no issue doling out advice on authoring the Codex—

"Or detailing whatever mess of relationships the six of them got into." Dain nods, cracking a huge yawn.

"Exactly." I glance over at him. "You should get to bed."

"You should, too." He glances over at the nearby clock. "It's almost midnight. I'm sure Riorson is wondering—"

"He's not here." I shake my head and sigh with entirely too much self-pity. "His squad is watching over Draithus this week. But you really should get some sleep. I'm only going to stay another few minutes."

His brow knits.

"Go," I urge him with a reassuring smile. "I'll see you tomorrow."

He sighs but nods and pushes his chair back, standing, then stretching his arms above his head. "Don't tell him I said so"—he drops his arms—"but the way I've heard he wants to reorganize the combat squads by strengths, since the active riders don't have a full wing to pull from, is brilliant."

"I'll be sure not to tell him," I promise, a corner of my mouth tugging upward.

Dain takes his pack off the table. "See you tomorrow."

I nod, and he walks out.

The library is comfortably quiet as I pour over the next entry, translating into what we call our draft journal. "The air has grown cold enough," I say out loud as I write the words into the draft journal, "to see my blood in the mornings."

I blink, then stare at the symbol for "blood." My mind spins at the possibility, and then I turn back to earlier entries, just to be sure. Every single time we translated the symbol "blood"…the word *breath* fits even better. We have the wrong word.

The blood of life is actually the *breath* of life, and setting the stone ablaze in an iron flame…

I close the journals and sit back in my chair. The *six* doesn't refer to riders.

"They're dragons," I say out loud in the empty library. Dain. I should tell—

No. He'll act only on the rules, not taking the ethics into account. There's only one person I trust to *always* do the right thing.

I stuff my things into my pack, sling it over my shoulders, and race out of the library, then climb four flights of stairs. My heart races as I knock on Rhiannon's door.

"Hey," she says when she opens the door, her bright smile faltering when I don't return it. Without another word, she steps back, ushering me into her room.

I glance at the spartan decor as I start to pace the length of the room, taking in two plain desks, two doorless armoires, and two beds with simple black sheets that have been awkwardly shoved into a space obviously meant for one—the result of the fliers' arrival. A single window illuminates the room with morning light. We're due in formation shortly.

"That one is supposed to be yours," Rhi says, gesturing to the bed on the right. "Just in case you ever want a night away from Riorson."

I press my lips between my teeth, searching for the right words as I wear a path in Rhiannon's floor. "I need to tell you something."

"All right."

Stopping suddenly in the middle of the room, I turn toward her. "I know how to raise the wards. I'm just not entirely sure we *should*."

The breath of life of the six and the one combined and set the
stone ablaze in an iron flame.

—THE JOURNAL OF WARRICK OF LUCERAS
—TRANSLATED BY CADETS VIOLET SORRENGAIL AND DAIN AETOS

CHAPTER
FIFTY-TWO

Rhiannon slides a mug of warm apple cider across her sister's dining room table the next day, then takes the empty seat between Ridoc and Sloane. The house has the same scent as most of the barracks in Riorson House—newly cut wood and a faint hint of stain. The carpenters have been working around the clock to turn out serviceable furniture.

I refuse to believe that it could all go up in flames if those dark wielders decide to test their wyvern at altitude. Four hours. That's all it would take for them to reach us from Draithus.

"Thanks." I take the mug and lift it to my face, breathing in the comforting scent before drinking. Looking over my mug, into the connected living room of the townhouse, I smile at the sight of Sawyer sitting with Jesinia on a blanket near the fire, an intense look of concentration on his face as he signs—

Shit, he might have just told her that he thinks her turtle is blue, but I'm not getting in the middle of that.

It's the second time this week Raegan has opened her home to our squad at Rhi's request, and the first time Jesinia's joined us. I have to give it to Rhi—her idea was genius. Getting our entire squad—eighteen of us—together outside the academic setting of Riorson House hasn't solved the tension between riders and fliers, but it's a step in the right direction.

Even Cat, who's sitting as far away from me as possible in the corner of the living room, isn't sneering as she and Neve talk to Quinn. She still hates being in Second Squad, but at least she's civil about it to everyone but me.

We've fallen into a routine over the last couple of weeks of November—now the first of December—adjusting our formation to include the fliers, attending classes together within our years, and even making it through our first sparring session where no one spilled blood yesterday. Rhiannon laid down the law last week, and now we run together every morning and sit together at Battle Brief and meals. She even assigned us study partners hoping that proximity might lead to mutual understanding or at least tolerance. Thank gods Maren is my study partner, but I still feel shitty that Rhi took on Cat to spare me.

"Any chance you speak Old Lucerish?" I ask Aaric at the end of the table. His tutoring would only be second to mine, considering Markham was my mentor. I'd feel better if someone else quadruple-checked the translation, someone other than rule-following Dain, but I'm pretty sure we have it. Otherwise, why would we be here?

"Absolutely not." He shakes his head and focuses on his new ink pen, his forehead lined with concentration. All of our first-years are channeling, and though they have yet to manifest a signet, they have a bet going about who will be able to master the lesser magic needed to work the writing implement first. Pretty sure Kai—the lone first-year flier without Luella—is going to beat them all.

He's currently on the couch between a couple of first-years, his spiky black hair bobbing, a dimple forming in his bronze cheek as he laughs at whatever story Bragen—the driftleader and our new XO—is currently telling. Other than Maren, Bragen is the easiest of the fliers to get along with. He also spends a lot of time shooting longing looks Cat's way.

"Why would Aaric speak Old Lucerish?" Visia asks from the opposite end of the table, looking up from her physics homework. "Aren't you from Calldyr?"

My face freezes. Fuck, I need to be more careful.

"Yep." Aaric looks up at me, his features a perfect, polished mask. "You have me confused with Lynx. He's from Luceras."

"Right. Of course." I nod, thankful for his quick cover.

"At some point, you're going to have to actually get to know the first-years. They're people now," Ridoc teases, his smile tight. He agrees with us about what we're about to do, but he's understandably worried about the fliers' reactions.

"Can't blame her," Imogen says, carrying a mug out of the kitchen with Maren following close behind. "We've added six first-years and six fliers to the squad in the last six weeks."

"We've been in the squad since July," Visia argues.

"You didn't count before Threshing." Imogen shrugs, glancing across the room. "Guess I'll go save Quinn from Cat."

"No blood on my sister's floor." Rhiannon shoots her a look that says she means it.

"Yes, Mother." Imogen mock salutes with her empty hand and then heads toward Quinn.

Maren takes the seat next to me, and Rhiannon lifts her brows at me in subtle question.

My throat tightens. *Here we go.* This is the whole reason we planned tonight's get-together, so why am I suddenly anxious?

Because I haven't discussed my decision with Xaden, not that he's been around more than one day a week since he and Brennan decided to reorganize how the combat squads operate.

"You're doing the right thing," Andarna says.

"The honorable thing," Tairn chimes in.

"Do it," I say to Rhiannon, gripping my mug with both hands.

"Listen up!" Rhi calls out as she stands, quieting the house, her gaze touching on every cadet. "For riders, squads are more than a unit. We're family. In order to survive, we have to trust each other on the battlefield...and off it. And we're trusting you to do with this information what you will." She looks to me.

What we're about to do is borderline treason, but I can't imagine doing this any other way.

I take a steadying breath. "I've been translating Warrick's journal—one of the First Six, who built Basgiath's wards," I clarify just in case they're not familiar with our history. "In the hopes that we can get the wards up in Aretia before the approaching wyvern decide we're the next target... And I think I know how to do it. But that's why we wanted to talk to you, because it will mean you fliers wouldn't be able to wield."

The fliers stare, stunned. Even Cat's eyes flare wide with what almost looks like fear.

"We know two other Poromish towns have fallen in the last two weeks, leaving Draithus vulnerable, and the Assembly wants the wards up and functional *now*," Rhiannon continues. "Which we think you deserve to know."

"Know what?" Cat stands, her chair screeching against the hardwood floor. "That you're about to kill our ability to channel? Our gryphons are still struggling to adjust to altitude, and now you're going to make us *powerless*?"

"Protective wards were our goal long before you came here." Imogen pushes off the wall and casually sets her hand on her hip, near her favorite dagger, angling her body toward Cat, and Quinn sidesteps to flank the angry flier.

"But we're here *now*," Cat retorts. "If my uncle had known you would tie a hand behind our back, he never would have made that deal!"

"Control yourself, Cat." Bragen keeps his tone level, but his brown eyes are sharp as he stands, putting his left arm out to block Cat from advancing on us. "How long until they're up?" he asks me.

"As soon as I tell the Assembly what I've found." As of this morning, the stone has a distinct hum, a vibration in that chamber that reminds me of the way Xaden described the armory at Samara, housing the alloy-hilted daggers.

"And when are you doing that?" Cat snaps.

"If you weren't here, it would be done already," I retort in the same tone she's giving. No doubt the majority of the Assembly will condemn me as a traitor for this, and maybe they'll be right. "But you *are* here. You *do* matter."

Maren shifts in her seat beside me, and though I refuse to slip my hand toward my daggers, Ridoc doesn't hesitate, folding his arms to give him quick access to the sheath along his shoulder.

"And how long are you giving us?" Bragen asks me, tilting his chin and exposing the vertical silver scars down his neck that disappear into his collar.

Every gaze shifts in my direction.

"I won't lie to Xaden. The moment he's home, I'll have to tell him," I admit. Multiple curses ripple through the fliers. "But I'll also tell him that I think we should hold off as long as possible to give you a chance to decide if you still want to stay, knowing you won't be able to channel."

"And you honestly think he'll listen to you." Cat's hands curl at her sides.

"The good, the bad, the unforgivable." That's what he said to me when he put my safety above the best interest of the movement. And he may want the wards up because I'm here and he isn't, but he also has a province to think of.

"No." I shake my head slowly. "I think he'll act in the best interest of Tyrrendor"—I leave myself out of the equation—"and want them up as soon as possible, but I can still try."

"We're no good to our people if we can't channel," Maren says, looking past Aaric to the window and drumming her fingers on the table.

"Yeah, well you're no good to them if you're dead, either," Imogen counters, keeping an eye on Cat. "And by not raising those wards right now, we're exposing all of Aretia—the riots, the drifts—hell, all of *Tyrrendor* beyond Navarre's wards to danger that's no longer necessary. So you'd better decide if you're willing to stay, knowing that it can happen at any moment, or if you're better off taking shelter in Cordyn, where you'll have power *and* dark wielders."

I don't envy them the choice, but at least we gave it to them.

"And if you stay, we won't leave you powerless." I reach under the table and retrieve my pack, then set the black leather bag on the table and unbutton the top. "Turns out alloy isn't the only thing we can imbue." I take out the six conduits Felix gave me yesterday after I trusted him with the truth, each containing an arrowhead like the ones I've been imbuing for weeks.

"What's in that?" Bragen asks, two lines etched between his brows.

"The kind of ore we don't use to make the alloy. It's not quite as rare as

Talladium but it's about ten times as explosive. Trust me, I've seen this stuff blow sky-high raw, let alone imbued." I glance at Sloane, who slowly smiles before she responds.

"Maorsite."

I'm suspended again over that sunburned field, the death wave a heartbeat from overtaking me once the Sage releases me from his hold, and he will. He does it every time.

I recognize the scenario for what it is now—a recurring nightmare—and yet I'm still held powerless, still too slow to reach Tairn, still can't force my consciousness to snap me awake.

"I grow weary of this. Now wield," the Sage whispers, his robes purple tonight. "Rip free. Show me the power you used to slay our forces above the trading post. Prove me right that you are a weapon worth watching, worth retrieving." His hand hovers over mine but doesn't touch me. "The one who watched thinks you'll never yield, that we should kill you before you grow into your full abilities."

My stomach turns, my mouth watering with nausea as the bony hand drifts upward, pausing at my neck.

"Usually, jealousy sways the tongue of young wielders." He drags a single, long fingernail down my throat, exposing an expanse of tan arm under his robes, and I twitch, fear accelerating my heartbeat.

I force my mouth to open, but no sound comes out. Touching me is new. Touching me is *terrifying*.

"The rest turn for the power," he whispers, coming so close I can smell a hint of something sweet on his breath. "But you will turn for something much more dangerous, much more volatile." He wraps his hand around my throat loosely.

I manage to shake my head in denial.

"You will." His dark, eyelash-less eyes narrow, and the jagged fingernails slice into my skin with an all-too-real bite of pain. "You'll tear down the wards yourself when the time comes."

The temperature plummets, and my next exhale is visible in the frozen air. I blink and snow covers the ground. The only warmth is a quickly cooling trickle along my neck.

"And you won't do it for something as trite as power or as easily satiable as greed," he promises in a whisper, "but for the most illogical of mortal emotions— love. Or you'll die." He shrugs. "You both will."

He flicks his wrist, and a bone-jarring crack tears me from my sleep.

I jolt upright in bed, reaching for my throat and gulping lungful after lungful of air, but there's no cut, no ache, and when I turn the mage light on with lesser magic and a twist of my hand, I see there's no blood, either.

"Of course there isn't," I whisper aloud, the raw sound cutting through the silence of my bedroom as the first hints of sunlight lighten the sky to purple beyond my window. "It's just a fucking nightmare."

There's nothing that can touch me here, Xaden asleep beside me.

"*Stop talking to yourself,*" Tairn grumbles, as though I've woken him. "*It makes us both seem unstable.*"

"*Do you see my dreams?*"

"*I have better things to do than monitor the machinations of your subconscious mind. If a dream bothers you, then leave it. Stop allowing yourself to be tortured like a hatchling and wake yourself like an adult.*" He cuts off conversation before I can tell him that human dreams don't always work like that, and the bond dims, a sign that he's already gone back to sleep.

So I lie back down, curling my body around Xaden's, and his arm wraps around my back and pulls me closer like it's a reflex, like this is the way we'll sleep for the next fifty years. I settle in against his warmth and lay my head on his chest, above the most comforting rhythm in the world besides Tairn's and Andarna's wingbeats—Xaden's heart.

Six days later, there are six new names on the death roll. The December snow makes flying absolutely miserable outside the valley, and at Basgiath, the dragons would simply refuse to train due to discomfort—theirs, of course, not ours—but we can't afford not to fly at every available opportunity, so here we are in the flight field, waiting for orders, facing off against Claw and Tail Sections for the squad exercises Devera and Trissa have organized.

"You'd think we were in the Barrens, it's so fucking hot in this valley," Ridoc mutters, unbuttoning his flight jacket to my right. "And it's only eleven."

A bead of sweat races from the hairline at the nape of my neck to the collar of my flight jacket, so it's not like I can disagree with him. Winter flight leathers aren't exactly meant for the Vale…or the valley.

"It won't be the second we're in the air." Sawyer's eyes briefly narrow, staring ahead of us, where Rhiannon, Bragen, and the other squad leaders meet with Devera and Trissa.

"You all right?" I ask quietly, so the first-years ahead of us can't hear.

"It's for the good of the squad, right?" Sawyer forces a tight, closed-lipped smile. "If they can stay and tolerate knowing we might strip their powers away at any second, I can deal with losing my position as executive officer."

"I want to go with you," Andarna says for the tenth time in the last fifteen minutes, and I look over my shoulder to see her flexing her claws beside Tairn, her talons digging into the earth. Her black scales shine with a green hue this morning, reflecting the grass around her. Maybe it's the result of lingering gold, and breathing fire will steal the last of the shimmer.

"I have no clue how far they'll want us to fly." I keep my voice as gentle as possible.

"Longer than you're capable of, Little One," Tairn adds.

"I made it an hour yesterday," Andarna argues, because *that* is what she does now. Tairn could tell her the grass is green, and she'd eviscerate yet another sheep on it just to change the color.

I lift my brows at Tairn, who simply huffs—whatever the hell that means.

"Trouble in double dragon land?" Ridoc asks, and Cat glances my way from his other side, Maren following suit now that we stand in rows of four.

"She wants to fly with us," I answer.

"I am flying with you," she insists, digging more than just her physical claws in. *"And this matter isn't up for debate amongst your human friends. Dragons do not consult humans."*

"I'm starting to wish I'd protested your right of benefaction when you asked the Empyrean to bond," Tairn grumbles.

"Good thing you're not the head of my den, then, isn't it?"

"Codagh should have known better—" he starts.

"What are the other adolescents doing today?" I interrupt, hoping to distract her. The last thing I want to do is climb to any altitude she can't handle and have her wing fail. Gods, the consequences of such a mistake would be incomprehensible.

"The other adolescents are not bonded and do not *understand me."*

I swear I can *feel* Tairn roll his eyes.

"You'd rather risk all the work you've done with your wing to play war than actually…" Shit, what do adolescent dragons do all day, anyway? *"Play?"*

"I would rather test my wing on a training mission, yes."

Rhiannon and Bragen head back our way, locked in discussion, both gesturing with their hands in motions that look like maneuvers. There's a sheen of excitement in Rhiannon's quick smile, and I find myself mirroring it. "She looks happy."

"Maybe they're finally going to let us fly farther than a half hour…you know, without making us hike up the Cliffs of Dralor after," Ridoc remarks. "Gods, I miss *flying*."

"That would be nice," Sawyer agrees, shooting me a teasing smirk. "Not all of us get to take a pleasure flight to Cordyn, you know."

"Hey, that joy ride got us a luminary." I glance meaningfully at the sheath at his side, which holds an alloy-hilted dagger. One for one. That was the deal Brennan struck with the Assembly when it came to supplying the drifts, and we've finally made enough to equip every rider in Aretia with multiple daggers.

"Listen up, Second Squad," Rhiannon says, looking over our group. "Our mission is simple. You know the summoning runes Trissa has been working on with us?" Even the first-years nod. They might not be able to weave runes, but at least they know what they are, which means they're a step ahead of where we were last year. "There are thirty of them hidden within twenty miles along the western range. This isn't just a test for us, but for our dragons to sense them."

"Can you—"

Tairn growls in response.

Point made.

"Winner gets a weekend pass. No training. No homework. No limits." She glances at Bragen, whose lips twitch into a smile.

"We've been given permission to fly wherever we want. If your gryphon feels comfortable flying the cliff wall, that means you can go anywhere." He looks at Cat. "Even Cordyn, though you'd only have a few hours there before you'd have to start the flight back. If you win, of course."

"Oh, we're winning," Maren says, shoulder-bumping Cat the same way Rhiannon does me.

"Good. You want that pass? We'll need to find and close more of those runed boxes than they do." She nods back toward Claw and Tail Sections.

"They return," Tairn says as wingbeats fill the sky.

I look up, a slow smile spreading at the sight of Sgaeyl soaring overhead with Chradh and eight other dragons, but I only recognize the three bonded to Heaton, Emery, and Cianna. Xaden's home…with a full riot of ten.

"I'm guessing you got your way with the new structure?" I ask Xaden as they land behind our line of gryphons and dragons.

Tairn breaks away as if we aren't about to be sent on a training mission.

"Bragen and I will divide you up into groups of four according to your abilities," Rhiannon continues.

"In a way," Xaden answers, executing a perfect dismount and walking toward us. My pulse leaps and the worry that seems to live in my chest lifts a fraction when I don't see any new injuries or blood.

"Sorrengail, you paying attention?" Rhi calls me out.

My head swivels back to the front of formation, where she's arching an eyebrow at me.

"Teams of four. Split by ability," I repeat with a nod, then give her a blatantly beseeching look that absolutely abuses her status as my best friend.

"We'll have an hour once we launch," Bragen says.

Go, Rhi mouths once the squad's attention is on him.

I smile in thanks, then step out of formation and walk past Andarna and Feirge, over the trampled grass, straight to Xaden. The scruff on his jaw is thick with days of growth, and there are circles under his eyes as he reaches forward, surprising me by tugging me against his chest in front of all of Fourth Wing.

The cold beard tickles as he buries his icy face in my neck and breathes deeply. "I've missed you."

"Same." I wind my arms around his torso, sliding my hands in the space between the swords he wears crossed at his back and his flight jacket, then hold tight to help warm him. "I need to talk to you."

"Bad news?" He pulls back and searches my eyes.

"No. Just news that's best shared when there's time to discuss."

His brow knits.

"Good to see you, Vi," Garrick says as he walks by, tapping me on the shoulder. "You definitely need to make him tell you about the venin he took down just outside Draithus."

"You what?" My stomach pitches sideways.

"Thanks for that, asshole." Xaden glares at Garrick.

"Just doing my part to help your communication skills thrive in a stable relationship." Garrick turns and walks backward, lifting his hands in a shrug.

"Like you have any room to talk about stable relationships," Imogen counters from behind him, the squad formation obviously having broken to ready for the mission.

"I'm going to skip the obvious pun to be made about plenty of mares in my stable." He flashes a grin, then turns and heads toward the path at the end of the valley. "Seeing as I'm no longer a cadet but a mature, responsible officer."

She scoffs as he walks by. "We need to go, Sorrengail."

"You took down a venin?" I pivot, keeping my attention on Xaden. "Outside *Draithus*?" It's the last Poromish stronghold before the Cliffs of Dralor.

"You have lengthy news to discuss?" he replies, lifting his brows.

"Are you all right?" I slide my hands to his face, scanning him like that tiny bit of exposed skin will tell me if the other ninety-five percent is unharmed. Being able to raise the wards won't mean anything if he isn't safe—at least it won't mean anything to me.

"News?" His eyes narrow.

"Violet!" Rhiannon calls.

"I have to fly out." I drop my hands reluctantly, and he catches one in his as

I retreat a step. "We'll talk when I get back."

"Tell me now."

"The wingleader voice doesn't work on me." I squeeze his hand and let go.

His eyes flare. *"You figured out how to raise the wards."*

I blink, then scowl. *"I hate it when you do that. Is my face really that easy to read?"*

"To me? Yes." He looks toward the rocky path that leads down to Riorson House. *"We should go now. How long will it take to raise them?"*

"No." I shake my head and turn toward my squad, seeing Sloane, Visia, and Cat clearly waiting for me. Guess I don't need to ask where I've been assigned. *"We'll talk about it later. Discussion paused."*

"At least tell me what was missed the first time." Xaden quickly catches up to me.

"Dragons." I pat Andarna's foreleg as we approach the trio of waiting cadets. *"'The six most powerful' refers to dragons, not riders."*

"In that case, I can have them up before you get back."

"No, you can't." I shoot him a glare.

"Are you two fighting silently?" Cat asks, glancing between Xaden and me, her perfectly arched brows rising slowly.

"They do that," Sloane informs her.

Xaden ignores them both completely, keeping his gaze locked onto mine as we reach them. *"And just why can't I?"*

I lean up and brush my lips over his cool cheek. "Because you'll need Tairn. Now go warm up. I have a mission to fly." Without another word to him, I turn to my squadmates. "Let's go."

The art of imbuing comes naturally to only a handful of signets, and automatically only to *one*: the siphon.

—A Study on Signets
by Major Dalton Sisneros

CHAPTER
FIFTY-THREE

Forty minutes later, the four of us are hiking *down* a steep, snow-covered ridgeline to a cave only accessible by foot in the sector our group has been assigned to, and Lucky Me is in the lead, which leaves Cat at my back.

At least Andarna's there to protect it should the flier get any stabby ideas about how to get me out of Xaden's bed.

"This is not what I had in mind when I said I wanted to fly with you." Andarna huffs at the powdery snow, scattering a portion in a shimmering cloud of frozen misery.

"This is what the mission called for, and you need your strength to fly back," I tell her, trudging forward through the knee-high layer of fresh hell and hoping I don't fall through into any older strata.

The only one who isn't struggling is Kiralair, Cat's silver-winged gryphon, who walks at Andarna's side. Only those two are light enough not to cause an avalanche on the nonexistent path.

"Anything?" Tairn asks as he flies to the next peak, his voice tense.

"We haven't even made it to the cave you selected," I respond, spotting the mouth of the cave about twenty yards ahead only because Tairn pointed it out under the camouflage of the snowy outcropping above. The riot left us at the only fully stable section of terrain, an outcropping of rock left bare by the vicious wind.

"I still find this plan lacking," he lectures. *"Leaving you on one peak to explore another for a possible energy signature leaves you in unacceptable danger."*

"From whom?" I tug my fur-lined hood closer to ward off the wind when it shifts, stinging the tips of my exposed ears. *"Do you really think any wyvern could—"*

"I'm coming back."

"It's entirely too easy to rile you." I laugh, and the sound echoes off the snow-covered bowl, making us all take pause.

"For fuck's sake, Sorrengail," Cat hisses once it's clear the snow around us is staying put. "Are you trying to get us buried in an avalanche?"

"Sorry," I whisper over my shoulder.

Her eyes widen. "Did you just apologize to me?"

"I can admit when I'm wrong." I shrug and continue forward.

"I'm fully present and capable of protecting her," Andarna snipes at Tairn.

"You do not yet breathe fire."

"Fire would only serve to melt the mountain," she reminds him, and I glance back to see her carefully picking her path, her scales reflecting the snow in an almost silvery sheen in places. *"I still wield teeth and claw should the aristocrat bare her vitriol."*

"Are you insinuating that I don't?" Cat asks.

"Do you even think you're wrong? Ever?" I ask, pushing forward. "I honestly think you might be worse than a dragon when it comes to confidence."

"Arrogance," Andarna corrects me. *"The flier doesn't have the skills to back up a word like 'confidence.'"*

I snort, but bite back the laugh before it can endanger us. Ten more feet and we'll be at the cave. If Tairn locates a second while we're retrieving the first, we'll be ahead of Claw Section, who has already found three to our section's two, according to Tairn.

Dragons are nothing if not competitive.

"What?" Cat asks.

"Andarna thinks you're arrogant, not confident," I tell her.

"She is," Sloane agrees.

"Just because your brother didn't like me doesn't mean you know me," Cat whispers at Sloane.

"No." I turn to face Cat, making her pause in the footsteps I've carved in the ridgeline. "You want to pick a fight? You come at *me*."

Cat cocks her head to the side and studies me. "Because you feel guilty for her brother's death." It's not an accusation or even a dig. Just the truth.

"Because I promised him I'd take care of her. So, you can aim all that hatred right here." I tap my gloved hand to my chest.

"He was wrong to ask that of you." Sloane catches up, Visia close behind.

"Because Imogen would have been a more capable protector?" I ask, only able to hold her too familiar blue gaze for a heartbeat before looking away.

"No. Because you already carry the weight of protecting Xaden's life. It was unfair of him to burden you with mine, too." She huffs a breath into her cupped, gloved hands to warm them.

I blink as my eyes sting from something other than the wind, then turn to continue trudging through the snow toward the cave, whose entrance is nothing but a narrow, icy ledge. *"It looks bigger than we thought from the air."* But still not wide enough for any dragon bigger than Andarna to squeeze into.

"There was a time my kind dwelled in every mountain of this range," Tairn tells me. *"That cave is undoubtedly part of the network of chambers that runs throughout this range for a wintering den. This entrance would have been inhospitable to any approach but direct flight—to protect the young…and the adolescent."*

"I heard that," Andarna quips.

"Kiralair says our squad has another box in hand," Cat tells us as I finally reach the cave's entrance, stepping out of the wind.

"We're *so* winning that pass." Visia grins, and Cat walks out of the snow and onto the rocky floor of the cave.

"Does every gryphon have *lair* in their name?" I ask Cat, hoping the subject change might change the aim of her sharp tongue from Sloane.

"Of course not. Is every rider named Sorrengail?" She folds her arms and bounces back on her heels like she's trying to stay warm.

"That right there is why I don't like you." Sloane crosses into the cave. "You're—"

Visia slips and I lunge forward, catching her hand and tugging her into the cave as snow crumbles where she'd just been standing.

"You all right?" I ask, pulling her farther into the cave and scanning her startled face.

"Of course she is. You never seem to have a problem saving *her*," Cat mutters.

"I'm fine." Visia nods, dropping her hood and revealing the dragonfire burn scar down her hairline. "That's going to make it hard to leave."

I shoot Cat a withering look, but she's too busy watching her gryphon, Kira, stretch across the hole in the path, then safely squirm her way in to notice.

"Reason number two." Sloane holds up two fingers and walks past Cat into the dark cave. "Needless to say, there are no mage lights in here."

And I've never been that good at producing them. Anything I wield with lesser magic is going to be swallowed up in this darkness. I rest my hand over my stomach as if that will help the instant rise of nausea from the smell of earth around us. At least it's missing that damp scent from the interrogation chamber, but it's close enough to make me pause.

"You ended the one who kept you prisoner," Andarna reminds me, following Kira in, tucking her wings tight to fit through the opening.

"Fear isn't always logical." I glance at the other riders. "Any chance either of you is a fire wielder? Because I don't think you want me wielding in here." Keeping the energy strung between my hand and the conduit for fifteen feet puts me into a sweat every time, and I can only keep it going for a few seconds.,

"No signet yet," Visia responds.

"Me, either," Sloane answers, peering into the darkness.

"You brought a *dragon*." Cat gestures wide, motioning toward Andarna.

"She can't breathe fire yet." I offer Andarna a smile. "But she will."

"Remind her that I can sever her head with one bite," Andarna growls, the sound higher than Tairn's menacing rumble.

"I will not. What does Tairn tell us?"

"We don't eat our allies," she mumbles, but there's a distinct tap of her talons against the rock floor.

"Great. Why they stuck me with you three, I'll never know. You'd think one of us would have a good mage light down." Cat removes her bow, then swings her pack from her back and rummages past the full quiver to pull out a small, unlit torch.

"Are you kidding me?" I gawk as she brings a piece of wood no larger than my palm from the bag, shakes her head, and reaches for another. "You carry one of those around with you?"

"Obviously." Cat digs into her bag again. "The fact that you don't says that you haven't been appropriately scared of the dark yet. Shit, I can't find the fire rune Maren made."

"You all trade runes?" Visia stares in open shock.

"And you call yourselves a *family*. Of course we share. Whoever can make it, does. Then we all trade so everyone is equally equipped." Cat shakes her head and stands, muttering a curse. "I can't find it."

"That's…brilliant," I admit. "Why didn't you tell us?"

"You're used to hoarding power," she says with a dismissive shrug. "Not sharing it. Now, unless someone has an idea for fire—"

"Got it." I yank off my gloves, then stuff them into one pocket and pull my conduit from the other, beckoning a trickle of my power to rise. It tingles, then burns as it flows down my hand, through my fingers, and into the conduit. The tendrils of energy light our immediate surroundings.

"That's so awesome." Visia smiles. "Can all of you do that?"

"No. It just hums for most of us. Glad to see you'll have all the light *you* need." Sarcasm drips from Cat's voice.

"Take it," I order Sloane.

"I'd rather live." She puts her hands up.

"If I thought it was going to kill you, I'd hand it to Cat." I hold the conduit out to her.

Cat snorts, but I think there was a note of laughter there.

"Good point." Sloane takes the conduit, and I concentrate on keeping the energy connected.

"Back up three steps. Good, another two," I tell her, and my fingers tremble as she does, stretching my signet.

"Wow," Visia whispers.

"Stick the torch into the energy, Cat."

"You think that's safe?" she asks.

"I have no clue, but I'm game to try if you are." I keep focused on the conduit, on the flow of energy, on the heat I keep checked by controlling the door to Tairn's power.

Kira clicks her tongue in a series of sounds I've become accustomed to but have no hope of ever understanding.

"Fine, I'll do it," Cat mutters, then lowers the torch until it catches fire.

I immediately drop my hand, cutting off the power, and I send a prayer of thanks to Dunne that it worked. Felix is probably going to have my head on a pike tomorrow at lessons. "I'll take it. Thanks, Sloane."

Sloane hands the conduit back like it might explode.

"Damn," Cat says, glancing from the torch, to the conduit, to me. "I hate that you're so…"

"Badass?" Sloane suggests, smiling in a way that reminds me of her brother.

"Powerful," Cat admits, looking away before slipping her pack back on, changing hands with the torch instead of passing it off.

"It's not the power making that possible," I tell her, channeling into the conduit so it lights up again and marching into the darkness. "It's the control."

"Yeah, well, I kind of loathe that, too," she mutters, catching up to walk at my side.

"A rare moment of honesty. I'll take it." We move into the cave, which seems to widen with every step we take. "They paired us because I'm supposedly the most powerful rider in the squad," I tell her, ignoring her muttered response. "But you're better at runes. We might not compliment each other, but we *complement* each other." I smile despite the darkness we're walking into. "Get it? With an E instead of the I."

Cat looks at me like I've just grown a third arm, and the torch starts to flicker.

There's a breeze.

"Are you telling scribe jokes?" Sloane asks, a couple of steps behind us, Visia at her side.

"Jesinia would think it's funny," Visia offers like she's trying to save me.

"Jesinia is a scribe," Sloane notes.

The cave opens up about twenty feet in, a vast tunnel forking to the left.

"Apparently there's a much easier way to get into this cave," Cat mutters.

"It's part of a network that runs through this range," I explain.

"Should we split up?" Visia asks.

"No!" All three of us respond at the same time.

"Which way do we go?" Sloane voices the question we're all wondering.

No one answers.

"Any help?" I ask Tairn, feeling our bond stretch. He's not far but definitely not close, either.

"There's an energy signature in that cave. That's all I can tell."

"I vote right. If it doesn't work, we'll come back and go left." I look to the others.

Cat nods, and we head farther in.

"So do you think you'll get a second signet?" Visia asks, breaking the silence. "Two dragons, two signets, right?"

"I don't know," I answer, glancing back at Andarna. I actually figured because she bonded me so young and lost the ability to stop time, the signet of lightning wielding was all that I would be blessed with. But now I wonder... *"Will I?"*

"Why are you asking me? Signets manifest according to the person wielding." Her eyes blink gold, her black scales blending in with the darkness.

"Second signets only happen when a dragon bonds a rider in the direct familial line as its previous," Sloane says, misunderstanding Visia's question. "But there's an equal chance of it causing madness. From what Thoirt told me, that's why Cruth wasn't punished for bonding Quinn. She's only the great-niece of her previous rider. Her signet's more powerful but not entirely different."

"Thoirt shouldn't be telling you matters resolved within the Empyrean," Visia lectures, then does a double take when she glances my way.

Gravity shifts. That can't be right. That would mean—

"Violet, are you okay?" Visia asks.

I shake my head but say, "Yes." How do you explain your heart is sinking past the rock floor of the cave? I take a deep breath, flex and unflex my hand as I grip the brightly glowing conduit. Andarna growls to my right, and I quickly assure her, "I'm fine." But we both know I'm anything but fine—I'm also equally certain now isn't the time to let my mind wander down that path.

"Holy shit, there it is," Sloane says, forcing me to pay attention as she walks past us to pick up the plain metal chest that's locked into an open position by the rune on the front.

"It's...plain," Visia notes.

"Are you going to counter the summoning rune?" I ask Cat. When she raises one brow, I add, "You're better at runes, remember?"

"I am." She nods, a genuine smile curving her mouth for the first time since I met her. "I just wanted to see if you'd say it again."

Kiralair's wing brushes my shoulder as she walks past us into the darkness, as if Cat needs to be guarded from the unseen.

Cat glances between the three of us with an uncertain—and unhappy— tense set to her mouth, then hands the torch to Visia in what looks like a painful sacrifice.

No, not a sacrifice: a gesture of trust.

She weaves the unlocking rune with a speed I envy, her hands moving quickly, confidently, as Andarna shifts her weight behind me.

"What's wrong?"

"The scent of others grows stronger."

"Wyvern?" Every muscle in my body clenches.

"No. They smell of stolen magic when you get close enough." She lifts her head, taking up three-quarters of the tunnel. *"This smells of…dragons."*

"Got it!" Cat says, and I turn at the sound of metal clicking shut. The chest is closed and latched.

"We'd better hurry," I tell them. "Andarna smells other dragons, which means the other sections might be closing in on us."

"I'm not losing this pass." Visia trades Cat, taking the chest and returning the torch. "It will give me time to fly home and convince my cousins to leave the border if my aunt and uncle won't."

"You're going to fly into Navarre?" Sloane damn near shouts.

"It's right on the border. They won't even know." Visia adjusts her grip on the chest and hurries past Andarna. "So let's get out of here."

"Bold choice to go back to Navarre." Cat jogs to catch up to Visia, lighting the way. "I respect it."

The effort, the consideration for Visia, thaws a small chunk of my heart toward Cat. Maybe she's not horrible to everyone…just me.

"It's the only thing to do," Visia starts as we approach the fork in the tunnel.

A low growl vibrates the very ground beneath our feet, making all four of us halt, and the hair rises on the back of my neck.

"What the—" Cat starts.

Another growl makes the pebbles around my feet bounce, and a full-grown orange dragon comes around the corner, its back scraping the top of the cave as it snaps its head our direction, glaring at us through its only remaining eye.

Oh. *Fuck.*

Visia shrieks.

"Tairn!" I mentally scream, forcing my body past the shock, the fear, the nauseating hopelessness of our situation. The orb falls from my hand, shattering on the ground at the same moment I reach for the women in front of me, but my hand only grasps the leather of Cat's pack.

I yank her backward with all my strength just as Visia is swatted out of the way by a sharp, jagged claw. Cat's body collides with mine, knocking us both to the ground, and the torch falls from her hand as Visia hits the side of the cave with a cracking sound that sickens my stomach.

The angle, the impact…gods…she's…she's dead.

"Silver One?" Tairn's voice roars in my head as the dragon blocking our way out focuses his narrowed eye on me and opens his jaw wide.

Fetid breath fills the air a second before he curls his tongue, and his throat glows orange with rising fire.

"Solas found us!"

I'll say one thing for dragonfire. It kills quickly.

—Colonel Kaori's Field Guide to Dragonkind

CHAPTER
FIFTY-FOUR

A dark shape flies at us from the left, sweeping Cat and me into a spinning tangle of limbs and propelling us backward. I grab onto her in the chaos, forcing her body in front of mine as we come to a skidding halt, knowing the shelter of facing my back to Solas won't be enough but trying anyway.

She has to live. She's third in line to the throne of Poromiel. If she dies in Tyrrendor, Cordyn will hunt Xaden down and execute him...if he survives my death.

Survive. Survive. Survive. I push the demand down every mental bond I have just in case we aren't out of range. Xaden's too far, but Tairn will hear it, and Andarna—gods, Tairn has to get here in time to save her.

Kiralair and Sloane fly into us next, swept in by an unseen force, pushing Sloane and me backward, toward Solas, but my back hits a hard, rough surface as the cave walls illuminate with the eerie glow of impending fire a heartbeat before we're overtaken by darkness.

"Take a breath!" Andarna demands. *"Don't argue!"*

Not darkness. Wings. It's her belly at my back and she's wrapped her wings around us.

"Breathe in and hold it!" I shout, then fill my lungs with sulfur-scented air.

Heat blasts, roaring past us in a stream that shakes Andarna's wings, and the temperature soars. I force my eyes closed to keep them from cooking as my skin *burns* as though we've been thrown into an oven. How can she survive this?

"She's fireproof," Tairn reminds me, but the panic in his voice doesn't do much to soothe the terror clamping down on my heart.

"Do not breathe!" Andarna demands, and I know it's because I'll singe my

lungs if I do, if *any* of us do. I count my heartbeats. One. Two. Three.

The blast feels like it goes on forever, like it's become my eternity, like my soul has done exactly what Sloane asked in the first part of the year and gone straight to the depths of hell without being commended to Malek. Eight. Nine.

On ten, it ends, and Andarna's wings fall away. Air rushes in, and I wait until I feel its cool brush across my cheek before I drag in a breath, hearing the others do the same.

I open my eyes and see Cat lunge in the torchlight across the small space, using her gloved hands to put out the burning tips of the feathers along Kira's far wing. It must have been exposed to the flames. Sloane races to help as Andarna gains her feet, and I narrowly avoid her tail as she faces down Solas.

"No! He's nearly twice as big as you are!" I lift my hands and throw the floodgates open on Tairn's power, letting it burn through me as Solas's blast failed to do, until I'm pure fire. But I can't wield in here, not when there's every chance I could hit one of us.

Andarna's roar fills the cave, and my heart stops when she goes for Solas's throat. He bats her away like she's nothing but a nuisance, and I muffle a cry as she slides into the wall, right over the charred remains of Visia's bones.

"I'm fine." Andarna shakes it off as Solas sizes me up.

"Three minutes," Tairn tells me. *"You will not die today!"*

Three minutes. We can make it three minutes. But time isn't our issue. Tairn can't fit through the opening of the cave. He'll have to find whatever entrance Solas used.

"How the fuck do you kill a dragon?"

"Let me go!" Cat shouts. "You're…you're draining my power!"

What the fuck? I chance a look backward, but all I see is Cat disengaging from Sloane's panicked grip.

"Go for his other eye."

"Get out of the way," I order Andarna, and this time, she listens, scrambling back to my side as I grab two knives from their sheaths and flip them, pinching at the tips for a heartbeat before loosing them.

The first misses as he swivels, but the second finds the mark.

His bellow of pain is followed by rage, and he stumbles backward into the forked tunnel, leaving a small, precious opening between his head and the wall.

Cat and Sloane are closer. They can make it.

"Get her out!" I yell at Cat. "Now!"

"Violet!" Sloane shouts, but Kira's beak closes softly around her pack, and she hoists her into the air as Cat scrambles to mount.

They rush by on the left, making it through just before Solas's claws come out swinging, his talons raking furrows into the stone of the cave.

I hit the floor, pain flaring up my shoulders. There's no *pop* as talons swipe over us, but something bites into my palm. Glass from the conduit.

I spread my bleeding fingers wide in the dim light of the dying torch, locating the remnants before it goes out. The top of the metal joint has broken, leaving four jagged prongs and one secured piece of alloy.

"*I don't have fire,*" Andarna tells me, following my thoughts.

But I have power.

"*It's about to get really dark in here.*" It's our only shot, and I'm taking it. "*You have to run as soon as there's an opening.*"

"*I'm not leaving you,*" she stubbornly argues.

"*One minute!*" Tairn announces.

How the hell am I going to get close enough to stab the remains of the conduit into him? There's no time to tie it to a dagger, and the force of a throw isn't enough to—

Solas roars in pain, his head swiveling back toward his shoulder, and through the opening, I see Cat poised in the dim light, nocking another arrow.

There's no time to ruminate on her sticking around to save me. I'm already moving, grabbing hold of the dying torch in my empty hand, then running toward the soft spot under Solas's foreleg, where his scales separate a few inches at a time to allow the movement of the joint.

He roars again, fire illuminating the cave in a short blast as he aims without sight, hitting the wall in front of him instead of Cat. I race into the deadly space underneath him and change my target when I realize he'll crush me if he falls, charging toward his right shoulder.

I shove the prongs of the conduit into the soft joint between his scales as Andarna sinks her teeth between his neck and shoulder, distracting him, and then I *wield.* Energy sizzles up my arm and into my fingertips where they meet the metal.

Control. This is all about *control.*

With one hand raised, wielding the delicate strain of energy, I back away from Solas as quickly as I dare, feeding more and more power into the stream, and then I pour everything—

Solas roars, swinging his hind end around. A shape comes swinging for me, and I make out the thicker part of his tail in the dim light a second before it slams into my stomach, sending me flying and breaking the stream of lightning.

I'm airborne, nothing more than a projectile as I fly backward, hitting my ass, then my back, and lastly my head against the ground with a crack. But I hold my power tight instead of striking, letting it burn me from the inside out. Better me than accidentally hitting Andarna.

The only sound is a loud ringing in my ears, and sight only comes in quick, flashing blasts. Fire. It flares as I struggle to sit up through the fog of my own heartbeat, revealing Andarna latched onto Solas, hanging on even as he thrashes, slamming her smaller body against the cave wall.

"NO!" I think I yell, but the incessant peal of bells in my head blocks it out, and suddenly I'm moving, being dragged backward by a pair of arms. My head falls back, and I recognize those eyes.

Liam. I *must* be dead.

"She's not clear!" someone shouts as the ringing fades slightly, and then another blast of fire shows two more arrows in the bloodied hole that used to be Solas's shoulder.

Cat. She's beside me, already drawing another arrow, and her lips move silently.

And the eyes above me aren't Liam's. They're Sloane's.

We're plunged back into darkness momentarily, and the ringing fades enough to hear Cat's voice clearly.

"Ninety. One hundred. One hundred and one." Her voice *shakes*.

Light flares again as I'm dragged backward, and Cat fires, hitting Solas in the same wound. Andarna flies free, taking a chunk of Solas with her as I'm hauled from the returning darkness into the growing light from the mouth of the cave.

"Andarna!" I claw at Sloane's grip, but the harder I fight, the weaker I feel, and the insufferable heat of my power lessens as Sloane starts to scream, letting me fall to the ground.

"Silver One!"

I feel the steady beats of air at my back and know Tairn is there, hovering, but I can't rip my eyes away from the darkness of the cave as I stumble to my feet near the entrance.

A dragon *screams*, then falls horrifyingly silent.

She isn't. She can't be.

"She lives," Tairn promises, but I don't breathe until I reach mentally and find my bond with Andarna gleaming and strong.

"I drained you." Sloane holds up trembling hands, staring at them like they don't belong to her. "I drained you!" She grasps my shoulders, yanking my focus from the dark as my head *swims*.

"For fuck's sake, Sloane, give her a second. She just hit her head," Cat barks, still aiming into the darkness as we stand in the glaring light but not firing an arrow without a target.

"Are my eyes red?" Sloane shakes me, or maybe *she's* shaking and simply holding on to me. "Are they red? I swear I didn't reach, Violet. I didn't take anything from you on purpose! Oh gods, am I turning venin?"

"She is as Naolin was," Tairn says.

"You're not turning." I take her hands from my shoulders and stare into the darkness as footsteps sound, talons clicking along the rock.

"I'm not?"

"Your signet manifested," I whisper, my eyes straining to see into the cave opening. "You're a siphon."

Andarna walks into the light, but it's not the blood covering her mouth that catches my attention—it's the blood dripping from the poisoned barb on her tail.

"You killed him." My shoulders dip in relief. "You killed Solas."

Pride and worry assault me at the same time, but I can't force my shields up before Tairn's voice fills my very existence.

"Slayer."

X aden bursts into our room as the healer finishes checking my eyes, shading my vision, then exposing me to light.

"Violet—" He halts a few feet away from where I sit on the edge of our bed. "Cat? What the hell are you doing in here?"

"She saved my life. Making sure she was seen by a healer was the least I could do," Cat answers.

"She *what*?" Xaden moves forward as the healer stands upright.

"You heard me. She put herself between that giant orange dragon and me." She rises from her seat—the same chair Xaden sat in while I slept in here for days after Resson, poisoned by the venin's blade. "Thank you, Sorrengail." She chokes on the words a little before passing by Xaden on her way out.

"Solas—" I start to explain.

"Oh, I already know," he seethes. "Sgaeyl told me."

"You were in a meeting. I didn't want to bother you." I follow the healer's fingers upon direction.

"Bother me?" Shadows flood the floor.

The healer notices, blinking quickly. "You'll be all right. I don't think you're concussed, but that's quite a lump on the back of your head, and I'll ask that you mind the stitches in your hand." She arches a silver brow at me.

"Of course." I lift my wrapped left hand. "Thank you."

She nods, then dismisses herself, disappearing into the hallway.

I stare at Xaden, and he stares right back, tension emanating from every line of his body. "If you want to fight about the wards, that's fine, but I'm not taking the blame for fighting my way out of a cave."

He stalks forward, then bends down into my space and kisses me, soft and slow. "You're alive," he whispers against my lips.

"So my heartbeat says."

"Good." He stands, folding his arms. "Now we can fight. What the fuck were you thinking, saving *Cat*?"

I blink. "I'm sorry, you're mad at *me*? I fight my way out of a cave against a dragon, and you're mad at *me*? For saving a woman in the line of succession to the throne of Poromiel?"

He reels backward, horror flashing into his eyes a second before anger swamps them. "You saved Cat because she's *third* in line?"

"First, I would have fought to save anyone—"

"You selfless, reckless—" he accuses, backing away slowly.

"And second, her death would have triggered yours, so hell yes I saved her!" My feet hit the ground and my head swims for a heartbeat, but my pulse steadies as I breathe deeply. "Tecarus would have had you executed if she'd died under your care."

"Un-fucking-believable." He laces his hands on the top of his head. "You hate her, and yet you refuse to raise the wards, no doubt so her power won't be stripped away, and then you put your life in front of hers—"

"For you!"

"All I want is *you*!" He flicks his hands, and shadows shut the door a little harder than necessary, sealing us in behind the sound shield. "If she dies, then I'll take the consequences. If they can't channel, I'll take those consequences, too. But not you. Never you. Gods, Violet. I'm doing everything in my power to both respect your freedom and keep you safe, and you're…" He shakes his head. "I don't even know what you're doing."

"Keep me safe." I laugh, sarcasm biting into my eyes and making them sting. "Is that what you do? I get it all mixed up with just not killing me."

"There it is." He retreats until his back hits the wall, and then he folds his arms and leans against it, crossing an ankle casually. "You finally ready to ask me about the deal I made with your mother?"

Nothing kills powerful, unshakable love faster than
opposing ideologies.

—The Journal of Warrick of Luceras
—Translated by Cadets Violet Sorrengail and Dain Aetos

CHAPTER FIFTY-FIVE

My mouth opens. Then shuts. "You knew…that I knew?"

"Of course I knew." He arches a dark brow as if *I'm* the problem here. "I've just been waiting for you to work up the courage, the trust, whatever you want to call it, to fucking *ask* me."

My hands fist at my sides, and I shove my power back behind the Archives door and slam my shields up. Without a conduit, there's every chance I'll set the curtains on fire for the entirely wrong reason. "You let me stew in it for *months*?"

"You didn't ask me!" He pushes off the wall but stops himself from taking more than a step. "I've been begging you for *months* to ask me what you want to know, to break down that last insurmountable wall you're keeping between us, but you didn't. Why?"

He has the nerve to put this on *me*?

"You're the one who said you'd never be entirely truthful with me. How am I supposed to know what you will and will not answer? How am I supposed to know what there is to ask?"

"The second you have a question, you ask it. Seems pretty simple."

"Simple? Brennan is alive. You made a deal with my mother for my life. She put those scars on your back. Tell me, Xaden, is it only the secrets about my family you want me to dig out of you? You holding anything about Mira?"

"Shit." He shoves a hand through his hair. "I didn't want you to know about the scars, that's true, but I *would* have told you if you'd asked."

"I asked last year," I challenge, walking toward the windows to look out over the rebuilt city, my anger heating my blood…but not my skin yet, thank the gods.

"I'm sorry. I can't change last year, and though you've said you understand why I kept you in the dark, I don't think you've actually forgiven me."

"I…" Have I? Wrapping my arms around myself, I watch a riot of ten fly overhead, my mind racing with the deal he made, with him *knowing*, him testing me with his ridiculous questions. And he still hasn't told me everything about the scars on his back or what I suspect from the cave about Sgaeyl bonding him. How much more can there be?

"As for the scars, I said you didn't want to know how I got them. You can't honestly tell me that you're happy knowing, are you?"

My stomach twists.

"Of course not!" I spin to face him. "She cut into you over and over!" I shake my head, truly unable to fathom her actions, let alone how he endured it.

"Yes." He nods as if it's just a fact, a piece of history. "And I didn't offer the information because I knew you'd find some way to blame yourself just like you've assumed guilt for everything that's gone wrong in the last few months."

I stiffen. "I have not—"

"You have." He walks forward, stopping at the edge of the bed. "And the scars on my back are *not* your fault. Yes, your life was the unnamed price for the marked ones entering the quadrant." He shrugs. "Your mother called in her favor, and I gave it. Do you want me to apologize for a deal I made before I knew you? Before I loved you? A deal that kept us alive? Started the flow of weaponry to the fliers? Because I won't. I'm not sorry."

"I'm not mad about the deal." How does he not understand? "I'm pissed that you kept it from me, that you insist on making me *ask* for things you should openly share. How the hell am I in love with you when I feel like I barely know you sometimes?"

"Because I let you live long enough for us to fall in love," he says. "Without that deal, gods know what I would have done in my need for revenge. Ask me why I don't regret it. Ask me about the first time I saw you. Ask me about the moment I almost killed you despite the deal and decided not to. Ask me *why*. Ask me something! Fight back like you would have done last year before I broke your trust. Stop being so scared of the answers or waiting for me to give them to you. Demand the truth! I need you to love all of me—not just what you decide to see."

"How are we still having the same fight five months later?" I shake my head. He can tell me or he can choose not to, but I'm done having to guess which questions to ask.

"Because it wasn't just me who shattered your trust last year. Because you were too pissed about my refusal to answer the superficial questions about the revolution to ask the real ones about *us*. Because you didn't have a chance to find your feet before you were tortured. Because I came for you, told you that I love you, and you decided you could admit to loving me, even be with me, but we skipped over the step where you admit to fully trusting me. Take your pick. It's like we're still on that parapet last year, but I'm not the one worried you'll find something unlikable if you dig a little deeper. *You* are."

"That's bullshit." I shake my head. "And how am I supposed to fully trust you when battle-axes are flying out of armoires left and right?"

He lifts his scarred brow. "I'm not sure I understand—"

"It was an analogy I used with Imogen. Never mind." I wave him off.

"About battle-axes in armoires?" His head tilts as he studies me.

I rub the center of my forehead. "I basically said that if a battle-ax came flying out of an armoire and almost killed you, you'd want to check out the armoire to make sure it wouldn't happen again."

"Hmm." He glances out of the corner of his eye to where our uniforms hang side by side, and his brow furrows in thought. "I can work with this."

"I'm sorry?"

"What's in our armoire right now?" He crosses his arms over his chest.

My mouth opens, shuts, then opens again. "Uniforms. Boots. Flight leathers."

"How many uniforms? Which pairs of boots?" Shadows curl along the floor, stretching from beneath our bed to the armoire doors. "Do you actually *know* what's in there? Or do you just trust that I haven't moved your belongings and everything's where you left it?"

"It's an analogy." This is ridiculous. "And I open that armoire every single day. I know where things hang because I see them."

"What about the blanket my mother made me that's tucked back on the top shelf?" Two strands of shadow reach for handles and open the armoire doors.

"I didn't go snooping." I shake my head, my eyes narrowing at him.

A corner of his mouth rises. "Because you trust me."

"Analogy." I enunciate every syllable.

"So ask the question, Violet," he says softly, in that calm, controlled tone that makes me lift my chin. "Humor me."

"Fine," I grit out through my teeth. "Do you happen to have a battle—"

Shadows surge from the armoire, and I catch the glint of metal a heartbeat before the bands of darkness hold a dagger to within inches of my chin.

I gasp, then lock every muscle. "What the fuck, Xaden?"

"Am I going to hurt you?" The carpet makes his bootsteps nearly silent as he crosses the room, giving me plenty of time to object or retreat, but I don't.

"I'm going to hurt *you* if you don't get that away from me." I keep my eyes on him.

"Would I ever let this knife hurt you?" His boots touch the tips of mine, and he leans into my space.

"Of course not."

The shadows slowly take the blade closer to Xaden's throat, and I grab for the hilt, yanking it away and tossing it to the desk before he can accidentally nick himself.

His smile flashes, then fades. "Hey, Violence?"

"What?" I snap.

"There's a knife in the armoire." His hand slides to the nape of my neck, and he leans in, narrowing the world to just the two of us. "All you had to do was ask, and even if you weren't aware it was coming, you know I'd never let it hurt you. I'm not the one you don't trust."

I scoff. "What is that supposed to mean?"

"Love, you're the smartest person I know. If you actually wanted the answers, you'd ask the right questions." His voice softens as his thumb sweeps along my jawline. "You knew about the deal. Maybe the question you need to be asking is *why* you didn't confront me about it."

"Because I love you!" My voice breaks into a mortifying whisper that's almost half as embarrassing as the thoughts I can't keep from spinning in my brain. The thoughts that I've fought to hold at bay ever since my mother told me about the deal she made with him. Heat flushes my cheeks as he holds my stare, and frustration curls my hands into fists. "Because I want to think you kept me alive those first few months before Threshing because you were intrigued or impressed by me or attracted to me like I was to you, and not because you made a deal with *my mother*. Because it's horrifying to think that the only reason you fell in love with me is because of *her*. Because maybe you're right and I didn't want that particular truth, since I know there's a thin line between devotion and obsession, between cowardice and self-preservation, and I'm walking it when it comes to you. I love you so fucking much that I ignored every warning signal last year, and now half the time I don't know what side of that line I'm standing on because I'm too busy looking at you to watch my own feet!"

"Because you don't *want* yourself to know where your feet *are*," he says softly.

My mouth snaps shut. How *dare* he.

Someone pounds on the door.

"Fuck off!" Xaden yells over his shoulder, then sighs as if remembering the sound shield.

"Let's put your theory to the test. You want me to demand the truth? To ask you something real?" I hold his gaze and steel my heart.

"Please, do," he challenges.

"What's your second signet?"

His eyes widen, and the blood drains from his face as his hand falls away. For the first time, I think I've actually managed to shock Xaden Riorson.

"I know you have one," I whisper as the pounding continues. "You told me that Sgaeyl was bonded to your grandfather, which makes you a direct descendant. If a dragon bonds a family member, it can strengthen a signet, but a *direct descendant* will either produce a second signet…or madness, and you seem pretty sane to me."

He inhales sharply and forces his features into a mask.

I shake my head and scoff. "So much for *asking*. I just can't figure out why Sgaeyl was allowed to choose you, how she got away with it. How you *both* did."

The pounding only increases. "We have an emergency out here!"

Brennan?

Both of our heads turn toward the door, and Xaden quickly moves to open it. He listens to my brother's hushed words, then looks over his shoulder at me. "A horde of wyvern has been spotted flying from Pavis toward the cliffs."

Xaden says something else to Brennan, then turns to me again. "You ready to raise those wards? Or would you like to wait until they're actually at the gates?"

Fuck.

CHAPTER
FIFTY-SIX

"Dragons," Brennan says as we skip the path that leads to the wardstone chamber and instead climb the one that leads to the top of the hill with the other members of the Assembly, Xaden and Rhiannon walking up behind us in the afternoon light.

The wind howls as storm clouds roll in above us. Even the weather holds a sense of urgency, and if I'm wrong? If I missed a symbol? A meaning? We'll be fighting for our lives in the next few hours. But I can feel the distinct, powerful hum of the wardstone from here, so that must mean I have part of it right.

The time Dain, Xaden, and I have put in imbuing the wardstone has paid off. It's not creating wards on its own, of course, but it's at least holding power.

The chaos inside Riorson House bleeds onto the trail that leads to the valley as riders and fliers alike hike for the flight field, armed to the teeth with swords, battle-axes, daggers, and bows. My own daggers are sheathed—all but the two I left in the cave with Solas's body—and my pack is strapped to my back. Most third- and second-years are headed to the outposts along the Navarrian border, and then there's me.

I'll be with Xaden, since Tairn and Sgaeyl can fly faster than the rest of the riot to confront the approaching horde. The last thing we want is to let them get to Aretia.

If we hurry and the translation is accurate, we might get the wards working just as the horde reaches the height of the cliffs. I try not to focus on what will happen if I've translated wrong again, my heart racing in my chest as we hurry up the path.

I glance over my shoulder at Xaden, his jaw clenched, eyes not quite meeting mine. Maybe he and I keep having the same fight because we never get to actually finish it. What in Malek's name could his signet be if he went that pale?

"Dragons," I repeat to Brennan, pulling my attention back to my brother and handing the journal over on the page I'd mistranslated originally. "That line?" I point with a gloved finger. "It's more loosely interpreted as political power, not physical, which would be a lower placement on the symbol. Dain caught that one. The stone needs a representative of each den." Which is exactly why Rhiannon is trekking up the path behind us with a stone-silent Xaden. We need Feirge. "And it took reading the entire beginning to know that once a dragon fires a wardstone, their fire can't be used on any other, and reading the entire end to know they created two wardstones. But it doesn't say why they never activated this one. It's dragonfire that triggers the imbedded runes, and they obviously had enough dragons, so why wouldn't they protect more of Navarre if they could?"

My entire body aches from today's attack, especially my head and shoulders, and I fight to lock the pain away so we can get this done. It won't matter if I'm hurting if we're dead in the next few hours. Gently, I probe the swollen knot on the back of my head and wince.

"Let me mend it," Brennan says, worry creasing his forehead as he looks up from the journal.

"We don't have time right now. Later." I shake my head and tug my hood up over my head to ward off the cold.

He shoots me a disapproving look but doesn't try to talk me out of my choice. "Not only did you translate it, but you went back and did it again when most people would have quit. I'm really impressed, Violet." His mouth curves into a smile.

"Thanks." I can't help but smile back with a little bit of pride. "Dad taught me well, and Markham picked up where he left off."

"Bet you disappointed the hell out of him when you stayed in the Riders Quadrant."

"I'm definitely his biggest failure." Just a few more steps.

"But Dad's biggest success." He offers the journal back.

"I think he'd be proud of all of us. You should keep that." I nod at the journal as we finally reach the top. "It needs to be preserved."

"Any time you want it, it's yours," he promises, tucking it into his jacket for safekeeping before heading left toward where Marbh stands next to Cath, his tail flicking as Dain waits in front of him, shifting his weight impatiently.

Six dragons surround the top of the chamber, standing wing to wing, and I make my way to Tairn, who stands beside Sgaeyl, as I would expect.

"How is Andarna?" I ask him, taking my place between his forelegs and peeking over the stone-rimmed edge into the chamber where the wardstone sits a hundred feet below. *"She's not responding when I reach out."*

"She's been questioned by the elders, and her actions were found justifiable," he answers. *"But to slay another dragon is a heavy mark upon the soul, even when in defense of yourself or your rider."*

"That's why you only took his eye instead of killing him." I stiffen as Xaden approaches, refusing to look his way as he moves into position with Sgaeyl.

"I should have ended him then. I will not hesitate when faced with a similar predicament in the future. She now suffers with a burden that should have been mine."

"I'm proud of her."

"As am I."

Rhiannon stands with Feirge, and Suri does the same with her Brown Clubtail.

"Let's get this done." Suri shoots a glare my way, obviously still angry that I've hidden my discovery for the past week. I'm definitely not winning any points in the trust department.

All six of us exchange glances and quick nods.

"It is time," Tairn says.

The dragons inhale as one and then exhale fire into the chamber in six separate streams, instantly warming the air around us. This is exactly why they built it open to the sky—not as some kind of worship of the stars but because the dragons needed access for *this*.

I look away, turning my head to the side when the heat triggers my hypersensitive skin, still stinging from Solas's assault. A heartbeat later, a pulse of magic vibrates through me in a wave, dredging my power to the surface with a feeling slightly softer than the one that had rippled out at the emergence of Aretia's first hatchling.

The fire ceases, and the blazing heat dissipates into the winter air, leaving us all staring at the stone, at our dragons, at one another.

That leveled, anchored sensation I've only felt within the wards at Basgiath has returned, and the wild, unleashed magic that's crawled under my skin since leaving Navarre seems to sit back, not weaker but infinitely more…tame. I lean over the edge to look, but the stone looks exactly the same as it did before.

Maybe the fire is more symbolic?

I glance over at Dain, and he smiles wider than I've seen in years, nodding to me. My quick grin mirrors his, and my chest swells with excitement. We did it. All the long nights and the cold days spent imbuing, all the squabbles over translation, and even my initial failure are worth it for this moment.

"Is that it?" Brennan asks, looking across the chamber's opening at me.

"We don't exactly have time to test it." Xaden points upward, where the drifts have already taken to the sky, then locks his gaze with mine. "Let's fly."

Tairn has never flown faster, leaving Sgaeyl and Xaden behind as he surges for the cliff with the best vantage point for spotting wyvern—the edge of the high plains—usually a two-hour flight for Tairn, but this evening we make it a few minutes under that mark.

"They're fifteen minutes behind us," he tells me as he sails over miles and miles of agricultural fields, gradually descending until we land fifty yards from the edge of the cliffs. *"Use it to center yourself."*

"Don't tell me you're taking Xaden's side of this argument." I unbuckle from the saddle and wince as I climb out of my seat. *"I need to stretch my legs."*

"I don't take the lieutenant anywhere." He chuffs. *"As if I have nothing better to do than listen to your romantic issues."*

"Sorry. Didn't mean to jump to conclusions." I navigate his spikes, and he dips his shoulder.

"Though I do take offense at your insult," he notes as I slide down his leg.

"Insult?" My knee protests when my boots collide with the frozen ground, but the wrap holds tight.

"You doubt your judgment as if I did not choose you for it."

"But you weren't listening. Right." Rolling my shoulders, I walk toward the edge of the cliff and summon just enough of my power that my skin warms even though my breath puffs out in clouds of steam.

There's a hum here, too, and I instinctively know that this is where the wards end, twenty feet short of the cliff's edge. This point is a four-hour flight from Aretia for average dragons—if such a creature exists.

Would this be the natural border of Basgiath's wards if they weren't extended by the outposts? That distance would leave Elsum, Tyrrendor, and even most of Calldyr unwarded.

Gods, we're not even shielding most of Tyrrendor if this is the wardstone's natural range.

"What's the news?" I ask Tairn.

"The nearest riot of three is twenty miles to the north, and the same to the south."

"No sightings?" We don't have the strength Xaden wants in each unit tonight, but we can cover more of the border in groups of three, or in our case, two. Deploying in smaller but closely spaced units gives the stronger dragons a better chance at communicating as well.

Every bonded pair has been recalled from the lines across Poromiel to defend the cliffs, but there's no hope of those stationed in Cordyn, or beyond at the border with the Braevick province, making it back in time.

"Not from the cliffs."

"But beyond?" I look out across the darkening landscape, searching for any sign of gray wings.

"I'd estimate we have a quarter hour." He huffs a hot breath of steam that billows past me. *"Prepare yourself. Sgaeyl approaches."*

"Do you think he's right?" I ask, folding my arms across my chest as wingbeats break the relative silence of the night.

"I know he thinks he is."

That's helpful.

Sgaeyl lands close to Tairn, and I breathe in my last moments of peace and prepare myself for the battle to come before the actual war reaches us.

It isn't long before I hear his familiar footsteps coming my way.

"No sightings on this side of the cliff," I tell him as he reaches my side, keeping my shields firmly in place. "Tairn thinks we have fifteen minutes."

"There's no one else out here." His words are clipped.

"Right. We're the only pair." I shift my weight, energy tingling in my fingers, slowly filling my cells, saturating me in preparation instead of drowning me as usual. "I know that goes against your full riot—"

"That's not what I mean." He shoves his gloves into his pockets, leaving his hands bare and ready to wield, the perfect picture of composure and control. "There's no one within miles to hear us."

My eyebrows shoot up, and I turn toward him in sheer incredulity. "I'm sorry, are you suggesting that the reason you didn't answer my question back in Aretia was because you don't trust your own sound shield on our room?"

"There is always someone better at something than you, including wards." He winces. "And maybe that wasn't the entire reason."

"Spare me from whatever bullshit you're about to impart." My stomach twists, and I lower my voice into my best Xaden impression. "'Ask me.'" I shake my head. "Yet, the first real question I pose, you duck out the door like a coward."

"It never occurred to me that you'd *ask* about a second signet," he argues.

"Liar." I whip my gaze forward, studying the sky for movement and fighting the scalding anger that tests the Archives doors of my power. "You wouldn't have told me that Sgaeyl bonded your grandfather if you never wanted me to know. Whether it was a conscious or unconscious choice, you made it. You *knew* I'd figure it out. Was it just another one of your *ask me* tests? Because if so, you failed this one, not me."

"Don't you think I know that?" he shouts, the words coming out strangled, like they had to be ripped from his throat.

The admission earns him my full attention, but his outburst is quickly smothered by his self-control, and we fall into strained silence as he stares off into the distance.

"Sometimes I feel like I don't know you." I study the harsh lines of his face as his jaw flexes. "How am I supposed to really love you if I don't know you?"

I can't, and I think we both know it.

"How long do you think it takes for someone to fall out of love?" He studies the skyline. "A day? A month? I'm asking because I don't have any experience with it."

What the fuck? I fold my arms to keep from giving in to the impulse to jab him with the sharp point of my elbow.

"I'm asking," he continues, his throat working as he swallows, "because I think it will take you all of a heartbeat once you know."

Apprehension slides up my spine and knots in my throat as I slightly lower my shields just enough to feel ice-cold terror along my bond with him. What the hell could his signet be that I wouldn't love him?

Oh shit. What if he's like Cat? What if he's been manipulating my emotions this whole time? I swallow back the bile inching its way up my throat.

"I would never do something like that," he retorts, sending a sideways, wounded glare at me as he continues to watch the sky.

"Shit." I rub my hands over my face. "I didn't mean to say that out loud."

He doesn't respond.

"Just tell me what it is." I reach for him, curling my fingers around the back of his arm. "You said that you trust me to stay because even if I don't know your darkest deeds, I know what you're capable of, but I don't if you won't tell me." Somehow, we're right back where we were months ago, neither of us fully trusting the other.

His mouth opens, but he snaps it shut, as if he was going to talk, then thought better of it.

"Signets have to do with who we are at our core and what we need," I think out loud. If he won't tell me, then I'll figure it out my damn self. "You are a master of secrets, hence the shadows." I gesture at the ones curled around his feet. "You're deadly with every weapon you pick up, but that's not a signet." My brow furrows.

"Stop."

"You're ruthless, which I guess could have something to do with an ability to shut off your emotions." I shift my weight and study his face, watching for even the most minute sign that I'm onto something, and keep guessing, trusting Tairn to spot the wyvern before we do. "You're a natural leader. Everyone gravitates toward you, even against their better judgment." That last part comes out as a mutter. "You're always in the right place—" My eyebrows rise. "Are you a distance wielder?" I've only read about two riders in all of history who could cross hundreds of miles in a single step.

"There hasn't been a distance wielder in centuries, and don't you think if I was one, I would have spent every night in your bed?" He shakes his head.

"But what do you need?" I ponder, ignoring the tense set of his jaw. "You need to question everyone to make your own impressions. You need to be a quick judge of character in order to know who to trust and who not to in order to have run those smuggling missions at Basgiath for *years*. More than anything, you need control. It's woven into every aspect of your personality."

"Stop," he demands.

I ignore the warning completely, just like I ignored Mira's warning last year to stay away from him. "You need to fix— Never mind, if you could mend, you wouldn't have brought me to Aretia. Let's try eliminating signets instead. You can't see the future, or you never would have led us to Athebyne. You can't wield any element, or you would have done so in Resson—" I pause as a thought pushes past the others. "Who knows?"

"Stop before you go somewhere we can't come back from." Shadows move across the inches that separate us, winding up my calves as if he thinks he's going to have to fight to keep me at his side.

"Who knows?" I repeat, my voice rising with my temper. Not that it matters. There's no one else for miles, and there are no sound-seekers in Aretia capable of hearing across miles of distance like Captain Greely in General Melgren's personal unit, hence why our communication times lag. "Do the marked ones know? Does the Assembly? Am I the only person close to you who *doesn't* know, just like last year?" My hand falls away from his arm.

It's *impossible* to have a signet that no one has detected, no one has trained. Has he played me for a fool *again*? The space between my ribs and my heart shrivels and shrinks, my chest threatening to crumple.

"For fuck's sake, Violet. No one else knows." He turns toward me in a move so fast it would intimidate someone else, but I know he's incapable of hurting me—at least physically—so I merely tilt my chin and stare up into those gold-flecked eyes in blatant challenge.

"I deserve better than this. Tell me the truth."

"You've always deserved better than me. And no one knows," he repeats, his voice dropping. "Because if they did, I'd be dead."

"Why would—" My lips part, and my pulse jumps as my head starts to swim.

He has to have full control. He has to make snap character judgments. He has to intrinsically know who to trust and who not to. In order for the movement to have been as successful as it was within the walls of Basgiath, he has to know...everything.

Xaden's most pressing need is information.

Tairn shifts, angling his body toward Sgaeyl instead of beside her.

Oh gods. There's only one signet riders are killed for having. Fear churns in my stomach and threatens to bring up what little I've had to eat today.

"Yes." He nods, his gaze boring into mine.

Shit, did he just—

"No." I shake my head and take a step backward out of his shadows, but he moves as if he takes the step *with* me.

"Yes. It's how I knew I could trust you not to tell anyone about the meeting under the tree last year," he says as I retreat another step. "How I seem to know what my opponent has planned on the mat before their next move. How I know exactly what someone needs to hear in order to get them to do what I need done, and how I knew if someone remotely suspected us while we were at Basgiath."

I shake my head in denial, wishing I'd stopped pushing like he'd demanded me to.

He crosses the space between us. "It's why I didn't kill Dain in the interrogation chamber, why I let him come with us, because the second his shields wavered, I knew he'd had a true epiphany. How would I know that, Violet?"

He'd read Dain's mind.

Xaden is more dangerous than I ever imagined.

"You're an inntinnsic," I whisper. Even the accusation is a death sentence among riders.

"I'm a *type* of inntinnsic," he repeats slowly, like it's the first time he's ever said the words. "I can read intentions. Maybe I would know what to call it if they didn't kill everyone with even a hint of the signet."

My eyebrows jolt upward. "Can you read thoughts or not?"

His jaw flexes. "It's more complicated than that. Think of that breath of a second *before* the actual thought, the subconscious motivation you might not even be aware of in your mind, or when instinct drives you to move or you're looking to betray someone. The intention is always there. Mostly they come across as pictures, but some people *intend* in *really* clear pictures."

Tairn growls low in his throat and lowers his head at Sgaeyl as a rush of something bitter and sick floods our bond. *Betrayal.* I slam my shields up, blocking him out before I'm lost to his emotions, already struggling with mine.

He didn't know.

Another rumble of anger vibrates his chest scales, and my heart lurches with pangs of sympathy.

Sgaeyl draws back in retreat, shocking me to the core, but holds her head high, exposing her throat to her mate.

The same way Xaden just metaphorically exposed his to me. All I have to do is tell someone—anyone—and he's dead. A soft roaring fills my ears.

"There are some secrets even mates can't share," Xaden says, his eyes locked on mine, but his words are meant for Tairn. "Some secrets that can't be spoken of even behind the protections of wards."

"And yet you know everyone's secrets, don't you? Everyone's *intentions*?" That's why inntinnsics aren't allowed to live. The implications of his signet hit me with the force of a battering ram, and I stagger backward like the blow is a physical one. How many times has he read me? How many pre-thoughts has he eavesdropped on? Do I actually love him? Or did he just say what I wanted to hear? Do the things I needed in order to—

"Less than a minute," Xaden whispers as Sgaeyl moves toward him—toward us. "That's how long it took for you to fall out of love with me."

My gaze flashes to his. "Don't read my...whatever!"

Tairn stalks toward me, his head low and his teeth bared as he places himself at my back.

"I didn't." The saddest smile I've ever seen tugs at Xaden's mouth. "First, because your shields are up, and secondly because I didn't have to. It's all over your face."

My heart struggles to beat regularly, torn between slowing and sluggishly admitting defeat, and racing—no, rising to *fight*—in defense of the simple yet agonizing truth that I love him anyway.

But how many more blows can that love take? How many more daggers are there in that metaphorical armoire? Gods, I don't know what to think. Nausea washes over me. Has he ever used it on me?

"Say something," he begs, fear streaking through his eyes.

The roaring grows louder, the sound like a thousand soft drops of rain on a roof.

"My love isn't fickle." I shake my head slowly, keeping my gaze locked on his. "So you'd better live, because I'm ready to ask you *all* the fucking questions."

"Silver One, mount!" Tairn bellows, demolishing the barrier of my shields like they're thinner than parchment. *"Wyvern!"*

Xaden and I both spare a single glance to the edge of the cliffs. My stomach drops as I realize that the approaching gray cloud isn't a storm and that roaring in my ears is actually wingbeats. One heartbeat, that's all I wait, and then I'm turning, moving, sprinting across the frozen ground and racing up the ramp Tairn makes of his foreleg to his shoulder.

"How many?" I lower my flight goggles and blast the question down the mental pathway that connects the four of us as I climb into my saddle.

"Hundreds," Sgaeyl answers.

"That's unfortunate." I force air through my lungs in measured breaths to keep calm, but my hand still trembles as I buckle the belt across my lap. The second I'm secure, Tairn swings his body parallel to the cliffs and launches, throwing my weight back into my seat as he climbs rapidly with heavy, forceful wingbeats.

When we have enough altitude for air superiority, Tairn banks left, flying in a tight circle until we face the flying horde. Then he pushes his wings back against the wind, abruptly halting our momentum and sending my body forward into the pommel as he hovers a hundred feet above the frozen field, leaving twice his body length between us and the cliff's edge. *"A little warning next time?"* I use our private bond.

"Did you fall?" he challenges along the same, his wings rising and falling only often enough to keep us relatively in place.

I decide to keep my retort to myself as Xaden and Sgaeyl arrive on our right, keeping a noticeable distance from the edge of Tairn's wing. *"I'm sorry she didn't tell you."*

"We will settle matters of emotion after matters of life."

Noted.

My stomach twists when I can make out individual shapes in the horde, then outright sours as evening sky appears between their wingbeats.

"Thirty seconds," Tairn estimates.

I release the pommel and turn my palms up, opening the Archives door to Tairn's power and letting it fill every cell in my body until the hum of energy I pick up on at the edge of the wards is replaced by the hum of energy that I've become.

"They're slowing," Xaden remarks as the horde spreads into a grouping I'm terrified to acknowledge looks like a formation.

Bile rises in my throat as I count one, two, three, four— *"I count at least a dozen venin."*

"Seventeen," Tairn corrects in a growl.

Seventeen dark wielders and a horde that rivals the riot at Aretia against…us. *"We're dead if the wards aren't up, if I messed up the translation."*

"You didn't," Xaden replies, sounding infinitely more confident than I feel.

Heat flushes my skin as my power seeks an outlet, but I keep it contained, ready to be wielded as three wyvern break away from the grouping and fly closer. They hover a tail's length beyond the edge of the cliffs, their scales dull and gray, holes peppered through their wings as though they hadn't quite finished forming.

"They can feel the wards," I manage to say before my stomach abandons my body, plummeting like a rock. The rider on the center wyvern…

"Then they can die in them, too," Sgaeyl replies.

I can only make out vague facial features from this distance, but I know in my very bones it's *him*. The Sage from Resson, the one who's taken up residence in my nightmares.

His head turns noticeably from me…to Xaden.

"He was in Resson," I tell him.

"I know." White-hot rage shimmers along the bond.

The Sage lifts his staff, then swings it like a club, pointing toward us.

"I love you," Xaden says as the wyvern closest to me banks away from the wards, falling into a turning dive, only to gain speed and climb again, leveling out behind the lead two before flying straight for us. *"Even if you believe nothing else I ever say, please believe that."*

"Do not speak to her as if death is a possibility," Tairn snaps, slamming his own shields around us both, an impenetrable wall of black stone, blocking out Xaden and Sgaeyl.

I breathe deeply, using every ounce of concentration to keep my power contained and my emotions under control as the wyvern accumulates speed and flies past the lead two, heading for the wards.

Time slows to heartbeats, my breath freezing in my heated chest.

Then the wyvern crosses the invisible barrier, and my heart stops beating altogether as its wings flap once. Twice.

"Prepare to dive." Tairn swivels his head, his jaw opening as the wyvern closes the distance to less than a body length, and I brace for the maneuver. *"Never mind."*

The wyvern's wings and head sag, and its body follows suit—as though someone plucked out its life force—and then it falls, propelled only by its previous momentum, passing forty feet beneath us and crashing into the field below, leaving a deep furrow before stopping.

"We should check—"

"Its heartbeat ceased," Tairn tells me, his attention already redirected to

the other two wyvern along the border and the horde behind them. *"The wards work."*

The wards *work*. Relief restarts my heart.

The Sage swings his staff again and lets out a furious shout, sending the wyvern on the right, who meets the same fate a few seconds later, impacting a short distance from the first one.

Tairn doesn't look when Sgaeyl dives for the carcasses, but he does lower his shields.

"They're dead," Xaden confirms a moment later, and I glance down to see Felix arriving on his Red Swordtail.

We're safe. I throw out my hands and release the searing energy within me, letting it snap free as I wield. Lightning cracks open the sky, striking a few feet from the remaining wyvern, and I curse under my breath.

Close, but I didn't hit him.

It's enough for the Sage to call off the attack, and though I can't see his eyes from here, I feel the hatred of his stare locking onto me as he looks back before joining the rest of the horde.

"That's it?" I ask Tairn as he holds position, watching the wyvern become a cloud of gray once again. How...anticlimactic. *"Now what?"*

"Now we stay long enough to be sure, and then we go home."

We wait another three hours before flying back, long enough for Suri to arrive and tell us of three similar incidents along the cliffs. We weren't the lucky recipients of a lone horde. It was a coordinated, simultaneous attack.

But we survived.

The joyous atmosphere is contagious when we walk into Riorson House a few hours later, accompanied by Felix, and I'm promptly pulled into Rhiannon's hug.

"You got the wards up!" Her flight leathers are still cold from the night air, meaning she's just returned, too.

"*We* got the wards up," I counter before I'm yanked out of her arms and smooshed against Ridoc's chest, then Sawyer's, as riders and fliers celebrate around us, the noise filling the cavernous space of Riorson House's foyer and somehow making the area feel smaller in the best way, less like a fortress and more like a home.

"We're needed in the Assembly chamber right now," Xaden says, leaning past Sloane and raising his voice to be heard over the cacophony.

Our eyes lock and I nod, keeping my shields firmly in place to block him out, which feels not only unnatural but...wrong. How ironic to celebrate a monumental victory and still feel like I've lost something precious. There hasn't been a second alone to discuss the fact that if my shields were down, he'd already know how fucked up my head is about the signet he's hidden.

I can't imagine walking away from this, from us, but that doesn't mean that we don't have some serious issues we need to discuss—nor that I am not pissed as hell that he's given me *another* reason to doubt my own ability to trust my own judgment. And just because I can't imagine walking away doesn't mean I won't do it if we can't find some healthy ground. I'm quickly learning it's possible to love someone and not want to be with them at the same time.

The second we walk into the Assembly chamber and a guard shuts the door behind us, the noise outside falls away and eight pairs of eyes turn in our direction. None of them appear as happy as they should be, given what we've just accomplished.

Syrena and Mira break away from the Assembly and walk toward us as Felix calls Xaden over from the dais with an urgent tone.

"We need to find time to talk," Xaden says quickly and quietly, and I know he only says it out loud because I won't let him into my mind.

"Later," I agree just to end the conversation before Mira and Syrena hear us. There isn't enough time in the world to process what he's told me.

He walks away as they approach, and I peel my gaze from his back to give my attention to my sister. The tension in her face has power rising within me swiftly, my body preparing for battle. "What's wrong?"

"As soon as the attack was over, a missive was delivered to Ulices," she tells me. "He was at the Terria outpost—"

"On the border with Navarre," I finish for her, anxious to get to the heart of the matter.

"Melgren has asked us to meet with him tomorrow. He requested whomever represents our movement—no more than two marked ones allowed—along with Violet and Mira Sorrengail." She reaches for my hand and squeezes gently. "You can say no. You *should* say no."

"Why would the commanding general of all Navarrian forces ask for a cadet and lieutenant?" My voice trails off and I glance over to the dais, where Brennan is locked in a quiet, heated discussion with the other six. "Our mother will be there."

"And if a fight breaks out, we know it ends in his favor—otherwise, he would never summon us. He's already seen the outcome."

I stick that predicament on the growing list of things I'll have to deal with.

"There's something else you need to know," Syrena says, drawing a dagger and placing it on her outstretched palm. With a flick of the flier's wrist, the dagger rises a few inches, then spins when she twirls her index finger.

It's a simple, lesser magic, something I learned last year—

"You can still wield." My heart sinks at the wider implications, and my shoulders sag.

She nods solemnly. "As glad as I am to not be stripped of my power, I'm sorry to say there's something wrong with your wards."

Fuck.

The day Augustine Melgren manifested his signet changed warfare
for the kingdom of Navarre forever.

—NAVARRE, AN UNEDITED HISTORY
BY COLONEL LEWIS MARKHAM

CHAPTER
FIFTY-SEVEN

The irony of meeting at Athebyne is not lost on me, nor is the fact that this is
the second time I'm visiting the outpost on the edge of the Esben mountain
range after finding out Xaden Riorson has hidden pertinent information from
me.

I spent last night in the library, which was probably in the best interest of
everyone as I continue to muddle through my thoughts. Intentions. What-the-
fuck-ever.

Today, I'm bleary-eyed and restless, with more questions than answers. But
as I glance over at Xaden landing on Sgaeyl's back, his face tense and drawn,
I can recognize that telling me, whether or not he wanted to, was the ultimate
gesture of trust.

And this time, I'm not the last to know. I'm the first. Maybe it makes me
completely, utterly foolish, but somehow that makes a difference, even if I
haven't had the opportunity to tell him that…or the opportunity to interrogate
his ass about how many of *my* intentions he's read.

I'm just not sure how many *this-times* I have in me, no matter how much I
love him.

Our riot of ten lands in the clearing over the ridgeline from the outpost
at noon—a full hour before we're due to meet—and four of the dragons back
into the cover of the forest immediately, hiding in the shelter of the enormous
evergreen trees that surround the field. The other six stand wing to wing, ready
to launch at a moment's notice.

"You're sure they won't be able to tell they're here?" I ask Tairn, putting my flight goggles into my pack before sliding down Tairn's foreleg. Landing on the frozen ground makes me wince. I'd woken up this morning with a hundred-year-old text stuck to my cheek and a throbbing ache in my neck.

"Not exactly, but there's no snow at this elevation to carry tracks. Dragons only sense each other mind-to-mind when we allow it. As long as they stay downwind, the others will know they're here but won't be able to identify how many or who has come."

"That's not exactly comforting." Especially given who insisted on traveling with us. I stretch my arms up at the sun and roll my neck carefully to ease the stiffness in my muscles. After fighting Solas yesterday and accidentally sleeping on a table in the library last night, my body has had it with me, and I can't blame it.

"You are not a child in need of comfort."

True, which only serves to remind me of the enraged adolescent I have waiting for me at home in Aretia. After telling her there would be no logical way to explain her presence even if Tairn carried her, which she was adamantly opposed to, Andarna cursed Tairn's entire family line, then blocked us both and went to practice with the elders.

Tairn's only response had been a muttered expletive about the moods of adolescents.

It doesn't escape my notice that Sgaeyl stands between Teine and Fann, Ulices's cantankerous Green Swordtail, not next to Tairn, which either explains or is a result of his surly mood this morning.

Mom and Dad are fighting, and everyone knows it.

Xaden crosses in front of Fann, completely unbothered by her snort of insult at his proximity, and peels off his gloves as he approaches me.

"You didn't come to bed last night." His brow furrows as he makes a quick study of my face, then shoves the gloves into his pocket, and I mirror his motions just in case we'll need to wield.

Then I reinforce my shields.

"I was in the library with Dain, poring over Warrick's journal to see what I got wrong. We both fell asleep on one of the tables, until Jesinia and a few others joined us for more study." I meet his gaze, then look away before I start pelting him with questions or do something even more foolish like forgive him before getting answers.

"I thought Jesinia didn't speak Old Lucerish?" He barely glances at the riders who walk by and gather in front of Fann. We've brought three from Mira's unit in addition to members of the Assembly.

"She doesn't, but Sawyer's smitten, and the others were determined to help in any way they could." Even Cat, Maren, and Trager had joined in a show of support.

"Did you find anything?"

The dragons raise their heads at a sound coming from the other side of the clearing, and the way they quickly lower them tells me everything I need to know. Early or not, this meeting is about to start.

"No," I answer, keeping my eyes on the trees and fighting the apprehension trying to knot in my throat. *The breath of life of the six and the one combined and set the stone ablaze in an iron flame.* What did I miss? "If I had, you'd know it."

"Would I?" His tone tightens.

"You would." My gaze jumps to lock with his. "I appreciate you not trying to talk me out of coming."

"I learned my lesson at Cordyn." He searches my face but doesn't reach for me. "Let me in. If only for a second, please let me in."

My chest tightens with every heartbeat as I hold his gaze. Exactly how much of this is mine to forgive? It's *his* secret. But I can't help wondering how much he's read into my own intentions. That's the part that has me hesitant, no matter how much I love him.

"Violet?" It's the blatant plea in his tone that has me lowering my shields just enough to feel our bond connect, and the resulting relief on his face is palpable. *"If you decide to tell them what I am as punishment for the crimes I've committed against you, I'll understand."*

"You want to discuss this now, of all times?" I lift my eyebrows at him.

"I wanted to discuss this last night, but apparently you were busy working to save Tyrrendor." His attention shifts to the trees, and Tairn's shadow races across the brittle prairie grass, winding around us.

"Are you complaining?" Our hands brush as we both turn to face whomever is coming through those trees.

"About you choosing the safety of my home over fighting with me?" He scowls but laces his fingers with mine. *"No, but—"*

Mira approaches from behind Xaden, her stride confident, though two lines of worry are etched between her brows.

I squeeze his hand, then let go.

"I need to know something." I run my hands down my hips, counting the blades sheathed there, all six of them. *"Did you ever use your signet to glean information to influence my feelings in any way?"*

"Never." He shakes his head, but his hands clench at his sides and the muscle in his jaw pops. *"But I have always lacked a certain element of self-control when it comes to you, and our bond makes it way too easy for you to send your intentions without even realizing it."*

Death would be preferable to the embarrassment that accompanies that revelation.

"I could torch him if you would like," Tairn offers. *"But you do seem attached."*

Heat flushes up my neck and stings my cheeks, reminding me of the times my scalp would prickle in his presence. *"You knew I wanted to kiss you that night by the wall…"*

Gods, I can't even finish the question.

The tops of the trees begin to sway.

They've brought dragons.

"Yes." He glances at me. *"And you have my most sincere apology. Had I known what we would become"*—he shakes his head—*"fuck, I probably still would have done it."*

"Do you still do it?" I have to know.

"No. I stopped the moment you were more to me than the general's daughter, the moment I realized the harm Dain had done—and that I was no better than he was."

Except Xaden hadn't brokered the information he'd stolen and been responsible for killing Liam and Soleil. Yet I've made some kind of peace with Dain, haven't I?

Maybe I'm becoming complacent with betrayal because it's fucking *everywhere.*

"I'm not going to turn you in," I say quickly, looking up at him as Mira comes within hearing distance. *"But we'll be fighting about this later."* I lift my brows.

The muscle in his jaw ticks like he wants to say more, but he only adds, *"I will make myself available to you."*

"You ready for this?" Mira asks, crossing in front of Xaden to stand beside me.

"No," I reply to Mira. "Are you?"

"No." She rests her hand on the pommel of the shortsword sheathed at her hip. "But she'll never know that."

"I want to be you when I grow up." A smile tugs at my lips despite the anxiety quickening my breaths.

"You'll be better than me," she counters, then looks over the top of my head to talk to Xaden. "By the way, you couldn't convince him to stay in Aretia?"

"I don't wield emotions, and members of the Assembly don't take well to being tied down and restrained." He reaches back over his shoulder and draws one of the swords strapped to his back with his left hand, leaving his right free to wield. "If you're looking to influence mindwork, find a flier."

I barely keep myself from jabbing him at his clever semantics, because the man clearly specializes in mindwork.

"Here we go," Mira mutters as seven figures dressed in black step into the clearing.

I palm a dagger in my right hand and crack open the door to the Archives, letting power trickle into me.

Melgren walks at the center, his beady eyes shifting down our line of Aretian riders. I don't need Cat's gift to heighten his anger. He wears rage like it's a part of his uniform.

I force myself to glance at the other members of their chosen party, only recognizing three, two of whom were Mom's aides at one point or another.

"Colonel Fremont—second on the left—is a very powerful air wielder," I tell Xaden. *"He can suck the air straight out of your lungs."*

"Thank you." Shadows rise in front of the three of us, curling in blade-like fingers at the level of our knees.

Then my gaze falls on Mom.

She walks at Melgren's side, cutting through the field with quick, efficient steps, her attention split between Mira and me. The closer she comes, the more apparent her exhaustion. Deep bruises mark the space under her eyes, contrasting with her paler-than-normal complexion, even though the lines from her flight goggles indicate she's spending time in the sky.

Mira tilts her chin and smooths her expression into a mask I envy and do the best to emulate.

The dragons follow, led out of the forest by Melgren's dragon, Codagh. The utter nightmare of a black dragon immediately lowers his head as he stalks forward, and his golden eyes narrow at me—no, at Tairn standing behind me. Fuck, I'd almost forgotten just how big he is, easily five feet taller than Tairn, numerous battle scars marking his chest scales and wings.

Mom's dragon, Aimsir, follows, prowling toward us at the same time the other five make their appearance, an orange, two reds…and a blue.

Tairn steps forward and lifts his head to hover over mine, a menacing rumble working its way up his throat.

"Don't drool on me," I joke, but it falls flat.

The Navarrian riders walk to the center of the field, and when Ulices moves, so do we, leaving ten feet of empty field between our lines. Swords and daggers gleam within easy reach on both sides.

"And here I was thinking you were dead, Ulices," Melgren starts, forcing a smile that's mostly bared teeth.

"And here I was hoping *you* were," Ulices counters, using his height to look down his nose at Melgren.

"No such luck," Melgren replies. "What happened to meeting at the outpost?" He gestures back toward the trees. "We have refreshments waiting if you'd care to—"

"Probably poisoned," Tairn adds, but he sounds slightly distracted, as if

holding more than one conversation at once, probably because he is.

"We don't," Xaden interrupts. "Speak your piece, Melgren."

Melgren's gaze jumps to Xaden. "We never should have let you into the quadrant."

"Regrets are truly a bitch, aren't they?" Xaden cocks his head. "Let's get to it. You may have nothing better to do with your day, but we're busy fighting for our Continent."

"Nothing better?" Melgren snaps, his face blotching. "Do you know the destruction you caused by dropping those wyvern on the outposts? The lengths we went to in order to keep it quiet? The civilians we had to—" He stops himself, breathing deeply and straightening his shoulders. "You almost tore down centuries of work, of tightly woven defensive strategy designed to protect the people within our borders."

"But only the people within your borders," Mira accuses. "Fuck everyone else, right?"

Mom's eyes flash with barely leashed reprimand.

"Yes." Melgren turns that unnerving stare on my sister. "When you abandon ship in the middle of a hurricane, you save those you can in the dinghy, then cut the hands off anyone else who tries to climb aboard so they don't pull you under."

"You're a callous asshole," she fires back.

"Thank you."

"Are we here for a reason?" Xaden asks. "You know, besides the evil villain lecture?" Sunlight glints off the blade of his sword as he shifts his grip.

"We *let* you go," Melgren answers, glancing between Ulices and Xaden. "Let you take half the Riders Quadrant cadets without so much as a fight. Let *her* go"—his withering gaze slides over mine, and I lock my muscles to keep from shuddering—"after she brutally murdered the vice commandant. Ever stop to think about why?"

My stomach clenches.

"I personally try *not* to think about you," Xaden replies, outright lying, but damn does he pull it off.

"You can't afford to lose the riders necessary to fight us," Ulices answers. "We're too expensive to keep, especially with the number of riders—and the riot—who chose to leave you."

"Perhaps." Melgren tilts his head. "Or perhaps I let you."

My grip tightens on my dagger.

"Perhaps"—the general draws out the word—"I knew we'd need you for a coming battle."

Highly unlikely. Who would they possibly be fighting behind the wards?

"I'll meet Malek before I fight for Navarre again," Ulices snarls.

"You were always too quick to make important decisions," Melgren says with a sigh, patting his chest. "That's why I didn't mourn your loss."

Damn. That was harsh.

"This meeting is over—" Ulices starts, red rising up his neck and splashing onto his cheeks.

"They're going to overrun us at Samara," Melgren interrupts.

Everyone quiets.

I struggle to draw my next breath. Surely he didn't mean to say that. I look at Mom, and my knees weaken at the subtle nod she gives me. Even Mira tenses.

"I've seen it," Melgren continues. "They come for us on solstice, and they win."

Shit, he said *exactly* what he meant. A chill races up my spine as the blood drains from my face. If Samara falls, if *any* of the outposts do, wyvern would have unfettered access to parts of Navarre the ward extensions have protected for the last six hundred years.

Without the outposts, Basgiath's wards would rebound to their natural limits, only a few hours' flight, reaching nowhere near the border.

"How?" Ulices challenges, and the riders from Mira's unit exchange disbelieving looks.

"Do me a favor," I say to Xaden. *"Forget feeling guilty about reading my intentions and please read theirs."*

"Everyone but the major on the right is shielded, but she's scared shitless and intends to do whatever she needs to get us to agree," he answers, shifting so his hand brushes the back of mine. *"Oh, and she wants to eat after this meeting, and argue with your mother over her supposed affection for her daughters. Now put your shields up and block me—and everyone else—out."*

Holy shit. No wonder inntinnsics aren't allowed to live. Xaden is both a jaw-dropping weapon and a frightening liability. I do as he suggests, only leaving space for Tairn and the opaque, glimmering bond I feel with Andarna, even at this distance.

"How isn't how it works." Melgren folds his arms across his chest, and Codagh bares his dripping teeth. "All that matters is that we lose on solstice."

They *lose.* If the wards are breached, there's no way to estimate the death toll. Every Navarrian civilian between the border and the wardstone's natural limitations will be in mortal danger.

"Silver One?"

"I'm fine." But I'm not.

"If you've already seen the outcome, then what the hell do you expect us to do about it?" Ulices challenges, lifting his hands as he shrugs.

My head turns in his direction, but I bite my tongue before I can reply that he obviously expects us to *help*.

"Change the outcome by fighting at our side." Melgren frowns like he's being forced to swallow rotten fruit. "In the battle I see, none of you are there." He glances at Xaden.

"And we're not going to be." Ulices shakes his head. "We don't fly for you."

No, we fly for... Wait, who *do* we fly for? Not just Aretia, or even Tyrrendor. And if we're willing to fight to defend the civilians of Poromiel, why wouldn't we fight to defend Navarrians, too?

"No, but you do fly for the Empyrean," Mom interjects. "Dragonkind won't stand aside if the hatching grounds in the Vale are compromised."

"Your mother is presumptuous to speak on behalf of dragonkind," Tairn mutters.

"If the hatching grounds are compromised. Losing one outpost won't take down the entire system, and half your riot left with us," I remind her.

"And you're proud of that? What you caused may very well be the reason we lose this battle!" the box-framed captain beside Mom snarls, lifting his shortsword in my direction.

I flip my dagger, pinching the tip in readiness to throw, but shadows jolt forward, knocking the sword from the captain's hand and putting him on his ass.

Xaden clicks his tongue and wiggles his pointer finger. "No, no. I'd hate to lose the spirit of civility, wouldn't you? We were all getting along so nicely."

"Godsdamned traitor," the captain spits out, fumbling for his sword before finding his feet. "Malek will meet you for your crimes."

Mom sheathes a dagger I never saw her draw, her focus flicking between the captain and Xaden.

"Tried that. He didn't want me—or any of us, remember?" Xaden scratches his relic with his empty hand.

"Enough," Melgren shouts. "I don't expect you to ally yourself with us for nothing. Fight for us at Samara, and I have it on King Tauri's word that we will respect the independence of your riot...and the city you've taken refuge in."

The breath freezes in my lungs. *"Does he know about Aretia?"*

"I can't tell."

"We will not conscript your citizens for our army, nor will we drag your people into a border war you have no chance of winning." Melgren shrugs.

"If you truly thought that, you would have invaded the second we left." Mira sounds like she's bored. "Unless you saw the battle didn't go your way."

"This is the only offer." Melgren ignores Mira, focusing on Ulices. "If you are not our allies, then you are our enemies."

Allies. That's the logical answer.

"I think we'll sit this one out," Ulices says dismissively, as though he's rejecting an offer of tea. "A kingdom who never comes to the aid of others doesn't deserve aid in their time of need. Personally, I think you all deserve whatever the dark wielders do to you."

I blink, everything in my body rebelling at the sentiment that civilians deserve to die because their leadership failed them, no matter who that leadership is.

"And you speak for your *rebellion*?" Melgren's attention slides to Xaden. "Or does the heir apparent?"

Xaden doesn't rise to the bait, nor does he argue against Ulices's statement. But he's going to, right?

The color drains from Mom's face as she looks between Mira and me, *past* us, and for the first time in my life, I see her wobble, like someone has knocked her off her center.

Bootsteps sound behind me, but I can't tear my gaze away from the emotions crossing Mom's face in rapid succession long enough to look to see who it is, and honestly, I don't need to.

"We rule by committee," Brennan announces, his arm brushing mine as he stops between Mira and me. "And I think I'm safe in speaking for the quorum when I say that we do not defend kingdoms who sacrifice neighboring civilians" — his head turns toward Mom, and her eyes bulge — "let alone their own *children* so they can hide safely behind their wards. You will not escape the suffering you've forced the rest of the Continent to endure."

"Brennan?" Mom whispers, and the urge to cross the line and hold her upright is almost too strong to fight.

"For fuck's sake, Brennan," Mira whispers.

"When all three of your children stand against you, perhaps the time has come for self-reflection. This *meeting* is officially over," Brennan states, his gaze locked on our mother. "Your hatching grounds are *not* in danger, and our riot has their own to protect now." He places his hand over his heart. "I mean this with every fiber of my body. We deny your offer of peace and happily accept war, since it sounds like you won't survive another two weeks to fight it." He pivots and walks away, leaving our mother to stare slack-jawed at his retreating back.

Is that all there is to it? With Suri and Kylynn in the woods behind us, the Assembly truly has a quorum, but Xaden hasn't spoken.

"Right." Xaden nods, tension straining the muscles of his neck. "If I were you, I'd try calling on the allies who helped win the Great War in the first place — oh, wait. You cut off contact with them centuries ago. I suppose this really is farewell."

I glance up at him and quickly school my features to mask my surprise. They're really going to leave them to die. *We* are going to leave them to die.

Wrath shines in Melgren's narrowed eyes. "We're done here. Do what you need to say goodbye," he says to my mother before leaving the field, walking toward the trees as Codagh moves with him, slinking backward and baring his teeth in warning for anyone foolish enough to attack his rider's back.

All the Navarrian riders beside Mom follow.

"Brennan," Mom whispers again, her shoulders folding inward as she covers her mouth with her hand. Her eyes water, and the pain I see there makes me look away.

Our riders make quick work of mounting, leaving only Xaden, Mira, and me on the field.

"Why did you want to see Violet and Mira?" Xaden asks, his tone devoid of sympathy.

"He's alive?" Mom asks Mira, her voice faint in what I think has to be shock.

"Obviously," she replies, folding her arms.

Mom's gaze shifts to me, like I'm going to give her a different answer. "He's the one who mended me after I took a venin blade in my side."

Her eyes sharpen. "You've known for *months*?"

"It's appalling to be left in the dark, isn't it, Mom?" Mira snaps. "To feel lied to, perhaps even betrayed, by your own family no less."

"Mira," I chastise.

"She sacrificed you, too, Violet," Mira reminds me. "Maybe she put you into the Riders Quadrant to save you from being killed as a scribe once you learned the truth, or maybe she did it to kill you before you could learn the truth and tear her precious war college to the ground"—she glances sideways at me—"which you did, if you remember."

Mom straightens her shoulders and lifts her chin, pulling herself together with astonishing, enviable speed. "I need a word with my daughters," she says to Xaden.

He arches his scarred brow, then looks to me for my decision.

I nod. If what Melgren says is true and she's called to the front lines, this might be the last time I see her. The thought sickens my stomach. It's one thing to leave her, to cut any and all contact, and quite another to leave her to her *death*.

Xaden backs away without another word, only offering his back once he passes by Tairn's claw.

"What do you want?" Mira asks.

"I'm not sure that matters at the moment." Mom unbuttons her flight jacket with trembling fingers. "But I want most—what I've always wanted—is for my children to live. Whatever wards you've raised from the instructions in Warrick's journal will fail."

Mira stiffens. "Our wards are fine."

She lies just as effortlessly as Xaden.

"They're not." Mom delivers a full lecture with a simple look. "Cut open the bodies of the wyvern who died crossing your border yesterday."

My lips part.

"Whyever would you think I'd be ignorant of activities on your border, Violet? Ignorant of where my daught—children are?" She shakes her head and dresses me down with a quick, cutting glance that makes me instantly feel like I'm five again before turning to Mira. "You remember what the carcasses of the wyvern looked like at Samara? The ones Riorson so kindly delivered?"

Mira nods.

"The stones used to create them were nothing but cold, marked rocks."

Stones? Do dark wielders have *runes*?

"Yes. I was there." Mira's tone sharpens.

"If you don't believe me, then check the wyvern you killed yesterday."

"And then what?" I ask.

"Fix your wards." She pulls a leather notebook from her jacket, and my eyes widen with recognition. "If you don't, they'll decline over time to nothing. Your father told me once that his research showed that Warrick never wanted anyone else to hold the power of the wards. He wanted Navarre to eternally hold the upper hand. But Lyra thought the knowledge should be shared."

"Warrick lied," I whisper. But about *what*?

She hands me the journal I'd been tortured for stealing, then nails my soul to the ground with the intensity of her gaze. "You have the heart of a rider but the mind of a scribe, Violet. I'm trusting you not only to protect yourself, but to protect Mira and"—she swallows hard—"Brennan."

I open the journal long enough to recognize the language as Morainian. My heart sinks for a second, but I close the journal, undo the buttons of my jacket, and slide it into my inner pocket. Translating this one will be all on Jesinia. Morainian is one of the dead languages I *can't* read.

She looks longingly over my shoulder, then glances at both Mira and me in turn. "You don't have to understand my choices. You simply have to survive. I love you enough to bear the weight of your disappointment." Before either of us responds, she turns on her heel and walks past Aimsir and disappears into the woods.

"Think she's full of shit?" Mira asks.

"I think the fliers can wield."

"Good point."

On the flight back to Aretia, Mira and I break away from formation and head for the nearest wyvern carcass within our borders. Xaden stays true to his lesson-learned proclamation and doesn't argue when we separate from the riot.

A half hour—and some creative knife work on Mira's part—after locating the pair of wyvern bodies, Mira draws back a polished chunk of what appears to be onyx marked with a complex rune I couldn't even begin to replicate.

And the damned thing is humming.

Oh *shit*. Is this why wyvern have suddenly reappeared? Did someone give the venin runes?

As if the stone has called to its partner, the carcass twenty feet away shudders, and our heads whip toward the giant, golden eye that blinks open.

"Fuck, no," Mira whispers, drawing her sword.

But I'm already an open gate to Tairn's power, and when I throw out my palms, it rips free, unleashed by my panic. Lightning cracks, flashing my vision to white and hitting its mark.

The blast knocks Mira and me backward, slamming us against the cold, stiff body of the wyvern behind us. Pain ripples down my spine, but everything seems to be where it's supposed to as my ass hits the ground beside my sister.

We both sit in stunned silence, watching the now-smoking, charred wyvern for signs of movement.

"You're sure lightning kills them?" Mira asks after a few tense minutes.

"Certain," I answer. "Thank Dunne the dark wielders didn't stick around longer to see that." The cliffside would be littered with reanimating wyvern.

She slowly turns her head to look at me, keeping an eye on the body. "No pressure, but if you don't figure out what Warrick lied about, we're all fucked."

"Right." *Because I did such a great job the first time*. And I don't even know Morrainian. I'll have to rely fully on Jesinia to translate and compare the two. I draw a shaky breath. "No pressure."

The combined hatching grounds at Basgiath is our generation's greatest asset...and our greatest liability.

—THE JOURNAL OF WARRICK OF LUCERAS
—TRANSLATED BY CADETS VIOLET SORRENGAIL AND DAIN AETOS

CHAPTER FIFTY-EIGHT

"**S**tubborn asshole," I mutter, turning just before the auditorium and heading to the sparring gym. Talking to Brennan has gotten me exactly nowhere over the last week, and his quick, effective dismissal of my genuine plea for him to reconsider the Assembly's position on the Samara problem has my blood boiling.

I push the doors open a little harder than necessary and find the sparring gym to be as empty as I'd expect at ten at night in the middle of a weekend, and dimly lit by the cool glow of mage lights hovering above each individual mat.

Xaden stands on the mat in the very center of the gym, feet apart and arms folded across his chest, wearing sparring gear and that carefully constructed mask of indifference he's known for.

"I thought you were kidding when I got your note." I close the door behind me, then focus on the lock and turn my hand in midair, channeling just enough power to hear the bolt slide home with a satisfying click. "I haven't seen you in a week, and this is where you want to meet?"

He'd been sent to monitor Draithus right after our return from Athebyne.

"Figured we'd be fighting. What better place for that than the sparring gym?" He stands completely still, waiting for me to come to him. His usual swords are missing, but he has two daggers strapped to his hip.

"You now have a warded bedroom," I remind him, stepping onto the mat. Though I'm not sure how strong those wards are given that our method for raising Aretia's wards was obviously flawed.

"*We* now have a warded bedroom," he corrects me, his gaze sweeping over me hungrily as I walk forward, stopping only a couple of feet away from him.

I can't blame him when I'm doing exactly the same, drinking in every detail of his appearance. Whether or not I'm still pissed about his latest reveal, I've missed him every minute he was gone, just like always. "What exactly are we fighting about? The Assembly voting to leave Navarre to fend for itself? Or the secret you kept from me *again*?"

His jaw flexes. "The majority voted once we returned, and though the details of that vote are classified, I'll break regulation and tell you that I *lost*."

"Oh." The sharpest edge of my anger dulls. "And you'd rather discuss the second issue in here? Where anyone can walk in and hear us?"

"*Unless there's a full inntinnsic around, no one can hear us like this.*" He gestures to the empty gym. Extending a hand, he crooks his fingers at me. "Come on. I know you're pissed, and no, I don't need the bond between us to catch on to that. It's in every line of your face, the purse of your lips, the tension in your shoulders."

I purposefully relax my posture. "You're right, you *don't* need the bond."

"See? Still pissed." He moves so quickly I barely have a chance to get my hands up before he sweeps my feet out from underneath me.

Shit.

He topples with me, bracing my fall with one hand and catching his weight with the other. The wind may not have been knocked out of me, but I'm breathless all the same. My hands brace on his chest, and his face is inches from mine, filling my vision and blocking out the world around us.

"I'm not sparring with you."

"Why?" His brow knits in confusion. "You have a better teacher? I have heard that Emetterio is teaching you a variety of new techniques, since venin adapt to our fighting styles so quickly."

"He is. But I'm not sparring with you because I *really* want to kick your ass." I shake my head, my braid catching slightly on the mat beneath me.

"Oh, you think you can hurt me." His slow grin makes me narrow my eyes.

I shift a hand and whip a dagger from a sheath at my ribs, putting it against the warm skin of his throat, right along the swirling lines of his relic. "I don't need to dignify that comment with a response." *Fuck him.* I make sure my shields are down so he hears it.

His eyes flare with something that looks like pride, and he leans into the blade.

I retreat just enough that it doesn't draw blood.

Guess we both just proved our point.

"You're capable of hurting me in ways I'm not sure you've even begun to fathom, Violet. I might be skilled enough to land a death blow, but you alone have the power to fucking *destroy* me." His hand slides out from behind my back to help bolster his weight. "Now, we can talk here, or we can see if Sgaeyl and Tairn are done fighting and fly through this snowstorm to the nearest vacant peak, but make no mistake, we're going to work this out."

I slide the blade back into its sheath, then lift my hand to his chest again. "On a sparring mat?" His heart beats beneath my fingertips, strong and steady, unlike mine, which pounds like a drum. I've had a week to process, a week to wish he was around so I could yell at him, but also a week to ruminate on the logical reasons why he wouldn't have told me.

The foremost of them being that he values his life.

"Sure as hell not in our bedroom." His knee separates mine. "We don't fight in there."

"Since when?" That's the most ludicrous thing I've ever heard. It's the only private space we have in this entire house.

"Since right now. I just made that rule. No fighting in our bedroom."

"That's not how this works."

"Sure it is." He drops his gaze to my mouth. "We make the rules when they come to us. Go ahead, make one."

"A rule?" I draw my leg up, bracing my foot on the ground so I'll have leverage if I want it, but the movement also drags my inner thigh up the side of his hip, and damn if that doesn't instantly summon an ache he's in prime position to ease.

"Anything."

"We don't keep secrets. No more *ask me.* No more tests to see who's in and who's out of this relationship. It's full disclosure between us…" I take a steadying breath and map out the golden flecks in his eyes just in case it's the last time. "Or it's nothing."

"Done."

"I'm serious." My hand slips up his chest to the juncture of his shoulder and his neck. "Even though I know you were right. I wasn't asking the right questions because I was afraid of the answers—and maybe I still am, given the fact that you're never completely open with me. Almost everyone in my life has kept secrets from me because I didn't ask the *right* questions, didn't look further than face value, and I understand that there will be times you can't tell me everything—that's the nature of what we do as riders—but I need you to stop setting me up for failure by insisting I figure out what there *is* to ask."

"Done." He nods. "I just…" A muscle in his jaw flexes.

"You just?" My fingers slide up the warm column of his neck and into his hair.

"I need to know you'll be here. That no matter what happens, you'll come back so we can talk it out or fight it out." His gaze drops to my mouth, then skims over my features.

My heart clenches, and I slide my hand along his chest, around his ribs, to his back, and then I hold on. "Done."

The lines between his brows smooth. "I need *you* to know that no matter what information I hold, you trust me, love me enough to realize I'd never let it hurt you. I'm not the easiest person to know, but I've learned my lesson, believe me. Even if it's classified, I won't withhold any information that affects your agency." He swallows, then balances his weight on one arm and runs the back of his hand down the side of my cheek. "I need to know you won't run, that you know you'll never have to."

"I love you," I whisper. "You could throw my entire world into upheaval, and I would still love you. You could keep secrets, run a revolution, frustrate the shit out of me, probably *ruin* me, and I would still love you. I can't make it stop. I don't want to. You're my gravity. Nothing in my world works without you."

"Gravity," he whispers, a slow, beautiful smile curving his mouth.

"The one force we can never escape," I tease. Then my smile falls. "I mean it, though." I lift my brows at him. "You have to let me all the way in, or all the love in the world won't hold this together. I am a person who *needs* information to center myself."

"Done," he whispers. "Want to know about my father? My grandfather and Sgaeyl? The rebellion?"

Maybe something easier. "Where's your mother?"

He startles but quickly masks the reflex.

"No one talks about her," I continue. "There are no paintings, no references to her being at the Calldyr executions. Nothing. It's like you were hatched and not born."

The moment stretches between us.

"She left when I was young. Their marriage contract said an heir had to survive to the age of ten, and then she was free to go, which is what she did. I haven't seen or heard from her since." His voice sounds like he dragged it across broken glass.

"Oh." My hand splays wide on his chest. "I'm sorry." Now I feel like shit for asking.

"I'm not." He shrugs. "What else do you want to know? Because I can't do this again. I can't go through months of uncertainty fighting to get you back, not knowing if I've fucked up the only thing that really matters in my life." His eyes close briefly. "Not that I won't if that's what you need."

"*When did it manifest?*" I slide my hand up to his neck. "*The signet?*"

"About a month after the shadows did. I'd already seen Carr kill another first-year for reading minds, so when it hit, I held my shit together and went to Sgaeyl, and when Carr asked if I'd had any other strange abilities emerge, since they knew Sgaeyl had bonded one of my relatives, I lied my ass off. And when my ability to control shadows seemed stronger than they'd expected, they had no reason to dig deeper." A corner of his mouth tilts upward. *"It helps that rider of record was thought to be a great uncle, not my grandfather."*

"She's really the only one who knows?"

"She's it. She made me promise not to tell anyone. She thinks anyone who knows will have me killed—or use me as a weapon."

"Shit, isn't that exactly what I did?" The second we were with Melgren, I'd asked—

"No," he whispers, lifting a hand and brushing the backs of his fingers along my cheek. "You asked me for the good of the mission, but you'd never use it for personal gain." He leans in, resting his forehead against mine. "Tell me we're all right. Tell me this didn't break us."

"Promise you won't use it on me again." I hold his gaze and curl my fingers into the fabric of his shirt.

"I promise," he whispers, then kisses me softly. "Now, do you want your presents?"

"Presents?" I arch my body up against his.

"You lost two of your daggers fighting Solas. I had two new ones made." A slow smile spreads across his face. "Just have to disarm me, and they're yours."

I slide my hand down his chest and do just that.

December nineteenth. I write the date on the next blank sheet of parchment in my notebook, then stare. We're two days away from solstice, and still the Assembly won't budge. But it's only an eight-hour flight to Samara, so I'm holding on to the hope that we'll do the right thing.

"Anything in Lyra's journal?" Rhiannon asks as she slides into the seat next to me at Battle Brief.

Nearly every head in our squad turns toward me, and the weight of their expectations forms a pit in my stomach. It's the same question every day, and I don't have an answer.

"I told you guys, once she finishes, I'll let you know." It only took one frustrating day trying to translate and failing before I handed it over to Jesinia.

I haul my new conduit out of my pack and set it in my lap. Felix gave them to every second- and third-year last week, and theirs are out, too, the riders imbuing shiny pieces of alloy for daggers with every spare second and ounce of energy they have. But mine has a special addition I asked him for after our battle with Solas: a strap of a bracelet to keep from losing it in combat. It's long enough to let the orb slide into my palm, but keeps it strapped to my arm in case I need to free myself for hand-to-hand.

The fliers have been working on carving shimmering maorsite arrowheads to fill their quivers as well.

Over the last two weeks since our meeting with Melgren, the atmosphere has changed from war college to straight up *war*. There's a nervous energy in the house that reminds me of the charge in the air just before a storm. All second- and third-years are being instructed in runes, and even I can admit, Cat is still the best of our year. She's the only one of us who's mastered a tracking rune, capable of tracking someone *else's* rune. *Mind-blowing.*

Our forge is glowing nonstop to produce weapons, and every rider has been pulled from the coastal outposts and pushed to the border regions, both with Navarre and Poromiel.

"Settle down!" Professor Devera orders from the center of the stage as Brennan joins her, and the theater quickly falls quiet. "That's better."

Ridoc puts his feet up on the chair ahead of him, and Rhiannon swats them down, leveling a behave-or-else look at him.

"What?" he grumbles, sitting up straight. "You've heard the death roll for the last week. No losses to discuss."

"As most of you know, we have no new attacks to report," Devera begins, and Ridoc shoots Rhi an I-told-you-so raise of his brows. "But what we do have is an updated map we think is over ninety percent accurate, thanks to flying patrols."

She turns toward the giant map of the Continent and lifts her hands. Red flags begin moving in an undeniable pattern, pulling away from known strongholds and gathering to the east.

Most settle directly across the border from Samara, while a few red flags spread out along our border.

"They've left Pavis," Ridoc notes, leaning forward.

"They've left...everywhere in the south," Sawyer adds. "And the Tyrrish border, too."

The north, in the provinces of Cygnisen and Braevick, is still spattered with red.

"But not Zolya." Maren sighs a few seats down on the left, and Cat presses her lips in a tight line next to her.

They obviously don't know our wards aren't operating at full strength.

"What can you ascertain from their reported movements?" Devera asks, turning back around to face us.

Brennan folds his arms in front of his chest and looks down at his feet before lifting his gaze to us. I know that look. He's feeling guilty.

Good.

"They're preparing for the battle Melgren foresaw," a rider from Third Wing calls out.

At least the Assembly isn't keeping Melgren's request a secret—just how they individually voted in regard to taking action on it.

"Agreed," Devera says, nodding in his direction. "It's hard to get an accurate count, but we estimate upward of five hundred wyvern." She glances at Brennan and, when he doesn't speak, continues. "And there are dark wielders among them."

A litany of swear words is mumbled throughout the theater.

"And why is it we're not engaging?" someone from First Wing asks.

"Because we're spiteful," Quinn says from behind me.

"What was that, cadet?" Devera calls her out.

Quinn shifts in her seat, but when I glance back, her head is held high. "I said because we're spiteful," she repeats, louder this time.

"Nailed it," Rhi says under her breath.

Brennan clears his throat. "We're not engaging because the Assembly voted and decided that the casualty rate among riders and fliers would be far too great. A battle this size could annihilate our forces, leaving the rest of the Continent undefended."

I shake my head at just how familiar that reasoning sounds.

"Some of us have family in Navarre," Avalynn says, a row in front of me with the other first-years in our squad. "Are we supposed to just sit back and wait to hear if they die?"

"They should have left," a rider retorts from somewhere in the vicinity of Second Wing.

"Not everyone has the means to pick up their entire lives and move just because a war is coming, you elitist prick," Avalynn counters, her voice rising.

She has a point, and the mutters of agreement throughout the wings rise in volume and pitch.

"This is *not* what Battle Brief is for!" Devera shouts.

We quiet down, but the energy has shifted, and it's not in a positive direction.

"Let's spin this another way," Brennan says. "If you were Melgren, what would you be doing right now?"

"Shitting myself," Ridoc answers.

Brennan rubs the bridge of his nose. "Other than that?"

"Bolstering the wards," Rhiannon offers. "As long as they remain at full power, this is all just bluster on the part of the enemy."

"Excellent point, Cadet Matthias." Brennan nods.

"So he has to choose between arming his forces or keeping the power supply concentrated in the armory?" That question comes out of First Wing.

"Another excellent point," Brennan agrees. "What's the problem with arming the forces?"

"Spreading out the daggers lessens the efficacy as a power supply for the wards," Rhiannon replies. "Even if the energy isn't actively being spent killing dark wielders, the wards are still weaker."

"Right." Brennan looks straight at me. "And what would you choose to do, Cadet Sorrengail?"

"Besides actually fight to defend innocent civilians?" The words are out of my mouth before I can think twice about calling my brother out in public.

"If you were Melgren." His head tilts, and from that look, I know I'm going to get the mother of all lectures after this.

I study the map for a heartbeat. "I'd have pulled every dagger from the coastal outposts to reinforce and boost the power supplies at the border outposts. They're powerless once they cross the wards. Wyvern die. Venin can't channel. That leaves them with hand-to-hand combat—"

"Or artillery," Cat adds.

"Exactly." I glance at her and nod. "As long as the Navarrian forces can physically repel the dark wielders and keep them from scattering the power supply in the armory, then there's no real danger of incursion."

"And that's exactly my point."

"But Melgren saw them being defeated," a flier from Second Wing says.

"Let's run with that thought." Devera gestures at the map. "Should the wards at Samara fall, what would happen?"

"They'd have a direct line to the hatching ground," someone answers.

"No," I reply. "That portion of the wards would fall back to its natural distance, about a three- or four-hour flight from Basgiath, just like ours. The power supplies in the outposts extend the wards, they don't create them, so while a large piece of Navarre would be unprotected—" Blinking, my gaze finds my brother's.

He nods.

Melgren was bluffing, banking on us not fully understanding how the wards work. He used a scare tactic to get us to agree to fight.

"Did you want to finish that thought, cadet?" Devara asks.

My mind spins as my heart lurches into my throat. I stare at the map, at the thin line of the border that remains uncrossed by what appears to be an undefeatable legion of the enemy, and a thought so terrifying I can barely reach for it begins to take hold. "How old is this information?"

"I'm sorry?" Devera's brows rise.

"How long have they been sitting on the border?" I clarify, my nails biting into the palms of my hands as I tighten my fists, pushing down the fear threatening to consume me.

She glances at Brennan, who replies, "They've been there for three days. This morning's report confirms they haven't moved."

Oh *gods*.

"*We act now.*" Tairn's voice rumbles through my head.

I stuff everything into my bag as Devera calls on another rider to answer a question.

"What are you doing?" Rhi asks in a whisper, and I notice almost every member of my squad has turned to watch.

"I need to find Xaden." I sling my pack over my shoulders and slip my arms through the straps, preparing to stand. "It's not Samara."

"All right." Rhiannon puts her things away, and the rest of the squad follows her lead. "We're coming with you."

There's no time to argue, so I nod and we all file out, earning us a few shouted protests from Devera, but the sound only blurs into the roaring in my ears as my thoughts spin faster and faster.

The hallway is relatively empty, since every cadet is at Battle Brief, making for a quick exit from the western wing of the house.

"*Where are you?*" I ask down the bond.

"*In a strategy meeting in the Assembly chamber,*" Xaden answers. "*Why?*"

"*I'm headed your way. I need you.*" We pass the doors to the history classroom and then the great hall.

"Is anyone going to tell us why we just walked out of Battle Brief?" Cat asks, a few steps behind me.

"Violet has a look in her eyes," Rhiannon explains, keeping up at my side.

"The same one she had before the Squad Battle last year," Sawyer says.

"She's onto something, and from our experience, you just roll with it," Rhiannon finishes.

Xaden walks out of the Assembly chamber and heads straight for me, meeting us in the middle of the hallway. "What's wrong?"

"It's not Samara we have to worry about."

"Why?" He keeps his eyes on me despite the shuffling of my squadmates.

"Because they're sitting there *waiting*," I explain. "They've been waiting for three days. Why?"

"If I knew their thought process, this war would be over," he replies.

"Melgren says they're overrun on solstice. That's the day after tomorrow."

Gods, we're going to have to move quickly.

He nods.

"Wyvern aren't going to take down the wards at Samara. They can't fly past them. Plus, smaller hordes were moved along the full border. I think Samara is just a distraction. I think they're waiting for them *all* to fall."

His eyes flare for a heartbeat.

"The battle can't take place somewhere else," Sawyer argues. "Melgren would see it."

"Not if we're there," Sloane counters. "Melgren can't see the outcome if three of us are there, remember?" She holds up her forearm, where her relic winds above the edge of her sleeve.

"Exactly." My fingernails bite into my palms. "He can't see the real fight if we're there. He has all his forces concentrating on Samara, when they should be—"

"At Basgiath," Xaden finishes my thought, his eyes searching mine. "The Vale."

"Yes."

"Do you want to go back?" he asks.

"Of course we do," Ridoc answers.

"I wasn't asking you." Xaden holds my gaze. "Do you want to go?"

Do I? Navarre has lied to their people—lied to *us*—for six hundred years.

"They would never come to our aid," Sloane says.

"They've definitely never come to ours," Cat agrees.

They've let Poromish civilians die time and again, safely tucked behind their wards, pulling the blindfold over Navarrian citizens' lives.

"The hatching grounds are there," Rhiannon argues.

"We have our own here," Trager counters. At least I think it's Trager, since I can't seem to look away from Xaden.

He's the stable ground beneath my feet as my mind spins faster and faster, my squadmates voicing contradicting opinions that match my own thoughts.

"My family is in Morraine," Avalynn pleads.

The voices behind me blur as they truly begin to argue.

"*We'd have to leave almost immediately,*" Xaden says, his voice cutting through the noise.

"*They lied to us. Executed your father. Tortured me.*" I force myself to stop counting their transgressions before they overwhelm my conscience.

"*Yes.*"

"*I keep thinking about the infantry cadets, and the healers, and even the scribes. People like Kaori stayed behind, those who just want to defend their homeland.*" Reaching forward, I grasp onto his arms to hold steady as the argument rages around us, and I get the distinct impression by the increase in volume that we're not the only squad out here anymore.

"Yes."

"If we don't go, we're no better than they are, leaving their civilians to die when we might be the very weapons they need." My grip tightens on him.

"Do you want to fight?" he asks, leaning down as the argument lessens around us, everyone waiting to hear what I say next, probably. "Say the word, and I'll take it to the Assembly. And if they won't support it, we'll go with whomever will. I go where you go."

The thought of risking my friends, losing them, has my stomach churning. I don't want to put Tairn and Andarna into danger. I would rather die than gamble with Xaden's life. But is there really a choice? Going might risk death, but staying risks us becoming just like our enemy.

"We have to."

We do not eat our allies.

—Tairn's personal addendum to the Book of Brennan
as quoted by Cadet Violet Sorrengail

CHAPTER
FIFTY-NINE

"*I can make it on my own,*" Andarna argues three hours later as cadets scurry into our hasty and unauthorized formation in the center of the valley.

"It's an eighteen-hour flight," I remind her, checking all the joints of her new harness. Thank gods she's still only half the size of Sgaeyl now, so Tairn can still carry her. "I respect your decision to come, but this is the only way." She can only fly for an hour or two before her wing muscle completely cramps.

"*And you think I should be carried like a juvenile?*" She huffs a breath of steam as I walk underneath her and fit my fingers between her scales and the smooth metal that curves under her shoulders.

"I think Tairn is capable of bearing your weight. You can fly until you tire or hold back the riot, but wearing a harness for quick clipping in is the only way I'm letting you come. I'm not risking you getting left behind if you fall out of formation." I tug at the steel just to be sure it doesn't give like mine did when we flew back to Basgiath last summer. "I get it. You don't want to be carried. Sometimes I don't want to fly in a saddle, but it's what I need in order to ride. It's your choice. You can come in the harness, or you can stay behind."

"*Dragons do not answer to humans.*" She bristles, straightening her posture.

"*No, but they do answer to their elders,*" Tairn grunts, his claws flexing in the green grass beside us.

"*Only to the eldest of our den,*" she counters as I walk out from under her, careful not to step on my flight jacket and pack that I've left on the ground. It's too damn hot up here to be dressed for the reality of December.

"Sure, I'll just go ask Codagh really quick," I quip sarcastically, jumping backward when a gryphon barrels by at full speed. They might be slower than dragons in the sky, but they're frighteningly fast on the ground.

They're also less than happy about being left behind, according to Maren.

"Try not to get killed before we get there, Vi. I think we might need you," Ridoc teases from my left, waiting in front of Aotrom, who snaps at the next gryphon who races by a little too close. I half expect to see feathers fall from between his teeth when he draws back his head.

"Perhaps I will be the eldest of my own den." Andarna arches her neck, tracking a flock of birds in the sky. I follow her line of sight, then quickly look away when the brightness of the sun stings my eyes, burning into my vision for a second and making her scales look a shiny, sky blue before I blink the spots away.

"I'm still in my middling years," Tairn grumbles. *"You'll be waiting awhile."*

"Really?" She shimmies the harness into a more comfortable position. *"I figured you were decades into your elder era. You certainly act like it."*

Tairn turns his head slowly, his eyes narrowing on Andarna.

"You don't act a day over a hundred," I reassure Tairn, then offer a smile to Maren as she approaches with Cat.

"I hate that we can't come," Maren says, swinging her leather rucksack from her shoulders. "We're supposed to stick together as a squad, right?"

"You wouldn't be able to wield," I remind her as she crouches, digging through her pack. "The second you crossed Navarrian wards, you'd be defenseless and targeted by riders and venin alike. That's not a great combination."

"And we'd slow you down. We've heard it." Cat folds her arms in front of her chest, surveying the chaos as Feirge lands ahead of us, flaring her wings before touching down near Rhiannon. "Doesn't mean we don't feel like shit that you're all rushing off to battle while we…study."

"I'm not so sure about the study part, since I think that's Devera's Red Clubtail up there," Ridoc adds, pointing toward the head of the formation.

"Here." Maren pulls out a small crossbow and leather-capped quiver from her pack, then stands. "Hate to tell you this, but you're awful with a longbow."

"Ummm. Thanks?"

"This will give you a secondary weapon if you run out of daggers. Just pull back the string until it catches here, then nock the arrow in the flight groove"—she points to the center of the bow—"and pull the lever with your forefinger."

It's compact and won't take too much strength to operate. The gesture is so kind that a lump grows in my throat. "It's perfect. Thank you." I take the weapon from her, but she pulls the quiver just out of reach.

"These are all maorsite arrowheads, imbued and runed to explode on impact." She lifts her dark brows. "They're cushioned in the quiver but do. Not. Drop. This."

"Got it." I take the quiver from her, then slip them both into my pack.

"The Assembly won't budge," Xaden says. He's dressed in full flight gear, his swords strapped across his back as he walks with my siblings.

"Stubborn assholes." Mira's also dressed for flight, her sword sheathed at her side, but Brennan isn't, and the anger simmering in my brother's narrowed gaze is aimed straight at me.

"They won't fight even knowing the hatching grounds are at risk?" Ridoc challenges, heading our way with Sawyer, Imogen, and Quinn.

"They think we're wrong," Xaden answers.

"*They* think that rushing into enemy territory with untrained cadets is a mistake," Brennan snaps. "And I agree. You're going to get cadets—including yourself—killed."

"It's not like we're taking the first-years," Rhiannon says, fastening the straps of sheaths around her flight jacket.

"Which is bullshit," Aaric bites out, Sloane and the other first-years walking up with him, all wearing flight leathers and determination. "We have just as much right to defend the hatching grounds as second- and third-years." The pleading yet accusatory look he gives me sinks my heart. He has just as much right—maybe more so—to defend Navarre as anyone here.

"None of you are going—" Brennan starts.

"You'd rather stay here, knowing there's every chance Mom will die?" I step toward my brother, and Mira pivots to my side, facing Brennan.

He flinches, his head drawing back like I hit him. "She had no trouble sending any of the three of us to our deaths." Brennan's gaze jumps between Mira and me, looking for understanding that neither of us gives him.

"We don't have time for this," Xaden lectures. "If you aren't coming, Brennan, then that's on you, but if we don't leave now, there's a chance we'll be too late to defend Basgiath." He turns, pointing a finger at the first-years. "And absolutely not. Most of you haven't even manifested a signet, and I'm not serving you up with your dragons as another energy source."

"I've manifested," Sloane protests, grasping the straps of her rucksack.

"And you're still a first-year," Xaden counters. "Matthias, get your squad ready to launch, then find your wingleader for further orders. We'll need to fly straight through. I'll take Violet with the—"

"With all due respect"—Rhiannon straightens her posture and stares him down—"unlike War Games, Second Squad, Flame Section, Fourth Wing will remain intact, though you're welcome to join *us*."

Sawyer and Ridoc move to my sides, and I know if I fall back, Quinn and

Imogen will be there waiting.

Xaden lifts his scarred brow at me, and instead of contradicting Rhiannon, I glance at my sister. "Same goes for you. You're welcome to join, but I stay with my squad."

The wind blows bitterly cold against my face nearly eighteen hours later as we cross into the Morraine province and follow the Iakobos River through the winding mountain range that leads to Basgiath. I've never been so thankful that my body heats when I channel. Everyone else in our party must be frozen to the core.

It's a testament to General Melgren's certainty about Samara that we aren't stopped by any patrols…because there are none. Even the mid-guard posts are devoid of riders as we fly over in a riot of fifty led by Tairn and Sgaeyl.

We may have left the first-years behind, but we also gained some of the active riders who hadn't been stationed along the cliffside border, like Mira, who's flying with Teine directly behind me as if she's scared to let me out of her sight.

"Aimsir is indeed within the Vale. Teine will relay communications for the squad while you locate your mother." Tairn finishes telling me the plan devised by leadership midflight that will allow us to recon, then adjust to whatever we find waiting for us.

My assigned task is to get through to my mother. No pressure or anything.

"When we reach the upcoming bend in the river, you'll release your harness from mine," Tairn tells Andarna. *"Fly to the Vale and stay there. An adolescent black dragon will raise human suspicion at Basgiath. Hide among our kind until it's over."*

"What if you need me? Like last time? I can stay hidden right at your side."

My heart clenches at the memory of how she'd appeared on the battlefield even after I'd begged her to stay hidden. She'd risked her life to help us and nearly lost it in the process. *"Stay with the feathertails—they'll need all your protection if the wards fall—and report anything the second it feels off."*

If we're too late, then gods help us all.

At the bend in the river, Andarna detaches and flies alongside us until the beats of her smaller wings can't keep up, then dives toward the ice-crusted river beneath us.

"The Vale," I remind her.

"I will be where I am needed," she counters, banking left, leaving the trail of

the river in favor of the snowcapped ridgeline that leads back behind the flight field and up into the Vale.

"That didn't sound like she intends on listening," I tell Tairn, watching her until she fades from view.

"I warned you what adolescents are like." He tucks his wings and dives, leaving my stomach behind as we drop a thousand feet in altitude in a matter of breaths, then levels out once we're only a hundred feet above the tall oak trees that line the river, approaching Basgiath from the south.

Everything looks as it should in the dying evening light, identical to when we left six weeks ago, simply covered in a fresh coat of snow. I look over my shoulder to see half the riot—First, Second, and Third Wings—break off, heading toward the flight field.

As long as everyone sticks to the plan, the next quarter will land in the courtyard of the quadrant while the rest of us continue onto the main campus.

"Can you sense anything off?" I ask as the walls of the Riders Quadrant come into view. Only half the windows in the dormitory are lit from within. An ache settles in my chest. No matter what cruelty transpired here, there's an enormous part of me that considers this place home.

It's where I studied, where I climbed trees with Dain, and where my father taught me the wonder of the Archives. It's where I fell in love with Xaden and learned just how much had been omitted from those very Archives.

"The wards are still up. We've made our presence known to the Empyrean, and I can definitely sense their displeasure, if that's what you mean." We cross over the courtyard, and Tail and Claw Sections peel off the formation with Devera in the lead, causing untold damage to the masonry as they land wherever they'll fit along the walls. *"But Greim is in residence, and she's reaching out to her mate, who is at Samara to contact Codagh."*

"At what point will you and Sgaeyl be able to cover distances like that?" We pass the parapet in nothing more than a heartbeat, and then Tairn banks left.

"Years. Greim and Maise have been mated for many decades." He races over the bell tower of the main college of Basgiath, then flares his wings and beats them backward, halting our momentum to the sound of alarmed cries from the watchmen in the four towers, shouting down their warnings.

"There are people down there," I tell him as he sinks gracefully into the main campus's courtyard.

"They'll move."

Sure enough, people scurry, scattering out of his way as he lands. *"Should you change your mind, I'll simply claw through the roof to reach you."*

I unbuckle quickly, unstrap the bag of daggers I was assigned to carry—each of us has one—and climb out of the saddle. "I'll be all right," I promise, working to his shoulder without so much as removing my flight goggles or tightening the straps on my pack. Speed matters, since only one dragon can land here at a time. I'll be alone until Sgaeyl follows.

My muscles protest the sudden movement after hours of riding, but I make it to his shoulder, then slide down the familiar ridges of his scales until my feet touch ground at Basgiath.

The second I'm clear, slipping the strap of my bag to my shoulder, Tairn launches skyward. He's strong but also heavy, and his talons barely clear the roofline of the infantry quadrant as he flies off.

Officers stand in stunned silence against the walls, staring at me with blatant shock, and I open the Archives doors just a crack to fill my body with enough energy to wield just in case one of them decides to make a move. Hands up, I scan the threats around me, taking note of the one captain in navy blue reaching for his sword. I retreat toward the wall beside the stairs leading up to the administration building until I feel frozen stone against my back.

Sgaeyl lands an instant later, momentarily obscuring my view of my would-be enemies, and Xaden dismounts, shadows in one hand and a sword in the other as he echoes my previous movements, giving only me his back as he retreats to my side. When Sgaeyl launches from the courtyard, Teine sweeps down, taking her place in perfectly timed coordination.

Movement up the stairs catches my attention, and I pivot, putting myself between Xaden and my mother as she descends with slow, deliberate steps, her hand on the hilt of her sheathed shortsword, Nolon a few steps behind her.

Here we go.

Shadows stream around me, racing across the cobblestones and stopping at the first step just as my mother reaches it. Her sigh is pure annoyance, and twin bruises lie in half circles beneath the eyes she narrows at us.

"Mom." Power crackles, lifting the loose tendrils of my hair as I glance back at the man who helped hold me prisoner.

"Really, Violet? You couldn't use the front door?" She glances at Mira, and then her gaze turns upward as Cath descends. Her face falls, but she holds her posture rigid as ever.

"He's not with us," Mira says, holding her sword pointed at the captain who's been working his way out. "In fact, he's pretty pissed we came."

Mom's head tilts slightly in a movement I know means she's talking to Aimsir. "Seems we've been fully invaded."

"We're not here to fight you. We're here to fight *for* you," I tell her. "You might not believe me, but your wards are in danger."

"Our wards are perfectly fine, as I'm sure you can feel." Mom crosses her arms as Dain joins us. "Oh, for fuck's sake." She calls across the courtyard,

"Hollyn, open the damned gates before one of these dragons takes off the roof." She looks pointedly at the shadows blocking her path.

They lift, retreating to the tips of my boots.

"Let the others know the gates are opening," I tell Tairn.

"I will position myself accordingly."

A full minute later, the guards throw open the gates, revealing the rest of our squad dismounting.

"Trust me, Mom. The battle you're expecting isn't at Samara: it's here." I explain my line of thinking in the few minutes it takes for my squadmates to reach us. "Someone is going to take down your wards."

"Not possible, *cadet*." She shakes her head as night descends in true around us. "They're heavily guarded every moment of every day. The biggest threat to the wards would be *you*."

"Let us check," Xaden says at my back. "You know your daughters would never strip Navarre of its protection."

"I know exactly who my daughters are. And the answer is no." Her dismissal is curt. "You're lucky to be alive crossing enemy airspace. Consider retaining your lives a personal gift."

"I think not." Mira's gaze sweeps the courtyard. "This courtyard should be full at this hour with soldiers returning from mess, and yet I only count five soldiers. One captain and four cadets, and no, I'm not counting the healers in the corner. You've sent every available body to Samara, haven't you?"

The temperature in the courtyard plummets from freezing to nearly unbreathable.

"The guards behind you have signets in mindwork, Mother. In fact, I'd bet money that the most powerful riders on campus are you and…who? Professor Carr?" Mira moves forward fearlessly. "Our forces can render aid or conquer. It's your choice."

Mom's nostrils flare as tense seconds pass.

"If you won't take them to the wards," Dain says from somewhere behind me, "I will. My father showed me where they are last year." Which is precisely why he's with our squad.

"Who do you want to be? The general who saves Basgiath, or the one who loses it to the very cadets who rejected your lies?" I lift my chin.

"Black really does suit you, Violet." It might be the nicest thing she's ever said to me.

"Like Captain Sorrengail said, it's your choice. We're wasting time," I retort. With night fallen, it's officially solstice.

Mom's gaze jumps to Mira, then slides back to me. "By all means, let's inspect the wards."

My shoulders dip in relief, but I keep my power at the ready as we climb the steps into the administration building, swallowing the knot of apprehension in my throat as we approach Nolon.

"Violet—" he starts.

Just the sound of his voice makes bile rise in my throat.

"Stay the fuck away from Violet, and I'll *consider* letting you live, if only to mend riders if there's a battle coming," Xaden warns the mender as we pass him near the entryway.

Mage lights glow above our heads as we walk into the familiar halls, a pair of healers scurrying by, coming from the direction of the mess hall where another group of cadets in pale blue peer out of the doorway.

"Chradh is worried," Tairn remarks, his voice tense.

"What would Garrick's dragon be worried about?" Xaden asks on the pathway shared by all four of us.

"Runes," Sgaeyl answers.

That's right. The Brown Scorpiontail found the lure in Resson because he's highly sensitive to them. *"Basgiath was built on runes,"* I remind them.

"This is different. He senses the same energy that he detected in Resson." Tairn's tone shifts. *"His rider officially has control of the dormitory with Devera."*

Garrick's in place.

Mom leads us down the hallway and into the northwest turret, then descends the spiral staircase that reminds me so much of its southern counterpart that my breath catches at the scent of earth.

Drip. Drip. Drip.

I hear the sound in my mind as clearly as if it were real, as if I were back in that interrogation chamber. Xaden's hand takes mine, lacing his fingers through my own.

"You all right?" he asks, shadows wrapping around our joined hands, their touch as soft as velvet.

For a second, I debate playing it off, but I was the one who demanded full disclosure, so it only seems fair that I give it. *"It smells like the interrogation chamber."*

"We'll set that room on fire before we leave," he promises.

At the base of the stairwell is…nothing. Just a circular room paved with the foundation stones.

Mom looks to Dain, and he walks past her, examining the pattern, then pushing on a rectangular stone at his shoulder height. It gives, and stone scrapes stone as a door swings open in the masonry, revealing a mage-lit tunnel so cramped it would give even the bravest person claustrophobia.

"Just like the Archives," I tell Xaden.

Mom orders her accompanying soldiers to stand guard. In return, Rhiannon orders Sawyer and Imogen to guard *them* as we walk into the tunnel. Mom goes first.

"What happened to being guarded?" Xaden asks, walking ahead of me.

Mira's at my back.

"The wards *are* guarded," she says, turning sideways when the tunnel narrows even farther. "Wouldn't you find it suspicious if guards were stationed at the bottom of an empty stairwell?" she challenges. "Sometimes the best defense is simple camouflage."

I walk sideways, breathing in through my nose and out through my mouth, and try to pretend I'm somewhere—anywhere—else.

We're going to have fun, you and I. Varrish's words slide over me, and my heart rate jumps.

Xaden's shadows expand from our hands to my waist, and the pressure there feels like his arm is around me, making it bearable to get through the passage for the twenty feet it takes to open up wide again. The tunnel runs for what looks like another fifty yards before ending at a glowing blue archway, and the hum of energy from what I assume is the wardstone vibrates my very bones, tenfold the intensity of the one at Aretia.

"See, it's guar…" Mom's words die, and we see them the same moment she does.

Two bodies in black uniforms lie on the ground, pools of their blood slowly expanding toward each other. Their eyes are open, but they're glazed and vacant, freshly dead.

My heart lurches and the shadows fall away with Xaden's hand as we both reach for weapons.

"Oh, shit," Ridoc whispers as the others file through the bottleneck behind us, drawing swords, daggers, and battle-axes.

Metal slides against metal as Mom pulls her sword, then breaks into a run, sprinting down the tunnel.

"No chance you'd stay here if I—" Xaden starts.

"None," I say over my shoulder, already racing after my mother down the long expanse. The vague sound of barked orders echoes off the tunnel walls as Mira catches up quickly, then passes me to run at my mother's side while Xaden keeps pace with me.

"Do you know where the ward chamber opens to the sky?" I ask Tairn as my boots pound the stone floor of the corridor. It has to, if it's constructed anything like Aretia.

"According to you, I cannot supply fire to more than one—" He pauses as though taking stock of my situation. *"On my way."*

"No!" Mom's shout sends chills down my spine as she and Mira make it to the chamber ahead of us, both charging left, weapons high.

The rest of us reach the chamber, and before I can assess the situation, Xaden's shadows jerk me off my feet and into his chest as he spins us backward, pressing my spine against the wall of the archway as the points of an orange's scorpiontail swing through the very place I'd been standing.

There's a fucking *dragon* in there?

"Are you…" His eyes fly wide.

"Didn't get me," I assure him.

He nods, relief shifting his gaze from worried to alert, and we both turn into the entrance, quickly joined by Ridoc, Rhiannon, and Dain.

My mouth drops, and power charges through my veins, so potent my hands buzz.

The wardstone is twice as large as the one in Aretia, as is the chamber that houses it, but unlike Aretia's, the rings and runes carved into it are interrupted by a diamond pattern. And unlike our wards in Aretia, this wardstone is on *fire*, lit on top by black flames that sputter and flare as a dragon emerges from behind the left side of the stone, driving Mom and Mira back toward us.

Not just any dragon. Baide.

"Get out of there!" Tairn orders as Baide lowers her head, and I get a single glimpse of her eyes—opaque instead of golden—before Mom charges toward her nose, lifting her sword to swing.

Baide knocks her aside with a single swipe of her head, and Mom flies into the stone wall of the chamber, cracking her head before falling into a heap.

Xaden throws his hand out, and shadows stream past, grasping both Mira and Mom, pulling them back to us as Baide roars, steam and spit flying from her mouth.

She stalks forward, her talons clicking on the floor as she maneuvers around the stone, revealing Jack Barlowe in his seat on Baide's back. The smile he gives me twists my stomach. "You're right on time, Sorrengail."

"Anytime you want to show up would be very appreciated," I tell Tairn as Xaden's shadows release Mira at my side but drag my mother's unconscious body back through the archway.

I can't wield in here, not without endangering everyone. Besides, the charge of the stone would draw every strike to it.

"It's not exactly an easy location to get to," Tairn growls in reply.

"What the hell are you doing, Barlowe?" Dain snaps.

"What I promised," he answers, glee shining in his eyes.

Xaden sends another stream of shadows, this one shooting toward Barlowe, and Baide drops her jaw, her eerie eyes flashing as fire glows up her throat.

"Xaden!" I yell as Ridoc pushes past me—past all of us—and throws his arms forward, palms out.

"Get down!" Ridoc shouts, and I glimpse a wall of ice rising before us as Xaden pulls me into the shelter of his body and crouches. The chamber glows orange for a heartbeat, then two, as fire rages against the stone walls. Ridoc screams as the blast dies.

The second the fire ceases, we're on our feet to face Barlowe and Baide, but the dragon has disappeared behind the wardstone again.

"I've got him!" Rhiannon rushes forward and hooks her arms under Ridoc's, then hauls him back from where only a puddle marks where the wall of ice had stood. Nothing prepares me for the sight of Ridoc's burned hands, blistered and bleeding.

"We'll take the left," Xaden says, glancing at me.

"Taking right," Dain agrees, shooting a look at Mira, who nods.

Xaden and I run to the left, and I flip the dagger in my hand, pinching it by the tip in readiness to throw as we round the corner.

What the fuck?

Baide is up on her back legs, her front claws grasping the top of the flaming wardstone, and Barlowe isn't in his seat. It takes a precious second we don't have to spot him holding on to the top of Baide's neck, clutching one of her horns.

Not even Xaden is fast enough to stop the downward plunge of Jack's shortsword between the scales alongside Baide's neck. The dragon's cry shakes the foundation of the chamber and stops abruptly when Jack pushes the blade all the way through the front of her throat.

Jack's head swings in our direction, and he wields with an outward-facing palm, throwing a shield that deflects Xaden's shadows as blood sprays from Baide's throat onto the wardstone. The black flames extinguish an instant before Baide collapses, her weight pitching forward.

The wardstone tips and Jack fumbles to hold on, giving me the perfect opportunity to flick my wrist and release the dagger.

I hear a satisfying cry as Xaden grabs hold of my waist, throwing up a wall of shadow that blocks out the chamber around us but doesn't shield us from the noise of the stone crashing. Cracking.

The humming stops.

The wards have fallen.

At its core, magic demands balance.
Whatever you take will be recouped, and it is not the wielder who
determines the price.

—MAGIC: A UNIVERSAL STUDY FOR RIDERS
BY COLONEL EMEZINE RUTHORN

CHAPTER
SIXTY

Xaden drops the shadows, and we both turn at the same time to survey the damage.

My heart seizes, and I reach for Xaden's hand reflexively. The wardstone lies in two pieces on the ground, and there isn't a flame in sight.

Holy Dunne, Navarre is *defenseless*.

There's no seeing over Baide's body to check on Mira, so I whip my gaze to the right, meeting Rhiannon's wide eyes where she stands at the front of the archway, protecting Ridoc and my mother.

Jack stumbles backward from the blow of my dagger, a dazed but elated look twisting his face as he wrenches it from his shoulder and drops it to the floor.

"He only has minutes," I whisper to Xaden.

Barlow has just *killed* his own dragon. It's unfathomable. Impossible. And yet Baide is most certainly dead as Jack falls to his knees and laughs up at the sky fifty feet above us.

Mira appears, moving silently around Baide's corpse, and Xaden gives her a subtle shake of his head when she lifts her sword. She keeps it poised for attack but doesn't continue forward.

"You know you're about to join your dragon, don't you?" Xaden asks, his voice low as shadows move in riotous swirls at our feet.

"What are you doing?" I palm another dagger.

"Getting whatever information we can." The utter calmness of his tone is unnerving.

"That's the thing," Barlowe says, his blond hair covering his forehead as he falls forward onto a hand. "I'm not. They have us thinking we're the inferior species, but did you see how easily I controlled her? How easily the energy she bonded us with is replaced?" His eyes slide shut as his fingers splay on the stone.

"Jack! Don't do this!" Nolon storms past Rhiannon, his features slackening when he takes in the destruction around him. "You…you're better than this! You can choose!"

My chest tightens. *"The way he said that is almost like he expected this."*

"Because he did," Xaden answers, his gaze locked on Jack. *"He wants to mend him. He's been trying to mend him since May. He's too weak to shield his intentions now."*

"Mend what? The injuries from the fall?"

Xaden's brow furrows in concentration. *"Jack's turned venin. Somehow, he managed it within the wards."*

I think I might be sick.

"There is no choice!" Jack shouts. "And if there was, I made mine the second I saw her"—he shoots a glare my way—"bond the most powerful dragon available at Threshing. Why should *they* determine our potential when we're capable of reaching for fate all on our own?"

Oh. Gods. His eyes have been bloodshot for *so* long. When did it happen? Before the fall. It had to have been before I wielded that first time. Back in the gym that day…

And I've thrown the *wrong* dagger.

"Baide," Tairn growls, and I glance up to see his silhouette block out the stars far above us.

"I'm so sorry."

"Magic requires balance," Nolon argues. "It does not give without a price!"

"Does it?" Jack inhales, and the stones around him turn from a dark, slate gray to a dusky beige. "Do you understand how much power is beneath your feet?"

One block pales, then another, and another.

"Xaden—"

"I know." Shadows shoot forward, knocking Jack backward and driving him across the floor before lifting him from the ground, pinning him in midair with an X across his torso. "When did you turn?" Xaden asks.

"Wouldn't you like to know?" Jack fights the binding, but Xaden closes his fist and the shadows snap even tighter.

"I know you're going to tell me." Xaden walks forward. "Because I have nothing to lose by killing you. So tell me when. Earn yourself a little good will."

"Before his challenge against me," I answer when Jack refuses to. "He forced power into my body. I just didn't recognize it for what it is. How? The wards—"

"Do not block *all* power like the dragons want you to think they do! We can still feed from the ground, still channel enough to survive. Enough to fool them. We might not be at full strength, capable of wielding greater magic under your *protections*, but make no mistake: we are already among you, and now we're free." Jack gestures at Baide, his glare alternating between Xaden and me. "I'll never know why it's you he wants. What the fuck makes you so special?"

"This changes everything," Tairn urges.

"You have no idea what's coming for you." Jack grasps at the shadows, his feet kicking against only air, but Xaden wraps another band around his throat, and he stills. "They're faster than you think they are. *He's* coming with a horde of greens. They all are."

"Might take them a minute to read the map." Xaden's tone shifts to taunting. "And you'll be long gone before they arrive."

"We need to keep him alive for questioning as long as possible." I shift my weight carefully to avoid Jack's attention.

"And what's your solution for that?" Xaden asks.

We have to cut him off from his power. My gaze swings wide, and I see Nolon creeping up on the left. He's kept him under control all these—

"The serum," I tell Xaden. *"He must be why they developed the signet-blocking serum."*

Motion near Mira makes me glance her way as Dain edges past her.

"They don't need a map. Not when I showed them the way. While you were busy smuggling weapons out, we were busy smuggling them *in*." Jack's motions grow weaker, his breaths more labored, just as Liam's had been. "This whole place will be ours in a matter of hours." He splays his palms wide and reaches the wall, then shudders as color leaches from the stone.

My heart jolts. We're underground.

Xaden pulls his alloy-hilted dagger and strides forward, but Dain gets there faster.

"Not yet!" Dain grabs hold of Jack's head and closes his eyes as stone after stone loses its color.

One. Two. Three. I start to count heartbeats as the desiccation expands.

On the fourth beat, Jack wrenches his hands from the wall and grasps Dain's forearms.

"Xaden?" It's a request, and we both know it, but he doesn't act.

Dain begins to tremble.

"Xaden!" I shout. "Jack's draining him!" Power ripples up my fingertips, ready to strike.

Only when Dain screams in pain does Xaden take the final step and slam the hilt of the dagger against Jack's temple, knocking him unconscious.

I rush to Dain as he stumbles backward, ripping at his flight jacket, tugging it off and shoving the fabric of his uniform up his arms to reveal a matching set of gray handprints burned into his skin in the same place where Jack grabbed him.

"Are you all right?" Gods, the skin is *crinkling*.

"I think so." Dain runs his hands down his arms in turn, then flexes his fingers in appraisal. "Hurts like a fucking ice burn."

"I'm assuming you know what to do with him? Seeing as you've been doing it since May?" Xaden shoots Nolon a withering look.

Nolon nods, reaching Jack and pouring a vial of serum into his mouth. Xaden withdraws his shadows, allowing Jack to crumble to the floor, then leans over and cuts away Jack's First Wing patch.

"How many riders are here?" Dain asks Nolon, who stares at Jack with a mix of disbelief and horror. Suddenly, I understand why he was always so exhausted this year. He wasn't mending a soul in the figurative sense, but the literal. "How many riders, Nolon?" Dain snaps.

The mender lifts his tired gaze.

"A hundred and nineteen cadets," my mother answers, holding her hand to her bleeding head. "Ten leadership. The rest have all been sent to midland posts and Samara." She glances at me. "Plus the ones you brought."

"I saw his memories. It's not enough." Dain shakes his head.

"Well, it has to be," Mira counters.

"Gather everyone. They're faster than dragons," Dain says to my mother. "We have ten hours. Maybe less. Then we're all dead."

A half hour later, nearly every seat in Battle Brief is full, and the lines are clearly drawn between those of us who chose to fight for Poromiel and those who chose to stay to defend Navarre. The Aretian cadets hold the right side of the terraced classroom, and for the first time, I don't pull out pen and paper to take notes when my mother and Devera take the stage with Dain.

The nervous energy in the room reminds me of those moments on top of the turret in Athebyne, where we decided to fight in Resson. Except there's no choice to make today; we're here.

This battle began in the wardstone chamber, and we've already lost. We just happen to still be breathing. Greim relayed to Tairn that Melgren and his forces won't arrive until *after* the approaching horde does, and word came in about an hour ago that there are other wyvern flying in a second wave.

As if the first won't be enough to destroy us.

Glancing over my shoulder, toward the top seats, I see Xaden standing next to Bodhi with his arms folded across his chest, listening to whatever Garrick tells him. A painful ache erupts in my heart. How can we only have hours left?

As if he senses the weight of my gaze, he looks at me, then *winks* like we're not facing certain annihilation. Like we've transported ourselves back to last year and this is just another Battle Brief.

"How are the hands?" Sawyer asks Ridoc as leadership confers about something onstage.

"Nolon mended them right after he took care of General Sorrengail." Ridoc flexes his fingers, showing off unblemished skin. "Dain?" he asks me.

"Nothing he can do for him." I shake my head. "Not sure if it's because it's an unmendable wound or because Nolon's too exhausted from trying to mend Jack over and over."

"Fucking Jack," Rhi mutters.

"Fucking Jack," I agree.

Devera starts the briefing. Intel reports a thousand wyvern headed this way. The good news? They didn't even bother stopping at Samara, which means casualties are low. The bad news? They don't seem to be stopping *anywhere*, which means we won't get a delay.

Dain steps forward and clears his throat. "How many of you have mastered a tracking rune?"

Not a single hand rises among the Aretian cadets, including Rhi's and mine. The Basgiath cadets look like Dain is speaking Krovlish up there.

"Right." Dain shoves his hand into his hair, and his face falls before he masks it. "That complicates things. Dark wielders know exactly where we are because, according to Barlowe's memories, he planted lures all over the college and up the path to the Vale."

Guess Dain's done keeping his signet classified.

My lips part. That's the energy Chradh picked up on when we arrived, the same energy that summoned the venin to Resson. Destroying the lures is our best chance of buying time, or at least throwing off further waves.

"I saw where Barlowe put most of the lure boxes but not all of them," Dain continues as footsteps sound in the doorway.

Every head turns as infantry cadets pour in wearing uncertain, anxious faces. I spot Calvin, the leader of the platoon we were paired with for maneuvers, gawking at the space, his gaze landing and remaining on the map of Navarre. He's wearing the same insignia as the rest of them, leading me to believe they've only sent their quadrant's leadership.

"The Infantry Quadrant will spend the next few hours trying to hunt them down for us while also preparing themselves…" Dain's voice drops off, and he swallows.

Devera takes mercy on him, stepping forward. "You'll be working within your squads tonight. Remember that wyvern are the distraction and the weapon. You take down one of the venin, and you kill the wyvern they've created. No one takes on a dark wielder alone. That's how you get killed. Work together, rely on each other, complement each other's signets just like it's the Squad Battle."

"Except it's real battle," Rhiannon says under her breath.

Where real cadets will *really* die.

"Remember that venin will mimic your fighting style, so change it up if you have no choice but hand-to-hand," Devera continues, the lines of her mouth tense with worry and perhaps a little dread.

The Basgiath cadets murmur among themselves and shift in their seats.

"I'll bet you all the daggers we've brought with us that they didn't teach them how to fight venin." Sawyer shakes his head, drumming his fingertips along the desk.

"First-years who haven't manifested, I expect you packed and ready to fly should we fall. Healers are stocking the infirmary and are preparing. Scribes are in the process of evacuating with our most important texts." Devera glances at my mother.

Of course they are. I can only wonder which texts they'll consider valuable enough to save, and which they'll conveniently leave behind to burn.

Mom looks up to my right, where Mira stands with a few of her friends, then drops her gaze to me. "The assignments given tonight have been decided with the best interest of Basgiath and the Vale in mind. There are incredibly powerful signets among you. Gifted riders." She looks in the first row, where Emetterio sits. "And even combat masters. But I will not lie to you—"

"That's a first," I mumble, and Rhiannon scoffs softly under her breath.

"—we are outnumbered," Mom continues. "We are underpowered. However, the odds may be against us, but the gods are with us. Whether you left after Threshing or stayed, we are *all* Navarrian riders, bonded for the purpose of defending dragonkind in the darkest hour, and this is it."

The darkest hour on the longest night of the year. My stomach churns as I fight off the spiraling weight of hopelessness.

"I want you to leave for Aretia," I tell Andarna. *"Get out before they arrive. Hide where you can and make your way back to Brennan."*

"I will be where I am needed, and it is with you," she counters.

Every argument I could make to keep her alive doesn't matter, and we both know it. Humans do not give dragons orders. If she's determined to die with Tairn and me, there's nothing I can do about it. I press my lips between my teeth and bite down to ward off the sting that comes to my eyes.

My fingernails bite into my palms as Mom assigns the active riders to cadet squads, splitting the experience among the group. Garrick is assigned to First Squad, Flame Section, and Heaton to First Squad, Claw Section, while Emery is assigned to a squad in First Wing. "Captain Sorrengail." Mom looks up at Mira. "You'll be with Second Squad, Flame Section, Fourth Wing."

Our entire squad looks over at Mira, and my eyes widen at the fear that flares in her eyes.

Anger simmers along my bond with Xaden. *"Fuck that."*

"With all due respect, General Sorrengail," Mira replies, rolling her shoulders back, "if we're to truly use our signets to their best advantage, then I should be paired with you as a last line of defense, since I can now shield without the wards."

Mom's eyebrows rise in surprise, and my gaze jumps between them like I'm watching a sporting match.

Mira swallows, then locks eyes with me. "And Lieutenant Riorson should be placed into Second Squad, as his signet has previously proven in battle to complement Cadet Sorrengail's." She looks at me like we're sitting across the dining room table from each other and not in the midst of a pre-battle briefing. "As much as I would love to be her shield, he gives us the highest probability of keeping our most effective weapon alive."

A tense second passes as I look to our mother.

"So be it." Mom nods, then finishes the unit changes.

The heat along the bond recedes, and my posture sags in relief. At least we'll be together.

"We get both of you?" Ridoc offers a quick smile. "Maybe we have a shot of lasting an hour."

"My money's on two," Sawyer chimes in with a nod.

"Both of you shut up before I knock your heads together," Imogen warns from a seat behind us. "Anything less than four hours is unacceptable."

How long did Resson last? One? And there were ten riders and seven fliers against *four* venin.

"Now that that's settled," Mom says as Kaori steps onto the floor, throwing up an illusion in the form of a top-down map of Basgiath and the surrounding area. "We're dividing Basgiath, the Vale, and surrounding areas into a grid of sectors."

Kaori flicks his fingers, and gridlines appear on the map.

"Each squad will be responsible for a sector of airspace while infantry covers the ground," Mom continues, nodding to Kaori. Squad insignia appear on different grids, and it takes me a second to locate ours on the side of the Vale, paired with a squad from First Wing. No patches are inside the space, but there are plenty of unbonded dragons no doubt ready to defend their hatching grounds. "Memorize these grids, because you're not going to have time to pull out a map when you're up there. If it's in your airspace, you kill it. If it crosses into another squad's airspace, you let *them* kill it. Avoid leaving your airspace at all costs, or it will turn into a disorganized melee, and that leaves us with inevitable weak grids. We'll reassign you as necessary as casualties are reported."

Not *if* they're reported.

The grid behind the main campus, where the ward chamber is located, is horrifyingly bare, as though they've already surrendered the space.

"This is wrong," I whisper. "We should be defending the wardstone."

"The broken one?" Sawyer questions quietly.

"Say it," Rhiannon urges.

"You have a better chance of living through it," Ridoc mutters, shifting in his seat.

I clear my throat. "It's a mistake to abandon the wardstone."

My mother levels a disapproving look on me, and the temperature drops a few degrees. "Why is it that only my daughters speak out of turn?"

"We get it from our mother," Mira snipes in a dry tone, and that lethal look pivots to her.

"It's a mistake," I push on. "We don't know what power remains in the stone, and it was placed in that exact location because it's over the strongest natural flow of power, according to Warrick."

"Hmm." It's not my mother looking my way this time. It's General Sorrengail. "Your opinion is noted."

Hope surges in my chest. "So you'll assign a squad?"

"Absolutely not. Your opinion, as noted as it is, is *wrong*." She dismisses me without another word, without the reasoning we would have been given had this been a Battle Brief, leaving me half my original size, shrinking in my chair.

A wave of warmth floods the bond, but it doesn't dim the chill from her rejection.

"You have your orders for the morning," Mom says. "Riders, find the nearest bed and sleep for as many hours as you can. Most of you who left Basgiath will find your rooms have not been commandeered, and most still contain your bedding. We need you rested to be effective." She looks over the briefing room like it might be the last time she sees us. "Every minute we hold out gives us a shot at reinforcements making it back. Every second counts. Make no mistake, we *will* hold out as long as possible."

I glance up at the clock. It's not even eight yet, which means I can keep my mantra for the next few hours. I will not die today.

I can't say the same about tomorrow.

The stars still wink in the night sky as Xaden and I dress in the relative silence of my room. Turns out the remaining cadets had left all but the wingleaders' quarters untouched, as if we'd see the error of our ways and return.

What few hours of sleep we'd gotten had been sporadic at best, leaving me at less than full strength and a little dizzy, but at least I wasn't plagued with nightmares.

Or maybe my imagination really is that overactive.

Xaden kisses a path down my spine, his lips brushing every inch of skin as he laces me into my armor over the cross-body wrap on my left shoulder that stabilizes the aching joint. My eyes slide shut when he reaches my lower back, and the desire he'd more than sated last night flares anew, flushing my skin. A few simple kisses are all it ever takes, and my body is instantly attuned to his.

"Keep doing that, and you'll be taking this right off," I warn him, glancing down over my shoulder.

"Was that a threat or a promise?" His eyes darken as he stands and ties me in, tucking the laces so they don't come loose. "Because I have no problem spending our last quiet minutes this morning tangled up in you." He slides his hand over the curve of my hip as he moves to face me, trailing his fingers along the waistband of my flight leathers, then dipping them between the buttons and my stomach.

We can't do this, can't hide away and pretend war isn't coming for us. Can't ignore that more than a dozen lures haven't been destroyed—or even found—when just *one* was enough to lead the venin to Resson, and we've only found half of what Jack left around campus. Can't deny that the last reports from the few riders brave enough to stay at the midland forts along the route from Samara relayed that attack is imminent in the next couple of hours. But *gods* do I want to.

"We can't." Regret saturates the words, and yet I can't stop myself from winding my arms around his neck. "No matter how much I would rather lock the door and let the rest of the world burn around us."

"We can." He lifts a hand to the back of my neck and tugs me closer, until our bodies meet from thigh to breast. "Say the word, and we'll fly."

I stare up into his eyes, marking each fleck of gold just in case I won't get another chance to. "You could never live with yourself if we abandoned our friends."

"Maybe." His brow knits for less than a second, so quick I almost miss it as he leans into my space. "But I know I can't live without *you*, so trust me when I say there's a very real, very loud part of me screaming to carry you out of here and fly for Aretia."

I know the feeling all too well, so before I dare to give it voice, I rise up on my toes and kiss him. At the first touch of our mouths, heat ignites between us, and he grabs ahold of my ass, lifting me. I sense that we're moving, turning as I part my lips for his tongue and throw all logical thought out the door.

My ass hits the desk and I hold tighter, kiss him harder as he slants his mouth over mine again and again, taking everything I offer and giving it right back. This isn't the slow exploration we'd shared last night, lingering on every touch, knowing it might be the last time. It's frantic and wild, hot and desperate.

My hand spears into his hair, holding him closer, like I still have Andarna's ability to stop time, like I can hold us in this moment if I just keep kissing him.

He groans into my mouth and his fingers work the buttons on my pants at the same moment I reach for his.

"We'll be quick," I promise between soul-consuming kisses, flicking open the first button.

"Quick," he repeats, sliding a hand down my stomach and into my pants, "isn't usually what you beg me for." His fingers brush—

Someone knocks.

We both freeze, panting hard against each other's mouths.

No. No. *No.*

"Don't stop." If this minute is all we have left, then I want it. Gods, if he would just move his hand a fraction of an inch lower…

His eyes search mine, and then he takes my mouth like the outcome of this kiss will decide the battle we're facing.

"I know you're in there!" Rhiannon barks through the door, and the knock changes to a pound. "Stop ignoring me before this becomes the most awkward situation known to Navarre."

"Five minutes," I beg as Xaden's mouth slides down my neck.

"Now," a deep, familiar voice demands, and Xaden puts a step between us, muttering a curse under his breath.

There's no way. Is there? But just in case there *is*, my hands fall from Xaden's pants and quickly redo the button on mine before I hop off the desk and rush to the door, sparing a second to check that Xaden's clothes are in place, too.

"Disengage your body parts or whatever you're doing—"

I unlock my door with a flick of my hand and yank it open to find not only every second- and third-year flier in our squad but a few of our first-years, including Sloane.

And Brennan.

Without thought for regulation or decorum, I fling myself into his arms, and he catches me, pulling me tight against his chest. "You came."

"I left you and Mira here to fight this on your own once before, and I'll never do it again. I knew I'd fucked up as soon as you left, but gryphons don't fly as quickly as dragons." He squeezes harder for a second, then lets me down. "Tell me where I can be of use."

"Are those *fliers?*" Every head turns down the hall as my mother approaches with two of her aides, but her steps falter when her gaze shifts toward my brother. "Brennan?"

"I'm not here for you." He dismisses her without another word in her direction. "Matthias is going to send the fliers to hunt the lures. They're faster on the ground and better with runes, anyway."

"We are," Cat agrees with a casual shrug, assessing the hallway like she's searching for structural weaknesses. Which she probably is. "And we don't abandon our drifts. We'll fight."

I might not like her, but damn do I respect her. Finding those lures will give us precious time to—

I grab onto Brennan's arms, and a spark of hope lights within my chest. "Have you ever encountered something you can't mend?"

"Magic," he answers. "I can't mend a relic or anything. Probably not a rune, either."

If he can do it, we'll just have to hold on long enough for Codagh to arrive.

"What about a wardstone?"

Brennan's eyebrows shoot up, and I glance past him to Rhiannon. "We have to guard the chamber, at least let him *try*."

Rhi nods, then turns to my mother, who's still staring at Brennan like he's a hallucination. "General Sorrengail, Second Squad, Flame Section, Fourth Wing officially requests permission to guard the airspace above the wardstone chamber."

Mom doesn't take her eyes off Brennan. "Granted."

Though there is some debate, it is greatly believed that turning venin heightens one of the dark wielder's senses. It is this scholar's belief that the one responsible for the death of King Grethwild developed keener eyesight. For not even the best of His Majesty's royal fliers could see through the darkness the venin hid within to slay our beloved king.

—MAJOR EDVARD TILLER'S UNACCREDITED STUDY OF THE VENIN PROPERTY OF THE LIBRARY OF CORDYN

CHAPTER SIXTY-ONE

Dawn is still an hour away as the riders in our squad stand on the ridgeline above the main campus of Basgiath, our dragons lined up behind us. The horizon holds a vague outline, the promise of light, but it winks in and out of my vision as the skyline shifts, the wavering shape on constant approach growing larger with every minute.

Hundreds of feet below, in front of the gates of Basgiath, my mother waits upon Aimsir, with her personal squad, including Mira and Teine, slightly behind her. She's in front of us *all*, her three children and the place she's sacrificed us—and her very soul—for.

"They're coming," Tairn tells me, his posture stiff while the others shift their weight or dig their talons into the snow-covered decomposed granite of the mountainside.

Squads from Third and Fourth Wings stand in formation up and down the mountains around us, but both First and Second Wings—half our forces, now that we're back with the Basgiath cadets—have been sent to the edge of the Vale. while our squad guards the airspace above the hundred yards between the back of main campus and the steep ridgeline we stand on, including the very well-hidden entrance to the ward chamber hundreds of feet below, where Brennan is working. Sloane, Aaric, and the other first-years are with him under the guise of fetching whatever he needs, but Rhi ordered them to Brennan's side mostly to keep them safe.

"I know." I glance over my shoulder at where Andarna nips at her harness between Tairn and Sgaeyl. She showed up an hour ago and refused to leave.

"Is this how it felt in Resson?" Rhiannon asks from my right, her hands nervously flitting over her sheaths and scabbard.

"How are you feeling?" I ask.

"So scared I'm pretty sure either my heart's going to give out or I'm about to shit myself," Ridoc answers from her other side.

"I was going to say horrifyingly scared, but sure, that works, too." Rhiannon nods.

"Yes. That's exactly how it felt." I do the customary checks again, not that I'd have time to get back to my room if I left anything. Xaden retrieved the dagger I'd put in Jack's shoulder, which gives me a full twelve, plus two alloy-hilted ones and the handheld crossbow strapped at my right thigh. I'm fully armed.

Thanks to the daggers we brought with us and the forge here at Basgiath, every cadet is armed.

"Does it ever get easier? Going into battle?" Sawyer asks beside Ridoc, peering down at the college. Infantry has been deployed into every courtyard, every hallway, and every entrance, the last line of a very fragile defense.

"No," Xaden answers from my left. "You just get better at hiding it. Everyone clear on the plan?"

"Riders answer to Rhi, fliers answer to Bragen," Quinn recites to our squad from down the line to the left. "When they arrive."

The fliers are still hunting down the boxes. Without the lures, maybe the wyvern would have waited until daylight. Maybe it would have taken them longer to get a feel for where the hatching grounds are. Maybe destroying the lures will deter the next horde that inevitably follows. But a thousand maybes won't change what we're facing now.

"We stay in our sector," Imogen says from Quinn's side, braiding the longer pink strands of her hair to keep it out of her eyes. "Should a wyvern leave our airspace, we let it become another squad's responsibility, so that we don't accidentally leave our sector unguarded. We maintain our airspace at all costs."

"Rhiannon is on dagger duty," Ridoc says, rubbing his hands together even though it's uncharacteristically warm this morning. I can't even see my breath. "She'll fetch and distribute should any venin fall from their wyvern and take our dagger with them."

"Any reason you can't just drag them all down with all that shadow power?" Sawyer glances Xaden's way like there's any possible chance he hasn't already considered that, the look mirrored by Rhi and Ridoc.

"Other than the reason that I almost burned out holding forty of them back in a narrow space like a valley, and there are what looks to be ten times that amount on an open plain?" Xaden counters, arching his scarred brow.

"Right. That." Sawyer nods to himself.

"Getting caught up in the wyvern is a mistake," I warn them as the downslope breeze becomes noticeable wind, but it, too, lacks the icy chill of December. "Yes, they'll try to kill us, but don't let them distract you from their creator. Kill the venin who created them, and those wyvern will fall. In our experience, they stick close to their creations during a battle."

"You know your pairs?" Rhi asks, glancing down the line.

Everyone nods. Our goal is always two against one in our favor.

"Mount up," Rhiannon orders.

I turn quickly and gather her into a hug, and she grabs for Sawyer and Ridoc, yanking them in, too. "Don't freeze," I tell them. "No matter what happens, just keep moving. And stay in the air. They can kill you if they drain the ground you're standing on. No one dies today."

"No one dies today," Ridoc repeats, and Sawyer nods as we break apart.

"Did you see Jesinia?" Rhi asks Sawyer.

My eyebrows rise. "She's here?"

"Flew in with Maren," Sawyer says, his head bobbing. "Guess gryphons are a little more easygoing in that department than dragons. She's in the Archives, comparing Warrick's journal to Lyra's to see if she can figure out why the wards in Aretia are faulty. Once you said you were scared the wards would fall here, she started worrying we wouldn't be able to get them back up without knowing what went wrong in Aretia. Turns out she's right."

"She shouldn't be at Basgiath." I shake my head, and my heart races to a gallop. "She's completely defenseless down there."

"She was worried she'd figure out the difference between the journals and be too far away to help. And if Brennan mends that stone, she's our only chance at raising the wards here successfully," Sawyer replies, backing away to follow Ridoc to their dragons.

"She has just as much right to risk her life as we do," Rhi reminds me over her shoulder, heading toward Feirge. "Now, warm up those wielding hands or do whatever it is you need to do to set this place on fire."

I turn to Andarna while Xaden finishes talking to Quinn and Imogen. "Promise me you'll stay hidden."

"*I can hide.*" She backs up a step, and I blink... It's almost as if she's faded straight into the darkness.

"*Benefit of being a black dragon,*" Tairn chuffs. "*We're born for the night.*"

I follow Andarna and scratch the scales between her nostrils when she lowers her head. "Stay put. Marbh is below you, keeping watch over Brennan. If the tide of the battle turns, he'll watch after you, but you have to go. Promise me."

"I will stand. I will keep watch. But I will not leave you this time." She huffs a breath that scents lightly of sulfur, and my heart sinks. She's seen too much for someone her age.

"It was easier when you were a juvenile." I give her one last scratch. Every dragon in our squad knows to take care of her if Tairn and I fall. But only she can make the choice to let go.

"I didn't listen then, either."

"Good point."

"It's almost time," Tairn announces, and my heartbeat accelerates as I turn toward the rising sun, a strip of orange illuminating not only the horizon but the massive cloud of wyvern that's nearly here.

Another gust of warm wind blows, and the stars wink out above us as dark clouds billow from over the mountains, charging the air with an energy that calls to my own.

Xaden meets me between Tairn and Sgaeyl, a scenario that reminds me entirely too much of Resson. He reaches for me, his warm hand cupping the back of my neck. "I love you. The world does not exist for me beyond you." Leaning down, he rests his forehead against mine. "I couldn't tell you that the last time we flew into a fight, and I should have."

"I love you, too." I grasp his waist and force a smile. "Do me a favor and don't die. I don't want to live without you." There are so many of them and so few of us.

"We don't die today."

"If only we all felt that kind of certainty," I try to joke.

"You keep your focus on the enemy and your life." He kisses me hard and quick. "Even Malek himself couldn't keep me from you."

I pull back at the first splatter on my head.

"Rain?" Xaden looks up. "In December?"

Warmth. Rain. The charge in the air.

"It's my mother." A slow smile spreads across my face. "It's her way of imbuing her favorite weapon." Me.

"Remind me to thank her afterward." He pulls me into another quick kiss, then turns away without another word, mounting Sgaeyl at a run.

I glance up at the sky and breathe deeply to carry the pressure my mother has just put on me. The storm will help me, but if the rain increases, it will cost us the help of the gryphons. They can't fly in anything much heavier than a drizzle.

"They'll guard the ground and ferry the wounded," Tairn says as he lowers his shoulder. I walk up his foreleg, rain splattering against his scales. Settling into

the saddle, I buckle the strap across my thighs and check to be sure the quiver Maren gave me is securely fastened to the left side of the saddle, within easy reach. I don't want to risk my shoulder slipping out by strapping it to my back. Then I grab the conduit from my pocket and slip the new steel bracelet attached to the top of it over my wrist.

Only then, when I'm certain I'm as prepared as I can be, when power flows through my veins with a heat that doesn't quite burn, do I look forward to the approaching enemy.

My heartbeat stutters.

Gods, they're *everywhere*, their horde larger than any riot I've ever seen. Flying at multiple altitudes—most equal with our position—the sea of gray wings, straining necks, and gaping jaws devours the sunrise.

We've grossly underestimated their numbers, and knowing there's another wave following this? My throat tightens as I glance down the line of my squad. There's no chance all of us are getting out of this alive…if any of us do.

But we just have to hold out long enough for Brennan to mend the wardstone. If we can raise the wards, even if Jesinia doesn't find what we missed in Aretia, we can stun the wyvern long enough to kill them.

Within a few breaths, the wyvern are close enough that I can make out which of them bears a rider, and when I reach two dozen in the count, I stop for the sake of my own sanity. Terror slides up my spine, and I breathe deeply to force it back down. I'm no good to Tairn and Andarna—to anyone in my squad—if I give in to panic, and I'll be even worse, a liability, if I don't keep fully in control.

They'll be within range in only minutes.

"Maybe we should have ridden out. Engaged them over the plains." I can't help but second-guess our plan as fear tightens my chest and speeds my heart rate.

"There are too many of them. They could have flanked and surrounded us easily. Here, we know every canyon, every peak, and they cannot circumvent us," Tairn answers.

They'll have to go through us.

"They're spreading out," Tairn says, his head swiveling. *"Their formation indicates they'll engage all our forces instead of targeting the Vale as we'd planned for."*

My stomach plummets. We've allocated ourselves poorly. *"Then we'll just have to be sure they never reach the Vale, won't we?"*

"You'll only have a clear firing field for a matter of seconds," Tairn reminds me.

"I know." Once the dragons engage, I'm just as likely to strike one of our own as I am a wyvern. This first strike counts for *everything*. I lift my hands and

open the Archives door to a steady but manageable flow of power, savoring the quick sizzle along my skin that comes with the rush of energy.

"Tell Aimsir I need Mom to move that cloud—"

"Yes," Tairn says, following my stream of thoughts to its conclusion before I even voice them.

I let the conduit rest against my forearm and concentrate on the cloud above us, blinking the steady fall of rain from my eyes.

The dragons beside us begin to shift their weight, their shoulders rolling in preparation to launch, but Tairn remains as still as the mountain we stand on. I spare a single glance over my shoulder for Andarna, but— *"Where are you?"* The battle hasn't even started yet and she's already left her position.

"Hiding like I promised." She peeks out from a cluster of boulders.

"Get ready," Tairn orders as the clouds roll overhead at a supernatural speed, rushing toward the enemy.

I focus on the horde. Without an outlet, power builds within me, so hot I start to think I might breathe fire, and I let it gather, let it burn, let it threaten to consume me.

"Violet…" Xaden says.

"Not yet," I answer. They'll be on us in *seconds*, but it has to be the right second. Sweat beads on my forehead.

"Violet!"

My mother's storm overtakes the wyvern at the highest altitude, and I release the torrent of scalding power, aiming it skyward.

Lightning cracks, jolting upward from the very ground of the ridge beneath ours in a blast of light so powerful it stings my eyes as it strikes into the cloud.

I drop my arms as the bodies fall. *"Maybe this will be easier than—"* Never mind. The wyvern's tactics adjust within seconds, just like the riders who control them, and they fly under the cloud cover, swerving to dodge plummeting carcasses of their horde.

"Holy shit!" Ridoc shouts as wyvern crash into the four roads that lead to Basgiath, their bodies leaving deep furrows in the ground.

That won't work again, so I slide the orb into my palm and summon power once more, drawing a faster, more concentrated stream as I target the nearest rider-bearing wyvern.

Fire whips through me as I wield, missing that wyvern but hitting another.

Shit.

"Focus on the next strike, not the last," Tairn says.

"Hold!" Xaden shouts, keeping the field clear long enough for me to fire off another strike.

I lift my hands again, giving Tairn's power dominion over my bones and muscles, then draw another strike to wield. Energy tears through me, and instead of flaring my palms, I concentrate on the intent of my fingers just like Felix taught me, drawing them downward with the strike, directing it to the target as though I am the composer and the lightning is my orchestra.

It strikes true, the wyvern and rider falling in separate, lifeless descents. A handful of other wyvern fall from the sky with the death of that dark wielder, but there's no time for relief or joy at the accomplishment when there are countless more.

And they're here.

My mother's squad launches to attack the first wave that intrudes upon their assigned sector. Aimsir rips the throat from one wyvern before I lose sight of my mother and Mira as the horde passes through their sector and into the next.

"*Focus on your sector,*" Tairn orders, and I rip my gaze from the area I'd last seen my family.

Second by second, each of the squads around and below us launch to defend their sectors, and when the first menacing gray snout crosses our line—the end of Basgiath's structures and the beginning of the mountain—I brace.

Tairn rears back, then hurtles forward, beating his wings as he runs for the edge of the ridgeline, then flying off it. I yank my goggles over my eyes at the first sting of wind, then quickly shove them back up when rain makes the glass impossible to see through.

"*That one's ours,*" Tarin tells me, flying directly for the fastest of the horde to enter our airspace.

Quinn and Imogen bank left, heading toward other targets, and I see the rest of the squad in my peripherals, but I keep my focus on the wyvern Tairn has claimed as we fly toward a head-on collision.

I grasp the conduit with one hand and lift my other as the space between us narrows to heartbeats. There's no need to reach for power; it's already there, both racing through my veins and charging the sky overhead.

Energy sizzles at the ends of my fingertips, and just as I aim to wield, the riderless wyvern drops his jaw and breathes out a stream of green fire. My heart lurches into my throat as the flames barrel toward us, and Tairn rolls left, narrowly missing the blaze.

I throw my weight right to keep level as we pass the wyvern, keeping my focus on the creature, and then strike, drawing lightning from the cloud above. It hits the wyvern just above the tail—I didn't calculate my strike closely enough to account for speed, but the charge is more than enough to drop it.

"*Below,*" Tairn growls, plunging into a dive.

I blink furiously into the wind, noting three wyvern trying to get through at a lower altitude. "*I can't strike here. I chance hitting someone above if I draw from the sky, they're too far to pull from myself, and if I miss from the ground up—"*

"Hold on."

I throw both hands on the pommel and do just that, spotting the rider on the center wyvern as we drop hundreds of feet in seconds, power a constant buzz in my ears.

Tairn strikes from above, flying directly into the wyvern on the left, and the impact whips my body forward as he sinks his teeth into the neck of the beast, dragging it down under us as we continue to fall.

The wyvern screeches, and I reach for one of my alloy-hilted blades, pivoting in my seat to watch Tairn's back and squinting into the rain as two massive shapes give chase. *"They're coming."*

A sickening crack sounds beneath us, and Tairn releases the wyvern, its neck broken as it falls the last hundred feet to the terrain below, somewhere behind the administration building.

Banking right, Tairn begins to climb with hard beats of his wings, but there's no way we'll have the high ground in time. They're less than fifty feet away, and at the angle of the remaining two wyvern's descent, we have seconds before Tairn becomes a chew toy. I check beneath us—we're clear—then grasp onto the conduit and take a steadying breath to calm the racing beat of my heart and the wild rush of adrenaline in my veins. Control. I need complete control.

There's only time for one strike. I release power, drawing it upward with my blade, and lightning streaks into the sky, hitting the closest wyvern in the chest.

"Yes!" I shout as the creature tumbles from the sky, but my joy is short-lived as its counterpart, complete with dark wielder, surges forward, opening its jaws to reveal rotten teeth and a green glow in its throat. "Tairn!"

The warning is barely past my lips when a band of shadow winds around the wyvern's throat and jerks it backward like a rabid dog at the end of a leash, its teeth missing the tip of Tairn's wing by mere feet as we continue to fly upward.

"Sgaeyl has claimed that one. We'll have to find our own," he tells me, climbing faster than ever into the driving rain.

I use precious seconds to scan our surroundings. Every sector is overwhelmed, ours included. Only flashes of color appear through the swarm of gray as we soar toward the conflict above us, but the majority of the wyvern still hover in the distance, held back on the edge of the thunderstorm.

"They only sent the first wave," Tairn explains. *"Probably to probe for weaknesses."*

Falling toward us, Aotrom has his claws raked into the belly of a wyvern, and I catch a glimpse of Ridoc as they spiral past, Imogen and her Orange Daggertail, Glane, on their heels.

"Ridoc!" I shout at Tairn.

"Focus on your mission or the plan falls apart. Trust the others to do theirs." He flies straight through the mayhem of gray, bursting into the airspace above it before he levels out.

He's right, we have a job to do, but trusting my friends to do their part feels a lot like ignoring them, too. Rain soaks my scalp and runs off my leathers as I survey the battlefield beneath us, forcing my breath in through my nose and out through my mouth to lower my heart rate.

This isn't the melee of Resson. This is a coordinated defense, and I need to focus so I can do my part.

Feirge is locked in close combat with a greenfire—a blast of blue fire erupts from its mouth—make that bluefire wyvern, and my heart clenches when Rhi narrowly misses the fire stream by leaping from Feirge's back to Cruth's. Quinn grabs hold of her forearm as the Green Scorpiontail stabs hard with her tail, and I rip my gaze away when I realize they have it under control and there's nothing I can do.

But Sawyer is outmatched fifty feet below as Sliseag goes head-to-head with three wyvern, one of whom bears a rider. I grip the conduit, then flood my body with another wave of power and lift my hand.

"Don't miss," Tairn warns.

I focus on the wyvern farthest from Sliseag just in case, then wield, drawing the power to my target with full focus and intention. Energy rips through me, and lightning strikes from the cloud above, white-hot and fatal to the wyvern below.

The rider looks up and locks eyes with me for a heartbeat before the pair dives, falling out of the battle. My stomach sours. There's only one reason to go to ground. To feed.

"Xaden—"

"On it," he assures me, and when Aotrom and Glane arrive to help Sawyer and Sliseag, I turn my attention to the other sectors.

"Three," Tairn notes, using the hands of the clock like we'd discussed, and I look right, where wyvern overrun a squad in Third Wing. The body of a dragon lies beneath them on the mountainside, but I look away before I take note of who they've lost.

If I focus on tomorrow's death roll, I'll be on it.

"Hold as steady as you can." I throw open the floodgates of his power as he banks right, flying toward their sector but not into it, and I wield, heat prickling my skin as I take down one wyvern.

Then I aim again for another.

And another.

Again and again, I wield in targeted, precise strikes for the sectors around us, hitting two-thirds of my targets but never striking a dragon, which I count as the ultimate win. Rain sizzles as it hits my skin, but I don't dare remove my flight jacket when my daggers are strapped to it, so I put the heat, the pain, into my mental box and slam the lid shut on it, forcing my mind to ignore the agonizing burn and wield again.

"Twelve."

I face forward and find the target, missing twice before I hit it. There are no venin left in our sector, but my hand trembles on the conduit as Tairn locates another wyvern, another threat, and I pull lightning from the sky so quickly that I no longer feel like I direct the storm.

I *am* the storm.

"You tire," Tairn warns.

Fuck exhaustion. *"People are dying."* A quick glance over the sunrise-lit battlefield reveals more and more spots of color among the gray carcasses littered on the ground, but I only stop quickly enough to note my squad is still fighting, handling each wyvern that crosses into our sector with teamwork and efficiency.

"Nine," Tairn rumbles but doesn't argue with me as he rolls left, keeping us above the battle, as I wield for the next squad, taking only the targets I'm certain of hitting without endangering our own riders.

Beneath me, shadows streak into other sectors as Xaden does the same.

Gods, the *heat* is going to cook me alive. Even the wind and rain aren't enough to cool the inferno growing inside my chest. I slip the conduit's bracelet from my wrist, then wedge it between my thighs long enough to strip my flight jacket off and slide it under the strap of my saddle, leaving me six daggers short, but they're in easy reach and the other two are the only ones that matter any—

"Twelve!" Tairn shouts, and I whip my head toward the plains to see another wave of wyvern soaring over my mother's sector, dangerously close to the clouds but not in them, leaving me unable to strike, given who's under them.

My heart stutters as they pass my mother without stopping, then barrel through the next without engaging.

Flying on top of the battle has given me the needed vantage point to wield, but it's also made us an undeniable target, and they're coming for *us*. I shove my hand through the strap of the bracelet so I don't lose the conduit. *"We should lead them away—"*

"We will follow the plan." Tairn dives, and my weight lifts against the straps of the saddle as we plunge toward my squad. The Second Squad dragons turn their heads toward the oncoming threat, all of us rising or falling into formation. *"Prepare."*

There are three venin on this assassination mission, their blue tunics standing out in stark contrast to the gray, bleary-eyed wyvern they ride. We've got ten seconds. Maybe.

One. Ridoc waves his hands at my right, holding a dagger that's been snapped in two. Shit, if his only remaining blade is broken—I blink when the pieces disappear. He wasn't waving at me.

Two. Snapping my head to the left, I find the pieces already in Rhiannon's hands as Feirge dives to where Sliseag hovers beneath.

Three. Feirge flies alongside Sliseag, and Rhiannon tosses the pieces.

Four. To Sawyer's credit, he catches them.

Five. Sgaeyl rises to take Feirge's place, and I lock eyes with Xaden only long enough to see that he's unharmed. Blood both drips from Sgaeyl's mouth and runs in rain-driven rivulets down the side of Xaden's face, but I instinctively know it's not his and focus on the imminent threat.

Six. Breathe. I have to *breathe* through the firestorm in my chest or I'll burn out. It's not that I don't recognize the signs: the trembling, the heat, the fatigue. It's just that they don't matter. Everyone I love is on this field.

Seven. They're almost on us, and I look down at the ward chamber, where Marbh stands watch with a Blue Clubtail I don't recognize and a vague shape I hope is Andarna, and when a flash of sunlight reflects on the dagger in Sawyer's hand, it disappears again, Feirge already on the move.

Eight. *"Dajalair is frustrated by the unflyable conditions,"* Tairn relays as Feirge rises alongside Aotrom.

Nine. *"Tell them they're more efficient guarding the courtyard and incoming wounded than struggling with waterlogged wings,"* I note. *"They'd be a liability up here right now, not an asset."*

The dagger changes hands, and Ridoc is once again armed.

I grin at how seamlessly we work as a team, then face the coming tidal wave.

Ten. *"You're beginning to think—"* Tairn starts.

"Like Brennan?" I suggest as the wyvern enter our airspace.

"Like Tairn," Sgaeyl answers, surging toward the enemy, her neck outstretched as shadows streak from under her, grasping a wyvern at the jugular and dragging it with them as Sgaeyl drops away from formation.

Tairn lunges toward another, throwing me back into the saddle as he takes the wyvern head-on. I jolt forward upon impact, blood spraying as Tairn's jaw locks on the throat of the wyvern.

Its screech rattles my brain as their claws grapple between them, forcing us into a vertical position that's nearly impossible to maintain, even with Tairn's wings beating this hard.

A flash of blue is all the warning I need to palm an alloy-hilted dagger and drop the conduit against my forearm to reach for my buckle, preparing to release it. I've seen this play before. I know this role. And this time I'm not coming away with a stab wound.

"Can you level out?" My heart jolts as the dark wielder jumps from the wyvern's neck to Tairn's, ignoring the menacing roar that vibrates Tairn's scales as he holds the wyvern in a death grip.

"Stay in your saddle!" he demands but rolls us horizontal.

The venin grabs a horn and holds on, his eerie, red-rimmed eyes never leaving mine during the maneuver or the seconds after when we fall into a rapid descent, the wyvern's weight pulling us downward. No spiderwebbed veins—he's just an asim, and I can handle him.

"You're the one he wants," the dark wielder announces, shoving his wet, stringy blond hair out of his eyes and striding down Tairn's neck as I yank at the belt with my left hand, but the buckle doesn't give.

He looks so…young. But so did Jack.

Tairn releases the wyvern, his shoulders bunching to push off the dying creature, but it snaps at his neck, and Tairn retaliates with a stronger bite, bleeding the life out of it as we fall and fall and fall.

"Your Sage?" I wrench on the leather, but the belt is stuck, and so am I.

Fuck.

I flip the dagger to its tip, catching the water-slick blade between my thumb and forefinger, and flick my wrist, firing the dagger toward him when he reaches the spikes between Tairn's shoulders.

He catches the blade, and pure panic floods my bloodstream as I pull my spare.

"You'll meet them all soon enough," he promises, raising my own blade as he marches toward me.

A green blur comes at us from the right, and we both look as Rhiannon jumps from Feirge to Tairn, landing in front of my saddle in a crouch.

The easiest way to defeat a dragon is to kill its rider.
Though the creature will most likely survive the blow, it will be
stunned long enough to be felled.

—CHAPTER THREE: THE TACTICAL GUIDE TO DEFEATING DRAGONS
BY COLONEL ELIJAH JOBEN

CHAPTER SIXTY-TWO

No. No. No. This is too familiar.

Losing Liam was… I can't lose Rhi. I just can't.

She surges forward as the wyvern screams, our rate of descent so fast that blood appears to fall upward. I yank on my belt again, but the leather is swollen with rain, wedged tight, and I watch, my heart launching into my throat, as she engages the dark wielder in a series of moves that would have had me on the mat.

He knocks her blade loose with a backhand to her wrist, and it flies from her hand as he kicks her. She skids backward along Tairn's rain-slick scales, and I reach for her, wrapping my left arm around her waist to steady her and pressing my dagger into her palm with my right hand.

She looks over her shoulder and nods at me, gaining her feet when he's almost on us. I force myself to look away as their blades clash and mountains rise, alerting me to how low our altitude is as I unstrap the crossbow at my thigh, then quickly open the quiver strapped at my left and slip the arrow into the flight groove. At this range, the wind and rain shouldn't matter.

"I need you to roll this fucker off you in three—" I start. "Rhi!" I shout out loud, taking aim. *"Two."*

She glances back, then throws her body flat between Tairn's shoulders, and I reach forward, grasping her ankle and pulling the lever without hesitation. *"One!"*

The arrow hits true, striking the venin in the sternum as Tairn banks hard right.

The dark wielder falls, but the sound of an explosion comes from behind us as I grip Rhi's ankle, ignoring the screaming protest of my shoulder as the wrap fights to keep the joint in place.

Rhi holds fast to Tairn's spikes, and he levels to horizontal quickly, pumping his wings to climb as she works backward toward me, then turns, wrapping her arms around me in a tight hug.

I hold on to her, still clutching the crossbow, and breathe deeply as Feirge mirrors Tairn's wingbeats just beneath us, keeping pace. She's all right. They're both all right.

This isn't Resson, and I didn't just lose my best friend.

"You reckless, irresponsible—" I yell.

"You're welcome!" she shouts, rain streaming down her face when she pulls away and hands back my blade. "Fix your saddle. I'll retrieve the dagger from the ground." She stands, then gives me a flash of a smile before *jumping* from Tairn's shoulder.

I track her fall, breathing a sigh of relief when she lands effortlessly on Feirge.

"My saddle is stuck!" I tell Tairn as we climb back to the battle.

"Good. Maybe you'll stay in *it."*

Sunlight glints off Quinn's labrys as she swings the double-sided battle-ax from Cruth's back into the shoulder joint of a wyvern trying its best to sink its teeth into Glane.

"Melgren is ten minutes out, but only two of his aides could keep up, and there's a general consensus that most of the dark wielders are holding back for a second wave." Tairn passes Cruth, and I look up into a sea of gray and barely suppress the urge to vomit. There have to be at least six riderless wyvern up there. How long can we keep this up? Pivoting in my saddle, I note Xaden beneath us on Sgaeyl, dragging wyvern by the throat into the side of the mountain one by one at speed as they dive toward them.

"Sgaeyl's outnumbered!"

"If she wants help, she'll ask for—"

A pain-filled roar joins the cacophony above, and my chest tightens. *"Andarna?"* I reach out, my gaze sweeping the blurred mountainside as we fly upward.

"I'm quite annoyingly safe and hidden," she responds.

"Aotrom!" Tairn bellows, and my stomach sinks.

Ridoc.

Tairn sweeps right, avoiding the plummeting body of a wyvern, but there's another above us with its teeth locked onto Aotrom's hindquarters, and three more closing in for the kill.

Sawyer and Sliseag fly from the opposite side of our sector, tracking to intercept at the same time, but everyone else is beneath us. I sheathe my dagger at my hip, then load the crossbow and strap that at my thigh as we surge upward.

Tairn's roar shakes his entire body as we approach, and I hold on to the pommel, bracing for the jarring collision, but he flies past as Sawyer and Sliseag reach the fray, then swings his massive tail into the trio of approaching wyvern.

I pivot as much as the saddle will let me at the crunching sound of bone shattering. A wyvern falls from the fight, half its head bashed in. One down. Three to go.

Tairn pulls the steepest turn I've ever experienced on his back, and my vision dims at the edge as he brings us nearly vertical before tipping his wing left and falling into a dive. I blink furiously into the wind and rain as we fly to Aotrom and Ridoc's aid.

Ridoc's doing all he can from Aotrom's back to dislodge the wyvern, stabbing his sword into its snout, but the dammed thing won't let go.

Sliseag gets there first, slashing out at the wyvern with his swordtail and cutting into a foreleg. When it doesn't let go, he pivots to close his jaw over its neck, but unlike Tairn, he isn't strong enough to snap a neck with a bite and loses precious seconds, leaving himself exposed to the remaining pair of wyvern.

We're not going to make it in time.

The pair changes course, veering from Aotrom at the last second and aiming for Sliseag.

We're almost there, but everything happens so *fucking* fast that it's as if the rest of the world slows down.

In one heartbeat, the closest wyvern opens its jaws.

In the second, it blasts green fire across Sliseag and Sawyer dives backward out of the seat, narrowly avoiding being burned to death and rolling down Sliseag's spine with a smoking boot.

In the third, it completes its assault, snapping at Sliseag's exposed side. Sawyer kicks at the gaping jaws to save his dragon from the bite, but in the next, he takes it himself, his leg disappearing between the wyvern's massive teeth.

"Sawyer!" Ridoc yells.

Sawyer's scream rips into my soul, and I nearly echo it when the wyvern's jaw locks with an audible *click* as Tairn slows his descent directly overhead, only a dozen feet above Aotrom as the remaining wyvern ducks under the fight.

Tairn's weight shifts, and I know he's chosen an angle of attack and is about to dive, but in this position, there's only time to save Sawyer or Sliseag, not both. Sawyer bellows in pain as the wyvern half drags him off Sliseag, wrenching away its ugly gray head before snapping again.

My stomach twists and my breath threatens to seize.

Fuck, there's nothing left below Sawyer's knee.

He's losing blood *and* his grip.

No. I'm not going to stand by and watch another one of my friends die. I refuse.

Grasping the dagger in my left hand and the crossbow in my right, I slice through the leather strap of my belt as Tairn dips his right wing, giving me the perfect angle for one. Single. Second. *"Forgive me."*

"Don't you dare—"

"Kill the other one quickly for both our sakes!" I'm already moving, sheathing my dagger and lunging from the saddle, gaining one, two, three running steps before I leap.

Andarna. Xaden. My sister. Brennan. They all flash through my mind as my arms swing through the fall, finding only air, but it's my mother's face I see in my mind when I land on Aotrom's back, the soles of my boots finding purchase at the edge of one of his spine scales.

"Silver One!"

"How's that for a running landing?" Holy shit, I made it.

Ridoc must think the same, because he stares at me in pure shock for a good second before he yanks his sword free of the wyvern's nose, then moves to plunge it again as I start running toward him. "I can't get the fucking thing off him!"

My heart pounds as hard as my feet as Tairn completes the dive to my right, a patch of black filling my peripheral vision. Ignoring the self-preservation instinct that tells me this is a *bad* idea, I race to Ridoc and shove the crossbow into his hands. "Fire it once I'm on Sliseag and get back in your seat!"

"Once you're *what*?"

I don't pause to answer the question, too busy running onto the nose of the godsdamned wyvern that's currently having part of its throat ripped out by Sliseag.

I run up the slope between the shrieking wyvern's eyes as it sinks its teeth deeper into Aotrom, then onto the flat of its head between its horns as Sliseag tears his jaw away.

"I'm going to throttle you myself once"—Tairn growls, and I hear the distinct sound of bone crunching in the distance—*"I get you on the ground!"*

I nearly roll my ankle on a spike halfway down the wyvern's gyrating neck and catch myself as Sliseag swings his head back to the wyvern attacking his rider, but Sawyer's grip along his spine scales is too tenuous for Sliseag to maneuver quickly. The dragon can't defend his rider without losing him.

He lets loose a skull-shaking roar as the wyvern takes another snap at Sawyer, swinging his tail with no effect.

"Hurry, Vi!" Ridoc yells.

"Sliseag!" I shout, breaking the cardinal rule of all riders. "Let me help him!"

The red swivels its head toward me, pinning me with furious golden eyes, and I nod, praying to Dunne he understands, that he holds still, and then leap from the wyvern's neck, my feet kicking for distance.

I land just above Sliseag's eyes and wrap my left arm around one of his horns, using it to both stop my momentum and hold my balance as his head swings toward the wyvern attacking Sawyer, snapping at the wyvern and coming up short.

"Now, Ridoc!" Using Sliseag's horn for leverage, I hurtle down his neck as an explosion sounds behind me, heat flaring along my back.

Sawyer scoots himself across Sliseag's spine, and I run faster, passing the seat. If he falls to that side, there's nothing Tairn can do. We're too close to the ridgeline below.

"Where are you?" I ask Tairn as Sawyer's eyes meet mine in a double take.

I ignore the snaps and snarls above me and keep moving.

"Where I'm supposed to be, unlike you*!"* he bites out just as his gargantuan frame turns in the sky ahead of me, dropping the lifeless body of the fourth wyvern from his jaws.

"Good. Now do me a favor." I charge past Sliseag's wings and alongside the enormous, gnashing teeth of the wyvern poised to devour Sawyer.

"Which would be?" Tairn asks, already flying toward us.

"Violet?" Sawyer's eyes widen with shock as blood pumps out of his leg in sickening rhythmic spurts. He needs a healer *now*.

I hit my knees, sliding the last few feet and slamming into Sawyer, knocking him farther down Sliseag's spine toward the dragon's hindquarters. Wrapping my arms around Sawyer, I clasp my hands behind his back. "Hold on!" I shout as we slide over countless red scales, seconds away from the edge.

Sliseag banks away from the ridgeline, giving us a few hundred much-needed feet of altitude for the inevitable fall, and tips us over.

"Silver One!"

Sawyer's arms close around me as we tumble off Sliseag's back and fall into the open air.

"Catch me." Wind tears at my hair, my face, my leathers, but I hold on to Sawyer as we drop in total free fall. I can save him. He doesn't have to die today. He *won't*.

One. Two. Three. Four. I count my heartbeats as we clear the ridgeline.

"What are you doing?" Xaden roars, and there's a faint, familiar brush of velvet at the base of my neck, as if Xaden's power has been extended to its limits. Our fall slows, but not by much as a dark wing blocks out the sky.

"What the hell does it look like I'm—" The breath is knocked from my lungs as an iron vise closes around us, halting our fall with a whipping change of momentum. *Tairn.*

"What part of 'stay in your saddle' did you not understand?" Tairn bellows, holding us in the precarious grip of his claw and banking left, toward Basgiath.

"You couldn't be in two places at once," I argue, fighting to draw breath as Sawyer goes limp above me, his chin falling against my shoulder. *"You had to kill the fourth wyvern, and Sliseag wouldn't defend himself if it meant losing Sawyer, so I took Sawyer."*

"And you just hoped I'd catch you?" He flares his wings, slowing our speed to a glide.

"As if you wouldn't." Air flows into my lungs in a trickle, then a stream.

He scoffs. Then changes the subject with, *"Your brother has mended the stone into one piece but does not feel...hopeful."*

My heart rises just to fall. Well, that's...great.

"Why? Can it not be imbued?"

"Marbh is not keen on details." Tairn lands on three claws in the small field between the back of the school and the cliff, gently opening the one that holds us.

What the fuck does *that* mean? Icy slush greets me as rain continues to fall, and I push Sawyer to his back and roll to my knees, putting my fingers to the pulse of his pale, freckled neck.

"Somebody help us!" I scream, my voice echoing off the stone walls of the administration building. The sluggish beat of his pulse jolts my own. He's losing too much blood too quickly, and there's no help in sight, though it's obvious we're not the first wounded to have landed here.

"I will call for aid," Tairn replies.

You can't have him, I tell Malek, shifting to kneel in the scarlet snow. *You took Liam. You may not have Sawyer.*

"Sawyer?" I wrench the buckle on the belted sheath around my left thigh, and mercifully, it gives. Knives and all, I wrap it over the wrecked leather beneath Sawyer's knee, inches above raggedly torn flesh, thread the leather through the buckle, and pull as hard as I can, crying out when pain sings through my left shoulder. "You have to wake up! Open your eyes!"

The bitter taste of fear floods my mouth as I force the metal prong through a smooth section of leather by sheer will. "Please?" I beg him, my voice breaking as my fingers search for his pulse at his wrist, then his neck, leaving crimson fingerprints on his bloodless skin. "Please, Sawyer, please. We said we'd all live until graduation, remember?"

"Aid comes," Tairn announces.

"I remember," Sawyer whispers, his eyes fluttering open.

"Oh, thank the gods!" I smile down at him, my lower lip trembling uncontrollably. "Hold on—"

"Violet!" Maren calls from across the field, and I look up to see her on Daja's back, the gryphon sprinting forward through the rain, covering the distance quickly with Cat and Bragen on foot a bit behind.

Tairn's head snaps upward toward the battlefield. *Sgaeyl—*

"Go!" If she's in danger, so is Xaden, and given the giant tendrils of shadow emanating from within a wall of gray on the edge of our sector…

Tairn crouches, then springs upward, launching with heavy beats of his wings against the morning sky as Daja reaches us, dragging a litter behind her.

"What happened?" Maren slides from Daja's back, her tan leathers streaked with blood.

"Wyvern took his leg." I glance between them as Bragen and Cat arrive. "Are you all right?"

"It's not ours," Bragen says, crouching on the other side of Sawyer. "You're going to be all right," he assures him. "Just need to get you to the healers." He slides his arms under Sawyer, then lifts and carries him to Daja.

The healers. Because mending isn't an option, not without his leg.

"We've been ferrying the wounded," Maren says over her shoulder, rushing back to Daja as Cat helps Bragen lower Sawyer to the litter.

"Thank you." I sit back on my heels and look to the sky, letting the strength of my bond with Xaden assure me that he's well instead of possibly distracting him by asking.

"Don't thank us," Maren says, mounting quickly and settling between Daja's shoulders before taking off for the Healers Quadrant, Bragen following after her.

"You look like shit." Cat crouches in front of me, her braid as sodden as mine as she looks me over. "I heard what you did up there. Well, Kira saw, and she told me. That took guts."

"You would have done the same." Exhaustion sweeps in, my shoulders drooping as adrenaline fades.

"I would have run faster." She slips one of her alloy-hilted daggers free and hands it to me. "Looks like you're missing one. I have another."

"Thank you." I take it like the peace offering it is.

"I'll look after Sawyer," she promises as she stands. "And don't you dare thank me for that," she calls back over her shoulder, walking toward the southwest tower without another word.

The conduit falls along my forearm as I wipe the rain from my eyes. I'd completely forgotten the damned thing was even there. Glancing left, then right,

I note the scattered wyvern bodies, and one Green Clubtail that makes my heart stumble—

Teine?

"Is alive," Tairn promises, already flying back to me. *"They are holding the last wave back, and your mother— Behind you!"*

I stumble to my feet and whip around to face the cliff…and the venin who stands about twenty feet away, watching me with a curious look on a heart-shaped face that had at some point been undeniably beautiful.

My stomach twists, and my grip tightens around the dagger Cat left me.

Cat. I don't want to draw attention to the retreating flier if the venin doesn't already see her.

"There's no point running," the dark wielder says, walking forward slowly, as if I'm no more of a threat than a butterfly. "We both know I'll drain the very ground underneath you, and then this all will have been for nothing." She throws her arms out, gesturing to the mayhem around us.

"Sorrengail!" Cat yells, and I hear the sloshing sound of her running toward me.

"Run, Cat!" I shout, glancing up at Tairn and spotting him mid-dive, about a minute out, but the footsteps don't slow.

The dark wielder's eyes flare as she spots Cat, and she drops to a knee, splaying her hand out over the icy ground.

"Stop!" I yell, my heart lurching into my throat and lodging there. This is so much worse than my nightmare. Even if I could run, there's no telling what she'd do to Cat. Flicking my wrist, I grasp the conduit in my left hand and lift my right—dagger and all—throwing open the doors to Tairn's power I'd never fully closed.

Slush melts at my feet and steam lifts from my skin as Cat reaches my side. "You have to get out of here."

"Shut up." She pulls a dagger from her thigh sheath.

"Oh, you are a powerful one, aren't you?" The dark wielder cocks her head to the side, a slow, insidious smile curving her mouth as she rises, studying me. "The lightning wielder."

Thunder booms in the cloud above us as energy gathers in my veins, hot and crackling. I don't have to run. I can wield.

"Her, I don't care about." She glances at Cat. "But you, I'm under orders not to kill, so let's not make this difficult."

"Me?" What the hell?

She takes a step forward, and I release a strike, hitting the ground right in front of her, stopping her in her tracks. "You'll be so much fun for *him* to wield."

The nightmare comes back full force, the Sage's words tumbling over me just enough to make my hand tremble.

A wild look comes over her narrow-set eyes. "And I will be his favorite for delivering you. I will be more than just an asim soon." Her words flow faster and faster. "I will be given the Vale when this is over!"

Delivering *me*?

"You can kill her at any time now," Cat reminds me, her gaze locked on the dark wielder.

"I want to know what the hell she means about delivering me," I murmur under my breath.

"You will turn for something much more dangerous…" Wasn't that what he said in the nightmare?

"It will be me! Me!" The venin shoves her shaking hand into her scraggly red hair.

Cat's doing this, heightening the woman's greed, spinning her out on her own emotions. Have to admit, it's a pretty badass ability when she's not using it on me.

"Enough, Wynn." A dark wielder in leathers the same color as the pulsing veins beside his eyes appears from the left, walking around the body of the fallen green and throwing out his hand.

Cat flies backward with a shout, slamming into the ground behind me.

Shit. No more time for curiosity. I wield, heat erupting from every inch of my skin as I draw the strike from the cloud above, hitting *Wynn* instantly. She falls where she stood, her eyes open and vague, smoke rising from her corpse.

"Fascinating." The new one strides for me, closing his fist.

The conduit flares with intolerable heat.

I drop it, watching in horror as it disintegrates, leaving nothing at the end of the bracelet. He flips his hand, palm upward, and I'm lifted off my feet, suspended in midair, completely immobilized.

Just like the dream, but that isn't the Sage.

My throat closes. I can't lift a hand to wield or even yell for Cat to run while she can. This isn't a dream. There's no waking up from this.

"Stay calm!" Tairn orders, nearly on us but not close enough.

"I'm on my way!" Xaden shouts as the venin steps over the body of his counterpart like she's a feature of the landscape and continues toward me.

They won't make it in time.

I won't, either.

Which means I've killed us all.

But Andarna can live. She just has to hold on, has to choose to survive.

"He's almost here, so let's move this along, shall we?" the dark wielder says, less than a dozen feet away now. "The horde tires of hovering, waiting for permission to attack."

A shape moves in the cliff behind the dark wielder. No, not a shape; part of the cliff itself; a giant…boulder?

A boulder with slivers of golden eyes.

It springs forward from the cliff like a projectile, expanding, changing colors, sprouting wings and claws and *black* scales.

I am alone in thinking the knowledge of wards, the protections
they provide, should not solely benefit Navarre,
and it has cost me everything.

—JOURNAL OF LYRA OF MORRAINE
—TRANSLATED BY CADET JESINIA NEILWART

CHAPTER SIXTY-THREE

The dark wielder turns, but he isn't fast enough.

Andarna lands directly in front of him, then opens her mouth and breathes *fire* down upon him, roasting the dark wielder before she snaps her jaws down and rips his head straight off his body.

I fall into the melting slush at the same time his corpse does, and she spits out the decapitated, smoking head, then huffs a hot breath of sulfur-laced steam.

What. The. Actual. Fuck.

"You…" I scramble to my feet and stumble toward her. "You just…"

"*I breathe fire.*" She preens, flaring her wings.

"Did you just *eat* him?" Cat stands but keeps her distance.

"*You do not speak to dragons you do not ride, human.*" Andarna snaps her teeth in Cat's direction.

"You looked like a part of the *cliff*." I stare at Andarna like I've never seen her before. Maybe I never have.

"*I told you I could hide.*" She blinks at me.

I open my mouth, then shut it, searching for words where there are none. *That* wasn't hiding. Her scales are as black as Tairn's now. Maybe I'm seeing things?

Tairn lands to the right, sending slush flying, then looks over our small battlefield with quick appraisal. "*You made quick work of it.*"

"She did." I point to Andarna as Sgaeyl and Sliseag land behind Tairn.

"You breathe fire," Tairn acknowledges, a note of pride in his voice.

"I breathe fire." Andarna extends her neck to the fullest.

"Melgren orders us to the Vale." Tairn's eyes narrow, and his head swivels toward Sgaeyl.

"They're pulling the whole squad to the Vale?" I glance upward, noting there are only two wyvern left in our sector.

The horde tires of hovering, waiting for permission to attack. That's what the dark wielder said. The final wave hasn't struck yet.

"Not the whole squad. Just us," Xaden clarifies, walking around Tairn. Tiny tendrils of steam rise where rain meets the exposed skin of his arms. He looks as tired as I feel, and there's a laceration on his forearm, but the lack of any other visible damage makes my shoulders dip in relief.

"They haven't sent their last wave yet, and Sawyer and Aotrom are already wounded. Moving the two of us leaves the squad and Brennan and the wardstone too exposed." I shake my head. We can't let that happen. Brennan's our best chance at surviving this.

"Exactly," Xaden says as he reaches my side. *"You're all right?"* His arm winds around my shoulders as he presses a hard kiss on my temple. "They're holding their own up there while this wave recedes. We need to go argue our point quickly."

"I'm all right," I promise. "Let's go."

"They're out front. We'll meet you there," Tairn says.

"Go to Marbh," I tell Andarna, pushing on my left shoulder and rotating the joint to try and ease the sharp, pulsing pain deep within the joint.

"I will be where you need me," she huffs.

"Fine, as long as that's with Marbh." I lift my eyebrows. At a dragon.

She flicks her tail twice, then walks off, but at least she's headed in the direction of the wardstone chamber safely below.

The halls of Basgiath teem with chaos as we pass by a line of gryphons and enter the guarded side door beneath the bell tower. My stomach drops. Wounded infantry and riders sit against the wall near this level's entrance to the infirmary in various states of injury, but mostly burns, their cries of pain filling the stone corridor as second- and third-year healers race from patient to patient.

"They ran out of beds twenty minutes ago," Cat tells us quietly. "Infantry is the heaviest hit so far."

"They usually are," Xaden notes, keeping his gaze focused across the hall on the door that leads to the courtyard and off the dozens of wounded to our right.

We stop abruptly as a platoon of infantry races by. The insignia on their collars show them as first-years.

"Violet." Cat grabs hold of my elbow, and I turn toward her, pausing as

Xaden pushes open the door. "Tell your mother we'll fight in the air if she can stop the rain, and if not, deploy us like the infantry. We have more experience fighting venin than almost anyone here, and gryphons are exceptionally quick on the ground."

There's only sheer determination in her brown eyes, so I nod. "I'll tell her."

She drops her hand, and Xaden and I walk into the courtyard.

It's pure fucking mayhem as we make our way through the lines of squads in dark blue being briefed by trembling second-years. It's as though their ranks have broken and they're cobbling together units with whoever hasn't been injured.

Once we reach the center, we have a clear view of the leadership meeting going on just in front of the open gate.

"At least they could shut the damned gate!" one of the infantry cadets shouts at Xaden and me as we pass.

"Shutting the gate isn't going to help you," Xaden replies, pointing left to the dead body of a wyvern poking through the partially demolished roofline. "Even if they were on foot, the five seconds it will take for them to get through isn't worth losing the necessary egress."

I shoot the second-year a sympathetic look and follow Xaden out. "You could be a little…"

"Nicer? Softer?" he counters. "Kinder? How the hell is that going to help them?"

He's not wrong.

"Hey," a second-year in dark blue says from a squad on the right, her gaze flicking over my shoulder.

"I'm sorry, but he's right. Shutting the gate isn't going to help." I say it as gently as I can.

"That's not why I stopped you." She points behind me. "There's a *scribe* chasing you down."

I turn to see Jesinia jogging toward me in the rain, her hand hidden beneath her robes.

She's keeping the journal dry.

"See if you can talk her into getting somewhere safe," Xaden suggests. "In the meantime, I'll start picking the fight without you." He walks into the thirty-foot-thick archway that serves as Basgiath's gate, crossing under the first portcullis and continuing on, immediately gaining the attention of my mother, General Melgren, and three of his aides standing at the edge of the second portcullis. The tails of their dragons swing just past them, forming a wall half the height of the fortress itself, even more in the case of Codagh.

"You should be—" I start signing to Jesinia, then drop my hands when I realize there's nowhere safe for her to be.

She grasps my elbow with her free hand and pulls me into the archway, under the portcullis. Leaving the journal within the robes, she pulls her other hand free to sign. "I think I found the difference between the two, but I think Lyra's journal is the lie."

"What did you find?" I sign, keeping my back turned toward Melgren and raising my shields, blocking everyone out, even Tairn and Andarna.

"I think it's a seven." She lifts her brows at me. "But it can't be."

"I don't understand." I shake my head. "Seven what?"

"That's the only difference between the two journals. I thought at first maybe it meant runes, that we'd mistranslated that part, since there are seven runes on the wardstone in Aretia," she signs, two lines furrowing in her forehead. "But I've checked and double-checked."

"Show me."

She nods, then pulls Lyra's journal free and flips to the middle, tapping a symbol in the middle of the page and handing it to me, freeing her hands. "That symbol there, it's a seven. But Warrick's says six, remember."

My heart sinks, and I nod slowly.

She has to be wrong.

"This reads, '*The breath of life of the seven combined and set the stone ablaze in an iron flame.*'"

Shoulders drooping, I sigh. Seven dragons is impossible. There are only six dens: black, blue, green, orange, brown, and red.

I hand her the journal. "Then maybe it's not a seven. Maybe you mistranslated?"

She shakes her head, flipping to the very first page of the journal, then gives it back. "Here." She taps the symbols, then lifts her hands. "'Here is recorded the story of Lyra of the First Six.'" She taps the six, then turns the pages to the previous spot in the middle. "Seven."

My lips part. Shit. Shit. *Shit.*

"They're close," she signs. "But that's a seven. And there are seven circles on the wardstone in Aretia. Seven runes. Seven," she repeats that last word, as if I could have possibly misunderstood.

Seven. Thoughts spin in my head too quickly to grab ahold of just one.

"This journal has to be…wrong," she signs when I remain silent.

I close the book and hand it to her. "Thank you. You should go to the infirmary. Sawyer is there, and if we—"

She shoves the journal into her robes and begins signing before I finish. "Why is Sawyer in the infirmary?" Her eyes fly wide.

"A wyvern took his leg."

She inhales swiftly.

"Go. If we evacuate the wounded, Maren said she'd watch over him, so if we evacuate, that's the safest place for you to be. She'll get you both out."

Jesinia nods. "Be safe."

"You, too."

She picks up her robes and sprints across the courtyard, cutting toward the southernmost door.

My head swims as I turn toward leadership gathered at the end of the archway and begin walking.

Could it mean a gryphon? Is that what it meant by six and the one? No. If a gryphon contributed to the wards, flier magic would work within the boundaries. But there aren't seven breeds of dragon—

I stumble, catching myself with a hand along the stone wall, while my brain trips down the path that makes the *only* sense. Even if that path is ludicrous.

But…

Holy shit.

I immediately shut the thoughts down before anyone connected to me can break through my shields and catch me thinking them.

"Absolutely not," Xaden snaps at Melgren, who stands between two of his aides.

I put myself in the middle of my mother and Xaden.

"You think cadets will be able to defend *all* this?" Colonel Panchek gesticulates wildly at the air as a Green Clubtail—

My heart seizes as Teine takes down the last remaining wyvern in their sector. The gray carcass tumbles from the sky and lands somewhere to the northeast, behind the line of dragons.

"What are you doing here?" Mom asks me as my gaze drifts upward to the line of wyvern hovering in the distance. Up until now, we've been wounded, but they're undeniably the kill shot, and in the center of their line rests a gaping hole, as if they're waiting for someone.

"She's never far from *him*," Melgren quips.

Those wyvern are waiting just like the dark wielder implied, and my stomach churns at the thought of *who* they're waiting for.

"We're not taking Tairn and Sgaeyl to defend the Vale," Xaden announces, folding his arms over his chest. "They already have First and Second Wings, plus every unbonded dragon."

Sgaeyl and Tairn land to the right, near the tower that leads to Parapet, and all I can do is hope Andarna isn't hiding over there with them, since I don't dare lower my shields to check. For the first time, I'm the one holding what might be the ultimate secret.

"You're the reason I can't plan effectively," General Melgren snaps at Xaden. "You're the reason I didn't even *see* this battle occurring." He tries to look down his hawkish nose at Xaden, but he's at least an inch shorter.

"You're welcome for flying to your aid," Xaden replies, earning a sneer.

"The Vale is the only thing that matters," Mom interrupts, shifting slightly so her shoulder is between Melgren and me. "The Archives are already sealed. The rest of the fortress can be rebuilt."

"You're going to abandon it," Xaden says softly, using that cold, menacing tone that used to scare the shit out of me. From the way Panchek steps back, it hasn't lost its edge.

Their silence is damning. My gaze jumps from face to face, looking for someone—anyone—to argue.

"They can launch that line at any moment." Melgren points to the waiting horde. "We have over sixty injured pairs, be it dragon or rider that's wounded. That horde right there will take us as spread out as we are now."

"Then why not move *every* cadet to the Vale?" Xaden challenges.

Melgren narrows his beady eyes. "You might lead a revolution, Riorson, but you know nothing about winning a *war*."

At least he called it a revolution and not a rebellion.

"You're using them as a distraction." Xaden drops his arms. "A delaying tactic. They'll die while those in the Vale have time to prepare. Prepare for *what*, exactly?"

My jaw drops. "You can't do that." I pivot, putting myself in front of Mom. "You won't need to. Brennan has mended the wardstone."

"Even Brennan can't mend magic, Cadet Sorrengail." There's no give, no room to stray from the course in her eyes.

"No," I admit. "But he doesn't have to. If the stone is mended, it could hold power. We could still raise the wards. I know how."

A curious caress of shimmering shadow slides down my shields, but I don't let him in.

"You weren't entirely successful in Aretia, were you?" she asks, lowering her voice so only I hear. "'Could' isn't good enough." That part is for a wider audience, and the rebuke heats my cheeks.

"I can do it," I whisper back just as quietly, then raise my voice to be heard. "If you put Xaden and me in the Vale, you leave the wardstone unprotected, and that is the *only* solution to keep everyone on this field alive today."

"You don't know if it works after being mended," she says slowly, like there's any chance I might misunderstand her. "And even if it did—"

"Their leader has arrived," Tairn tells me, and by the way every rider's face pivots skyward—including mine—he's not the only dragon who's noticed.

There, in the center of the horde, now flies a wyvern slightly larger than the others, bearing a rider in royal blue. The pitch of my stomach says that if he comes closer, I'll recognize his dark, thinning hair and the annoyed purse of his lips, even if logic argues that I won't, that it's just a fucking *dream*.

My heart rate soars as fear soaks into my skin, colder than the rain and melting snow around us.

"As you can see," Mom says, tearing her gaze from the horde. "It's too late for wards now."

"It's not!" I argue.

"Cadet—" Mom starts.

"I can get them up," I promise, putting myself in her way when she tries to sidestep me. "If they can hold power, then I can get the wards up!"

"Cadet," Mom snaps, her cheeks turning ruddy.

"At least *see* if the stone can hold power before you sentence all of us to death!" I push.

"Violet!" Mom shouts.

"Listen to me!" I yell right back. "For once in your life, listen to what I'm telling you!"

She draws her head back.

I forge on. "For once in *my* life, trust me. Have faith in *me*. I can get the wards up."

There it is, the slight narrowing of her eyes that says I have her attention.

"If we raise the wards, every wyvern on this field is dead. Every dark wielder is powerless—" I swallow, thinking of Jack. "Nearly powerless. Name one other weapon capable of managing that feat. Just go down there with me and see if it will hold power. Help me imbue it," I plead with my mother. "If it won't hold power, then I'll do whatever you want, but I can do this, General. I know how."

"Enough of this. We're wasting time." Melgren waves me off, then walks toward Codagh, his aides following after.

"Wait!" my mother calls out, and my heart stops.

"I'm sorry, General?" Melgren snaps, pausing to face us just outside the archway.

"This is my school." Mom lifts her chin. "I said wait."

"It's *my* army!" he barks. "And there is *no* waiting!"

"Technically, half of it is your army," Xaden says, his gaze pinned on the wyvern horde. "The other half is mine. And seeing that you had no problem having my father executed, I have no problem leaving *you* to die if you refuse her help."

Melgren stares at Xaden, the color slowly draining from his face.

"That's what I thought." Xaden sticks out his hand. "You want to walk with me, Violet?"

Something in his tone—maybe it's resignation—makes me twine my fingers with his, following him as he walks out of the archway, past Melgren, and toward the dragons.

"Where are you going? They're about to attack—" Melgren starts.

"I'm buying her the time she needs," Xaden answers, and my stomach sinks. "And they won't attack. Not yet. They're still waiting."

"What the fuck for?" Melgren snaps.

Xaden's hand tightens around mine. "Me."

You're going to love Violet. She's smart and stubborn.
Reminds me a lot of you, actually.
You just have to remember when you meet her:
she's not her mother.

—RECOVERED CORRESPONDENCE OF
CADET LIAM MAIRI TO SLOANE MAIRI

CHAPTER
SIXTY-FOUR

"What do you mean, they're waiting for you?" I ask once we're in front of Codagh, facing an open battlefield littered with the corpses of wyvern and dragons alike. A pulsing ache of dread erupts in my chest.

There's already been so much death, and we haven't yet faced the worst of their forces. From the look of that line, they've held almost all of their dark wielders back.

"That's one of their teachers," Xaden says, his eyes locked on the venin riding front and center. "The one who escaped Resson."

"He was at the cliffs, too." I fight to keep my voice as calm as possible despite the palpitations of my heart. I need to get those wards up *now*. They're the best chance we have of getting out of here alive. But each dragon can only contribute their fire to one wardstone, which means—

"He thought we'd be at Samara. Figured we'd do the honorable thing and answer Melgren's call."

"How do you know that?" My brow furrows.

"Do us both a favor and don't ask."

Tairn and Sgaeyl prowl out past Aimsir, monitoring the threats both on the ground and in the sky as they head this way. Heart pounding, I glance between them and the slowly lowering figure of the Sage a hundred yards away. He's coming to the *ground*.

Shit. I have to be quick.

"If you had to choose to correctly raise the wards here at Basgiath or ours at…" I can't say it. Not here. "What would you choose?"

Xaden's brow knits as he tears his gaze from the Sage to look at me.

"You have to choose. I only have the resources to fully raise the wards here or…there." There's a blatant plea in my tone. "I could never take that choice from you." He's already given so much.

He flinches, then glances toward the hovering horde and the theatrically slow descent of the Sage on his wyvern before bringing his eyes back to mine quickly. "You ward wherever you are, which is here."

"But your home…" It's softer than a whisper.

"*You* are my home. And if we all die here today, then the knowledge dies with us anyway. Ward Basgiath."

"You're sure?" My heart beats like the second hand of a clock, ticking down what time we have left.

"I'm sure."

I nod, then slip my hand from his and pivot, facing down the biggest dragon on the Continent. "I need to talk to you."

"Holy *fuck*, Violet." Xaden turns, putting himself at my side as Codagh slowly lowers his head, tilting toward the end to glare at me with narrowed golden eyes, because even level, I won't come past his nostrils. "You know what you're doing?"

"If I don't, we're all dead." And I'd better be quick, because Tairn is almost here. I can feel him dismantling my shields. No rider can keep their dragon out for long if they want in.

Codagh's nostrils flare, and his lip curls above very sharp, very long, very close teeth.

"You *know*." It comes out like the accusation it is. "And you didn't tell your rider because dragonkind protects dragonkind."

A blast of steam hits me in the face, and Xaden swears under his breath, shadows curling at his feet.

"Yes. I figured it out. I've already used Tairn's fire on the second wardstone, so if I power the stone at Basgiath, will you come?" I ask, my fingernails cutting into my palms to keep from shaking. This is the one dragon on the Continent besides Sgaeyl who doesn't fear Tairn on one level or another.

"You don't need him as the black dragon for Basgiath," Xaden argues. "You have Andarna."

"Will. You. Come?" I hold Codagh's menacing glare. "We're all dead if you don't. The Empyrean will end."

He huffs another breath of steam, softer this time, then dips his chin in a curt nod, lifting his head as Tairn approaches from the left and Melgren appears on the far side of Codagh's foreleg.

"You court death?" Tairn asks, pushing past my shields.

"I needed to confirm a secret that isn't mine to share," I answer. *"Please don't push."*

Tairn's talons flex in the icy slush beside me.

I turn to Xaden. "I don't want to leave you, and I have about a million questions as to why you think they're coming for you, but if I don't…" Every fiber of my being rebels at the notion of leaving him.

Leaning in, he lifts his hand to the nape of my neck. "You and I both know you can't raise the wards and stay to fight. When we were in Resson, I held them back while you fought. I trusted you to handle yourself. Now trust *me* to handle myself while you get the wards up before more people die. End this." He kisses me hard and quick, then looks at me like this will be the last time he ever sees me. "I love you."

Oh…*gods*. No. I refuse to accept the goodbye in his tone.

"You will stay alive," I order Xaden, then glance to the waiting horde, the figure of the Sage who is nearly to the ground, taking his time as if this is all a game he's already won, and finally to Tairn. "Stay with him."

Tairn growls, raising his lip over his fangs.

"Stay with him for me. Don't you dare let him die!" Turning on my heel, I break into a run without saying goodbye to Xaden. Farewells aren't needed when I'll see him shortly. Because there's no chance I'm going to fail.

"The fliers want to fight," I say to Melgren. "Let them!"

I pretend I haven't been in a battle for the last two hours, haven't wielded to exhaustion, haven't pushed my body to the breaking point and *run*.

"Cut the storm so the gryphons can fly!" I shout at my mother as I pass by, sprinting under the archway. Fuck her permission or her understanding. If the wardstone can hold power, I'll imbue it on my own.

My arms pump and I force my legs to *move*, despite the jarring pain in my knees. I run through the courtyard, dodging infantry squads, and I run up the central steps. I run through the open door and down the hall with a pounding heart and burning lungs. I run like I've been training for it since Resson.

I run because I couldn't save Liam, couldn't save Soleil, but I can save the rest of them. I can save *him*. And if I give myself even a moment to linger on the possibilities of what he might be facing, I'll turn around and run straight back to Xaden.

Taking the spiral steps at breakneck speed has me dizzy when I reach the bottom of the southwest tower, and I don't waste my gasped breaths on our first-years standing guard at the doorway as I sprint through, into the tunnel that smells like Varrish and pain.

"Move!" I shout at Lynx and Baylor. Because I remember their names. Avalynn. Sloane. Aaric. Kai, the flier. I know all the first-years' names.

They dive to opposite sides, and I force my body sideways, shuffling through the narrowest part of the tunnel.

My chest tightens, and I think of Xaden.

Xaden, and the scent of thunderstorms, and books. That's all I let in as I force my way through the passage. And as soon as it opens up, so do I, pushing myself harder than I ever have, racing down the rest of the tunnel and into the ward chamber lit by morning sunlight.

Only then do I skid to a halt and brace my hands on my knees, breathing deeply to keep from puking. "Does. It. Work?" I ask, looking up at the stone that is miraculously in one piece *and* standing where it should be.

"Damn, Sorrengail, I don't think I've ever seen you run that fast!" Aaric lifts his brows.

"Here." Brennan stumbles out from next to Aaric, his reddish-brown waves damp with sweat, and the first-year catches him, slinging his arm over his shoulder to keep my brother standing. "It took everything I had to mend it."

"Will it hold power?" I ask, forcing myself to stand through the nausea.

"Try," Brennan suggests. "If it doesn't, this was all for nothing."

Every second counts as I step up to the stone. It looks exactly how it did when we arrived last night, with the exception of the powerful hum of energy and the flames.

"Looks just like ours did before we imbued and fired it," Brennan observes.

"Right, except this stone was actually on fire when we got here," I tell him, lifting my hand to the black iron.

"Iron doesn't catch fire," Brennan argues.

"Tell that to the wardstone," I counter. Without a conduit, this is harder than I imagined, but I have to know. Opening up the Archives door again, I welcome Tairn's power in a focused trickle, just like Felix taught me, but instead of powering the conduit, I rest my fingertips on the wardstone and let it flow.

"How long did it take for three to imbue the wardstone at home?" Brennan asks.

"Weeks," I answer, my fingers tingling painfully, like they've just had circulation restored after a lengthy period of numbness, and I watch with more than a little satisfaction when energy streams past the tips. I pull my hand back an inch, just enough to see the white-blue strands connect my fingertips to the stone, and then I increase the power.

Heat prickles my skin, and I push myself to the edge to imbue, which isn't as far as I'd like it to be after hours of wielding. Sweat pops on my forehead, and my skin flushes red.

"We don't have weeks," Brennan says softly, as though talking to himself.

"I know."

Roars sound in the distance, and I look up through the chamber's opening to the sky so far above us. My throat closes at the sight of gray clashing with green. With orange. My squad is up there fighting without me. Xaden is battling at the gates. We're out of time.

I cut my power, then rest my palm on the stone. There's a tiny vibration, like the ripple of water after a pebble has been skipped into a vast lake. We don't have enough pebbles. "It can hold power, but we don't have enough riders who can imbue down here."

"I'll have Marbh put the word out," Brennan says, and we both look skyward when a flash of red is quickly followed by one of gray.

"We need every rider who can make it." But who the hell is going to stop fighting and risk the battle on a hunch? My heart careens. It looks exactly like what my mother warned us not to let happen—a full-on melee. A dark shape moves at the top edge of the chamber, and I lower my shields for the first time since speaking to Jesinia.

"Get down here," I say to Andarna, walking around to the back of the stone so no one coming to help imbue will see her.

"I'm not fond of pits—"

"Now." There's no room for argument in my tone.

I put my hand on the stone and call my power to rise while she descends, blacking out the sun momentarily on her way down, where no one else can see. Power flows out of me in a steady drip, buzzing the ends of my fingertips as I feed it into the stone.

She lands, sticking to the shadows the morning light doesn't yet touch.

"Why didn't you tell me?"

Her golden eyes blink in the darkness. *"Tell you what?"*

"I know." I shake my head at her. *"I should have known earlier. The second I saw you after Resson, I knew something was different about the sheen of your scales, but I figured I'd never been around an adolescent, so what would I know?"*

"Different." She cocks her head to the side and steps out of the darkness, her scales shifting from midnight black to a shimmering deep purple. *"That's exactly how I've always felt."*

"It's why you feel like you don't fit in with the other adolescents," I note, my hand shaking as I hold the power steady, giving the stone what I can until others arrive to help. *"It's why you were allowed to bond. Gods, you told me yourself, but I thought you were just being…"*

"An adolescent?" she challenges, flaring her nostrils.

Nodding, I try to ignore the sounds of battle high above so I can concentrate on saving us, even as anger barrels down the bond from Tairn, and fury… I can't think about what Xaden's doing. *"I should have listened when you said you were the head of your own den. That's why no one could fight your Right of Benefaction last year. Why the Empyrean allowed a juvenile to bond."*

"Say it. Don't just guess," she demands.

Even a slow breath won't calm my racing heart. *"Your scales aren't really black."*

"No." Even now, her scales are changing, taking on the grayish hue of the stone around us. *"But he is, and I so badly want to be just like him."*

"Tairn." It's not hard to guess.

"He doesn't know. Only the elders do." She lowers her head, resting it on the ground in front of me. *"They revere him. He is strong, and loyal, and fierce."*

"You are all those things, too." I wobble under the strain of wielding but keep my balance, keep the power flowing into the stone. *"You didn't have to hide. You could have told me."*

"If you didn't figure it out, you weren't worthy of knowing." She huffs. *"I waited six hundred and fifty years to hatch. Waited until your eighteenth summer, when I heard our elders talk of the weakling daughter of their general, the girl forecasted to become the head of the scribes, and I knew. You would have the mind of a scribe and the heart of a rider. You would be mine."* She leans into my hand. *"You are as unique as I am. We want the same things."*

"You couldn't have known I would be a rider."

"And yet, here we are."

A thousand questions go through my head, none of which we have the time for, so I give her exactly what I wanted—to be seen for who and what she is. *"You are not a black dragon, or any of the six that we know of. You're a seventh breed."*

"Yes." Her eyes widen in excitement.

I suck in a quick, steadying breath. *"I want you to tell me everything, but our friends are dying, so I need to ask if you are willing to breathe fire for the stone."* Sweat pops on my forehead as my temperature rises, and yet I pull more and more power, my arm trembling with the effort to keep it leashed, keep it trickling instead of striking.

"It is why I was left behind." She cocks her head to the other side. *"At least from what I remember. It has been centuries."*

"Nice to see you, Cam. Your father's been looking for you." I hear Mom's voice from the other side of the stone.

"I'm a bonded rider. There's nothing he can—"

"Don't really care. It holds power?"

Mom? What the hell could she be doing here? She should be on the battlefield. *"Fly,"* I order Andarna, my voice weakening. *"I don't trust her to see you."*

"It holds power," Brennan replies.

Andarna hesitates, then launches, flying for the top of the chamber. My fingers scrape across the stone as I slowly make my way around the side.

"You are pushing the limits," Tairn warns, distress tightening his tone.

"I have no choice." Taking a few staggered steps, I reach for Xaden lightly, not to distract but just to feel— His shields are up, blocking me completely out.

"He fights," Tairn says, and my vision darkens momentarily before clearing again…with a view of the battlefield. I'm seeing through his eyes just like I had Andarna's last year.

A swath of gray blocks out the world a second before the sky appears again, red flowing against the clouds in a stream, and then Tairn glances beneath him, watching the wyvern fall with a burst of satisfaction before he scans the ground, spotting Xaden near the edge of the ravine.

My heart beats erratically as I watch the Sage easily block each of Xaden's shadows with blasts of blue daggers of fire, then stops completely when the dappled sunlight catches on two blades imbedded in the ground behind the staff-wielding venin.

Xaden must have thrown his daggers and *missed*. I know he carries a third, but will he get to use it? Because the Sage isn't losing territory. He's gaining on Xaden, coming closer step by step, backing Xaden against the edge of the ravine.

Green fire streams from overhead, and Tairn jerks his attention upward to Sgaeyl and the three wyvern moving in to attack, one blasting cherry-red fire. Oh *gods*, there are even more breeds than we know about. Terror floods the pathway, and my vision darkens again, my ears ringing as if I've just been hit.

I blink and breathe deeply, forcing air through my throat as it constricts, and the chamber comes back into view. Stumbling one step, then another and another, I drag my hand along the slowly warming stone as I turn the corner to the front of the wardstone chamber, catching sight of Mom, Brennan, and Aaric in the middle of a conversation I can't hear over the ringing in my ears.

The power not only burns but scorches my veins, my muscles, my very bones.

"You're burning out," Andarna warns, her voice pitching high with worry.

The next breath I take singes my lungs.

"Silver One!" Tairn roars.

The wards *have* to go up. *"You both have to live. Promise me you'll choose to live."*

Because I'm starting to realize the price of imbuing this wardstone in time to save everyone I love, and it's my life. My power feels so insignificant to a stone this size. It would take *all* of Tairn's power—his very life—and I won't give that. But I can give enough that the riders who make it can finish the job.

I fall to my knees, but I don't lose contact. I pour and pour, opening my Archives door and taking on the full force of Tairn's power, shaking with the effort to keep it controlled, focused, constructive instead of violent.

"Violet?" Brennan's voice sounds from far away.

Heat surges through me in waves as I push power into the stone, and my world narrows to pain, heat, and my racing heartbeat.

"Violet!" Mom rushes to me, her eyes wide with fear as she reaches for my free hand, then gasps, drawing back a red, blistered palm.

The ground rises toward my face, and I throw that hand out to catch myself against the stone floor and keep channeling. So what if my skin sizzles, my fingers redden, my muscles give out, and I surrender to the fire? Nothing matters beyond imbuing this stone, raising the wards that will save my friends, my siblings, *Xaden.*

"What's your signet?" Mom shouts, but I lack the strength to lift my head.

"*You can't do this,*" Andarna argues in a shriek.

"*You have your purpose.*" Even my mental voice is a whisper. "*Maybe this is mine.*"

"Hasn't manifested," Aaric answers in a panic.

"What about the others out there?" Mom's voice rises.

He starts to answer the ones he knows of, and I tune him out to stay focused on control, on lasting long enough to be the most use.

Brennan hits the ground to my left, crouching a few feet away, his lips moving, but I close my eyes and reach for *more* of the power that's slowly killing me.

"*You will cease!*" Tairn orders.

"*I'm so sorry.*" The muscles in my arm lock from exhaustion. Finally. Now I won't have to hold it in place. I'm entering the final stages of burnout, just like I had on top of the mountain with Varrish. "*You shouldn't have to lose two riders this way.*"

Forcing my eyes open, I stare at the pattern of rock beneath my fingers, and I get it. I finally understand why someone would turn to stealing magic. All of the power in the world is beneath my fingertips, and if I channel, if I take from the earth instead of from Tairn, I'll have enough power to save—

"*You must save yourself,*" Tairn demands. "*I chose you not as my next, but as my last, and should you fall, then I will follow.*"

"*No.*" Steam rises from my skin.

"*Let go,*" Andarna pleads, and the rush of air in the chamber paired with the slight tremble of the ground tells me she's landed.

"I won't do it!" Sloane's shout echoes off the walls and breaks through the haze.

Inch by painful inch, I force myself to raise my head, just in time to see Brennan's eyes widen and Mom's boot rising toward my shoulder. She makes impact softly, and before I can open my mouth, she kicks with her full strength, sending me sprawling across the chamber floor and breaking my hold on the wardstone.

Power flies into the air with the crack of lightning as I hit my back, and a scream tears from my throat, the sound echoed by Brennan as his face fills my vision and he grasps my hand. Cool relief streaks up my arm, the burn fading, my muscles mending from the strain and releasing.

If I don't cut the power, he'll die. He can't mend me that fast over and over, and the next wave of heat pushes forward—

I shove the Archives door closed with the last of my mental strength, and the power cuts off. The relief from Tairn and Andarna is instant, but all I taste is the sour bite of defeat as I lie there, my brother kneeling next to me as he mends the body I've been so reckless with.

And above me, I see a flash of green before the swarm comes into view, the sky darkening with beating gray wings.

"It's the only way," Mom yells, and I turn my head as my muscles knit and my skin cools. "You can't imbue something this big in an instant. Not without hundreds of riders, which we don't have. If you want to save your friends, you'll do this!" she shouts at Sloane, her fingers wrapped around the first-year's wrist as she drags her to the wardstone.

"Mom?" I croak, but she doesn't answer.

"You're a Mairi," Mom says to Sloane.

"Yes." Her bright blue eyes meet mine, wide with uncertainty.

"I killed your mother." Mom taps on her chest.

"Mom!" I shout.

Brennan collapses next to me, pale and sweating, and I haul myself to my knees.

"I tracked her down and hauled her to her own execution, remember?" Mom says to Sloane, pushing her against the stone. "You were there. I made you watch. You and your brother."

"Liam," Sloane whispers.

Mom nods, picking up Sloane's left hand and putting it on the lowest circle of the massive rune carved into the stone. "I could have stopped his death, too, if I'd just paid a little more attention last year to what my own aide was doing."

"No!" I shout, lunging forward. Aaric runs in from the side of the ward chamber, not only catching me but *stopping* me. "Let me go!"

"I can't," he says apologetically. "She's right. And if I have to choose between her life and yours, I choose yours."

My life or…*hers*?

"Andarna!" I scream.

"I'm so sorry. I choose your life, too. You are mine. I can't let you die." Andarna shifts around my side, moving forward so she's poised to step between my mother and me.

Oh *gods*. No. Sloane is a siphon.

"Can you hear them up there dying? That's what's happening," Mom says, her tone softer than she's ever used with me. "Your friends are dying, Cadet Mairi. Tyrrendor's heir is fighting for his life, and you can stop it. You can save them all." She picks up her free hand, and to my dread, Sloane doesn't drop the other from the stone.

"Don't do it!" I cry. "Sloane, that's my *mother*." This isn't happening. Maybe Sloane won't listen to me, but she'll listen to Xaden. I throw down my shields—

Pain. Agonizing, blistering pain roars down the pathway. Hopelessness and… helplessness? It hits me from every angle, stealing my breath, overwhelming my senses and my strength. My body sags—my full weight in Aaric's arms—as my mind fights to separate Xaden's emotions from mine.

He's… I can't think around the pain, can't breathe for the tightness in my chest, can't feel the ground beneath my feet.

"Xaden's dying," I whisper.

Sloane's gaze snaps to mine, and that's all it takes.

"You don't have to do anything but stand there," my mother promises somewhere in the distance. "Your signet will take over for you. Think of yourself as nothing more than a conduit for power. You're simply facilitating mine flowing into the stone."

"Violet?" Sloane whispers.

I drag my gaze to hers, but I'm not here. Not really. I'm dying on the battlefield, the last of my strength fading, burning, consuming my body. But it will be worth it to save the one I love. *Violet*.

"Fight!" I scream down the bond at all three of them, shouting past blood and vengeance. Wrath and fire. The sour taste of wyvern flesh between her teeth.

"You can do this," Mom says, her voice soothing.

"Mom!" My voice cracks as she laces her fingers with Sloane's.

"It's all right," Mom says to me, her eyes softening as Sloane's body goes rigid. "As soon as my power—Aimsir's power—lives within the stone, fire it. Raise the wards. There's nothing I wouldn't do to keep you safe. Do you understand? Everything was to get you to this moment, when you'd be strong enough—" She falls to her knees but doesn't let go of Sloane.

"No, no, no." I fight Aaric's arms as my chest threatens to collapse, to crumple in on my heart. Mom blinks in and out of my vision, blurry one second, then clear.

"I'm so sorry," Aaric whispers.

"You're everything we dreamed you would be," Mom says quietly, her skin paling even as Sloane's flushes scarlet. "All three of you." She looks down at Brennan. "And I'll get to see him soon."

Our father. My eyes flare as I struggle to break free from Aaric.

"Don't," Brennan begs, shaking his head. "Don't do this." He staggers to his feet, stumbling her direction, but doesn't get far before falling.

"Live well." Her head bobs and her eyes roll as her skin takes on a waxy pallor that's an obscene contrast to her flight leathers as her chest rises and falls slower, in a stuttered, incomplete breath.

Brennan crawls toward her.

Footsteps sound from behind me, coming at us at a run.

"No!" I scream, tearing my throat, ripping into my soul.

A distinct, hair-raising hum emanates from the wardstone as Mom falls forward into Brennan's arms.

Sloane staggers backward, staring at her palms like they belong to someone else, and Aaric finally lets me go.

I fly forward, hitting my knees in front of where Brennan sits with Mom's body draped across his lap, his hand trembling as he reaches for her face. My fingers find her neck, but there's no pulse. No heat. No life.

The only beat I hear are bootsteps racing into the chamber.

She's gone.

"Mom," Brennan whispers, his face crumpling as he looks down at her.

"What did you *do*!" Mira drops to her knees and pulls Mom's body from Brennan, her hands furiously seeking what mine just had, any sign of a heartbeat. "Mom?" She shakes her violently, but Mom's head rolls onto her shoulder. "Mom!"

I can't breathe. She's the tide, the storms, the very air, a force too big to be extinguished without ripping the world itself apart to the core. How can she just be gone?

"I'm so sorry." Sloane cries softly.

"What did you do?" Mira yells again, the full force of her wrath turned on Brennan.

"Xaden needs you," Andarna says, but I can't move. *"Tairn and Sgaeyl wait with him."*

"We need to get them out," Aaric says, and there are hands—his, I think—on my shoulders, pulling me up off the floor and guiding me backward.

Mira follows, hooking her arms under Mom's and dragging her from the chamber. Sloane helps Brennan, and then we're all in the tunnel. Someone else carries Mom. One of the first-years?

Mira's hands are on my face, searching my eyes, as a shape blocks the entrance to the tunnel. "Are you all right?"

"I couldn't stop her." Was that my voice? Or Brennan's?

Heat flares, intense enough to suck the oxygen from my lungs, but it doesn't touch us.

Andarna is in the doorway, her wings flared to stop the flame that circles the chamber, flowing in from six above and the one who makes all the difference. A pulse of energy runs through me in a wave. The wards.

When Andarna moves, my gaze wanders up the mended wardstone to the iron flame that burns black on top.

It's all that's left of my mother.

Most generals dream of dying in service to their kingdom.
But you know me better than that, my love.
When I fall, it will be for one reason only: to protect our children.

—RECOVERED, UNSENT CORRESPONDENCE OF GENERAL LILITH SORRENGAIL

CHAPTER SIXTY-FIVE

Thud. Thud. The sound echoes down the ward chamber.

"Wyvern bodies," Andarna tells me, pivoting to peek her head through the doorway. *"Please forgive me."* Her golden eyes blink.

Forgive her?

"She made a choice," I whisper, but the tears falling down my cheeks aren't quite as resigned, nor are the sobs racking Mira's body, and the blank stare on Brennan's face is anything but peaceful as he removes his flight jacket in slow, jerky motions and drapes it over Mom's body.

I'm not sure how much time passes as we're ushered down the tunnel and through the narrow passage. The stairs are a blur.

"You are alive. You will live today. You will wake tomorrow," Tairn promises me as I force one foot in front of the other.

"Xaden?" I reach through the bond, but his shields are up.

"He lives."

Thank you, Dunne.

That's gravity, right? He's enough to keep my feet grounded. To keep the sun rising.

"He'll put her body in the quadrant," someone tells Brennan. A dragon must have brought Mom's body out of the ward chamber.

We emerge from the southwest tower to the sounds of victory. Cheers and cries of thanks to the gods. Infantry, healers, riders, and fliers alike clog the hallway with their hugs, but we make it through.

Mira, Brennan, and I stand in the doorway of the courtyard, watching the celebration break into full force. None of us seem able to move.

A face appears in front of mine. Brown eyes. Brown hair. Dain.

"Violet?" He lifts a blood-soaked arm to reach for me, then thinks twice. "Are you—"

"Move!" Rhiannon pushes him out of the way, her grin tired and so very beautiful. "You got the wards up!" She cups my face with both hands.

"Yes." I manage a nod, my gaze skimming over her face. There are a few tears in the thighs of her leathers that might be stab wounds, but I can't tell. "Are you hurt?"

"It's nothing," she assures me. "You should have seen it! The wyvern started falling from the sky like dead weights, and the venin panicked and ran. Leadership is hunting them down."

"Good. That's good." I keep nodding. "The others?"

"Ridoc is all right. Imogen took a swipe on her side, but she's barely complaining. Quinn has a busted cheek, but I think it's mostly swelling, and I was just headed to check on Sawyer and the fliers. Want to..." She studies my expression. "Xaden?"

"Alive," I croak. "According to Tairn."

She glances at Brennan, then Mira before turning back toward me, understanding dawning as her face falls.

"My mom," I try to explain, but my throat closes. "She. The wardstone didn't have any power, and my mom..."

"Oh, Vi." Rhi takes the step that separates us and pulls me in a hug.

It doesn't matter that I shouldn't, that it's a shameful display of emotion, or that she wouldn't want it. I break down and sob against Rhiannon's shoulder, my breaths coming in heaving gasps. With every tear, I feel my feet gain traction on a spinning world, feel the first waves of shock start to pass.

When I look up, Brennan is sitting on the steps that lead into the administration building, looking ready to pass out as he gives orders, and Mira is nowhere to be seen.

"What do you need?" Rhi asks.

I reach out to Xaden, but his shields are still locked up tight, so I drag the backs of my hands across my face and try like hell to pull myself together. "I need to lay eyes on Tairn and Xaden."

In the front," Tairn tells me, and I head in that direction, passing the negotiations between Melgren and Devera and pausing when I hear him laying out terms for our return. An attack, a horde that big? Bodies dropping all over the kingdom? There's no chance leadership can hide this. It's only a matter of hours before every Navarrian citizen knows they've been lied to. No wonder they want us to return.

I'm not even sure I *want* to come back. I make my way through the courtyard and then the archway, into the open air.

Open…graveyard.

Bodies of wyvern litter the ground with a few colors mixed in, but I don't recognize any of the dragons I pass as I make my way to the looming shapes of Tairn and Sgaeyl near the edge of the ravine.

"Are you harmed?" I ask him.

"You would know if I were," he says, his head swiveling as Andarna approaches, her right wing trembling as she flares them just before landing.

"You two need to catch up. Right now."

Tairn turns a golden eye on me.

"Right. Now," I repeat.

His attention fully shifts to Andarna, and I walk toward Sgaeyl, feeling Xaden beyond where she sits guard.

"Are you going to let me pass?" I ask her, keeping my eyes on hers and not the blood beard she's sporting.

"You fought well today."

"Thank you." A reluctant smile tugs at my lips. "You did, too."

"Yes, well, I'm *expected to."* She shifts her forelegs, revealing Xaden standing at the edge of the ravine, his back turned toward me. *"Be careful of your words."*

"That's ironic coming from you," I mutter but move forward, surveying him. There's a laceration across his upper back, but that's all I see as I walk to his side, keeping my toes a few inches from the edge, where his damn near hang over. "What happened?"

"I killed him." His voice is flat, and so is his expression, the noon sun cutting away almost every shadow from his face. "Snapped whatever tether he had on me and killed him. His body fell into the ravine, and now I keep watching the river like it's going to pop back up, even though I know he's miles downstream by now."

"I'm sorry I wasn't here." I reach for his hand, but he tugs it away.

"I'm not. You saved us."

"My mother saved us." My voice cracks. "She had Sloane siphon Aimsir's power and both their life energies into the wardstone. She's gone."

His eyes slide closed. "I'm so fucking sorry."

"She killed your father. Why would you be sorry?" I swipe at another tear that leaks out.

"I didn't want her dead," he says softly. "I could never want anyone you love dead."

Silence falls over us, and it's not the comfortable kind.

"Melgren wants us to come back," I throw out there, looking for some reaction, *any* reaction.

"Then we come back." He nods. "Aretia's wards are already weakening, and these are intact. Which you'll explain to me later, right?" His gaze flicks sideways at me but quickly leaves, like I'm painful to look at.

"I'll explain," I promise.

"Good." He nods. "It's safer for you here. This is where we should be." He drags in a shaky breath, then laughs. "You won't be as scared under the full wards."

My brow furrows. "I just fought an entire wyvern army, dark wielders, and raised wards, losing my mother in the process. Please, do tell me what could possibly be scarier than that?"

"You love me," he whispers.

"You know I do." I grab hold of his hand, and my stomach twists when he turns toward me but lowers his eyes. "What's out there that I should be scared of, Xaden? What did he tell you? What did you see?" What could he know that has him this shaken?

Slowly, he drags his gaze up my body, and it feels like it takes years for him to just *look* at me.

When he finally does, I gasp, my hand tightening on his in reflex.

No. That single word is all I can think, feel, scream internally as I stare up at the man I'm hopelessly in love with.

"Me," he whispers, a faint, almost indistinguishable red ring emanating from his gold-flecked onyx irises. "You should be scared of *me*."

We have tried every method we know of, as you requested.
There is no cure. There is only control.

—MISSIVE FROM LIEUTENANT COLONEL NOLON COLBERSY
TO GENERAL LILITH SORRENGAIL

CHAPTER SIXTY-SIX

XADEN

Every note of Sgaeyl's terror plays down my spine as I hang suspended mere feet above the battlefield, my muscles frozen, my power locked uselessly inside of me. Even if he let me go, I'm not sure I'd have enough strength left to wield. He wore me down for fucking *fun*.

I was never a match for him. None of us are.

Every nerve in my body screams from the pain of incineration, the heat from wielding too much for too long burning me alive. But worse than the pain is the *defeat*.

"It hurts, doesn't it? Nearing burnout?" The Sage walks a slow circle around me, his blue robes darker at the hem from the melting snow, mere feet from the ravine I had to cross to prove I could cut it in this place. "Magic does like everything in balance. Take too much and she'll consume you for overstepping."

I tear at the bonds he has wrapped around me, invisible strings of power that bind me like a trussed chicken.

"You strike. I block. You throw. I dodge." He sighs, dragging his staff in the dirt behind him.

Just like my fucking nightmares.

Except the sweat dripping down the back of my neck reminds me that this is very much my reality. That Violet is beneath Basgiath, fighting to raise the wards; that Tairn is picking off the wyverns tearing at Sgaeyl above me to keep her from my side. What is it about me that fails the females in my life?

"So, I'm going to give you one last chance to make the right choice so we can get this over with," the Sage says, stopping in front of me and smiling up at me with those eerie red-rimmed eyes and spider-webbed veins. He retreats a handful of steps, then taps the staff on the ground.

Gravity claims me, and I fall, passing my feet and slamming into the ground on my hands and knees.

"I told you once that you'd turn for love," he says, holding his arms out. "And so you shall."

"You don't know shit about me." I stumble for my feet and fall again, landing on my knees as Sgaeyl roars in pure fury overhead.

"I know more than you think." He lowers his staff and leans on it like a walking stick.

"Because you're a Sage?" I spit, grounding my feet on that hillside in Tyrrendor and reaching for my power.

"A Sage?" He laughs. "I am a *general.*"

Fire races down my arms and shadows stream from beneath me, wrapping around the arrogant asshole's torso. Satisfaction courses through me in a high better than churram. "Generals die the same as soldiers." I fight with my own arms to get them to move, but they don't obey, having gone into muscle failure long before he hefted me into the sky.

"Do they?" He laughs again, wrapped in darkness. "Come on, shadow wielder. Turn. It's the only way to save her."

"Fuck you." I throw myself down the bond and feel Violet slipping, burning, intending to... My shadows slip, but the *general* doesn't move.

She's going to sacrifice herself to save *me.*

She intends to die.

My heart vaults into my throat, and I taste it again, the same as it was when I sat by her bedside after Resson—fear.

"You know what will happen when you fail?" the general taunts, flicking at the weak bands of shadow that curl around his throat. "I'll step over your dead body and find her. Then I'll wrap my hands around her delicate little neck—"

Fury surges in my veins, the blast of adrenaline enough to solidify the bands of shadow and yank them tight, but no matter how hard I tug, he won't move.

"—and drain her."

I slam one hand onto the ground and clench my other fist, my arm shaking with the effort it takes to hold him there as I delve to the depths of Sgaeyl's power and let the fire consume me.

"Hold him!" she demands.

But I can't.

He's too strong, and I have *nothing left*. But I'll be damned if Violet suffers the consequences. He won't get his hands on her. Not today. Not ever. The slush beneath my palm melts, and I feel… There's something beneath me.

A steady flow of unmistakable…*power.*

"You cannot!" Sgaeyl shrieks. *"I chose you!"*

But Violet chose me, too.

I reach.

My heart stammers and I gasp for air, jolting upright in bed. I check the back of my neck, but it's dry. No dripping sweat. No aching muscles. No exhaustion.

Just Violet, sleeping beside me, her cheek resting on the pillow, her breaths deep and even thanks to the exhaustion that's left bruises under her eyes, her arm bent as though reaching out for me even in her dreams.

I watch her long enough to calm my racing heart, my gaze skimming over every part of her I can see from the silvery lines of her hard-won scars to the silvery half of her hair on the pillow. She's so fucking beautiful I can barely breathe. And I almost lost her.

My fingertips trail over the smooth, soft skin of her cheek, spotting the tracks her tears left. She lost her mother today, and while I won't mourn the loss of Lilith Sorrengail, I can't stand the pain Violet's suffering.

And yet I'm about to be the biggest cause of it.

"I love you," I whisper, just because I can, and then I climb from the bed as quietly as possible and dress quickly in the moonlight.

Silently, I leave the room, then make my way down the hall and to the staircase, surrounding myself in the warmth of my shadows as I descend floor by floor to the tunnels of Basgiath.

I don't bother reaching for Sgaeyl. She's been eerily silent since the battle ended.

The doors to the bridge open at my command, as do the ones on the far side when I reach them, keeping myself wrapped in darkness as I pass the overflowing clinic where we'd spent hours waiting for Sawyer to come out of surgery earlier.

I sidestep two drunken infantry cadets and keep walking down the tunnel, only turning when I reach the guarded staircase that leads to my target. The guard cracks a yawn, and I slip by unnoticed thanks to the increase in my signet… or whatever this is.

The last time I walked these stairs, I'd just murdered everyone who stood between me and Violet. It's ironic that's the cell I end up standing in front of now, peering through the barred window at Jack-fucking-Barlowe.

"You look good," the second-year says, sitting up on the reconstructed bunk and smiling. "You here to dose me? Pretty sure I'm not due until tomorrow morning."

"What's the cure?" I fold my arms across my chest.

"For the serum?" He scoffs. "The antidote."

"You know what I fucking mean." Shadows scurry in from the edges of the walls in his cell. "Tell me what the cure is, and I won't send for the Rybestad Chest that will hold you in the air until you mummify."

He stands slowly, cracking his neck before he moves to the center of the room, where the chair they'd tortured Violet in had been bolted. "Cures are for diseases. What we have is power, and that, dear Riorson, isn't curable. It's enviable."

"Bullshit. There's a way to get rid of this," I seethe.

His smile grows even wider. "Oh no. There's no cure. You can never give back what's taken—you'll only hunger for more."

"I'd rather die than become one of you." Fear flavors the words because I *feel* it, the power beneath the college, the craving to sate the need for it.

"And yet, you just did." Jack laughs, and the sound curdles my blood. "All this time, you've been convincing everyone you're the hero, and now you'll be the villain…especially in her story. Welcome to our fucked-up family. Guess we're brothers now."

ACKNOWLEDGMENTS

Thank you to my husband, Jason, for being the best inspiration an author could ever have for the perfect book boyfriend and for your endless support in what can only be described as years of utter chaos. Thank you for holding my hand when the world went wonky, getting me to every doctor's appointment, and managing the overwhelming calendar that comes with having four sons and a wife with Ehlers-Danlos. Thank you to my six children, who are quite simply my everything. To my sister, Kate, who never complained when we were holed up in a London hotel room with edits instead of sightseeing: love you, mean it. To my parents, who are always there when I need them. To my best friend, Emily Byer, for always hunting me down when I disappear into the writing cave for months.

Thank you to my team at Red Tower. Thank you to my editor Liz Pelletier, for giving me the chance to write my favorite genre. To Stacy Abrams for what shall be called the July all-nighter. You are an absolute goddess. Hannah, Lydia, Rae, Heather, Curtis, Molly, Jessica, Toni, Nicole, Veronica, and everyone at Entangled and Macmillan for answering endless streams of emails and for bringing this book to the marketplace. To Julia Kniep and Becky West for all the incredible notes and support. To Bree Archer for this phenomenal cover and Elizabeth and Amy for the exquisite art. To Meredith Johnson for being the GOAT. Thank you to my phenomenal agent, Louise Fury, for always standing at my back.

Thank you to my business manager, KP, for holding my sanity in your hands and never dropping it. Thank you to my wifeys, our unholy trinity, Gina Maxwell and Cindi Madsen—I'd be lost without you. To Kyla, who made this book possible. To Shelby and Cassie for keeping my ducks in a row and always being my number one hype girls. To every blogger and reader who has taken a chance on me over the years, I can't thank you enough. To my reader group, The Flygirls, for bringing me joy every day.

Lastly, because you're my beginning and end, thank you again to my Jason. There's a little bit of you in every hero I write.

RED TOWER
BOOKS™

THE CONTINENT

EMERALD SEA

NAVARR

LUCERAS PROVINCE

JAKOBON RIVER

MORRAINE PROVINCE

ELSUM PROVINCE

THE VALE ✧ ✧ BASGIATH

CALLDYR CITY ✧

CALLDYR PROVINCE

DEACONSHIRE PROVINCE

TYRRENDOR PROVINCE

LEWELLEN ✧

ARETIA ✧

ATHEBYN

CLIFFS OF DRALOR

MEDARO PASS

DRAITHUS ✧

ARCTILE OCEAN